There was no time.

The horsemen had reached a full gallop, trampling the tender, radiant green grass the way they would trample Kip. They finally split, one switching his vechevoral to his left hand so they could cut Kip down simultaneously.

Kip lashed out, jumping, determined to at least punch one stupid grin to oblivion before he died. It was a poor jump, and far too early. But as Kip's body rose to meet the extended lances, a radiant green mass rose through him. He felt energy rush out from his body. A dozen blades of grass rose through his hand, with his punch, tearing his skin as they ripped out of him. They thickened to the width of boar spears as green light poured from him, and became blades in truth. As he threw them into the air, Kip was thrown back down to the ground. The butts of a dozen radiant jade spears thunked into the ground around him.

Praise for the novels of Brent Weeks:

"Weeks manages to ring new tunes on...old bells, letting a deep background slowly reveal its secrets and presenting his characters in a realistically flawed and human way."
—*Publishers Weekly* on *The Black Prism*

"...A solid, entertaining yarn."
—The Onion A.V. Club on *The Black Prism*

"All in all *The Black Prism* is an A++ from me while the series has the potential to become one for the ages. The main flaw of *The Black Prism* is that it ends—despite 600+ pages and a reasonable ending point, I still wanted another 600 at least!"
—Fantasy Book Critic on *The Black Prism*

"Weeks has written an epic fantasy unlike any of its contemporaries. It is a truly visionary and original work, and has set the bar high for others in its subgenre."
—graspingforthewind.com on *The Black Prism*

"[*The Blinding Knife*] places Brent Weeks on comfortable footing beside contemporaries like Brandon Sanderson and Joe Abercrombie, if not a step above...one of the best Fantasy books of 2012."
—Aidan Moher on *The Blinding Knife*

"Weeks creates a rich blend of politics, culture and character...then throws in magic-using assassins. Brent Weeks is so good it's starting to tick me off."
—Peter V. Brett, *New York Times* bestselling author of *The Desert Spear*

"What a terrific story! I was mesmerized from start to finish. Unforgettable characters, a plot that kept me guessing, non-stop action and the kind of in-depth storytelling that makes me admire a writer's work."
—Terry Brooks on *The Way of Shadows*

"Kylar is a wonderful character—sympathetic and despicable, cowardly and courageous, honorable and unscrupulous...a breathtaking debut!"
—Dave Duncan on *The Way of Shadows*

The
Black Prism

Books by Brent Weeks

THE NIGHT ANGEL TRILOGY

The Way of Shadows
Shadow's Edge
Beyond the Shadows

LIGHTBRINGER SERIES

The Black Prism
The Blinding Knife

The
Black Prism

Lightbringer: Book 1

BRENT WEEKS

orbitbooks.net

*To my wife, Kristi, who's spent the better part
of a decade proving me right.*

Copyright © 2010 by Brent Weeks
Excerpt from *The Blinding Knife* copyright © 2011 by Brent Weeks
Map by Chad Roberts Design

Orbit
Hachette Book Group
1290 Avenue of the Americas, New York, NY 10104
www.HachetteBookGroup.com

First trade edition: July 2013

Orbit is an imprint of Hachette Book Group, Inc. The Orbit name and logo are trademarks of Little, Brown Book Group Limited.

The Hachette Speakers Bureau provides a wide range of authors for speaking events. To find out more, go to www.hachettespeakersbureau.com or call (866) 376-6591.

The publisher is not responsible for websites (or their content) that are not owned by the publisher.

Library of Congress has cataloged the hardcover edition as follows:
Weeks, Brent.
   The blinding knife / Brent Weeks.—1st ed.
      p. cm.—(Lightbringer series ; bk. 2)
   ISBN 978-0-316-07991-4
   1. Emperors—Fiction. 2. Brothers—Fiction. 3. Secrets—Fiction.
4. Magic—Fiction. I. Title.
   PS3623.E4223B575 2012
   813'.6—dc23

                                        2012009016

Printing 14, 2021

LSC-C

Printed in the United States of America

ISBN 978-0-316-24627-9 (pbk.)

Contents

Chapter 1

Kip crawled toward the battlefield in the darkness, the mist pressing down, blotting out sound, scattering starlight. Though the adults shunned it and the children were forbidden to come here, he'd played on the open field a hundred times—during the day. Tonight, his purpose was grimmer.

Reaching the top of the hill, Kip stood and hiked up his pants. The river behind him was hissing, or maybe that was the warriors beneath its surface, dead these sixteen years. He squared his shoulders, ignoring his imagination. The mists made him seem suspended, outside of time. But even if there was no evidence of it, the sun was coming. By the time it did, he had to get to the far side of the battlefield. Farther than he'd ever gone searching.

Even Ramir wouldn't come out here at night. Everyone knew Sundered Rock was haunted. But Ram didn't have to feed his family; *his* mother didn't smoke her wages.

Gripping his little belt knife tightly, Kip started walking. It wasn't just the unquiet dead that might pull him down to the evernight. A pack of giant javelinas had been seen roaming the night, tusks cruel, hooves sharp. They were good eating if you had a matchlock, iron nerves, and good aim, but since the Prisms' War had wiped out all the town's men, there weren't many people who braved death for a little bacon. Rekton was already a shell of what it had once been. The alcaldesa wasn't eager for any of her townspeople to throw their lives away. Besides, Kip didn't have a matchlock.

Nor were javelinas the only creatures that roamed the night. A mountain lion or a golden bear would also probably enjoy a well-marbled Kip.

A low howl cut the mist and the darkness hundreds of paces deeper into the battlefield. Kip froze. Oh, there were wolves too. How'd he forget wolves?

Another wolf answered, farther out. A haunting sound, the very voice of the wilderness. You couldn't help but freeze when you heard it. It was the kind of beauty that made you shit your pants.

Wetting his lips, Kip got moving. He had the distinct sensation of being followed. Stalked. He looked over his shoulder. There was nothing there. Of course. His mother always said he had too much imagination. Just walk, Kip. Places to be. Animals are more scared of you and all that. Besides, that was one of the tricks about a howl, it always sounded much closer than it really was. Those wolves were probably leagues away.

Before the Prisms' War, this had been excellent farmland. Right next to the Umber River, suitable for figs, grapes, pears, dewberries, asparagus—everything grew here. And it had been sixteen years since the final battle—a year before Kip was even born. But the plain was still torn and scarred. A few burnt timbers of old homes and barns poked out of the dirt. Deep furrows and craters remained from cannon shells. Filled now with swirling mist, those craters looked like lakes, tunnels, traps. Bottomless. Unfathomable.

Most of the magic used in the battle had dissolved sooner or later in the years of sun exposure, but here and there broken green luxin spears still glittered. Shards of solid yellow underfoot would cut through the toughest shoe leather.

Scavengers had long since taken all the valuable arms, mail, and luxin from the battlefield, but as the seasons passed and rains fell, more mysteries surfaced each year. That was what Kip was hoping for—and what he was seeking was most visible in the first rays of dawn.

The wolves stopped howling. Nothing was worse than hearing that chilling sound, but at least with the sound he knew where they were. Now...Kip swallowed on the hard knot in his throat.

As he walked in the valley of the shadow of two great unnatural hills—the remnant of two of the great funeral pyres where tens of thousands had burned—Kip saw something in the mist. His heart leapt into his throat. The curve of a mail cowl. A glint of eyes searching the darkness.

Then it was swallowed up in the roiling mists.

A ghost. Dear Orholam. Some spirit keeping watch at its grave.

Look on the bright side. Maybe wolves are scared of ghosts.

Kip realized he'd stopped walking, peering into the darkness. Move, fathead.

He moved, keeping low. He might be big, but he prided himself on being light on his feet. He tore his eyes away from the hill—still no sign of the ghost or man or whatever it was. He had that feeling again that he was being stalked. He looked back. Nothing.

A quick click, like someone dropping a small stone. And something at the corner of his eye. Kip shot a look up the hill. A click, a spark, the striking of flint against steel.

The mists illuminated for that briefest moment, Kip saw few details. Not a ghost—a soldier striking a flint, trying to light a slow-match. It caught fire, casting a red glow on the soldier's face, making his eyes seem to glow. He affixed the slow-match to the match-holder of his matchlock and spun, looking for targets in the darkness.

His night vision must have been ruined by staring at the brief flame on his match, now a smoldering red ember, because his eyes passed right over Kip.

The soldier turned again, sharply, paranoid. "The hell am I supposed to see out here, anyway? Swivin' wolves."

Very, very carefully, Kip started walking away. He had to get deeper into the mist and darkness before the soldier's night vision recovered, but if he made noise, the man might fire blindly. Kip walked on his toes, silently, his back itching, sure that a lead ball was going to tear through him at any moment.

But he made it. A hundred paces, more, and no one yelled. No shot cracked the night. Farther. Two hundred paces more, and he saw light off to his left, a campfire. It had burned so low it was barely more than coals now. Kip tried not to look directly at it to save his vision. There was no tent, no bedrolls nearby, just the fire.

Kip tried Master Danavis's trick for seeing in darkness. He let his focus relax and tried to view things from the periphery of his vision. Nothing but an irregularity, perhaps. He moved closer.

Two men lay on the cold ground. One was a soldier. Kip had seen his mother unconscious plenty of times; he knew instantly this man wasn't passed out. He was sprawled unnaturally, there were no blankets, and his mouth hung open, slack-jawed, eyes staring unblinking at the night. Next to the dead soldier lay another man, bound in chains but alive. He lay on his side, hands manacled behind his back, a black bag over his head and cinched tight around his neck.

The prisoner was alive, trembling. No, weeping. Kip looked around; there was no one else in sight.

"Why don't you just finish it, damn you?" the prisoner said.

Kip froze. He thought he'd approached silently.

"Coward," the prisoner said. "Just following your orders, I suppose? Orholam will smite you for what you're about to do to that little town."

Kip had no idea what the man was talking about.

Apparently his silence spoke for him.

"You're not one of them." A note of hope entered the prisoner's voice. "Please, help me!"

Kip stepped forward. The man was suffering. Then he stopped. Looked at the dead soldier. The front of the soldier's shirt was soaked with blood. Had this prisoner killed him? How?

"Please, leave me chained if you must. But please, I don't want to die in darkness."

Kip stayed back, though it felt cruel. "You killed him?"

"I'm supposed to be executed at first light. I got away. He chased me down and got the bag over my head before he died. If dawn's close, his replacement is coming anytime now."

Kip still wasn't putting it together. No one in Rekton trusted the soldiers who came through, and the alcaldesa had told the town's young people to give any soldiers a wide berth for a while—apparently the new satrap Garadul had declared himself free of the Chromeria's control. Now he was King Garadul, he said, but he wanted the usual levies from the town's young people. The alcaldesa had told his representative that if he wasn't the satrap anymore, he didn't have the right to raise levies. King or satrap, Garadul couldn't be happy with that, but Rekton was too small to bother with. Still, it would be wise to avoid his soldiers until this all blew over.

On the other hand, just because Rekton wasn't getting along with the satrap right now didn't make this man Kip's friend.

"So you *are* a criminal?" Kip asked.

"Of six shades to Sun Day," the man said. The hope leaked out of his voice. "Look, boy—you are a child, aren't you? You sound like one. I'm going to die today. I can't get away. Truth to tell, I don't want to. I've run enough. This time, I fight."

"I don't understand."

"You will. Take off my hood."

Though some vague doubt nagged Kip, he untied the half-knot around the man's neck and pulled off the hood.

At first, Kip had no idea what the prisoner was talking about. The man sat up, arms still bound behind his back. He was perhaps thirty years old, Tyrean like Kip but with a lighter complexion, his hair wavy rather than kinky, his limbs thin and muscular. Then Kip saw his eyes.

Men and women who could harness light and make luxin—drafters—always had unusual eyes. A little residue of whatever color they drafted ended up in their eyes. Over the course of their life, it would stain the entire iris red, or blue, or whatever their color was. The prisoner was a green drafter—or had been. Instead of the green being bound in a halo within the iris, it was shattered like crockery smashed to the floor. Little green fragments glowed even in the whites of his eyes. Kip gasped and shrank back.

"Please!" the man said. "Please, the madness isn't on me. I won't hurt you."

"You're a color wight."

"And now you know why I ran away from the Chromeria," the man said.

Because the Chromeria put down color wights like a farmer put down a beloved, rabid dog.

Kip was on the verge of bolting, but the man wasn't making any threatening moves. And besides, it was still dark. Even color wights needed light to draft. The mist did seem lighter, though, gray beginning to touch the horizon. It was crazy to talk to a madman, but maybe it wasn't too crazy. At least until dawn.

The color wight was looking at Kip oddly. "Blue eyes." He laughed.

Kip scowled. He hated his blue eyes. It was one thing when a foreigner like Master Danavis had blue eyes. They looked fine on him. Kip looked freakish.

"What's your name?" the color wight asked.

Kip swallowed, thinking he should probably run away.

"Oh, for Orholam's sake, you think I'm going to hex you with your name? How ignorant is this backwater? That isn't how chromaturgy works—"

"Kip."

The color wight grinned. "Kip. Well, Kip, have you ever wondered why you were stuck in such a small life? Have you ever gotten the feeling, Kip, that you're special?"

Kip said nothing. Yes, and yes.

"Do you know *why* you feel destined for something greater?"

"Why?" Kip asked, quiet, hopeful.

"Because you're an arrogant little shit." The color wight laughed.

Kip shouldn't have been taken off guard. His mother had said worse. Still, it took him a moment. A small failure. "Burn in hell, coward," he said. "You're not even good at running away. Caught by ironfoot soldiers."

The color wight laughed louder. "Oh, they didn't *catch* me. They recruited me."

Who would recruit madmen to join them? "They didn't know you were a—"

"Oh, they knew."

Dread like a weight dropped into Kip's stomach. "You said something about my town. Before. What are they planning to do?"

"You know, Orholam's got a sense of humor. Never realized that till now. Orphan, aren't you?"

"No. I've got a mother," Kip said. He instantly regretted giving the color wight even that much.

"Would you believe me if I told you there's a prophecy about you?"

"It wasn't funny the first time," Kip said. "What's going to happen to my town?" Dawn was coming, and Kip wasn't going to stick around. Not only would the guard's replacement come then, but Kip had no idea what the wight would do once he had light.

"You know," the wight said, "you're the reason I'm here. Not here here. Not like 'Why do I exist?' Not in Tyrea. In chains, I mean."

"What?" Kip asked.

"There's power in madness, Kip. Of course…" He trailed off, laughed at a private thought. Recovered. "Look, that soldier has a key in his breast pocket. I couldn't get it out, not with—" He shook his hands, bound and manacled behind his back.

"And I would help you why?" Kip asked.

"For a few straight answers before dawn."

Crazy, and cunning. *Perfect*. "Give me one first," Kip said.

"Shoot."

"What's the plan for Rekton?"

"Fire."

"What?" Kip asked.

"Sorry, you said one answer."

"That was no answer!"

"They're going to wipe out your village. Make an example so no one else defies King Garadul. Other villages defied the king too, of course. His rebellion against the Chromeria isn't popular everywhere. For every town burning to take vengeance on the Prism, there's another that wants nothing to do with war. Your village was chosen specially. Anyway, I had a little spasm of conscience and objected. Words were exchanged. I punched my superior. Not totally my fault. They know us greens don't do rules and hierarchy. Especially not once we've broken the halo." The color wight shrugged. "There, straight. I think that deserves the key, don't you?"

It was too much information to soak up at once—broken the halo?—but it *was* a straight answer. Kip walked over to the dead man. His skin was pallid in the rising light. Pull it together, Kip. Ask whatever you need to ask.

Kip could tell that dawn was coming. Eerie shapes were emerging from the night. The great twin looming masses of Sundered Rock itself were visible mostly as a place where stars were blotted out of the sky.

What do I need to ask?

He was hesitating, not wanting to touch the dead man. He knelt. "Why my town?" He poked through the dead man's pocket, careful not to touch skin. It was there, two keys.

"They think you have something that belongs to the king. I don't know what. I only picked up that much by eavesdropping."

"What would Rekton have that the king wants?" Kip asked.

"Not Rekton you. You you."

It took Kip a second. He touched his own chest. "Me? Me personally? I don't even own anything!"

The color wight gave a crazy grin, but Kip thought it was a pretense. "Tragic mistake, then. Their mistake, your tragedy."

"What, you think I'm lying?!" Kip asked. "You think I'd be out here scavenging luxin if I had any other choice?"

"I don't really care one way or the other. You going to bring that key over here, or do I need to ask real nice?"

It was a mistake to bring the keys over. Kip knew it. The color wight wasn't stable. He was dangerous. He'd admitted as much. But he had kept his word. How could Kip do less?

Kip unlocked the man's manacles, and then the padlock on the chains. He backed away carefully, as one would from a wild animal. The color wight pretended not to notice, simply rubbing his arms and stretching back and forth. He moved over to the guard and poked through his pockets again. His hand emerged with a pair of green spectacles with one cracked lens.

"You could come with me," Kip said. "If what you said is true—"

"How close do you think I'd get to your town before someone came running with a musket? Besides, once the sun comes up...I'm ready for it to be done." The color wight took a deep breath, staring at the horizon. "Tell me, Kip, if you've done bad things your whole life, but you die doing something good, do you think that makes up for all the bad?"

"No," Kip said, honestly, before he could stop himself.

"Me neither."

"But it's better than nothing," Kip said. "Orholam is merciful."

"Wonder if you'll say that after they're done with your village."

There were other questions Kip wanted to ask, but everything had happened in such a rush that he couldn't put his thoughts together.

In the rising light Kip saw what had been hidden in the fog and the darkness. Hundreds of tents were laid out in military precision. Soldiers. Lots of soldiers. And even as Kip stood, not two hundred paces from the nearest tent, the plain began winking. Glimmers sparkled as broken luxin gleamed, like stars scattered on the ground, answering their brethren in the sky.

It was what Kip had come for. Usually when a drafter released luxin, it simply dissolved, no matter what color it was. But in battle, there had been so much chaos, so many drafters, some sealed magic had been buried and protected from the sunlight that would break it down. The recent rain had uncovered more.

But Kip's eyes were pulled from the winking luxin by four soldiers and a man with a stark red cloak and red spectacles walking toward them from the camp.

"My name is Gaspar, by the by. Gaspar Elos." The color wight didn't look at Kip.

"What?"

"I'm not just some drafter. My father loved me. I had plans. A girl. A life."

"I don't—"

"You will." The color wight put the green spectacles on; they fit perfectly, tight to his face, lenses sweeping to either side so that wherever he looked, he would be looking through a green filter. "Now get out of here."

As the sun touched the horizon, Gaspar sighed. It was as if Kip had ceased to exist. It was like watching his mother take that first deep breath of haze. Between the sparkling spars of darker green, the whites of Gaspar's eyes swirled like droplets of green blood hitting water, first dispersing, then staining the whole. The emerald green of luxin ballooned through his eyes, thickened until it was solid, and then spread. Through his cheeks, up to his hairline, then down his neck, standing out starkly when it finally filled his lighter fingernails as if they'd been painted in radiant jade.

Gaspar started laughing. It was a low, unreasoning cackle, unrelenting. Mad. Not a pretense this time.

Kip ran.

He reached the funerary hill where the sentry had been, taking care to stay on the far side from the army. He had to get to Master Danavis. Master Danavis always knew what to do.

There was no sentry on the hill now. Kip turned around in time to see Gaspar change, transform. Green luxin spilled out of his hands onto his body, covering every part of him like a shell, like an enormous suit of armor. Kip couldn't see the soldiers or the red drafter approaching Gaspar, but he did see a fireball the size of his head streak toward the color wight, hit his chest, and burst apart, throwing flames everywhere.

Gaspar rammed through it, flaming red luxin sticking to his green armor. He was magnificent, terrible, powerful. He ran toward the soldiers, screaming defiance, and disappeared from Kip's view.

Kip fled, the vermilion sun setting fire to the mists.

Chapter 2

Gavin Guile sleepily eyed the papers that slid under his door and wondered what Karris was punishing him for this time. His rooms occupied half of the top floor of the Chromeria, but the panoramic windows were blackened so that if he slept at all, he could sleep in. The seal on the letter pulsed so gently that Gavin couldn't tell what color had been drafted into it. He propped himself up in bed so he could get a better look and dilated his pupils to gather as much light as possible.

Superviolet. Oh, sonuva—

On every side, the floor-to-ceiling blackened windows dropped into the floor, bathing the room in full-spectrum light as the morning sun was revealed, climbing the horizon over the dual islands. With his eyes dilated so far, magic flooded Gavin. It was too much to hold.

Light exploded from him in every direction, passing through him in successive waves from superviolet down. The sub-red was last, rushing through his skin like a wave of flame. He jumped out of bed, sweating instantly. But with all the windows open, cold summer morning winds blasted through his chambers, chilling him. He yelped, hopping back into bed.

His yelp must have been loud enough for Karris to hear it and know that her rude awakening had been successful, because he heard her unmistakable laugh. She wasn't a superviolet, so she must have had a friend help her with her little prank. A quick shot of superviolet luxin at the room's controls threw the windows closed and set the filters to half. Gavin extended a hand to blast his door open, then stopped. He wasn't going to give Karris the satisfaction. Her assignment to be the White's fetch-and-carry girl had ostensibly been intended to teach her humility and gravitas. So far that much had been a spectacular failure, though the White always played a deeper game. Still, Gavin couldn't help grinning as he rose and swept the folded papers Karris had tucked under the door into his hand.

He walked to his door. On a small service table just outside, he found his breakfast on a platter. It was the same every morning: two squat bricks of bread and a pale wine in a clear glass cup. The bread was made of wheat, barley, beans, lentils, millet, and spelt, unleavened. A man could live on that bread. In fact, a man *was* living on that bread. Just not Gavin. Indeed, the sight of it made his stomach turn. He could order a different breakfast, of course, but he never did.

He brought it inside, setting the papers on the table next to the bread. One was odd, a plain note that didn't look like the White's personal stationery, nor any official hard white stationery the Chromeria used. He turned it over. The Chromeria's message office had marked it as being received from "ST, Rekton": Satrapy of Tyrea, town of Rekton. It sounded familiar, maybe one of those towns near Sundered Rock? But then, there had once been so many towns there. Probably someone begging an audience, though those letters were supposed to be screened out and dealt with separately.

Still, first things first. He tore open each loaf, checking that nothing had been concealed inside it. Satisfied, he took out a bottle of the blue dye he kept in a drawer and dribbled a bit into the wine. He swirled the wine to mix it, and held the glass up against the granite blue sky of a painting he kept on the wall as his reference.

He'd done it perfectly, of course. He'd been doing this for almost six thousand mornings now. Almost sixteen years. A long time for a man only thirty-three years old. He poured the wine over the broken halves of the bread, staining it blue—and harmless. Once a week, Gavin would prepare a blue cheese or blue fruit, but it took more time.

He picked up the note from Tyrea.

"I'm dying, Gavin. It's time you meet your son Kip. —Lina"

Son? I don't have a—

Suddenly his throat clamped down, and his chest felt like his heart was seizing up, no matter that the chirurgeons said it wasn't. Just relax, they said. Young and strong as a warhorse, they said. They didn't say, Grow a pair. You've got lots of friends, your enemies fear you, and you have no rivals. You're the Prism. What are you afraid of? No one had talked to him that way in years. Sometimes he wished they would.

Orholam, the note hadn't even been sealed.

Gavin walked out onto his glass balcony, subconsciously checking his drafting as he did every morning. He stared at his hand, splitting sunlight into its component colors as only he could do, filling each finger in turn with a color, from below the visible spectrum to above it: sub-red, red, orange, yellow, green, blue, superviolet. Had he felt a hitch there when he drafted blue? He double-checked it, glancing briefly toward the sun.

No, it was still easy to split light, still flawless. He released the luxin, each color sliding out and dissipating like smoke from beneath his fingernails, releasing the familiar bouquet of resinous scents.

He turned his face to the sun, its warmth like a mother's caress. Gavin opened his eyes and sucked in a warm, soothing red. In and out, in time with his labored breaths, willing them to slow. Then he let the red go and took in a deep icy blue. It felt like it was freezing his eyes. As ever, the blue brought clarity, peace, order. But not a plan, not with so little information. He let go of the colors. He was still fine. He still had at least five of his seven years left. Plenty of time. Five years, five great purposes.

Well, maybe not five *great* purposes.

Still, of his predecessors in the last four hundred years, aside from those who'd been assassinated or died of other causes, the rest had served for exactly seven, fourteen, or twenty-one years after becoming Prism. Gavin had made it past fourteen. So, plenty of time. No reason to think he'd be the exception. Not many, anyway.

He picked up the second note. Cracking the White's seal—the old crone sealed everything, though she shared the other half of this floor and Karris hand-delivered her messages. But everything had to be in its proper place, properly done. There was no mistaking that she'd risen from Blue.

The White's note read, "Unless you would prefer to greet the students arriving late this morning, my dear Lord Prism, please attend me on the roof."

Looking beyond the Chromeria's buildings and the city, Gavin studied the merchant ships in the bay cupped in the lee of Big Jasper Island. A ragged-looking Atashian sloop was maneuvering in to dock directly at a pier.

Greeting new students. Unbelievable. It wasn't that he was too good to greet new students—well, actually, it *was* that. He, the White, and the Spectrum were supposed to balance each other. But though the Spectrum feared him the most, the reality was that the crone got her way more often than Gavin and the seven Colors combined. This morning she had to be wanting to experiment on him again, and if he wanted to avoid something more onerous like teaching he'd better get to the top of the tower.

Gavin drafted his red hair into a tight ponytail and dressed in the clothes his room slave had laid out for him: an ivory shirt and a well-cut pair of black wool pants with an oversize gem-studded belt, boots with silverwork, and a black cloak with harsh old Ilytian runic designs embroidered in silver thread. The Prism belonged to all the satrapies, so Gavin did his best to honor the traditions of every land—even one that was mainly pirates and heretics.

He hesitated a moment, then pulled open a drawer and drew out his brace of Ilytian pistols. They were, typical for Ilytian work, the most advanced design Gavin had ever seen. The firing mechanism was far more reliable than a wheellock—they were calling it a flintlock. Each pistol had a long blade beneath the barrel, and even a belt-flange so that when he tucked them into his belt behind his back they were held securely and at an angle so he didn't skewer himself when he sat. The Ilytians thought of everything.

And, of course, the pistols made the White's Blackguards nervous. Gavin grinned.

When he turned for the door and saw the painting again, his grin dropped.

He walked back to the table with the blue bread. Grabbing one use-smoothened edge of the painting, he pulled. It swung open silently, revealing a narrow chute.

Nothing menacing about the chute. Too small for a man to climb up, even if he overcame everything else. It might have been a laundry chute. Yet to Gavin it looked like the mouth of hell, the evernight itself opening wide for him. He tossed one of the bricks of bread into it, then waited. There was a thunk as the hard bread hit the first lock, a small hiss as it opened, then closed, then a smaller thunk as it hit the next lock, and a few moments later one last thunk. Each of the locks was still working. Everything was normal. Safe. There had been mistakes over the years, but no one had to die this time. No need for paranoia. He nearly snarled as he slammed the painting closed.

Chapter 3

Three thunks. Three hisses. Three gates between him and freedom.
The chute spat a torn brick of bread at the prisoner's face. He caught it,
almost without looking. He knew it was blue, the still blue of a deep
lake in early morning, when night still hoards the sky and the air dares
not caress the water's skin. Unadulterated by any other color, drafting
that blue was difficult. Worse, drafting it made the prisoner feel bored,
passionless, at peace, in harmony with even this place. And he needed
the fire of hatred today. Today, he would escape.

After all his years here, sometimes he couldn't even see the color,
like he had awoken to a world painted in grays. The first year had
been the worst. His eyes, so accustomed to nuance, so adept at pars-
ing every spectrum of light, had begun deceiving him. He'd halluci-
nated colors. He tried to draft those colors into the tools to break
this prison. But imagination wasn't enough to make magic, one
needed light. Real light. He'd been a Prism, so any color would do,
from those above violet to the ones below red. He'd gathered the very
heat from his own body, soaked his eyes in those sub-reds, and flung
that against the tedious blue walls.

Of course, the walls were hardened against such pathetic amounts
of heat. He'd drafted a blue dagger and sawn at his wrist. Where the
blood dripped onto the stone floor, it was immediately leached of
color. The next time, he'd cupped his own blood in his hands to try
to draft red, but he couldn't get enough color given that the only light

in the cell was blue. Bleeding onto the bread hadn't worked either. Its natural brown was always stained blue, so adding red only yielded a dark, purplish brown. Undraftable. Of course. His brother had thought of everything. But then, he always had.

The prisoner sat next to the drain and began eating. The dungeon was shaped like a flattened ball: the walls and ceiling a perfect sphere, the floor less steep but still sloping toward the middle. The walls were lit from within, every surface emitting the same color light. The only shadow in the dungeon was the prisoner himself. There were only two holes: the chute above, which released his food and one steady rivulet of water that he had to lick for his moisture, and the drain below for his waste.

He had no utensils, no tools except his hands and his will, always his will. With his will, he could draft anything from the blue that he wanted, though it would dissolve as soon as his will released it, leaving only dust and a faint mineral-and-resin odor.

But today was going to be the day his vengeance began, his first day of freedom. This attempt wouldn't fail—he refused to even think of it as an "attempt"—and there was work to be done. Things had to be done in order. He couldn't remember now if he had always been this way or if he'd soaked in blue for so long that the color had changed him fundamentally.

He knelt next to the only feature of the cell that his brother hadn't created. A single, shallow depression in the floor, a bowl. First he rubbed the bowl with his bare hands, grinding the corrosive oils from his fingertips into the stone for as long as he dared. Scar tissue didn't produce oil, so he had to stop before he rubbed his fingers raw. He scraped two fingernails along the crease between his nose and face, two others between his ears and head, gathering more oil. Anywhere he could collect oils from his body, he did, and rubbed it into the bowl. Not that there was any discernible change, but over the years his bowl had become deep enough to cover his finger to the second joint. His jailer had bound the color-leaching hellstones into the floor in a grid. Whatever spread far enough to cross one of those lines lost all color almost instantly. But hellstone was terribly expensive. How deep did they go?

If the grid only extended a few thumbs into the stone, his raw fingers might reach beyond it any day. Freedom wouldn't be far behind. But if his jailer had used enough hellstone that the crosshatching lines ran a foot deep, then he'd been rubbing his fingers raw for almost six thousand days for nothing. He'd die here. Someday, his brother would come down, see the little bowl—his only mark on the world—and laugh. With that laughter echoing in his ears, he felt a small spark of anger in his breast. He blew on that spark, basked in its warmth. It was fire enough to help him move, enough to counter the soothing, debilitating blue down here.

Finished, he urinated into the bowl. And watched.

For a moment, filtered through the yellow of his urine, the cursed blue light was sliced with green. His breath caught. Time stretched as the green stayed green...stayed green. By Orholam, he'd done it. He'd gone deep enough. He'd broken through the hellstone!

And then the green disappeared. In exactly the same two seconds it took every day. He screamed in frustration, but even his frustration was weak, his scream more to assure himself he could still hear than real fury.

The next part still drove him crazy. He knelt by the depression. His brother had turned him into an animal. A dog, playing with his own shit. But that emotion was too old, mined too many times to give him any real warmth. Six thousand days on, he was too debased to resent his debasement. Putting both hands into his urine, he scrubbed it around the bowl as he had scrubbed his oils. Even leached of all color, urine was still urine. It should still be acidic. It should corrode the hellstone faster than the skin oils alone would.

Or the urine might neutralize the oils. He might be pushing the day of his escape further and further away. He had no idea. That was what made him crazy, not immersing his fingers in warm urine. Not anymore.

He scooped the urine out of the bowl and dried it with a wad of blue rags: his clothes, his pillow, now stinking of urine. Stinking of urine for so long that the stench didn't offend him anymore. It didn't matter. What mattered was that the bowl had to be dry by tomorrow so he could try again.

Another day, another failure. Tomorrow, he would try sub-red again. It had been a while. He'd recovered enough from his last attempt. He should be strong enough for it. If nothing else, his brother had taught him how strong he really was. And maybe that was what made him hate Gavin more than anything. But it was a hatred as cold as his cell.

Chapter 4

In the early morning chill, Kip jogged across the town square as fast as his ungainly fifteen-year-old frame would allow. He caught his shoe on a cobblestone and pitched headlong through Master Danavis's back gate.

"Are you okay, boy?" Master Danavis asked from his seat at his work bench, his dark eyebrows rising high above cornflower blue eyes, the irises half filled with the stark ruby red that marked him a drafter. Master Danavis was in his early forties, beardless and wiry, wearing thick wool work pants and a thin shirt that left lean, muscled arms uncovered despite the cold morning. A pair of red spectacles sat low on his nose.

"Ow, ow." Kip looked at his skinned palms. His knees were burning too. "No, no I'm not." He hitched his pants up, wincing as his scraped palms rubbed on the heavy, once-black linen.

"Good, good, because—ah, here. Tell me, are these the same?" Master Danavis put out both of his hands. Both were bright red, filled with luxin from the elbow to his fingers. He turned his arm over so that his light *kopi*-and-cream-colored skin wouldn't interfere as much with Kip's examination. Like Kip, Master Danavis was a half-breed—though Kip had never heard anyone give the drafter any trouble for that, unlike him. In the dyer's case, he was half Blood Forester, his face marked with a few strange dots they called freckles, and a hint of red in his otherwise normal dark hair.

But at least his lighter than normal skin made what he was asking Kip easy.

Kip pointed to a region from the dyer's forearm to his elbow. "This red changes color here, and this one's a bit brighter. Can I, uh, talk to you, sir?"

Master Danavis flicked both hands down with disgust and ruby luxin splashed onto ground already splattered a hundred shades of red. The gooey luxin crumpled and dissolved. Most afternoons, Kip came to sweep up the remnants—red luxin was flammable even when it was dust. "Superchromats! It's one thing for my daughter to be one, but the alcaldesa's husband? And you? Two men in one town? Wait, what's wrong, Kip?"

"Sir, there's ah..." Kip hesitated. Not only was the battlefield forbidden, but Master Danavis had once said that he thought scavenging there was no different than grave robbing. "Have you heard from Liv, sir?" Coward. Three years ago, Liv Danavis had left to be trained at the Chromeria like her father before her. They'd only been able to afford for her to come home at the harvest break her first year.

"Come here, boy. Show me those hands." Master Danavis grabbed a clean rag and blotted up the blood, dislodging the dirt with firm strokes. Then he uncorked a jug and held the rag over its mouth. He rubbed the brandy-soaked rag over Kip's palms.

Kip gasped.

"Don't be a baby," Master Danavis said. Even though Kip had done odd jobs for the dyer for as long as he could remember, he was still scared of him sometimes. "Knees."

Grimacing, Kip pulled up one pant leg and propped his foot on a work bench. Liv was two years older than Kip—almost seventeen now. Not even the lack of men in the village had made her look at Kip as anything more than a child, of course, but she had always been nice to him. A pretty girl being nice and only accidentally patronizing was pretty much the best Kip could hope for.

"Let's just say that not all sharks and sea demons are in the sea. Chromeria's a tough place for a Tyrean since the war."

"So you think she might come home?"

"Kip," Master Danavis said, "is your mother in trouble again?"

Master Danavis had refused to apprentice Kip as a dyer, saying there wasn't enough work in little Rekton to give Kip a future, and insisting he only was a halfway decent dyer himself because he could draft. He'd been something else before the Prisms' War, obviously, because he'd been Chromeria trained. That wasn't cheap, and most drafters were sworn to service to pay the expense. So Master Danavis's own master must have been killed during the war, leaving him adrift. But few adults talked about those days. Tyrea had lost and everything had gotten bad, that's all Kip or the other children knew.

Still, Master Danavis paid Kip to do odd jobs and, like half the mothers in town, would give him a meal anytime he wandered by. Even better, he always let Kip eat the cakes the women in town sent, trying to attract the handsome bachelor's attention.

"Sir, there's an army on the other side of the river. They're coming to wipe out the town to make an example of us for defying King Garadul."

Master Danavis started to say something, then saw that Kip was serious. He said nothing for a moment, then his whole demeanor changed.

He started asking Kip questions rapid-fire: where were they exactly, when was he there, how did he know they were going to wipe out the town, what had the tents looked like, how many tents had he counted, were there any drafters? Kip's answers were unbelievable even to his own ears, but Master Danavis accepted it all.

"He said King Garadul is recruiting color wights? You're certain?"

"Yessir."

Master Danavis rubbed his upper lip with thumb and forefinger, like a man would smooth his mustache, though he was clean-shaven. He strode to a chest, opened it, and grabbed a purse out. "Kip, your friends are fishing this morning at Green Bridge. You need to get out there and warn them. The king's men will seize that bridge. If you don't warn them, your friends will be killed or taken for slaves. I'll warn everyone here in town. Worse comes to worst, use that money to get to the Chromeria. Liv will help you."

"But—but, my mother! Where—"

"Kip, I'll do my best to save her and everyone here. No one else is going to save your friends. You want Isabel taken as a slave? You know what happens, right?"

Kip blanched. Isa was still a tomboy, but it hadn't escaped him that she was turning into a beautiful woman. She wasn't always very nice to him, but the thought of someone hurting her filled him with rage. "Yes, sir." Kip turned to go, hesitated. "Sir, what's a superchromat?"

"A pain in my ass. Now go!"

Chapter 5

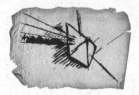

This was not going to be pretty. The note, the you-have-a-son note, hadn't been sealed. Gavin could pretty much guarantee that the White's people read all of his correspondence. But Karris had laughed after giving him the note, which meant *she* hadn't. So she didn't know. Yet. But she'd gone to report to the White. Where Gavin was expected.

He rolled his shoulders and stretched his neck to one side and then the other, each giving a satisfying little pop, then started walking. His Blackguards fell in step behind him, each carrying a wheellock musket and wearing an ataghan or other weapon. He climbed the stairs to the open roof balcony of the Chromeria. As always, he noticed Karris first. She was short, with a naturally curvy figure now carved into too-hard planes and veins by years of strenuous training. Her hair was long and straight and platinum blonde today. Yesterday it had been pink. Gavin liked it blonde. Blonde usually meant she was in a good mood. Her hair color changes were nothing magical. She just liked to change frequently. Or maybe she figured she stood out so much that she might as well not even try to blend in.

Like the other Blackguards protecting the White, Karris wore fine black trousers and blouse, cut for fighting and plain except for the embroidery of her rank on the shoulder and at the neck in gold thread. Like the others, she carried a slim black *ataghan*—a slightly forward-curving sword with a single cutting edge for most of its length—and rather than a shield, a metal parrying stick with a punch dagger in the middle. Like the others, she was extensively trained in the use of both, and a number of other weapons. Unlike the others, her skin wasn't the deep black of a Parian or an Ilytian.

Nor was her mood dark, apparently. There was a mischievous little twist to her lips. Gavin raised a brow at her, pretending to be mildly peeved about her earlier prank with the shades in his room, and came to stand before the White.

Orea Pullawr was a shrunken old woman who was taking more and more to the wheeled chair she sat in now. Her Blackguards made sure that every guard rotation had at least one burly man in case she needed to be carried up or down stairs. But despite her physical infirmity, Orea Pullawr hadn't needed to fend off a challenger for the white robe for more than a decade. Most people couldn't even remember her real name; she simply *was* the White.

"Are you ready?" she asked. Even after all these years, she still had trouble accepting that this wasn't hard for him.

"I'll manage."

"You always do," she said. Her eyes were clear and gray except for two broad arcs of color surrounding each iris, blue on top and green below. The White was a blue/green bichrome, but those arcs of color were washed out in her eyes, desaturated now because she hadn't drafted in so long. But each arc was as thick as possible, extending from the pupil out to the very edge of each iris. If she ever drafted again, she'd break the halo: the color would break through into the whites of each eye, and that would be the end of her. That was why she didn't wear colored spectacles. Unlike other retired drafters, she didn't even continue the pretense of carrying around her unused spectacles to remind everyone of what she once was. Orea Pullawr was the White, and it was enough.

Gavin headed to the dais. Above it, mounted on arcing tracks so it could be adjusted for any time of day or month of the year, a great polished crystal hung. He didn't need it. Never had, but it seemed to make everyone more comfortable to think he required some crutch to handle so much light. He never got lightsick either. Life just wasn't fair. "Any special requests?" he asked.

How exactly the Prism felt the imbalances in the world's magic was still a mystery. Shrouded in religious hokum about the Prism being connected straight to Orholam and therefore all the satrapies, the subject had not even been studied before Gavin became the Prism. Even the White had been quite nearly fearful when she asked about it, and she was as brassy a woman as Gavin had ever met.

Not that they'd made much progress, but long ago he and the White had struck a bargain: she would study him intensely and he would cooperate, and in turn she would allow him to travel without Blackguards dogging his every step. It worked, mostly. Sometimes he couldn't help but tease her, since it seemed they hadn't learned anything in the sixteen years he'd been the Prism. Of course, when he pushed her too far, she'd bring him up here and say she really needed to examine how the light moved through his skin. So he'd balance. In the open air. In the winter. Naked.

Not pleasant. Gavin being Gavin, he'd learned pretty much exactly where the line was. Emperor of the Seven Satrapies indeed.

"I'd like you to start allowing the Blackguard to do their jobs, Lord Prism."

"I meant about the balancing."

"They train their whole lives to serve us. They risk their lives. And you disappear, every week. We agreed you could travel without them, but only during emergencies."

Serve us? It's a little more complicated than that.

"I live dangerous," Gavin said. They fought about this all the time. Doubtless the White figured that if she didn't make a show here, he would push for more freedom. Doubtless she was right. Gavin looked at the White flatly. The White looked at Gavin flatly. The Blackguards were very, very quiet.

Is this how you would have handled them, brother? Or would you have simply charmed them into submission? Everything in my life is about power.

"Nothing special today," the White said. Gavin began.

A Prism, at core, did two things no one else could do. First, Gavin could split light into its component colors without external aids. A normal red drafter could draft only an arc of red, some a wider arc, some a lesser arc. In order to draft, they had to be seeing red—red rocks, blood, a sunset, a desert, whatever. Or, as drafters had learned long ago, they could wear red spectacles, which filtered the sun's white light to deliver only red. It gave less power, but it was better than being utterly dependent on one's surroundings.

The same limitations applied to every drafter: monochromes could draft only one color; bichromes could draft two colors. Generally, it was colors that bordered each other, like red and orange, or yellow and green. Polychromes—those who controlled three or more colors—were the rarest, but even they had to draft from the colors they could see. Only the Prism never needed spectacles. Only Gavin could split light within himself.

That was convenient for Gavin, but it didn't help anyone else. What did help was this: standing atop the Chromeria, light streaming through his eyes, filling his skin with every color in the spectrum, bleeding out of every pore, he could feel the imbalances in magic in all the world.

"To the southeast, like before," Gavin said. "Deep in Tyrea, likely Kelfing, someone's using sub-red, and lots of it." Heat and fire usually meant war magic. It was the first place most non-drafting warlords or satraps went when they wanted to kill people. No subtlety. The amount of sub-red being used in Tyrea meant either they'd been having a quiet war, or the new satrap Rask Garadul had set up his own school to train battle drafters. It wouldn't be something his neighbors would be happy to learn. The Ruthgari governor who occupied Tyrea's former capital Garriston definitely wouldn't be happy to learn it.

In addition to the surfeit of sub-red, more red magic than blue had been used since Gavin last balanced, and more green than orange. The system was self-regulating, initially. If red drafters around the world used too much red, it would begin to get harder for them to draft, and simultaneously easier for the blues. Sealed red luxin would unravel more easily, while sealed blue would seal better. At that level, it was an inconvenience, an annoyance.

Legends spoke of an era before Lucidonius came and brought the true worship of Orholam when the magic centers had been spread throughout the world: green in what was now Ruthgar, red in Atash, and so forth, all worshipping pagan gods and mired in superstition and ignorance. Some warlord had massacred almost all the blues. Within months, they said, the Cerulean Sea had turned to blood, the waters choked of life. Fishermen on every side of the sea had starved. The few surviving blue drafters had heroically worked to bring the balance back by themselves—using so much blue magic that they'd killed themselves. The seas cleared, and the red drafters returned to drafting as before. But this time there were no blue drafters left. Anything using red luxin failed, the seas turned bloody again, famine and disease descended.

And so it went. Nearly every generation huge natural disasters wiped out thousands who believed they'd done something to offend their capricious gods.

Prisms prevented that. Gavin could feel what was out of balance long before there were any physical signs, and fix it by drafting the opposite color. When Prisms failed, as they inevitably did after seven, fourteen, or twenty-one years, the Chromeria had to prevent disasters the hard way—in addition to running around putting out fires (sometimes literally), they would send missives throughout the world, perhaps urging blues not to draft unless it was an emergency, and reds to draft more than usual. Because everyone could only draft a finite amount in their lives, that meant hastening the reds to their death, and keeping the blues from doing useful work in all of the Seven Satrapies. So at such times, the Chromeria sought a Prism's replacement with great fervor. And Orholam was faithful to send a new Prism every generation, or so the teaching went.

Except for Gavin's generation, when in his ineffable wisdom, Orholam had somehow sent two—and torn the world apart.

Gavin spun in a slow circle, spreading his arms wide and releasing gouts of superviolet light to balance the sub-red, then red to balance blue, then orange to balance green. When the world felt right once more, he stopped.

He turned and smiled at the White. Her expression, as usual, was a cipher. Her Blackguards—every one of whom was a drafter and thus had an idea of how much power Gavin had just handled—looked similarly unimpressed. Or perhaps they were simply habituated. He was the Prism, after all. It was his job to do the impossible. If anything, they relaxed slightly. Their job was to protect the White, even from him, if it came to it.

Gavin was the Prism, and thus ostensibly the emperor of the Seven Satrapies. In reality, his duties were mostly religious. Prisms who became too much more than just figureheads found themselves forcibly retired. Often permanently. The Blackguard would die to protect him from anyone else, but the White was the head of the Chromeria. If it came to it, they'd fight for her, not him. If it did, they knew they would likely all die, but then, that was what they trained for. Even Karris.

Gavin wondered sometimes, if that ever happened, would Karris be the last to try to kill him, or the first?

"Karris?" the White said. "There's a ship waiting for you, heading for Tyrea. Take this. You can read it once you set sail. When you can, scull the rest of the way. Time is of the essence." She handed Karris a folded note. It wasn't even sealed. Either the White trusted Karris not to even open it before her ship sailed, or she knew she'd read it immediately whether it was sealed or not. Gavin thought he knew Karris well, and he didn't know which she'd do.

Karris took the note and bowed deeply to the White, never even glancing at Gavin. Then she turned and left. Gavin couldn't help but watch her go, her figure svelte, graceful, powerful, but he kept his glance brief. The White would notice regardless, but if he stared, she'd probably say something.

She waved her hand as Karris disappeared down the stairs, and the rest of the Blackguard withdrew from earshot.

"So, Gavin," she said, folding her arms. "A son. Explain."

Chapter 6

Green Bridge was less than a league upstream from Rekton. Kip's body screamed at him to quit running, but every time he slowed his pace, he imagined the soldiers coming up the opposite side of the river. He had to get there first.

About twelve nightmares of enslavement and death later, he did. Isabel and Ramir and Sanson were relaxing against the bridge, fishing. Isabel was bundled against the cold, watching while Sanson tried to tease out rainbow trout and Ram told him how he was doing it wrong. They all looked at Kip as he bent over, puffing. No sight of soldiers anywhere.

"Gotta go," Kip said in between breaths. "Soldiers coming."

"Oh, no, oh, no! Not *soldiers*!" Ram said in mock panic.

Sanson jumped to his feet, thinking Ramir was serious. Sanson was bucktoothed and gullible, good-natured, always the last to get a joke and the most likely to be the butt of it.

"Relax, Sanson. I'm joking," Ramir said, punching Sanson's shoulder, too hard.

When they'd first heard about the recruiters demanding levies, it had taken them about a second to conclude that if one of them were pressed into King Garadul's service, it would be Ram. At sixteen, he was a year older than the rest of them, and the only one who seemed remotely like a soldier.

"I'm not," Kip said, still bent over, hands on his knees, breathing hard.

Still uncertain, Sanson said, "My ma said the alcaldesa had a big fight with the king's man. She said the alcaldesa told him to stick those orders in his ear."

"If I know the alcaldesa, she didn't say *ear*," Isa said. She grinned wickedly, and Sanson and Ram laughed. They just weren't getting it.

Kip saw Isa look at Ram—just a quick glance, looking for his approval. As she found it, Kip saw her pleasure double, and he felt sick in his stomach. Again.

"What's going on, Kip?" she asked. Big brown eyes, full lips, full curves, flawless skin. It was impossible to talk to her and not be aware of her beauty. Prettier even than Liv, really, and infinitely more *here*.

Kip tried to find words. People are coming to kill us, and I'm worried about some girl who doesn't even like me.

From Green Bridge, it was three or four hundred paces to the nearest orange grove. There was precious little cover between the bridge and the trees.

"There are—" Kip started, but Ram ran right over his words.

"If they conscript me, I'm going to volunteer to become a battle drafter," Ram said. "It's dangerous, I know, but if I have to leave everything I love here, I'm going to make something of myself." He looked into the distance, off to a grand future. Kip wanted to punch him in his handsome, heroic face.

"Why don't you and Sanson run off?" Ram asked. "You know, hide from the big bad army? Isa and I want to say goodbye."

"Why can't you say goodbye with us here?" Sanson asked.

Isa blushed.

Ram's eyes flashed. "Seriously, you two, don't be assholes, huh?" he said, pretending to be joking.

"Ram, listen," Kip said. "The army is coming to make an example of us. We need to leave. Right. Now. Master Danavis said they'd seize the bridge." In fact, Green Bridge itself was a relic from the last army that came through. It was all green luxin—the most durable luxin: when sealed, it broke down more slowly than any other kind. They said that when Gavin Guile had led his army through here on his way to crush his evil brother Dazen Guile's army, Gavin Guile, the Prism himself, had drafted this bridge. By himself. In seconds. The army had pushed through without slowing, though its foragers had stolen all the food and livestock still in town. All the men in the town had been pressed into service on one side or the other.

It was why they had all grown up without fathers. No one in Rekton should treat an army passing through as a light matter. Not even the children.

"Do me a favor, Tubby. I'll make it up to you," Ram said.

"If you go with the soldiers, you won't be *here* to make it up to me," Kip said. He wanted to kill Ram when he called him Tubby.

An ugly look passed over Ram's features. They'd fought before, and Ram won every time. But it was never easy. Kip could take a lot of punishment, and sometimes he went crazy. They both knew it. Ram said, "So do me a favor, huh?"

"We have to go!" Kip nearly shouted. He didn't know why he was surprised. It was no mistake they always called Ramir Ram. He picked a goal and went straight at it, bashing down anything in his path, never veering right or left. His goal today was to take Isabel's maidenhead. That simple. No mere invading army was going to stop the stupid animal.

"Fine. Come on, Isa, we'll go to the orange grove," Ram said. "And don't think I'll forget this, Kip."

Ram took her hand and pulled her into a walk. She went with him but turned, looking over her shoulder at Kip, as if expecting him to do something.

But what could he do? They were actually going the right direction. If he went over there and punched Ram in the face, Ram would beat him bloody—and worse, they'd both be out in the open. If Kip followed on their heels, Ram might assume he was trying to start a fight even if he wasn't, with the same result.

Isabel was still looking at him. She was so beautiful it hurt.

Kip could stay. Do nothing. Hide under the bridge.

No!

Kip cursed. Isa looked back as he emerged from Green Bridge's shadow. Her eyes widened, and he thought he saw the shadow of a smile touch her lips. Real joy at seeing Kip pursue her and be a man, or just venal delight in being fought over? Then her gaze shifted up and left, to the opposite bank of the river. Surprised.

There was a man's yell from above, but over the hiss of the waters Kip couldn't understand what he said. Ram stumbled as he reached the top of the riverbank. He didn't catch himself. Instead, he dropped to his knees, tottered, and fell backward.

It was only when Ram's limp body rolled over that Kip saw the arrow sticking out of his back.

Isa saw it too. She looked at whoever was on the bank, glanced at Kip, and then bolted in the other direction.

"Kill her," a man commanded in a loud clear voice, on the bridge directly above Kip. His voice was passionless.

Kip felt sick, helpless. He'd wasted too much time. His mind refused what his eyes reported. Isa was running along the bank of the river, fast. She'd always been fast, but there was nowhere to hide, no cover from the arrow Kip knew was coming. His heart hammered in his chest, roared in his ears, and then, suddenly, its rate doubled, tripled.

The barest shadow flicked at the corner of his eye: the arrow. Kip's arm spasmed as if he himself had been struck. A flash of blue, barely visible, thin and reedy, darted from him into the air.

The arrow splashed into the river, a good fifteen paces away from Isa. The archer cursed. Kip looked down at his hands. They were trembling—and blue. As achingly bright blue as the sky. He was so stunned he froze for a moment.

He looked back to Isa, now more than a hundred paces away. There was the same flicker of a shadow as another arrow passed from the periphery of his vision to the center of it—right into Isa's back. She pitched face first onto the rough stones of the riverbank, but as Kip watched, she got back up to her knees slowly, the arrow jutting from her lower back, hands and face streaming blood. She was almost to her feet when the next arrow thudded into her back. She dropped face first into the shallows of the river and moved no more.

Kip stood there stupidly, disbelieving. His vision narrowed to the point where crimson life swirled from Isa's back into the clear water of the river.

Hoofbeats clopped loudly on the bridge above them. Kip's mind churned.

"Sir, the men are ready," a man said above them. "But... sir, this is our own town." Kip looked up. The green luxin of the bridge overhead was translucent, and he could see the shadows of the men—which meant that if he or Sanson moved, the soldiers might see them too.

Silence, then, coldly, the same officer who had demanded Isa die said, "So we should let subjects choose when to obey their king? Perhaps obeying my orders should be optional, too?"

"No, sir. It's just..."

"Are you finished?"

"Yes, sir."

"Then burn it down. Kill them all."

Chapter 7

"You're not even going to pretend that you don't read my mail?" Gavin asked.

The White barked a laugh. "Why insult your intelligence?"

"I could think of half a dozen reasons, which means *you* could probably think of a hundred," Gavin said.

"You're avoiding the question. Do you have a son?" Despite her dogged determination to get the answer—and Gavin knew she wouldn't let him dodge this, artfully or not—she kept her voice down. She understood, better than anyone, the gravity of the situation. Even the Blackguards wouldn't hear this. But if she had read his unsealed mail, anyone else could have too.

"To the best of my knowledge, it's not true. I don't see how it could be."

"Because you've been careful, or because it's actually impossible?"

"You don't really expect me to answer that," Gavin said.

"I understand that a Prism faces substantial temptations, and I appreciate your temperance or discretion over the years, whichever it's been. I haven't had to deal with pregnant young drafters or irate fathers demanding that you be forced to marry their daughters. I thank you for that. In return, I haven't joined your father in pressing you to marry, though that would doubtless simplify your life and mine. You're a smart man, Gavin. Smart enough, I hope, that you know you can ask me for a new room slave, or more room slaves, or whatever you require. Otherwise, I hope that you are...very careful."

Gavin coughed. "None more so."

"I don't pretend to be able to track all your comings and goings, but to the best of my knowledge, you haven't been to Tyrea since the war."

"Sixteen years," Gavin said quietly. Sixteen years? Has he really been down there for sixteen years? What would the White do if she found out my brother is alive? That I've been keeping him in a special hell beneath this very tower?

Her eyebrows lifted, reading something else in his troubled expression. "Ah. A great many things may be done during war by men and women who think they may die. Those were wilder days for you. So perhaps this revelation is a *particular* problem."

Gavin's heart stopped cold. For all of a thousand things that had happened sixteen years ago, the one that was most important now was that during the time the child must have been sired, Gavin had been betrothed to Karris.

"If you're absolutely certain that this isn't true," the White said, "I'll send a man to take the note from Karris. I was trying to do you a favor. You know her temper. I figured it would be best for both of you if she learned about this while she is away. After her head cools, I imagine she'll forgive you. But if you swear it isn't true, then there's no need for her to know at all, is there?"

For a moment, Gavin wondered at the old crone. The White was being kind, no doubt, but she had also orchestrated this situation to happen right in front of her—and the only reason for her to do that was so she could see Gavin's most honest reaction. It was kind and cruel and cunning all at once, and by no means accidental. Gavin reminded himself for the hundredth time not to get on the wrong side of Orea Pullawr.

"I have no recollection of this woman. None. But it was a terrible time. I, I cannot swear it." He knew how the White would take that. She thought he was admitting to cheating on Karris during their betrothal, but that he believed he'd always been careful. But young men make mistakes.

"I should go," he said. "I'll get to the bottom of it. This is my mess."

"No," she said flatly. "Now it's Karris's. I'm not sending you to Tyrea, Gavin. You're the Prism. It's bad enough that I have to send you after color wights—"

"You don't *send* me. You just don't stop me."

It had been their first titanic clash of wills. She refused to let a Prism endanger himself, called it madness. Gavin hadn't made any arguments at all, just refused to be stopped. She'd confined him to his apartments. He'd blown the doors off.

Eventually, she gave in, and he paid for it in other ways.

A moment passed, and she said very quietly, gently, "After all this time, Gavin, after all the wights you've killed and all the people you've saved, does it hurt any less?"

"I hear there's some talk of heresy," Gavin said brusquely. "Someone preaching the old gods again. I could go find out."

"You're not the *promachos* anymore, Gavin."

"It's not like any fifty of their half-trained drafters could stop—"

"What you *are* is the best Prism we've had in fifty, maybe a hundred years. And they might have fifty-one drafters, or five hundred at their little heretical Chromeria, so I won't hear of it. Karris will check on this woman and her son and see what she can learn as she investigates this 'King' Garadul. You can expect her return within two months. And speaking of color wights, an unusually powerful blue wight was just seen on the outskirts of the Blood Forest, heading toward Ru."

A blue wight heading toward the reddest lands in the world. Odd. And blues were usually so logical. It was a distraction, but it was a good one, and it left him almost no time to reach Karris. "By your leave, then, High Lady," he said, his good manners always partly ironical. He didn't wait for her approval before he gathered his magic and jogged toward the edge of the tower.

"Oh no you don't!" she said.

He stopped. Sighed. "What?"

"Gavin!" she scolded. "Surely you didn't forget you promised to teach today. It's a high honor for each class to meet with you. They wait months for this."

"Which class?" he asked suspiciously.

"Superviolets. There's only six of them."

"Isn't that the class with the girl always spilling out of her top? Lana? Ana?" It was one thing when women pursued Gavin, but that girl had been throwing herself at him since she was fourteen.

The White looked pained. "We have spoken with that one a few times."

"Look," Gavin said, "the tide is going out, I have to catch Karris. I'll teach that class next time you see me. No excuses, no fight."

"You give me your word?"

"I give you my word."

The White smiled like a sated cat. "You enjoy teaching more than you admit, don't you, Gavin?"

"Gah!" Gavin said. "Goodbye!"

Before she could say anything else, he sprinted for the edge of the tower and leapt into space.

Chapter 8

Kip was staring at Isa's body. After she'd seen the soldiers kill Ram, she'd looked back at Kip. She'd been looking for safety, for protection. She'd looked at him, and she'd known he couldn't save her.

A sound and a sudden absence next to him made Kip tear his eyes away from Isa. Sanson was running toward the village. Sanson wasn't smart, but he'd always been practical. He hadn't done anything so dumb in his life. But Kip couldn't blame him. They'd never seen anyone die, either.

But there was no way the soldiers could fail to see Sanson, and now he'd die too if Kip didn't do anything.

Kip had stood around enough, doing nothing while his friends died. He didn't think. He acted. He ran—the other way.

Kip hated running. When Ram ran, it was like watching a hunting hound speed after a deer, all hard lean muscles and flowing strength. When Isa ran, it was like watching the deer flee, all easy grace and surprising speed. Kip running was like a milk cow lumbering out to pasture. Still, no one was expecting him.

He made it to Ram's body and to full speed before he heard a shout. He crashed up the bank of the river, barely slowing. Once he got his mass moving, it took a lot to stop him.

A dead tree, its trunk rising to shin level, mostly hidden in the long grasses, counted as a lot. Kip's shin cracked into wood in midstride, and he pitched forward. He skidded on his face and then flopped over like a fish. Pain blurred his vision black and red. For a second, he thought he was going to throw up, then he went lightheaded. He looked down, fully expecting bone to be jutting out of his leg. Nothing. Wimp.

Tears streamed from his eyes. His hands were bleeding again, fingernails torn. He heard the men on the bridge shouting. They'd lost him for the moment, but horsemen were coming. He wasn't fifty paces away. The grasses were only knee high. The horsemen would see him any second now, and then he'd die. Just like Isa.

He staggered to his feet, his shin afire, tears blurring the world. He hated himself. Crying because he fell down. Because he was clumsy. Because he was weak.

The horsemen gave a yell as he stood. Kip had seen King Garadul's horsemen pass through town before, but never in full battle harness. When they passed through Rekton, their harnesses were always stowed. Rekton wasn't even big enough to be worth showing off for. The two horsemen galloping toward Kip were both part of the lower cavalry. Barely able to afford their own ponies, weapons, and armor, they served only during the dry season. Amateur warriors, hoping to bring home loot and lies before the harvests. Both were dressed in mail-and-plate jackets. Lighter and cheaper than the full plate worn by the lords and King Garadul's Mirrormen, these long jackets bore six narrow rows of thin, overlapping plates down the front, with four-to-one riveted mail for the sleeves and back. Each wore a *toep*, a round helmet with a spike on top and vulture plumes sticking up beside them. A mail aventail draped down over the shoulders, protecting the neck and giving double-thickness mail over the upper chest. Neither carried a lance. Instead, they bore *vechevorals*, sickle-swords. The weapons had a long handle like an ax and a crescent-moon-shaped blade at the end, with the inward bowl-shaped side being the cutting edge. The horsemen were jostling each other for the better line, laughing, competing to see who would hack the child.

The laughter did it. It was one thing to give up and die, it was something else to let some giggling morons murder you. But there was no time. The horsemen had reached a full gallop, trampling the tender, radiant green grass the way they would trample Kip. They finally split, one switching his vechevoral to his left hand so they could cut Kip down simultaneously.

Kip lashed out, jumping, determined to at least punch one stupid grin to oblivion before he died. It was a poor jump, and far too early. But as Kip's body rose to meet the extended lances, a radiant green mass rose through him. He felt energy rush out from his body. A dozen blades of grass rose through his hand, with his punch, tearing his skin as they ripped out of him. They thickened to the width of boar spears as green light poured from him, and became blades in truth. As he threw them into the air, Kip was thrown back down to the ground. The butts of a dozen radiant jade spears thunked into the ground around him.

The horsemen barely had time to jerk on their reins before they rammed into a wall of spears. Their vechevorals went flying out of their hands as their horses were impaled, lifted off the ground by the angle of the spears, snapping those in front with the force of their impact, only to find more behind those and be impaled further. The riders were thrown from their saddles into the waiting green spears. The lighter of the two caught and was held, five feet off the ground. The heavier rider snapped off the spears and fell flat on his back beside Kip.

For a long, stupid moment, Kip had no idea what had happened. He heard a shout from the bridge: "Drafter! Green drafter!" He looked at his hands. Radiant green was slowly leaking from his bloody fingertips—the exact shade of the grass, and the spears. There were cuts at his knuckles, wrists, and under his nails, like something had ripped the skin on its way out. A scent like resin and cedar filled the air.

Kip felt woozy. Someone was cursing in a low, desperate voice. He turned.

It was the soldier, bleeding on the ground near him. Kip had no idea how the man was still alive. There were four spears through his body, but they were disappearing now, bowing under their own weight, shimmering as if on some tiny level they were boiling away into nothingness. The soldier sucked in a breath. The movement made the two spears through his chest shift. The soldier whimpered and cursed, and slowly the spears disappeared, leaving only chalky green grit to mix with his blood. Despite the mail hanging askew across the man's face, Kip could see the gleam of his dark eyes, shining with tears.

For a few moments, Kip had felt *connected*. The green was unity, growth, wildness, wholeness. But as it slipped from his fingers, the great spears bowing like wilting flowers, he felt alone once more. Scared. The smaller rider who'd been held off the ground was released with a thump and the clanging of mail as he hit the ground. The spears shimmered, dissipated, and blew apart like heavy dust.

Kip heard weeping. It was the bigger rider, still cursing. The man drew in a great breath and abruptly coughed, spitting blood all through the mail over his face. He turned over onto his stomach, and more blood poured out of his broken toep.

Kip turned away. He looked toward the bridge. The king's soldiers were gone. Kip could only guess that they had assumed that some trained drafter had shown up to rescue him. Maybe they would wait until dark to come after him, or maybe they had their own drafter back at camp. Either way, Kip had to run, fast.

He turned on wobbly legs, fingers stinging, his brain thick with grief and exhaustion, and stumbled toward the orange grove.

Chapter 9

Gavin Guile plunged past classrooms and barracks and knew that not a few people would rush to the windows to see what came next. In fact, this was the first day of drafting classes for the dims, so he was probably about to be a perfect illustration of one of the primary lessons every magister taught.

The magister would light a candle and instruct the students to comment on what was happening. This always gave the magisters plenty of opportunities to abuse the bewildered children, who would invariably say, "It's burning." "But what do you mean by this word, 'burning'?" "Uh, it's burning?" The eventual point was that every fire began on something tangible and left almost nothing tangible. When a candle burned, where did all the tallow go? Into power— power we experience as light and heat, with some residue—whether much or little depended on how efficiently the candle burned.

Magic was the converse. It began with power—light or heat—and its expression was always physical. You made luxin. You could touch it, hold it—or be held by it.

Halfway down, Gavin drafted a blue bonnet and a harness from the cold blue of the sky with some green added for flexibility. It unfurled with a pop and slowed his fall. When he was a few paces from the ground, he threw down blastwaves of sub-red that slowed him enough that he could land lightly in the street. The bonnet dissolved into blue dust and green grit and a smell like resin, chalk, and cedar. He strode toward the docks.

He found her within minutes, just arriving at the docks herself, a bag slung over her shoulder. She'd changed from her Blackguard uniform, but was still wearing pants. Karris only wore a dress once a year, for the Luxlords' Ball, where it was required. She'd also somehow dyed her hair almost black so as not to stand out so much in Tyrea.

Of course, it was impossible not to stand out with those eyes, like an emerald sky adorned with ruby stars. Karris was a green/red bichrome—almost a polychrome. It was an "almost" she'd hated all her life. Her red arc extended into the sub-red so far that she could draft fire, but she couldn't draft stable sub-red luxin. She'd failed the examination. Twice. It didn't matter that she could draft more sub-red than most sub-red drafters, or that she was the fastest drafter Gavin had ever seen. She wasn't a polychrome.

But on the other hand, polychromes were too valuable to be allowed to join the Blackguard.

"Karris!" Gavin called out, jogging to catch up with her.

She stopped and waited for him, a quizzical look on her face. "Lord Prism," she said in greeting, ever proper in public—and still, evidently, not having read the note.

He fell in step beside her. "So," he said. "Tyrea."

"The armpit of the Seven Satrapies itself," she said.

Five years, five great purposes, Gavin. He'd given himself purposes since he'd first become Prism as a focus and distraction. Seven goals for each seven-year stint. And the first was—the first had always been—to tell Karris the whole truth. A truth that might ruin everything. What I did. Why. And why I broke our betrothal fifteen years ago.

And you can rot in that blue hell forever for that, brother.

"Important mission," he said.

She shrugged. "How come the important missions never take me to Ruthgar or the Blood Forest?"

He chuckled. Ruthgar was the most civilized and prosperous

nation in the Seven Satrapies, and of course, as a green drafter, Karris would feel a strong fondness for the Verdant Plains. Alternately, the Blood Forest was where her people were from, and she hadn't walked among the redwoods since she was young. "Why don't you make it a quick trip, then? I can scull you there."

"To *Tyrea*? It's on the opposite side of the sea!"

"It's on my way to a color wight I've got to deal with." And I may not have many more chances to be near you.

She scowled. "Seems like there've been a lot of wights recently."

"It always seems like there've been a lot recently. Remember last summer, when there were six in six days, and then none for three months?"

"I guess so. What kind?" she asked. Like most drafters, she felt a special outrage when a wight had come from her own color.

"A blue."

"Ah. So I'm guessing you'll be right on your way." Karris knew about Gavin's special hatred for blue wights. "Wait, you're hunting a blue wight…in Tyrea?" she asked, turning to look at him with her haunting green eyes with red flecks.

"Outside Ru, actually." He cleared his throat.

She laughed. At thirty-two, she had the faintest lines on her face—more frown lines than smile lines, sadly, but she still had the same dimples. It just wasn't fair. After years of knowing her, a woman's beauty shouldn't be able to reach straight into a man's chest and squeeze the breath out of him. Especially not when he could never have her. "Tyrea's a thousand leagues from Ru!"

"Couple hundred at most. If you stop wasting daylight arguing with me, I might be able to get you there before nightfall."

"Gavin, that's impossible. Even for you. And even if it were possible, I couldn't ask you—"

"You didn't. I volunteered. Now tell me, would you really prefer to spend two weeks on a corvette? It's clear today, but you know how those storms come up. I heard the last time you sailed, you got so green you could draft off your own skin."

"Gavin…"

"Important mission, isn't it?" he asked.

"The White's going to kill you for this. She's got an ulcer named after you, you know. Literally."

"I'm the Prism. There's got to be some advantages. And I like sculling."

"You're impossible," she said, surrendering.

"We all have our special little talents."

Chapter 10

Kip woke to the smell of oranges and smoke. It was still hot, the evening sun slipping through the leaves to tickle his face. Somehow, he had made it to one of the orange groves before collapsing. He looked down the long, perfect rows for any soldiers before he stood up. His head still felt foggy, but the smell of smoke drove away any thoughts of himself.

As he approached the edge of the orange grove, the stench grew stronger, the air thick. Kip caught flashes of light in the distance. He emerged from the grove and saw the sun setting behind the alcaldesa's mansion, the tallest building in Rekton. As he watched, the sun went from a beautiful deep red to something darker, angry. Then Kip saw the light again—fire. Thick smoke billowed suddenly into the sky, and as if on signal, smoke billowed up from a dozen places in the town. In moments, the smoke blossomed to raging fires towering dozens of paces above the roofs.

Kip heard screams. A ruin of an old statue lay in the orange grove. The townsfolk had always called it the Broken Man. Much of it had dissolved in the centuries since its fall, but the head mostly remained. Someone had long ago carved steps into the broken neck. The head was tall enough to watch the sun rise over the orange trees. It was a favorite spot for couples. Kip clambered up the steps.

The town was on fire. Hundreds of foot soldiers surrounded the town in a vast, loose circle. As the flames drove some townsfolk from their hiding place, Kip saw King Garadul's horsemen set their lances. It was old Miss Delclara and her six sons, the quarrymen. The biggest one, Micael, was carrying her over one burly shoulder. He was shouting at the others, but Kip couldn't hear what he was saying. The brothers ran together toward the river, apparently hoping to find safety there.

They weren't going to make it.

The horsemen lowered their lances as they reached a full gallop, maybe thirty paces away from the fleeing family.

"Now!" Micael yelled. Kip could hear it from where he stood.

Five of the brothers dropped to the ground. Zalo was too slow. A lance punched through his back and sent him sprawling. Two of the others were skewered as their pursuers quickly adjusted their aim and caught the men low to the ground. Micael's pursuer dipped his lance too, but missed. He caught the ground instead, and the lance stuck.

The horseman didn't release his lance in time, and was slammed out of his saddle by the force of his own charge.

Micael ran over to the fallen soldier and drew the man's own vechevoral. With a savage chop, despite the layers of mail, he nearly cut the man's head off.

But the other horsemen had drawn rein already, and in seconds there was a forest of flashing steel blocking Micael, his brother, and his mother from Kip's view.

Kip felt like he was going to throw up. At some signal he didn't see or hear, the horsemen formed back up and charged off toward new victims in the distance. Kip was only glad that they were far enough away he couldn't recognize them.

Around the rest of the town, the foot soldiers were moving in.

Mother! Kip had been watching the town burn for several minutes, and he hadn't thought about anything. His mother was in there. He had to go to her.

How was he going to get into the town? Even if he could get past the soldiers and the fire, was his mother even still alive? The king's men had seen the direction he had run away, too. They would think that the "drafter" they'd seen earlier was the only threat in the whole area. Surely they would be watching for him. In fact, they might have men out hunting him now.

If so, perching on the highest point in the orange grove was probably not the smartest thing to do.

As if on signal, Kip heard a branch snap. It might have been a deer. Evening was coming on after all. There were lots of deer in the orange groves after—

Not thirty paces away, someone cursed.

Talking deer?

Kip dropped to his stomach. He couldn't breathe. He couldn't move. They were going to kill him. Just like they killed the Delclaras. Micael Delclara was big. Tough as old oak. And they'd slaughtered him.

Move, Kip, just move. His heart was a riot in his chest. He was shaking. He was taking tiny breaths, way too fast. Slow down, Kip. Breathe. He took a deep breath and tore his eyes away from his trembling hands.

There was a cave not far from here. Kip had found his mother there once, after she'd disappeared for three days. There'd long been rumors of smugglers' caves in the area, and whenever his mother ran out of haze and money she went looking for them. She'd finally gotten lucky about two years ago and found enough of the drug that she hadn't come home. When Kip had found her, she hadn't eaten for days. She'd nearly died. He'd overheard someone saying aloud that they wished she had, for his sake.

Reaching the ground, Kip started jogging, trying to keep the ruin between himself and the man he'd heard. He ran about as fast as Sanson would run if Sanson carried another Sanson on his back. So Kip jogged, trying to be quiet, zigzagging through the straight rows of trees. Then he heard a sound that froze his bones to the marrow: dogs barking.

Fueled by fear, Kip found a flat-out run. He ignored the burning in his legs, the stabbing in his lungs. He was already headed toward the river; the cave was on its banks. He heard a soldier shouting curses, maybe two hundred paces back, maybe less. "Keep those dogs on the lead! You want to find a drafter while it's still light out?"

It was getting darker by the minute. So that was why he was still alive. With all colors muted by darkness, drafters weren't nearly as powerful at night. And between the smoke and a bank of black clouds rolling in, the sky was darkening faster than normal. If they'd let the dogs go, they'd have run him down already. But with darkness coming on so fast, they might feel safe to let them go at any minute.

Suddenly, Kip was on the riverbank. He stepped on one pant leg and almost fell down, barely catching himself with one hand. He stopped. The cave was upstream, away from town, not two hundred paces away. He picked up two stones that fit nicely in his hands. If he had the cave to protect his sides and back, he could...What? Die slowly?

He looked at the rocks in his hands. Rocks. Against soldiers and war dogs. He was stupid. Insane. He looked at the rocks again, then threw one onto the opposite bank of the river, downstream. He threw the second rock farther. Then he grabbed two more, rubbed them against his body, and threw them as far as he could. The last one crashed through the branches of a willow tree. Lousy throw.

No time to mourn his ineptitude. Kip's scent trail already was headed upstream—the direction he did need to go. He'd just have to hope. It was a pathetic attempt, but he had nothing else. He kept moving upstream up the bank, trying to ignore the sound of the barking dogs closing in. Then he stepped into the river, careful not to let his clothes touch any dry rocks. The place where he had come to the river was a bend, so soon he was out of the line of sight.

"Let the dogs go!" the same voice shouted.

Then Kip was opposite the cave entrance. It was invisible from the river, obscured by boulders that had fallen in front of the opening. But as soon as he stepped out of the river, he'd be leaving scent for the dogs, and a visual trail of wet rocks for the soldiers. He couldn't get out of the water. Not yet. He looked up at the black clouds.

Don't just sit there. Give me some rain!

"What's the problem? What's wrong with them?" the soldier demanded.

"They're fighting dogs, sir, not trackers. I'm not even certain they're on the drafter's trail."

Kip kept pushing upstream another hundred paces where the bend in the river straightened out and a tree had fallen down the bank into the water. It wouldn't do anything for the scent trail, but it would hide the water he was dripping. He cut up the bank and then stopped. If he headed back downstream, he'd be going closer to the men hunting him. But the soldier's mention of other trails had put a small desperate hope in Kip's breast. Other trails meant maybe other fresh trails. And if it weren't for the dogs, the cave would be the safest place to spend the night.

Swallowing so his heart didn't jump out of his throat, Kip turned downstream, toward the cave. He thought he felt a cool prick on his skin. Rain? He looked up at the black clouds, but it must have been his imagination. He came to the spot overlooking the cave's entrance.

Two soldiers were standing almost directly below him. Two others were on the opposite bank. There was one war dog on each side. Either dog's head would have come up to Kip's shoulder, easily. They both wore studded leather coats like horse armor without the saddle. Kip dropped to the ground.

"Sir, if I may?" one of the men said. Apparently getting permission, the soldier said, "The drafter came straight to the river, then veered sharply upstream before going into the water? He knows we're following him. I think he doubled back and went downstream."

"With us so close behind?" the commander asked.

"He must have heard the dogs."

Which made Kip think of something else: dogs can smell scents on the wind too. Not just on the ground. Kip's throat tightened. He hadn't even thought about the wind. It was blowing from the southwest. His path had taken him east and then north when the river turned—the perfect direction. If he'd gone downstream, toward town, the dogs would have smelled him immediately. If the commander thought about it, he'd surely realize that too.

"Rain's coming. We might only have one shot at this." The commander paused. "Let's make it fast." He whistled and gestured for the men on the other side of the river to head downstream. They took off at a jog.

Kip's heart started beating again. He slipped down the bank beside two great boulders. There was a narrow space between the two. It looked like it went in for about four paces and then stopped, but Kip knew that it turned sharply. He never would have discovered it the first time if it hadn't been for the pungent, sickly sweet odor of haze floating out. Orholam knew how his mother had ever found it.

Now, even knowing it was there, Kip almost didn't have the courage to push between those rocks. There was something wrong, though. It wasn't as dark as it should be. It was fully night outside and Kip was blocking the entrance, so someone was already inside, and they had a lantern.

Kip froze again until he heard the sound of the war dogs change pitch. They'd found the rocks he'd thrown across the river. That meant it was only a matter of time until they discovered his fraud. The darkness and tightness were suffocating. He had to move, one way or the other.

He pushed around the corner and into the open space of the smuggler's cave. There were two figures sitting in the wan light of a lantern: Sanson and Kip's mother. Both were covered in blood.

Chapter 11

Kip couldn't help but cry out. His mother was seated against the wall of the cave, her once-blue dress dyed black and red with blood dried and fresh. Lina's dark hair was matted, darker than normal, stringy with blood. The right side of her face was pristine, perfect. All the blood was coming from the left side of her head, traveling down her hair like a wick, blooming on her dress. Sanson sat next to her, his eyes closed, head back, clothes almost as gory.

At Kip's cry, his mother's eyes fluttered. There was a huge *dent* in the side of her head. Orholam be merciful, her skull was shattered. She stared in his direction for several moments before she found him. Her eyes were a horror to behold, the pupil of her left eye was dilated, the right a tight pinprick. And the whites of both were completely bloodshot. "Kip," she said. "Never thought I'd be so happy to see you."

"Love you too, mother," he said, trying to keep his tone light.

"My fault," she said. Her eyes fluttered and closed.

Kip's heart seized. Was she dead? Before today, he'd never seen anyone die. Orholam, this was his mother! He looked at Sanson, who looked healthy, despite all the blood on his clothes. "I tried, Kip. The alcaldesa wouldn't listen. I told her—"

"Even his own family didn't believe him," Kip's mother said, her eyes still closed. "Even when the soldiers rode down his mother and split his brother open, Adan Marta stood there, arguing how our satrap wouldn't possibly do such a thing to his own people. Only Sanson ran away. Who would've thought he was the smart one in that family?"

"Mother! Enough!" Kip's voice came out whiny, childish.

"You came back, though, didn't you, Sanson? Tried to save me, unlike my own son. Too bad he didn't try to help me like you tried to help your family, or I might still have a chance."

Her words touched some deep well of rage. Potent, but uncontrollable. He pushed it down, pushed the tears back. "Mother. Stop. You're dying."

"Sanson says you're a drafter now. Funny," she said bitterly. "All your life you're a disappointment, and you learn to draft today. Too late for any of us." With effort, she took a deep breath, then opened her eyes and fixed her gaze on Kip, taking a little while to focus. "Kill him, Kip. Kill the bastard." She lifted a narrow, filigreed rosewood jewelry case as long as Kip's forearm from the floor of the cave beside her. Kip had never seen it before.

Kip took the case and opened it. There was a dagger inside, double-edged, of an odd material, starkly white like ivory, with a thread of black winding down the center to the point, and no other adornment save for seven diamonds embedded in the blade itself. It was the most beautiful thing Kip had ever seen, and he didn't care. He had no idea what the blade was worth, but the case it had come in alone would have paid for a month of his mother's binges. "Mother, what is this?"

"And I thought Sanson was slow," she said, hard, sneering, dying, afraid. "Put it in his rotten heart. Make that bastard suffer. Make him pay for this."

"Mother, what are you saying?" Kip asked, despairing. Me, kill King Garadul?

She laughed, and the motion made a fresh wash of blood spill down her head. "You're a stupid, stupid boy, Kip. But maybe a dull sword can go where a sharp one wouldn't be allowed." Her head bobbed. Her breathing was getting labored. Her head drooped to her chest, and Kip thought she was dead, but her eyes opened once more, only one focusing, locking Kip in her glare. Her fingernails dug into his forearm painfully. "You go, go train to be a drafter, go to the..." She seemed to be searching for the word "Chromeria," but couldn't find it. She noticed, looked furious, afraid. It was evidence she really was dying. "You learn what you need, but don't you forget me. Don't you forget this. Don't listen to him, you hear me? He's a liar. You will not fail me in this, Kip. You learn, and then you kill him, you understand?"

"Yes, mother." She was talking like she knew King Garadul. How could she have known him?

"Kip, if you ever loved me, avenge me. Swear it by your worthless soul, Kip. Swear it, or I swear to Orholam I'll haunt you. I won't... let..." She lost her train of thought.

Kip looked over at Sanson, who stared back silently, horrified. Kip's mother's fingernails dug in deeper, and her seeing eye seemed almost aflame, demanding his attention, his promise. He said, "I swear to avenge you, mother, by my very soul."

Something like peace stole over her features, softening the hard planes. Then she laughed quietly, satisfied, somehow cruel—until her laughter stopped. Her hand dropped from Kip's forearm, leaving bloody tracks. "I won't let you down, mother, I'll go right—"

She's dead.

Kip stared at her woodenly, inexplicably numb. He closed her awful, bloodshot eyes. "Are you hurt?" Kip asked.

"Huh?" Sanson asked. "Me?"

Kip stared at him, "No, genius, I'm talking to the dead person." It was cruel, thoughtless.

Sanson's eyes welled up with tears. "I'm sorry, Kip. I tried to get her out. I was too late." He was right on the verge of breaking down. Kip was an ass.

"No, Sanson. No, I'm sorry. Don't talk like that. It's not your fault. Listen to me. We need to act right now, not think. We're in danger. Are you hurt?"

Sanson's eyes cleared and his chin lifted. He met Kip's gaze. "No, this blood is all—no, I'm fine."

"Then we need to go right now, while it's dark and raining. They've got dogs. They can track us. It's our only chance."

"But Kip, where are we going to go?" Odd. Just like that, Kip was the leader. Was it that he'd found some new well of strength, or was Sanson just that weak? No, don't even think like that, Kip. He trusts you. Can't that be enough?

What if I'm not worthy of trust?

"I'm going to be a drafter," Kip said. "I guess. So we need to get to the sea. We should be able to find a ship in Garriston that's going to the Chromeria."

Sanson's eyes widened, obviously thinking about what Kip's mother had sworn him to, but he said nothing but, "How do we get to Garriston?"

"We float the river first." Kip realized then that he'd lost the purse Master Danavis had given him. He didn't even know when. So even if they made it down the river, they wouldn't be able to pay for the trip to the Chromeria.

"Kip, the soldiers were in a big circle around the whole town. If they're still like that, we'll have to cross through their line twice. And the town's still on fire. The river could be blocked."

Sanson was right, and for some reason that made Kip suddenly furious. He stopped himself. This wasn't Sanson's fault. Kip's eyes felt hot. It was so hopeless. He blinked rapidly. "I know it's stupid, Sanson." He couldn't look his friend in the eyes. "But I don't have any other ideas. Do you?"

Sanson paused for a long moment. "I saw some dead wood on the bank that might work," he said finally, and Kip knew it was his way of telling Kip he trusted him.

"Then let's go," Kip said.

"Kip, do you want to...I don't know, say goodbye?" Sanson nodded in the direction of Kip's mother.

Kip swallowed, holding the knife-case in a white-knuckled grip. And say what? I'm sorry I was a failure, a disappointment? That I loved you, even if you never loved me? "No," he said. "Let's go."

Chapter 12

The boys crept out of the cave. Kip went first. Apparently that was the price of becoming the leader. Kip had been under these same stars on the river dozens of times, but tonight there was hunger in the cool air. The wind had changed direction, and now the smells of the light, misting rain opening the earth mingled with woodsmoke and the faint, fresh fragrance of the oranges ripening on the trees. Always before, that scent had cheered Kip. Tonight it was faint, ephemeral, as fragile as Kip's chances.

They made it to the river's edge without seeing any soldiers. They'd floated the river before, all four of them grabbing a few planks of wood for extra buoyancy, but mostly just lying back and letting the current carry them. But they'd always waited until late fall, when the river was lower. Even then, they'd all sported dozens of scrapes and bruises from the rocks they couldn't avoid. It was the middle of summer now, and though the river was lower than in the spring, it was still high and swift. That meant they would be able to float over rocks that would scrape them in the fall, but the rocks they couldn't avoid they would hit much faster.

Sanson found the sticks he'd seen before while Kip waited anxiously, trying to peer downriver for any hint of the soldiers. The clouds over the village were glowing orange, lit by the fires below them. Sanson returned with a few branches, not enough for both of them. The boys looked at each other. "You take them," Kip whispered. "I float better than you."

"What do we do if they see us?" Sanson asked.

Kip's nerve almost failed him as he thought about it. What could they do? Run away? Swim away? Even if they made it to the banks of the river, where could they go? The town was on fire and there were only fields around town. Men on horses with dogs helping them would find Kip and Sanson in no time.

"Play dead," Kip said. After all, we shouldn't be the only bodies in the water. Actually that wasn't true; this far upstream, they *should* be the only bodies in the water. If any of the soldiers realized that, the boys would quickly become real corpses.

The water was cold even this far from the mountains, but it wasn't freezing. Kip sat down in it, and the current began pulling him toward town. Sanson followed. They were pulled around the first bend and approaching the spot where Kip had first come to the river when he saw the flaw in his plan.

To play dead meant that in the sections of river that were most dangerous, the places where he and Sanson would most want to see or listen to find out if they'd been discovered, they'd have to keep their ears submerged and their eyes fixed on the clouds above. If they were discovered, Kip's plan guaranteed that they wouldn't know it until too late.

They should get out of the water. He couldn't do this. Kip glanced back. Sanson was already lying back, floating on his back, ears covered, limbs loose. He'd been pulled over to the other side of the river, and the current had already brought his lighter body even with Kip. Kip's heart hammered. If he got out now, Sanson wouldn't know it. Kip wouldn't be able to grab his friend without making so much noise that it would rouse anyone within hundreds of paces.

A voice spoke out of the gloom on the riverbank. "Yes, Your Majesty. We think the drafter climbed up into that tree. The dogs tracked him that far and lost him."

Kip saw the torch first. Someone was approaching the bank of the river, not five paces downstream. His first thought—to run like hell—would get him killed. He swept his arms once, twice, paddling downstream, then he lay back. The cold water closed over his ears, muffling all sound except the desperate thumping of his pulse.

The bank here was raised a pace and a half, high enough that even lying back, Kip could see the man. Kip wasn't two paces away, and the torch the man held illuminated an imperious face in its flickering orange light. Even warmed in torchlight, there was something fundamentally cold about that face, an unpleasant smirk hiding in the corner of that mouth. The king—for Kip had no doubt, even in half a second of seeing him, that this man was King Garadul—was not yet out of his twenties but already half bald, with the rest of his hair combed to his shoulders. He had a prominent nose over a tight, immaculate beard and thick black brows. The king stared upstream, a vein on his forehead visible even in the torchlight, gazing at the opposite bank where Kip had crossed. His angry question was barely more than a murmur through the water closed around Kip's ears.

Then the king turned just as Kip was starting to get downstream of him. And he turned left, toward Kip. Kip didn't move a muscle, but it wasn't because he was being smart. He felt warmth blooming in the cold water between his legs.

It was only the torch directly between the king and Kip that saved the boys. His eyes went right over them, but blinded by that light in the darkness, he saw nothing. He turned, swore something, and disappeared.

Kip floated down the river, head back, almost disbelieving that he was alive. The water was cold around him, the stars were pinpricks in Orholam's mantle above. They were more beautiful than he'd ever realized. Each star had its own color, its own hue; brilliant rubies, startling sapphires, and even here and there an elusive emerald. For perhaps twenty paces, Kip floated in utter peace, enrapt by the beauty.

Then he hit a rock. It struck his foot first and spun him around so he was floating sideways. Then another rock, mostly submerged, caught his shirt and flipped him facedown in the water. He gasped and flailed, freezing with fear as his head came clear of the water and he realized how loud he'd been.

A little way down the river, Sanson had pulled his head out of the water and was staring at Kip with horror. How could Kip make so much noise? Kip looked away, ashamed. They floated in silence for a long minute, staring into the darkness, waiting to see if any soldiers would appear. They did their best to avoid the rocks, legs pointed downstream, hands paddling in little circles to keep themselves afloat. But no one came.

They floated as close together as they could, though Kip knew it was unwise. Two bodies floating separately might not be remarkable, but two floating side by side? Still, he didn't move away. Silence settled over the boys as they came closer and closer to the bridge where their friends had died that morning. It seemed so long ago now.

And then Kip saw her, lying on the riverbank. The soldiers who'd murdered Isa had pulled their arrows out of her body. But aside from turning her over, they hadn't moved her corpse. She lay on her back, eyes open, head turned left toward Kip, dark hair waving in the river. One arm was raised over her head, not drifting in the current but instead stiff as a felled tree. The underside of her arm and even her face was a horrific dark purple with pooled blood.

Kip put his feet down on the slick rocks of the riverbed to go to her. He was about to stand when some sixth sense stopped him. He hesitated and, still lying in the water, looked around as much as he could.

There! Standing on the bridge, with only his head visible, the soldier kept watch. So they weren't stupid. They'd figured that whoever this *drafter* was that they'd run into earlier, he'd have the decency to come back and bury his friends.

The current was carrying Kip downstream. No decision *was* a decision.

But what could he do? Face soldiers? If there was one, there might be ten, and if ten, maybe a hundred. Kip was no fighter, he was a child. He was fat, weak. *One* man would be one man too many.

Kip turned away from Isa's corpse and lay back in the water once more. He didn't want to remember her like this anyway. A knot formed in his throat, so hard and so tight it threatened to strangle him. Only his fear of the soldier above kept him from crying as he floated under Green Bridge.

He didn't even think of the dagger in its ornate case strapped to his back until they were far downstream. He could've tried; he could've at least gotten out of the water and taken a look. Isa deserved more.

Soon they were drifting into town, where the river flowed in a narrower, deeper channel, lined on each side with great rocks and crossed at intervals by sturdy wood bridges.

Parts of the town were still on fire, though Kip didn't know whether that was because they were built of materials that were less flammable or because the fire had spread more slowly through some areas and was only reaching some buildings now. Soon they encountered their first corpse. A horse. Still harnessed to a wagon full of late-season oranges, it had been trapped in a section of the town that was now smoldering. Maddened by the fire, the mare had leapt into the river. The wagon had followed and either crushed or drowned it, spilling oranges everywhere.

Kip thought it might be the Sendina family's horse and wagon. Sanson, never overly sentimental, grabbed a few oranges from the wreckage of the wagon and stuffed them in his pockets.

Sanson was probably right. Kip hadn't eaten all day, not that he'd noticed until now, but he was starving. Despite feeling like he might throw up, he reached over the half-submerged horse and grabbed a few oranges too.

They came closer to the water market, and it kept getting hotter. Kip heard strange screams. There were fires still burning ahead. The water market was a small, circular lake that was dredged regularly to keep a uniform depth. It was said that once both river and town had been much larger. The river, supposedly, had been navigable from below the falls all the way to the Cerulean Sea, and then from Rekton all the way to the mountains, bringing traders from all of the Seven Satrapies, hungry for Tyrea's famous oranges and other citrus fruits. Now, only the smallest flat-bottomed boats could make the trip downstream and the number of robbers happy to relieve traders of anything valuable convinced most farmers to send their oranges on the slower, heavily armed, and much less profitable caravans. Even the smallest, hardest, and thickest-skinned oranges sent by caravans over land would rot long before they could reach the distant courts where nobles and satraps would pay a fortune for such a delicacy. So almost every year some young farmer tried the river, and a few times they got through, all the way to Garriston, and came home with a fortune—if they managed to avoid the robbers again on the way back.

But for the most part, the trade for which the water market had been built was long dead. The townsfolk kept it for pride and for their own use. All the roads were already built around the water market, all their storehouses surrounded, so they maintained the barges and floated around the circle every market day according to rules and an etiquette that no outsider could hope to understand. In the middle of the water market was an island, connected by a drawbridge to the north shore.

As they came fully in sight of the island, Kip saw where the screams had come from. The drawbridge was down, and the island was filled with hundreds of animals trapped by the fires closing in around them. Even the drawbridge, straining with the weight of dozens of horses, sheep, pigs, and a grotesque carpet of rats, was smoking at one end. Eyes rolling in fear, the brick-maker's draft horse looked like it was on the verge of bolting, though where it would go was impossible to say. The animals filled the island to overflowing; they were packed shoulder to flank over the entire little circle and the bridge.

Kip was so absorbed in the spectacle that he began floating right into the middle of the river between the docks and the island.

"Master, it's so hot," a young voice said behind and above Kip.

Kip thrashed and turned. On the raised bank of the market circle stood a young man a little older than Kip. The young man wore only a red loincloth. His curly black hair and bare chest glistened with sweat. He was looking over his shoulder, apparently to a man behind him. Kip could see nothing of that man, but he didn't wait. Kip thought they must have heard him when he thrashed, but apparently the roar of the fires drowned out the sound.

Motioning to Sanson, Kip swam toward the wall. Sanson followed. The young man's master said something, but it was lost in the noise. Kip and Sanson clung to the wall with their bodies pressed as close to it as they could, looking up.

"Watch this," they heard the man say. A whirling lasso of fire spun into view over their heads and then flicked forward. It wrapped around one post of the drawbridge and stuck there. The rest of the rope flared out of existence, but that length stayed, smoldering, little wisps of flame escaping against the wood, splinters turning black and curling back, smoking.

Kip was at once horrified and captivated. In all the years he'd spent helping Master Danavis, the drafter had never done anything like this.

"Now you try," the man said.

For a moment, nothing happened. Kip looked over at Sanson. Both of them were stuck to the wall, arms spread wide to get good holds on the stone so they wouldn't have to tread water. Kip had the sudden feeling that they'd been set up. The drafter knew they were here; he'd just told his apprentice that so Kip and Sanson would stay in place. They were going around. He should swim, right now, as fast as he could.

He tried to breathe deeply, swallowing on his fear. Sanson returned his gaze, his own eyes worried, but not understanding what Kip was thinking.

Then a wheel of flame spun out above them. The animals on the bridge and the island shrieked in a hundred different ways. The wheel drew back and unraveled, becoming a whip, somewhat like what the master drafter had sent out just a minute before—but much, much larger. This was the youth's work?

The whip snapped out, but not at the post of the drawbridge. Instead, it cracked audibly as it snapped on the flank of the brick-maker's draft horse. Crazed with pain and fear, the old beast surged forward. Kip heard the boy laughing as the horse rammed directly into the rail of the drawbridge. The rail cracked and broke open. Several pigs and thin-coated sheep fell into the water.

The draft horse tried to stop, suddenly aware of the drop, but its hooves scraped wood for only a moment before it plunged headfirst into the water. Water splashed all the way over to Kip and Sanson.

"What was that?! Was that what I told you to do?" the master drafter demanded.

Quickly, Kip looked from the animals in the water to the bridge. The bridge post was just starting to catch fire in earnest now. Once it climbed up to the drawbridge, the animals would go crazy, just as the horse had. Kip didn't think the drawbridge itself would catch fire quickly, but he couldn't be sure.

If he and Sanson wanted to get out of the water market and out of the burning town, the fastest way was to go under the straining bridge in front of them and directly over the waterfall to head downriver. The other way would be to go the long way around the circular lake, exposed to the eyes of the drafter and his apprentice above them the whole time. Either way they went, at some point they would be visible.

Of the animals that had fallen into the water, the big horse was the only good swimmer. It was kicking toward the other side of the water market, away from the boy and the fire. The sheep were screaming, little legs churning frantically. The pigs were squealing, lunging at each other, biting.

There was a meaty slap and a cry of pain from above the boys.

"You never go beyond my orders, Zymun! Do you understand?!"

The drafter kept yelling, but Kip stopped listening. The drafters were distracted. It was now or never. Kip drew a few quick breaths, nodded at Sanson—who looked bewildered—and launched off the wall, swimming toward the drawbridge.

Chapter 13

Gavin drafted a blue platform, thin, barely visible against the water it floated on.

"You did that just to make me nervous, didn't you?" Karris asked.

Gavin grinned and stepped onto the scull. He extended a hand to Karris, giving her a little bow. She ignored his hand and hopped aboard.

He pulled up the keel as she landed, so the scull zipped out from under her feet. She yelped—and he caught her with a cushion of softer green luxin that quickly morphed into a seat. He lifted the seat and placed it on the front of the scull, then bound both of their packs to the scull near his feet.

"Gavin, I am not going to sit while you—" She tried to stand, and he threw the scull forward. With nothing to hold on to, she tumbled back into the chair with another yelp. Gavin laughed. Karris was one of the best warriors the Chromeria had—and she still squeaked when surprised.

She shot a look back at him, peeved and amused at once.

"I thought you'd like being swept off your feet," he said.

"You had your chance for that," she shot back.

His grin dropped into the waves like so many other treasures and disappeared.

Karris looked dismayed. "Gavin, I…"

"No, I deserved that. Please, go ahead and stand."

Sixteen years. You'd think we'd have both have moved on. Not that we haven't both tried.

"Thank you," she said, but her voice was contrite. She stood up, feet wide, knees slightly bent.

The scull was propelled by banks of little oars jutting out from each side. Through generations of study, green and blue drafters had figured out how to use gears and wheels and chains to drive the oars, each drafter customizing his craft to fit his own body so that he could propel it with whatever combination of arm and leg movements he preferred, and making whatever tweaks he thought made it more efficient. Because the craft had so little friction with the water, an athletic drafter could go the speed of a sprinting man for an hour.

That was fast. Very fast. But it wasn't nearly as fast as Gavin had promised. Still, he leaned fully forward, his body suspended in a web of luxin, arms and legs pumping. He elongated and narrowed the scull so it became a dagger knifing over the water's face. They attained full speed as they left the harbor.

Gavin was sweating, but it was a good, clean feeling. The wind blew in his face, carrying away any words either he or Karris might have said, and without words, there was simply her presence, the sight of her dark hair whipping in the sea wind, the strong lines of her face, skin glowing in the morning light, chin lifted, neck extended, enjoying the freedom as much as he was.

Karris was facing forward, so she didn't see him draft the luxin scoops into the water. Gavin had always thought there had to be a better way. After all, a drafter could throw a fireball at any speed, it was only dependent on will—if he threw something too big or too fast, of course, he might hurt himself from absorbing the kick—but sculls didn't take advantage of will. They were instead perfect rowing watercraft that used muscle power more efficiently than any other machine. Gavin wanted to do better; he wanted to use magic the way a sail used wind.

That had only led to ripping off a mast or two. But he refused to give up. It had been one of his seven goals when he'd still had seven years left to live: learn to travel faster than anyone thinks is possible.

The solution had come to him from when he was a child, shooting seeds through a reed at his brothers. Air, trapped between a plug and the walls of the reed, could shoot a seed with much greater force than if you'd simply tried to throw it with your hand. After a lot of trial and error, he'd put the whole reed in the water, opening it at both ends so it traveled fully underwater. He attached another reed diagonally and shot plugs of magic down into the water and then out the back of the reeds.

He let the oars drop and the whole mechanism fell away with barely a splash, luxin dissolving even as it hit the waves. He put his hands to the reeds.

At the first thump, Karris jerked. She squatted deeper to lower her center of gravity and her hand went instinctively to her ataghan—except that it was in her pack. Then the scull leapt forward. The first great thumps shook everything as Gavin strained to get up to speed, his muscles knotting with effort. But within moments, the scull leveled off, and the tension on Gavin's arms and shoulders eased somewhat. The plugs hit the water at a steady *whup-whup-whup*. The modified scull—what he called his skimmer—barely kissed the waves.

There was still physical effort. Gavin was throwing a lot of force into the water, and his arms and shoulders were basically lifting all of his own weight plus Karris's. But magic could be drafted from the whole body, so it was like carrying a heavy pack with the straps distributing the weight perfectly—strenuous, but not crushing. Still, in the last year of doing this every day, his shoulders and arms had gotten bigger than in his entire life.

Karris turned. Her mouth literally hung open. She stared at the entire contraption, the scoops of blue luxin given flexibility throughout with green, with the super-flexible, sticky red where the plugs shot into the reeds so they wouldn't be shattered. She straightened slowly, leaning into the wind, her back against Gavin so that she wasn't creating another windbreak.

He felt her shaking, and realized she was laughing with delight, though he could barely hear it. The wind blew away the smell of her hair too, but for a moment he imagined he could smell it again. It made him ache.

"Watch this," he shouted. In the distance, an island appeared. He leaned and the skimmer veered hard toward it. Indeed, he'd quickly learned that the skimmer was capable of maneuvering much faster than he could. The real limit was how quickly he could change direction without tearing himself in half. He leaned right and then left, carving beautiful turns on the calm seas. He angled the reeds down and the skimmer popped over one of the bigger waves and suddenly they were airborne.

For more than a hundred paces, they flew, silent except for the sound of the wind, right over the little island. Then they landed like a skipping stone and were off once more.

In the speed and wind and the closeness of Karris, Gavin finally felt free once more. Despite the warmth of the day, the wind was cold, and if Karris didn't quite burrow into him, she did let her body fully relax against his, grateful for his warmth. If she got too cold, he knew, she would draft sub-red, but she was saving her strength. She didn't know what waited for her in Tyrea.

That he did—at least in part—lent sweetness to the moment. She would read the White's letter and learn that he'd fathered a child while they were betrothed. Though she now professed no interest in his love life, it had been one of the questions she'd asked when he broke it off: Is there another woman? No. Have there ever been any other women while we've been betrothed? No, I swear it.

Karris wouldn't forgive him this time. It had taken years for her to forgive him for breaking their betrothal and refusing to answer why. But this, this was betrayal.

Orholam, how he'd miss her.

He avoided the shipping lanes and stayed far from shore. Around noon, he saw clouds ahead. It didn't look like a storm, so he guessed that it was the island satrapy of Ilyta. It was a country of many ports and more pirates. The central government had collapsed decades ago, and now parts of it were ruled by whatever pirate lord was powerful at the moment. Most of the Seven Satrapies paid tribute to one or another of the pirate lords, enriching them and enabling them to do more piracy.

Gavin had no fear of them, but he didn't want to be seen either.

While it might be good for the pirates to have another reason to fear the Chromeria, he'd prefer to keep his little invention secret for as long as possible. Besides, he was only using Ilyta as a landmark. It was a lot of trouble to use an astrolabe, and in the time it took him to calculate their position he could just skim around until he found it. Garriston was at the mouth of a large river. It was the busiest port in Tyrea, but that wasn't saying much. He turned south.

Karris said something to him, but he couldn't hear her, so he slowed the skimmer.

"Can I try too?" she asked.

"I thought you were saving your strength."

"You can't have all the fun." Because he was behind her, he couldn't see her whole smile, but he saw one dimple and one raised eyebrow.

He widened the skimmer's hull so they could stand side by side, and handed over the starboard reed. Karris always preferred to draft from her right hand.

At first they were out of synch, and the craft shuddered and strained as they threw the plugs at different speeds and times. He looked over at her, but before he could say anything she took his right hand in her left. She squeezed a tempo to keep him on the beat as she used to do when they danced.

The memory hit him as if the skimmer had clipped a reef and smashed him into the sea: Karris, fifteen years old, before the war, at the yearly Luxlords' Ball on top of the Chromeria. Her light blonde hair was long and straight and as fine and shiny as her green silk dress. Their fathers were in discussion on which of the Guile brothers she would marry. Gavin, the elder brother and likely to become the next Prism, was of course the richer prize. His father, Andross Guile, didn't care about Karris's beauty.

"You want a beautiful woman? That's what mistresses are for." But though he didn't care for the boys' preferences—alliances were to be bought as cheaply as possible, and the marriage of his firstborn was the most valuable stone he had to play—Andross Guile was well aware that other families weren't always so calculating. Some fathers were loath to marry their daughters to men they didn't care for.

Andross Guile had ordered the younger Dazen to seduce Karris.

"There's a servant's room one floor down. Here's the key. Twenty minutes after you leave with her, I'll make some pretext for her father and I to speak privately, and we'll come down. I expect to catch you in the act. I'll be surprised, dismayed, furious. I'll most likely strike you. But what is one to do? The passions of youth and so forth. You understand?"

Both brothers did. Luxlord Rissum White Oak was reputed to be hot-tempered. Andross Guile would strike Dazen first and get himself between the two so White Oak didn't try to kill Dazen. But the real point was that if Karris were caught making love with Dazen, her father would have no choice. So as not to shame the White Oaks, Karris would quickly be married to Dazen. The families would be allied, and Andross Guile would still have his more valuable elder son to play.

"Gavin, I expect you to be pleasant but not encouraging with the girl. If your brother fails the family in this, you *will* have to marry her."

"Yes, sir."

But then the ball had begun. Gavin had taken the first dance with Karris and the worst possible thing had happened. Holding her petite form against him, her hand in his squeezing out the beat, and looking into her jade green eyes—at the time, she had had only the tiniest flecks of red in her irises—Gavin had been enchanted. By the time Dazen came to dance with her, Gavin was in love. Or lust anyway.

I've been betraying Karris since before we even met.

Karris squeezed his hand harder than she had been. He looked over. Her eyes held a question. He must have tensed, and Karris had caught it. She'd always been deeply physical. She hugged or brushed or touched those she loved all the time. Dancing was as natural to her as walking. She didn't touch Gavin often anymore.

He gave a dismissive smile and shook his head. It's nothing.

Karris opened her mouth to speak, paused. "Make the tubes bigger!" she shouted, and laughed, the barest edge on it. A forced laugh.

So she remembered the dance, squeezing out the beat into his hand. Of course she did. But she was letting it go, and he was grateful for it. He widened the reeds as far as they could handle, and soon they were going faster than he'd ever gone by himself. He hadn't meant to show her this next trick, but he couldn't help himself. He knew it would bring her real joy. And what fun is it being a genius if no one appreciates you?

He released Karris's hand. This part was the most dangerous. At this speed, running into something deliberately was stupid. And yet...

"Brace yourself!" he shouted. Throwing his right fist forward, Gavin threw green luxin out as far in front of them as he could. It landed on the waves with a splash. A moment later, the skimmer hit the green luxin ramp.

In an instant, they were airborne. Flying, twenty paces above the waves.

Gavin released the whole reed apparatus and drafted. The luxin of the platform shot up his and Karris's backs and then shot out from his arms. They were falling now, fifteen paces from the waves, and even if hitting them at this speed meant they would skip rather than just splash, they were still falling twenty paces. The luxin spun out in every color, trying to form despite the gale-force wind.

Ten paces to the waves. Five. At this speed, hitting the water would be like hitting granite.

Then the luxin hardened in its shape, which was as much like a condor's wings as Gavin had been able to manage. The wings caught the air, and Karris and Gavin shot into the sky.

The first time Gavin had attempted it, he'd tried to hold one wing in each hand. He'd learned then why birds have hollow bones and weigh almost nothing. The lift had nearly torn his arms off. He'd gone home wet, bruised, and angry, with most of the muscles in his arms and chest torn. By making the condor all one piece instead, he'd taken away the need for muscle at all. The whole thing flew on the strength and flexibility of the luxin, speed, and wind.

Of course, it didn't really fly. It glided. He'd tried to use the reeds, but it hadn't worked so far. For the time being, the condor had a limited range.

Karris wasn't complaining. She was wide-eyed. "Gavin! Orholam, Gavin, we're flying!" She laughed, carefree. He'd always loved that about her. Her laughter was freedom for both of them. She'd forgotten about the dance. That made it worth it.

"Get in the middle," he said. He didn't have to shout. They were completely inside the body of the condor. There was no wind. "I'm not very good at turning; mostly I lean one way or the other." Indeed, because he was heavier, they were already turning toward his side. Together, they leaned toward her side until the condor straightened.

"The White doesn't know about this, does she?" Karris asked.

"Only you," he said. "Besides..."

"No one else could do the drafting required," Karris finished for him.

"Galib and Tarkian are probably the only polychromes who could handle all the colors necessary, and neither of them is fast enough. If I can make it easy enough for other drafters, I might tell her."

"Might?"

"I've been thinking about the ways this could be used. In war, mostly. The Seven Satrapies already fight and scheme over the few polychromes there are. This would make it a hundred times worse."

"Is that Garriston?" she said abruptly, looking north and west. "Already?"

"The real question is whether you want to crash onto land or into the water," Gavin said.

"Crash?"

"I'm not very good at landing yet, and with so much extra weight—"

"Excuse me?" Karris said.

"What? I haven't tried flying with a manatee aboard either, I'm just—"

"You did not just compare me to a sea cow." Her expression made ice look warm.

"No! It's just that all the extra weight..." What is it you're supposed to do when you're in a hole? Oh. "Um." He cleared his throat.

She grinned suddenly, dimples flashing. "After all this time, Gavin, I still get you." She laughed.

He laughed ruefully, but the pain went deep. And I still don't get you. Maybe she would have been happy with Dazen.

Chapter 14

It felt like years before Kip reached the bridge post. He paused, looking back toward the drafters as Sanson caught up with him. The master was still striking his apprentice, who'd curled into a ball, screaming. They definitely hadn't seen Kip or Sanson, but they were also turned toward them, and if they looked up, the bridge post wasn't big enough to hide both boys.

The bridge groaned, and Kip looked up. The opposite post, on the island side, was aflame, and the animals were pushing away from it, but too scared to go back into town, which was also burning. That pushed them against the rail directly above the boys—and against the gap in the rail the horse had made—mere paces to their left.

Half a dozen rats splashed into the water, kicked by the other animals. Each of them began swimming in a different direction, including several right at the boys.

Kip's stomach knotted in visceral fear. It was ridiculous that a rat should freeze him while two drafters didn't—but he hated rats. Hated hated hated them. Sanson yanked on his sleeve, pulling him away. Kip launched off the post, splashing awkwardly. He turned back, making sure none of the rats latched onto his clothes. His eyes flicked up to the apprentice drafter Zymun, the boy's head tucked between his arms as his master beat him. But then Zymun stiffened.

Zymun shouted something and stood, and his master stopped hitting him. Kip got his first good look at the boy. He couldn't have been more than a year older than Kip, with unruly black hair, dark eyes, and a wide, fleshy mouth curved into a triumphant grin. Even in the moment Kip saw him, Zymun's and his master's skin were filling with red, the swirls like smoke being inhaled, but then compacted until it filled their bodies.

Kip turned and swam as hard as he could. There was one metal screen in front of the waterfall to keep boats or swimmers from going over, and a dock and stairs next to it. Sanson was already to the screen, more than ten paces ahead of Kip.

After a few more hard strokes, Kip glanced back. The bridge and the jostling animals blocked much of his view of the two drafters, but as he looked, he saw the master run a few quick steps forward. He jumped, spread his arms wide, and slapped his hands together. A shimmering ball of red luxin formed between his hands, and as they slapped together it rocketed forward. The drafter was blasted back by the force of what he'd thrown, but still landed on his feet.

The ball caught fire in midair, right before it plowed through the animals on the bridge. Sheep, horses, and pigs exploded in every direction, body parts flying. Wild shrieks filled the air, sounding almost human. The burning missile tore off the railing and blasted a chunk out of the middle of the bridge itself, and then it streaked over Kip's head with a fiery roar and smashed the wood stairs above the dock. Kip didn't think the drafter had missed, and for a moment he thought the man was trying to trap them.

The drawbridge cracked, and all the animals on it stumbled toward the sagging middle.

Now Zymun ran forward. He slapped red hand to red hand, but this time Kip couldn't even see the ball of luxin—because it wasn't aimed at him. One moment, Zymun was falling back, completely bowled over from the force of what he had thrown, and the next, the entire wood bridge exploded.

Flames and blood and spinning, detached body parts leapt into the sky. One great flaming section of the bridge streaked toward Kip, tumbling and filling his vision. It hit the water beside him with a great hissing splash.

When Kip could see again, he was pressed against the metal screen in front of the waterfall, surrounded by scraps and shards of wood, some sections still burning, one great section of the bridge slowly sinking, and hundreds of rats, some burnt to charcoal, others wounded, others simply wet, but all the living desperate to get out of the water. The larger animals hadn't been blown so far by the explosion, but they were coming, thrashing, kicking, splashing, biting each other in their fear and pain.

"Kip! Climb over! We've almost made it!" Sanson shouted. He was already on the other side of the metal screen.

"Don't move!" the older drafter shouted. His skin was already filling with red swirls. "Don't move or the next one's coming for your head!"

Kip grabbed the screen, but as soon as his hands touched it, he felt little claws scratching on his legs, then more on his back. He froze. Rats. First one or two, then half a dozen.

His eyes clamped shut as he felt the claws scramble onto his neck, and then over his head. In holding on to the screen, his body had become a bridge—the only way out of the water—and the rats swarmed him.

In moments, it wasn't half a dozen rats. It was hundreds.

Kip's muscles locked. He couldn't move. Couldn't think. Couldn't breathe. He didn't dare even open his eyes. Rats were in his hair. A rat had fallen down the front of his shirt and was clawing his chest. Rats were running up his arms.

"Move, Kip! Move or die!" Sanson shouted.

Suddenly, Kip felt detached from his own body. He was nearly drowning, the town was on fire, almost everyone he knew was dead, two drafters were trying to kill him, and he was worried about rats. Even as he clung here, the drafters were preparing the death blow, and he was too frightened to move. Ridiculous. Pathetic.

He felt a hand grab him, and his eyes snapped open. It was Sanson. Sanson had climbed back up the grate and was braving the rats to try to help Kip over. Kip shook like a dog, dislodging perhaps a dozen rats, but leaving many more. Still terrified, he began climbing up the grate.

He threw one leg up onto the top of the grate, but he couldn't pull himself up. He was too heavy. A rat fell into his gaping pant leg and began scurrying up against his bare skin.

Sanson grabbed Kip's clothes with both hands and yelled with the effort. Kip pulled one last time, and felt his body rising, rising—and finally rolling over the top of the grate. He crashed into the water on the other side.

The current pulled at him immediately. When he surfaced, Sanson was yelling something, but Kip couldn't even make out the words. He reached down into his pants and grabbed the struggling rat and threw it away.

Then he was at the waterfall. There were ledges running perpendicular to the falls, and the town daredevils would sprint along those and leap over the falls. It was too late for Kip to try that. There were sections where the water was shallower than others. Kip turned desperately and his feet caught an underwater rock. The force of the current pushed him forward, and he squatted on the rock, gathering his feet underneath him, flailing his hands to right himself. The pool at the base of the falls was plenty deep, but if he didn't jump far enough, he'd hit rocks on his way down.

He jumped as hard as he could. To his surprise, he actually went the direction he was trying. For a moment, there was perfect freedom. Peace. The roar of the water drowned out all other sound, all other thought. It was beautiful. Somehow, he and Sanson had been floating in the river all night, and now the sun was just peeking above the horizon, beating back the midnight black of one horizon to deep blue, to icy blue, to pinks and oranges that lit clouds like halos.

Then Kip realized how fast he was falling. His body was at an angle to the fast-approaching water below. From watching the bolder youths, he knew he had to hit feet first or headfirst with arms extended or he would be hurt badly.

There was no way he was going headfirst, so he arched his back and wheeled his arms.

Whatever he'd done, it seemed to be the exact wrong thing, or maybe he'd already been twisting forward, because he found himself parallel to the water. He was going to land the most colossal belly-flop ever seen. From this height, it might well kill him.

Not only that, but he realized that he was falling with the water— all the divers he'd ever seen had jumped out beyond it. The water always glanced off one rock on the way down.

He didn't even have time to think a curse before a rock smacked his foot, hard. He threw his arms out—

—as he crashed into the water headfirst, feeling like someone had just hit him over the top of the head with a board. His arms felt like they'd been torn off. And he'd forgotten to take a breath before he hit. Kip opened his eyes underwater in time to see something big streak down into the water beside him in a gush of bubbles. Sanson!

Sanson had hit feet first, but had been spun when he hit the water so he was upside down. He seemed stunned for a moment, unmoving, then his eyes opened, but he was looking away from Kip. Obviously disoriented from the fall, Sanson began swimming—down. Kip grabbed his foot to get his attention.

But Sanson panicked. He thrashed and kicked Kip square in the nose. Kip yelled—and watched the last of his air go rushing toward the surface.

Sanson turned, saw Kip, saw the direction the bubbles were going, and then saw the blood blossoming in the dark water. He grabbed Kip, and together the boys swam for the surface.

Kip barely made it. He gasped, inhaling water and blood, and then coughed it out. He coughed again, then retched. Sanson tugged on his arm. "Kip, help me! We've got to get to shore before we get to the rapids."

That woke Kip up. Within fifty paces of the deep, still area where the waterfall landed, there was another set of rapids so steep they were almost a series of waterfalls themselves. And already the current was getting swifter. Foot aching, head splitting, nose streaming blood, he swam with Sanson.

They made it to shore with ten paces to spare. The boys hauled themselves onto a grassy bank and inspected the damage, exhausted. Sanson was uninjured, and he looked sheepish. "Sorry, Kip. I mean, about your nose and all. I never liked swimming. Always thought there were things in the deep that'd grab me."

Pinching his bleeding nose, Kip looked at his friend. "Oo sabed my life ub dere," he said. "Oo din't eben break ma nose." Kip was more concerned about the foot he'd struck on his way down. He unlaced his shoe with one hand and tugged the shoe and stocking off. His foot was sore, and there were some nice scrapes along the top, but when he rubbed it he didn't think any bones were broken. He began tugging his wet stocking back on, which was hard to do while still pinching his nose with one hand.

"I can't believe we got—" Sanson started.

"Away?" Kip asked. He had abandoned trying to tie his shoe with one hand and was sniffing hard, trying to keep blood from dripping all over him. Even as he finished the knot, though, he knew why Sanson had stopped speaking. They were bathed in a harsh red glare.

Looking up, Kip saw a red flare hanging in the sky above them, marking their location for the rest of the king's army—who had to be nearby. The flare's smoke trail led back to the top of the falls, where the two drafters stood, looking at them.

Kip and Sanson had escaped two drafters. Now they had to escape the rest of the army.

Kip hopped to his feet, sniffing hard. He thought he was going to hyperventilate. Then he saw a horseman on the ridge that wound from above the waterfall down to the Sendinas' farm. He abruptly forgot about his bleeding nose. The horseman would have to go farther to go around, but he had a horse. Kip and Sanson had to make it down the trail along the rapids and get to the farm before the horseman did.

Then Kip saw three other horsemen join the first. And then another, and another.

He and Sanson started running.

The waterfall kicked up huge clouds of mist, day and night, and the valley stayed dark for hours longer than the surrounding country. When the flare winked out, Kip lost sight of both the horsemen and the trail.

He stopped, terrified. Broad-leafed plants, slick with the mist, obscured both sides of the tiny trail. One foot set on those, and he would plunge down the rocky incline to the river. In the rapids, he'd be battered to death.

He needed to see. He tried to look at things out of the corners of his eyes, the way Master Danavis had taught him. The part of your eye that focused on things was best at seeing colors, but outside the focus area was better at seeing light and dark.

"Move!" Sanson said.

Kip looked over his shoulder. Sanson's face looked like it was on fire. Kip took a step back and tottered on the sharp edge of the trail. Everywhere Sanson's skin was exposed, he looked hot. Kip could even see the steam evaporating off his arms in little orange whorls.

"What's wrong with your eyes?" Sanson asked. "Never mind. Move, Kip!"

Sanson was right again. It didn't matter what Kip was seeing, or how. He turned and started forward. Somehow, the wonder of it all crowded out his fear. The plants were like torches lighting his way, even gently illuminating the trail between.

One hand still hitching up his wet, heavy pants, Kip began jogging as fast as he could, fearless despite the slick rocks, narrow trail, and death beckoning from every side.

There were bodies in the river, caught up in the rapids. Dear Orholam, there were bodies at the Sendinas' farm, little lumps nearly as cold as the surrounding ground. Smoldering, ruined buildings burned hot in Kip's vision. More important for him and Sanson, he saw a flat-bottomed punt tied at the Sendinas' dock. He and Sanson hit the bottom of the trail at a full run. They rounded a corner and in the morning sun saw thirty mounted Mirrormen, drawn up in battle formation.

"We wanted to take you alive," the red drafter said. His skin was crimson, and fury tinged his voice. "A drafter with your potential doesn't come along every day. But you've killed two of King Garadul's men, and for that, you die."

Chapter 15

"You're not really going to crash us," Karris said as Gavin brought them over the scrub desert.

"Oh, I see. When I'm flying, *we're* flying, but when we're crashing, *I'm* crashing."

Gavin banked the condor to the right so they wouldn't be seen from Garriston. There was still a good chance some farmer or fisherman would spot them, but who would believe a lone fisherman who said he'd seen a giant flying man-bird? If a whole city saw them, it would be a different story. Garriston, despite being the most important port in Tyrea, wasn't much. The bay was overfished, the land was hot and dry with bad soil, the Ruthgari governor corrupt, his men worse.

It hadn't always been this way. Before the False Prism's War, there had been a vast system of irrigation canals that had brought this scrub desert into bloom, with two or even three harvests a year. There had been locks that fed trade to dozens of small cities up and down the Umber River. But canals and locks required drafters and maintenance. Without either, this land had withered, punished for the sins of dead men.

"Gavin, I'm serious. Are we really going to crash?"

"Trust me," he said.

She opened her mouth, then shut it. He guessed what she hadn't said: Because that's worked out so well for me before?

"Got anything fragile in your bag?" he asked.

"How bad is this going to be?" she asked, real concern in her voice.

"Sorry. I should have waited until we were closer to the ground."

"Wait, what's that?" Karris asked.

Gavin looked west, following her eyes, but didn't see what had made her curious. The land around Garriston was plains and dry farmland, but to the west it quickly yielded to steep, tall, impassable mountains that abutted almost directly on the sea. The Umber River was just on the other side of those mountains. If it could go straight to the sea—through the mountains—it would have been only ten leagues long. Instead, it had to go east to Garriston, separated from the ocean by fencelike mountains, almost a hundred and fifty leagues from origin to outlet.

"There," Karris said, pointing. "Smoke."

Gavin wasn't sure that the black wisp was anything more than Karris's—and now his—imagination. Regardless, it was on the other side of the mountains, so it didn't matter. He was just opening his mouth to tell Karris that when the condor passed over one of the foothills. A powerful updraft shot them higher into the air.

It took Gavin's breath away. He'd only experimented with the condor over water. He hadn't even thought about how the ground beneath where he was gliding would affect the air above it. Now that he had experienced it, it made sense. Why else did birds of prey spiral so often in the same places? Gavin had assumed they were good hunting grounds. Now he knew. Updrafts.

"Can we make it over the mountains?" Karris asked.

From this new height—Gavin looked down, gulped, and immediately looked back to the horizon—he was certain that what they had seen was smoke. And for it to be visible from this far away, it could only be one of two things.

Let it be a forest fire. Please, Orholam.

"We can. But if we do, you're not going to meet the man who was supposed to get you into Garadul's army. And I can't get the condor back into the air without the sea. I'll have to float all the way down the river."

"Gavin, when I see that much smoke, I think red wight. A Torch could be burning down an entire city. You're heading out to stop a color wight near Ru? These people aren't worth any less than the people of Ru. If it comes to it, there are a lot of drafters in Ru who could work together against the blue wight. These people have no one."

In his mind's eye, Gavin was comparing the land below him to the maps he knew of Tyrea. It was surprisingly easy, given that he was closer to the perspective most maps were drawn from than most people ever got. He looked at the mountains, the not-quite-pass through them, and the position of the rising smoke. A thought struck him with a greater force than mere intuition. He wasn't here on acci-dent. It wasn't coincidence that he was gliding in the one place where he could see this fire, or that he had Karris with him. That was no forest fire. It wasn't a red wight either.

That fire was rising from Rekton. It had been a beautiful town before the war. It was the town where Gavin's "son" was. Gavin knew it, even though they were so far away there was no way to know it. If Orholam had actually existed, this was the kind of pun-ishment he would devise for Gavin. Or test.

Whatever it was, it was a choice.

Five years left, and five great purposes still to accomplish. And one of those actually was mostly selfless: to free Garriston, which had been crushed because of him. Which was suffering still, because of him.

If Gavin went to Rekton, he'd have to face that crazy woman, Lina. He'd have to face her son Kip, and tell him that he wasn't his father: Sorry, you're still fatherless. I have no idea what your lying slut mother is talking about.

That would doubtless go over well. They would also be close to Rask Garadul's army, so Karris would open her orders, and every-thing would get messy fast.

All Gavin had to say was, "I've got my orders." Karris would understand. She'd always been dutiful. To a fault.

But you aren't Karris. This isn't her test.

He opened his mouth to say it, and it tasted like cowardice. He couldn't force the words past his gritted teeth.

"Let's go see," Gavin said. He banked the condor, and saw that he hadn't made his decision a moment too soon. It would be a near thing to clear the gap between the mountains.

Karris squeezed his hand and her eyes sparkled, those jade green eyes with red diamonds in them. For some reason, her joy struck him more deeply than any disappointment could have. That joy was a reminder of sixteen years of joy he should have given her, joy stolen. He turned away, his throat tight.

The mountains loomed, and Gavin realized for the first time just how fast they were going. There was no hope of a splashing wet landing here. If the updrafts he'd expected didn't catch them soon, he and Karris were going to paint a large crimson blotch across the face of these rocks.

Orholam, if there isn't any wind at all, then there isn't any wind to get thrown upward, is there?

He was beginning to draft a red cushion—hopelessly, knowing no matter how big he made it, it would be too little at this speed—when the updraft caught them. They were hurled skyward, the wings of the condor straining.

Karris shouted with exultation.

The force was incredible. It was hard to estimate how fast they were rising, but Gavin shortened the condor's wings both to take stress off them and because Rekton wasn't so far away that they would need that much height. The higher they were, the more visible they were. But it did make him think. With all the height he could get off of mountains, the condor's range was vastly greater than he had assumed.

It was a thought for another time. Right now the problem was to stay low so they weren't visible to all of Tyrea, and to lose some of the tremendous speed they'd built up. He drafted a bonnet of the same blue luxin he'd used for himself when he jumped from the Chromeria. It popped open instantly, throwing both him and Karris forward, then ripped away almost as fast.

When they regained their balance, Gavin tried again. Green this time, and much smaller. He sealed the bonnet to the luxin of the condor so it didn't tear him apart. It worked, sort of. They slowed a little.

Now they were headed downward at merely ridiculous speeds. Gavin struggled to expand the wingspan again.

"What can I do?" Karris shouted.

Gavin cursed. He'd barely begun to experiment with changing the condor's wings. In all his trials, he'd merely leaned to one side or the other and caught himself before hitting the ground or the water. Grunting with the strain, he lifted the front edge of the wings skyward. Point up to go up, right?

It was exactly the wrong thing to do. They pitched sharply downward. By the time he leveled off the wings, they were heading straight down. Worse, the suddenness of their drop meant his feet weren't even touching the floor. He had no leverage to push against to continue to manipulate the wings. He threw luxin up to the ceiling to force his body down, and began locking his feet to the floor, but the eucalyptus trees were looming huge. He was too slow.

Then he was slammed to the floor. The condor dipped below the height of the trees, in a meadow, and then began to rise. It wasn't going to make it.

Gavin reached into the luxin as the condor crashed through the branches. The blue luxin cracked and would have shattered if he hadn't grabbed it. For another instant, he couldn't see anything as they knifed through the trees, then again they were airborne. Heading up and up, steeper and steeper.

He finally looked at Karris. Her skin was a war of green and red. Her hands were braced against the ceiling and the luxin lines traced from both hands to the back of the condor. She'd taken control of the tail. It was flared, green, bent up. She'd saved their lives, but her eyes were closed with the effort, muscles straining to hold the tail up against the force of the wind.

"Karris, level it off!" Gavin shouted.

"I'm trying!"

"You've already gone too—"

Then they were upside down, heading back the opposite direction. Gavin's shirt fell in front of his face, and when he pulled it out of the way they were leveled off—upside down.

"Don't level off *now*!"

"Make up your mind!" she shouted. She was standing on her hands on the ceiling. Gavin locked her in again and together they turned the wings and tail once more. They were crushed to the floor as the great luxin bird swooped out level once more, only twenty paces above the trees.

Gavin breathed freely for the first time in what seemed like hours. He checked the condor. It seemed well enough.

"Did they see us?" Karris asked.

"What? Who?" How was she able to see so many things at once?

"Them," she said, nodding.

Gavin looked toward Rekton. They were only a few leagues east of the town now, and it had indeed been burned. All of it. That meant either an incredibly strong red wight, or something else entirely.

And they were looking at the something else. There was a small army encamped around the town. It could only be Garadul's men.

Orholam have mercy.

"No," Gavin said. "They'd have to stare almost straight into the sun to see us."

"Huh. Lucky, I guess," Karris said.

"You call this lucky?" Gavin asked.

"What's that?" she interrupted.

Below the town, after the falls fed into rapids and the Umber River's rage finally cooled, there was a group of homes. Almost a village, but all the buildings were smoldering. There was a green drafter, skin filling with power, facing several of King Garadul's Mirrormen.

"That's a child!" Karris said. "Two! Gavin, we've got to save them."

"I'll bring us down as close as I can. Roll when we hit." They leveled off ten paces above a plain of rock and brush and tumbleweeds. Gavin threw out a small bonnet to slow the condor again. It snapped open, but this time they were both ready for the whiplash and braced themselves. Gavin threw out another and another. They slowed down faster than he'd expected. The condor pitched toward the ground.

Gavin flung his hands out, blasting the condor to pieces. As they fell, he wrapped Karris and then himself in an enormous cushion of orange luxin, rimmed with a shell of segmented flexible green, with a core of super-hard yellow.

They slammed into the ground, the orange and green luxin slowing them before exploding from the force of their landing. The yellow luxin was formed into a more rigid ball around each of them. Gavin crashed through some bushes, bouncing and rolling half a dozen times before the yellow luxin cracked and spilled him unceremoniously onto the ground. He wiggled his fingers and toes. Everything worked. He jumped up.

"Karris?"

He heard a yell. Not a good one. He ran.

Karris sprang to her feet, twenty paces away. Her hair was askew, but he didn't see any obvious injuries. He came to stand by her. "What is it?" he asked.

She glanced down. There was a rattlesnake at her feet, as long as Gavin's spread arms. A dagger through its head pinned it to the ground. Karris's dagger.

As Gavin stood there, mouth open, Karris put a foot behind the snake's head and pulled the dagger out—with her hand, for Orholam's sake, not with drafting. Sometimes Gavin forgot how tough Karris was. She wiped the blood off on a black kerchief the Blackguards carried for such purposes—black didn't show hard-to-explain bloodstains. She shook slightly as she tucked the kerchief away, but Gavin knew it wasn't fear or nerves. It took a body time to relax from the amount of adrenaline imminent death triggered.

Karris didn't blame him for nearly getting her killed. She grabbed her bag and bowcase, strapped her ataghan belt around her narrow waist, checked to make sure neither blade nor scabbard had been damaged in the fall, and threw her bag on her back. It was like the sudden violence had reminded her of what she was—and of what they weren't. Back on the ground, back to reality.

"Sorry 'bout that," Gavin said. "I should have gone for the sea."

"If we had, there could have been sharks." She shrugged. "And now I'd be wet." She smirked, but it didn't touch her eyes. He wasn't going to reach her now. Work loomed—and her work was dangerous, a job that might well lead to war, a job that might require her to kill or to die. She had to ruthlessly cut away any entanglements that would distract her.

"Karris," he said. "What's in that note ... it isn't true. I don't expect you to understand or maybe even believe me, but I swear it isn't true."

She looked at him, hard, inscrutable. Her irises were jade green, but now the flecks of red were like starbursts, flaring, diamond-shaped. One way or another, through means magical or mundane, luxin or tears, Gavin knew that soon those eyes would be red. "Let's save those children," she said.

Karris ran, and he followed her. They cut back and forth down a hillside dominated by eucalyptus trees, peeling bark scattered on the ground, brush slapping them. Karris cut toward the skinny child, leaving Gavin to save the one facing the red drafter.

But it didn't matter. Neither of them was going to make it in time.

Chapter 16

It was too far to run for the punt, even for Sanson. A cool realization settled on Kip: he was going to die. He was surprised at his own reaction. No panic. No fear. Just quiet fury. Thirty elite Mirrormen in full harness against a child. A trained red drafter against a child who'd first drafted yesterday.

"When I tell you, run," Kip told Sanson.

Out of the corner of his eye, he saw something flash over the trees hundreds of paces to his left, but when he looked, there was nothing there. He saw that the Mirrormen were looking back and forth at each other, as if they'd caught the same glimpse he had.

"Now, Sanson. Run." Kip didn't take his eyes off the drafter.

Sanson ran.

The Mirrormen hesitated until the red drafter gestured, a quick sign, with military efficiency. One Mirrorman from each side of the line peeled off and circled around Kip, digging their heels hard into their horses. The red drafter himself rode forward alone.

Everything Kip had done with magic so far had been instinctive. Now he needed to do something on purpose. Light was pouring over him. There was green everywhere. The two Mirrormen circling him were each keeping an eye on him, but they were going after Sanson. The wildness surged through Kip once again and he felt the skin under his fingernails tear open again as luxin poured into his palm. A javelin formed in his hand. He hurled it at the Mirrorman nearer to

Sanson, but the throw was pathetic. It flew maybe fifteen paces, not even half the distance it needed.

The red drafter laughed. Kip ignored him.

Kip had seen the other red drafter and his apprentice Zymun throw fireballs from a standstill. They'd been thrown back from hurling something with so much force, but they hadn't fully thrown it physically. Kip imagined the magic streaking from him as the reds' had done. The air in front of him coalesced, sparkling, coruscating greens, from sea-foam to mint to evergreen, taking on the outline of a spearhead.

With an explosion of energy, it leapt away. Kip felt as if he had fired an overcharged musket. He tumbled to the ground. Worse, he missed. The green spear cut the air behind the galloping Mirrorman. It crashed into one of the few standing walls of one of the burned-out homes. The wall went down in billows of ash.

Kip scrambled to his feet to try again, but even as the air began sparkling green in front of him, he caught something red out of the corner of his eye. He turned toward the red drafter—too slowly. Something hot blasted through his hands, scattering the green luxin he'd been gathering, burning him.

The red drafter was advancing toward him, dismounted now, walking calmly, red swirling down into his hands again. Kip held his hands up, just as he had a hundred times when Ram was threatening to hit him. This time, a green shield formed, translucent, covering him from head to toe, its weight supported on the ground.

The red drafter flicked a finger forward. A spark shot out, trailing a long red tail. It stuck to Kip's shield, burning faintly, its red trail going all the way back to the drafter. Kip panicked and, only carrying the shield because it was stuck to his arms, dodged to one side. A much larger red missile roared out from the red drafter. It followed the tail toward the spark, curving in midair along that line.

Kip was blown off his feet and thrown back a dozen feet. He felt the green shield crack with a report, as if it had been his own bones snapping.

He lifted himself from the dirt in time to see one of the Mirrormen pursuing Sanson raise his long, sweeping cavalry sword and slash downward in midcharge. Kip couldn't see Sanson, but the Mirrormen reined in and the second horseman reversed his grip on his lance and stabbed downward hard, once, twice, professionally, coolly.

Both Mirrormen relaxed like men who've finished their work, and Kip knew Sanson was dead.

He rolled over. The red drafter was standing over him. Kip was faintly surprised by how ordinary the man looked. A long face, dark eyes, roughly cut hair, crooked teeth revealed by his grimace. He was going to kill Kip, but without passion. Just a man following orders.

Before Kip could gather magic one more time, the drafter imprisoned Kip's arms in red sludge, sticky and thick. Kip couldn't move.

The drafter raised his bespectacled eyes toward the sun once more, magic spiraling like smoke down into his arms, filling him with power for the killing blow. A dense indigo dot appeared on his ear, then over his temple as his head moved, as if someone with a lantern letting out a single ray of light from somewhere in the forest was somehow focusing that little beam right on his—

There was a roar, for just a fraction of a second, as if Kip were standing at the base of the waterfall once again. Something huge and yellow blasted into the red drafter so fast and hard it seemed the man disappeared. His body was thrown into the air, torn in half by the force of the collision. The red luxin sludge holding Kip fell into dust.

Kip stood and looked in horror at what had been a man. The red of the drafter's clothes now mingled with his blood, magic and violence mixed. But his entire upper body had been reduced to jelly. Kip looked to the forest.

With the boy saved for the moment, Gavin ran toward the Mirrormen. Karris had headed down the hill to save the other boy running for the river, but she was already too late. The Mirrormen formed up with surprising discipline and speed. None of these men had bothered to bard their horses. Barding was heavy and awkward and tired the horses quickly, and the Mirrormen obviously hadn't expected to run into any real opposition, much less drafters. That meant the horses were easily the most vulnerable targets. But Gavin didn't like killing innocent beasts. Their masters? That was a different matter.

He swept a hand in a sharp, hard arc, the air crackling like a succession of rocks exploding in a fire. A dozen blue globes, each half the size of his fist, shot out. The mirrored armor, working like a mirror reflecting light, reflected part of any luxin thrown against it, making it unravel. That was a big problem for a drafter trying to cut down a horseman with a luxin sword, but it was only protection, not invulnerability. The thin-walled luxin globes smashed against mirror armor—and sheared open, dumping out flaming red goo that splashed all over the Mirrormen, up and down their chests, into their visors, down the seams into their groins.

With fire and screams and the sizzle of burning skin, the charge faltered. Gavin swept his other hand out and another dozen globes shot out. Men were crashing to the ground from their saddles, trying to roll and put out the fires. Others clawed at their flaming helmets, cooking. Still others were trying to continue the charge, half a dozen men lowering their lances—until the second wave of globes caught them.

More than a dozen horses continued the charge, though. Even without their riders' guidance, these horses were bred to war, and they ran toward Gavin.

Gavin threw green wedges around himself like a clamshell and braced himself. The horses jostled him hard as they charged past, but left him standing.

There were only three Mirrormen left uninjured, all of them men on the ends of the line who'd broken off the charge early. They were sawing their reins, turning tail to flee. Cowards, perhaps. But smart cowards. Gavin flicked fingers at each in turn. Superviolet luxin was fast, light, and invisible to almost everyone. Like a spider, each dot stuck to one of the men and then climbed up to the joint in their armor at the back of their necks.

Three spiked missiles of yellow luxin sped along the superviolet spiderwebs trailing from those spiders to Gavin a moment later. With a meaty crunch, each missile punched through mail and into a spine. Three riders toppled from their galloping horses.

With all the riders around him dead or dying, Gavin looked down the hill to see how Karris was doing against the last two Mirrormen. One was already down, and if anything, Gavin was surprised to see that the other was still alive—a fact that would no doubt change shortly.

Four hundred years ago, when it had been founded, the Blackguard had been an Ilytian company, chosen as much for their proud relation to Lucidonius as for their martial skill. But when Ilyta lost influence in the Spectrum, the Blackguard had been forced to abandon choosing on the basis of province and instead had justified their elite position on function: when a drafter drafted, his skin filled with the color he was about to use. That meant in a fight, a paler-skinned Atashian or Blood Forester drafter was easier to predict. That justification had satisfied the Parians, who were also darker-skinned, just fine. Since then, Blackguards had been mostly Parians or Ilytians, with Parians gradually becoming the majority as their political power waxed.

But having based their protected status on their fighting prowess, the Blackguard had been forced to accept more than a dozen elite warrior-drafters from countries other than Paria and Ilyta over the last two centuries.

Karris had joined them because it was impossible to deny her. She'd sparred with every member of the Blackguard and defeated all but four of them. She was simply the fastest drafter Gavin had ever seen, and after her Blackguard training, one of the most dangerous. And it meant nothing to her. At the rate she pushed herself, Gavin thought she'd be lucky if she lasted another ten years. Probably closer to five. It was like she was racing him to Death's gates. But she wouldn't die today.

The other horseman charged her, his sword drawn. Karris stood her ground, only moving at the last second so that she was directly in the horse's path. The horseman, expecting her to move the other way, was too surprised to change his course. Karris dropped to the ground just as the horse was about to trample her. With flexible fingers of green and red luxin extending from her own hands and crossed, she grabbed the cinch strap as the horse passed over her.

The horse thundered past and for a moment Gavin thought she'd been trampled. Then he saw her flipped into the air. The luxin uncrossed and whipped her back toward the still-galloping horse. She crashed into the back of the horseman and almost spilled out of the saddle, but she scrambled and managed to maintain her seat behind him.

The horseman flailed, having no idea what had just happened or what had hit him from behind. Karris drew her knife as she reached around his head with her other hand. She tore open his visor and buried the knife deep in his face. The man spasmed hard and both of them fell.

Karris tried to push the horseman down so she'd land on him, but his foot never cleared the stirrup. Instead of a cushioned landing, she was spun hard backward by his body being yanked from under her, and then hit the ground and abruptly rolled forward. She had the good fortune to land on grass, though.

Gavin looked at the boy they'd just killed thirty of Satrap Garadul's elite bodyguards to save. He was maybe fifteen, chubby, awkward, with eyes round at what he'd just seen. The child turned and ran toward the river. At first Gavin thought he was fleeing in fear, but then he realized the boy was going to check on his friend, the one Gavin and Karris had come too late to save.

"What is the meaning of this?" a man shouted.

Gavin turned—and cursed himself. He'd been so concerned about the boy and Karris and what was happening down toward the river, he hadn't been paying attention to what was happening up the road. The roar of the rapids and the waterfall had muffled the sound of hooves, but there was still no excuse. The man who'd shouted had the same weak chin that seemed to beg someone to stick a fist in it that he'd had sixteen years ago, the last time Gavin had seen him. His whole body was quivering with outrage as he took in the carnage that was all that remained of thirty of his supposedly invincible Mirrormen.

But Satrap Garadul's face changed the moment he saw Gavin. He drew rein even as half a dozen of his drafters and a score of his Mirrormen surrounded him. "Gavin Guile?"

Chapter 17

The White was going to kill him.

Gavin deserved killing. The presence of Satrap Garadul himself changed everything. If these had merely been Satrap Garadul's soldiers, as Gavin and Karris expected, Gavin could have killed the men and left. Satrap Garadul would be furious and would hunt the drafters who had done it, but he would have had no idea who he was after. It might have simply been that there was a powerful drafter living in—what was this worthless little town called? Rekton, that was it. Oh, the irony.

It was too late to grab the spectacles Gavin kept in a pocket against such eventualities. With spectacles, with what he'd done, he was a mysterious polychrome. Without them, he could only be the Prism.

So now the Prism himself had moved against Satrap Garadul, and there was no denying it. Rask Garadul knew him.

"Gavin?" Satrap Rask Garadul said again. There was something odd in his tone of voice, an intensity, maybe a trap. He was dressed in mail with segments of plate worked in. Smaller segments, not requiring articulated joints. His was a poor country.

He'd changed his seal. It used to be his family's moon and two stars on a field sable, his personalized with a snarling fox. Now both fox and field had been done away with. The king's new seal was a white chain, broken, on a black field. Gavin knew instantly that the symbol was important. Rask wasn't merely repudiating his name and his father, whom he'd always despised as weak. This was new. Had he fallen under the sway of the heresy of the old gods that Gavin had heard rumors about? What was he doing? Why was he asking Gavin's name when he already knew it was him? Was he giving Gavin an opportunity to lie, to say that he wasn't the Prism?

If Gavin did so, what would Rask Garadul do? Kill him and explain later to the Chromeria that it had been a mistake; through no fault of his own, he'd killed an attacker who'd disavowed being Gavin Guile. If Rask thought he was going to kill Gavin with a handful of drafters and a score of Mirrormen, he was wrong, but what else could it be? Maybe Satrap Garadul was simply as surprised to see Gavin as Gavin was to see him, and he didn't know how to play this.

If Gavin lied and Rask attacked, Gavin would have no choice but to kill him. If he killed Rask, he'd have to kill all of Rask's men. And what would the satrapies make of that? More men were coming down the path behind the satrap even now. Gavin couldn't kill them all. No matter how strong he was, if a hundred men fled in a hundred directions, some of them would get away. Word would get out that the Prism himself had come to Tyrea and assassinated the satrap without provocation.

It didn't matter that Satrap Garadul was massacring everyone in this town. It was his town; he could do with it as he saw fit. At one time, a Prism could have destroyed or killed one of his satraps at will, but that time was long past. Perhaps back when the Seven Satrapies had really been satrapies. No longer. His power was ceremonial, religious only. The Prism wasn't supposed to interfere in the internal affairs of a nation—and Gavin had already more than just interfered. If he killed everyone here, and skimmed back to the Chromeria so he got home within a few days of having left, the Chromeria could plausibly deny that he was responsible. It was too far away for him to have come and gone.

He would kill a man he'd never liked; he would stay out of trouble, and the only people to pay for it would be a bunch of soldiers in the most backward of the Seven Satrapies. Well, the boy might have to die too. Otherwise he could blackmail Gavin. And what would Karris think? Well, what did it matter what she thought? She was an impossibility for him already. He'd known he was going to lose what little he had with her today regardless.

The man he'd once been wouldn't have hesitated.

What would you do, brother?

It had been so long, Gavin wasn't even sure anymore.

"I am the High Lord Prism Gavin Guile," Gavin said, bowing slightly, putting one hand behind his back and trying to wave off Karris.

"So, Lord Prism," Satrap Garadul said loudly, "is this how the Chromeria declares war?"

"Strange that your thoughts should so quickly go to war, Satrap."

"Strange? No, it's strange you should call me a satrap. You expelled the rightful satrap, my father, from Garriston, stole that city, our capital and only port, and have denied Tyrea's people access to the Chromeria. Tyrea is a satrapy no more, and hasn't been since your war, Prism. I am King Rask Garadul of Tyrea. You have murdered my personal guards. And you call it strange that war should occur to us?" Rask's voice rose. "Perhaps you think Tyreans are bred to be slaughtered by the Chromeria's lackeys?"

There was a rumble among the Mirrormen that told Gavin this kind of talk was nothing new.

"But surely the Chromeria wouldn't send the Prism himself just to kill a few of my men." Rask pretended to be thinking, but didn't wait long enough for Gavin to get a word in. "No. The Prism would only come if there was something much more important to accomplish. Something that would ensure the Chromeria's stranglehold on the Seven Satrapies continued. Tell me, *Lord* Prism, have you come to assassinate me?"

One doesn't send a lion to kill a rat.

So help him, Gavin almost said it out loud.

There was a rattle of armor and stomping of hooves as the Mirrormen and drafters pressed in closer to Rask Garadul. Gavin only heard it; he was looking down the hill. He'd avoided looking until now to avoid drawing attention to Karris. By now, she'd probably decided whether she was going to stay or go.

She was almost gone, already starting down the swift-flowing river on a little punt. If Gavin knew Karris, though, she would stop and try to see what happened to him. After all, she was a Blackguard, and though their first responsibility was always to the White, his protection came in a close second. He wondered if she'd left because she trusted him, because she thought he could fend for himself, or because she had her own mission to accomplish and nothing could be allowed to interfere with that.

The stout boy, on the other hand, was now almost directly behind Gavin. After Gavin had saved him once from Mirrormen, apparently he thought Gavin was his best hope to survive.

"You misunderstand me, King Garadul," Gavin said, turning once more, committed, letting the title stand. "I saw these men slaughtering the innocent citizens of your satrapy. I intervened to save your people. I believed I was doing you a favor."

"Doing me a favor by murdering soldiers in my uniform?"

"Renegades, surely. Bandits. What sort of madman would burn his own town to the ground?"

Many of the Mirrormen looked away or down and threw furtive glances at King Garadul. Clearly, not all of them had been happy to murder their countrymen. The king flushed. "I am king," he declared. "I will not have my choices questioned. Especially not by the Chromeria. Tyrea is a sovereign nation. Our internal conflicts are no business of yours." The soldiers went back to being stony-faced.

"Of course not. It's simply...novel to find a king burning his own town and people. Murdering children. You can understand my confusion, I'm sure. My apologies for this misunderstanding. The Chromeria serves the Seven Satrapies. Tyrea included."

It was, perhaps, as well played as Gavin could manage. If they'd been standing before fifty nobles versed in the interplay of nations and respectful of diplomacy, it might have been enough. Rask Garadul would demand some monetary consideration, allowing it had been an honest and understandable error and preserving his own right to have been outraged, and Gavin would be understood to have won. Elegant and clean.

But Rask Garadul was a young man and a new king. He was not standing in front of nobles, but in front of his men. He saw that he was losing, but with the bloody corpses piled on every side and his men looking askance at him, he didn't think he could afford to lose. "Surely you haven't come hundreds of leagues simply to patrol our kingdom for bandits? And unannounced, no less. One would think you'd snuck into our kingdom under cover of darkness, like some sort of spy."

Ah, not stupid either. When on a losing path, take a new one, quick. Gavin glanced once more at the boy, to see how he was holding up. Not well. He was practically quivering with terror. He had eyes only for Rask Garadul. Or was that rage?

"A spy?" Gavin said lightly. "How droll. No no no. One has people to do that sort of thing. One doesn't do it oneself. Surely you've been king long enough to know this?"

"What are you doing here?" King Garadul demanded. Again, shockingly rude if they'd been in a court in any capital in the Seven Satrapies. He glanced at the boy, and Gavin knew he was lost. He could leave—he was the Prism, after all, and even killing thirty of Garadul's Mirrormen wasn't enough to justify his seizure or murder. Especially not under questionable circumstances. Rask would risk uniting the satrapies against Tyrea. Killing a satrap would be an outrageous breach; killing the Prism would be an unconscionable one. But Rask felt he was losing, and he was going to make Gavin pay for that. He was going to hurt him as badly as he could.

Gavin would be released; the boy would be killed.

"I saw smoke," Gavin said. "One of the ways I serve the Seven Satrapies is by dealing with color wights. I came to help."

"What are you doing in our kingdom?"

"I wasn't aware you'd closed your borders. Indeed, I wasn't aware of this new 'kingdom' at all. This seems needlessly...hostile. Especially to wish to bar a servant of the realms like myself." The myth of polite dialogue between disinterested, reasonable neighbors, that myth upon which so much of diplomacy rested, was clearly dead, so to turn the attention away, Gavin stepped right over its corpse. "Are you hiding something, King Garadul?"

"You're from Rekton, aren't you, boy?" King Garadul asked. He wasn't going to play Gavin's game. "What's your name? Who's your father?"

"I'm Kip. I've got no father. Most of us don't. Not since the war." It sent a lance through Gavin's guts. He'd almost let himself forget. The False Prism's War had wiped out dozens of these little towns. All the men, from boys who couldn't grow a mustache to old men who had to use their spears as canes, had been pressed into service by one side or the other. And he and Dazen had sent them against some of the most talented drafters the world had known. Like lumber to a mill.

"What about your mother, then?" King Garadul asked, irritated.

"Her name was Lina. She helped at a couple of the inns."

Gavin's heart stopped. Lina, the crazy woman who'd sent him the note, was dead. This boy, this fearful boy, was supposed to be his son? The only survivor from a town burnt to the ground stood here, and he was the only one who could cause Gavin grief. If Gavin had believed in Orholam, he'd have thought it a cruel prank.

"Lina, yes, I think that was the name of the whore," King Garadul said. "Where is she?"

"My mother was no whore! And you killed her! You murderer!" The boy looked near tears, though of rage or grief Gavin couldn't tell.

"Dead? She stole something from me. You'll take us to your house, and if we can't find it, you'll work for me until you pay it off."

Rask Garadul wasn't going to have the boy work off his mother's debt. Gavin had no doubt Rask was lying about the whole thing. It was merely an excuse to take the boy—who, if Rask was a king, was one of the king's subjects. Most likely, Rask would kill him right in front of Gavin, just to salve his own pride. The boy meant nothing. He could have been a dog or a nice blanket for all Rask cared. He'd become a chit. Part of Gavin was sickened, and part of him reveled in it.

Put me in a situation where I can't win? Really? You think this is impossible for me? Let's play.

"The boy goes with me," Gavin said.

Rask Garadul smiled unpleasantly. He had a gap between his front teeth. He looked more like a bulldog baring its teeth than a man smiling. "You're going to risk your life for this thief? Hand him over, Prism."

"Or what?" Gavin asked, deliberately polite, curious, as if he really wondered. Threats so often withered when you pulled them out into the light, naked.

"Or my men will say how there was a big misunderstanding. We had no idea the Prism was here. If only he'd announced his coming. If only he hadn't been confused and attacked my soldiers. We simply defended ourselves. It was only after his unfortunate death that we discovered our error."

Gavin smirked. He put a fist to his mouth to cover his chuckle. "No, Rask. There's a reason I don't travel with Blackguards: I don't need them. You were just a snot-nosed boy during the False Prism's War, so maybe you don't remember what I can do, but I can tell that some of your men do. They're the ones who look nervous. If your men attack, I will kill you. The White will be furious with me for a month or two. It will be a diplomatic problem, to be certain, but do you really think anyone cares what happens to the *king* of Tyrea? 'King,' not satrap, and thus a rebel. They'll only want assurances that it won't happen to them. We'll make promises and apologies and pay the tuitions of all Tyrean students for a few years, and that will be the end of it. Your successor will doubtless be less belligerent."

Rask moved to speak, but Gavin wasn't about to let him.

"But let's pretend for a moment that by some chance you actually killed me without being killed in turn. I see what you're doing here: razing a town so you can raise an army. Founding your own Chromeria. The question is, do you think you're ready, right now, for war? Because if I go back now, armed only with words, the Spectrum might not believe me. But if you kill me, that will be a more elegant testimony than any I could muster. And do you really think your version of what happened is the only version that's going to get out? You *are* a young king, aren't you? And here you were talking about spies just moments ago."

Silence stretched cool hands between them. Gavin had won as completely as he'd probably ever won a pure argument.

"The boy is my subject and a thief. He stays." Garadul's whole body was quivering with fury. He wasn't calling Gavin's bluff. He was simply refusing to lose.

Gavin hadn't been bluffing. Nine times out of ten, he could probably kill every one of these soldiers and drafters—depending on how good the drafters were. And he'd probably emerge with nothing more than a singed eyebrow. Protecting the child during such a fight was another matter. Is it better that the guilty should perish, or that the innocent should live?

And not all of the Seven Satrapies would be quite as quick to forgive as he'd pretended.

"He's no thief," he said, looking to redirect the conversation from a pure I-win/you-lose bifurcation. "He's got nothing but the clothes on his back. Whatever his mother may or may not have done, it's nothing to do with him."

"Easy enough to test, isn't it?" Rask asked. "Search him."

From the look on his face, apparently Kip *was* a thief. Unbelievable. Where was hiding whatever he'd stolen? Between rolls of fat?

"No! It's the last thing she gave to me! You took everything else. You can't have it! I'll kill you first!" There was a wildness in the boy's voice that Gavin recognized immediately, even before Kip's irises were flooded with jade green. The boy was going to attack King Garadul, his Mirrormen, and his drafters. Very brave, but more stupid.

King Garadul's drafters would see it too.

Gavin threw his left hand up in a quick arc, forming a wall of red, green, yellow, and blue luxin intertwined between Kip and King Garadul's men. With his right hand, he drafted a blue cudgel and clubbed Kip over the back of the head. The boy crumpled. Only Karris, Gavin thought, could have done it faster.

A single red luxin fireball thrown by one of Garadul's drafters hit the wall and sizzled as it plunged into Gavin's shield, instantly extinguished.

Everyone else stood stunned. Gavin released the shield. A few of the Mirrormen were looking again at the corpses of their comrades, maybe thinking that their deaths were no fluke. Rask Garadul alone seemed unfazed. He dismounted, walked over to the unconscious boy, and searched him roughly.

Rask Garadul produced a slender rosewood case that had been tucked inside the back of Kip's belt. He opened it a crack, shot a satisfied smile at Gavin, and tucked it in his own belt. He walked back to his horse and mounted.

"A thief and an attempted assassin. Thank you for your service in foiling the attack, Lord Prism." King Garadul motioned one of his men toward Kip. "I think that tree should support a noose. Will you be staying for the execution, Gavin?"

So this is where it ends. This is the cost of my sins.

"There was no attempt on your life, King Garadul. We both know that. The boy didn't even draft. I was merely disciplining him as a Chromeria student for considering drafting without permission. You have the box, and you've already murdered the supposed thief, his mother. A harsh punishment to be sure, but this is your satrapy—er, 'kingdom.' It's obvious he knew nothing of it except that his mother gave it to him. Whatever claim you have to him pales in comparison to mine."

"He's my subject, and therefore mine to do with as I will."

Only one card left. Gavin said, "You asked earlier why I came to this boiling latrine you call a country. Kip is the reason. My claim to him is greater than yours. He's my bastard."

Rask Garadul's eyes went stony, and Gavin knew he had won. No man would publicly claim a dishonor if it weren't true. He also knew from that look, before the man even spoke, that he was going to have to kill Rask Garadul. But not today.

"Your time is finished," Rask Garadul said. "Yours and the Chromeria's. You're done. Light cannot be chained. Know this, Prism: We will take back what you've stolen. The horrors of your reign are almost at an end. And when it ends, I will be there. This I swear."

Chapter 18

Karris floated the punt downstream until she rounded a corner and disappeared from sight. She didn't think the soldiers had seen her leave, so she beached the punt on the opposite side of the river and found a hill from which she could see Gavin. She climbed the hill on her hands and knees. There were several trees and bushes and long grasses between them. Ideal. What wasn't ideal was the distance. One hundred and twenty paces. She was a great shot, but the bow she'd brought was a simple recurve, not a longbow. Good and portable, very accurate to seventy paces. One twenty was a different question. She shuttled the mental abacus. She should be accurate within four feet, and she could shoot rapidly. If Satrap Garadul stood still, she could shoot four arrows within a few seconds, correcting for her mistakes. Good enough. At least, better than any of her other options. She scooted back from the top of the hill and strung her bow, checked the fletching and trueness of her arrows, and crawled back into position, hidden and deadly.

When Gavin and the satrap talked for a few minutes, Karris relaxed. In conversation, Gavin could tie anyone in knots except maybe the White. Though Gavin was standing amid piles of Rask Garadul's dead, now it was probably just a matter of how much the satrap would pay *Gavin* for troubling him.

Making sure she could still see Gavin and that her weapons were close, Karris opened her pack. The White had told her not to read her orders until she'd left for Tyrea, so Karris had put the orders in the bottom of her pack, beneath a change of clothes, spare spectacles, cooking implements, a few flares and grenadoes—thank Orholam those hadn't ignited when she fell during the fight, but they were worth the risk. She pulled out the folded note. As sensitive orders always were, it was made of the thinnest paper possible, the outer folds covered with scribbles so the translucent paper couldn't simply be held up to the light to read what was within. The seal had a simple spell trigger: anyone who simply broke the seal would bring two luxin contact points together, and there would be a small but instant fire. It wasn't foolproof, of course: any careful drafter could disarm it, or any non-drafter could simply cut around the seal, but sometimes simple precautions worked where more elaborate schemes did not.

Karris checked on Gavin. Still talking. Good.

Drafting a bit of green from the grass she was sitting on, she unhooked the trap on the seal. Gavin had told her not to believe what was on this note, which had been written by the White herself. So who was more likely to lie to her? Gavin, ten times out of ten. The thought made her sick to her stomach. No, she was getting ahead of herself. She almost put the note away—she could deal with this later.

But her orders had to do with Tyrea, maybe even with Satrap Garadul, and the satrap was standing in her sight. The orders could be to kill him—or to make sure no one else did. She had to know right now.

She opened the note. The White's script was a little shaky, but still expressive and elegant. Karris translated the thin code automatically. "Inasmuch as purple may be the new color, we'd all be gratified to know the new fashions." Infiltrate and ascertain the satrap's intentions. The Seven Satrapies and the Chromeria are nervous about the new satrap and what he wants.

There was a curlicue on the last "s" to let her know the formal code was ended, but the note continued. "I also have news of a fifteen-year-old boy in a town called Rekton. His mother claims he is G's. If you have the chance, find out. I'd love to meet them." Gavin had a bastard in Rekton. Bring mother and son to the Chromeria.

Karris looked toward Gavin in time to see him draft a cudgel and crack it over the back of the boy's head. It would have been either funny or alarming, except that she felt like she'd been hit the same way. She watched, dumbfounded, as Gavin threw up a luxin wall, quenched an attack, and kept talking—cool to the end.

She was so stunned, she didn't pick up the bow, didn't draw. This was Rekton. That boy could draft. It was too much of a coincidence. *She* had been the one who insisted Gavin turn the flying contraption here. She felt a chill. For them to be here now was nothing less than Orholam's hand moving. Karris knew Orholam didn't care about her. She wasn't important enough. So what was this? A test for Gavin?

Fifteen years old. Son of a *bitch*. That child had been conceived while she and Gavin were betrothed.

Gavin picked up the boy, straining—the boy was both tall and chubby—and threw him over a shoulder. Then he walked toward the river, as if he didn't have a care in the world. The man really was walking away from a satrap, leaving thirty of the satrap's bodyguards dead. As always, Gavin was audacious, unstoppable, unflappable. The ordinary rules just didn't apply to him.

Never had.

For a single, perilous moment, Karris was sixteen again, with everything she had known, everyone she had loved torn away. She'd wept that day, wept until she realized no one was going to comfort her. She'd drafted red to take comfort from its heat and fury. She'd drafted so much red it had almost killed her. Today, she didn't even need to draft. The fury was there in a heartbeat. "Don't believe what's in your orders," Gavin had said. Of course he had. The liar. The son of a bitch.

That was why the White had told her not to open her orders immediately. She'd wanted Karris to cool off before she had to face Gavin. To not cause problems.

Nice to see that the two most important people in her life were both manipulating her.

Gavin drafted a scull onto the river and set the boy down. He didn't hurry, merely let the current take him, not so much as turning.

It must have been a near thing, then. He was treating Satrap Garadul like he was a dog and eye contact might provoke him. Being treated like a dog, well, Karris knew all about that, didn't she?

She found herself on her feet, striding back toward the river. Her spectacles had mysteriously found their perch on her nose. If Satrap Garadul weren't just two hundred paces away, Karris thought she'd have hurled a fireball at Gavin's head. He rounded the corner on the punt and saw the look on her face.

He blanched. And, for once, said nothing.

Karris stood on the bank of the river, trembling as he floated nearer and nearer.

Gavin didn't ask if she'd read her orders, he could tell. "Get in," he said. "If you have that black cloak, cover yourself. Better that they don't get a good look at you."

"Go to hell. I'll make my own way," Karris said.

He extended a hand and blasted a fist-size hole in her punt with a bullet of green luxin. "Get in!" he commanded. "King Garadul's coming any minute."

"King?" She drafted green luxin to cover the hole. It was petty and dumb, and curse Gavin for making *her* seem unreasonable. She hated him. She hated him with a passion that made all the world fade. Just let the horsemen come on her now.

"He's rejected the Chromeria, the Prism, the Seven Satrapies, Orholam himself. He's set himself up as a king." Gavin swept a hand toward her punt. Hundreds of tiny fingerling missiles flew from his hand and stuck quivering in the wood along the entire length and breadth of the punt, and then they burst all at once. Woodchip shrapnel and sawdust sprayed over both of them. Gavin said, "Slap me and be done with it, but get your ass in the boat."

He was right. Karris got in. This was not the time. She rummaged through her pack for the cloak and threw it on, pulling up the hood despite the heat. The boy was still unconscious. Gavin didn't wait, as soon as she was in, he drafted the oars and straps. They hit the water, and the scull sped forward almost immediately. Karris looked back and wasn't much surprised to see a dozen horsemen crest a hill, coming after them.

But it was a hopeless pursuit. The land along the river wasn't smooth, and Gavin's scull was fast. Gavin and Karris said nothing, not even when the scull entered a long section of rapids. Karris helped widen the platform with flexible red luxin and stiffer green, giving it a wide and high lip. Gavin drafted slick orange onto the bottom of it so when they did hit rocks, they slid right over them.

Within half an hour, they were certainly safe. Still Karris said nothing. How many times could one man hurt you this badly? She couldn't even look at him. She was furious with herself. He'd seemed so different after the war. His breaking their betrothal had left her with nothing. She'd left for a year, and he'd seemed overjoyed when she came back. He'd respected her distance, never said anything when she had a few affairs to try to purge him from her mind. That had somehow made her more furious. But eventually, she'd been drawn back to the mystery of him, and slowly won over by this man who seemed so completely changed by the war.

How many men come back from war better?

None, apparently.

And how many women come back smarter?

Not this one.

The river was joined by another tributary and widened considerably and Karris's place at the prow, looking out for rocks, became unnecessary. It was a beautiful day. She took off the cloak and felt the sun's rays—Orholam's caress, her mother had told her when she was a little girl. Right.

"They say there are bandits on this river who rob anyone who comes through," Gavin said lightly. "So maybe we'll find someone for you to kill."

"I don't want to kill someone," Karris said quietly, not meeting his gaze.

"Oh, you had that look in your eye—"

She looked up and smiled sweetly. "Not *someone*. I want to kill you."

Chapter 19

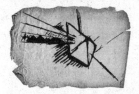

"Ah." Gavin cleared his throat.

The boy twitched, and then sat bolt upright. Maybe hearing "I want to kill you" wasn't the best way to be awakened after your village had been massacred. Gavin raised an eyebrow at Karris. You really need to do this now?

She huffed out a breath and turned away while the boy rubbed his head and moaned. The boy squinted at her, but she kept her back to him. She busied herself unstringing her bow and stowing it. The boy turned his royal blue eyes to Gavin. Interesting, with his light brown skin and kinky hair. Blue eyes were blue because they were the deepest, and thus the most light-sensitive and best light-collecting. It was far from the only criterion, but people with blue eyes were disproportionately represented among the most powerful drafters. More light to use, more power to burn.

Right now, those deep eyes were narrowed in pain. Apparently Gavin's swat had left the boy with a nice headache.

"You saved me," Kip said.

Gavin nodded.

"Who are you?" the boy asked.

Straight to the gut, huh? Karris turned to see what Gavin would say. She folded her arms.

Gavin stopped rowing. "This is Lady Karris White Oak, who, despite the sometimes humorously juxtaposed conjunctions of name and skin color and title, is a member of the Blackguard." Karris's look of fury didn't shift in the slightest. Apparently the old jokes still weren't funny. "And I..." He'd introduced Karris first to give himself a moment to think. It hadn't worked. *Five years and five purposes left, Gavin. This might be your last chance.*

The boy had been unconscious when Gavin had claimed his patrimony. He didn't know. He didn't have to know. Better for him not to know, in many ways. But better still for him not to hear it from Karris first, in a burst of rage. This boy was not his son, but without Gavin and Dazen's war—the Prisms' War or the False Prism's War, depending on which side you'd fought—none of the children of Rekton or a hundred other villages would be fatherless now. Gavin fantasized again for a moment about telling Karris everything she didn't know, and letting the chips fall where they may. But Karris wouldn't believe a partial truth and couldn't handle it whole.

At least this lie would give an orphan a father. It would give a child who'd lost everything one thing back. Gavin shouldn't care, but he did.

"I'm Prism Gavin Guile. I'm... you're my natural son."

The boy looked at him like he didn't understand what Gavin had said.

"Perfect," Karris said. "Why don't you just drop everything on him at once? Why don't you *think*, Gavin? I swear you're as impulsive as Dazen ever was."

Impulsive? Pot, meet kettle. Gavin ignored Karris, looking only at the boy. He'd just admitted to cheating on her years ago, lying to her about it afterward, and then—just an hour ago—lying to her again. She was doing cold rage, and it didn't fit her. Hot rage was more her style.

The boy glanced at her, confused by her anger, then glanced back. He was still squinting, though Gavin couldn't tell how much of that was from his headache from being cracked across the back of the head, how much might be lightsickness from drafting, and how much was confusion from his rapidly changing situation.

"You're what?" Kip asked.

"You're my natural son." It was too hard, for some reason, to say, "I'm your father."

"And you come *now*?" Kip asked, sick despair painting his face. "Why didn't you come yesterday? You could have saved everyone!"

"I didn't know you *existed* until this morning. And we came as fast as humanly possible." Faster, really. "If your town hadn't been on fire, we wouldn't have known to come."

"You didn't know about me? How could you not know?" Kip asked plaintively.

"Enough!" Gavin roared. "I'm here now! I saved your life, probably at the cost of a war that will make ten thousand more orphans. What more do you want?"

Kip withered, shrank in on himself.

"Unbelievable. You bully," Karris said. "You're given a son, and the first thing you do is scream at him. You're a brave man, Gavin Guile."

The unfairness of it all made Gavin's fists curl. Justice and injustice and the insanity of this life he'd chosen boiled over. "You want to lecture me about bravery? Is this the woman who ran away from a noble house to become a *guard*? Trying to get yourself killed through work or using too much magic isn't bravery, Karris; it's cowardice. What do you want from me? You want me to bring back your dead brothers?"

Karris slapped him. "Don't," she said. "Don't you ever—"

"Talk about your brothers? Your brothers were vipers. Everyone breathed a sigh of relief when Dazen killed them. The best thing he ever did was kill them, and the best thing they ever did was die."

Karris's eyes went red, and luxin curled through her skin in an instant. Gavin felt a stab of fear—not for himself. He could stop whatever she threw his way. But every time a person drafted huge quantities, they hastened their own death. And they granted their color more sway over them. When he'd first met Karris, her jade green eyes had only the smallest ruby stars in them. Now, even at rest, when she wasn't drafting, those ruby stars dominated the green.

But Karris didn't attack. She said, "I'm a slow learner, but I finally got it. You've betrayed me for the last time, Gavin." She nearly spat his name. "I—"

"You damn stubborn woman! I love you, Karris. I've always loved you."

It was like the wind went out of her sails for a few heartbeats. Red luxin drained from her fingertips. Then, when Gavin was just starting to hope, she said, "You dare? You unbelievable—you—you—Gavin Guile, you've brought me nothing but misery and death. We're finished!" She grabbed her bag and jumped off the boat.

Gavin was too startled to say anything. He watched as Karris swam to shore and then dragged herself and her bag out of the water. She could travel to Garriston without him, of course, and she'd still arrive earlier than her contact had expected. There were, of course, bandits to worry about, and a woman traveling alone would make a prime target.

If the bandits got careless because of that fact, they'd be lucky to survive. But everyone had to sleep sometime. Karris was being rash, but nothing Gavin could say would make any difference. Not for a long while. This was why the White had tried to arrange it so he wouldn't be present when she found out about his bastard. He could go after her, but it would be useless. With her temper, he would only make things worse.

Five purposes, and I didn't even spit out the whole truth.

Kip was huddled to one side of the boat, trying to be small. He glanced up and met Gavin's eyes for a moment. "What are you staring at?" Gavin demanded.

Chapter 20

Though she had never drafted a drop of blue, Karris had always had an affinity for what were called the blue virtues. She liked having a plan. She liked order, structure, hierarchy. Even as a child, she enjoyed learning etiquette. Sitting at a Parian formal dinner and knowing the exact function of every tiny spoon and shell cracker, knowing how many times to flick the excess water from your fingers after washing in the water bowl between the first and second course, and knowing where exactly to set your three-tined *urum* to let the table slaves know you were finished eating brought her something akin to peace. Placing your goblet halfway over the lateral divisor meant you wanted exactly half a glass more wine. On the vertical meant you'd like to switch from white to red. Sign and countersign. The luxiat's call and the congregation's response. She loved dance and could perform most of the dances of the Seven Satrapies. She loved music and could play the gemshorn or accompany herself on the psantria while she sang. But nothing she'd learned was helping her now. There was no structure, no hierarchy, no order to direct her.

She was supposed to still be on a ship. She was supposed to meet with a Chromeria spy before she got this far into Tyrea. He was supposed to guide her up the river to King Garadul's army and give her a cover that would get her into the army without getting killed. Instead, she was dripping wet, alone, and less than a full day's walk from that army, with no introduction, no map, no guidelines, no plan. Gavin and his bastard had disappeared down the river not five minutes ago.

I'm getting reckless. The red is destroying me.

Karris wrung out her heavy black wool cloak and started looking for a place to make camp. On the hillside there were huge numbers of eucalyptus trees filling the air with their fragrance, mixing with the taller pines, blocking out the harsh rays of Orholam's bright eye. It took her only a few minutes to find a decent spot mostly obscured by brush. She gathered wood and made a little pyramid. She didn't bother with kindling: there were advantages to being a red. But she did look around carefully for several minutes before she drew out her spectacles from their little pocket up one sleeve. She was alone. She drafted a thin thread of red luxin into the base of her pyramid.

Even drafting that much red blew on the coals of her fury. She tucked away the red and green lenses and thought of smashing Gavin's grinning face. *I love you?* How dare he?

She shook her head and shook her finger out, flinging away deliberately off-center red luxin, getting rid of the excess. As with all luxin drafted imperfectly, it decayed rapidly, releasing a paired scent: the smell of resin that all luxin shared and the odd, dried-tea-leaves-and-tobacco smell of red in particular.

She took out a flint and her knife instead of drafting sub-red directly for a spark. She was already cold, so she struck the spark like a mere mortal.

I love you. That bastard.

While her wet clothes dried, she changed into the spare clothing that had been in her waterproof bag. Tyrean fashion had become mercifully practical in the last fifteen years. Though in social or urban settings women wore calf- or ankle-length dresses belted and often accompanied with a wrap or a full jacket for the evening, on the trail and in the countryside women often wore men's linen trousers, albeit with longer shirts than men wore as a nod to modesty, worn untucked but belted, like a tunic. The way Commander Ironfist had explained it to her was that after the False Prism's War, there hadn't been enough men and boys to harvest the oranges or other fruits. The young women who'd joined the harvesters had shortened their skirts to make it easier to climb ladders repeatedly. Clearly someone had objected to that. Probably not the young men holding the ladders.

Thus the addition of trousers.

Karris liked the clothing. She was used to wearing men's clothes from training with the Blackguard, and if this loose linen didn't move with her as nicely or feel as soft as the stretchy, luxin-infused Blackguard garb, it was still cool. It also did a better job of camouflaging her body than the tight Blackguard garb. No man would dare so much as whistle at a woman Blackguard on the Jaspers, even if she was flaunting a hard-earned figure a little. A woman traveling alone in a far country shouldn't tempt fate more than necessary.

As her little fire burned merrily, Karris distracted herself by arming carefully. Her ataghan would sit concealed and fairly accessible within her pack once the black cloak was dried and rolled up. A *bich'hwa*—a scorpion—was strapped to one thigh inside her trousers. It was a weapon with iron rings to fit the fingers, four claws for swiping, and a dagger—the scorpion's tail—for stabbing. It wasn't quickly accessible, but she always thought it was good to have more weapons than were visible. Another long knife was tucked into her belt. Her bifocal spectacles went into the bag. Their weight simply made them too obvious if she concealed them in these long, flowing sleeves. That left her with her eye caps. The caps, with horizontally streaked lenses of red and green, each fit onto an eye socket, as tight and close to the eye as possible. A thin ridge of sticky red luxin made sure the lenses would stay on her face—and, if she weren't careful, would rip off half her eyebrow when she removed them. The sticky red luxin was shielded with a little strip of solid yellow luxin that was to be torn off before you stuck the caps onto your eyes.

For all that the eye caps had saved her life a time or three, Karris didn't like them. Naturally long eyelashes were a nice accessory at the Luxlords' Ball, but not so much when you had a lens a finger's breadth from your eye.

Karris hid her caps in plain sight, on a necklace made of chunky multicolored stones, none so clear or interesting as to make the necklace seem valuable. The caps clicked together around one link and blended with all the other stones. Another pair of caps was tucked under her belt buckle.

I'm stalling, she thought.

From where she was now, she had only two choices. She could head down the river and meet up with her contact in Garriston and then come back up the river, or she could try to infiltrate King Garadul's army on her own. Going down the river would waste time, and she'd still be much too early. There was also the threat of bandits. She assumed her contact would have some good way of circumventing them on the way back up, but that wouldn't help her as she headed downriver. Going on alone would mean trying to join a hostile army without a proper introduction. And now that Gavin had clashed with King Garadul, the king knew that the Chromeria had already gotten one drafter here, so surely he would be doubly suspicious of anyone else showing up.

In fact, Gavin's little stunt in Rekton had probably made her work impossible. There were certainly Tyreans as pale as she was, but her accent was wrong, and she was a drafter. To a suspicious camp, everything about her would scream spy. The White's orders had never factored in the circumstances in which she found herself now. It was like sitting at what you thought was a dignified Parian dinner with its rules, and finding yourself seated with raucous Ilytian pirates feeding you blowfish instead. There were rules for that too, and if you broke them, you'd consume a nice tender morsel that contained a poison that would leave you in agony for ten minutes, at which point it would leave you dead.

And Karris didn't know the rules here.

Of course, Gavin would just eat the whole damned fish—and somehow, miraculously, it wouldn't harm him. Everything was effortless for Gavin. He'd never had to work hard for anything. Born with a monumental talent to a scheming rich father, he simply took what he wanted. Even the rules of being a Prism didn't constrain him—he traveled to and fro about the Seven Satrapies without so much as a Blackguard escort when he didn't want one. And now he could cross the Cerulean Sea in a few hours. For Orholam's sake, now he could fly.

Get out of my head, liar. I'm done with you.

The lines didn't fit. The tiny spoons were gone, and the urums had a thousand tines instead of three. Fine. Karris wasn't going home. She wasn't going to wait for some man to come hold her hand and get her into Garadul's camp. She wasn't going to fail. There was more than one way to find out what King Garadul's plans were.

Of course, she didn't know what those were, but she was going to figure it out. As for now, she remembered something her brother Koios used to say before he'd been killed in the fire: "When you don't know what to do, do what's right and do what's in front of you. But not necessarily what's right in front of you."

The town of Rekton had been burned to the ground. There had been one survivor. There might be more, and if there were, they would be in desperate need of help and possibly protection. Those, Karris could provide.

And if it involved lighting some jackass up with a fireball the size of a small house, so much the better.

Chapter 21

They practically flew down the river. Kip had never traveled so fast in his life. And the Prism didn't speak a word, sunk into his own dark mood. For most of the afternoon, Gavin Guile worked what the scull had in the place of oars—for a while, it would be almost like a ladder, then it would be like the bellows of a forge, then it would be oars, then it would be a rolling track. Gavin worked at one until he was exhausted, muscles quivering, sweat matting his thin shirt. Then he would draft a little, the oars would change to some new shape that gave his most weary muscles a rest, and he would keep going.

When Kip finally found his voice, he said, "Sir, um, he took my case?" He wasn't going to ask about Karris White Oak or what Gavin had said. Not now. Not ever.

Gavin looked at Kip, his mouth tight. Kip regretted speaking at once. "It was that or your life."

Kip paused, then said, "Thank you, sir. For saving me." That seemed like a better choice than saying, But that was mine! It was the last thing—the only thing—my mother ever gave me!

"You're welcome," Gavin said. He glanced back up the river, his thoughts obviously elsewhere.

"That man, he's responsible for killing my mother, isn't he?" Kip asked.

"Yes."

"I thought you were going to kill him right there. But you stopped."

Gavin glanced at him, weighing him. His voice was distant. "I wasn't willing for the innocent to die so I could kill the guilty."

"Those men weren't innocent! They murdered everyone I know!" Tears leaked down Kip's face. He felt ragged, wrung out, finished.

"I was talking about you."

It caught Kip short, but his emotions were still a jumble. His presence had kept Gavin from killing King Garadul. He didn't know words that could convey his feelings for that. He'd failed his mother again. He'd actually blocked her vengeance by his own incompetence.

I'll make good, mother. On my soul. I'll kill him. I swear it.

Half a dozen small villages passed, and dozens of boats. Fed by tributaries, the river widened. But Gavin stopped only once, to buy a roasted chicken and bread and wine. He threw the food to Kip. "Eat." Then they were off again. Gavin didn't eat. He didn't speak or even slow when they passed the fishermen startled by their appearance.

It wasn't until the sun set and Gavin shifted the oars again that Kip ventured to speak once more. "Can I help...sir?"

The Prism gave him an appraising glance, as if he hadn't even thought of having him help. But when he spoke, he said, "I'd really appreciate that. Here, stand on this and just walk." He'd been running. "You can use these hand oars to help if you want. Steer by dropping in the hand oar on the side you want to turn toward. Port for port, starboard for starboard, right?"

"Port is left?"

"Right."

Kip blinked. Uh... "Port is right?"

"Only if you're facing aft."

The panic must have been clear on Kip's face, because Gavin chuckled. "It doesn't matter. You just go until you're too tired, or if we hit rapids or bandits. I'm going to rest for a bit." Gavin sat in Kip's place and tore into the remains of the chicken and bread. He watched as Kip struggled with getting the scull up to a halfway decent pace. Kip turned a time or two—it actually was pretty simple—and looked at Gavin to see if he approved, but the Prism was already asleep.

The quarter moon was straight overhead as night fell and Kip began walking. Even driven only by Kip's walking, the scull was fast. Gavin had narrowed the hull even further when Karris had left, so the boat seemed more to hover over the water than plow through it. For the first few minutes, Kip was gripped with anxiety. Every turn he was sure they would confront bandits and the Prism wouldn't awaken. But soon he fell into the rhythms of the boat, the waves, and the night.

An owl was hooting in the distance, and little bats were swooping and diving, eating the insects that flew high above the water while trout leapt to eat those that flew too low. The scull startled a heron, which flew off into the night on great blue wings.

Gradually, the peace of the night seeped into Kip. The surface of the river became as smooth as a mirror, and the stars shone in it. He saw ducks huddled on the shore, their heads tucked into their wings. And then he looked once more at the man who was supposedly his father.

Gavin Guile was a muscular man, broad-shouldered but as slender as Kip was fat. Kip searched for any resemblance at all, some hint that this could be true. Gavin was lighter-skinned; he looked like a mix between a Ruthgari, who had green or brown eyes, dark hair, and olive skin, and a Blood Forester, with their cornflower blue eyes and flaming red hair and deathly pale skin. Gavin's hair was the color of burnished copper, and his eyes, of course, were those of a Prism. When he was drafting they looked whatever color he was using at the moment, and could change in an instant. When he wasn't drafting, Gavin's eyes shimmered as if they were prisms themselves, every little twitch sending a cascade of new colors through his irises. They were the most disconcerting eyes Kip had ever seen. They were eyes to make satraps squirm and queens faint. The eyes of Orholam's Chosen.

Kip's eyes were plain blue, which did nothing for him except mark him as a crossbreed. Maybe some Blood Forester lineage. Like most peoples, Tyreans had dark eyes. Kip's hair was dark as a Tyrean's, but tightly curled like a Parian's or an Ilytian's, rather than straight or wavy. Enough to mark him a freak, but nowhere near enough to mark him this man's son. Of course, his mother hadn't had the look of a Tyrean either, which just complicated things. Darker than either, with kinky hair and hazel eyes. Kip tried to imagine what the child of his mother and this man might look like, but he couldn't do it. Blend enough mutts, and who knows what you'll get? Maybe if he weren't so fat he might see it. Maybe it was simply a cruel trick. A lie.

The Prism. The Prism himself? How could such a man be Kip's father? He'd said he hadn't known Kip even existed. How could that happen?

The answer seemed pretty obvious. It had been during the war. Gavin's army had met Dazen's not far from Rekton. So as they'd come through town, Gavin had met Lina. He was the Prism, heading to what might be his death. She was a young, pretty girl whose town had been destroyed. She'd shared his bed. Then he'd gone on to kill his brother— perhaps the very next day—and in the aftermath of the war and the reconstruction and the work of putting down the rest of the rebellion and rebuilding alliances and administering the peace, he'd probably never thought of her again. Even if he had, Tyrea wasn't exactly the friendliest or safest of places for the Prism back then. It had sided with Dazen, the evil brother, and been treated cruelly as a result.

Or maybe Gavin had raped Lina. But that didn't make sense. Why would a rapist claim Kip? Especially because it obviously cost Gavin a lot to do so.

Kip could imagine his mother, pregnant, unmarried, left in the devastation that was Rekton. Of course she'd want to escape. Kip would have been her one hope. What would she have done? Travel, alone, to Garriston, where the victors were administering Tyrea? He could imagine that well enough. His mother, presenting herself to some governor, demanding to see Gavin Guile because she bore his bastard. She'd have been lucky if she got as far as a governor with that tale. So she'd been turned away, her dreams of anything good or easy in her life dashed.

Whenever she looked at Kip, she didn't see her own bad choices, she saw Gavin's "betrayal" and her disappointment. Kip was a dream dashed.

Within half an hour, Kip was tiring. His arms were burning. He thought of how Gavin had practically sprinted for hours. The thought of waking the Prism so soon shamed him. He'd always tired quickly, but if he pushed through his initial fatigue he had a lot of stamina.

He wasn't going to wake the Prism. Not at all. Let the man rest. He'd earned that much from Kip. Kip would keep going until Gavin woke. Even if it killed him. He swore it.

The oath made Kip feel good. He was insignificant. A nothing. But he could give the Prism himself a good night's sleep. He could do something. He could matter, in a small way, but a bigger way than he ever had in his whole life.

He kept going. The Prism had saved him today. The Prism himself! Gavin had faced down King Garadul. He'd killed a score or more of Garadul's Mirrormen—and walked away. And Kip had probably endangered it all by trying to attack the king. How stupid could he get? With all the drafters there, Kip had thought he could get to the king? Stupid!

Despite the coolness of the night, it wasn't long before Kip was covered in sweat. His fast walk had become a trudge, but that trudge still drove the scull as fast as a horse's canter.

Kip was so focused on just keeping going that he was on top of the camp before he noticed it. There were maybe a dozen men carousing around a fire, drinking and laughing as one strummed a badly out-of-tune lute. Kip kept trudging, his brain slow to take in what this had to be. The men were all armed, including one who looked like he was supposed to be on watch—that one still held his crossbow cocked and ready against his shoulder.

Kip thought of whispering to wake Gavin, but they were so close that anything loud enough to wake the Prism might be loud enough to carry over the river to the crossbowman who stood just at the edge of the firelight, his body turned toward the river but his head turned to his comrades.

The scull made only a slight hiss as it cut across the water. Surely it would be inaudible beneath the merry crackling of the bandits' fire. The bandits had partially dammed the river, with rocks pinching in from either side. They'd laid wood planks over the top to make a walkway with only a tiny gap in the middle. Any boat that tried to get through would be within range of at least their spears.

Kip could disengage himself from the oars and touch Gavin—but what could Gavin do? It was night. There wasn't much light for a Prism to work with. Maybe if Kip had woken him earlier. Now it was too late. He'd probably killed them. He'd have to shoot for the gap and hope for the best.

He aimed the scull at the gap and gasped as at the last second the moonlight cut through the water and revealed the bandits' last trap: a stout, sharpened pole was embedded in the riverbed and stuck up to within a few thumbs of the surface of the water. Anyone who tried to shoot the gap would find themselves hung up, with a gaping hole in their hull.

The scull's luxin hull barely brushed the pole and slid past.

Kip shot a glance at the crossbowman as the scull slipped through the teeth of the bandits' trap. The man was only a few years older than Kip. He was laughing, happy, hand extended to one of the other men, asking for a skin of wine.

Then Kip was through. The crossbowman turned, shaking his head, then froze as he saw Kip. In the dark, the translucent luxin must have been well-nigh invisible to the sentry's fire-spoiled night vision. He was seeing a fat boy running past him—on the river's surface. Impossible.

Kip smiled and waved.

The sentry lifted a hand and waved back. Froze. Looked back at his comrades at the fire. His mouth opened to shout an alarum, but nothing came out. He turned back to the river and looked for Kip.

Kip was still within easy crossbow shot. He knew that, but he didn't speed up, even though—at this moment—he had energy to spare. Anything he did might spook the sentry.

The sentry stared hard into the darkness at the disappearing ghost—and said nothing. He rubbed his forehead in consternation, shook his head, and turned back to his friends. Then Kip ran, not for long, but after a minute of running the scull was hundreds of paces downriver. Kip returned to his walk. He smiled. Stupid as it had been, he'd made it through without even waking the Prism.

He didn't know how long he walked. He tried to keep an eye on the shore, but weariness had sunk into his bones. He passed smaller camps—whether of bandits or just innocent travelers, he couldn't tell. But each time he saw them, he slowed to a crawl until he could see that all the men in the camp were asleep. He even did his trick again of unfocusing his eyes, and he could see the sleeping lumps of several more men than his focused eyes could, but never another sentry.

The sky didn't lighten for what seemed a thousand years. Kip's legs were burning. His lungs ached. He could barely feel his arms, but he refused to stop. Even at his bare trudge, the scull still moved twice as fast as a punt.

Finally, the sun touched the mountains. As always, daylight came long before the sun could climb the Karsos Mountains' backs to announce sunrise. And still the Prism didn't wake. Kip wouldn't stop walking. Not now. He'd gone all night. Surely the Prism would wake any moment and see what Kip had done. He would be impressed. He would look at Kip with new eyes. Kip would be more than a burden, a shame, a bastard to be quietly admitted and then avoided.

The Prism stirred, and Kip's heart leapt. But then the man settled back in, his breathing steady once more. Kip despaired. He looked to the rising sun. Was he going to have to wait until the light shone directly on the Prism's face? That would be another hour at least. Kip swallowed. His tongue felt thick and dry, raspy as a file. How long had it been since he'd had a drink? A river beneath his feet, and he was parched.

He needed a drink. He was past needing a drink. If he didn't drink, he was going to pass out. The Prism's wineskin wasn't even a full pace away. Kip stopped walking. His legs quivered. His feet were numb, and now they hurt as the blood leached back into them. He extricated himself from the oar mechanism and stepped over to grab the wineskin.

Or tried to. His numb feet got tangled up and he pitched forward, barely able to twist one way so he didn't crush the Prism. His turned shoulder slammed onto the scull's gunwale, and suddenly everything that had been good about the scull turned bad. The shallow displacement that had allowed the boat to slip over the bandits' trap meant no stability. The bowl-like flare of the slick hull that had allowed them to slide over rocks meant that the sudden shift in weight was cataclysmic.

One moment, Kip was staring at the river from thumbs away. The next, the entire scull flipped. Kip's head went in first. And yet despite the water closing over his ears and the thrashing of his own stupid clumsy limbs and the crashing of the rest of the scull hitting the water, somehow he was certain he heard a man's startled yell.

The river was warm. Kip was so mortified, he decided to just die and get it over with. He'd just dunked the Prism into the river. Orholam!

Oh, he'll be real impressed now, Kip.

Then his lungs started burning, and the idea of quietly dying to remove one ignominious blot from creation lost all appeal. Kip thrashed, weakly. His legs decided now would be a good time to cramp, and both did. Then his left arm. He flapped in the water like a lame bird, got one gulp of air, and plunged back down. Part of him knew he could float. He'd floated leagues down the river just yesterday, but panic had him fully in its grip. He floundered, took a breath at the wrong time, and sucked in water.

His head hurt. Orholam, it was like someone was ripping out all of his hair.

He spit and spluttered. He was in air! Sweet, precious air! Someone had grabbed him by the hair and pulled him out of the water. He coughed twice more and finally opened his eyes.

The Prism was winking at him—no, not winking. The Prism was blinking away the water that Kip had just spat up into his face.

Let me die now.

The man hauled Kip into the scull—now wider, with a keel, and much more stable than before. Kip hung his head and rubbed his arm and legs until they could move again. The Prism was standing over him, waiting. Kip swallowed, wincing, and braced himself to meet the great man's fury. He looked up sheepishly.

"Love a morning swim," Gavin said. "Quite bracing." And he winked.

Chapter 22

Dazen Guile woke slowly, senses bombarded with the stultifying blue blandness of his dungeon. Three thunks, three hisses, and his breakfast fell onto the dungeon floor. Ignoring the cold in his limbs, ignoring the stiffness and pain in his body from sleeping on blue luxin with only a thin blanket, he sat and folded his arms.

The dead man was whistling tunelessly, sitting against the opposite wall, bobbing his head to a nonexistent beat.

The madness of blue was a madness of order. A giist would understand every nuance of Gavin's prison. But every time Dazen sank into the madness, he was frightened that he'd never come out of it. The last time he'd tried must have been years ago. He'd drafted a lot of blue since then. Choosing a descent into the blue again might well be choosing annihilation.

"Dazen," the dead man said. "You are Dazen this morning, aren't you?" It was a favorite trick of the dead man's, pretending Dazen was the crazy one. "You aren't thinking of going giist, are you?"

He hated his brother for doing this, for forcing this choice. But there was no passion to his hatred. It was a bare fact, as naked as his own limbs, stripped of mystery.

Enough. Better oblivion chosen of his own will than torture forever according to his brother's.

Dazen drafted blue like he was taking a deep breath. His fingernails turned that hateful blue, his hands, arms. It spread over his chest like an icy cancer, and it cooled him. His hatred itself became an oddity, a mystery, something so irrational and powerful it couldn't be quantified or understood, merely accounted for approximately. The blue suffused his entire body.

"Bad idea," the dead man said. "I don't think you'll come out of it this time." He started juggling little blue luxin globes. He could handle five now. When Dazen had first met him, the dead man couldn't even juggle three.

Without passion clouding his study, he could appreciate the cell. His brother was brilliant. What had he said after imprisoning him? "I made this dungeon in a month, you will have as long to break out as it takes. Consider it a test." Every time he had given up, he'd returned to that statement. It was an admission of imperfection. The cell could be broken. There was a weakness; he merely had to find it.

"The hellstone isn't the weakness," the dead man said. "Didn't I tell you? He respects you too much. It won't go a few thumbs deep, it'll go two paces."

He was aware, briefly, of a human emotion barely at the threshold of his perception. Loss—fury at how he'd scrubbed piss and oil for years, years of degradation, for nothing. His brother had no interest in degrading him. That wasn't his way. All that effort, for nothing. He turned those feelings over like an odd stone in his hands, then tossed them aside. They only clouded his vision.

Something was sitting right in front of his face, and he wasn't seeing it. It had to be something obvious, something that simply required him to look at the problem from a new angle. His brother had been so good at that kind of thinking.

"Maybe the only question is, are you going to do this Gavin's way, or Dazen's?" the dead man asked. He had that little superior, mocking smile. Dazen wanted to smash his face in when he grinned like that.

But maybe he was right. That was the trap: trying to do this Gavin's way. If he did this his brother's way, it would only lead deeper.

He put his luxin-filled hands to the ground, feeling the outline of the whole structure. The cell was sealed, of course, hardened and guarded against simple magical tampering, but as before, it felt different to the south. Not that he was sure it was the south side, he'd merely decided that the one area that felt different would be the south for him, his lodestone. That was where his brother stood when he came to see him. It hadn't happened in a long time, but there was a room beyond the blue luxin walls there, where Gavin could come when he wanted to check on his brother, to assure himself that he was still a prisoner, still safely kept from the world, still suffering as much as he hoped.

That would be the weakness. The luxin there had to be thinner, simpler, so Gavin could manipulate it so that he could see through it. It would be warded, of course, but Gavin couldn't have thought of everything. He'd only had a month.

But Dazen's every attempt with fire had been a failure. Red luxin was flammable, so he'd thought that if he cut himself, he could draft red luxin. He could, a little. But that was good for nothing unless he could make it burn. A fire would give him full-spectrum light to work with—and he would be able to get out. But he had nothing to make a spark. Trying to leach heat from his own body had nearly worked—or at least he'd thought he was close, and he'd nearly killed himself the last time by cooling his body too much.

It just wasn't possible. He was going to die down here. There was nothing he could do.

He drafted a sledgehammer and, screaming, smashed it against the wall. It shattered, of course. It didn't leave so much as a scratch.

Dazen rubbed his face. No, the enemy was despair. He had to conserve his strength. Tomorrow he'd rub the bowl more. Maybe tomorrow would be the day.

He knew it wouldn't, but he held on to the lie anyway.

In the wall, the dead man was cackling.

Chapter 23

"We need to talk about your future," Gavin said. "You have some choices."

Kip looked at the Prism across their fire. Night was coming on fast in their little island. Kip had slept for hours, apparently, completely missing Garriston and only waking as their boat lurched, hitting the sand as night fell.

"How long will I live?" Kip asked. He was grumpy, hungry, and just starting to comprehend some of the implications of what had happened in the last two days.

"A question for Orholam himself. I'm just his humble Prism," Gavin said, a wry smile twisting his lips. He was looking out into the darkness.

"You know what I mean." It came out sharper than Kip meant. Everyone he knew was dead, and he was going to be a green drafter. He'd seen his future in the color wight: death or madness and then death.

Gavin's eyes snapped back to Kip. He moved to speak, stopped, then said, "When you draft, it changes your body, and your body interprets that change as damage—it heals what it can, but it's always a losing battle, like aging. Most male drafters make it to forty. Women average fifty."

"Then the Chromeria kills us or we go mad?"

Gavin's face went hard. "You're getting emotional. I don't think you're ready for this."

"Not ready?" Kip said. Gavin was right, Kip knew it. He was on edge. He should just shut up, but he couldn't help himself. "I wasn't ready for everyone I know to be murdered. I wasn't ready to impale some horsemen and jump over a waterfall. Words are nothing. What is it? Once we aren't useful anymore, we have to kill ourselves?" Why was he yelling? Why was he trembling? Orholam, he'd sworn on his soul to kill a king, was he mad already?

"Something like that."

"That or turn into a color wight?" Kip asked.

"That's right."

"Well, I guess we've talked about my future," Kip said bitterly. He knew he was being snotty, but he couldn't stop himself.

"That wasn't what I meant, and you know it," Gavin said.

"How would you know what I know, *father*?"

It was like watching a spring release. One second, the Prism was sitting across the fire from Kip. The next, he stood right in front of Kip, his arm drawn back. The next, Kip was hitting the sand, head ringing from Gavin's openhanded blow, ass scraped from sliding off his log, his wind taken by the fall.

"You've been through hell, so I've given you more slack than I give any man. You wanted to find the line? You've found it."

Kip rolled face up as he caught his breath. He had sand sticking to the wetness at the corner of his mouth. He rubbed it. Just slobber, not blood. "Orholam's balls!" he said. "Guess what I've found? A line! I'm the greatest discoverer since Ariss the Navigator!"

Gavin trembled, his face a mask. He rolled his shoulders, popped his neck right and left. Though his back was to their fire, Kip could see red luxin smoke-swirls curling into his eyes.

"What are you going to do? Beat me?" Kip demanded. It's just pain.

Sometimes Kip hated himself for how he saw weakness. The Prism threatened him and the first thing Kip saw was the threat's emptiness. Gavin couldn't beat him precisely because Gavin was a good man and Kip was defenseless.

Gavin's look darkened to murder for one moment, then cleared to simple intensity. The briefest flicker of amusement. "Take a deep breath," he said quietly.

"What?"

The Prism made a little backhanded gesture, as if whisking away a fly. A gob of red luxin flicked out of his hand and splattered over Kip's mouth. Kip took a deep breath through his nose before the luxin spread and covered that, too. Then it wrapped around the back of his head, spread over the top of his head, and solidified. Only Kip's eyes were uncovered, mouth and nose were covered, utterly blocked. He couldn't breathe.

Gavin said, "You remind me of my brother. I could never win against him growing up. And when I did, he'd give me some patronizing praise that made me wonder if he'd let me win. You see the cracks in things? Fine. It's proof enough that you're a Guile. Our whole family has it. Including me. Think about this, Kip: there are a lot of problems that would go away for me if I leave that mask on your face until you're dead. You might want to think twice before you try to use a man's conscience against him. It may turn out he doesn't have one."

Kip listened, conserving his strength against his rising panic, certain that after Gavin was done talking, he would take the luxin off his face. But Gavin stopped talking, and he didn't remove the mask. Kip's stomach churned as his diaphragm worked to suck in more air, pumped down to expel the dead air he held in. Nothing.

He reached up to his neck, trying to find the seam where luxin abutted skin. But the line was smooth, the luxin sticking close to the skin. He couldn't get his fingernails under it. He reached up around his head, his eyes. If he stabbed his fingernails into the soft skin next to his eyes, he could lift the edge of the mask and get one finger underneath it. His vision was darkening. He looked at Gavin, pleading, sure that the man would step in now.

Gavin watched him, pitiless. "If the only thing you're going to respect is strength, Kip, first, you're a fool, and second, you've come to the right man."

The panic came. He should have known better. Kip thrashed, tried to scream, reached up to that thin ridge of luxin by his eyes—but he barely touched it before his hands drooped. He should have known he couldn't trust...

Chapter 24

After traveling all day and into the night, Karris first became aware of Rekton in the distance as a great, unvariegated glow as she stalked through the forest. It was long after nightfall now, the air cool in the undergrowth. She was enough of a sub-red to use dark vision, but it wasn't perfect, and on a moonlit night like tonight she kept switching back and forth from normal to dark vision. Light below the visible spectrum was rougher; it didn't lend itself to fine differentiation of features. Even faces simply looked like warm blobs, brighter here and there, but it was much more difficult to make out expressions or fine movements—or even to identify a face from much of a distance.

The glow meant Rekton was still burning. Karris circled it slowly, climbing the last hill. She stayed off the road, admiring the waterfall just below the town in the silver moonlight. She hadn't seen anyone on the road all day, which she found odd. If no one was fleeing downriver from Rekton, it probably meant no one had made it out. But it was also strange to follow the river through arable land and not come across any other settlements. She'd seen orange orchards that clearly hadn't been tended since the war, but they were still growing fruit. The fruit was sparse and the trees leafy and chaotic and growing haphazardly in comparison to the paintings Karris had seen of orange harvests, but they were still here. With the price Tyrean oranges fetched, she found that hard to believe. Tyrean oranges were smaller but sweeter and juicier than Atashian oranges, and the Parian oranges didn't even compare. No one had moved back after the war?

Had the Battle of Sundered Rock really killed so many that even now, sixteen years later, the land lay fallow, bearing fruit for deer and bears alone?

Karris didn't see any bodies until she crept into the still-burning town, wrapped in her hooded black cloak. She was following the main road, its cobbles even and well maintained: a symbol in Karris's mind of a place well governed. A burned body lay in the middle of the street, facedown, one arm extended, a finger pointing deeper into the town. Only the hand and pointing finger were unburned. The head was missing.

She hadn't seen this kind of burn since the war. During the war, the armies had clashed a number of times in areas where the bodies couldn't be buried and where there wasn't enough natural fuel for funeral pyres. Corpses had to be disposed of to avoid losing even more soldiers to disease, so red drafters would spray a corpse with a quick stream of red jelly. A quick coating, even if drafted carelessly, could be lit quickly. Problem solved. It wasn't cremation, though. If bodies were burned singly, rather than in piles, the bones remained. If the drafter weren't thorough, certain body parts wouldn't be reduced entirely to bone. Rib cages and skulls ended up full of smoking meat—good enough for exigencies of war when you had to dispose of your opponents' corpses to avoid spreading disease, but never good enough for one's own countrymen.

King Garadul hadn't fought in that war, but he was aping the worst practices of it—on his own people.

As she suspected, that pointing hand led Karris to more bodies. At first they were spread widely, then one every thirty paces, one every twenty paces, one every ten. All were headless. Then bodies lined the sides of the main road now in a solid row, past smoking, crumbled homes and shops. The nicely maintained cobblestones here had cracked from the heat. There were tracks across the cobbles. At first she couldn't tell what they were, but as she got closer it became obvious: they were drag marks, streaks of dried blood perhaps a day old from the decapitated bodies being dragged from the square.

She paused amid the smoke and gore before she rounded the corner that would take her to the town square. She drew the short sword, but didn't put on her spectacles. If there was a trap, it would be here, but there was enough red and heat for her to fight magically if necessary. Even if she wasn't planning on a straight infiltration, there was no need to announce that she was a drafter if she didn't have to. When the moment came, she'd announce it with fire.

Karris rounded the corner.

Dear Orholam.

They hadn't melted the heads. They'd preserved them with a blue-and-yellow luxin glaze and stacked them in the middle of the town square. Eyes staring, faces mangled, blood cascading from the top to the bottom like a champagne pyramid at the Luxlords' Ball. Karris had half expected something like this from all the decapitated bodies, but expecting it wasn't the same as seeing it. Her stomach heaved. She turned and clamped her jaw shut, blinking rapidly, as if her eyelids could scrape the horrors off her eyes. She studied the rest of the square to give her stomach time to settle.

If Gavin had seen this, he would have killed King Garadul. Pitiless as the sea, righteous as Orholam, he would have hunted down every one of these monsters. Whatever he had done during the war and before—whatever he had done to her—since the False Prism's War, Gavin had traveled the Seven Satrapies meting out justice. He'd sunk Ilytian pirate fleets twice, killed the bandit king of the Blue-Eyed Demons, made peace when war had broken out again between Ruthgar and the Blood Forest, and brought the Butcher of Ru to justice. Other than the Tyreans, the people loved him. And he would have wreaked a mighty vengeance here, even for Tyreans. He wouldn't have stood for this.

Most of the buildings were piles of rubble, smoking in the predawn gray. Here and there a single wall stood, scorched and blackened and separated from its fallen fellows. The alcaldesa's residence, if such it was—it was the grandest building she'd seen here, with steps leading directly onto the square—was a total loss. The soldiers had flattened it; there wasn't one rock left sitting on another.

But the square itself was immaculate. Any burnt wreckage had either been pushed into the streets leading here or shoveled directly into the river, whose channel bounded the square to the west. King Garadul had wanted nothing to distract a visitor from his grisly trophy. Steeling herself, Karris looked back to the pyramid of human heads. All the drag marks, all the bloody streaks led here. The bodies—Karris hoped they'd all already been bodies by the time they came here—had all been decapitated here so that the pyramid would be as bloody as possible. This was a spectacle. King Garadul wanted everything to lead to this horror.

The pyramid was taller than Karris. The heads at the top, crowning the pyramid, were children: round-cheeked little boys and little girls with their hair in ribbons and bows.

Karris didn't throw up. There was something about this that simply left her cold. By their ages and her own, those children could have been hers. She found herself counting the heads. There were forty-five at the base, and the pyramid was as wide as it was tall, built with mathematical precision. The children's heads were smaller, and there was no way to tell if the pyramid was solid or if these heads had been stacked around the outside of a smaller pyramid made of something else. Karris's fingers moved as she mentally moved the beads of an abacus, shuttling them left and right.

If the pyramid was solid heads, there were somewhere in the neighborhood of a thousand heads here.

Cold tingles shot over her skin, the precursor to vomiting. She looked away. You're a spy, Karris. You have to find out everything important. Taking long, deep breaths, she examined the bottom corner of the pyramid, then looked edge-on at one face of the shape. It was made of multiple layers of different colors of luxin. King Garadul wanted this to last for years. Someone could attack the pyramid with a sledgehammer, and they might be able to crack it, but not break it open. There would be no burying these heads or removing this hideous monument.

The skill evident here meant King Garadul had access to a number—perhaps a large number—of fairly talented and skilled drafters. Bad news. Karris had heard Gavin express his belief that King Garadul was starting a pseudo-Chromeria to train his own drafters away from the Chromeria's oversight. This was pretty strong evidence that Gavin was right.

"Bastard," Karris said. She wasn't sure whether she meant Garadul or Gavin. How stupid was that? She was staring at a pile of heads and she was as angry at Gavin as she was at the monster who'd done this? Because he'd slept with some strumpet during the war?

Insanely, even after the great fire that had ruined everything in her life and killed her brothers, Karris had been more than half tempted to go over to Dazen's side during that time. If only to hear his side of what had happened. Maybe Gavin had known.

Or maybe it was the guilt of his illicit liaison that had caused Gavin to break their betrothal right after the war.

So he was unfaithful. Welcome to the common fate of women who love great men. For all you know, it was only one night of weakness on the eve of the last battle, some beauty throwing herself at him, and he didn't say no, just once.

Right. But for all I know, *every* night was a night of weakness.

It was years ago, Karris. Years! How has Gavin acted in all the years since the war?

Aside from breaking our betrothal and leaving me with nothing?

How has he acted toward you in the last fifteen years?

Decently. Damn him. Aside from lying and secrets. What had he said? "I don't expect you to understand or even believe me, but what's in that note, I swear it isn't true." Something about that niggled at her. Why would he compound the lie?

The wind shifted and blew smoke across the open square. Karris coughed, her eyes burning. But just as she finished coughing, she thought she heard a crack.

Another crack, and then, just a block away, a chimney came crashing down into the torched remains of a house. The dawn was red—a trick of the smoke and spectrums, not a heavenly mirror to all the blood spilled here.

Karris began searching the town, looking for survivors and surveying the damage. Do what's right, do what's in front of you. The town hadn't burned easily. The buildings were stone, albeit with wooden supports, and the trees were green, either from manual watering—the river ran right through town—or from their roots reaching deep enough. But every single building in the town center had burned down completely. That meant red drafters.

They must have walked through all the buildings, spraying red luxin on every wooden beam.

Karris searched for two hours, climbing over rubble in the streets, sometimes having to go around whole blocks. She wrapped a wet cloth around her face, but still got lightheaded, coughing frequently. She found nothing other than more corpses and a few mournful dogs. All the livestock had been taken. The town church had been the site of a small battle. A luxiat's body lay decapitated like the rest, outside the doors of the church. Karris could imagine him denouncing the soldiers outside, trying to protect those of his flock who'd sought sanctuary within the walls. Inside, she found pruning shears, an ax, and knives, and a pair of cleavers, and one broken sword, and decapitated bodies. And dried, burned blood everywhere. The beams here were seared but hadn't caught fire. Either clumsy drafting, or religious fear, or the fact that the ironwood beams, imported from the deserts of southern Atash, were so old and dense.

The pews, however, and the bodies had burned. Karris was in a daze, whether from inhaling smoke or just becoming inured to the tableau of death and suffering. In the back corner of the church behind the stairs, she found a young family, the father with his arms wrapped around the mother, who was sheltering a child. The soldiers hadn't found these. They'd died in each other's arms from the smoke. Karris checked each of them carefully, feeling for the faint tremor of life at each neck. Father, dead. The mother, a girl not yet out of her teens, dead. Karris took the swaddled babe in her arms last, a boy. She prayed under her breath. But Orholam turned a deaf ear; there was no life in his tiny breast.

Karris staggered. She had to get out of here. She put the dead babe down on the nearest table, only to see it was the altar. She careened up the main aisle of the church, past smoldering pews on her left and right, images of another time, another sacrificed babe, joining the horrors before her eyes.

She was almost out when the floor collapsed.

Chapter 25

"You need to make some choices, Kip," Gavin said.

From all he could tell, Kip had only been unconscious for seconds or minutes. It was still dark, the stars burning coldly overhead, the fire not yet scorching his clothes despite its nearness to where he'd fallen. The strangling red luxin mask was gone, though there remained a light coating of dust, gritty and sharp on his skin.

"I'll kill you!" Kip said. He couldn't trust anyone. Everyone was a liar. Everyone was just out for himself. Fear rose, and that made the anger flare as it sometimes did, hot and fierce and uncontrollable. He sat up, eyes locked on the Prism's face. The man looked at him coolly, unapologetic, merely curious about what Kip would do, ignoring his words. Kip wondered if he could conjure giant green spikes from the fire to impale the man.

Smart, Kip. In the middle of Orholam only knows where, you'd kill your guide? For what? For not tolerating your peevishness?

Not betrayal, Kip, a lesson. Kip shivered. He'd really thought Gavin was going to kill him. And that was the point. He had given Gavin no choice but to show that he couldn't be handled, not by a child. He was not only older than Kip, he was smarter, and harder, and more experienced, and he demanded respect.

And that was...appropriate.

But that didn't stop Kip's shivering. If only for a few seconds, he'd really thought he was dying—and there had been nothing he could do about it. But this was the one man who could show him how to never be powerless again. This was the man who could teach him how to avenge his mother and Rekton. And Kip was going to sit in silence and stubbornness?

With as much dignity as he could muster, Kip retook his seat on the log. His knees trembled, but he was able to sit without disgracing himself further. "Sorry," he mumbled, looking away. He cleared his throat so he wouldn't squeak. "What choices?" he asked.

He could tell Gavin was a little surprised and pleased that Kip didn't fight, but the man left it alone. "You're my natural son, Kip. That has consequences. For you." Kip was watching Gavin's face closely. He said the words "my natural son" without a grimace, without even his eyes tightening. Kip wondered if he'd rehearsed to be able to say that so blithely. Kip had seen something of what claiming his own patrimony had cost Gavin, and still the man claimed him without so much as a grimace at Kip's grimace-worthy existence. It had to be an act—who could be pleased about learning that he'd fathered a bastard?—but it was an act for Kip's sake.

Gavin was a better man than Kip would have expected. "Being known as my bastard has costs," Gavin continued. "You haven't been raised in privilege, but people who resent those raised in privilege will resent you. You haven't been educated, but those who have been will look down on you if you know less than they do. If I acknowledge you, you'll attract the wrong sort of friends. Those who hate and resent me can't often take it out on me, Kip, I'm too powerful, too dangerous. But they will take it out on you. It isn't fair, but that's how it is. You'll be under constant scrutiny, and both your successes and failures will have repercussions you can't even guess at now. My father may choose not to recognize you. Others will seek to prove you're a fraud. Others will attempt to use you against me. And still others will want to befriend you only in the hope that it will help them gain some favor with me. False friendship is a poison I'd like to protect you from."

Too late for that. Kip thought of Ram: Ram who was always in charge, who always liked smearing Kip's face in his own inferiority and claiming it was friendly teasing. Ram, whom Isa had loved. Ram, dead, lying with an arrow in his back. "So what are my options?" Kip asked. "I am what I am."

Gavin rubbed the bridge of his nose. "You could go as just another student for the time being. Then, whenever you like, I'll publicly acknowledge you. You'll have time to gain your bearings, to learn who your real friends are."

"By lying to them?"

"Sometimes lies are most necessary with our friends," Gavin snapped. He paused. "Look, I just wanted to give you the option—"

"No, I'm sorry. I'm not—I'm not mad at you. My mother...Do you remember what she was like? I mean, before me?" Kip asked.

Gavin's mouth worked. He wet his lips. Then shook his head. "I don't remember her, Kip. At all."

So, not exactly a love affair. Kip's emptiness doubled. There was no family to belong to. "You're the Prism; I guess a lot of women want to be with you," Kip said.

"It was war, Kip. When you expect to die, you don't think about the effects your actions might have on others ten years on. When you've seen friends die all around you, there's something about making love that makes you feel alive. There was far too much wine and spirits and no one who would rein in a young hothead who had the misfortune to be the Prism. But it's not an excuse. I'm sorry, Kip. I'm sorry for what my thoughtlessness has cost you."

So my mother had one night with you, and she pinned her hopes on that. Kip had no doubt she'd elbowed and schemed her way past a dozen other women who would have gladly shared the Prism's bed. And she'd filled years with bitterness for that?

Kip forced a laugh, his heart breaking. For all the times he'd dreamed about who his father might be, he'd never dared to dream that he might be the Prism himself. But in his dreams, his father had been called away by some emergency. He'd left them because he had to. But he'd loved Kip's mother and Kip. Missed them. Wanted to come back, and would any day. Gavin was a good man, but he didn't care about Lina. Or Kip. He would take care of Kip because he was dutiful. A good person. But there was no love. No family to belong to. Kip was alone, outside, staring through barred windows at what he would never have.

It was like being given a gift that was wildly exotic when you wanted something perfectly common. Still, what kind of an ingrate was he? Complaining? Feeling sorry for himself—because the Prism was his father?

"I'm sorry," Kip said. He stared at his fingernails, still torn from his luxin use. "This isn't right. My mother had...some problems. I guess she wanted to trap you by showing up with me." Kip couldn't maintain eye contact. He was so ashamed. How could you be so stupid, mother? So mean? "You don't deserve this. You saved my life, and I've been...awful." Kip blinked, but he couldn't fully stop the tears. "You can leave me wherever—well, preferably not on a deserted island."

Gavin smirked, then got serious. "Kip, your mother and I did what we did. I appreciate you trying to shield me from the consequences of my actions, but *you* are not trapping me into anything. People can talk. I don't care. Understand?" He expelled a breath. "Regardless, the only damage I care about has already been done."

For a second, Kip didn't understand. The damage was already done? No one even knew Kip was alive.

Except Karris. That was what Gavin meant. Kip had caused a rift with the only person in the world Gavin cared about. What had been intended to make Kip feel better hit him instead where he was weakest. His mother had made him feel guilty for simply existing for as long as he could remember. He'd ruined her life by being born. He'd ruined her life by having too many demands. He'd made people look down on her. He'd held her back from all the things she could have done. Mentally, he could try to shrug off her words. She didn't mean it. She loved Kip, even if she had never said the words. She didn't know how she was hurting him.

But Gavin was a good man. He didn't deserve this.

"Kip. *Kip.*" Gavin waited until Kip looked up at him. "I will not abandon you."

Visions of a locked cupboard, screaming—screaming—and no one answering. "Is there anything to eat?" Kip asked, blinking. "I feel like I haven't eaten in a week." He poked his chest. He could feel ribs sticking out.

Gavin pulled a rope of sausages out of his pack, cut one off—only one?—and tossed it to Kip. "Tomorrow, you start at the Chromeria."

"Oomowwow?" Kip asked, mouth full.

"I'm going to share a secret with you," Gavin said. "I can travel faster than anyone suspects."

"You can disappear and reappear somewhere else? I knew it!" Kip said.

"Um, no. But I can make a boat that goes really fast."

"Oh, that's...amazing. A boat."

Gavin looked nonplussed. "Point is, I don't want anyone to know how fast I am. There's war coming, and if I need to unveil it, I need it to be a surprise. You understand?"

"Of course," Kip said.

"Then I need you to tell me what you want. I'm going to go take care of some things while you're being initiated."

"Initiated?"

"Just some tests to determine the rest of your life. You're late, though, all the other students have already started, so we have to hustle you in. After initiation, you can stay and be trained."

Kip's throat tightened. Dropped alone on a strange island, knowing no one, and having little time to prepare for a test that was supposed to determine the rest of his life? On the other hand, the Chromeria was where he'd learn the magic he needed to kill King Garadul. "What's the other option?"

"You come with me."

It was light at the end of a tunnel. Kip's heart flipped. "And what are you going to do?"

"What I'm good at, Kip." Gavin stared up, his irises swirling rainbows. He smiled, but it didn't touch his eyes. When he spoke, his voice was cold and distant as the moon. "I'm going to make war."

Kip swallowed. Sometimes looking at Gavin, he felt like he was staring through trees, getting glimpses of a giant striding through a forest, crushing everything in his path.

Gavin turned his eyes back to Kip. His face softened. "Which mostly involves boring meetings to convince cowards to spend money on things other than parties and pretty clothes." He grinned. "I'm afraid you've probably seen more magic out of me already than most of my soldiers ever did." His eyes clouded. "Well, not quite. You look confused."

"It's not really about what you just said, but—" Kip stopped. It seemed like a pretty offensive question, now that it was halfway out of his mouth. "What do you do?"

"As Prism?"

"Yes. Um, sir. I mean, I know you're the emperor, but it doesn't seem like..."

"Like anyone listens to me?" Gavin laughed. "Seems like it to me too. The bald truth of it is that Prisms come and go. Usually every seven years. Prisms have all the foibles of lesser men, and huge shifts of power every seven years can be devastating. If one Prism sets up his family members to govern every satrapy, and the next Prism tries to set up his own in their places, things get bloody fast. The Colors, on the other hand, the seven members of the Spectrum, are often around for decades. And they're usually pretty smart, so Prisms have been managed more and more over time, given religious duties to fill their days. The Spectrum and the satraps rule together. Each satrapy has one Color on the Spectrum, and each Color is supposed to obey the orders of his or her satrap. In practice, the Colors often become co-satraps in all but name. The jockeying between Color and satrap, and all the Colors and the White, and all the Colors and the White against the Prism, pretty much keeps order. Each satrapy can do what it wants at home as long as it doesn't rile up any other satrapy and trade keeps flowing, so everyone has an interest in keeping everyone else in check. It's not quite that simple, of course, but that's the gist."

It sounded plenty complicated enough. "But during the war...?"

"I was appointed promachos. Absolute rule during wartime. Makes everyone nervous, in case the promachos decides that the 'war' lasts forever."

"But you gave it up?" It was a dumb question, Kip realized.

But Gavin smiled. "And wonder of wonders, I haven't been assassinated. The Blackguard doesn't only protect Prisms, Kip. They protect the world from us."

Orholam. Gavin's world sounded more dangerous than what Kip had just left. "So you'll teach me to draft?" he asked. It was the best of all worlds. He would learn what he needed to learn, without being set on a strange island alone. And who could teach drafting better than the Prism himself?

"Of course. But first there's some things we have to do."

Kip looked longingly at the sausage rope Gavin still held. "Like eat more?"

Chapter 26

By noon the next day, Kip had fully swallowed his teasing about a fast boat. They were flying across the waves at mind-boggling speed, and Gavin had enclosed the boat, muttering something about that woman and her ideas, so now, despite the speed, they could speak.

"So you've used green," Gavin said, as if it were normal for him to be leaning hard forward, skin entirely red, feet strapped in, hands gripping two translucent blue posts, throwing great plugs of red luxin down into the water, sweating profusely, muscles knotted. "That's a good color. Everyone needs green drafters."

"I think I can see heat, too. And Master Danavis said I'm a super-chromat."

"What?"

"Master Danavis was the dyer in town. Sometimes I'd help him. He had trouble matching the reds as well as the alcaldesa's husband liked."

"Corvan Danavis? Corvan Danavis lived in Rekton?"

"Y-yes."

"Slender, about forty, beaded mustache, couple freckles, and some red in his hair?"

"No mustache," Kip said. "But, otherwise."

Gavin swore quietly.

"You know our *dyer*?" Kip asked, incredulous.

"You could say that. He fought against me in the war. I'm more curious about you seeing heat. Tell me what you do."

"Master Danavis taught me to look at the edges of my vision. Sometimes when I do, people glow, especially their bare skin, armpits, and...you know."

"Groin?"

"Right." Kip cleared his throat.

"Blind me," Gavin said. He chuckled.

"What? What's that mean?"

"We'll see later."

"Later? Like what, a year or two? Why do all adults talk to me like I'm stupid?"

"Fair enough. Unless you're truly freakish, you're likely a discontiguous bichrome."

Kip blinked. A what what? "I said I'm not stupid; ignorant's different."

"And I meant later today," Gavin said.

"Oh."

"There are two special cases in drafting—well, there are lots of special cases. Orholam's great bloody— I've never tried to teach the early stuff. Have you ever wondered if you were the only real person in the world, and everything and everyone else was just your imagination?"

Kip blushed. Back home, he'd even tried to *stop* imagining Ram, hoping the boy would simply cease to exist. "I guess so."

"Right, it's one of a puerile mind's first flirtations with egoism. No offense."

"None taken." Since I have no idea what you just said.

"It's attractive because it validates your own importance, allows you to do whatever the hell you want, and it can't be disproven. Teaching drafting runs into the same problem. I'm going to assume here that you do accept that other people exist."

"Sure. I'm not much for lecturing myself," Kip said. He grinned.

Gavin squinted at the horizon. He'd rigged up two lenses separated by an arm's length and mounted on the luxin canopy so he could scan the seas. He must have seen something, because he banked the skimmer hard left—port! Hard to port.

When he turned back, he'd apparently missed Kip's quip.

"Anyway, where were we? Ah. The problem with teaching drafting is that color exists—it's separate from us—but we only know it through our experience of it. We don't know why, but some men—subchromats—can't differentiate between red and green. Other subchromats can't differentiate between blue and yellow. Obviously, when you tell a man that he can't see a color he's never seen, he might not believe you. Everyone else who tells him red and green are different colors could be just playing a cruel joke on him. Or he must accept the existence of something he'll never see. There are theological implications, but I'll spare you. To make it simple, if there are color-deficient men—incidentally, it is almost always men—why could there not also be those who are extremely color-sensitive, superchromats? And it turns out there are. But they're almost always women. In fact, about half of women can differentiate between colors at an extreme level. For men, it's one in tens of thousands."

"Wait, so men lose both ways? Blind to colors more often and really good at seeing them less often? That's not fair."

"But we can lift heavy things."

Kip grumbled. "And pee standing up, right?"

"Very useful around poison ivy. I was on a mission with Karris this one time..." Gavin whistled.

"She didn't," Kip said, horrified.

"You thought she was mad at me back on the river? Somehow, it was my fault that time, too." Gavin grinned. "Anyway, to wend my way back to my point, most of us can see the normal range of colors. Hmm, tautology there."

"What?" Kip asked.

"That's a digression too far. Just because you can see a color doesn't mean you can draft it. But if you can't see a color, you'll draft it poorly. So men aren't as accurate when drafting certain colors as superchromat women, which is half of them. Will can cover a lot of mistakes, but it's better if there aren't mistakes to begin with. This becomes vital if you're trying to build a luxin building that won't fall down."

"They make luxin *buildings?*"

Gavin ignored him. "The special cases that I started all this to tell you about are sub-red and superviolet. If you can see heat, Kip, there's a good chance you can draft it."

"You mean I can start a fire like whoosh?!" Kip made a grand sweeping gesture.

"Only if you say 'whoosh!' when you do it." Gavin laughed.

Kip blushed again, but Gavin's laughter wasn't mocking. It didn't make him feel stupid, just silly. There was plenty scary about the man, like Master Danavis was scary sometimes. But neither seemed mean. Neither seemed bad.

"And that would be very strange," Gavin said, "because you've drafted green." He looked like he was trying to figure out how to teach something. "Have you ever seen a rainbow?"

"A rain-what?" Kip asked, doe-eyed.

"It was a rhetorical question, smarty. The order of colors is superviolet, blue, green, yellow, orange, red, sub-red. Usually, a bichrome simply spans a broader arc. So they draft superviolet and blue, or blue and green, or green and yellow. A polychrome—much rarer— might draft green, yellow, and orange. A drafter who drafts colors that don't border each other is rare. Karris is one. She drafts green, but not yellow, not orange, and then she drafts most of red and into sub-red."

"So she's a polychrome."

"Close. Karris can't quite draft sustainable sub-red—what they call a fire crystal. Fire crystals don't last long regardless because they react to air, but—never mind that. Point is, she's just short of being a polychrome, and that matters."

"I bet that made her happy," Kip said.

"On the bright side, they wouldn't have let her become a Blackguard if she was a polychrome—polychromes are too valuable—and the pressure on her to bear children would have increased. Regardless, it's rare, and it's called being a discontiguous bichrome. Discontiguous because the arcs aren't touching. Bichrome because there are two. See? Everything in drafting is logical. Except what isn't. Like so: seeing sub-red is seeing heat, so seeing superviolet should be seeing cold, right?"

"Right."

"But it isn't."

"Oh," Kip said. "Well, that makes sense, I guess." Except that it doesn't.

"I have the strongest urge to ruffle your hair," Gavin said.

Kip grunted. "So how is this going to work?"

"There's a small island we use as an artillery station. There's a tunnel between there and the Chromeria, which is a secret so important that if you tell anyone, the Chromeria will hunt you down and execute you." He said it cheerfully, but Kip had no doubt that he was serious.

"Then why did you just tell me?" Kip asked. "I could let it slip."

"Because I've already shared a secret that I think is more important—the existence of this skimmer. But if you betray that secret to our enemies, the Chromeria might do nothing. But if you do betray us deliberately, you'd also tell them about the escape tunnel. So now if you betray me, you'll betray the whole Chromeria too. And they'll come after you and they'll kill you."

Kip felt a chill. This man was warm, personable. Kip had no doubt that Gavin liked him, but in Gavin's circles, you could like someone and still have to kill him. The casual way that Gavin prepared for Kip's possible betrayal told Kip he'd been betrayed before and been caught unaware by it. And Gavin wasn't the kind of man who had to learn a hard lesson twice.

"I'm going to dock on the island and put you on a boat to the main island. I'll send a Blackguard with you to take you to the Thresher. In a few days, you'll leave with me wherever I decide we have to go and I'll start teaching you to draft."

Kip hardly heard the last part, though. "The *Thresher*?"

Chapter 27

Karris only fell a few feet through the floor before she hit something soft. Her left foot sank to the knee while the rest of her body continued falling into the basement. The sticky whatever-it-was held her leg as she fell, so she swung upside down and the rest of her slapped into the side of something like a great red egg—a thin crust over gooey innards. She smacked into it, broke the side, and splatted into red luxin. Then her fall pulled her free and she fell onto a stone floor.

As she'd been trained, she flung her right hand down hard, the shock of slapping the floor hurt her hand—it always hurt—but that slap took the pressure off more vulnerable areas of her body and allowed her to guide the last part of her fall. She rolled instead of landing on her head.

In a moment, she popped up to her feet, and pulled the thin-hilted ataghan from her pack. There was no light in the chamber except what spilled down through the hole she'd made in the ceiling. Chunks of wood were still falling into the hole. The great red egg shone in the sudden light. Settling smoke, stirred by Karris's fall, climbed the shaft of light surrounding the egg. The entire room, perhaps twenty paces by thirty, stank of smoke and burnt red luxin, which was odd, because red luxin usually burned perfectly cleanly. For that matter, every surface illuminated in the weak light appeared to be blackened luxin as well.

But the great egg took all of Karris's attention. At least seven feet tall, it was seared perfectly black except where Karris had broken it. Red luxin now oozed out of that wound like tar. A half dozen tubes snaked away from the egg in every direction, disappearing into the ceiling, each also blackened. The seared corpses of a dozen of King Garadul's soldiers lay about the room.

"What in the hell?" Karris murmured. She lifted her sword to crack the egg open.

The egg exploded before she could touch it. A great section of the front flew into her, the blackened shell shattering over her barely raised left arm, her chest, stomach, and legs. Caught in midstep, she was thrown off balance. She stumbled and felt more than saw a form shooting backward out of the egg even as the shell splattered over her.

Instead of trying to catch herself, Karris flung herself into the fall. She rolled forward, tucking her ataghan in so she didn't skewer herself, and attacked. There was no hesitation. Ironfist had pounded that lesson into Karris for years: when attacked, you counterattack instantly. The speed of that strike was often the only advantage you had. Especially if you were small. Especially if you were a woman. Especially if you weren't wearing your spectacles and the other drafter was.

Karris's attacker had backed all the way up to the wall. He stood with living coils of red luxin like giant knots around his hands. Karris knew that construction. If you knew what you were doing, you could hold extra open luxin outside your body. Those knots of open luxin could be formed into anything you wanted and, held on your hands, you could actually fling them however you needed. The man stood like a trained fighter, too: left side toward Karris, left hand up to block but still with some springiness to throw out an attack, right hand higher and pulled back, right knee bent deeply, holding most of his weight. Even with Karris's speed with drafting and the amount of red luxin here to reflect red light to her eyes, it still took some time to ready an attack, and he had the drop on her. Her only hope was to close the distance between them before he killed her.

His left hand flicked out, right to left, low. Red luxin glommed on the floor to slow her. She was expecting it, and she stutter-stepped over the sticky patches. His right hand snapped forward in three sharp jerks. Three balls, each the size of a fist, whipped out right to left. Karris dodged the first and second, but the third caught her as she had to stutter-step again to miss another sticky patch on the floor. It thumped hard into the ribs on her left side, then splattered. She rolled with it, spun into range, and slashed with the ataghan.

The red drafter met her descending sword with layer after layer of red luxin. Held luxin, even red luxin, could gain a certain degree of rigidity from the drafter's will, and more from being woven, but red luxin could never stop steel. It was like pitting water against a sword.

But this wasn't just a bit of held red luxin. It wasn't like slapping a sword into still water. It was like standing below a dam when they opened the floodgates. It was only water, but the speed and volume of it would blow a man off his feet. Likewise, the red luxin hitting Karris slowed her, slowed her more, and finally brought her to a complete halt.

The red drafter's face paled as the luxin drained out of him. Next, his neck and chest went back to their natural hue as the torrent continued. Then his muscular shoulders, the luxin being bleached out of his body from eyes to extremities. They both realized he was running out of luxin at the same time.

Karris broke off her attack at the same time he did. She feinted to his right, expecting to meet more red luxin, and set up a killing blow. Instead, her sword clanged against something hard, but she didn't see any sword. He couldn't have drawn one without her seeing it, not even in this darkness.

Not hesitating, she lifted the ataghan and brought it down toward his head. It clanged and stopped as he lifted his hands in a V.

He shoved her hard backward and followed, keeping close. The shaft of light piercing the gloom of the room illuminated his hands and what he was holding as he shouted, "Enough! Damn you, stop for one second."

The drafter held a pistol in each hand, crossed, their barrels holding Karris's ataghan prisoner between them. His right pistol stared at her right eye, his left at her left eye. Karris had her other knives and the bich'hwa, of course, but there was no way she could draw any of them before he could pull a trigger.

The pistols staring at her were of Ilytian design. The Ilytian renunciation of magic usually meant their mundane tools were the best. With pistols, however, it was still dicey. This drafter had wheellock pistols. They negated the need to keep a fuse burning, but the flints failed to ignite the black powder at least one time in four.

Unfortunately, both pistols were double-barreled, and all four hammers were raised. Karris tried to do the figures—was it one time in sixteen or one time in two hundred fifty-six that all four shots would fail? Her heart despaired. She wasn't going to gamble on those odds, not even one in sixteen.

So...talking.

"What do you draft?" the man demanded, his voice strained.

"I don't know what you're talking—"

"What. Do. You. Draft?!" he screamed. He flung her ataghan aside and put one pistol directly against her forehead. It was too dark for him to see her irises, but he was going to figure out soon, anyway, so Karris said, "Green. Green and red."

"Then draft a ladder and get out. *Now!*"

Another time, Karris might have been irked that she obeyed so promptly, but her spectacles were on her face in an instant and she turned toward the light. Everything in this chamber was covered with either open red luxin or blackened, seared, closed red luxin. Finally, she found an ironwood beam up in the temple that reflected a pure enough white light to allow her to draft a good solid green.

Even as her body filled with green, she saw why the drafter was so urgent. This chamber was filled with red luxin. She shouldn't have put it together so slowly. There were two entrances to the room, and the dead soldiers were seared but not roasted to death—and the red luxin had remained, coating everything rather than burning as it should have.

And it still remained. This room was full of red luxin, old and new. They were inside a powder keg.

A burning pew fell over, spilling smoldering and flaming brands toward the hole. One tottered on the edge, promising death.

Karris ran forward, throwing down green luxin thick enough to stand on. She drafted what was effectively an impossibly narrow staircase, the steps only wide enough to hold her feet, only strong enough to hold her weight if she concentrated her will. But it only had to last for two seconds while she sprinted out—and it did. She stepped, stepped, stepped, fleet-footed as a hind, and vaulted, landing on the church floor. She felt a bit of the floor give way to drop into the chamber below, so she rolled again and kept running for the open front door. That much red luxin in the basement meant the whole thing could—

Whoomp!

The explosion made the floor jump beneath Karris's feet. It hit just as she was pushing off of a step, and it flung her like a spring. The yawning open doors of the church yawned wider and she was lifted and thrown forward. For a moment she thought she would make it through them and be flung harmlessly outside, but she'd been lifted high by the explosion—too high. The ironwood frame above the door loomed. Then her upper body smashed into it, and through it. The burned, weakened ironwood gave way after only an instant, but the instant it held was long enough for her to be spun viciously, upside down, flipping so fast she didn't even know how many times she tumbled.

Then she was skidding on cobblestones and gravel, not sure if she'd blacked out for a second or exactly how she'd come to the ground.

She turned over, ignoring the just-starting screams of protest from all too much of her body, and looked toward the mangled front door of the church.

A gigantic crimson snake, all aflame, stabbed its head out the front door. No, not a snake, a tube of pure red luxin, afire, the width of a man's shoulders. Then the serpent vomited, and just a little faster than fire could curl up the flammable red luxin, the drafter was shot clear of church and fire and luxin alike.

He landed not far from Karris, and far more gracefully, rolling to bleed off speed, and finally standing. He scanned the streets on every side and, seeing no one, only then allowed himself to relax a little. But once he did, Karris could see the bone-deep weariness steal over him. Drafting as much magic as she'd just seen left him looking about as bad as she felt, deathly pale and tottering on his feet.

"Come on," the drafter said. "I think Garadul's soldiers are all gone, but if not, they'll be here soon after what you just did. We need to go."

Karris stood, wobbled, and would have fallen if he hadn't grabbed her. "Who are you?"

"I'm Corvan Danavis," the drafter said. "And if I don't misremember, you're Karris White Oak, aren't you?"

"Danavis?" she asked. Orholam how she hurt. "You were Dazen's. A rebel. I can make it on my own, thank you." She shrugged off his help, leaned crazily to one side, then the other, and finally collapsed. He watched, arms folded, and didn't catch her. Her shoulder hit the ground and the world swam.

Karris saw Corvan's boots come close. He was probably going to leave her here for the soldiers. She deserved it, too. Stupid, stubborn girl.

Chapter 28

The dory Gavin drafted while they were still five leagues from Little Jasper Island was modeled on one he'd seen an Abornean wild drafter use, with high sides and a flat bottom, a pointed prow, and a flat bow plate. It was safer and far less efficient than the sculls Gavin preferred, but that was the point. Not many drafters dared to use a scull on the ocean, because if you were going to use a scull on the ocean, you had to be willing to fall in the water. That meant being confident of getting out of the water solely by drafting, and not many drafters had the skill or the will to swim in rough seas and draft at the same time.

Gavin's skill—or recklessness—meant his usual silhouette on the open sea was instantly recognizable. He didn't want that. Thus the dory.

Kip was sulking, nervous about the Thresher and Gavin's refusal to tell him anything about it.

Within a couple of leagues, they passed two merchant galleys and a galleass. Each time, a mate inspected them through a spyglass, saw Gavin's muddled clothes and no distress flags, and rowed past without a word. There was little wind today, so the sailors got to rest while galley slaves manned their banks of oars. Each time he encountered another ship, Gavin waved gamely when the spyglass came out, and returned to his own oars.

What people called the Chromeria was really two islands: Little

Jasper, covered entirely by the Chromeria itself, and Big Jasper, home to embassies, merchants' estates, shops, stalls, taverns, brothels, prisons, flophouses, tenements, warehouses, rope makers, sail makers, oar turners, fishermen, convict slaves, and far more than its fair share of graspers, schemers, and dreamers.

Big Jasper had two large natural harbors, one on the east that provided natural protection during the dark season, and one on the west for the light season, when the storms came from the east. As the island had grown in population and importance, breakwaters had been built on each side so both harbors could be used year-round. After several occupations, which had never touched the Chromeria but had purged Big Jasper in fire and blood, a wall had been built to encircle the entire island. Thirty paces thick and twenty high, it was now used mostly by the city's runners to spot and stop crimes in the streets below.

Gavin's business was on Little Jasper, but he couldn't dock in its single, smaller harbor without being seen by spies from every one of the Seven Satrapies. Even Tyrea would have a spy watching those who were important enough to dock there directly. So he rowed them between the two islands. Between the jaws of Little Jasper's U-shaped harbor was Cannon Island. Only twenty men were garrisoned there at any time, and there were always two drafters on duty, ostensibly because of the hazards of docking on the island when there was anything more than the gentlest tide and lightest wind. It was a loathed posting, and one from which not even the Blackguards escaped. It was thought that the White kept the rolls restricted to higher-ranked Chromeria guards in order to be able to teach humility to a certain class of men and women who tended to be a little more brash than was good for themselves.

And indeed, the White and the Black did use postings to Cannon Island as punishment, but only for trusted soldiers. The fiction worked better if it was half true. When other soldiers traded postings—I'll take your Cannon Island post next week if you'll just take my rounds this next weekend—the watch captain noted the names of anyone who switched. Those were then watched carefully while they were on duty, and more carefully afterward. Spies had certainly infiltrated the island, which was strategically important for purely mundane reasons, but none had yet—the White believed—penetrated Cannon Island's real importance.

Amid the crashing waves of high tide, Gavin brought the dory around the back of the island. With his drafted multitude of oars, he had far greater control than he would have had over a mundane boat, but it was still tricky business to line up with the rollers erected long ago so boats could be pulled clear of even storm-height waves. They'd been seen, of course, and two Blackguards—Blackguards were always given the boat duty—greeted them.

The men, imposing brothers with coal-black skin, recognized Gavin instantly. Each held up a hand—not in greeting, but to give Gavin a stable target. He aimed superviolet at each hand, stuck it there, and then flung a coil of green luxin along that stable thread. Like rope, the luxin stuck in each big man's hand. Gavin fastened the other ends directly to the boat with two small globs of red luxin. The men pulled him in expertly. The dory rattled as it settled awkwardly from the waves onto the rollers and then slipped smoothly up the ramp.

Commander Ironfist, the elder brother, spoke first, as always: "Sir." His eyes flicked down to Gavin's tattered clothes. The "sir" was his laconic equivalent of, *Of course I recognize you, but if this is supposed to be a disguise, I'm smart enough not to ruin it. What do you want us to call you today?*

"I'll need a Blackguard to take Kip to the Chromeria, Commander. I've told him about the escape tunnel, by the by, so keep an eye on him."

Both men absorbed that in displeased silence.

"We'll need to wait until low tide for—" Tremblefist began.

"Immediately," Gavin said, not raising his voice. "He's to be put through the Thresher. No rush, tomorrow will be fine. Report the results to the White. Tell her Kip is my...nephew."

Ironfist's eyebrow twitched, and Tremblefist's eyes widened. Kip, on the other hand, looked stricken.

Gavin looked at the boy, but Kip seemed suddenly shy.

"I'll see you tomorrow," Gavin said. "You'll do fine. After all, you've got my blood." He smirked.

Kip looked baffled. "You mean you're not...saying I'm not your, um, bastard?" Kip himself looked confused with all the negatives.

"No no no. I'm not disavowing you! When I say 'nephew,' everyone knows what it means. It's just more polite. And it pays to be polite where the White is involved."

Ironfist coughed. He could cough quite pointedly.

Gavin looked at him pointedly in return. Ironfist adjusted his *ghotra*, his checkered Parian headscarf, as if oblivious.

"But how do people know I'm not really your nephew?" Kip asked. He was still clutching the luxin oar Gavin had drafted for him.

"Because they'll pause like it's delicate, and not say your surname. 'This is Kip, the Lord Prism's...nephew.' Not, 'This is Kip Guile, the Lord Prism's nephew.' You see?"

Kip swallowed. "Yes, sir."

Gavin looked across the waves to the Prism's tower. He hated being gone overnight. His room slave Marissia would dye the bread and throw it in the chute for the prisoner, and he knew he could trust her. But that was different from doing it himself. He looked back to the frightened boy.

"Do me proud, Kip."

Chapter 29

Kip watched the Prism head out across the waves with something akin to panic. Gavin was so in control of everything, so fearless, and now he'd left him. With two unfriendly giants.

As Gavin finally disappeared from sight, Kip turned to look at the men. The scarier one, Ironfist, was putting on blue spectacles with large oval lenses wrapped close to his eyes. As Kip watched, the blue luxin filled the man, but it was almost invisible against his coal-black skin. The whites of his eyes already looked blue when you saw them through the blue lenses, so it wasn't until the skin under his finger-nails turned icy blue that Kip was sure he hadn't just imagined the Blackguard was drafting at all.

"Grab a rope," Ironfist told his brother. "With the float on it." Tremblefist disappeared, leaving Kip with his brother.

"I don't know why you've been trusted with this island's secret," Ironfist said, "even if you are his . . . nephew. But now that you know, you're a guardian of it like the rest of us, you understand?"

"He did it so if I betray him men like you will come kill me for him," Kip said. Was he never able to keep his mouth shut?

A look of surprise flitted across Ironfist's face, and was quickly replaced with amusement. "A deep thinker, our *friend*," he said. "And a young man with ice water in his veins. How appropriate."

From the "our friend," Kip understood that they weren't even to say the Prism's name here, not even now, with the wind whipping around them and the possibility of eavesdropping nil. It was that kind of secret.

"The story is you and your master, a scribe, came out on a friend's boat to...hmm."

"To study some local fish?" Kip asked.

"Good enough," Ironfist said. "He didn't account for the waves and had no skill with boats. He tried to bring you here for shelter. Your dory capsized and he was lost. We pulled you out of the sea."

"Oh, to account for why *he* isn't here if any of the others saw us coming in," Kip said.

"That's right. Hold tight."

Kip was holding a luxin oar up between himself and Ironfist, but he almost didn't get what the big man meant until too late. With a quick, snapping punch, Ironfist lashed a hand through the luxin and stopped it so close that Kip flinched. He barely even noticed the luxin crumbling to dust in his fingers. He had a sudden urge to urinate.

"I don't know if you've given your sire reason to suspect you," Ironfist said. "But if you betray him, I'll tear your arms off and beat you with them."

"Good thing I'm fat, then," Kip shot back.

"What?" Incredulous.

"Soft arms." Kip grinned, thinking Ironfist had been kidding. The stony, flat, willing-to-kill look on the big man's face made Kip's grin break and disintegrate like broken luxin.

"That fat'll make you float, too. Get in the water," a cold voice behind him said.

Kip flinched. He hadn't even heard Tremblefist approach. The man was carrying a hollow log with numerous knotted ropes and loops attached. The wood was carved with several handles too, so it would be easy to throw into the sea. A swimmer could then grab for whatever length of rope he needed.

Tremblefist handed the log to Kip and Ironfist rang a loud bell. "Man overboard!" Ironfist shouted. "We've got two in the water!"

"Move it," Tremblefist said. "And you'd better get completely wet. Fast. Help will be here in seconds."

Kip clutched the hollow log and jogged down the ramp between the rollers. The first big wave knocked him cleanly off his feet. His head smacked one of the great wooden rollers and he saw stars. Then the water was over him.

The water was shockingly cold at first. It was a cold that you quickly got used to—the Cerulean Sea was fairly warm—but Kip didn't have moments. He gasped and inhaled salt water as another wave passed over him. As he coughed his lungs clear, flapping his arms like an injured bird, he could feel the riptide grab him. Where was the log? He'd lost it. It was gone.

Someone was shouting, but he couldn't hear what they were saying over the crash of the waves. The swells were only a pace high, but it was enough to blot out Kip's vision. He turned in a circle.

There was a bell ringing, ringing. Kip turned toward it, and despite the swells, he could see the looming black of Cannon Island. It was still receding. He started swimming. A wave pummeled him, drove him under the water and spun him. He kicked, kicked, trying not to panic. Failing. He had no air. Orholam, he was going to die. He kicked, desperate.

He bobbed to the surface like a cork, but he was lost once more.

His panic receded. He'd floundered somehow to the side of the riptide, and now the waves were bringing him in toward Cannon Island, but not toward the boat ramp. He was headed for the rocks. He swam hard sideways toward the sound of the bell.

He was rising with one of the swells when he saw something impossible. Ironfist, with a rope tied around his chest, was running—through the air. He was wearing blue spectacles, and both of his hands were pointed down. He was hurling blue luxin toward his feet, sprinting, making a platform to stand on even as he ran.

As Kip watched, the blue luxin platform—anchored only somewhere back on Cannon Island—cracked with a report and began to crash toward the waves. Ironfist leapt as the platform fell, releasing the luxin and executing a perfect dive.

He surfaced right next to Kip, his spectacles and ghotra ripped off by the waves, and grabbed Kip with one arm. Then the men on the beach began pulling in the rope as fast as they could. In less than a minute, Kip and the big man were staggering up the ramp. Well,

Ironfist was striding, one hand holding a fistful of Kip's shirt in case he fell, and Kip was staggering on jellied, naked legs.

"We couldn't save your master, son. I'm sorry," Ironfist said. There were a dozen soldiers crowded on the narrow portico outside the back door of Cannon Island. One threw a blanket over Kip's shoulders. "Take this young man inside and take care of him," Ironfist commanded. "I've got business on Big Jasper, I'll take him with me and notify the family. Ten minutes."

As the soldiers ushered Kip inside, he heard Ironfist swear quietly, "Damn, those were my best blue specs."

Chapter 30

Liv Danavis walked briskly over the luxin bridge called the Lily's Stem that connected the Chromeria on Little Jasper Island to the markets and homes on Big Jasper Island, trying to ignore the tension knotting her shoulders. She was wearing rough linen pants, a cloak against the chilly wind of the bright morning, her dark hair pulled back in a ponytail, and the same sensible low leather shoes she'd worn when she'd first come to the Chromeria as a terrified fourteen-year-old. She always felt the temptation to dress up in her nicest things when she was summoned, but she always resisted. Her rich, imperious handler would make her feel shabby no matter what she wore, so she might as well be defiant. If Dazen Guile had won the Prisms' War, Liv would be Lady Aliviana Danavis, the daughter of the celebrated general Corvan Danavis. Being Tyrean would have been a badge of honor. She wouldn't have owed anyone anything. But Dazen had been killed, and those who sided with him disgraced, her own father narrowly avoiding execution despite being held in higher esteem than any general on either side. So now she was plain old Liv Danavis from Rekton, the dyer's daughter. And Ruthgar owned her contract. So what? She wasn't scared of being summoned.

Much.

Despite having been on the Jasper Islands for the last three years, Liv hadn't come over to Big Jasper very often. The other girls came every week to listen to minstrels, get food not made in the Chromeria kitchens, meet boys who weren't drafters, shop, and drink too much after examinations. Liv couldn't afford any of those, and didn't want to ask charity of anyone, so she begged off, always saying she needed to practice or to study.

The benefit of that was that she wasn't yet jaded to the wonders of Big Jasper. The entire island was stuffed with buildings, but nothing was haphazard, unlike back home or in Garriston. The buildings were white stucco, blindingly bright in the sun, rising in terraces with the shape of the land. Geometric shapes dominated: hexagonal buildings and octagonal buildings topped with domes. Every building large enough to justify one—and many that weren't—sported a dome, and the domes were every color in the rainbow. Blue domes the color of the Cerulean Sea, beaten gold domes on the homes of the rich, copper domes turning gradually green and scrubbed every year to gleam again at Sun Day, domes painted the color of blood, mirrored domes. And with the domes, the doors, too, were beautiful. It was as if all the irrepressible personality of the Jasperites rebelled against the conformity of their white walls and similar-shaped homes, but only in the decorating and designing of their doors. Exotic woods, chiseled patterns from every corner of the Seven Satrapies and beyond, doors apparently carved of living wood with leaves still growing from the Tree People, Tyrean horseshoe arches, Parian chessboard patterns, huge doors to small buildings, keyhole doors in huge edifices.

But at least as iconic as the colored domes and shining white walls of Big Jasper were the Thousand Stars. Every street was laid out perfectly straight, and at every intersection stood pairs of narrow arches, thin, looking impossibly spindly on their white legs, at least ten stories tall, connecting high above the intersection in a groin vault. Mounted on swivels at the pinnacle of the groin vault was a circular mirror, highly polished, flawless, as tall as a man. With the special layout of the streets, as soon as the sun conquered the horizon, light could be directed anywhere.

Long ago the builders had said, In this city, there will be no shadow that Orholam's eye cannot touch. Day was longer on Big Jasper than anywhere in the world.

The original purpose, as near as Liv could guess, had been to extend the power of drafters on the island. In other densely populated cities, the buildings eventually crowded out the sun. Not only did that make a city feel dark, but it meant drafters walking down those streets were vulnerable. The buildings here were separated carefully according to height and width, leaving lightwells, but with the Thousand Stars, a drafter could have as much power available to her as she could handle for hours longer than she would otherwise.

On Sun Day, every one of the Thousand Stars was slaved to the Prism. Everywhere he walked, every mirror turned, illuminating him. Obviously, some beams were blocked by buildings, but no matter where he walked—even in the poorest areas—at least a few had unobstructed views. Indeed, before anyone built a building, their plans had to pass inspection that they wouldn't interfere with the Thousand Stars. Only a very few had been able to circumvent the rules, like the Guile palace.

Of course, Liv thought, the same rules don't apply to the obscenely rich. Never do. Not here.

Every principality in the city was allowed to determine how it wished to use its stars when they weren't needed for defense, law enforcement, or religious duties. Some moved their stars in rigid schedules, making a light clock that everyone in the district could easily see.

Today, the first principality Liv walked through, the Embassies, was having a market day. They'd fitted diffuse yellow lenses over half of their stars, lighting an entire great square with cheery light. A half dozen yellow drafters, hired specially for the occasion, were—without spectacles—juggling brightwater, liquid yellow luxin. Dragons exploded in the air, great fountains of shimmering, evaporating yellow luxin shot skyward, drawing great crowds toward the market. The other half of the stars, fitted with lenses of every color, spun in great circles around the market in a dizzying display.

Liv pitied the tower monkeys—the petite slaves, often children—who had to work the ropes here today. Among slaves, they were well treated, even paid, their work for the star-keepers considered important, technically difficult, and even holy, but they spent their days in two-man teams in the narrow spindles, one spotting and one working the ropes with deft hands, often working from the first shimmer of dawn until the dark of night without reprieve except for switching with their spotter. When the Prism or a superviolet traveled and needed use of the stars, they could do so directly, magically. But every mundane purpose required the services of the monkeys.

Idly, Liv considered reaching into a superviolet control line embedded in the street and taking control of a star, just to wreak some havoc on the rich people's party. That was the beauty of being a superviolet. No one could tell you were drafting who couldn't also see superviolet.

Still, it wasn't like she would be the first student to do such a thing. Punishments for such pranks were swift and severe.

Liv's stomach was doing backflips, though. Despite the hubbub of the morning crowd and shouts of merchants and the singing of minstrels and the crackling of the brightwater fireworks, nothing could distract her from her upcoming meeting.

The Crossroads was a kopi house, restaurant, tavern, the highest-priced inn on the Jaspers, and downstairs, allegedly, a similarly priced brothel. It was centrally located in the Embassies District for all the ambassadors, spies, merchants trying to deal with various governments, and drafters having just crossed the Lily's Stem, because the Crossroads was housed in a former embassy building. As a matter of fact, it was in the old Tyrean embassy. Liv wondered if her handler had done that on purpose, or if she'd just chosen it because she knew it was far too expensive for Liv to afford.

Liv hiked up the grand staircase to the second floor where the kopi house was. A beautiful greeter met her with a dazzling bright smile. The Crossroads had the best staff in the city: every last man, woman, and table slave attractive, immaculately dressed, and unfailingly professional. Liv had always suspected that the slaves here earned more than she did. Not that that would be hard. Actually, it was Liv's first time inside.

"How may we serve you today?" the greeter asked. "We have some lovely tables by the south window." She politely didn't stare at Liv's rough clothing.

"A private table, if possible. I'll be meeting a...friend from the Ruthgari embassy, Aglaia Crassos."

"Of course, I'll be sure to send her over." The staff here knew everyone who was anyone, by name. "Will you be needing muting for your table?"

Muting? Oh. Liv tightened her eyes to see into the superviolet. Of course. She'd forgotten; she'd heard about this too. A third of the tables here were surrounded by superviolet bubbles. The bubbles had holes, of course, or the patrons inside would suffocate, so the sound couldn't be completely cut off, but it would certainly help make sure it was a hundred times harder to eavesdrop. Some of the bubbles even had small spinning superviolet fans to blow fresh air into them. Which, Liv realized, was eminently practical. Those patrons who had opted to have the bubble but not the fan looked uncomfortably warm.

Liv was going to go way out on a limb and guess that the fan was available for a small additional cost.

Now that she was looking, she realized the greeter was herself a superviolet drafter, her pupils bearing the halo barely a third of the way through her irises. No wonder Liv hadn't noticed right away. When a superviolet drafter got much further along, the color in their eyes began to bleed over into the visible range, lending a slight violet tinge that was difficult to see in brown eyes and made blue eyes astonishingly beautiful—not that Liv was ever going to get that, with her bland browns.

"Actually..." Liv said. She turned her cloak so the woman could see the back. It was common for superviolets to weave some extra pattern into their clothing so that other superviolets could identify them.

The greeter's pupils tightened to pinpricks in a heartbeat as she glanced at Liv's cloak. "Very finely done. Superviolets are welcome to draft their own muting, just let us know you're going to be using muting when you visit so our servers don't make any mistakes."

The woman took Liv to a table by the windows on the south side where she could get sunlight through open windows. There was plenty of sunlight here in the clerestory—the arches and flying buttresses supported all the weight of the roof easily, so the second story had windows from floor to ceiling—but one of the downsides of being a superviolet was that thick windows like those used here interfered with light collection. Any skilled drafter could still use magic, but it took longer and gave some drafters headaches.

Liv sat and watched how the staff worked, weaving effortlessly between tables, giving a wider berth to those surrounded by superviolet shells. A slender young serving man with short kinky hair and a gorgeous smile came to her table, pausing just outside where her bubble would have been if she had already drafted one. He was probably only a few years older than her, and devastatingly beautiful, his jacket expertly tailored to a leanly muscled body.

Somehow, she managed to give him her order. Just a kopi. Which would doubtless cost a full danar. When he brought it back, steaming hot and dark as hellstone, and gave her a long smile, Liv decided the kopi was definitely worth a danar. Maybe more.

Her good mood died at the sight of Aglaia Crassos climbing the stairs with her butt-puckered gait. The twenty-something-year-old Ruthgari was, as best Liv could tell, the youngest daughter of some important family. She had the prized, vanishingly rare Ruthgari blonde hair, but other than that, she was no beauty. She had the blue eyes that were wasted on non-drafters, a long, horsey face, and a huge nose. Stationed at the Ruthgari embassy to get some political experience before she married some fiancé she hadn't met back in the city of Rath, she had always acted like she was too good to handle Liv. She'd even told Liv that being assigned Liv's case had been her punishment for some indiscretion with the Atashian ambassador's son. Mostly, she handled bichromes and polychromes and real spies.

Catching sight of Liv, Aglaia came right over, giving a little wave to a few patrons and a wink to one.

"Aliviana," Aglaia said, coming to stand before her table, "you're looking so…active this morning." The pause said it all. The searching expression, as if she was really trying to find something good to say. From some women, it might have been an accident.

You want to play it like that? Fine. "Such a pleasure to see you, Aglaia. You wear petty malice so well," Liv said. Oops.

Aglaia's eyes widened momentarily, and then she faked a laugh. "Always were a sharp instrument to handle, weren't you, Liv? I love that about you." She sat across from Liv. "Or is it just that you're too stupid to understand your situation?"

My father told me not to come here. Sharks and sea demons, he said. I should have listened. I'm antagonizing the woman who holds my future.

"I..." Liv licked dry lips, as if a little lubrication would help her force submissive words out. "I'm sorry. How may I be of assistance, Mistress?"

Aglaia's eyes lit up. "Say that again."

Liv hesitated, clenched her jaw. Forced herself to relax. "How may I be of assistance, Mistress?"

"Draft us a bubble."

Liv drafted the muting bubble, complete with a fan.

"Such a proud girl you are, Liv Danavis. The next time I have a party, I'll have to remember to have you come serve the food. Or perhaps clean the chamber pots."

"Oh, I love cleaning chamber pots. And I love telling all my friends who haven't yet signed contracts how well the Ruthgari treat their drafters," Liv said.

Aglaia laughed. She really did have an unpleasant laugh. "Well played, Liv. That was an empty threat, and I deserved to be called on it. You're from Rekton, aren't you?"

Liv was instantly on her guard. Aglaia had let an insult pass? Liv would have expected that after being called on an empty threat, Aglaia would lay out a real one—and she had quite a few possibilities at her disposal. That she didn't should have made Liv feel better. It didn't.

"Yes," Liv admitted. There was no reason to lie. Nothing came from Rekton. Besides, Aglaia would have a record of where Liv was from. It was on her contract. "It's a small town. Inconsequential."

"Who is Lina?"

What? "She's a serving woman. Katalina Delauria. Takes odd jobs." An addict, a disgrace, and a nightmare of a mother. But Aglaia didn't need to know that, and Liv wasn't going to say anything bad about the folks back home.

"Any family?"

"None," Liv lied. "She settled in Rekton after the war, like my father did."

"So she's not Tyrean?"

"You mean originally? I don't know. Some Parian or Ilytian blood, maybe," Liv said. "Why?"

"What's she look like?"

Too skinny, with bloodshot eyes and bad teeth from smoking haze. "Tall, short kinky hair, mahogany skin, stunning hazel eyes." Now that Liv thought about it, Lina had probably been a real beauty once.

"And Kip? Who's he?"

Oh, hell, caught. "Uh, her son."

"Oh, she does have family, then."

"I thought you meant does she have any people around Rekton."

"Right," Aglaia said. "How old is Kip?"

"Fifteen now, I suppose." Kip was nice, though it had been obvious the last time Liv was home that he was terribly infatuated with her.

"What's he look like?"

"Why do you want to know all this?" Liv asked.

"Answer the question."

"I haven't seen him for three years. He probably looks totally different now." Liv threw up her hands, but Aglaia didn't relent. "A bit chubby. A little shorter than me, the last time I saw him—"

"For Orholam's sake, girl, his eyes, his skin, his hair!"

"Well I don't know what you're looking for!"

"Now you do," Aglaia said.

"Blue eyes, medium skin, not as dark as his mother's. Kinky hair."

"Half-breed?"

"I guess so." Though Liv couldn't have said what Kip's halves would be. Parian and Atashian? Ilytian and Blood Forester? Something else? Probably not simple halves, whatever he was. "Half-breed" was a mean description, though, and completely unfair. The finest families and all the nobles in the Seven Satrapies intermarried far more often than commoners, and *they* were never called half-breeds.

"Blue eyes, though. That's interesting. Not many people in your town with blue eyes, are there?"

"My father has blue eyes. There's a few among people who settled there after the war, but no, we're like the rest of Tyrea."

"Is he a drafter?"

"Of course he is. My father's one of the most famous red—"

"Not your father, idiot girl. Kip."

"Kip? No! Well, not the last time I saw him. He was twelve or thirteen then."

Aglaia sat back. "I should let you grope in the dark after your attitude today, but then you'd be even more likely to muss everything than you already are. I have an assignment for you, Liv Danavis. It turns out that my punishment of having to deal with you was Orholam's gift in disguise. We intercepted a letter this woman Lina wrote to the Prism."

"She what?"

"She claimed Kip was his bastard."

Liv laughed, it was so ridiculous. Aglaia's face said she wasn't kidding.

"What?!" Liv asked.

"She said she was dying, and she wanted Gavin to meet his son Kip. We don't know if it's their first communication or not. But she didn't ask for anything, or threaten him. Kip's the right age, and Gavin had blue eyes before becoming the Prism. The rest is inconclusive, but the note was written as if it were true. As if Gavin knows her." Aglaia smiled. "Liv, I'm going to give you an opportunity at a better life, and I hope I don't need to tell you that I can already make you have a much worse life, if I so choose. You tested as a superviolet and a marginal yellow. For obvious reasons, your sponsor chose not to train you as a bichrome."

Yes, Liv knew it well. A bichrome was expected to be kept in a certain style, or it reflected badly on the sponsor and the sponsoring country. And yellow was so hard to draft well that few who were trained in yellow passed the final examination. So supporting a yellow bichrome was a huge investment, with little possibility of a return. Liv's sponsor had pretended she wasn't a bichrome to save his money. It wasn't fair, but there was no one to speak up for Tyreans.

"Here's your assignment, girl. I've maneuvered things so that your class will be up next for the Prism's personal instruction. Get close to him—"

"You want me to spy on the Prism?" Liv asked. The very notion was nearly . . . blasphemous.

"Of course we do. He may solicit you for information about his son and this woman Lina. Use that opportunity. Become indispensable to him. Become his lover. Whatever you need to—"

"What? He's twice my age!"

"And that would be horrible—if you were forty years old. You're not. It's not like we're talking about someone old and decrepit. Tell me the truth, you've already dreamed about him tearing off your clothes, haven't you?"

"No, absolutely not!" Really she'd just admired him. Every girl did that. But for Liv, it had been completely abstract. Platonic.

"Oh, a saint you are. Or a liar. I guarantee every *other* red-blooded woman in the Chromeria has dreamed about it. No matter. You'll think about it now."

"You want me to seduce him?!"

"It is the easiest way to be in a man's room while he's sleeping. Then if he wakes while you're rifling through his letters, you can pretend to be jealous and say you're looking for letters from some other lover. Truth is, we don't care how you get close to him, but let's be honest: what do *you* have to offer the Prism? Witty conversation? Insight? Not so much. On the other hand, you're pretty for a Tyrean. You're young, not very bright, uncultured, not powerful, not a scholar or a poet or a singer. If you can get close to him some other way, great. I'm just betting the odds."

It was the most eviscerating way to be told you were pretty that Liv had ever heard. "Forget it. I'm not going to be your whore."

"Your piety's touching, but it's not whoring if you want to do it, is it? You've seen him. He's gorgeous. So you get a few extra benefits. You can enjoy him, you can bask in every woman's jealousy, you get everything that we offer—"

"I don't want anything more from you."

"You should have thought of that before you signed your contract. But that's in the past. Liv, if you can get even one private meeting with Gavin Guile, we will set you up as a bichrome. Get close to him, and we'll make your rewards even richer than that. But spit in my face, and everything in your life can turn to hellstone. I have full power over your contract, and I will use it."

The offer of setting up Liv as a bichrome seemed awfully generous just for getting one meeting with the Prism, but she saw the logic behind it. A Prism could do what he wanted, but sleeping with a Tyrean monochrome would seem questionable, tasteless. Slumming. A bichrome, on the other hand, at least had some standing. The truth was, the offer was still probably generous, and might make Gavin more suspicious of them, but the prize—having a spy next to the Prism himself—was worth so much that the Ruthgari were willing to risk it. They needed Liv to say yes.

"Besides," Aglaia said. "If you're smarter than I think you are, you can find out for yourself who gave the orders to burn Garriston. You could find out who's responsible for your mother's death."

Chapter 31

Gavin had hunted down hundreds of color wights, and this one didn't feel right.

The madness struck every color wight differently, but blue wights always reveled in order. They loved the hardness of blue luxin. Most eventually tried to remake themselves with it. Every one of them believed they could avoid madness if only they were careful enough, smart enough, and thought through every step. But what was a blue wight doing crossing the reddest desert in the Seven Satrapies?

Rondar Wit had been posted in one of the smaller coastal cities of Ruthgar. Married, four children, and a good relationship with his lord patron, who'd waited two weeks to report Rondar's disappearance—no one liked to believe that *their* friend might go mad.

Gavin trudged through the desert. He'd stopped briefly at one of his contacts on the coast, got dressed entirely in red, and armed, and still thought he should reach the wight before dark. Still, he was exhausted. Skimming was fast, but his arms and shoulders and stomach and legs ached. His will felt sapped. He didn't get lightsick when he drafted too much—but he did get tired and shaky.

Coming near the top of a dune, he stopped so as not to skyline himself and drafted a pair of long lenses. Tracking blues was usually easy because no matter how smart they were, most couldn't bear to be illogical. If you figured out where they were going, you could guess they would take the most efficient route there. Gavin had no idea

174 • Brent Weeks

where this one was going, but he was following the coast. Unless his objective was nearby, Gavin was going to assume that the giist would continue heading down the coastline, staying far enough from the coast to avoid farms and towns. Of course, this wight had made a mistake, coming in too close from the desert for the sake of speed and access to water, and had been seen by a boy herding the rangy desert cattle the nomads kept. The boy had told his father, and his father had told everyone, including Gavin's contact.

For a few days, the wight would try to put as much distance between himself and the herders as possible.

So Gavin made guesses, drafting blue to help himself think like one of them. Assuming the blue wight didn't have a horse that the boy hadn't seen—and horses usually hated color wights—a man pushing hard through this desert could only move so fast. Gavin had been through here before, and though he didn't know it intimately, there were a number of points where a man had to decide if he wanted to follow the coastal road or take a trader's route through the Cracked Lands. And there were places where the Cracked Lands were so broken and treacherous that there was no discernible traders' route at all. Gavin wasn't going to choose one or the other. He waited at one of the places where the roads met and diverged.

And waited. He untucked his shirt, pulled it askew, rebuttoned it offset one button, and tucked it back in. And waited. He drafted sub-red into fire crystals to bleed off heat from his body, watching the tiny crystals take shape, crinkle, and then flame out. Every ten minutes, he trudged back high on the great dune to poke his head over and scan the desert.

As the sun descended, he saw the telltale gleam. Aches forgotten, he was again a circling hawk, waiting for the marmot to step just *this far* from his hole. He felt the same spasm of black fury that he felt every time. He should kill it, kill it instantly, and not listen to its lies, its justifications, its haughty madness.

No, this time, he needed to listen. First.

This giist's skin was layered with blue luxin. It wasn't just armor: it was a carapace. Chromaturgy changed all men, but blue wights were seduced by the perfections of magic. They sought to trade flesh for luxin. This one had progressed further than most. Talented, then, not to mention meticulous and likely brilliant. It still wore blue pants and shirt, though both were dirty and, uncharacteristically for a blue's personality, torn. So it thought it was almost done with the need for clothing, but either the dangers of exposure in the desert or the possibility of needing just a bit more blue to draft from had convinced the creature to keep its clothing for a little longer. Its face, though, was the true wonder—or horror, depending on how you looked at it.

It had insinuated blue luxin beneath its very skin. Gavin had seen it before. The process had to be done slowly and carefully enough to not cause infections or rejection, but once begun, it had to be finished quickly. The skin lost feeling and began dying as soon as it was cut off from the body, so the wight began sloughing off rotting skin. This one's forehead had split open, revealing robin's egg blue beneath peeling, necrotic skin. It had drafted blue covers for its eyes arcing from brow to cheekbones in a solid dome so it would effectively *always* be wearing blue spectacles, but the result made it look like a bug with bulging blue eyes. It was, Gavin had always thought, one of the worst parts of giists trying to remake themselves. If all your skin died, your eyelids died. Even if you could draft a thin blue membrane every time you needed to clear your eyes—and it had to be held blue luxin, because rubbing blue glass against your eyeballs was never a good idea—even if you dealt with that, you could never close your eyes to sleep. Even wights needed sleep.

An hour later, as the sun was almost touching the horizon, burning the desert beautiful, Gavin put on his borrowed red spectacles, gathered the red cloak around himself, cracked open a white mag torch, and stepped out in front of the giist.

The blue wight convulsed. Blues hated surprises, hated not having foreseen something, hated having their plans disrupted. But they were also hard to read, the blue perfection of a luxin face preventing facial expression of emotions even as the magic in their veins slowly obliterated their capacity to feel them.

But the surprise lasted only a moment. The giist sprinted straight for Gavin, its skin afire with blue, its eyes literally aglow, buggy, lit from within with refracting blue light. Gavin tossed the mag torch down in the sand in front of himself and threw open his red cloak, taking a wide stance on the side of the dune as the giist charged.

Gavin's hand swept up past the weapons harness, little fingers of red luxin plucking all the tiny daggers from their sheaths. As he took one great step forward with his left foot, he drafted a dozen thin barrels along his arm. Then his right arm whipped forward with all the energy coiled in his body added to the force of his will. The dozen tiny daggers became steel missiles as he flung them. They flew at incredible speed, one after the other.

A blue shield sprang from the wight's left arm and blossomed huge, to catch the splashing fire it expected from a red drafter with a mag torch. Instead, the steel daggers hit with a sound like hail on a tin roof. The shield pitted, cracked, cracked wide, and gaped open. The last three daggers sailed cleanly through. The first struck its cheek and deflected off its carapace. The next cut only the air next to its neck, and the last buried itself in the wight's shoulder.

The giist had already begun its counterstroke, though. It flung its right fist forward and five enormous spikes formed in the air around its hand and stabbed for Gavin's stomach in a line so that even if he moved left or right, he'd still be skewered.

Gavin cheated, of course. He drafted a solid platform beneath the sand to give himself a solid surface to jump off of and dove down the dune, flipping and landing in a great slide down the dune's face.

The giist whipped around, dropping its luxin spears and drafting a blue great sword in their place. It saw that Gavin had lost his spectacles in his dive, and it twitched a smile. Its cheek had been sliced by Gavin's dagger, and a flap of skin peeled open, drooping toward earth, showing a crosshatched network of blood vessels and blue luxin, though the luxin was cracked and broken at the point of impact, capillaries oozing blood. The dagger in its left shoulder seemed to be hampering its motion, but it was nothing lethal.

"You reds," the giist said, its voice gravelly, as if it hadn't spoken in some time. "So impulsive. You thought you could take me, alone, just because it's sunset in a desert?"

Gavin glanced at his spectacles lying on the sand above him. The giist saw it and swung its great sword. The blade elongated in midair, closing the full five paces, and smashed the red spectacles to bits, then shortened again.

"You should leave murdering the Unchained to your Prism," the giist said.

The Unchained?

Gavin said, "They told us the Prism was too important for you. They told us we should be able to handle one blue wight in the middle of a desert. They said Rondar Wit wasn't that gifted."

The giist laughed. "Was that supposed to make me angry? I'm not Rondar any longer. The Prism's empire crumbles over your head, slave. Join us. See what it is to be free. You have, what, perhaps five years left? Not long, not even for a drafter in their world. Why die for their false god? Why die for their lies? Why die, ever?"

The giist was trying to *recruit* him? This was different. Gavin kept his eyes squinted. The less the giist saw his eyes, the less likely it was to notice how odd they were. "False god?" Gavin asked. Immortality?

Slimy held blue luxin swiped along the insides of its bug eyes, from the inner corner to the outer. Blinking. "Surely you don't believe in Orholam? Are you all corrupt, or just stupid? If Orholam himself chooses the Prism as the Chromeria has preached since Lucidonius, how could there be two Prisms in one generation? Or are you one of the mental cowards who shrugs and calls it a mystery, who says Orholam's ways are ineffable?"

It was one thing for a color wight to run: not even blues were immune to cowardice. But an attack on Orholam himself was a heresy that cut to the root of the world. If you called Orholam a fraud, and said everyone in power must know it, the Chromeria became the purveyor of lies, an oppressor who stole from you, not a friend who needed your help to sustain their worthy efforts. "I haven't believed in Orholam for years," Gavin said, honestly. "But why trade one superstition for another?"

The giist glanced at Gavin's shirt, noticing the buttons weren't done properly. Good. Any time it spent looking at his buttons was time it didn't spend looking at his eyes. "You stop believing lies so you can believe the truth, not so you can believe nothing at all. King Garadul has..." He trailed off, looking at Gavin suspiciously. Putting something together.

"King Garadul, is he who leads the Unchained?" Gavin asked.

"Who are you?" it demanded. "You aren't nervous. And you should be." It tore the dagger out of its shoulder, sealed the wound, and tossed the dagger aside. It drew a long, ball-handled matchlock pistol from the ragged pouch, began loading in a precise manner with the odd, quick, but absentminded mode blue wights sometimes had. It used blue luxin like an extension of its hands. Blue luxin ramrod, blue luxin fingers to hold the slow match, blue luxin to draw out the powder horn and a lead ball. It grabbed the still-burning mag torch from the sand and held it up to light the slow match. "Foolish, rash red drafter," the giist said, glancing down at Gavin's misbuttoned shirt. "You should always spend the extra to buy a mag torch in your own color."

"I did," Gavin said.

The giist's eyes snapped from the white torch to Gavin's eyes. Even through the buggy eye cover and the frozen luxin face, Gavin read realization in every line of the giist's body.

Before it could move, Gavin leapt forward with an insane scream.

Taken off guard, the giist lost concentration on the luxin hand holding the mag torch, and that hand disintegrated, dropping the flaming brand. The giist didn't forget its great sword or the pistol, though. It lifted the blade to impale Gavin, raised the pistol.

Drafting parrying sticks of blue luxin in each hand, Gavin slapped the blade aside. He flung the giist's hands wide. Letting the parrying sticks disintegrate, he drafted. A narrow blue blade sprang from his palm. He stepped close, inside the blue wight's arms even as the pistol's hammer clicked and the match slapped down. He slammed blade and palm into the giist's chest, its carapace yielding with a popping sound. Gavin shed the remaining blue luxin with a flick of his arms and pulled in the hottest sub-reds he could handle into each hand. Flames curled around his fists as he clenched them.

The pistol roared and went spinning harmlessly out of the giist's hand.

It staggered back, but Gavin stepped in close once again. He threw two quick jabs, left hand to the giist's right eye, right hand to its left eye. The blue bug-eye lenses cracked, melted, releasing a quick burst of resin and chalk smells. It all happened so fast the blue wight couldn't resist. Blues were slow to react when they found their presuppositions were wrong.

Broken, the giist sank, sat, tried to catch itself, and fell on the sand. Despite its solid blue lidless eyes, despite the burned skin and the crosshatched blue luxin through the cut on its cheek, to Gavin it looked abruptly human once more.

The startled look in those broken-haloed eyes.

The red red blood spilling down its chest.

And suddenly, the figure looked more like a man than like the monster that Gavin had found standing over Sevastian's bed all those years ago, the window broken open behind him, light gleaming off blue skin and red blood.

Gavin took a deep, unsteady breath. He'd stopped it this time. No innocents had died. And there was one decency left to extend, not because Rondar Wit deserved it, but in spite of the fact that he didn't.

"You gave the full measure, Rondar Wit. Your service will not be forgotten, but your failures are blotted out, forgotten, erased. I give you absolution. I give you freedom. I—"

"Dazen!" the giist shouted, hands clutching its wound, writhing.

Gavin was so startled he lost his place in the funerary rite.

"Dazen leads us, and the Color Prince is his strong right hand." The giist laughed, blood flecking his segmented blue lips.

"Dazen's dead," Gavin said, his gut twisting.

"Light cannot be chained, Prism. Not even by you. You're the heretic, not…" And then the darkness of death closed over the giist at last.

Chapter 32

Kip barely had time to get scrubbed down with towels, dressed in some soldier's pants and a dry shirt and heavy boots—surprisingly enough, it all fit; apparently they were used to big soldiers out here—and plopped in front of a fire before Ironfist showed up. His tightly curled hair was damp, but otherwise there was nothing to give away that he had just been in the ocean too. He wore a regulation gray uniform like Kip's, though with a gold seven-pointed star and two bars on his lapel, where Kip's uniform was blank.

"Up," Ironfist said.

Kip stood, rubbing his arms in what seemed a vain effort to get warm. "I thought you were a commander of the Blackguard. Why are you wearing a captain's uniform?"

Ironfist's eyebrow barely twitched. "So you know Chromerian ranks?"

"Master Danavis taught me all the military ranks of all Seven Satrapies. He thought—"

"That's nice. You have all your belongings?" Ironfist said.

Kip scowled, at being interrupted and dismissed and at the thought of belongings. "I don't have any stuff. I didn't have that much to start with, and—"

"So the answer is yes," Ironfist said.

So that was how it was going to be. "Yes," Kip said. "Sir." He was only a little sardonic with the sir, but Ironfist looked at him sharply, no humor at all in the one raised eyebrow. He really was very big. Not just tall, not just really tall. Rippling with muscle. Intimidating. Kip looked away. He cleared his throat awkwardly. "I'm sorry you had to dive in and get me. I'm sorry I made you lose your spectacles. I'll pay you back, I promise."

Suddenly, to his complete horror, Kip felt tears welling up from nowhere. Orholam, no! But the pull was as irresistible as the riptide. His stomach convulsed as he tried to choke back the sob, but it escaped anyway. He was so sick of being weak. He was the child who couldn't even hold on to the rope someone put in his hands. He hadn't been able to do anything. He hadn't saved Isa when she needed him. He hadn't saved his mother. He hadn't saved Sanson. He was powerless, stupid. When it had come down to it, he'd panicked. His mother was right about him.

Half a dozen expressions rushed over Ironfist's face in quick succession. He raised one hand awkwardly, lowered it, raised it again, and patted Kip's shoulder. He cleared his throat. "I can requisition another pair."

Kip started laughing and crying at the same time, not because Ironfist was funny, but because the big man thought Kip was crying about his spectacles.

"There you go," Ironfist said. He thumped Kip's shoulder with the side of his fist in what Kip thought was supposed to be a friendly manner—except it *hurt*. Kip rubbed his shoulder and laugh-cried harder.

"Let's go," Kip said, shrinking back lest Ironfist tap one of his namesakes on his shoulder again and leave a smoking ruin.

Ironfist's eyebrows twitched up in a momentary expression of relief.

"Almost as bad as dealing with a woman, huh?" Kip said.

Ironfist stopped cold. "How'd..." he trailed off. "You are a Guile, aren't you?"

"What do you mean?" Kip asked.

"Let's go," Ironfist said in a tone that brooked no argument. Kip didn't hesitate. He didn't know what precisely Ironfist would do to him if he didn't obey, but knowing was a logical process. Fear was faster.

Outside, he saw that they'd rigged up another boat on the ramp. He rubbed his clammy arms and stared at the sea. The tide was half-way in and getting worse, and the waves crashed powerfully over the rocks of Cannon Island. This boat was a small sailing dinghy. It didn't look even as stable as the dory. And it was smaller. Kip's stomach turned.

"Commander?" one of the men said. "You sure? I wouldn't want to go out on this even with experienced sailors. Especially if you're going the long way."

Kip didn't see the look that passed between the men, but he heard the soldier say, "Yes, sir," quickly afterward.

Cannon Island was in the middle of the current that flowed between Little Jasper and Big Jasper. Little Jasper Bay was calm, protected by a seawall, but Kip and Ironfist were headed the opposite direction, to circle three-quarters of Big Jasper in order to get to its bay.

"Aren't we going to the Chromeria?" Kip asked. He could see the tops of colored towers, only partially visible above the rocky body of Cannon Island. "Why can't we go to their bay? It's closer."

"Because we're not going straight there," Ironfist said. He gestured for Kip to get in and handed him an oar.

The men pushed them off and Ironfist began rowing hard. Kip did his best to keep up with the big man, but almost immediately they began turning toward Kip's side. Ironfist said nothing; he just switched sides and rowed hard a few times on Kip's side until they were straight, then returned to his own side. The commander aimed them so they quartered the waves. Kip's heart was constantly in his throat. The three- and four-foot-tall waves yielded to five- and six-foot-tall waves.

And then Ironfist raised their little sail a third of the way. "Keep us straight," he barked, working the lines. Kip felt like a headless chicken, flopping awkwardly from one side of the boat to the other, keeping them headed slowly forward, going up each wave with a lurch and swooping down the opposite side.

"Down! Get down!" Ironfist shouted. Kip dropped just as the wind shifted and the sail swung from one side of the boat to the other, the boom whipping over his head. It snapped so hard against the ropes that Kip thought it might tear off or break.

Orholam, that could have been my head.

The dinghy leaned over hard, even with the sail only a third of the way raised, and jumped forward. Kip had barely gotten back up to his knees, and the sudden forward motion made him tumble backward, splashing into the cold dirty water at the bottom of the dinghy.

"The rudder! Take the rudder!" Ironfist ordered.

Kip grabbed the rudder and held it straight for a long moment, though the dinghy was turned too far away from the wind—taking the waves almost side on. He blinked seawater out of his eyes. Throw the rudder this way, it turns at the fulcrum there, and the boat turns... Got it.

Part of the next wave sloshed over the gunwales as Kip threw the rudder hard toward the port side. A hard gust of wind made the dinghy bear down even farther in the water, then they popped up hard as they escaped the killing grip of the wave.

Kip whooped as they sped forward, riding the waves, plowing through them at times now, rather than simply being at their mercy. But Ironfist didn't share his joy. He was glancing up at the sky. He raised the sails a little more, and the dinghy picked up even more speed, leaning so hard to the port side that Kip thought they were going to capsize.

When they reached the west side of Big Jasper, they were able to run before the wind. It was like flying.

Ironfist kept glancing south, but the dark clouds there seemed to dissipate rather than gather, and by the time they turned into Big Jasper's wind shadow, Kip could tell from Ironfist's demeanor that they were out of danger.

"There's a small dock that we want, head straight," Ironfist told him, raising their sail all the way.

So Kip aimed them past galleys and galleasses, corvettes armed with a single gun mounted on a swivel, and galleons with fifteen cannons on each side. They stayed fairly far out so they wouldn't interfere with the constant stream of ships coming in and out of the bay, the dinghies taking crews ashore.

"Is it always like this?" Kip asked.

"Always," Ironfist said. "Bay's too small, so to accommodate the number of boats needed to keep trade flowing smoothly there's an elaborate system to determine who gets in first. It works..." He glanced up at a captain swearing loudly at the harborman standing on his deck with an abacus. The harborman looked singularly unimpressed. "For the most part."

Between having to veer sharply now and again to avoid other boats according to some ships' etiquette that he didn't understand, Kip didn't get to catch more than a few glimpses of the city covering Big Jasper. And from what he saw, it did cover Big Jasper. There was a wall just above shore around the entire island—leagues of walls—but even that couldn't hide the city as it rose on two hills. Aside from a few green patches—gardens? parks? mansions' grounds?—there were buildings everywhere. Soaring bulbous domes in every color, everywhere. And people, more people than Kip had ever seen.

"Kip. Kip! Port! Gawk later."

Kip tore his eyes off the island and turned to port, narrowly avoiding ramming a galleass. They sailed past under the evil eye of the galleass's knotted-haired first mate. He looked like he was going to spit on them, but saw their uniforms and spat on his own deck instead.

They proceeded into open water until they started to round the eastern side of the island. "Turn in here," Ironfist said. Kip turned toward a little dock with a few small fishing boats moored to it. They docked and headed up to the wall. Kip tried not to gawk, though the wall itself was easily the biggest man-made structure he'd ever seen.

Ironfist strode to the gate. The guards outside looked confused. "Captain?" Then they snapped sharp salutes, eyes wide. "Commander!"

A smaller door inset to the larger gate was open, and Ironfist walked through, nodding to acknowledge the men. The city inside was too overwhelming for Kip to comprehend even part of it. But the part that hit him first was the smell.

Ironfist must have noticed the look on his face. "You think this is bad? You should try a city without sewers."

"No," Kip said, looking at the hundreds of people in the streets, the three- and four-story buildings everywhere, the cobbled streets with tracks worn a hand's breadth down into the stones. "It's just that there's so much." And there was. Smells of cooking pork, spices Kip didn't know, fresh fish, rotting fish, a thin odor of human waste and a stronger one of horse and cattle manure, and, overwhelming it all, the smell of unwashed men and women.

The people parted naturally around Ironfist, and Kip followed in his wake, trying not to run into anyone as he shot glances at all the people. There were men wearing ghotras like Ironfist, but also bedecked in robes with checkered patterns and loud colors. There were Atashian men with their impressive beards: beads, braids, natural sections, and more beads and braids. There were Ilytian women with multilayered dresses and shoes nearly like stilts, making them a full hand taller. And a riot of colors everywhere. Every color in the rainbow, combined in every possible way. Ironfist looked back at Kip, amused.

"Those soldiers at the gate," Kip said, trying to take Ironfist's attention off his being a bumpkin. "Those weren't your men."

"No," Ironfist said.

"But they recognized you, and you didn't recognize them, and they were really excited that they'd seen you."

Ironfist looked at Kip again, scowling. "How old are you again?"

"I'm fift—"

"The commander," Ironfist said. As if that answered everything. He smirked as Kip scurried up beside him. "You're the genius. Let's hear it," he said.

Genius? I never acted like I thought I was that. But that was a distraction. This was a test. In fact, Ironfist had been testing Kip the whole time, Kip saw now. Putting him on the rudder had been a test, to see what he would do, how quickly he would figure it out, and if he would freeze up. Kip wasn't even sure how well he'd done on that count.

Ironfist was a commander. A commander, the commander. *The* commander. Oh. Oh my.

"There's only one company of Blackguards, isn't there?" Kip asked.

Like most of Ironfist's expressions, this one was quick and quickly muted: the full white of his eyes around dark irises visible for a bare moment, then a little smirk to cover. "Not bad, given the obvious hint, I suppose."

"So you're the sole commander of the most elite company in the Chromeria. That makes you like a general or something?"

"Or something."

"Oh," Kip said. "So that means I should probably be even more intimidated of you than I am right now, huh?"

Ironfist laughed. "No, I think you've got it just about perfect." He grinned.

"What were you doing pulling guard duty on that rock?"

"It is a bit more than a rock."

Put that way, it did make some sense. The Blackguard had to protect the Chromeria's most important people, and a secret escape tunnel was the kind of thing you had to check yourself. "Still," Kip said.

They came to a much wider road and Ironfist—Commander Ironfist—turned onto it, heading west, the opposite direction of almost all of the traffic. He sighed. "It's not a duty anyone wants, so it's sometimes used as punishment. Let's just say I've given the White reason to be displeased recently."

Kip said quietly, "Or that's a cover so you can go out and check the maintenance of the tunnel."

"Except that a tunnel is…a tunnel. Don't make things more complicated than they are, little Guile."

Huh? "Oh." Ironfist could come from the Chromeria side and make sure the tunnel worked. He didn't need to sail out to the island for that. Some genius I am. Embarrassed, Kip rushed to ask another question, and asked the question he knew he shouldn't. "So what did you do to make him mad at you? You know, the White."

"Him?" Ironfist asked.

"Her?"

Ironfist turned in at a little house with an oxidized copper dome, unlocked the door, and pointed for Kip to go in. "There's hard tack and cheese and olives in the kitchen. Latrine off to the left. Bed straight down the hall. You're not to leave until I come get you tomorrow at dawn."

"But we came across those huge waves instead of waiting, I—I thought we were going straight to the Chromeria."

"I'm going straight to the Chromeria."

"While I just sit here all day?"

"When you see what you have to do tomorrow, you'll be glad you had the rest." Ironfist moved to leave.

"But, what—what are you going to do?"

"I'm going to go get back in the White's good graces."

Kip scowled as the door closed. There was a click. He was locked in. "That's great," he told the closed door. "I'll just wait here. I've been meaning to catch up on my thumb-twiddling." Grumbling, he made his way to the olives and cheese. Ten minutes later, he was asleep.

Chapter 33

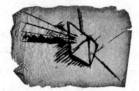

Karris woke beneath a lean-to constructed of tree branches and a man's cloak. It was either dusk or dawn. She guessed dawn from the dew on the ground. She examined herself with a soldier's efficiency, moving each limb and digit experimentally, trying to gauge her own potential for movement, violent or otherwise. All her fingers and toes worked properly, but her entire left side was bruised. She must have not only crashed through the doorframe with her upper body there, but also landed on her left side, because her shin ached, her knee ached, there were gravel scratches on her hip, her breast felt like someone had mistaken it for a sawdust-filled training bag and punched it for an hour, and her shoulder—Orholam, her shoulder. She could breathe without much pain, though, which she hoped meant there weren't any broken ribs, and she could still move her arm, although it almost made her black out to do so.

Her right side hadn't escaped undamaged either. She had long gravel scrapes on her right arm and her stomach, probably some to match on her back, and her neck was sore from Orholam knew what. She'd stubbed all the toes of her right foot—didn't remember doing that either—and her left eye was swollen, not enough to block her vision, but enough to look real pretty. There was also a scratch on her forehead, several attractive lumps on her head, and—what the hell, a cut right on the tip of her nose?

No, not a cut. A pimple. Unbe— A pimple? Now? Orholam hates me.

Every one of her cuts and scratches had been smeared with some kind of ointment that smelled of berries and pine needles. Someone cleared his throat. "There's more ointment to your right. I tended the more...obvious cuts."

Which Karris took to mean that Corvan hadn't stripped her naked.

"Thanks," she grumbled. "What happened back there?"

"Aside from the obvious?" Corvan asked, his voice flat.

"In the church, downstairs. I've never seen red luxin that didn't burn cleanly. If you drafted it wrong, it should have evaporated, not formed a crust. And what was that thing you were in?" Karris sat up, wincing. Her ankle hurt too. Ow, when had she twisted her ankle? She ignored it, and tried to remember all she knew about Corvan Danavis. He'd been a rebel, of course, but before he'd sided with Dazen, he'd been a scion of one of the great Ruthgari families. For nearly a hundred years, Ruthgar and the Blood Forest had been bound together in peace, the closest of allies. Noble families from Ruthgar had intermarried with the leading families of Blood Foresters, holding lands on either side of the Great River. Other peoples had begun referring to the countries as one, merging the Verdant Plains and the Blood Forest to call the joint country Green Forest. Vician's Sin had put an end to that, and by a generation before the False Prism's War, the countries were instead known as the Blood Plains. If one good thing had come from the False Prism's War, it was that it had given Gavin the clout to finally end the interminable small-scale war constantly simmering between Ruthgar and the Blood Forest.

Corvan was a product of that conflict. Born into a warrior family, with some ungodly number of brothers (eight? ten?), he was, Karris thought she remembered, the last one alive. Karris barely remembered him from before the False Prism's War. He was just another Ruthgari from old blood left suddenly penniless with little more than the fine weapons he carried and the fine clothes on his back. He'd been a monochrome, too, so his prospects of reclaiming wealth in some other land had been dismal. When the war had started, he'd joined Dazen immediately, like so many other dispossessed young lords with everything to gain.

Karris had been fifteen years old, and she couldn't remember Corvan personally at all. Which, she supposed, wasn't too surprising, given all the attention she'd been getting from the Guile brothers. He'd been an adviser only for much of the war, but near the end of the war, Dazen had made him a general. Karris had heard Commander Ironfist credit that fact with Gavin winning the war—not calling Corvan Danavis incompetent, but the opposite. Commander Ironfist had said that if Corvan Danavis had been a general for the whole war, Gavin's armies wouldn't have even made it to the Battle of Sundered Rock. Ironfist had further said that if General Danavis hadn't surrendered unconditionally after Sundered Rock, there might still be guerrillas fighting in half of the Seven Satrapies. Corvan's grace in defeat had convinced his men to go home.

Dipping her fingers into the bowl of ointment, Karris gave Corvan a look. He appeared confused. She began lifting her long shirt, ointment on her fingers, and he got it. He cleared his throat and turned away. Karris smeared ointment gingerly on the scrapes on her chest, giving herself time to think.

With all that history, Karris expected Corvan Danavis would be some graybeard. This man was in his mid-forties, shaven except for a day or two's stubble. His skin was lighter than most Tyreans, but much darker than Blood Forester pale, though he did perhaps have some freckles on his cheeks. His eyes were blue—no shock there, with the ludicrous amount of red he'd been able to draft. The luxin halo was only halfway through his irises—even less than Karris's, despite his being probably twelve or fifteen years older than she was. There were perhaps red highlights in his dark hair, too, and his hair was wavy rather than kinky. And the general had been famous for his red mustache, which he'd kept trimmed except at the ends that dangled below his chin, where he'd tied red and gold beads. Maybe this was some other Corvan Danavis, or some man who'd taken his name, hoping to profit from the general's good reputation. "They were on us before we knew what was happening," Corvan said. "I'd counseled the village to send a boy or two for the levies but even I didn't expect this kind of retribution. King Garadul came here not to teach us a lesson, but to teach the rest of Tyrea one. I've only run into his like once before." General Delmarta, the Butcher of Ru, Karris guessed.

"You saw the pyramid?" Karris asked, turning back to him.

Corvan Danavis got very still. The side of his mouth ticked up in a snarl for the briefest instant. But when he turned his gaze to Karris, it was cool, in control. There wasn't even a hint of fresh red luxin in his eyes, which spoke of astonishing control for a drafter his age. "I gathered those I could and pulled back to the church." Was he hoping Garadul's men would respect holy ground? "It's the least flammable building in town" Corvan said, answering the unspoken question. "We fought, and we lost. The Delarias and the Sworrins couldn't get the door to the basement open, and I was too busy fighting. Maybe I shouldn't have fought at all. I think the chromaturgy just drew more soldiers. They overwhelmed us. I retreated downstairs."

"Alone?"

He looked surprised at the question. "Everyone else was dead," he said.

Except for one young family, not ten paces from the stairs. Had Corvan fought at all, or had he immediately retreated downstairs and locked the door behind himself, dooming the townsfolk to fiery death? The soldiers had carried away their dead, and the fires had obscured most of the evidence of battle in the temple, so Karris couldn't know for sure.

"So this is where you tell me how you used the most flammable luxin to escape a fire," Karris said.

"Do you know why you blow on a flame when you're starting a campfire?" Corvan asked. He didn't wait for Karris to answer. "Because fire needs to breathe. I'm a monochrome, Lady White Oak. We have to be more creative than near-polychromes like you."

"Just tell me what you did," Karris said. How did he know she was nearly a poly? She was still trying to decide if it was even possible that this could be General Danavis. In this backwater? And from a Blood Forester family? The eyes and freckles spoke of Blood Forester heritage, but with that skin? Of course, he had grown up in a noble family, and a family breeding its sons for war. The perfect combination for a warrior drafter was black skin with blue eyes. Even caramel skin was far better than pale Blood Forester skin to give a warrior an extra fraction of a second before their opponents knew what color they were drafting. So it was possible. Noble families had certainly married off their daughters and sons for lesser reasons. Fearing that your children wouldn't look like natives of their own land might move far down the list of concerns when pure survival was at stake.

"When I went downstairs," Corvan continued, "I knew they'd come after me, so I covered every surface in the room with red luxin. I sealed the room completely and coated myself in the luxin as well. When the soldiers came in, I closed the door behind them and set it all afire. The conflagration devoured all the air in the room, and both the fire and the soldiers died." So that was why the red luxin had had a crust rather than burning away cleanly. No air.

"And the tubes?" Karris had crashed through some tubes when she'd fallen.

"They led outside. So I could breathe."

"So why didn't you leave after you killed them?"

He stared hard at her. "Because if I didn't wait until every last ember burned itself out, I'd be inviting the entire room to explode. As you might have noticed when you brought burning embers with you and made the entire room explode."

Oh.

"Why is King Garadul gathering an army?" Karris said. "Why now?"

"To assert himself, I'd imagine. New king, wants to show he's tough. Does it have to be more complicated? Rask Garadul was always a crazy little bastard."

"If you really are Corvan Danavis, you just lied to me," Karris said. A general of Corvan's standing would have been delving into the possible strategies Rask might be pursuing. A general with Corvan's record of success would have come up with a dozen already.

Corvan paused, and if anything, Karris thought he looked pleased. "So little Karris White Oak is all grown up," Corvan said. "Joined the Blackguard, and now a Chromeria spy."

"What are you talking about?" Karris said. She felt like she'd been hit in the stomach.

"The only question is, who wants to kill you, Karris? Not only are you more conspicuous in Tyrea than even I am, what with that fine hair and fair skin, but *you* of all people? They sent *you*? Here?"

"Why shouldn't I be here? I came to research the southern desert reds—"

"Seriously, Karris. Don't demean us both. At the very least, I'm an enemy of your enemy. You're here for information. I'll give it, but not if you lie to me. If you go unprepared against these people, you'll die."

He could have killed her in the church, Karris realized. Or he could have left her and let the fire do it. Corvan did have a sterling reputation, even among his enemies, and she needed to know what he knew. She surrendered, lifting her open hands. She winced. Ow, her left arm was killing her. "Why can't *I* be here?" she asked.

"Do you have any idea what happened to all the men and women who fought for Dazen?" Corvan asked.

"They went home."

"It's always harder for the losers to go home. Dazen's armies were a motley bunch. A lot of bad men, and some good ones who'd been wronged."

"Like you," Karris interjected sarcastically.

"This isn't about me. Point is, a lot of us couldn't go home. Some went to Green Haven; the Aborneans accepted a few small communities, and the Ilytians claimed to be willing to take anyone, but the only thing anyone got from them was a clipped ear."

Karris shuddered. It was how the Ilytians marked slaves. They heated shears red-hot and cut the slave's left ear nearly in half. The scar tissue kept the ear from ever fusing back together and made it easy to identify who was a slave.

"Some of us were more fortunate," Corvan said. "Our armies raged back and forth across this land for a few months, and the people here had no reason to love either side. We wiped out whole villages. Those that survived had nothing but young children, old men, and a few women. Most of the towns reviled the soldiers, and where former soldiers tried to stay by force, Rask's father, Satrap Perses Garadul, wiped them out. But a few towns realized that if they were ever going to rebuild, they needed men. The alcaldesa of Rekton was one of those. She chose two hundred soldiers and let us stay, and she chose well. A few nearby towns did the same. Other men, of course, became bandits, and even Perses Garadul couldn't hunt all of those down."

"How did you get to stay?" Karris asked. "As a general, you were more responsible for what happened to this country than most."

"My wife was Tyrean. We'd married a few years before the war. She was in Garriston when...when it burned. One of her retainers survived and saved our daughter and brought her to me. So I had a year-old little girl, and the alcaldesa took pity on me. The point is, people around here remember the war a little differently than Gavin's people do."

Not terribly surprising, considering they got the ass-end of the deal.

"They remember it as a fight over a woman," Corvan said blandly.

"That's—that's ridiculous!" Karris spluttered. Orholam have mercy.

"You're a great favorite of artists here. Not that we have many talented ones, but the fair-skinned, exotic beauty with fiery hair still inspires artists good and bad to raptures. Even if most men wouldn't dare believe you were the same woman—you're usually portrayed in a wedding dress, sometimes torn—Rask doubtless owns paintings by talented artists who'd actually seen you."

"It wasn't like that," Karris said.

"But it makes a good story."

"A *good* story?"

"Good tragic. Good interesting. Not good happy." Corvan cleared his throat. "I can't believe you don't know this."

"There are almost no Tyreans on the Jaspers now. And no one speaks to me of those days."

Corvan looked on the edge of saying something, but he held his tongue. Finally, he said, "So the question is, who would send *you* to our new King Garadul, knowing that he would surely recognize you, and what did they hope to achieve by delivering you into his hands?"

The White. The White betrayed me? Why?

Chapter 34

It had been a long morning already. Gavin had woken painfully early to reach the coast by the dawn, and then had skimmed as soon as he'd been able to draft the sun's first rays. Then he'd sculled to Cannon Island and made an unpleasant, claustrophobic trip through the escape tunnel, leaving him dirty, sweaty, sore, and deprived of sleep. But there was no other option than to push; not after what the color wight had told him.

The tunnel met the Chromeria at a disused storage room in the basement, three levels underground. There was a plain closet set in the back of one of the rooms, and a hidden door in the back of that closet. Gavin grabbed a lantern from a hook, twisted the flint, and was gratified to see it light instantly. He released the luxin he'd been holding into two puddles on the floor that quickly dissolved—no need to terrify anyone he ran into—and slipped into the closet.

The hidden door closed smoothly behind him. He opened the closet door. A hand's breadth, then it stopped, blocked. With the light of the lantern only cutting through the little crack, he couldn't see what the problem was. He reached through the crack into the darkness. Polished wood greeted his fingertips, smooth and straight, then more, right on top of it. Chairs.

Well, that was the problem of a super-secret door hidden in a disused storage room, wasn't it? Sometimes people saw a disused storage room and thought it should be used to store things.

Sighing, Gavin set down the lamp and braced his shoulder against the door. He pushed, hard, harder. The door slid another hand's breadth or two as the stacked chairs shifted, then stuck fast. He glanced at the lantern, drafted a green wand, and stuck a blob of red luxin to the end. He lit the red with sub-red and poked his narrow torch through the gap, holding it high. He poked his head through the gap after it.

The entire room was packed with furniture, as if half a dozen lecture halls and dining areas had been cleared out and everything put in here. Dear Orholam. Gavin swore quietly. The only clearance was down at floor level. The only way out was to crawl between the legs of the chairs and tables.

There was nothing for it. Unless Gavin wanted to start a fire, draft huge amounts, and obliterate everything in the room so he could simply walk out—not terribly discreet—he was going to be mopping the floor with his body. Great. He let the luxin torch disintegrate and started crawling.

Ten minutes later, he stood. He didn't try to brush the dust from his clothing. There wasn't much point. He was muddy with dust, that's how much dust there was, along with damp floors and sweat and dust he knocked off of the chairs and tables above him. He listened at the door for a full minute, heard nothing.

Stepping into the hall lightly, he closed the door behind himself. He extinguished his lantern with a puff; the halls were brightly lit. Even three floors below the sea, the cherry glims (the red-drafting second- to fourth-year students) were expected to keep the lamps fueled with red luxin. The storeroom, wisely, was set almost at the end of one of the long hallways. Gavin ducked down to the lift at the end, mere paces away.

The lifts had to serve the entire Chromeria, which meant they had to be serviceable by slaves or the dims, the newest students. So it was entirely mechanical. As anyone stepped into the lift, a scale would indicate how many counterweights were needed. If a drafter chose to use less counterweight, she would have to pull herself up the rope, albeit only lifting a fraction of her own weight. If she used more counterweight than her own weight, it could be difficult to stop at the correct floor. A central lift handled all the heavier loads and moved entire classes, while these side lifts took smaller loads. Additionally, each lift bay had numerous slots and ropes so that ambassadors wouldn't have to wait while dozens of dims made their way to class.

Gavin grabbed the second to the last rope. Secrecy meant he couldn't take the last one, though if someone saw and recognized him, they would wonder why he wasn't taking the lift reserved for a man of his rank, so it was probably a wash as to which way was more discreet. He drafted a brake, threw the lever to double his own weight, and kicked the release.

He flew upward at great speed. Though he started deep beneath the earth, the lifts were brightly lit. At the top of each chute were holes to the outside, and mounted there were highly polished mirrors from Atash that sent natural light down the chutes for as long as the sun was visible to that chute each day. Adjusting the mirrors every few minutes was another fun job for the dims, and every evening they would have to crank all the counterweights back into place. Gavin could remember doing that himself. As memories went, it wasn't a terribly pleasant one.

The lift didn't go all the way to his chamber near the top of the Chromeria, of course. That would be far too convenient—or, as the Blackguards preferred to say, insecure. No reason to give assassins a direct path to the Prism or anyone else important. Instead, after whizzing upward at high speed halfway up the Chromeria, zipping past students and magisters and servants and slaves so fast that they had no chance to see who was in such a hurry, Gavin threw the brake.

He stopped at the top of the chute and stepped out in front of the guard station that protected this floor. There were four men here, guards, not Blackguards, all looking up from their dice guiltily. Apparently they hadn't noticed the whizzing rope until too late. Their mouths hung open at the sight of him, Gavin Guile himself, sweaty, dirty, and *here*.

"Tell you what," Gavin said, tucking the brake into his belt. "You keep this quiet and I will too." He stared significantly at their dice and the coins on their table. Guarding the lift at this high a floor had to be boring, but Luxlord Black wouldn't be pleased to learn that his soldiers were gambling on duty.

Four heads bobbed as one. Gavin stepped into the next lift, which was right next to the one he'd exited, and got in his accustomed position. This time, he chose a more human speed.

There were two Blackguards guarding the lift at his level, and these men weren't dicing. They were barely even blinking. Both had their spears in hand, knees lightly bent, spectacles on.

When the Blackguards were on duty, they were on duty.

The men snapped salutes and slapped their spears crisply to their shoulders, swiveling smoothly back into their spots. Gavin walked past and slipped into his room. A bit of superviolet dropped all the shades, giving him light. He pulled a summons chain by his desk and walked over to his bathtub. Today was going to involve a lot of diplomacy, but most importantly, it was going to involve his brother, and there was no way he could appear before Dazen disheveled. It might be interpreted as weakness. He opened the tap, tested the water, and heated it with sub-red.

He was starting to take off his clothes when the door opened and his room slave Marissia walked in. She'd been captured during the war between Ruthgar and the Blood Foresters. Like most of her people, she was red-haired and freckled, eyes like jade. Karris had Blood Forester blood. Gavin had never thought it a coincidence that his room slave was a young, pretty girl from the Blood Forest. The White had hoped, doubtless, to dull some of his appetites that had caused so much trouble before the war. The girl had even been a virgin when she came to serve him ten years ago, which meant that the Ruthgari who'd captured her had had more of a taste for gold than flesh.

Marissia helped him strip off his filthy clothes and piled them to take them for laundering. Then Gavin stepped in the bath. "I have messages for you," she said. "Are you ready to take them?"

Gavin held a hand out, telling her to wait, then sighed as he slipped into the hot water. Messages, demands, barely a minute to think.

"Call a meeting of the full Spectrum. When do you think is the earliest possible, Marissia?"

Marissia had already loosened the laces of her dress, and now she pulled it and her shift over her head, folding them right side out next to the tub. If there was one skill Marissia hadn't mastered in her ten years serving Gavin, it was pretending that the rest of the world ceased to exist when there was the possibility of making love with him. She would bathe with Gavin, she would make love with Gavin if he wanted to, but she wouldn't let her hair get wet, and afterward she would pick up her perfectly folded dress, slip it on in a moment, and be on to her next duty. Marissia was many excellent things, but "abandoned to the moment" wasn't one of them.

"Luxlords Blue and Yellow are over on Big Jasper today," she said, picking up soap and a washcloth. "Yellow has family visiting and is hiding out in one of the taverns. Black is working on his ledger and swearing at anyone within a league, and Red is likely in the kitchens. So far as I know, the others are in their normal places on Little Jasper."

For as pretty as she was—and how the White had obviously chosen her because she looked like Karris—the most surprising thing about Marissia was how competent she was. She knew everything, and carried everything she knew right at her fingertips. Gavin had taken great care to win her full loyalty, knowing there was no way he could keep his prisoner's existence secret from his room slave—not forever—and knowing full well that she'd been sent to spy on him by the White.

Gavin's options had been simple: to let a succession of room slaves parade through his chambers, getting rid of each quickly, hoping that they didn't have enough time to discover his secret, or win one's loyalty completely. Karris didn't like Marissia, but she ignored her. It would have been ten times worse if Gavin had a new room slave every month—and doing so would doubtless also have meant that over time he was allowing a spy for every noble family to ransack his room and report the most intimate details about him to all the satrapies.

Besides, he needed someone to throw bread down the chute when he was gone.

Still, the White had shown impeccable taste in choosing Marissia. Though her body was nearly as familiar as his own after ten years, it was still a joy to see her lean curves. She slid into the tub behind him, holding soap and a washcloth, and began washing his back and shoulders.

"Tonight, then, after dinner. Let the White know I would like to see her in an hour."

"Yes, Lord Prism. Is there anything else before I give you the messages?"

"Go ahead."

"Your father wishes to speak with you."

Gavin gritted his teeth. "He'll have to wait." He lifted an arm as Marissia scrubbed his armpit.

"And the White wishes to remind you that you promised to teach that cohort of superviolets when you returned."

"Oh, hell." How'd she even know he was back?

"Would you like me to wash your hair, Lord Prism?"

Gavin wanted nothing more than to enjoy Marissia and then relax in a hot bath until evening, but there was something he had to do before he spoke with the White, before he met with the whole Spectrum, and definitely before he spoke with his father.

"No time," he said, trying to shut off the rising feeling of panic, ignoring the tightness in his chest at the prospect of what he had to do.

She soaped his chest, her body warm and slippery against his back. Soft, comforting. It was almost enough to relax him. She kissed the spot on the back of his neck that always made him shiver, and trailed her fingernails down his soapy chest, over his stomach, lower. She kissed his neck again, hesitated. A question in that pause.

He made a plaintive sound. "No, no time for that either." How well did Marissia know him? Often when there was no time for meetings or other duties, there was still time for that.

Often? Almost always.

She squeezed him under the water, hesitated for a moment more, as if to say, Your lips say no, but someone else says yes, please! But then she kissed his neck again, a peck, and began scrubbing the soap off his body. "I've missed you greatly, Lord Prism," she said quietly. She finished and stepped out of the bath. "I'll lay your clothes out," she said, toweling off briefly, then wrapping the towel around her waist, walking to a closet to select clothes for him.

He watched her appreciatively, then shook himself.

I'm not going to be able to lace my pants if I keep this up.

After she laid out his clothes, she came back to the bath as Gavin stood, but he waved her off, he could towel himself dry today. Marissia dried and dressed herself in about the time it took Gavin to pat his chest dry. Then she went out.

After getting dressed, Gavin opened the little service closet, carefully lifted the stacked, folded linens from the shelves, and walked them over to another closet where he stacked everything carefully. He then lifted out the shelves themselves and slid them into a nook on the other side of the room. The result was an open space in a closet that barely came up to his chest. The process was slow, but the point was that no one ever discover his secret. If someone came while he was gone, the room must simply look empty. If they searched the room, they should find nothing that appeared out of the ordinary. That was worth extra time and inconvenience.

Gavin drafted a blue-green board fit to his feet, shoulder width, with a hole in the center. Then, tucking a mag torch into his belt and clutching the board in one hand, he stooped and stepped into the closet. He closed the door behind him. The floor beneath his feet clicked. In order to keep it secret, he'd designed the floor not to open unless the door was shut. Hunched, he found the hook and pulled it up, threaded it through the hole in the board, and wrapped it around his belt. He dropped the board and slid his feet into the slots on it. His design was based on the tower's lifts, but simplified because he had no one to maintain it, and no space for counterweights. It was basically ropes into the darkness and a pulley at the top.

Now the terrifying part. Gavin edged the floor open farther—and dropped like a stone into the darkness.

The pulley whizzed, but its high-pitched protests disappeared within moments as Gavin fell. There was no resistance at all. He fell faster, faster. He drew the blue mag torch and broke it against his leg. The lift shaft, which he had cut himself into the Chromeria's heart, was barely a pace and a half wide. There was nothing to be seen except smooth cut stone and the rope, one side whizzing up and the other side speeding down with Gavin.

He reached to the rope brake at his belt, but his movement tilted the board strapped to his feet, making one side touch a wall. The friction yanked that side upward, slamming him into the rock on the other side. The brake went tumbling from his fingers—and landed on his board. He snatched for it. Missed. He drew his knees up, his back skidding along the smooth wall, and grabbed the brake.

As he stood back up slowly, he grabbed the hook, attached the board to the brake, and threw the brake onto the whizzing lines. He squeezed the brake, all too aware that if he didn't brake quickly he might hit the bottom of the shaft at incredible speed, but if he braked too quickly he could break either the board or his own legs.

His legs trembling from the strain of trying to remain standing as he rapidly decelerated, he passed five broad white lines painted on all walls of the shaft. It was the warning that he was almost to the bottom. A moment later, he passed four broad white lines. Still too fast. Three. Two.

Okay, not too bad. One.

He hit the ground with a surprisingly hard thump. His natural reaction was to try to roll with the impact—which didn't work well, given that there wasn't any slack in the rope. He flopped over onto his back and rolled on top of the mag torch. It burned through his shirt instantly.

Gavin jumped to his feet with a yelp. Mercifully, the shirt didn't catch fire. He examined the angry red burn on his ribs. Very painful, but not very serious. He unhooked himself from the lift.

The chamber at the bottom of the lift was only four paces square. Gavin saw none of it. In the blue light of the mag torch, he walked to one blue wall. At his touch, it became translucent, but there was nothing behind it. Not yet. Slowly, ever so slowly, the chamber opposite lifted from its resting place and spun into position.

This was Gavin's greatest work. He'd constructed it in one furious month, sinking everything he knew into it. But whenever he called the blue chamber forth, his heart seized. And it did so today. The slow speed of the blue chamber's lift and rotation was necessary so that the man inside wouldn't even know he was moving.

On the other hand, it gave Gavin five minutes with nothing to do but wait. It would be empty today. Dear Orholam. Gavin's chest tightened. It was hard to breathe. The chamber was too small. There was no air. Breathe, Gavin, breathe. Paint that nonchalance on thick.

Finally, the translucence revealed the smooth globe of the dungeon's interior. Opposite Gavin stood a man who looked much like himself, though thinner, less muscular, dirtier, and with longer hair.

"Hello, brother," Gavin said.

Chapter 35

"Now this," Ironfist said, "is how you should be introduced to the Chromeria. High tide and dawn." He'd arrived before dawn, waking Kip to the bewildered feeling of not knowing if it was morning or night. Kip had only slowly been able to get his bearings as the commander hustled him through the less-crowded streets, finally cresting this hill. "They call it the Glass Lily," Ironfist said. "A rather softer name than it deserves, but then steel isn't transparent, is it?"

As they crested the hill, on first glance, the Chromeria did look something like a flower. Six towers in a hexagon surrounded one central tower. Because Little Jasper rose in altitude from south to north, the towers farther away from Kip rose higher, though all were the same height from base to tip. And each tower was completely transparent on its south side. Completing the odd flower imagery was the bridge, if it could be called a bridge.

The bridge crossing the ocean between Big Jasper and Little Jasper was green, like a flower's stem, heading right to the flaring towers and the bulbous walls that actually hung past vertical. But not only was the bridge green, it wasn't supported by anything. It lay at the surface of the water. It wasn't floating, because it didn't move with the waves, and the sea was choppy on one side of it and much calmer on the other.

"Why green?" Kip asked, trying to kick his brain into working. Wasn't green flexible?

"It's blue reinforced with yellow. It only looks green," Ironfist said, resuming his walk toward the bridge. Kip hurried to keep up, having difficulty gawking and walking at the same time, all tiredness fled.

"Yellow?" Kip asked. "How does that work? The Pr—erm, my *uncle* hasn't told me anything about yellow."

Ironfist looked at Kip, his gaze heavy as a sledge. He didn't answer, not even when Kip shut up and walked quietly alongside him, looking expectantly up at the big man but not bothering him.

Finally, Ironfist glanced at Kip. "Do I look like a magister to you?"

"Just figured that you're not much good as a fighter without your blue spectacles," Kip said. Stop, you moron! Don't—"So we might as well put you to some use."

The Blackguard commander's head snapped toward Kip. Kip swallowed. You deserve the crushed skull you're about to get, Kip. You're begging for it.

Then a small, unwilling smile crept over the commander's face. He guffawed. "When Orholam hands out the brains, the folks at the front of that line have to go to the back of the common sense line, huh?"

"What?" Kip asked. "Oh."

He waited patiently, thinking that his joke would buy him an answer about yellow luxin, but Ironfist ignored him. The perverse little grin on his face told Kip that he knew Kip was waiting for an answer and was only holding his tongue because he didn't want to start another topic. But Ironfist wasn't going to give him the pleasure of winning an answer. Pudgy force, meet immovable mass.

Within minutes, though, they had made their way onto the Lily's Stem—or rather, into it—and Kip forgot whatever it was that he had asked. The bridge was fully enclosed, albeit with blue luxin so thin it was almost as colorless as glass. But beneath their feet, the bridge actually *glowed*. Kip shot a look at Ironfist.

"No matter how often you look at me, I'm still not going to be a magister," the big man said.

"How about a guide?"

"Nope."

"A polite host?"

"Uh-uh."

A jackass? Kip's mouth actually opened to say it when he noticed again how thickly muscular Ironfist's arms were. He closed his open mouth and scowled.

"You were going to say something?" Ironfist asked.

"Your name," Kip said. "Is that common, among Parians?"

"Ironfist? Far as I know, I'm the only one."

"That isn't what I—" Oh, he was teasing.

Ironfist smirked. "You mean to take a name that describes us? Very common. Some use our old tongue, but the coastal folk—my people—use words that outsiders can understand. But the Ilytians do it too. To a lesser extent, the whole Chromeria does it. Gavin Guile is almost never called Emperor Guile or Prism Guile. He's just the Prism. Orea Pullawr is just the White. A lot of people think that meaningless names are the true puzzle."

"Meaningless names. You mean like Kip?"

Ironfist cocked an eyebrow. Shrugged.

Thanks a lot.

The crowds heading to Little Jasper for the day didn't even seem to notice the wonder beneath their feet. The bridge was perhaps twenty paces wide and three hundred long from shore to shore. The surface was lightly textured, but that barely interfered with its transparency, aside from some dirt. Kip could see the water right under his feet, not even a foot away, swelling up with every wave and gapping in between them. They were on the side of the bridge with heavy seas, too—apparently here traffic traveled on the right, unlike at home, so waves crashed into the luxin right next to Kip. After having been pulled in and pounded by those same waves, it made him more than a little nervous. No one else seemed to even notice it.

Then, at about the time Kip and Ironfist reached the middle of the bridge, Kip saw a monster wave coming in. Just in time to meet the bridge, trough met trough, peak met peak, and the wave loomed high—its height easily half again as tall as the bridge. Kip braced himself and took a deep breath.

He didn't notice he'd clamped his eyes shut until he heard

Ironfist's quiet chuckle. He opened his eyes as the last of the water sluiced off the outside of the tube, harmlessly. The bridge hadn't groaned, hadn't shuddered, hadn't even acknowledged the power of the wave that had just fully passed over it.

A few passersby grinned knowingly. Apparently this was the kind of joke that didn't get old.

"Is this why—" Kip stumbled as he reminded himself to use the correct term. "Is this why my uncle wanted me to come this way?"

"Part of the reason, I'm sure. Anytime we have to deal with a recalcitrant king or satrap or queen or satrapah or pirate lord, we make sure they come across at high tide. It's a good little reminder of whom they're dealing with."

Little reminder?

The next wave crashed over the bridge as well, and soon even the wave troughs were higher than the bottom of the bridge. By the time Kip and Ironfist stepped off the bridge, it was half submerged in the sea. Unbelievable. Kip hadn't grown up on the sea, but even he knew that the tide coming in so hard and high and fast was unusual. It made him wonder if there was some magic to that too. And through it all, the bridge didn't even shudder. Some reminder.

The bridge curved up before it spilled them onto the shore, of course, but when it did, Kip was finally able to start paying attention to the Chromeria.

The first two towers, to the right and left as one stepped onto Little Jasper, were set narrower than the back two towers, either to help strengthen the wall near the huge gate where it was most likely to be attacked or—

Oh. It's all about the light.

As soon as Kip realized that, everything else made sense. Everything about the Chromeria was designed to maximize exposure to sunlight. Building on a slope meant that more sun could reach the lower levels of the northerly towers and the yard. Having the first two towers of the hexagon set narrower meant that they didn't cast shadows on the back towers. The "glass" northern walls and the north sides of each of the towers meant that every north-facing room got as much sunlight as they could use, while the southern rooms had opaque walls more amenable to privacy and comfort. Kip imagined that those with a stifling fear of heights might not do well in some of the Chromeria's rooms—minimizing its footprint, and adding to the flaring lily shape, all the towers except the central one leaned out. It was no accident either; despite the lean, the floors were all level. Perhaps it was that the Chromeria needed more space than was available on the island, so the only way to have more space was to make the towers extend beyond the island. Perhaps it was simply because they could.

Either for support or convenience, there was a lattice of translucent walkways between each tower and its adjacent ones. Encircling the central tower, halfway up, a clear walkway connected to the tower at two points and then radiated out to each of the other towers in turn. Kip could see that those enclosed walkways were filled with people making their way between towers. Doubtless it was much faster if you had business high in each tower to be able to travel directly rather than walk all the way down the stairs, cross the central yard, and then climb all the way back up. But the visual effect remained. The air around the central tower, like a flower's style, was kept uncluttered, prominent.

"Each color has its own tower," Ironfist said.

"Thought you weren't a guide," Kip said before he could stop himself. He blinked. If he didn't dislike pain so much, he would have physically bit his tongue to give himself a reminder.

Ironfist simply looked at him.

"Sorry," Kip squeaked. He cleared his throat and said, deeper, "I mean, sorry."

Ironfist still looked at him flatly.

"Let me guess," Kip said, squirming, wanting to deflect Ironfist's intense gaze. He pointed to the tower to the left of the gate they were approaching, then in a sunwise circle. "Sub-red, red, orange, yellow, green, and blue." Blue was the last one, just to the right of the gate.

"Good guess," Ironfist said reluctantly.

"So why do the superviolets get bent over the fence?" Kip asked.

"Excuse me?" Ironfist's voice pitched higher.

"You know," Kip said. What?

Ironfist's right eyebrow climbed.

"Like for a whipping."

"That expression doesn't mean what you think it means," Ironfist said.

Kip opened his mouth to ask what it did mean then, but could tell the commander wasn't going to tell him.

"There are never enough superviolets to fill an entire tower, and superviolets can draft best if they are higher up. The quality of light there is better for their work, plus a good majority of their work is directly for the White. So they inhabit the Prism's Tower, close to the top."

They walked to the great gates with hundreds of other people who were coming, to work or conduct business. The gates were covered with beaten gold, but were open, so Kip only caught a glimpse of the scene and figures depicted on them. The walls, however, were a wonder themselves. It became obvious that blue luxin was their main element, but the luxin itself could be lighter or darker, and it apparently had to be mixed with yellow. For strength? That had to be it, given that the entire bridge was made of that mix. But each wall of the hexagon was different. There were patterns of blue and yellow and green throughout, and that wasn't even including the towers. While the north side of each tower was as close to perfectly transparent as possible for maximum sun exposure, the rest was constructed to mark the buildings for their owners, so that even the untrained could tell which building belonged to whom. And, apparently, to show off.

Every surface of the blue tower was cut like a giant sapphire so that the entire tower gleamed off a thousand surfaces no matter what angle you saw it from. The sub-red tower, over its base of interwoven blue and yellow and green, seemed to burn. Illusory flames licked up the luxin for ten and twenty feet and occasionally threw sparks and flames even higher. All the rest of the tower seemed to ripple, like the air over a fire.

Kip stumbled as they entered the central yard. He looked at his feet. Great grooves cut the ground in a broad arc, connecting the gates. But the gates Kip had passed didn't slide shut, they just shut on hinges, like normal doors. He looked at Ironfist, confused.

"Glass flower," Ironfist said.

"Huh?"

"What do flowers do?"

Look pretty? "Uh..."

Ironfist looked pleased to have stumped him. "With regards to the sun."

"They open?"

"And how would that work with a group of buildings?"

Kip thought about it, and gave up.

"It wouldn't," Ironfist said.

"Oh. Then..."

"Try again."

"Do you ever answer questions straight?" Kip asked.

"Only to my superiors." Which was, Kip realized, a straight answer. He wrinkled his nose, too intimidated by Ironfist to point that out, but the twitch at the corner of the big man's mouth told him he knew. "Flowers follow the sun from morning to night," Ironfist said, perhaps by way of apology.

Kip looked at the tracks again as he and Ironfist approached the central building. Before the road came to the gate, it flared wide—so wide that most of it simply abutted the wall in a wide crescent. "You mean the *whole thing* turns?" It was the only thing that made sense, Kip realized. If the buildings were all transparent on the north side, they would only take full advantage of the sunlight in the middle of the day, but if the whole compound turned, they would get maximum light from dawn until dusk. But *all* of it? Impossible!

"Here we are," Ironfist said.

Kip swiveled his head back to the front as they stopped in front of a huge silvery gate. It was as plain as everything else here was ornate.

Two guards on either side of the gate, dressed in full mirror armor, each wearing a sword and holding a matchlock musket nearly as tall as he was. "Commander Ironfist," they said in greeting.

"Finally," Ironfist said, pushing Kip inside. "You are about to meet the Thresher."

Chapter 36

Meetings with Dazen were always a practice in deception.

Gavin's tightened chest didn't ease at the sight of his brother. He should have killed him years ago. How simple that would have been. How simple it still could be. All he needed to do was stop dropping bread down the chute. Just like that, his problem would go away. He thought of it every morning, after every sleepless night. But this was his brother. He hadn't killed him in the heat of battle, how could he kill him in cold blood?

Seven years, seven purposes.

Three times now, he'd put "Tell Karris Everything" on the list. Not just about loving her. About this. That Dazen wasn't dead, that he was here. That so much was built on lies. She deserved to know; she could never know. Because if she knew, it might bring them reconciliation and happiness together—or it might bring a new war to consume the Seven Satrapies.

"Hello, brother," Gavin said again. The air was cool on his skin, the scent of resin and stone inescapable. He braced himself for the response. His brother, after all, was a Guile too. And unlike Gavin, he had nothing else to think of except what he would say to Gavin the next time he came to visit. That, of course, and plot to escape. After sixteen years, most men would have given up, but not a Guile. That was their legacy: absolute, unreasoning faith in their supremacy over other men. Thank you, father.

212 • *Brent Weeks*

"What do you want?" Dazen asked, his voice rough from disuse.

"Did you know that during the war, I fathered a bastard? I just found out about a month ago. As big of a surprise to me as to anyone, but all sorts of things happen during war, don't they? Karris was furious, of course. She wouldn't share my bed for three weeks, but, well...making up with Karris has always been so good that I almost want to fight with her." He looked up and left and smiled for an instant, as if at a private memory.

It was important to layer the lies with a Guile. In Gavin's narrative to his brother over the years, he had established an alternate life. He and Karris were married, but had no children—a nagging heartache, and a source of conflict with Andross Guile, who wanted Gavin to put Karris aside and find a woman who could produce heirs. He leaked those details slowly, grudgingly, making his brother work to uncover them. Then, every time, Gavin could leak more information to see if his brother looked either confused by the lies or contemptuous of them.

Dazen had a nasty smile on his face. "So who was it? Do you even know her name? Did she have proof?"

He was fishing, hoping Gavin would give him something for nothing. And he would suspect Gavin if Gavin gave it to him. But Gavin went ahead. "His face is proof enough. He's the very image of Sevastian."

Dazen's face paled. "Don't you bring Sevastian into your lies, you monster, don't you dare."

"We've adopted the boy. His name is Kip. Good kid. Smart. Talented. A bit awkward, but he'll grow."

"I don't believe you." Dazen looked sick. He might not believe it, but he was close. "Who's the mother?"

Gavin shrugged, as if it didn't matter. "Lina."

"You lie!" Dazen snarled and slapped a hand against the blue luxin separating them. "Karris would never take that harlot's bastard!" It was real fury, after sixteen years bathing in placid blue light, something deep and hot and too instant to be false.

Which told Gavin three things. But some purposes are best achieved by misdirection. "She had a rosewood box," he said, "about this long. Do you know what was in it?"

The expression on Dazen's face told Gavin he'd made a mistake. Head pulled back, stunned, then confusion, hope, and finally laughter. There was genuine joy. Dazen kept laughing, shaking his head, prolonging the laugh, now, rubbing it in. He leaned against the blue luxin between them, but naturally, confident. "Here's what bothers me more than everything else," Dazen said. "More than your betrayal. More than your murders. More than the cruelty of imprisoning me rather than just killing me. More than you stealing Karris. More than all the rest of it together. How is it that no one has noticed?"

"We're not doing this again, dead man," Gavin said. "You don't want to trade, fine. I'll be going."

"This is my trade. Let me hear you say it, and I'll tell you all about the dagger."

Dagger? Dazen had dropped that tidbit deliberately. Oh, shit. Gavin had overlooked something. His chest tightened, throat clamped shut. It was hard to breathe, harder still to keep his face smooth.

There was no one here. No one who could overhear if he said it aloud. It wasn't new information. If he could get new information for old, it wasn't a loss. But it felt like one.

Gavin moistened his lips. "My name is Dazen Guile, and I stole your life."

"How'd you do it, Dazen? How did no one notice?"

I took your clothes and strode out of the flames at Sundered Rock. My face was swollen from our fight. I'd already given myself your scar and cut my hair like yours. I just started giving orders, and your people became mine. "I just acted like a selfish asshole, and everyone assumed I was you," he said, feigning nonchalance.

The prisoner laughed, ignoring the last part. "Well, it's a beginning. Feels good, doesn't it? They say confession is good for the soul."

Dazen—Gavin!—snarled, "Now...about that dagger."

"It's my vengeance, little brother," the prisoner said. "It is the sweet song of victory," the prisoner said. "It is the sting in the night. Dryness in your bones. Sleeplessness and terrors. It is your death and my freedom, Dazen. It is the end of all your lies."

"And apparently I've only heard the beginning of yours," Gavin said, sneering. His brother was lying. Had to be. He was just trying to make Gavin worry. He was chained, not witless. Confined, not toothless.

The real Gavin laughed. "No, you see, the beauty of it is that I don't have to lie. What are you going to do, little brother? You don't have the spine to starve me. No, you'll just watch it coming. Death will draw his sword and you will stand and do nothing. It's always been your way." He laughed again. "I have nothing more to say to you. Begone."

Dazen trembled. Every word his brother said touched some deeper well. The time Karris's elder brother Rodin had sworn to beat Dazen, and Dazen had stood still, waiting, not really believing Rodin would do it until it was too late. The terrible dreams Dazen had had as a child, and for which the elder Gavin had mocked him. Even being dismissed, as Dazen had always hated. Orholam damn him, Gavin had always known the cracks in his armor. Dazen shook his head.

No, *he* was Gavin now. The mask had to be total, even in his own thoughts. At all times. Dazen was another life. "Dazen" was the wretch on the other side of the luxin now. Dazen was the weak bastard trying to anger him so that Gavin would kill him. That's all this was. The prisoner was terrified, weak. He was a shell. He was trying to provoke Gavin to kill him because he couldn't summon the courage to suicide. That was all.

The man Gavin had once been would have killed the prisoner and been done with it. In the war, Dazen had become ruthless. Dazen loved the clash of arms, the splash of blood. Dazen loved his mastery over other men. Dazen would crush those who rose against him. Now, as Gavin, he wouldn't be pulled back to that. He wouldn't give his brother the satisfaction. "Well," Gavin said. "It was a pleasure as always, but it's getting late"—of course, it was barely noon, but he liked making the real Gavin wonder just how disoriented he was down here—"and Karris is eager tonight. She made me promise not to keep her waiting." That's for cheating on her and leaving me with the mess, you bastard. "So a good evening to you, *Dazen*."

The prisoner said, "Your lies are failing already, Dazen. You just keep wondering who already knows, and how they're plotting against you. Sweet dreams."

"There are worse things than waking from a nightmare to find yourself in the arms of the woman you love. Say, waking in a cell. Sweet dreams to you too, brother." Gavin touched the glass and it went dark, and once more the cell began its slow, slow rotation into the earth.

Gavin leaned against the cold wall, trying to calm his racing heart. It wasn't a loss; he'd learned some things from his brother. First, he had indeed been cheating on Karris. Kip was Gavin's bastard. Second, Gavin had known Kip's mother—and she wasn't a prostitute. If she had been, he would have said, "Karris would never take a harlot's bastard." Instead, he'd said, "That harlot's bastard," which meant he intended the word as a slur, not a description. Third—unless he was far, far smarter than Gavin gave him credit for, which was possible—the real Gavin still wasn't getting information from the outside.

That was why Gavin had put all of his lies in the past tense: Kip's discovery. A month of not sharing a bed with Karris, decisions already made about raising Kip. If someone were passing him news, the prisoner would be confused by the chronological disparity—which, because it didn't seem to serve a purpose, he wouldn't expect to be a lie. Gavin didn't expect his brother to voice his confusion, of course, but he was hoping to see it in his eyes. There had been none.

So Dazen wasn't getting information from the outside, which meant he wasn't plotting with this "Color Prince," whoever the hell that was. So the Color Prince was merely using a retelling of the Prisms' War to agitate dissent. All the world believed Gavin had won, and the Color Prince didn't like how things had turned out, so he was pretending to be in league with the losing brother—whom he had no idea was actually alive. This Color Prince was a liar and an opportunist then, not a zealot who knew the truth.

Which meant there was only one place the Color Prince could be: Tyrea. Either King Garadul was the Color Prince himself, or the two were connected.

Thank you, brother. Very helpful. And you used to be better at lying than I was.

But after the prison finally settled into place, he checked and double-checked all his chromaturgy. Nothing was out of place. And yet, even as he ascended up the shaft and out of the evernight he'd created down here for his brother, he trembled. He was as trapped as Gavin was.

I could just stop feeding him. I wouldn't even have to do anything. I could just take a vacation, tell Marissia not to drop the dyed bread down the chute while I'm gone. He'd simply...die.

He remembered when they'd been children and Dazen had climbed the lemon tree to prove he could do everything his older brother could—and fallen. They thought he'd broken his ankle. Gavin had carried him all the way home. A small thing, for an adult, but Gavin had been reduced to tears by the effort. But he refused to give up. His little brother had never forgotten it.

And now the little brother is going to kill that man in cold blood, without even having the courage to face him as he did it?

Enough. All the world knows your brother is dead. *You* are all they know. Besides, you need your wits about you. You have to tell the Spectrum you started a war. And then you need to convince them to fight it your way.

I do have a chance. Just as long as the White's in a good mood.

Unless...

Oh, Gavin Guile, sometimes you do play a deep game, don't you? He grinned to himself. Seven years, seven goals. One impossible prize. A small failure could serve his greatest success.

Gavin made it back to his room and was putting everything back in place to disguise the door in the closet again when there was a sharp rap at the door. He threw the closet closed as the White opened the door.

"Good to see you, Lord Prism!" she said.

Gavin was painfully aware of the mess in front of him and the burn on the back of his shirt—a burn he had no good way to explain if she saw it. "And you, High Mistress," he said, smiling. "Just the person I wanted to talk to, if we could meet in a few moments, perhaps in your chambers?"

Orea Pullawr looked at him sharply. "I'm afraid that's going to have to wait. There's a class waiting for you. A class you promised me you'd teach." Her nose twitched. "Did you burn something in here?"

"Um, yes?" Gavin said. It came out as a question. Damn it.

" 'Um, yes?' "

Gavin cleared his throat. "Yes."

She waited.

He said nothing more.

"Very well, then. Be like that. I thought you left to take care of that color wight."

Ah, she was angry because she thought he'd neglected a mission whose abandonment might mean people dying. And she would have been sure, it being a blue, that he would go immediately. And she didn't know why he'd summoned the Spectrum. The White didn't like to be left in the dark. "Consider it taken care of," Gavin said. Which she would interpret to be him blowing her off, but he didn't know how to not tell her about the skimmer if he was fully honest.

After showing it to the boy and Karris, it was a secret he couldn't expect to keep much longer, but that would be a big conversation, and he wasn't ready for it yet.

She lifted her eyebrows, like, You're going to be dismissive, to me?

A thought hit him. "The class is superviolets?"

The White nodded, suspicious.

"There's a girl from Tyrea in that class, isn't there? Alivia?"

"Aliviana Danavis, from Rekton."

So he'd remembered correctly. A girl from Kip's town. Perfect.

He hesitated. Kip had said Corvan was there, but… "No relation, surely?"

"Actually, she's General Danavis's daughter."

Gavin let the shock show as dull surprise, like he'd just heard about some minor tragedy on the other side of the world. He'd heard the girl's surname was Danavis before, but he'd assumed it was some distant relation, if any. Corvan's own daughter? And why had Corvan been living in the same town as Gavin's bastard? Coincidence? If so, that was a *heavy* coincidence.

Regardless, it required Gavin's attention, right away. "Huh. You're right, I need to go teach that class. It's a holy responsibility." Juggling, always juggling.

"I always distrust you when you get dutiful," the White said.

He smiled, blandly innocent.

Chapter 37

It seemed to Kip that the entire first floor of the Prism's Tower was a jungle of benches, desks, signs, queues, and clerks. Obviously, the whole business of the Chromeria passed through this room. There were queues for traders seeking contracts for food, queues for traders delivering contracted food, the same for every other trade good Kip could imagine, queues for redress of grievances caused by Chromeria residents, queues for laborers seeking work, queues for adjudicating fee disputes on Big Jasper. There were even queues for nobles— although there were many more clerks staffing that one than any of the others. The room had a busy hum, but despite the crowd, it was obvious that the Chromeria ran like a well-oiled mill. The people were impatient but not angry, bored but not surly.

Commander Ironfist led Kip to a desk with a single clerk, and no queue at all. "All the rest of this year's darks were admitted weeks ago."

"Darks?" Kip asked.

"That's what people like you are called. Unofficially. Supplicants, officially: you want to be part of the Chromeria, but you aren't yet. So you're a dark. Darks, dims, glims, gleams, beams. But you don't need to remember any of that right now."

Kip opened his mouth, shut it. Ironfist said nothing until they reached the desk. The clerk, obviously daydreaming, sat bolt upright when he noticed Commander Ironfist.

"Yes, Commander? How may I assist you?"

"I have a supplicant for immediate testing."

"Immediate as in..."

"Now."

The clerk's throat bobbed. "Yes, Commander. Supplicant's name?"

"Kip. Kip Guile," Ironfist said.

The clerk grabbed his quill, began writing, got halfway, froze. "Guile as in...?"

"As in, no one needs to hear it from you. Is that a problem?" Ironfist asked.

"No, sir. I'll just go talk to my superiors. You could go ahead up to the testing room. I'm sure the testers will be along presently." With a quick bob of his head, the clerk got up and ran to a back office.

"I understand the rest, but what's a glim?" Kip asked as they climbed the stairs together. He trod on his sagging pant leg, which had fallen lower as he climbed the stairs, and he almost pitched forward on his face. He cleared his throat and hiked up his pants. Life would be so much easier if he had a waist.

"A glimmer," Ironfist said.

Ah, dark, dim, glimmer, gleam, beam. A light progression, then.

Ironfist said, "Now quiet. This is supposed to be solemn. You go into the room and don't say anything until your testing is finished. Got it?"

Kip almost said yes, then nodded instead. This might be harder than he had thought. Ironfist gestured to the door, and Kip walked in. Ironfist closed the door behind him.

The room was utterly plain. One wall curved slightly inward, so Kip guessed that was the outer wall of the tower. Other than that irregularity, the room was a square, ten paces wide, all white stone with a single wood table and a single wood chair. The room was lit by a strange white crystal set into the wall, the same kind Kip had seen in all the halls and even, now that he thought of it, in the great room downstairs with all the queues. Kip flopped into the chair. It had been an exhausting week. Had it only been yesterday that he'd been skimming across the waves, that he'd tried to drown, tried to sail? Had it only been a few days since...No, Kip wasn't going to think about that. Too jagged. Too heavy. He'd be blubbering again if he wasn't careful.

He'd been waiting for several hours when he heard the muffled exchange of angry words from the hall. That was definitely Ironfist, laying into somebody. Kip swallowed hard. He wanted to get up and eavesdrop, but he knew that with his luck as soon as he got to the door it would open.

Whatever the argument had been about, it was over as quickly as it began. The door didn't open. Kip waited. And waited. He was just starting to get tired, eyes drooping, when the door popped open.

A man of perhaps thirty, wearing red spectacles hung from a red cord around his neck, came in. He was clearly furious. Apparently not the winner of the argument, then. "Darks will stand!" he snarled.

Kip shot to his feet. His chair skittered back, caught its legs, and went crashing to the floor. Kip flinched, smiled weakly in apology, and picked up the chair.

The man continued staring at him, his mouth a tight white line. He had a large hooked nose and the deep olive skin of an Atashian, though he was beardless, but it was the eyes that captured Kip's attention. The brown eyes were interrupted by a hard circle of royal red in the middle of the iris. Scarlet streaks like sunbeams pierced the rest of the brown irises. Kip put the chair back as he'd found it, looked back to the man, and got nothing, no hint of what he expected.

Kip moved away from the chair. The man stared liquid hatred at him. "Sorry," Kip mumbled, defensive.

"Darks will not speak! Ignorant Tyrean trash."

"Oh, kiss my blubbery butt cheeks," Kip said. Oops.

He squeezed his eyes shut to curse himself, so he didn't even see the blow coming. The fist cracked across his jaw, and the next thing he knew, he was on the ground, drooling blood.

Kip was slow to anger. Usually. But he popped up to his feet almost as fast as he'd fallen, and the rage was there, everywhere. Everyone he knew was dead. Everything he cared about was gone. He didn't care if the drafter tore him apart.

But as he bounced to his feet, he saw the light in the drafter's eyes. Do it! the man's eyes said. Give me the excuse. I will bounce you out of the Chromeria before you know what hit you.

And like that, Kip's anger dropped into a more familiar channel, and he had control again. There was a footstep in the hall. "Good," Kip said. "We've got something to build on there. A little clumsy for a kiss, but I understand your eagerness. I'm sure with that ugly face you don't get much practice. But I said kiss my butt cheeks. *Butt* cheeks. Butt cheeks, cheeks." He gestured. "They're different. Try again, this time with feeling."

The drafter's face went from incredulity to rage. He stepped forward and—just as the door opened—buried his fist in Kip's stomach. The drafter was distracted by the opening door and didn't put his full weight into the blow, but Kip doubled up as if it were the hardest blow he'd ever taken. He crumpled and coughed blood, retching.

"Magister Galden, what in Orholam's name is going on here?"

The drafter who'd hit Kip said, "I—I—He defied me!"

"So you *struck* him? Like the benighted do? Get out. Get out now! I'll deal with you later."

Magister Galden turned and stood over Kip. "I'll remember this, and I'll find you someday when there's—"

"So help me Orholam, if you threaten a student in my presence for your own malfeasance, Jens Galden, I will strip you of your colors and put you off Little Jasper this very hour. Test me. Please."

Magister Galden looked absolutely stricken. Like his life was falling apart without warning.

That embarrassment and pain could be turned to rage, oh so easily. Sometimes Kip frightened himself. Magister Jens Galden was standing between him and the man who'd come in the door. Kip couldn't see the man, and that man couldn't see Kip. All he had to do was give Jens Galden a big, triumphant smile and leave his stomach open. The magister would lose control—Kip knew all about losing control—and kick him. Kip would leave his stomach open, inviting it. Jens would kick him, and lose everything.

And for what, Kip? For having a temper and being an asshole? Kip hesitated. The man had made him furious, but that was too much.

But if Kip didn't smile, he'd have an enemy. An enemy he could destroy right now.

Wherever that thought was going, he didn't get time to follow it. The moment passed. Jens Galden snarled and wheeled out of the room. Kip was left on the floor, the inside of his lips still lacerated, bleeding and painful. He'd done what was right; maybe he should have done what was smart.

He picked himself up. The man who'd saved him was just poking his head out the door after Magister Galden. He said, "Arien, I need you to conduct the testing."

A woman said, "Luxlord, I'm not a tester."

"And I don't want to wait while a new one is summoned!" he said sharply. "I'm supposed to meet with the Prism in half an hour. We need to get started now."

The luxlord came back into the room. He was a tall man, wearing Ilytian hose and doublet though his skin was olive like Jens Galden's rather than deep black. He was balding; his fringe of dark, wavy hair was streaked with white and brushed out long, halfway down his back. He was somewhere in his fifties, fit, and wearing a heavy black woolen cloak embroidered with gold thread in intricate lattice. His fingers were burdened with wide gold rings and jewels of every color of the spectrum, oddly worn between the knuckles in the middle of his fingers rather than closest to his hand. But Kip was learning to look at people's eyes—and the odd thing about the luxlord's eyes was perhaps that they were normal. They were green; there was no foreign color shot through those eyes.

The luxlord smiled. "No," he said, "I'm not a drafter. The Black usually isn't. My name is Carver Black. Luxlord Black, for most purposes." The name didn't sound Atashian, so maybe he was Ilytian, but Kip guessed the man could just as easily have grown up here or anywhere. Obviously, there was a lot of trade and movement among certain nations. Just not Tyrea.

Kip moved to speak, stopped, pointed to his lips.

"Yes," the luxlord said. "You can speak. We'll begin momentarily, as soon as Arien is ready."

"Um, nice to meet you, Luxlord Black. I'm Kip."

"And you, Magister?" Luxlord Black asked. "Are you ready?"

"Yes, Luxlord," she said. She sat at the chair, and the Black stood beside the table. Kip came to stand in front of the table himself.

Magister Arien was short and skinny, nervous around the Black, but happy and cute. She looked up at Kip like she wanted him to succeed. He tried not to let her orange eyes disturb him. "Supplicant," she said, "I'm going to lay out a series of colored tiles, from one tone to another. You will arrange the tiles in order." She smiled suddenly. "We'll start easy."

With that, she opened a bag in her lap, rummaged through the tiles for a bit, and extracted a black tile and a white tile. These she laid at the edges of the table. Then she laid a dozen tiles in various shades of gray in between. Kip quickly moved them into place from lightest to darkest.

Arien said nothing, simply checked the backs of the tiles, made marks on a parchment, and swept the tiles off the table and back into the bag. Then she laid out brown tiles, from a tumbleweed to sepia. This was harder, but Kip swapped tiles quickly once more.

The test was repeated with blues, greens, yellows, oranges, and reds. When Kip got the reds perfect, Arien pulled out a black bag, checked the backs of the tiles carefully—shielding them from Kip's eyes with a hand as she did so—and lined up another series of reds, except this group had twice as many tiles, so the gradations of color were much much finer. Scarlets, vermilions, strawberry, raspberry, cerise. Kip lined them up and only had trouble with one. The color at the edge of that tile was slightly darker than the color on its face. Finally he put it in its spot by the color on its face.

She flipped the tiles over, and Kip saw that he'd put tile fourteen between tiles nine and ten. Arien winked at him apologetically, as if he'd done better than she expected, despite failing.

"That's not right," Kip said.

"Silence!" Luxlord Black said. "I know you don't know our ways, supplicant, but you will not speak during the testing."

"But it's wrong," Kip said.

"I'm warning you."

Kip raised his hands in silent protest.

Luxlord Black sighed. "Magister?" he asked. "Usually protests have to be lodged after the test results are finalized, but apparently nothing is going to go according to custom today. A judgment, please?"

Arien flipped the tiles back over as Kip had had them lined up. She cleared her throat awkwardly. "Luxlord, I'm sorry, I'm not a superchromat. I tried to tell you. I can't tell the difference myself. The key says that the—"

"The key is being challenged." Luxlord Black scratched an eye with one finger. "Half of women superchromats, and I choose... Never you mind. Go get a superchromat, Magister."

"Yes, Luxlord," she said meekly.

She left and the luxlord turned his green eyes to Kip. "Who are you, really? Why are you testing today? Why the special treatment? Where are you from?"

"I'm from Tyrea, sir. King Garadul wiped out my—"

"King? What's this about?"

The door opened and Magister Arien came in, followed by a woman who looked like a scarecrow. She was almost as tall as Luxlord Black, lean as a rail, with faded brown skin, bones sticking out at sharp angles, wrinkled, her kinky hair white and short with only a few wisps of something darker clinging to the tips, the natural mahogany of her eyes eclipsed by orange and red in jagged starbursts through her irises, reaching almost to the outer edge.

"Mistress Kerawon Varidos, I'm sorry to disturb you," Luxlord Black said. He shot a look at Arien.

"She was just in the hall; she asked what I was doing," Arien said defensively.

"Nearly bowled me over. What's this challenge?" the old woman asked. The tiles were lying face up the way Kip had left them. "How did the supplicant order them?"

Silence. The mistress looked from Luxlord Black to Magister Arien. "That is the way he ordered them," Arien said.

"So he's a freak to his gender. Are we done?"

"The key says it should be like this," Magister Arien said. She turned the tiles over and pointed to the numbers on the back.

"You come to me to differentiate the finest red chroma and you think I can't read?" Mistress Varidos asked sharply.

Magister Arien looked horrified. Her mouth opened and shut.

The old scarecrow picked up tile fourteen in her bony claws. She turned it and looked at the edges. "Strip your tester of her position," she said. "This tile has been left in the sunlight. It's been bleached. It's the wrong color. The boy's a superchromat." She turned to Kip. "Congratulations, freak."

"Freak?" Kip said.

"Simple, is he? Too bad."

"What?" Kip asked. He still hadn't figured out what everyone's titles meant, much less what he was supposed to do with all of this.

"Kip, you're forbidden to speak!" Magister Arien said.

"That's an injunction against cheating," Luxlord Black said. "For when hundreds of supplicants are testing in the same room."

"He just came today," Magister Arien told Mistress Varidos. "The Prism himself ordered that he be tested immediately. He doesn't know all the rules."

"Continue the testing," the mistress ordered.

Kip and Magister Arien glanced at Luxlord Black. Kip guessed that, technically, the luxlord was the highest-ranking person in the room, but the man gave the tiniest shrug, as if it wasn't worth fighting over. Go on, he waved.

Magister Arien sat once more, pulled out a set of tongs, and used them to lay out another dozen tiles—except these were all the same deep red. Kip blinked. Magister Arien handed him the tongs. Um, thanks?

Kip reached a hand out for a tile, and then he understood. He could feel the heat radiating off them. He was supposed to see the differences in heat? He stared as if by sheer willpower he could tear the truth out of the tiles.

Time crawled past. Kip started to daydream. He wondered if Liv Danavis was here. Oh, no, he'd have to tell her.

Hi, Liv, great to see you. Your father's dead.

Fantastic. Kip thought about the flames roaring through his town, about that drafter and his apprentice, throwing fireballs. Jumping over the waterfall, running down the waterfall path in the utter darkness, relaxing his eyes so he could actually see better than focusing directly. Oh, Orholam, I *am* simple.

"Okay, that's long enough," Luxlord Black said.

"No wait! Wait! I just—I just..." Kip stared at the tiles again. Relax, eyes, come on! He let his focus go soft, and abruptly it was clear. Using the tongs, he shuffled each tile into its correct place in moments from the hottest to the merely warm. This was what Master Danavis had been teaching him? The old dyer had never let on that what he was showing Kip wasn't normal. Unbelievable.

The thought of the dyer left a hollow in Kip's stomach. Master Danavis had been good to him. Inventing chores he probably could have done faster himself, just to give Kip a little money. And like everyone in Rekton, he'd been slaughtered.

Kip hoped Master Danavis had taken some of the bastards with him.

"Are we almost done?" he asked roughly. He wanted to be alone. He was too tired, his emotions erratic, the reality of what had happened in Rekton trying to rush in and overwhelm him now that he had a second where he wasn't running from soldiers or bandits or having magic thrown at him.

"No," the old scarecrow said. "Don't bother, girl," she told Arien, who'd only flipped over half of the tiles. "He got them all correct. Show him the superviolets."

Magister Arien put away the hot tiles with a glance at Luxlord Black, who seemed unfazed. Then she pulled out the last tiles, which were all the same deep violet.

Relax my eyes to see one side of the spectrum, so...Kip tightened his eyes as hard as he could, and the colors leapt apart. Someone had written a letter on each tile. It read: "Nicely done!"

Kip laughed. He slapped them into place.

Magister Arien looked at Mistress Varidos. "Why are you looking at me, you fool girl?" the old woman asked. "I can't see superviolets. I'm at the other end of the spectrum."

The younger woman blushed and flipped over the tiles. They were in the correct order.

"Congratulations, boy," Mistress Varidos said. "You can be some satrap's gardener."

"What?" Kip asked.

"It's one use for excellent color matchers, and a step up for you, Tyrean."

The door opened and Commander Ironfist stepped in. "What's this?" he asked.

"We've just finished testing the supplicant," Magister Arien said. "He's a full-spectrum superchromat!"

"You're wasting his time with tiles? I don't care what colors he can see, I want to know what he can draft. Where's that idiot tester I started with? I told him to put Kip through the Thresher."

"You're putting a raw supplicant through the Thresher?" Mistress Varidos asked.

"Wait, *this* wasn't the Thresher?" Kip asked.

"Do you feel threshed?" Ironfist asked.

"You're putting a raw supplicant through the Thresher?" the mistress asked again.

"He's leaving in the morning. The Prism demands to know his capabilities before they go."

"This is highly irregular," the mistress said. "Who is this boy?"

"I'm right here," Kip said, irritated.

"Regular or irregular is irrelevant," Ironfist said. "Can you and this magister assist in the testing or not?"

"Me?" Magister Arien asked, alarmed. "I don't think I—"

"We can do it—" the mistress began.

"Good, then—" Ironfist said.

"—but I demand to know who he is first."

"I'm right here!" Kip said.

"Don't you raise your voice to me, boy," the mistress said, stabbing the air in front of his nose with one bony claw.

"Who are you, boy?" Luxlord Black asked quietly, even as the voices continued to rise.

"I think I'd really prefer not to help with the Thresh—" Arien was saying.

"You have no standing to make demands, Mistress—" Ironfist was saying to the old woman.

"I'm Kip Guile!" Kip shouted. "I'm Gavin Guile's bastard, Kip."

Silence.

Kip looked from one face to another. Luxlord Black merely looked shocked. Magister Arien looked stunned to the point of tears. Commander Ironfist looked peeved. Mistress Varidos looked oddly satisfied. "Ah," she said. "Then we'll start the Thresher immediately. Girl," she ordered Arien, "go get the room ready. Summon the testers." She looked at Kip. "So, maybe not a gardener after all."

Go bend yourself over a fence, Kip said—but only to himself.

Chapter 38

Liv Danavis climbed the last steps to the top of the Chromeria, glancing around nervously. She was at the head of the short line of her classmates, carrying her chair awkwardly high so she didn't catch it on the steep stairs. At first she thought the deck was empty, then she saw him. Her target. Her last chance.

The Prism was standing right at the edge of the building, leaning out, looking east, past the red tower, studying the ships in Sapphire Bay. Though Gavin Guile was literally twice Liv's seventeen years, he cut a fine figure in the afternoon sun. A sharp V from broad shoulders to narrow waist, arm thick with muscle where the wind was blowing one sleeve up. His copper-colored hair streamed in the wind. He had that odd combination uncommon even among the high houses of the Seven Satrapies of red hair and—instead of the freckled skin that would mark him a Blood Forester—deeply tanned skin. Could it be true? Could this man be Kip's father?

"Liv! Move!" Vena hissed.

Liv started. She'd stopped right at the top of the steps, blocking the rest of the class. She hurried forward, blushing. She knew it was bad when oblivious Vena noticed something. Perfect. Liv was going to hear about this. If not from Magister Goldthorn, certainly from a few of the less friendly girls in the class.

As the six girls took their places—there were no boys in the class—the Prism saw them. He pulled himself away from the edge of the tower and walked to the head of the class. As when they sat in their normal class—though mercifully the days of solid book learning were mostly past—Liv took the second row, her Poor joining her friend Vena's Oblivious Artist and Arana's Plain Merchant's Daughter. The girls who somehow embodied beautiful, rich, connected, noble, preening, and gifted into only three bodies took the front row, as they always demanded. Magister Goldthorn, barely three years older than her disciples, did everything those girls wanted.

Gavin Guile came to stand in front of the class. "Hail, disciples," he said. It was the traditional teachers' greeting.

"Hail, Magister," they said in unison, answering without thinking about whether they actually should address him by some other title. He was the Prism, after all.

"Good," he said, giving a lopsided grin. Orholam, he was cute. "Today, I am only a magister. And you are only glims."

"Gleams," Liv corrected without thinking.

She shrank into her chair as Magister Goldthorn hissed and all the girls turned disbelieving stares at her. Correcting the Prism! He could say up was down and everyone should nod and smile. But he didn't look upset. He just stared at Liv for a long moment with those unsettling prismatic eyes.

"Ah, yes," he said. "Well, since you are advanced students, I suppose you have questions for me? What's your name?"

"Me?" Liv asked. Of course he meant me, he's looking right at me. "Um, Liv."

"Umliv?"

She blushed harder. "Aliviana. Liv. Liv Danavis." Had she added that last part hoping he would notice? Wouldn't she have just said Liv otherwise? Was she trying to ingratiate herself, just as her Ruthgari masters wanted?

"Well done," Beautiful whispered from the front row. "Only took you three tries."

"Related to General Danavis?"

Liv swallowed. "Yes, sir. He's my father." Committed now. Well done, Liv.

"He was a good man." He said it as if he genuinely respected the man who'd been responsible for so many of his own men's deaths.

"He was a rebel." She couldn't keep the bitterness out of her voice. Bitterness that her father had lost everything in the war, including her mother. Bitterness that she was always going to be different. Bitterness that her father never spoke of the False Prism's War, never even tried to justify fighting for the wrong side.

"And not many of the rebels were good men, making your father even more remarkable. Do you have a question, Aliviana?"

All the students were supposed to have prepared questions, but Beautiful, Rich, and Connected in the front row usually dominated any time the class had with important drafters, so Liv hadn't expected to get the chance to ask hers. She hesitated.

"I have a question," Beautiful said. Her real name was Ana, and she leaned forward eagerly, crossing her arms under her breasts. It was reasonably warm on top of the Chromeria, but Ana had to be cold, considering how little of her body that dress covered. The combination of Ana's frustratingly effortless natural beauty, short skirts, and deep cleavage was rarely lost on male magisters.

"Wait, I do have a question," Liv said. She'd already brought up that she was Corvan Danavis's daughter. The only way she could be more interesting to him—and make him suspect more that she was a spy—was by volunteering that she was from Rekton and knew Kip.

And the only way *out* was to go much, much further. Dear Orholam, please...

"Yes, Liv," Gavin said. But he didn't look at her. Face expressionless, he was staring hard at Ana. He glanced down at her propped-up cleavage then back to her eyes and shook his head just a fraction. Yes, I see. No, I'm not amused.

Ana blanched. Her eyes dropped, she sat up and shifted in her chair to pull her skirt down. Thank Orholam Liv was in the back row, because she couldn't suppress her grin, despite everything.

"Liv?" Gavin asked, turning those prismatic eyes on her. Entrancing.

She cleared her throat. "I was wondering if you could talk to us about uses of yellow/superviolet bichromacy."

"Why?" Gavin asked.

Liv froze. Her prayer was answered. A chance.

Magister Goldthorn interjected. "How about we talk about super-violet/blue bichromacy instead? It's far more common. Three of my disciples are bichromes. Ana here is nearly a polychrome."

Gavin ignored her.

Liv hadn't thought this moment would ever come. She'd been trapped so long in this class, with these girls. In one more year, she'd be finished. In fact, she'd mastered enough drafting that she could take the final examination right now and pass easily. She hadn't because there was nothing good waiting for her when she finished. A terrible position decoding official, non-secret communications for the Ruthgari noble who held her contract. She wouldn't even be trusted with secret communications. No matter that she'd been a babe in arms during the war and felt no loyalty to the rebels, she was Tyrean. It was enough to curse her in the Chromeria's eyes.

Each of the Seven Satrapies was responsible for the tuition of its own students. It was an investment every satrapy gladly made because drafters were so vital to every part of their economies, their armies, their construction, their communications, their agriculture. But Tyrea had nothing. The corrupt foreign governors of Garriston sent a pittance every year. Those students who came from Tyrea mostly had to pay their own way. The Danavises' wealth had been stolen during the war, so Liv had needed to pledge her services to a Ruthgari patron just to stay at the Chromeria.

If Liv were from any other satrapy, her ambassador would have forced her patron to pay for bichrome training for her or surrender her contract. But there was no Tyrean ambassador anymore. There was an official bursar's purse for "hardship" cases like hers, but it had long ago become a slush fund for bureaucrats to reward their favorites. Tyrea had no voice, no place.

"Liv asked because she's a yellow/superviolet bichrome," Vena said.

Gavin turned and looked at her. Vena was an artist and dressed like one. Boyishly short hair, artfully disheveled, lots of jewelry, and clothing she'd tailored for herself. Half the time you couldn't even tell what country's style she was borrowing from, if any. But despite not being pretty, she was always striking and—in Liv's opinion anyway—looked great. Today, Vena wore a flowing dress of her own invention, with silver embroidery at the hem reminiscent of the Tree People's zoomorphic designs. The designs in the visible spectrum were echoed cleverly in the superviolet.

"What a marvelous young woman you are," Gavin said to Vena. "And a good friend. I love your dress." As Vena blushed crimson, Gavin turned to Liv. "Is this true?"

"No, it's not," Magister Goldthorn said. "Liv's Threshing was inconclusive, and since then she's shown no further abilities."

Liv pulled out the broken yellow spectacles—really only a monocle—that she'd bought secretly two years before. She held it up, squinted through one eye, and stared at the white stone of the Prism's Tower. In a moment, yellow luxin filled her cupped hands.

It sloshed like water. Yellow luxin's natural state was liquid. It was the most unstable of any luxin, not just sensitive to light but also to motion. At its best, it could be used mainly for two things: if held with will in liquid form, it made great torches. Or, in a thin, sealed sheet, it would slowly feed light to other luxins, keeping them fresh the same way that lanolin and beeswax rejuvenated leather.

Liv threw the cupped liquid aside. It didn't even make it to the ground, instead flashboiling in midair into pure yellow light.

Magister Goldthorn spluttered, "This is outrageous! You are forbidden to draft—"

"You are forbidden," Gavin interrupted her, "to squander the gifts Orholam has given you. You're Tyrean, Aliviana?"

Magister Goldthorn stopped cold. One did not interrupt the Prism himself, not twice.

"Yes," Liv said. "Little town not far from Sundered Rock, actually. Rekton."

His eyes seemed to flash for a second, but it might have been Liv's imagination, because he said, "How long before you pulled the threshing rope?"

"Two minutes five seconds," she said. It was considered a very long time.

He looked hard at her. Then his expression softened. "As stubborn as your father, I see. I barely made it past one. Well done. So...superviolet and yellow. Watch this." He held out both of his hands.

Every girl's pupils tightened to tiny apertures. Superviolet luxin was invisible to normal sight. Even a woman who could draft superviolet wouldn't see it unless she was looking for it. "Your normal lessons have covered—doubtless to the point of your nausea—crafting missives with superviolet luxin."

Had they ever. Its invisibility was why superviolet drafters were used for communications. But on top of that, every satrapy was also looking into ciphers and methods of stacking, twisting, and obfuscating the superviolet-written messages, locking the messages into fragile loops that would be broken by any but someone who knew the exact method to open and read them. Fun, for a while. But they'd passed the fun place a long long time ago.

"You know what superviolet is great for?" Gavin asked. "Tripping people." Every girl in the class grinned guiltily. All had done that at one time or another. "No, seriously. The pranks are where you learn to apply your color in ways no one else has thought of. You have to be a little bad to make history. Sealed superviolet isn't as strong as blue or green, but it weighs almost nothing, and for Orholam's sake, it's invisible!" Gavin drafted a hollow superviolet egg the size of his hand. He winced for an instant, as if something was paining him. "The trick with yellow, Liv, is to understand how it releases its power. So, into the middle of this egg, draft liquid yellow." He did. "The important bit is to leave absolutely no air inside the container. It has to be solid." He closed it while looking at the girls, not paying attention. He'd just left an air bubble in the egg. He hadn't noticed.

"If it's solid, totally airtight, then even if you shake it—"

Liv raised her hand, opened her mouth, but she was too slow.

Gavin shook the egg. It exploded with a blinding flash.

Everyone hit the ground.

Before Liv even opened her eyes, she heard Gavin laughing. Was he insane? She looked up, but his hair wasn't even ruffled. "Now," Gavin said. "If that egg had been made of blue luxin, when it shattered we'd all have been cut to pieces. But as you all know in your heads—if not in your hearts or your bodies, apparently—sealed superviolet frays easily. Not that it can't be useful." With a speed and facility that stunned Liv, he drafted another egg and filled it with liquid yellow luxin.

"Get up," he told the class. Ana was crying quietly. She'd scraped her knee when she'd fallen, and it was bleeding. Served her right for wearing such a short skirt. The rest of the girls got up, righted their chairs, and sat. Ana stayed on the ground. "Get up," Gavin ordered her. "You're going to be a drafter in a few months. You want to act like a woman? You're not even ready to act like an adult."

The lash of his words hit Ana hard, but every girl in the class felt the sting. His statement was as true for Liv as it was for Ana. She looked away from Ana, realizing how easy it would have been to be in her place right now. She felt a momentary twinge of compassion for the girl, then irritation that she was feeling that. Ana had made her life miserable.

Gavin promptly ignored Ana. He flung a strand of superviolet skyward. It was so light, it was caught in the wind and drifted to the west off the tower, but as long as he held the luxin open and supported it and drafted more and more into it, he could send it higher, and he did, rapidly. Then he brought the yellow egg up to the thread of luxin, made loops to hold it on to the line, and then launched it into the air. His right hand snapped down with the recoil of the launch.

The egg zipped along the invisible line, curving out over the tower. At its apex, two hundred feet out, it exploded with a sharp report. Far below, Liv heard people in the yard crying out in wonder and surprise.

"Now, imagine I pointed that at a charging line of horses. It won't kill anyone directly, but horses don't like having things explode in their faces any more than prissy girls do."

Blanching and blushing filled the sudden, pained silence.

"There's a couple of other special ways you can use superviolet in dual-color drafting. Anyone?" Gavin asked.

Ana lifted her hand uncertainly. He nodded. "For distance control?"

"That's right. You have to leave your superviolet open, and the longer you make the line, the harder it is to control. It's like juggling when you can't see the balls. But..." He held out his hands, a swirl of colors went through his eyes, and he was holding a red ball, a yellow ball, a green ball, a blue ball, and an orange ball. (Liv saw him wince again, as if he had a pulled muscle in his back.) Then he started juggling. The girls—all of them, even Magister Goldthorn—gasped. First because the properties of the balls weren't right. Orange was slick, oily. Red was sticky. Yellow was liquid. Then, of course, because it was a different kind of impressive to see someone juggle five of anything.

Oh. Liv got it. Every ball had a very thin blue luxin shell, filled with luxin of a different color.

Gavin closed his eyes and kept juggling. Impossible. Was he just showing off? No, he *was* showing off, but he was also still teaching.

"Ah," Liv said, pleased.

"Someone got it," Gavin said, opening his eyes. "With my eyes closed, how am I juggling?"

"You're the Prism. You can do anything," someone mumbled.

"Thank you, my butt hasn't been kissed all day, but no."

Did he just say that?! "You're not juggling," Liv said, recovering first.

Gavin took his hands away from the twirling balls. They kept going in the same intricate pattern. Everyone tightened their eyes and saw the superviolet luxin connected in a track through the balls. The balls were simply following the invisible track. "That's right. If you give a visible reason, even if it's astounding, you can hide an invisible phenomenon right under people's noses. That is the power of superviolet luxin. Tell you what, Aliviana, will you do me a favor?"

"Sure."

He smiled. "Good. I'll hold you to that." He turned. There was a dark stain on the back of his shirt. Was that blood? Should Liv say something? "Magister Goldthorn, I'm sorry, but I have to leave. I still owe you half a class, and I'll make it up to you. In the meantime, if you'd notify the appropriate officials, Aliviana Danavis is hereby recognized as a superviolet/yellow bichrome. Her instruction will begin

THE BLACK PRISM • 237

immediately. I would be...*disappointed* if she were outfitted in a style less decent than the average Ruthgari bichrome's. Costs should be taken from Chromeria finances. If anyone has a problem with that, direct them to me."

Liv forgot about Gavin's shirt instantly. She couldn't believe what she'd just heard. With a few sentences, the Prism had changed everything. Freed her. A bichrome! In a word, she'd gone from a life writing letters for some backwater noble to a life of only Orholam knew what. She thought she was imagining it until she saw the exact same stunned expression on Magister Goldthorn's face. It was real. The second part of what he'd said took only a moment more to sink in. Liv was to be kept in a style equivalent to a Ruthgari bichrome *at the Chromeria's expense.* And the Ruthgari kept their drafters in more lavish apartments than anyone. It was all part of their strategy to attract the best talent.

If Liv played it halfway right, she could escape that hellstone harpy Aglaia Crassos.

Gavin smiled at her, a roguish, boyish joy mixing with something deeper Liv couldn't read. Then he left.

But watching him jog down the steps out of view, Liv was filled with a vague unease. She'd gotten everything she hoped today, and everything that she hadn't quite dared to hope. But something more had happened.

The Prism had just bought her. She didn't know why she was worth it, but it didn't strike her as a random gesture. She looked at Vena, who shrugged back, eyes wide. Gavin Guile had some purpose in mind for Liv, and she would perform it gladly. How could she not? But what was it?

Chapter 39

The cell's blue was trying to sink into his brain, make him passionless, logical. No room for hatred, for envy, for fury. The dead man was muttering in his wall.

Dazen stood and walked over to him. The dead man resided in a particularly shiny section of the blue luxin wall. He was, of course, Dazen's twin.

"The time has come," the dead man said. "You need to kill yourself."

The dead man liked to drop a fire in Dazen's lap and see what he did with it.

Dazen popped his neck left and right. The dead man popped his neck right and left. "What do you mean?" Dazen asked.

"You haven't been willing to do what you need to do. Unless you can cut deeper than Dazen, you—"

"I am Dazen now!" Dazen snapped.

The man in the wall smiled indulgently. "Not yet, you're not. You're still me. You're still Gavin Guile, the brother who lost. Dazen stole your life, but you haven't taken his. Not yet. You're not ready. Talk to me again in another year or two."

"You're dead!" Dazen snapped. "You're the dead man, not me. I am Dazen!"

But his reflection said nothing.

His son was out there. His son, not the real Dazen's. The real Dazen was stealing his son. Just like he'd stolen his entire life.

Gavin had decided long ago that if Dazen was going to steal his life, he would steal Dazen's in return. His younger brother had always been the smarter of the two, so the only way to escape would be to become Dazen—to outthink his brother, to dig a pace below the real Dazen's deepest trap and spring it back on him. So far, it hadn't worked.

"It hasn't worked because you're not willing to risk everything to win. That was Dazen's genius," the dead man said. "You remember the last time you two fought?"

"When he imprisoned me and stole my life?"

"No, the last time you fought with your fists."

Gavin couldn't ever forget it. He'd been the older brother. He *needed* to win. He couldn't even remember what they'd fought over. That hadn't been important. He'd probably started it. Dazen had been getting too big for his boots for a while, not giving Gavin the respect he deserved. So Gavin had punched him in the shoulder and called him something foul.

Though Gavin was older, Dazen had grown to be at least his size, if not bigger. Most days, Dazen would take the abuse with a complaint and a curse. Not that day. Dazen had attacked him, and suddenly Gavin had been struck with the fear that had been sneaking up on him for quite some time. What if he lost?

They were struggling, trying to throw each other, raining punches to each other's arms, stomach, shoulders. Many were blocked, but even those that got through were more painful than damaging. Fighting your brother had rules. You didn't try to break bones, you didn't hit in the face. It was about submission and dominance and punishment.

But if Dazen won one fight, things would never be the same between them. That couldn't happen. In his fear and desperation, Gavin punched Dazen in the face.

It rocked Dazen back on his heels, but more from shock than from the power of the blow. Dazen was usually pretty even-keeled, but as soon as Gavin saw his face, he knew he'd made a mistake. A big one. The pain didn't matter. The dominance didn't matter. Not to Dazen. He'd gone absolutely crazy. He didn't even need to draft red to utterly lose it. And lose it he did.

Dazen bulled into Gavin and swept him off his feet. Gavin tried to pull away, dance aside, pull loose. But Dazen wasn't jockeying for position; he was taking Gavin down. They fell. Gavin landed on top of Dazen, connecting a good shot with his knee.

It didn't matter. It was like Dazen didn't even feel it. He just absorbed the shot and pulled Gavin with the force of his fall. Abruptly Gavin's little brother was on top of him. Dazen grabbed his throat in both hands and squeezed.

Gavin's panic receded. They'd both been taught grappling. He slugged Dazen across the jaw. Nothing. Dazen took it. The next punch Dazen deflected with an elbow. He squeezed.

The panic came back with a vengeance. Dazen was going to kill him! Gavin punched and punched and punched, but Dazen just took the punishment.

Go ahead, hurt me, but I'm going to kill you.

The world was going dark when Dazen abruptly released Gavin. He staggered to his feet as Gavin coughed himself back to life. By the time Gavin stood, his little brother was gone.

After that, they hadn't fought again. It was enough. They'd known without saying a word that if they ever fought again, someone would likely get killed.

And if I'd won at Sundered Rock, someone would have been.

But Dazen had let him live. It was like that moment when he'd had Gavin's throat in his hands. He could have crushed me. He could have killed me, but he let me live instead. Because he was weak.

"If Dazen's weak," the dead man said, "what does that make you? You lost to him." He laughed.

"Never again. It's taken me this long, but I understand at last. I will take this lesson from my brother: win at any cost. Be ready to pay it all, and you won't have to." That was it. Simple. Now, *now*, Gavin was ready to become Dazen. He would take Dazen's strengths and leave his weaknesses.

He reached out a hand and touched his reflection. "You really are a dead man now," he said.

His previous attempts to draft sub-red had failed because he couldn't get enough heat. The only thing that generated heat down here was his own body, and he'd nearly killed himself last time when he'd taken too much heat. He'd gone delusional, and still it hadn't been enough. He hadn't been willing to risk everything. He hadn't been willing to die, if it took that. He was willing now.

"Thank you, brother. Thank you, son," he said aloud. He drafted a blade of blue luxin. It only held an edge if he concentrated hard, but over a course of days, he and the dead man shaved his long hair off. He would cut off a hank, separate the strands into narrow sheaves, and tie the ends of those so they wouldn't fall apart. When he had a good pile, smearing as much oil from his body on his makeshift yarn as he could, he began weaving. This had to be done first. Later he wouldn't be in any shape to try it.

For once, the blue helped him. The old him—back when he was free, back when he was Gavin—could never have done this. Threading the hairs over, under, over, under, making mistakes, starting over, fumbling and dropping the whole unfinished thing, trying to catch it and losing a week's work in one second when his fingers pulled the threads loose—it all would have driven him mad. But blue reveled in detail, in putting every hair in its place.

Dazen didn't even notice it at first, but one day he realized he had something he'd lost long long ago. He had hope. He *would* get out. He knew that now. It was only a matter of time. Vengeance was coming, and, if long delayed, it would be all the sweeter for it. Dazen sighed, contented, and continued his work.

Chapter 40

Gavin tore off the stained shirt and grunted as he scraped the cloth across his burn. Fifty danar shirt, and I ruined it in half an hour. Worse, he'd noticed some of the girls glancing at the spreading stain. That wasn't a disaster. They wouldn't ask about it. One of the Spectrum would. He liked to save up his lies for them.

He cursed under his breath.

Gavin knew that Marissia must have some sort of an organizational scheme to how she put away his clothing, but whatever it was, he'd never pierced its logic. He rifled through stacks of shirts and pants and breeches and cloaks and habias and robes and thobes and petasoi and ghotras, most of which he didn't think he'd ever worn. Orholam, he had a lot of clothes. And these were only his summer clothes. He supposed it was because, as Prism, he was supposed to be of all peoples, so if he met with an ambassador or needed to suddenly visit Abornea, he would already have local clothing that fit him.

He was still standing bare-chested, ointment smeared on his burn—at least he had the sense to keep aid supplies in his own room—when the door opened. Marissia slipped in quietly. She glanced at the burn on his ribs. Her jade green eyes lit with anger, though Gavin couldn't tell if it was at him or for him. Maybe a bit of both. She grabbed the ointment from his table and smeared more around to his back. Ouch. Apparently, he'd missed some spots. Then she bandaged him with a practiced hand. She wasn't gentle. "Does my lord need assistance finding another shirt?" she asked.

"Owww!" he yelped. He cleared his throat, lowered his voice an octave. "Please."

She went to a stack he swore he'd searched thoroughly and immediately plucked a shirt from its depths. He didn't think he'd ever worn it before, but it was a style he liked, and dark enough that if the ointment soaked through this one, no one would notice. Marissia had a certain magic of her own. He could swear that shirt hadn't been there before.

She began whistling quietly as she dressed him and fixed his hair; it was an old tune, pretty. Marissia was a good whistler.

Oh, the tune was "Little Lamb Lost." A comment on not being able to find his own clothes? Probably. He had bigger things to worry about. He'd dealt with his brother, how much trouble could the Spectrum be?

"I'll be leaving either in the morning or the next day," Gavin said. "There's a young man testing downstairs. Kip. He's my, uh, natural son." There was no need to use the "nephew" euphemism with Marissia. Marissia knew that Gavin had imprisoned his brother, but even she didn't know that Gavin wasn't Gavin. She hadn't known either of them before the war, so she didn't need to know. He trusted her completely, but the fewer people who knew that secret, the longer it would be before all this crashed down on his head. "He's sixteen—fifteen, I mean. Will you find appropriate clothes for him and pack for both of us for two weeks?"

"More for fighting or for impressing?"

"Both."

"Of course," she said flatly.

On his way out the door, Gavin grabbed his sword in its jeweled scabbard. He wasn't nearly the hand with a blade that even the least of the Blackguard was. He had been quite skilled once, but once he'd realized he could draft any combination of color and instantly have a weapon of whatever kind he needed, he hadn't practiced with plain steel as often as was required to compete with professional warriors like the Blackguard.

244 • *Brent Weeks*

Of course, that assumed a fair fight, and there was no such thing with a drafter. The Blackguards themselves would fight with whatever was at hand: blades, magic, a goblet of wine, or a faceful of sand.

He tucked the Ilytian pistols into his belt too. Just to be an ass.

When Gavin stepped out of his door, there were two Blackguards waiting for him. His escort. It was his compromise with the White. He got to travel without the Blackguard when he thought it was absolutely necessary—so, most of the time—as long as he agreed to have them around when he was in a place where assassination was more likely. The White wasn't pleased with how he'd interpreted their agreement, but he clung ferociously to what little freedom he had.

He strode quickly through the single hall that separated the halves of this level. He and the White each had one-half of the floor. Because of the Chromeria's rotation, Gavin's half was always pointed toward the sun. An odd irony that the White should be forever in shadow, though in her elder years this White had appreciated it. It minimized the temptations of drafting and hastening her own death. Gavin wondered again how she did it. Without drafting, he would feel empty, weak. Life wouldn't be worth living without chromaturgy. It defined who he was. Surely it had done the same for the White, and yet she lived on, her will still iron, her back unbowed.

Stepping past the Blackguards guarding her room, he knocked on her door.

"She's not here," the man on the left said. "The White has gone to meet with the Chromeria. She thought it would be rude to keep the full Spectrum waiting because of one man's tardiness."

This was how the Blackguards registered their displeasure. His own Blackguards knew where he was going as soon as he turned toward the White's room rather than toward the lift, but they didn't tell him. The White's Blackguards knew where he was going as soon as they saw him, but they didn't tell him the White was gone until he knocked, causing him to waste more time and be even later. One man's tardiness? What's the Spectrum going to talk about without me? I called the meeting.

As was typical, the Blackguards were careful in showing their irritation. There would be no more trouble from them for a while, Ironfist would see to that. If they peeved Gavin more than occasionally, he would do more to avoid them and they wouldn't be able to do their job of protecting him. Still, they wanted him to respect them. Which he did, after a fashion.

It's an odd person who volunteers to jump in front of an arrow when they don't even know if they'll like the Prism or White that they'll be assigned to guard. But he wouldn't be chained. Power was freedom. Power had to be maintained.

"If you can't serve me well," Gavin said to his own two Blackguards, "you can't serve me at all." He turned on his heel and started walking toward the lift.

Of course they said nothing. They simply accompanied him on his left and right. Commander Ironfist trained them to ignore orders that put their charges in danger.

Gavin waved his arms down, drafting bars of blue luxin strengthened with yellow down to his left and right. His Blackguards hesitated momentarily as he kept walking briskly, and he closed the gap in the middle. He kept walking, not even looking back as he threw up walls of solid blue, red, green, yellow, and superviolet.

It satisfied a small part of him. His brother really had gotten under his skin. The bastard.

But at the same time, this was necessary. The Blackguard had to know they couldn't control him. That was how smart bodyguards worked: impede your freedom a little, then a little more, and soon they had their way. Gavin wasn't going to let that happen. If he had the Blackguard hovering around him at all times—as they ultimately wished—they would learn not just his secrets like the skimmer and the condor, but his final secret. What would the Blackguard do if they found out that Gavin wasn't Gavin at all? They might decide he was the de facto Prism and that was enough. Or they might decide he was a threat to the real Prism. Or he might split the Blackguard into warring camps. Pleasant thought, a bunch of elite warrior-drafters trying to destroy each other. That was what made this necessary. The Blackguard must be taught and taught again to accept the crumbs Gavin let drop: You can protect me if you serve me wholeheartedly, and I'll withdraw that privilege whenever I please for any reason or none.

At first, years ago, Commander Spear had punished those Blackguards who let Gavin escape them. When that didn't work, he'd made the punishments public, shaming the Blackguards for that which wasn't their fault. Gavin had felt awful, and had not changed a bit. Commander Spear had escalated the punishments, publicly flogging several men, including a young Ironfist. Gavin had responded by yawning and not letting any Blackguards near him for a month. Then he'd walked through crowded markets, leaving bound and gagged the Blackguards that Commander Spear sent, and he'd done it in the aftermath of the war, when there had been not a few men who would have gladly killed him.

When there finally was an assassination attempt and no Blackguards present, Commander Spear had discharged the six Blackguards who were supposed to be protecting Gavin. The White had finally stepped in and discharged Commander Spear instead. Gavin hadn't felt sorry for the man. Once he'd learned that using Gavin's guilt against him wouldn't work, he should have tried something else. A man who couldn't change tactics shouldn't be in charge of the Blackguard in the first place.

The move hadn't made Gavin any friends, but it had left him in charge. Besides, he didn't need friends. The two Blackguards at the lift looked at each other as he approached. The woman on the left was short but as thick as a bull. She said, "High Lord Prism, I notice you don't have an escort. May I join you?"

Gavin grinned. "Since you ask so nicely," he said.

They opened the lift for him, and in moments he was on the next level below his and the White's floor. The Blackguards on watch blinked at his sole escort. Doubtless they knew the guard rotation, and knew she wasn't supposed to be on Prism duty, nor was the Prism supposed to be guarded by only one Blackguard.

"High Lord Prism," one of them said, a tall red/orange bichrome youth only twenty years old, thus quite talented. "May I accompany you?"

"Thank you, but no," Gavin said. "You can't protect me from what's waiting here."

Gavin had told Kip that the White tried to balance the Prism's power, but he didn't like it much when she did.

He stepped into the council room. The Colors were scattered around the table. For formal events, they would sit in order around the table: Sub-red, Red, Orange, Yellow, Green, Blue, Superviolet, Black, Prism, White. For meetings like this one, however, the pull of sitting by friends or the lure of grabbing one of the more comfortable chairs outweighed the natural tendency to sit in the same spot every time. Gavin found the last spot, between the Superviolet, a tall, skin-and-bones coal-black Parian woman named Sadah, and the soft, lighter-skinned Ruthgari man with the beaded beard, Klytos Blue.

Gavin had told Kip that each Color represented a country, and that was mostly true. Each satrap or satrapah appointed one Color. It was the most important decision most rulers ever made. But the system had begun to break down even before the False Prism's War, when Andross Guile had bribed and blackmailed his way into the Red seat, though the Blood Forest already had one Color. He'd been so audacious, he'd stolen that seat from Ruthgar, claiming that the Guiles' sliver of swampland in Ruthgar made him eligible for the Ruthgari seat.

Of course, after the war, similar logic had been used to deprive Tyrea of a seat.

There were so many interlocking and overlapping layers of loyalty it was dizzying. Both the Red and the Green were Ruthgari and thus likely to unite on any issue concerning Ruthgar. But the Green was also cousins with Jia Tolver, an Abornean woman who was the Yellow. The Aborneans strangled both Parian and Ruthgari trade through the Narrows, so anything to do with trade would see them at each other's throats, but on anything else they might try to form a bloc. The Sub-red was a Blood Forester, who were allies now with their stronger neighbors the Ruthgari, but her parents had been killed in the war by the Green's brothers. And on it went. Every noble family in the Seven Satrapies did everything it could to get at least one son or daughter into the Chromeria, if for nothing else than to try to watch their backs.

248 • *Brent Weeks*

In turn, everyone in the Spectrum did all they could to protect themselves. Family bonds, clan bonds, national bonds, color bonds, and ideological bonds cut every which way. The Colors were political creatures as much as they were magical. To be named a Color took a certain amount of chromaturgical aptitude—the White saw to that—but after that bar was reached, not a few of these seats had found inhabitants at the same time that donkey-trains loaded with gold had made their way into royal houses. Gavin knew it had been thus when his own father had joined.

The White, in her wheeled chair, said, "I call this meeting to order. Let the record show that all Colors except for Red are in attendance." They hated that. Hated that they couldn't get rid of Andross Guile. They hated that in defiance of all convention, he hadn't attended a meeting in five years but still insisted that his votes be counted. They hated what his having his vote delivered by messenger said about how little he valued their opinions. No eloquence would ever move Andross Guile. He would see and weigh every issue alone, and decide, regardless of the mummery of these Spectrum meetings. But they feared him, too. The White said, "Lord Prism, you have called this meeting, so I turn over the proceeding to you."

She thought she was thwarting him. That he'd grown too independent. That he might become dangerous if she didn't yank the leash.

Careful, Orea. When choked, dogs go docile—but wolves go wild.

Gavin's relationship with the Spectrum had always been thorny. Of course, when he'd been recuperating after Sundered Rock, they'd stripped him of his title of promachos, taking control of the armies away from him, as custom dictated. But they hadn't known whether he would allow it. Still learning his new guise, he had, but he didn't care much for any of the Colors personally. Nor did they care for him. He'd lived too long, become too powerful. He didn't need them, and that scared them.

They hated his father. They hated the Guiles, and they stymied Gavin whenever they could.

Patience, Gavin. Plenty of time for purpose six. Plenty of room to maneuver. You are Andross Guile's son.

"We need to release the city of Garriston immediately, pull out all of our men, and give it back to King Garadul," Gavin said. "Preferably with an apology that we didn't do it sooner."

Silence. Followed by awkward silence.

Klytos Blue chuckled uncertainly. When no one else joined him, he fell silent.

"King?" the White asked.

"That's what he's calling himself." Gavin didn't elaborate.

Sadah Superviolet said, "Surely you're not serious, Lord Prism. The governorship transfers to Paria in a few weeks. It's our right. People have made plans. Ships are sailing already. If we must have this conversation, let us have it two years from now."

"Absolutely not," Delara Orange said. She was a forty-year-old bichrome, with great sagging breasts and the red and orange in her eyes pushing to the very edge of her irises. She was an Atashian. Atash got the governorship right after Paria's. "Paria took the very first rotation, when there were actually a few treasures left in the city. And you looted it all."

"We also had to repair a city that had been burned to the ground and care for its injured and ill. We took only what was an appropriate recompense."

"Stop," Gavin said, before it could go any further. "You're having the wrong fight. This isn't about who has the governorship, in what order, or for how long. It's been sixteen years since we crushed Tyrea. They still don't have a representative in this room. There are fewer Tyreans in the Chromeria every year. Why is that? Have they suddenly stopped bearing drafters there? Or is it because we have demanded a tribute from them so ruinous they can't support their drafters, which in turn impoverishes their land further? Then we hold Garriston, their main port and their largest city, and your governors tax every orange and pomegranate and melon. I've been to Garriston, and it's a shadow of its former greatness. The great irrigation canals are full of sand. The fields are worked by women and children or no one, and there's not a drafter to be found."

"You pity them?" Delara Orange asked. "When my brothers rise from the dead and the Castle of Ru is rebuilt, I'll feel pity for Garriston. They joined Dazen. It was their war that killed tens of thousands. I saw them cast Satrapah Naheed's two-year-old son down the Great Steps. I saw them cut open her pregnant belly, take her babe, and make bets on how far down the steps one of their men could throw the screaming child. They cut off the satrapah's nose and ears and breasts and arms and legs and threw her down after. While we watched. The babe made it all the way to the last step, in case you're curious. I got some of its brain on my dress. I wanted to try to catch it, but I didn't move. No one did. Those are the people you wish us to have mercy on? Or maybe it's the people who sank the entire refugee flotilla, which had not a single drafter or armed man on board?"

That was Gavin's fault. As Dazen. He'd sent a young, new general, Gad Delmarta, who had always been efficient and direct. Gavin had told Gad to secure Ru. General Delmarta had taken that to mean to secure it so that there could never be any resistance ever again. He'd exterminated the royal family—all fifty-six members of it and scores of their male retainers—publicly, one at a time, in the order of their succession, and burned down their great castle, the pride of Atash. When the people had fled, General Delmarta had sent fire drafters after the flotilla. Gavin had only found out about it afterward, and then what could he do? It was war, and his general had followed his orders, and when General Delmarta marched on the great city of Idoss next, it had surrendered without a fight because of their fear of the man, because of his cruelty.

"Maybe," Gavin said, "we could count how many children died when you burned Garriston in retaliation and barred the gates so no one could escape? I seem to recall that all the Tyrean drafters and all but two hundred of the Tyrean soldiers were a hundred leagues away at the time. How long did it take for the river to clear of bodies? So many little corpses bobbing in the water. Even with all those hundreds of sharks turning the bay to bloody foam with their thrashing, it was weeks, wasn't it?"

Gavin had never learned whose idea it was, but when Garriston had been burned, someone had stationed red drafters all around the walls. Soldiers shielded the drafters while they hurled red luxin back and forth in swathes throughout the city. Red luxin was used as fuel for lamps. Spread throughout a city, it had made a hell for the residents of Garriston. Tens of thousands had jumped into the river, and thousands more had jumped in on top of them. Their bodies themselves had almost been enough to dam the river in places. And then some of his older brother's cleverer drafters had floated red luxin down the river in little boats of green or blue luxin, or mixed red and orange luxin to make a concoction so flammable it would burn even underwater, or mixed it with superviolet to make it float burning on the very water itself. Between the fire, the smoke, the water, the press of the crowds, the crushing deaths as whole buildings fell into the packed river, and the fire floating down the river itself, there had been death on a scale no one had imagined before.

Before the war, Garriston had been home to more than a hundred thousand people. His own conscriptions had thinned that to perhaps eighty thousand. After the fires, only ten thousand remained, and after the first winter, only five thousand.

"Enough," the Black said. Carver was no drafter, and so in some respects he was the weakest member of the Spectrum. As the Black, he was responsible for most of the mundane aspects of ruling Little Jasper: importing food, managing trade, awarding contracts, recruiting and paying soldiers, maintenance for buildings and the docks, building ships, and everything else that the White ceded to his control so she could focus on managing the Chromeria itself. But he was a formidable man, and Gavin respected him. "We could list horrors all day, Lord Prism. What's the point?"

The point is, out of my five great purposes left, the only purely altruistic one is to free Garriston. Those people are suffering because of me, and you bastards have stopped every attempt I've made to help them.

"The point is," Gavin said, "that the Tyreans have as much reason to hate us as we have to hate them. We've been punishing them for the war for sixteen years. Most of the people paying the price now were children when the war started. They see no reason they should continue paying for what their dead fathers did or didn't do. They hate us, and the fact is, none of us—none of the Seven Satrapies—want to go back there with an army."

"What are you saying?" Luxlord Black asked. "Do you have specific intelligence of a threat?"

"I'm saying if we don't pull out of Garriston and end the tribute on our terms, King Garadul is going to take Garriston by force and end it on his." That's what King Garadul had meant when he'd told Gavin, "We're going to take back what you stole from us." But Gavin couldn't tell them about that without revealing more secrets, and they wouldn't believe it anyway.

"I'm failing to see the humor here," Klytos Blue said nervously. He was a coward in a dozen ways, but Ruthgar wasn't going to give up Garriston easily, Gavin knew. "We've got a thousand soldiers and fifty drafters there. The drafters alone could hold off whatever army this 'King' Garadul could raise."

"Knuckling under to a rebel, a man who declares himself a king—it's unthinkable," the Orange said. "He deserves death."

Oh, father, it's too bad you never come anymore. You would enjoy this. I can do one thing that you never could.

"First," Gavin said, "us leaving is the right thing to do. We're punishing people who have suffered too much already, and they hate us for it. We've been planting the seeds of another war for the last sixteen years. They started the war, yes. General Delmarta was born in Garriston, yes. But that doesn't excuse us from what we've done, which is not just wrong, but also stupid."

"Excuse me?" Delara Orange said. Her predecessor to the Orange—her mother—had been the architect of the rotating occupation scheme.

"You heard me," Gavin said. "We get almost no Tyrean drafters. You think that's because none are born there anymore? Ha! What if, instead of training here, where they are poor and reviled and suspected as traitors, what if someone decided to train them closer to home? A new school, a Chromeria dedicated to vengeance, started because of our pettiness and stupidity."

"Nonsense," Delara said. "We would have heard of such a thing."

"But what if you hadn't?" Gavin asked. "The quality of instruction might not be as good as ours. I hope it wouldn't be. But even with a few rudimentary fire spells, how long could your fifty drafters stationed in Garriston hold out against several hundred? How long could your soldiers hold out against thousands of rebels who could hide in plain sight among the locals? The fact is, King Garadul *will* take Garriston. He will demand it, on terms that he knows are insufferable, and then he will seize it. The only question is, will we lose and lose face and make King Garadul seem like a winner, and finally get drawn into a war your satrapies don't have the stomach for, or will we forgo a tribute which—after it's divided six ways—is insignificant, and give away that which we can't keep? If we give Garriston to King Garadul before he even asks, we look magnanimous. If we give him an apology, we look moral, and if we do both before he asks, we deprive him of a victory and a cause."

"Do you have evidence of all this?" Delara asked. She was slippery, as oranges tended to be, but drafting red luxin made a drafter more aggressive and reckless over time, too. "Because it seems to me that you would like us to give away an entire city for little reason otherwise. We don't know this new *King* Garadul. He has only recently taken power. He hasn't sent us a single emissary, much less made demands."

"You're telling me none of you have spies at Garadul's side?" Gavin shot back.

A few sardonic smiles and silence. No one was going to admit that, of course. They didn't trust each other enough. There had been no wars in the last sixteen years, but that didn't mean that everyone's interests were aligned. The Chromeria and every capital was as full of spies as it had ever been.

"If you don't," Gavin said in an imperious tone sure to needle them, "get some."

"High Luxlord, we take your advice to the satrapies very seriously, of course—" Klytos Blue started to say. The Ruthgari hated Gavin, and had since he'd ended the war with the Blood Forest.

Gavin cut him off. Time to play the hothead. "Listen, you morons. I don't know how you didn't see this coming. Or maybe some of you did. Your loyalty is noted. The fact remains, this is rebellion and it's heresy. King Garadul is talking about overthrowing the satrapies and the worship of Orholam himself. I would have thought Orholam would command better service from his Colors."

"Enough! Enough, Lord Prism!" the White barked. She looked at Gavin like she couldn't believe what he'd said.

Nothing like calling powerful men and women idiots, ingrates, disloyal, and impious all at once. Looking around the room, Gavin saw shock on some faces and hatred on others.

In the silence, Klytos Blue spoke first. He was a blue. It was only natural he should think things through faster than anyone else. "I believe that we should take the Lord Prism seriously. It's only prudent that we serve the satrapies and Orholam as zealously as he does every day." The words were delivered straight, but the malice couldn't have been more evident. "I move that we send a delegation to Garriston, to assess the threat from the alleged rebel Garadul and report back to us directly."

"A delegation?! Are you blind or stupid or corrupt?" Gavin demanded. "By the time they—"

"Gavin!" the White said. "Enough!"

She took the vote for a delegation to be sent and report back in two months' time. It passed, five to zero, with two abstentions.

Gavin sat back in his chair, as if stunned, defeated. In the silence before anyone stood to leave, he shook his head. Said grimly, "I ceded power after the war, gave up the *promachia*. I became an adviser, when many wanted me to be an emperor in truth. And now you ignore me. Very well. But tell your satraps and satrapahs this: Prepare for war. King Garadul won't stop at taking Garriston. I guarantee it."

You see, father, this is the one thing I can do that you never could: I can handle appearing to lose.

Chapter 41

Liv had barely seen her new apartments in the yellow tower before she'd gone out. Not to celebrate, not because she was impulsive, but because her courage had been fading with every passing second. She'd been to half the moneylenders on the islands before she found one willing to do business with her.

Stepping inside her new room, she found that the tower's slaves had brought all her meager belongings over from the closet she'd called home for the last three years. And there was a woman sitting on her bed.

"Salvé, Liv, been out celebrating?" Aglaia Crassos asked.

"What are you doing in my apartments?" Liv asked. "How'd you get in here?"

"It's not good to forget your friends, Aliviana." Aglaia stood and came to stand a hand's breadth from Liv's face.

"What? You're here to threaten me? I'm shaking."

Something ugly crossed Aglaia's face, but then was replaced by that smooth mask again, and that disingenuous laugh. "Careful with that sharp tongue, girl. You may cut your own throat."

"I'm done," Liv said. "Gavin Guile has—"

"Bought you to be his bed slave. I heard."

"Go to hell!" Liv said.

"You're the one who'll do that, seeing how you're throwing yourself at the man who murdered your mother and destroyed your country."

It was a tremendous slap. Liv took a step back.

Aglaia had made a reference to the burning of Garriston before, but Liv had never heard anything remotely like that. In truth, Liv had no idea, but considering the source, she was willing to bet it was a lie. "The Prism didn't have anything to do with that."

"And you know that because he said so? Your mother died in those fires. Your father led the fight against Gavin Guile."

"What do you care about Garriston? Ruthgar fought on the Prism's side. Your father fought beside Gavin."

"And my brother is the governor of Garriston, so I'm in a position to know things," Aglaia said. She lowered her voice and leaned in. "And maybe now you are too."

So that was what this was about. "No," Liv said. "I'm finished with you, with Ruthgar, and with your lies." Fealty to One. That was the Danavis motto, with strong suggestion that it was fealty *only* to one. And Liv wasn't about to serve this one.

"Welcome to your new life, Liv. You're important now. You are a player in the great game, and your hand isn't all bad. You see, Liv, you might be Tyrean, but no one's going to hold that against you anymore. It will only make you more remarkable for overcoming such a handicap. The good life can be yours."

"You can't buy me," Liv said.

"We already did."

"Things are different now. By the Prism's own command."

Aglaia's eyebrows rose slowly, making her horsey face seem even longer. It was a practiced gesture, but then, nothing about her was genuine. "I've been working with you for, what, three years now? And I went back through my notes. I never thought you were a thief, Aliviana Danavis. But now you're abandoning your duty after three years of schooling. Three years we've supported your every need—"

"Oh so generously, too!" Liv said.

"If it had been more generous, your debt would be that much greater now. Here's my question, Liv. What kind of woman are you?"

It was the same question that had put a quill in Liv's hand to sign away a fortune. With her new friendship with Gavin, she could probably tell the Ruthgari to go bugger themselves. What could they say against the Prism's decision? And though Liv had gone from a nothing—a monochrome talented in a minimally useful color—to a bichrome, she still wasn't worth fighting over. Plenty of each nation's investments went bad. Drafters died or burned out, or switched loyalty in the last year of their training. Every nation tried to steal drafters, and the Ruthgari were more successful at it than anyone else, so surely they wouldn't fight too hard to keep Liv.

But to be a Danavis was to act with honor. Always.

"What do you want?" Liv asked.

"You've been an embarrassment to me, Liv. The hardly talented daughter of a rebel general. But now you're going to be a jewel in my crown. You will be my vengeance on those who thought to slight me. And for that, I need you to be a success. You'll already be collecting a generous allowance from the bursar out of the Chromeria's general fund. Keep that, and we'll pay you double as well. We'll forgive your debt and the years of service you already owe us. Hell, if you play your cards right, you can draw allowances from three or four nations before you leave the Jaspers. Indeed, you won't need to leave the Chromeria at all, if you serve us well. Think about that: you can have a life here, at the center of the world, where everything important happens. Bed who you want, marry who you want, give your children every advantage you were denied. Or you can go serve some lordling somewhere, writing letters and examining his wife's bed to see if she's faithful to him, hoping he'll give you permission to marry someone you can tolerate. Out of all the nations, Ruthgar is the best to serve. And the worst to offend."

"But why do you want me to spy on the Prism? He's never done anything to offend Ruthgar."

"We like to keep an eye on our friends. It helps us remain friends—"

"And yet you were just telling me how I could do this to hurt the man who killed my mother. Which is it, Aglaia? Do you want me to betray him to hurt him, or it's not really a betrayal at all because you aren't going to hurt him?"

"Well said," Aglaia said. But then she continued, unflappable, "The point is, you may be able to damage the man personally who is responsible for so much havoc in your country, but your interference, your betrayal—perverse girl, insisting on calling the service of your own country a betrayal—your 'betrayal' won't result in war. These lands have seen enough of that."

It took Liv a moment to digest. It did make sense. In a way.

"But this is impossible. I don't know the Prism. He's talked to me once. Once."

"And he liked you."

"I don't know that I'd go that far."

"Do you have any idea how hard it is to get someone next to that man? We're going to give you all this just for *trying*. Besides, we know he has a weakness for Tyreans." A tiny, quick lift of her eyebrows showed that she was honestly surprised that the Prism would have such bad taste. "Maybe you can use this son of his to get close to him. We don't care."

It was bad enough to be asked to betray the Prism, but to use Kip to get to him? No. Kip was a good boy. Liv wouldn't do it. There was only one way out of this, and she'd known it all along.

Liv pulled out three coin sticks. "This is how much the Ruthgari government has spent on my upkeep for the last three years. With interest. Here, take it. I'm done with you. I'm free. I don't owe you anything."

Aglaia Crassos didn't even look at the coins. She didn't ask how Liv had gotten so much money. In truth, it had taken signing over a writ to an Abornean moneylender that would allow him to receive her allowance directly, and a ruinous interest rate. Liv was a pauper once more. She'd have to sell some of the marvelous dresses they'd given her just to stay afloat. "Liv, Liv, Liv. I don't want to be your enemy. But now that you're finally worth something, I'd swive a horse before I'd let you go. You have a cousin who was here when you first arrived. Showed you how things work here, yes?"

"Erethanna," Liv said.

"She's a green serving Count Nassos in western Ruthgar. She just petitioned to marry some blacksmith. The count has put a hold on it—at my request."

"You..." Liv said, trembling.

"Lovely couple, apparently. So happy together. Tragic if the count decided the land needed Erethanna to marry another drafter to increase her odds of having gifted children."

"Go to hell!"

"And your own studies can be opposed. And rumors can be started from dozens of corners about all sorts of despicable things you've done. We can poison any well when you finish your studies and are looking for work. You can't stay under the Prism's patronage forever. The second his eyes turn elsewhere..."

"I'm not worth that much to Ruthgar," Liv said, real fear constricting her throat.

"No, not to Ruthgar. But to me you are. Your attitude has made you worth my full attention. And if you make me look bad, I will make you mourn the day you ever met me."

"I already do." Liv felt deflated. "Get out. Get out before I kill you with my bare hands."

Aglaia stood, grabbed the money sticks, and said, "I'll take these for my troubles. After you've reconsidered, you know where to find me."

"Get out!"

Aglaia walked out.

Liv was left trembling. Not thirty seconds later, there was a knock on the door. That was it. Liv was going to kill her. She strode to the door and threw it open.

It wasn't Aglaia. A beautiful woman stood there. A Blood Forester, with the oddly pale, freckled skin that still seemed strange to Liv even after years at the Chromeria, and red hair like a flame. The woman was dressed in a slave's dress, but it was tailored to her lean figure, and a finer cotton than Liv had ever seen any slave wear. A nobleman's slave?

The slave handed Liv a note. "Mistress," she said. "From the High Lord Prism."

Liv Danavis stared at the note, feeling stupid, off balance. It read, "Please come see me at your earliest convenience." Her heart leapt into her throat. A summons from the Prism. So here it was, the beginning of her paying her debt to Gavin Guile. She didn't fool herself by hoping it would be the end of it, too. When you owed a luxlord, you owed them forever.

She just hadn't thought he'd ask for her so soon.

Oddly, the first thing she thought of was, What do you wear for an audience with the Prism? Liv didn't usually pay much attention to her choice of clothing. Maybe that was because when you only have a few changes of clothes, you wear what's clean and despair of ever wearing what's fashionable. That, of course, had changed instantly. Gavin had ordered that she be kept in an equivalent fashion to a Ruthgari bichrome, and that meant lots of clothes, a few jewels, and this huge apartment—literally five times larger than the one she'd lived in for the last three years. And though she might not have any money, now she had *makeup*. Now she had options, and she wasn't sure she liked it. The idea of turning into a prissy girl like Ana made Liv's stomach turn.

The slave was still standing at the door, waiting to be dismissed with the pleasant, neutral expression of a woman ignoring the cluelessness of her superior.

"Pardon me, *caleen*," Liv said, "but would you help me?" Liv always felt awkward when it came to dealing with slaves. No one in Rekton had been rich enough to afford one, and the few slaves that came through working with the caravans were treated the same as other servants. Things were more formal at the Chromeria, and most of the other students had grown up having slaves or at least being around them, so Liv always felt like everyone else knew what to do, while she was all thumbs. She still felt weird calling a woman ten years her senior by the diminutive "caleen."

Of course, now that Liv was a bichrome, she was going to have to get used to it fast, or she was going to look like an idiot even more often than usual.

The slave cocked an eyebrow like any twenty-eight-year-old would at any seventeen-year-old being foolish.

"I don't know what to wear," Liv said in a rush. "I don't even know what 'at your earliest convenience' means. Does that mean actually at my earliest convenience, or does it mean go right this moment, even if I were just wearing a towel?"

"You can take a few minutes to dress appropriately," the slave said.

Liv stood paralyzed. Was what she was wearing now appropriate?

"Most women called to the Prism's room wear something more... elegant," the slave said, eyeing Liv's plain skirt and blouse.

Maybe the fitted blue dress, then. Or that odd Ilytian black silk sheath. But that was more of an evening dress, wasn't it? Or should she wear the shockingly small... Liv wrinkled her nose. There was something about the slave's statement that made her nervous. She could just imagine a procession of beautiful women queued up outside the Prism's door. Liv had never heard any gossip about who the Prism took to his bed, but she wasn't exactly in the middle of the juicy gossip circles, and she could certainly imagine more than a few girls willing to dress or undress any way the Prism wanted. In addition to basically being the center of the universe, he was gorgeous, commanding, witty, smart, young, rich, and unmarried.

Whoever had packed her drawers with cosmetics had bought mostly skin lighteners or darkeners. But with Liv's kopi-and-cream-colored skin, she didn't have a hope of looking as light as a west Atashian. Her eyes were too dark anyway. And with wavy hair, even with a darkener on her skin, she wasn't going to look Parian. There was no hiding that she was Tyrean.

All those other girls and women would look fantastic in their fancy dresses and perfect makeup. They'd feel comfortable, beautiful. Liv would feel like a fool and look like a tramp.

How many of the women called to the Prism's room had gone with ulterior motives? How many had been acting for one country or another? How many of the ones who hadn't been co-opted had gone with their own agenda anyway? All of them? She wasn't going upstairs to seduce Gavin Guile—to hell with Aglaia and her ilk—so why should she make herself look like she was?

"To hell with it," Liv said. She didn't swear much, but it felt good right now. She threw down a dress that probably cost as much as she'd spent all last year. "It's convenient for me to go right now."

The slave looked like she wanted to speak, but she stopped herself. "This way, ma'am."

After they headed up the luxlords' lift, the slave led Liv to the Blackguards stationed there. The woman of the pair searched Liv for weapons. Thoroughly.

Liv couldn't help but feel a little violated. "They take their job seriously, don't they?" she said as they finally led her to what Liv assumed was the Prism's door.

"Do you have any idea what it would mean for the world if the Prism died? He's not always an easy man, but he's a much better man than Prisms usually are. And there are many of us who would do anything for him. Anything. Remember that…ma'am."

Orholam's prickly beard, but the slave woman was protective.

The slave stopped at the door, knocked three times, and opened it. Liv stepped into the Prism's room and found him sitting behind a desk, staring at her. His eyes were entrancing. Right now, they looked like diamonds, scattering light everywhere. He gestured to the chair across from him, and Liv sat.

"Thank you, Marissia, you may go," Gavin said to the slave. Then he turned his diamond eyes on Liv and said, "It's time for that favor."

Chapter 42

"Scout!" Corvan called. "She's seen us. Sonuvabitch!"

After Rekton, Corvan and Karris had decided to travel together. Both wanted to go after King Garadul's army, if for different reasons: Karris to join it somehow, and Corvan to see if he could find some way to exact vengeance. It was a risk to trust Corvan Danavis, of all people, but he had saved Karris and his reputation from the war was sterling. Truth was, it was more dangerous to travel alone.

They'd been following King Garadul's army south for days, and not once had he put out scouts. He'd seemed so careless that now Karris and Corvan had walked right past a scout in a tree stand.

As they stood at the edge of a wood, half a league behind the rear guard, the scout was sprinting to the east, down a slight hill, rather than going straight for the rear guard.

"She'll have a horse down in the gully there. You might be able to cut her off," Corvan said. He was unslinging his great yew bow. "Shot's too far. But I might get lucky."

Karris was already running. Away from the Umber River, Tyrea had rapidly become a scrub brush desert. In a few spots fed by underground springs, there were clumps of pine trees like the one she and Corvan had just left, but for the most part this land was rolling hills, often broken, something between a desert and a badland. It had made their pursuit of King Garadul's army more and more difficult, because even though they were traveling by foot and thus didn't kick up the huge quantities of dust that Garadul's men and wagons did, they still could be seen. They had to decide at every hill whether they should go straight over and risk being seen, or go around and lose even more ground. An army didn't travel fast, but it did travel straight.

The scout was a good two hundred paces in front of Karris. Judging from the slight slope of the hill, and making a guess, Karris angled off to the right. Probably the scout would make it to her horse, but if Karris were within a hundred paces when the scout mounted, she wouldn't be mounted for long.

Something dove out of the sky and pierced the ground not five paces behind the fleeing scout. She didn't even notice. Damn. Corvan had nearly hit a sprinting target at two hundred fifty paces. That close and he couldn't have gotten just a little closer?

The woman turned and angled more to the right. Corvan's second arrow missed by a good fifteen paces, flying where she might have been if she'd run straight.

Karris barreled on, heedless of the ground, hurdling tumbleweed and praying that she not step on the infrequent tough cactus that grew so low to the ground here that you never saw it until its spines stabbed through your shoes. And that wasn't as bad as the rattling snakes. At the speed Karris was running, of course, there would be no warning rattle, just a strike. She pushed harder. Maybe if she ran fast enough, even a striking snake might miss her.

Out of the corner of her eye, she saw Corvan's next arrow streak into view. The shot was more than three hundred paces now, albeit with no wind, so Corvan was having to shoot halfway between the horizon and vertical simply for the arrows to make the distance. But this shot looked perfect.

It dove and the scout crashed into the ground, full speed. Karris couldn't believe her eyes. An impossible shot. Three hundred paces at a running target? She cut left, heading straight for the woman.

Almost as soon as Karris turned, she saw Corvan's arrow. Sticking out of the ground. Back where the scout had fallen. It hadn't impaled her. It had *tripped* her.

Even as Karris saw it, she saw the woman standing, her head

swiveling toward Karris. She looked shaken, her palms bloody, a cut down the side of her face, but the woman started running regardless.

Karris had easily covered a hundred of the two hundred paces between them, and as the scout had to go from a dead stop to sprinting, Karris made up more than half of that. She wasn't even thirty paces back.

No more arrows fell. They were out almost four hundred paces now. Even with a yew longbow this was an extreme distance. There was no way Corvan would risk an errant shot with Karris so close to their quarry.

Karris fumbled with her necklace, trying to grab her eye caps. Even breaking stride that much gave the scout an edge, and she pulled away. Curse her, the woman ran like an antelope. But with the patience born of experience, Karris let her take the extra distance. Once she got the green-and-red eye caps on, the fight was over.

She cracked apart the appropriate link of her necklace, watching the ground in front of her, ripped the luxin off, and slowed for a few steps to get the caps stuck perfectly around each eye socket.

The scout cut hard left as the hill descended rapidly, shouting. Karris came after her, filling her right arm with red luxin and her left with green as she ran.

The scout was shouting? To whom?

Maybe she was shouting to her horse.

Sure she is, Karris.

In an instant, Karris was over the hill and barreling down the steep path straight into a camp. There were a dozen men waiting for her. At least two with nets. Two with catchpoles. Cudgels, staves. Swords sheathed. Not wanting to kill, but capture. A trap.

Karris felt sick horror, the shot like a fist in her gut. Like she was sixteen again, her father dragging her to a boat, sailing away from Big Jasper. Her father's boat had sailed past the family mansion, where she'd secretly—she thought—agreed to meet Dazen. Her brothers were there, lying in wait. They'd said they were going to teach Dazen a lesson for trying to destroy their family. But she'd seen murder in their eyes.

She had been standing on the deck when an explosion had blown out all the windows of her room on the second floor of the mansion. She saw figures limned in fire, fighting.

Something ripped off half the roof and explosion followed explosion. Bodies were hurled a hundred paces out into the water. Standing next to her on deck, her father paled. "You said he was coming alone, you stupid slut. Look what you've done! He must have brought an army!" Her father didn't strike her, just grabbed her head and made her watch what she couldn't have torn her eyes away from if she tried. In minutes, the only home she'd ever known was engulfed in flames.

She'd been a child then. She'd been unable to think, unable to act. She wasn't a child any longer, and she had pools of rage to draw from that that innocent hadn't known.

Karris used the height disparity of coming down the steep trail to leap at the first of the two horsemen who were side by side. He was holding a catchpole in both hands and he brought it up sideways, trying to block. He caught her extended foot, but she just let her kick collapse and slammed into him with both knees.

Ribs crunched as she swept him out of his saddle. She rolled as she hit the ground, but had to catch herself with her right hand, which was holding her narrow ataghan, so she drafted a thin blade of green luxin from her left hand as she passed under the second horse. The blade passed through its belly easily.

Karris was on her feet before the horse even reared in pain. She let the green luxin disintegrate as she charged one of the net men, switching her sword to her left hand. He was too stunned. He didn't move, not even as she lunged full length, stabbing at his face, her right hand flinging a weak arc of fire behind her for distraction. The net man still didn't move, and her lunge connected. The blade caught him between the eyes, skidded off the bone, and dove deep through his eye.

Turning to follow the arc of fire she'd thrown, Karris saw a weighted net spinning toward her just as the arc of fire faded from the air. Perfect throw.

But she waited, *waited*, switching sword hands again, until the net was between her and a man swinging a staff overhead at her.

With a snapping *pop-pop*, Karris shot out two horseshoes of green luxin. One whistled harmlessly through the twisting, expanding net. But though it missed the net, the horseshoe did catch the staff-swinger in the cheek, blasting him off balance. The second horseshoe snagged the net as it passed through and whipped it back into several men, its leaden weights suddenly becoming a flail.

The horse was rearing now, screaming in pain, a hideous sound. Its entrails spurted out in a bloody, ropy mass. But Karris barely heard it, barely saw it. She saw only chaos, and chaos was her friend, chaos was her advantage when fighting these odds.

Men were falling away from her on every side. Karris flung little balls of fire at the tents nearest her, blocking her view, curse being short! Where was the man shouting orders? The tents went up in flames, but it didn't seem to faze anyone but Karris. Everyone was fleeing.

She was just beginning to get a sense of how many men were in this camp—there were dozens of tents, maybe a hundred men? Orholam, she had to get out! Then she heard a thunderous roar. The ground around her feet jumped into the air as musket balls struck and the concussion of their fire rolled over her.

She looked up and saw a wide half-circle of musketeers, at least forty of them. Half were reloading in smooth, practiced motions. Unhurried. Well trained. The other half had their muskets, still loaded, trained on Karris.

"The next volley takes your life, Karris White Oak!" a man shouted. He was lean, mounted, wearing rich garments that announced he was King Rask Garadul, if the smug expression on his face hadn't. "The sword and the luxin. Now," he said.

Karris looked at the semicircle of blasted dirt in front of her, trying to gauge the accuracy of the king's musketeers. Pretty damn good. They were only twenty paces away. It would take a miracle. King Garadul's armor was, of course, mirrored, and he had Mirrormen and drafters to his left and right. What about Corvan?

If Corvan ran as fast as she had, he might get here at any time—Karris always lost track of time once fighting started. Maybe he'd already seen what she had gotten into. Either way, not even he could do anything against these odds. He certainly couldn't save Karris from twenty musketeers with an easy shot at her.

Karris pulled off her eye caps and dropped them and threw her sword away and let the green and red dribble from her fingertips. Usually, when she let the luxin go, she felt less wild, less angry. Not this time.

"Galan?" King Garadul said, gesturing to someone behind her.

Karris was starting to turn when something heavy cracked her over the head.

Chapter 43

Kip followed Commander Ironfist up another flight of steps, which disgorged them in front of the biggest double doors Kip had ever seen. The doors were a slightly smoky glass filled with slow waves of every hue, a great lake of color.

Commander Ironfist lifted one great silver knocker and pounded it onto the door three times. It was as if he'd thrown three rocks into a pond of light. Though the door itself didn't move, the light within it cratered and threw ripples out in every direction. It took Kip's breath away. He put a hand on the door, and where his fingers touched, tiny ripples formed.

"Don't touch," Ironfist barked.

Kip pulled back his hand as if burned.

"There are a few things you need to know before you go in, Kip," Ironfist said. "First, it's all real. We lose one out of every ten supplicants."

"Lose as in . . ."

"They die. Second, you can make it stop whenever you want. There will be a rope put in your hand. Pull the rope, and it will ring a bell. They'll stop immediately. Third, if you quit, you're finished, you can't stay. It costs a lot of money for a satrap to maintain a drafter, and not one of them will waste money on a coward. Gavin has instructed me that should you fail, I'm to give you enough silver to buy a small farm and put you on a ship to the destination of your choice. It's better than most failures get, but you'll not be allowed to return here ever again. You're a shame enough as it is."

Apparently tact wasn't part of the test. "I'm shameful?" Kip asked, a lump rising in his throat. Gavin hadn't treated him like that.

Ironfist blinked. "The life of a drafter is hard and short. I don't have time for lies, no matter how comforting. You're a bastard. That's a common enough shame for a great man, but it's a shame nonetheless. Anyone who can do simple arithmetic will know that you were sired while the Prism was betrothed to Karris White Oak, a woman most of us hold in high regard. Prisms are held to a higher standard, so you're a greater shame than usual. Even if you're excellent in every regard, you'll be a shame. If you're a failure, it's worse. That's the truth. Dressing it up in silk and lace isn't going to change it.

"Now, fourth, they say Orholam himself watches every initiation. Failing means failing him, farmboy. Ready?"

If Kip failed, he'd be put off the island. Not only would he shame the man who'd saved his life, but he would lose his only chance for retribution on the man who'd taken his mother's.

Kip wasn't going to fail. He'd die first.

Ironfist saw the look on his face. "Good."

The great doors in front of Kip rippled once more, the molten iridescent hues undulating gently and then seeming to spill left and right. It was as if something huge were surfacing from unimaginable depths. Kip's heart seized as a great face appeared, so fast he couldn't even comprehend all the details, just white hair, eyes like stars, and water of every shade bursting away from his features as he burst free—and opened his mouth, a yawning cavern of blackness that overwhelmed the doors. Kip flinched as it seemed the mouth would swallow him.

The doors burst open from within as if a giant had smashed them. A gust of air rushed over Kip.

"Enter," Ironfist commanded.

Kip walked in alone to a round chamber. The walls and floor were the same smoky-clear crystal as the door. Seven figures stood in a crescent around a black disk inlaid in the floor. Kip hesitated, and none of them moved. No one told him where to go.

THE BLACK PRISM · 271

The figures were robed, one for each color. The superviolet wore violet robes and sub-red wore deep red robes for the benefit of those who couldn't see into their spectra, but as Kip widened and then tightened his eyes, he saw that the sub-red was indeed radiating heat and the superviolet was clad in his color, hard pieces of superviolet luxin hooked together like rings of mail.

Still uncertain, Kip walked toward them. As he got closer, he could see beneath their hoods. His fists balled. The sub-red had blackened skin. No eyebrows. No hair. Little flame wisps escaped from its head. The green's face was gnarled as an old oak, its eyebrows like moss, hair strung with lichen. The blue looked like cut glass, features either smoothed out to planes or sharpened to jewel-like points.

Dear Orholam, were these all color wights? Then, from within his sleek goo, the orange blinked. Kip noticed the eyes. All of their eyes.

These were drafters in masks and makeup. They represented the wights of each color. Seven different varieties of death and dishonor. Kip started breathing again, though he couldn't control a little tremble. He stepped onto the black disk facing them.

"I am Anat, I am wrath," the sub-red said. "I am consumed with rage."

"I am Dagnu, I am gluttony," the red said. "I can never be filled."

"I am Molokh, I am greed," the orange said. "I can never be satisfied."

"I am Belphegor, I am sloth," the yellow said. "I withhold my talents."

"I am Atirat, I am lust," the green said. "I desire ever more."

"I am Mot, I am envy," the blue said. "I cannot bear others' good fortune."

"I am Ferrilux, I am pride," the superviolet said. "I would usurp Orholam's own throne."

They were the names of the old gods. Kip had barely even heard of them.

"These are the distortions of our nature."

"The temptations of power." The voices spoke out in turn, smoothly, overlapping, like one consciousness.

"For without mastery of ourselves, we become monsters."

"Shameful and ashamed, hiding in the darkness."

"But we are the sons and daughters of Orholam."

"We are Orholam's gift, expressions of his love."

"His law."

"His mercy."

"His truth."

"Thus we stand unashamed, clothed in his righteousness."

The sub-red stepped forward, pulled off his mask, and stepped out of his robe. He was a young man, muscular, handsome, and naked. "Casting off wrath, I am patience," the sub-red said. He lifted his hands and, even without looking into the sub-red, it was clear that he was drafting. The air shimmered with heat around his whole body. "Orholam's will be done."

The red stepped forward, pulled off her mask, and stepped out of her robe. She was young, athletic, beautiful, and also naked. Kip's eyes widened. He tried to hold them to her face.

Somber ceremony, Kip. Orholam's watching, Kip. Straight to hell, Kip.

"Casting off gluttony, I am temperance," the red said. She lifted her hands and red luxin blossomed through her entire body, eyes, face, down her neck to her breasts, nipples, firm tight stomach, breasts, nipples—*Kip!* In an instant, she was like a statue, every bit of her skin dyed a perfect red. "Orholam's will be done," she said.

The orange stepped forward. A man, mercifully. "Casting off greed, I am charity," he said. Lifting his hands, he turned a gleaming orange. "Orholam's will be done."

Yellow said, "Casting off sloth, I am diligence. Orholam's will be done." Her body filled with sparkling yellow light.

The green was a disconcertingly if appropriately curvaceous woman who looked Kip hard in the eye. That helped as she disrobed. He thought she might slap his head off if he looked at her generous— oops. "Casting off lust, I am *self-control*," she said. "Orholam's will be done."

The blue disrobed. "Casting off envy, I am kindness," she said softly. "Orholam's will be done."

The superviolet was the last man, and he was enormously muscular. "Casting off pride, I am humility," he said in a booming voice. "Orholam's will be done."

As one, they brought their hands down and pointed them at Kip's feet. Sprays of pure color blasted the black circle he stood on. It began to rumble and rattle beneath his feet. Then, abruptly, the disk of rock began sinking into the floor—and Kip with it.

In moments, Kip was down to his butt. But the hole was too narrow. His fat caught on the sharp sides of the floor. He had to shimmy just to fit, and as the hole deepened, either his stomach or his butt was pressing against a wall.

"Raise your right hand," the superviolet said.

As Kip did, swallowing convulsively, he saw a rope dropping all the way from a ceiling so high above that he couldn't see past the glare of its brightness. The superviolet caught the rope and put the knotted end in Kip's upraised hand.

"Pull the rope, and it ends," the man said. He had something akin to kindness in his voice.

Then Kip was fully in the hole, and still going down. He stopped below the floor. The light high above in the testing chamber went out. Kip could see nothing.

He tried to take a deep breath, but the chamber was so tight he couldn't even draw a full breath.

There were whispered voices above him. "Dees, will you run this test for me?"

A man's voice replied, awkward, "I've never run one before, my lord. You know, I think we set the tube too narrow. He's fat. He could suffocate."

"He's the Prism's bastard."

"So? He's not here."

"So accidents happen. But I can't be here when they do. The Prism knows I hate him. He doesn't know you. So if an accident happens on your watch—"

Kip couldn't hear the rest because water started pouring over his head. Cold, first a dribble, then a steady stream. It ran down the back of his neck to where his back was pressed tight against the walls. The walls around him pulsed an intense blue. Dear Orholam, they were going to kill him to get back at his father. Just like Gavin had warned him.

The water pooled around his middle. He was too fat for it to drain down to his feet, he sealed the whole tube. Kip's heart was pounding. The intense light emanating through the walls burned from blue down into green, through the whole spectrum in order, even through heat, and then faded into nothing again as the water reached Kip's neck.

Up to his ear. He pushed his body hard against the side of the chamber, and a gap opened between his hip and the wall. The pooled water poured down to his feet. But it kept coming from above.

For a few moments, he was able to intermittently push against the wall and make it drain once more, but soon he was awash, nearly floating. He pushed against the wall again, and the water didn't drain at all. There was nowhere for it go.

The water rose once more to his left shoulder, which was trapped down even as his right was trapped up. Then up to his neck. His left ear.

He didn't notice when the walls pulsed superviolet, but then they passed through blue, to green as the water rose to his chin, to yellow as it touched his lips, orange as it covered his lips—was the water falling more slowly on his head now? He took deep breaths through his nose, wriggled to try to use his body's wedged-in position to climb higher in the tube, and found that there were straps above his shoulders, keeping him down.

This was insanity. Someone was trying to kill him. Kip had to ring the bell. His fingers were claws around the rope. He could try again when there wasn't a murderer around.

No. Quitting meant being put out. It meant failing.

There was barely time to take one last deep breath before the water covered Kip's nose.

The falling water pelting his head abruptly ceased. Kip could imagine it now: "He was so fat, he trapped the water. It wasn't supposed to be that high. We didn't put too much water in...he just panicked. You know, a child, trapped and afraid. He must not have even thought to pull the rope."

So that was it. He either quit and shamed his father more than his very existence already did, or his father's enemies did their best to kill him.

Holding his breath, his lungs just beginning to burn, there was a sudden, stark clarity to the world: pull the rope, go home.

But, there *was* no home. So, pull the rope, and go farm...somewhere. Or stay, and maybe die. Fail here, and he failed his father and his mother. Fail here, and he was a failure forever.

I'm *not* pulling the rope.

The chamber went black. The water got hot from the sub-red light, but then even that faded.

I don't like farming. Kip coughed out some of his air, laughing, the thought was so inane. But the pain rapidly squelched wry humor. He couldn't make his heart slow. He couldn't stop his throat from swallowing convulsively, his chest from pumping on nothing. I'm not pulling the rope, damn you. I'm not pulling the rope.

Something shifted. At first, Kip thought it was the water pouring out, but it wasn't. The ground below him was rising, but the stops above his shoulders stayed in place, crushing him in place. The water, far from draining, simply rose up his raised arm. In moments, he squatted down, pushed against his own knees. It squeezed him and he coughed, the last of his breath bubbling out.

He was trying to hold on to nothing. Breathing the water in would be worse than breathing nothing at all, he knew it. He knew it and yet his body overwhelmed him and he sucked a breath in. The water was hot, sharp, acrid in his lungs. He gagged, hunched even tighter against his own knees, his body ripping itself apart. He coughed and, miraculously, water shot out of his mouth into air, blessed, glorious, free, beautiful air!

Gasping, spitting, retching, and still compressed into a ball, Kip breathed. He could breathe! Mostly. His knees hurt from being squashed tighter than his not-so-flexible joints would allow. His back hurt. His ribs hurt. But Orholam, the air was good. If only he could get a full breath.

Nothing happened. It was still utterly black. Kip was sweating now. He was packed in here. It was getting hotter by the second and he was still dripping wet. The colors flashed past him, through the whole spectrum again.

So that's how it was. They saw that he wasn't going to quit, so they weren't going to give him another chance with the colors.

It didn't matter. I'm not pulling the rope. "I'm not pulling the rope!" Kip shouted. Or tried to shout; he wasn't very loud with only a half a breath.

In response, the floor rose even more, crushing him harder against the stays on his shoulders. Kip screamed. He sounded like a coward.

He couldn't even push back against the stays. His knees were bent too far to get him any leverage. If he just pulled on the rope a little, he could get a breath, and then he could go on fighting.

No! Kip deliberately relaxed his fingers, his arm. He concentrated on breathing. Tiny, quick little breaths.

It was enough. It would be enough. He was making it enough.

A succession of colors blurred past. Kip didn't care. Was he supposed to do something? What? Draft? Right. Go bugger yourselves.

The pressure eased suddenly and the floor dropped. Then the walls eased wider. Kip almost fell, but after a moment his rubbery legs were able to take his weight. The walls pulled back farther, farther. He tried to take a wider stance, but there was nothing beyond his little disk except air.

Reaching one hand out, Kip couldn't feel the walls at all. A breeze blew across his skin, giving him the sensation that he was standing on some high place. It had to be an illusion, though, he was in the middle of the school. No way was there a big hole here.

Colors flashed through distant walls, illuminating the chamber for a brief, terrifying moment. Kip stood over an abyss. His disk was the tiny round top of a pillar: a pillar standing alone in the middle of nothingness. The walls were thirty paces away. The ceiling over his head had a single hole, through which only his hand was poking.

Wind buffeted him, and Kip felt his grip go white-knuckled on the rope. He clamped his eyes shut, but then he couldn't tell if he was swaying with the wind or against it or staying still. His heart was beating so hard he could hear his own pulse in his ears between gasping breaths. He screamed words, but he didn't even know what they were.

After an eternity, the walls came back. They closed firmly around him, but comfortably now, and he felt a surge of relief. He'd made it. He'd passed. He hadn't given up. He'd hadn't pulled the—

Something touched his leg.

What was that?

It curled around his ankle, twisted around his calf. A snake. Kip looked up and some many-legged thing dropped on his face.

He reached a spastic hand up to sweep a spider away, but felt a manacle snap over his wrist and pull his left arm away, lock it into place. He tried to kick the snake away from his feet. *Snap, snap.* Shackles closed around his feet and yanked them wide apart.

Kip screamed.

The spider fell into his mouth.

Before he even knew what he was doing, Kip bit down fiercely on it, crushing it in his teeth, sour goo squirting into his mouth. He screamed again, sheer defiance. Something landed in his hair. Dozens of slithering things roped around his feet, climbed his legs. He was going crazy.

"I'm not pulling the rope!" he shouted. "You bastards, I'm not pulling the rope!"

Kip convulsed. Orholam have mercy. His whole body was covered with loathsome things. He was weeping, screaming—and salvation lay in his hand. There was nothing wrong with farming. No one would hold failure against him. He didn't need to see these people ever again. And what did he care what they thought of him anyway? The whole game was stacked against him. He was finished. It was over.

With an inhuman cry, Kip took the rope, with all his loathing and fury and despair rising in him, totally overwhelming him, failure calling his name—and threw it out of the hole. He sank against the wall, burying his face in the rock, crying.

Colors flashed past once more, but the snakes and spiders didn't go. They covered his body.

Still the oppressive darkness continued. Something heavy and hairy landed on his back. Little claws stabbed him through his shirt. A rat. Then one on his thigh. Another landed on his head, scratching him as it slid off his wet hair.

Kip froze. Fear like lightning flashed through his entire body. He was in a cupboard, helpless, starving, parched. He shivered uncontrollably.

His motion disrupted the nasties and something bit him. He yelped, humiliated, furious. He twisted. More prickly bites, stinging bites, savage bites covered his arm, his legs, his groin, his back. Kip thrashed, throwing himself against one wall and then the other, trying to crush the beasts. Rats were climbing up his body on every side, and they refused to let go. He was weeping. He was so ashamed. There was something about the spider. The spider he'd bitten.

It was too much. He couldn't take it anymore. He was finished. Kip couldn't stop himself. He reached for the rope. He was a failure, a shame, a fat, blubbering coward. A nothing.

He felt the rope pressed back into his hand. "Here you go, Tubby," a satisfied voice whispered. The taste, Kip. The taste was wrong, a kind voice said.

What the woman had said didn't quite register. They were all over him.

Kip pulled the rope. Failure.

A distant clang, high overhead. At once, the stinging ceased. Every slithering, crawling, clinging, stinging thing evaporated, disappeared. They weren't real. They hadn't been real rats. Kip should have known from the spider he'd bitten. Would have known, if he hadn't been such a coward. That goo inside hadn't been guts, it had been luxin. It was all illusions, fake fears. He'd been tricked.

He'd failed. As the platform rose, Kip's brain—no longer fogged with terror—realized what the woman had called him: "Tubby." It was what Ram used to call him. Kip died a little. He'd proved Ram right. Again.

As he emerged, though, the men and women were now dressed in festive robes of their own colors, dazzling sapphire blues, emerald greens, diamond yellows, ruby reds. They appeared jubilant.

"Congratulations, supplicant!" Mistress Varidos said, coming to join the circle.

Kip stared at her, dumbfounded.

"Four minutes and twelve seconds. You should be very proud. I'm sure your father will be."

She was speaking some language Kip didn't understand. Proud? He'd failed. He'd shamed himself, shamed his father. He'd given up. The rage and frustration that had been building up suddenly had nowhere to go, leaving him feeling stupid.

"I failed," Kip said.

"Everybody fails!" the incredibly muscular superviolet said. "You did great! Four minutes twelve! I only lasted a minute six."

"I don't understand," Kip said.

The nymphish yellow laughed. "That's how the test is designed. We all *failed*."

They surrounded him, men pounding him on the back, women touching his arms or shoulder, all congratulating him. It was a bit intoxicating to be so wholeheartedly welcomed by people who were so beautiful. Now that his brain was working again, he noticed that they hadn't necessarily chosen men to represent the old gods and women for the goddesses. Was that because they'd come so far that it simply didn't matter anymore, or was it deliberate disrespect?

"Is it true?" Kip asked Mistress Varidos, who had stood back some lest the jostling crowd knock her over. "Everyone fails?"

She smiled. "Almost everyone. It's not to see if you can make it through the test, it's to see what kind of a person you are. And fear widens your eyes. Those colors you saw flashing past were the real test. Those will tell us what you can draft. Are you ready to see your results?"

"Wait. 'Almost everyone'? Who doesn't fail?" Kip asked.

The jubilant men and women quieted.

The old woman said, "The only person in my lifetime who didn't take the rope was..."

Gavin. Kip knew it. Of course. His father had been the one man who did what no one else could do, what no one else had ever done. Kip *had* failed him.

"Your uncle," the mistress said.

My "uncle" Gavin, or my uncle Dazen?

Apparently registering his confusion, she said, "Your uncle Dazen Guile, who nearly destroyed our world. Good footsteps not to follow, hm?"

She was speaking that other language again. After all Kip had seen Gavin do, it was Gavin's *brother* who'd passed?

"Four minutes is wonderful, Kip, but that's just bragging rights. Are you ready to see your colors?"

Chapter 44

Liv dropped into a curtsey, glad for the excuse to break eye contact with the Prism. When she straightened, Gavin Guile was looking at her critically. Obviously she'd been right, not many women answered his summonses in their work clothes and no cosmetics.

"It's been a long time since I've seen a proper Tyrean curtsey," the Prism said.

After your armies left, there weren't many women left to curtsey. "How may I serve you, High Luxlord Prism?" Liv asked instead.

"Lord Prism is sufficient," Gavin said.

"Thank you, Lord Prism."

He was obviously weighing her, thinking. But thinking what? Whatever else that wretched woman Aglaia Crassos had done, she'd made Liv think of the Prism as Gavin Guile—a man, and a good-looking one at that. His eyes were—quite literally—the most entrancing eyes in the entire world.

Magister, Liv. Tutor. Lord. Luxlord. Noble. General. Twice as old as you. Way too old for you. Not a broad-shouldered, muscular man—just another magister. You can go to hell, Aglaia Crassos.

"Have you chosen who you want to be your magister in yellow?" he asked.

Thank you!

See, I'm a disciple. Purely academic. A child in comparison to him. Hopelessly young and ignorant. She pursed her lips. "Honestly, I'd like to study under Mistress Tawenza Goldeneyes." She could barely believe she'd dared say it out loud. The woman only took three disciples a year—and she already had three. The three best yellow disciples in the Chromeria.

Gavin laughed. "That prickly she-bear? A bold choice. She's the best, and she probably won't hate you as much as you think she does for the first year. I'd have you send my compliments to her when I assign her a fourth student, but she'd doubtless take it out on you. Consider it done. How are your apartments?"

She paused. It was almost a personal question. No, he's simply worried—no, not worried, he's checking that his orders have been carried out. Generals do that sort of thing. "They're better than anything I thought I'd ever have, Lord Prism. And the clothes? I used to have three dresses. Now I've got more than fifty and my worst is nicer than my old Sun Day best." Wait, maybe clothes weren't the best topic.

"And yet you decided to come in this," Gavin said, noticing. Oops. His voice didn't intone disapproval. If anything, there was a thin thread of amusement. But his face didn't give her any expression to know if he was irritated. She should have listened to that slave, Marissia. It wouldn't have killed her to freshen up a little. He glanced past her, and she followed his gaze, but the room was empty except for the two of them, and there were no unusual decorations on the walls, just the normal testing crystal.

"You said to come at my earliest convenience." She couldn't keep a defensive tone out of her voice. "I thought you'd not want to be kept waiting." That was better. Nicely assertive, Liv.

"I think you'll do perfectly."

"Lord Prism?"

"You're perfect because you refuse to be impressed, Aliviana. I like that. It—"

"I wouldn't exactly say I'm not impressed!"

He grinned. "You say, interrupting me."

And proving his point.

Liv decided to shut up. Maybe differentiating herself from all the other women who came here—and were unsuccessful in their attempts to seduce Gavin—had not been a good plan.

"It seems every time I summon a woman between the ages of thirteen and sixty, she comes dressed like a Ruthgari courtesan, either overly eager or completely terrified. Like I run a brothel up here."

Oh, Orholam strike me, what if I've done the one thing that makes me more attractive to him? "You're Gavin Guile," Liv said, like that explained everything. It did. Not only would snaring the Prism totally change a woman's own life, but it would change her entire family's life. Immediately and for generations to come, and for the better. Add gorgeous and virile to "Prism," which already meant powerful, respected, and rich, and Liv had no doubt that hemlines soared and necklines swooped. It was a wonder that women didn't come to the Prism naked. How much would Ana have worn if the Prism had summoned her?

On second thought, Liv didn't want to think about that.

"Yes, I am," Gavin said, smirking as if at some private joke. "And I need your help, Aliviana."

Liv swallowed. The truth was, he could ask anything, and there was no way she could say no. "Liv, please."

"Right." Gavin cleared his throat. Why is he clearing his throat? He feels awkward? Does he feel awkward starting an affair with a girl half his age?

Gavin glanced over Liv's shoulder again. "A number of years ago—it feels like quite a number of years ago...I have a...*nephew*. His mother was Tyrean. I want you to tutor him. It might make him feel more comfortable to learn from another Tyrean. I know you Tyreans don't have it easy here. What do you say?"

Liv spluttered. A "nephew"? A tutor? Kip! Of course! Orholam, she'd gone completely the wrong direction! Idiot! The Prism hadn't even been thinking anything remotely... "W-well, of course, Lord Prism. Is there...why do..." What was she saying? She'd already been impertinent enough. Asking the wrong question about a man's bastard might be a good way to ruin everything. "What color is he gifted with?" She only remembered at the last second to say "he" and not "Kip." She wasn't supposed to know Kip was the Prism's bastard at all.

I would make a lousy spy.

"Green. Possibly blue. He's being initiated right now."

"Right now?" Liv asked. The year's initiations had been completed long ago. Liv had never heard of someone being initiated at any other time of year. "How long has your—how long has he been here?"

"He arrived yesterday."

"And he's being initiated already?!" Liv asked. Poor Kip.

Gavin glanced behind her again. This time, she knew what he was looking at. Throughout the tower, for reasons Liv had never comprehended, there were plain crystals set into the walls. For the whole year, they simply sat and sparkled, dully refracting whatever light they caught from their surroundings, but during initiations at the beginning of each year, they glowed brilliantly. As the supplicants passed through the Thresher, invariably there was the wash of one color after another as each test progressed, the same wash each supplicant saw. As soon as they drafted, the crystal turned a brilliant hue in whatever color they drafted. For Liv it had been superviolet first, then yellow weakly.

The whole time Liv had been here, the Prism had been watching to see how his bastard son was doing.

Come to think of it, if the test had been going on since the first time Gavin Guile had glanced behind Liv, it was taking a really long time. Usually it took less than a minute.

They both turned to look at the crystal. "What did the tester say when they lowered you into the Thresher?" Gavin asked.

"He said something about the only good rebel being a dead rebel, and how he still owed my father blood," Liv said. The point had been, as it always was, to scare the person being tested. Fear made the eyes dilate. Fear made a supplicant draft to the utmost of her abilities. It also helped even the most arrogant young lady or lordling begin their studies with a bit of humility.

"How about you?" Liv asked. Neither of them turned from the crystal.

"Something about my brother," Gavin said. "Turned out to be more right than they knew."

"I'm sorry," Liv said. She wasn't sure if she was apologizing for asking, for the tester, or for the real-life nightmare Gavin had gone through later in having to kill his own brother.

"I never liked that part, scaring them. The chamber is terrifying enough, and the thought of failing is scary enough. They don't have to make supplicants think they're really going to die. It breaks people. It breaks children."

Liv had never thought about it that way. The Thresher just was. Everyone went through it. It was inextricable from drafting, from the Chromeria. If nothing else, every drafter had the Thresher in common.

"The noble girls all knew what was coming," Liv said. "Unlike the rest of us. They knew the test itself wouldn't hurt them, so that bit of talking outside the test was the only thing that made them afraid. Because even if they'd been warned, hearing a tester who claims to belong to your enemy's family say that accidents happen is terrifying."

"Hadn't thought of that," Gavin said. "All my friends were nobles. I thought everyone knew what was coming."

Of course you did. It's just another way the Chromeria's stacked to favor your kind.

Gavin cleared his throat. "Liv, my son might be special, really gifted. We'll find out presently, but I wouldn't be surprised if he's a polychrome. He's Tyrean, his mother just died, he's going to face false friends and unearned enemies just for being my son; he won't fit in anywhere and yet people are going to be watching him all the time. If he's truly powerful on top of that ... he could turn into a monster. He wouldn't be the first in my family to handle great power poorly. The gift isn't a pure gift, you know."

"What do you want me to do?" Liv asked. Was she really going to be tutoring the Prism's son? Bastard son, but still. She felt like a huge weight had been lifted off of her. The Prism was just the Prism—well, maybe there was no such thing as being *just* the most powerful man in the world—but he was a lord to whom she owed service. Normal service. Something not terribly hard, given how completely he'd changed her life.

"Maybe he'll be a monochrome. Probably will be. I'm getting ahead of myself," Gavin said.

"But if he's not?" You've got to let me know what your expectations are or I'm going to fail—and then you'll be mad at me for that.

Typical nobleman. Liv felt good that she was able to be irritated. She was regaining her bearings.

"Pretend he's normal. In all ways. I know he'd figure it out pretty quickly if we stay, but I'm going to take him away from here as soon as I possibly can. Until then, give him some normalcy. If he makes you mad, yell at him. Smack his knuckles with a stick if he misbehaves, you understand? But if he masters something difficult, pretend it's good but nothing out of the norm. I want him to know that those who matter aren't going to be impressed by who his father is or how much he can draft."

"And who are these people?" Liv asked sarcastically. She hadn't really meant to say it out loud, but Gavin was being ridiculously idealistic. Of course who he was and how much he could draft mattered. Maybe when you were born on the top of the mountain you could pretend the mountain didn't matter, but those who climbed it and those born at its base who could never climb at all knew differently.

"Me and Orholam," Gavin said, ignoring her tone. "If we're the only ones whose approval he cares about, he's got a chance."

Liv didn't know if that was the most arrogant or the most profound thing she'd ever heard. Maybe both. Whatever else it did, though, it reminded her who and what Gavin was. By Orholam's scowling brow, she'd been glibly sarcastic to the Prism, the man closest in all the world to Orholam himself. And thank Orholam that Liv had turned down that awful woman. Even if it was going to cost her dearly. Spying on the Prism himself? It was practically sacrilegious. As bad as Liv's stupidity and awkwardness and horrifying sliver of infatuation was, how awful would it have been to be a traitor too? She swallowed. "I'm sorry, Lord Prism, I was out of—"

Gavin raised a hand and stood abruptly.

Liv glanced at the crystal but saw nothing. The crystal hadn't changed. She looked over at Gavin in time to see the Prism blanch—then his face was lit up like the sun had just come out from behind the blackest clouds.

A wash of colors flashed through his skin and he threw out a hand toward the crystal. A crackling, shimmering tube of luxin shot from his hand and stuck to the crystal on the opposite wall like an iridescent spiderweb on fire. More and more gushed out of the man, pushing deep into the crystal.

And then, as abruptly as he started, Gavin stopped. A moment later, the crystal glowed a brilliant jade green, and then a less intense blue.

Gavin sighed with relief.

"What was that?" Liv asked.

"A secret!" Gavin barked. He gestured, and Liv felt a gust of cold wind and heard the windows drop heavily into their slots.

"Come here," the Prism ordered. His body filled with every color in the rainbow and beyond. A rope of green luxin wrapped around a chain of yellow-infused blue ran from his hand. "Now, girl! I have to be there first to contain this, and he's going to need you."

In a daze, Liv hurried over to the Prism. She didn't even know what he was talking about.

"Get on my back," he said.

"What?"

"On my back, now! Hold on tight."

She jumped on his back. His body was unnaturally hot from the sub-reds he was holding along with every other color. What was he doing? She looked at the chain he was holding again. Then he turned and faced the void outside his window. She squeaked and held on with a death grip.

"Nna tha igh!" the Prism said.

"What?" Liv asked, loosening her grip around his neck.

"Not that tight," he growled.

Even as she apologized, bands of luxin whipped around her body, holding her tight against him. Gavin took a run toward the window and leapt.

Liv's view, at first, was only of the luxin spooling out of Gavin's hand like spider's silk, perfectly matching the rate at which they were falling. She realized she had no idea how far exactly they would have to fall to get to the level of the Threshing Chamber, or how Gavin would know when to stop them. For that matter, how did he mean to get back into the tower from the outside? Hope someone left a window open?

Oh, dear Orholam!

They were falling an awfully long time. Liv's eyes disobeyed her and jumped from the luxin above to the ground below. It was rushing up at them with incredible speed.

Then she was crushed into Gavin's back as he solidified the rope. The pressure threatened to sweep her off of him and straight into the courtyard. They whipped around backward and she saw the rope-chain spooled out to the distant top of the Prism's Tower, and the tower itself was looming bigger and bigger as as they swung back toward its sheer, unbroken face.

Three sharp jerks pushed her and Gavin backward, but with nowhere near enough force to slow them down. Briefly, Liv saw three missiles streaking out from Gavin's outstretched left hand toward the tower in front of them.

She didn't see what the missiles did, because whatever else they accomplished, with Gavin shooting them out of his left hand while his right held the rope, he absorbed the recoil with his left arm. So as soon as the missiles were out of his hand, Gavin and Liv were sent spinning sharply widdershins.

Glass and stone exploded on every side around Liv. She was sliding along a floor, zipping straight and smooth for a fraction of a second, abruptly cut away from the Prism. Then something caught the hem of her skirt. Her momentum and the friction with the floor yanked it up hard, and then her bare skin squeaked on naked stone. She flopped over sideways and rolled a few times. When she stopped against the wall, all she could think was that she couldn't believe she was still alive.

There were half a dozen drafters in the suddenly breezy hallway, looking at the Prism and her in disbelief. The Prism was already up, giving sharp orders.

Why is my butt cold? Liv followed the drafters' stares and looked down. Her skirt was bunched around her waist from the slide, exposing her to all the world. She squeaked, yanked her skirt down, and jumped to her feet.

"You, get Luxlord Black. Tell him I want this repaired. Today. Go immediately. You, take the names of everyone in this hall and everyone in the testing chamber," the Prism was saying. Liv, seeing everyone's attention was on the Prism, shifted her hips. She hadn't noticed until after she jumped up, but her butt cheeks had been cold because her underclothes had been yanked up too. Now they were cleaving the moon in a serious way. She shimmied, trying to fix her underclothes without fishing after them with a hand. "Aliviana, what are you doing?" the Prism asked.

Liv froze, transfixed.

"Never mind, stay here. I'll call for you in a moment." Gavin opened the door to the testing chamber and slipped inside. All the drafters in the hall, including one of the best-looking young magisters in the whole Chromeria, Payam Navid, turned to look at Liv, obviously wondering why she was so important—and killing her chance to quickly tug her underclothes down. Not having any idea what she was going to find or what the Prism was going to expect of her, she smiled nervously at the young magister.

Chapter 45

Gavin moved quickly, hearing the old bichrome say, "Are you ready to see your colors?" to Kip.

"I know I am!" Gavin said. "Mistress Varidos, may I?" Family members of supplicants weren't allowed in the testing chamber for fear that it would lead to cheating. The rule, at least theoretically, even applied to the Prism. There's a reason theory and practice are two different words.

"I wasn't even aware that you'd begun your testing. How long did they say you lasted?" Gavin asked.

"Four minutes, I guess," Kip said.

"Four twelve," the old mistress said.

Gavin physically stopped. It had seemed like a long time up in his room, but he'd supposed it had only seemed long. Four minutes was astounding. Passing had only taken him five.

Mistress Varidos drew close to Gavin and whispered, "There was some irregularity that I think you should know about."

Gavin smiled at Kip. "Well done, we'll just be a moment." He came aside, leaving Kip with the men and women who were asking him which part he thought was hardest, how he'd managed to hold out so long, and generally treating him like the center of the world. It was pretty intoxicating for a young drafter, and it was supposed to be.

Grinning, Gavin walked toward the tester's table with Mistress

Varidos. They came to stand right over the stone table. A black samite cloth was spread over a hole in the middle of the table. The testing stone would be right in there. Gavin tried to remember exactly how it was positioned. He'd only get one shot at this. "What was the irregularity?" he asked. The samite blocked out any outside light that would interfere with the testing stone.

The old woman exhaled slowly. "He threw the rope out of his hand at about three thirty. Before I could stop her, one of the women put it back in his hand."

"Are you joking?" Gavin said.

"They send the beautiful ones for the testing. Half of them barely have the brains to remember their lines, much less remember some of the more obscure rules governing situations that have never arisen in living memory. Even Dazen didn't throw the rope aside."

"Which one did it?"

"The green."

Of course it was the green. Wild, unpredictable, chafing at the slightest restriction. "Get her over here!"

The green tester saw the mistress's summons and walked right over. All the testers were beautiful, and if being light-skinned was a detriment on the battlefield, it was favored for this and a few other ceremonies. The visual effect of a man or woman whose skin was green or blue or red was more muted the darker their natural skin tone. Even the Parians chose coastal, lowland, or mixed-blood countrymen to represent them in this ceremony. This woman was Ruthgari, and light-skinned even for them. She moved with the easy grace of a dancer. Her thin green robe, thrown on during the ceremony so that all the testers would be clad in their colors when the supplicant emerged—which might be only ten or fifteen seconds after their testing began—was, in her case, open deep between her large breasts. She walked up eagerly, throwing her hair back, back straight, standing just on the other side of the table.

The nudity and near-nudity of some of the ceremonies were shrouded in religious and cultural symbolism that made them almost non-erotic. Almost, because no matter how high-minded you might be, you couldn't completely ignore the fact that you were looking at someone who was naked and astoundingly attractive. But the parties afterward, especially at initiations, were always a gray area. Everyone beautiful, everyone half-clad, everyone with the fresh memory of everyone else stark naked, the atmosphere jubilant, the wine flowing freely, and the somber ceremonialism suddenly removed.

This green knew exactly what she was doing. Gavin was taller than the woman, so he could barely help but stare down her barely closed robe. Instead, he looked at her heart-shaped face, hazel eyes, the pupils barely haloed in green. She looked familiar.

"Over here," he said, pointing next to him, between himself and Mistress Varidos. She stepped around the stone table to where he'd pointed, but closer in than necessary.

"Who are you?" he asked, his voice cool.

"My name's Tisis," she said, her smile showing off great dimples.

"Tisis what?"

"Oh," she said, as if she didn't have a thought in her head. "Tisis Malargos."

"What happened, Tisis?" he asked, pretending not to recognize the name. Her father and uncle had been his friends—that was, his *Dazen's*. They'd disappeared after the war. Killed by bandits or enslaved by pirates, most likely. She had the family look. No doubt she hated him. She'd seen that Kip had a chance of passing the test, so she'd sabotaged him. Gutsy. Foolish and infuriating, but gutsy.

"The supplicant cheated," she said. "He threw out the rope. I put it back in his hand."

"You're not to touch the supplicant in any way during the testing. Is there something about that rule that's unclear?"

"I didn't touch him— Pardon me, High Luxlord Prism, I put the rope back in his hand without touching his skin. I was trying to preserve the integrity of the test."

"Malargos," Gavin said. "You're Ruthgari, right?"

"Yes, Lord Prism."

Gavin looked at her flatly. "When your own Blessed Satrap Rados crossed the Great River to fight the Blood Foresters who outnumbered him two to one, do you remember what he did?"

"He burned Rozanos Bridge behind his army," she said.

"Was *that* cheating?"

"I—I don't follow," she said.

"He burned the bridge so his men knew they couldn't flee. He gave them no way out. Every last man knew he had to win or die. It's where we get the expression 'burning your bridges behind you.'"

"But I saw him reaching for the rope," she complained weakly. She swallowed, suddenly unnerved to have contradicted the Prism to his face.

"And you gave it back to him."

"Of course."

"So you would have built a new bridge behind Blessed Satrap Rados?"

"Of course not, that would be..."

"And doomed him. How long did you last before you pulled the rope?" Gavin asked.

She flushed and looked away. "Seventeen seconds." She pulled her robe tighter around herself, finally covering up.

"And you destroyed a young man's chance at passing."

"We could retest—" she started.

"You know we can't. Once supplicants know it's not real, the Thresher doesn't work. Everyone would say it was because he got special favor for being my nephew—"

"I didn't mean—"

"And you know it!" Gavin said, only keeping his voice down with effort.

"It doesn't matter what you *meant*," Mistress Varidos hissed.

While the mistress was speaking, Gavin split some superviolet from the light of the torches. Just a little. The beauty of superviolet was its invisibility. Even though there were at least half a dozen people in this room who could see superviolet luxin if they tightened their eyes, Gavin was betting that none of them was tightening her eyes at this very moment. And even if someone was, what Gavin was about to do was so small and so quick that even someone looking might miss it. Magical sleight of hand. The superviolet settled into his fingertips.

"You broke the rules, Tisis," the mistress said. "You botched your duties, and you may have destroyed a young man's future."

"But nobody *passes*!" the young woman protested. It had become a mark of pride just to hold on for a long time. Conspiracies, the dark, tight spaces, heights, spiders, snakes, rats—the Thresher hit all of the most common fears. Usually, believing that failure would mean the loss of everything and with their eyes dilated from fear, the applicant drafted any and all colors before they pulled the rope. It wasn't perfect, of course, but it was the best test they had.

"Get out of my sight," Gavin said.

She went, huffing, furious, crossing between Gavin and the mistress, just as Gavin had planned. He pulled a stone from his pocket, holding the short rod behind his wrist, slid the samite off the hole, flicked invisible superviolet out of his fingertips and used it to snatch the testing stone out of its grooves. He snapped the luxin back to his wrist, binding the testing stone to his forearm with bands of superviolet, and with the last of the superviolet in his finger dropped the false testing stone into place.

It had all taken less than a second, and Gavin hadn't so much as leaned over. "Well, let's see what we have, shall we?" he said, still drawing the rich samite cloth away from the hole.

In full view of Mistress Varidos, Gavin set the samite aside and reached into the receptacle, leaning over, grabbing the testing stone, and pulling it out. The testing stone was an ivory bar—either from sea demon washed ashore or from elephants deep within Ruthgar—tipped on each end with obsidian. The ivory was precious, but the obsidian was the real wonder. No one knew where the obsidian extant in the world had been harvested, or mined, or made. Obsidian was rarer than diamonds or rubies, so after every testing the obsidian ends of each testing stone were removed to be reused.

The superstitious called it hellstone. Most drafters were just happy that it was rare, because it was the only stone that could draw luxin directly out of a drafter! Gavin had heard that in the ancient world kings and satraps—and in more mythic tales, the assassins of the Broken Eye—had created entire daggers or even swords of obsidian.

But obsidian only evinced its magical properties when two very special conditions were met. First, it had to be in near-total darkness: that is, a total lack of light in the visible spectrum—for some reason superviolet and sub-red didn't interfere with it. Second, it needed the drafter's blood, an open cut at that. There had to be a direct physical connection between the obsidian and the luxin for the luxin to be drawn out of the drafter. When that connection was made, however, the pull was quite strong. Cut a drafter's shoulder with obsidian while he was holding luxin in his hand and hold the stone against the cut, and within maybe ten seconds the luxin would be gone. Scholars speculated that was because drafters had luxin throughout their bodies at all times, so the connection was direct, even if it was distant within the body.

Because the rates at which obsidian pulled colors out of a person were different for the different kinds of luxin, they made nice lines as they were pulled out of the body and into the ivory. If a color formed and stayed and was thick enough, the supplicant was deemed worthy of receiving training in that color. If there were two colors, of course, the supplicant was deemed a bichrome, and more than two made them a polychrome.

Gavin took the testing stone. He caught a faint whiff of cloves that was the scent of superviolet luxin. He held it for just a moment, willing the scent to disperse, and handed the stone to Mistress Varidos. As the head tester, it was her place to declare the findings. As he did, everyone else gathered around. She carefully removed the obsidian tips and stowed them in a special box, and then held the testing stone over her head. There was a clear, thick green bar, peaking toward the blue side, and next to it a less full blue. Yellow was faint. There was a tiny bit in the superviolet. It was a classic bell, the most common pattern in drafters.

The mistress said, "I hereby declare Kip of Rekton gifted of Orholam in the colors green and blue, with superviolet undecided and to be tested further at a later date. Kip, congratulations, you're a bichrome."

A cheer went up.

Only Kip still looked confused.

Gavin walked around the table, put an arm around Kip's shoulder, and squeezed. "Well done, Kip."

Kip was limp in Gavin's embrace. "So I passed?" he asked quietly.

"You passed. You made me proud."

Another cheer went up, and within no time, wine and brandy and special cakes and fruits and meats and sweetmeats were being produced by slaves who flooded the chamber.

Gavin released the boy, who was looking at him like he was utterly befuddled, like he couldn't believe the words Gavin had just said. Some of that, too, was the magic. The emotional effects of every part of the spectrum had just passed through Kip for the very first time. He didn't know yet what to do with the residue. It took time. Gavin gestured toward the door, beckoning Aliviana.

"Kip," Gavin said. "I've brought you someone special. A surprise for you. She'll be your mentor. She'll explain how things work and teach you some of the basics until we leave. Kip, may I present—"

"Liv?!" Kip said as the girl stepped out from behind Gavin.

"Kip!"

"Why don't you go ahead and take him up to his room, Liv," Gavin said. "And remember what I said."

Kip was still in a daze, so Liv took his hand and turned to lead him toward the main door. There would be a crowd there, no doubt. No need for Kip to think anything was out of the usual.

"Why don't you go the back way?" Gavin said. He turned and flung superviolet at the opposite wall. A section of the wall popped open on previously hidden hinges.

Liv took Kip out the back door.

Commander Ironfist and Luxlord Black came in the front door.

"Luxlord, Mistress, Commander, Magisters," Gavin said, waving a friendly hand to show he was simply too busy just now to speak with Ironfist or Luxlord Black. He walked toward the back door himself. He needed to get Kip now. He should have commanded the boy to wait outside the room instead of sending him upstairs.

Gavin stepped through the back door, already composing the letter he would leave for the White, and almost ran over a dark, demure little man in a slave's robe. He recognized the man and his heart dropped.

"Greetings, Lord Prism," the little man said, his headscarf so starched it barely moved as he bobbed his head. He'd been a Parian legalist before being captured by Ilytian pirates, enslaved, and eventually sold to Andross Guile. Brilliant and discreet, he'd been Andross Guile's right hand for twenty years. "Your father tires of your delays. He demands you come to his chambers immediately."

With Andross Guile, "immediately" meant yesterday. Gavin cringed inside, popped his neck right and left, and said, "Take me to him."

Chapter 46

Kip followed Liv Danavis through a narrow hall and then out to a lift. His head was still awhirl and his emotions were a riot that seemed not completely internal, as if somehow, additional emotions were being pressed onto him. It felt alien. Maybe it was just seeing Liv. He'd known she was at the Chromeria, and he'd hoped to see her ever since he'd known he was coming here, but actually seeing her was different.

Master Danavis had shared many of Liv's letters with Kip, so in some ways it didn't feel like it had been two full years, but she'd been fifteen then. He'd been thirteen. Apparently, he'd grown since then, because he was finally taller than she was. Of course, he was still also about three times wider than she was. If anything, she was even more beautiful than she had been.

As she led him through a hall and finally to a lift, she didn't say anything. Kip was glad for the silence. He didn't think he could have found his tongue. An odd, quiet joy and peace settled over him at seeing her. He remembered when she was fourteen years old and the rumor had run around town that she was going to be betrothed to Ged, the alcaldesa's son. Shortly thereafter, she'd left for the Chromeria. Kip had been relieved. She'd seemed too good for little Rekton. But though he was sure she hadn't thought of him since, he'd missed her. She had been like the sun passing overhead, and he'd turned his face as she passed, warmed by her presence, but never daring to hope for more. When Master Danavis had shared that Liv was having a hard time with some girl at the Chromeria, Kip had wanted to leave immediately and kill the offender, then come home.

Seeing her wavy hair swish and bounce around her shoulders as she led him was like standing in the sunlight again after a long winter. Kip didn't want words. Once he opened his big mouth, he'd surely spoil everything. He just watched her walk, hiking up his own pants gracelessly as she strode ahead, purposefully, at home, at ease, in command of her environment.

"I think I'm lost," Liv said. She looked to each side, down halls that looked exactly the same. She bit her lip.

Eyes locked on that full, slightly moist lip, Kip gulped.

"Kip?" she said. "No, never mind, of course you wouldn't."

She headed off again, and Kip followed. Liv had turned into a woman in the time she'd been away. She was as slender as he was fat. Her eyes large lucid brown, her skin smooth and clear where his was cursed with pimples around his neck and jaw as his beard was only just coming in. Thank Orholam, at least her chest was bigger than his.

Kip barely glanced there, though, and now as he followed her, he barely looked at her body. Her skirt did swoosh back and forth in a most pleasing manner as she walked, revealing slim, well-turned calves. But aside from a glance or two, or maybe three—Kip glanced again. Ah! Four. Aside from that, he didn't look at her the way he'd look at some other beautiful woman. It just didn't seem respectful.

Oops, five.

She stopped when they got into the lift. "I just realized," she said, laughing at herself, "that I have no idea where I'm supposed to take you. Uh, tell you what. You can come to my room until I get this figured out. If you're like I was after the Threshing, you'll probably need to go straight to bed. Right?"

Kip wasn't sure how he hadn't noticed before, but he *was* tired. He felt as if someone had taken the bottle of his energy and shaken it all out. He nodded his head.

"Don't feel like talking?" she asked, giving him a little grin. It was the kind of grin you gave a little child who'd missed nap time and was fighting to stay up to get dessert. But Kip couldn't even summon the passion to despair at seeing that indulgent grin on her.

I'm cute to her. *Cute*. Ugh.

She set the counterweights on the lift, paused for a moment—she must have been surprised how much weight she needed to add to account for Kip—and added more. In moments, they were speeding up the tower, passing other students going both up and down. They stopped and stepped into a wide lobby area that dimpled out to one of the clear tubes that connected the central tower to all the others.

Kip looked at Liv, eyebrows up.

"My apartments are over in yellow. Yellow's in the middle of the spectrum, so bichromes and polychromes include yellow more often than other colors, so the yellow tower has more bichrome apartments. They don't have the space for those in the Prism's Tower. Are you afraid of heights?"

"Not *usually*," Kip said uneasily.

"Oh, so you can talk!"

"I can fall too," he mumbled.

"You'll be fine, I promise," she said. She walked out into the tube. It was four paces across and enclosed with blue luxin so thin it was almost clear. The bottom of the walkway was thicker blue reinforced with thin bars of yellow. It looked impossibly thin. As Kip had seen from far, far below, the walkway attached to the Prism's Tower only at two places: on the east side and here, on the west. After going straight out about halfway to the green tower that was directly west of the Prism's Tower, this walkway met a great almost clear luxin circular walkway. From that circle, there were spokes out to each of the six towers.

Liv led Kip out to one of those intersections between circle and spokes, the point farthest from any support. She jumped up and down. "See, totally safe." She laughed. "Now you try it."

"I don't know," Kip said. If he could ever overcome his fear, the view from up here was magnificent. Of course, it was hard to look at mere magic towers when he had Liv right here. "Okay," he said weakly. He didn't want to let her down.

Of course, if I break this spindly walkway, I'll be letting us both down. The quick way.

Trying to be a good sport, Kip hopped a little, landing as lightly as possible on his toes and absorbing all the shock in his knees.

"Oh, seriously," Liv said.

Kip sighed and jumped so high he thought he was going to touch his head on the canopy. As he landed, he heard a loud crack.

He threw his hands out looking for something to grab, his heart seizing up. He was about to throw himself at the handrail when he saw Liv's face.

She laughed and covered her mouth. "I am so sorry," she said. "I shouldn't have. It's kind of a tradition for new students, and the Prism wanted me to give you the whole experience." Kip looked at her hands. They seemed to be clenched around something invisible. He tightened his eyes, and sure enough, she had a bar of superviolet luxin snapped in her hands.

Kip chuckled. It only sounded a little forced. "Give me the traditional mop, would you? I think I left a traditional puddle."

She laughed. "Thanks for being a good sport. If it makes you feel better, I almost fainted when my magister did it with our whole class. Come on, it's just a little farther now."

They walked together around the spindly circle, then turned toward the yellow tower. The yellow tower had been at the back right when Kip had entered the Great Yard, so he hadn't really seen it. Now it loomed both above and below.

"I think my eyes are full," Kip said.

"What?"

"I've seen too many amazing things today. Either this is just not as impressive, or I've lost my ability to be amazed, because to me, this looks like a plain yellow tower. No flames, no jewels, no twisty movement." The tower was luminous, but otherwise it looked like cloudy yellow glass, translucent, but not transparent. Maybe it was hard to see because the sun was going down beside the tower.

Liv smiled. He didn't know how he'd forgotten her dimples. "The yellow is amazing because it's made entirely of yellow luxin."

"And the others aren't," Kip said, not understanding. He blinked. "I mean, they're not made of their own colored luxin?"

"No, no, no. The others have magical façades built over traditional building materials. The yellow is made entirely of yellow."

From his admittedly brief instruction with the Prism, Kip thought that yellow was used like magical lanolin or something—it nourished other luxin, but otherwise degraded back into light easily. "Uh, I thought yellow was kind of a bad choice for a building material, being unstable and all." Kip was just remembering why he had been keeping his mouth shut. The more he talked with Liv, the more natural it would be for him to talk about home. And the more *unnatural* for him not to say anything about home. The moment they went there, he was going to have to tell Liv her father was dead, and the pleasant ease of being in her company would be shattered. She would go from this bright, glowing, dimpled young woman to a bereaved orphan.

"It *is* a bad choice," Liv said. "That's why this is so amazing." She pulled him toward the tower's entrance. Suddenly Kip didn't know if he wanted to leave the solidity of the blue-yellow spindles.

Sure, a minute ago, I was worried to step out on these, and now I don't want to leave.

"Yellow is usually the least stable luxin. It shimmers right back into light at the least movement, like water boiling away in a moment. That's why they call it brightwater. But do you remember when that harper played a few years ago back in Rekton, and he stopped between every song to retune his harp?"

Kip nodded. "It didn't seem to make any difference to me." Dangerous ground, talking about anything back home, but if he could keep her talking until he collapsed from exhaustion, he might avoid telling her the news for one more day.

Liv said, "The thing was, *he* could tell when his harp was even a fraction out of tune. No one else could, though. There are people who can do that with light. To make luxin of any color, you have to hit the right note within the color or the luxin won't form. If you are only approximately on pitch, the luxin is much more likely to fail. You can cover some mistakes with more will, but you need someone really special to do work like this."

"Does this have something to do with superchromats?" Kip asked. He felt like he was finally starting to put together some pieces.

"Yes." She seemed surprised that he'd heard of that. "You're not really going to stand out there all night, are you?"

"Oh." Kip followed her into the tower.

"Superchromats can see finer gradations in colors than most people."

"Are you one?" Kip asked.

"Mmm-hmm. About half of all women are."

"But not that many men."

"There are only ten male superchromats in the entire Chromeria."

Ah, thus Mistress Hag calling Kip a freak. "That doesn't seem fair," Kip said.

"What does fair have to do with it? Because you're blue-eyed you'll be able to draft more than I can. It's not a matter of fair."

Kip frowned. "So you've got to be a superchromat to make yellow stay?"

"Short answer? Yes. In truth, even superchromacy has degrees to it. You took that superchromacy test and there were maybe a hundred blocks with fine gradations? Imagine there were a thousand blocks, with the gradations of color that much finer. To make solid yellow that will stay, you'd have to pass *that* test—and then have the control to draft yellow in that tight, tight spectrum. The result, though, is the strongest of any luxin."

"Can you do it?" Kip asked.

"No."

"Uh, that was probably a rude question, huh?" Kip asked, wrinkling his face.

"I'm the last person here who's going to hold the minutiae of tower etiquette against you."

"Which is a yes."

"Yes," she said, smiling. Why were dimples so beautiful, anyway? "I still can't believe you're the Prism's... nephew, Kip."

"You're not the only one," Kip said. So Gavin had been right. They all did pause before they said nephew. He guessed it should have felt better than hearing that he was a bastard all the time. It didn't.

They got on another lift and went down. Apparently there was some sort of order of precedence for who got what rooms. When they got into Liv's room, Kip was surprised. It was not only large, but it was a suite of rooms—and facing the sunset. This had to be the kind of room most drafters would kill for.

"I just moved here," Liv said apologetically. "I'm a bichrome. Barely. I'm sure you're exhausted. You can sleep in my bed."

Kip looked at her, flabbergasted, sure that she wasn't saying what he thought she was saying, trying not to let his expression say anything at all.

"I'll sleep in the next room, silly. These new carpets are so thick I can sleep on them like a Parian."

Kip swallowed. "No, I didn't think you were—I mean, I was just—um, I was thinking I shouldn't take your bed. I should sleep in the next room."

"You're my guest, and you've got to be exhausted. I insist."

"I'm, uh, I don't want to get your bed all dirty. I'm sweaty and gross. From the testing." Kip was looking at her bed. It was beautiful. Everything here was beautiful. At least they'd been treating her well.

"The Thresher does that to people. I'll get you a basin and you can sponge off a little before you pass out, but really, I insist."

Liv disappeared into the next room. Kip felt a lump growing in his throat. He hadn't said anything so far about her father, but he could practically feel the subject growing between them. Liv came back in the room with steaming hot water, a sponge, and a thick towel. She set them down and then sat in a chair, facing away from Kip.

"You don't mind if I sit here and chat while you wash, do you?" she asked. "I won't turn around, swear."

"Uh." Of course he minded. She'd turn around when he was half naked and run screaming from the room, for Orholam's sake. It was one thing for someone to know you were rotund, but it was something else entirely for them to see your fat rolls. At the same time, he was her guest and she hadn't asked anything else of him. And he'd been rude.

"So, Kip...how's my father? You haven't said anything about home."

For a long moment, Kip couldn't say anything. Just start talking, Kip. Once you start, you'll be able to tell her everything.

"You're sighing," Liv said. "Is something wrong?"

"You know how the satrap would send messengers to Rekton every year asking for levies?"

"Yes?" Liv said her voice rising more with concern than asking a question.

"You can turn around, I'm not naked."

She turned.

"When Satrap Garadul's son Rask took power, he declared himself king. He sent another messenger. The town sent that one away empty-handed too, so he decided to make an example of us." Kip heaved a deep breath. "They killed everyone, Liv. I'm the only one who got away."

"My father? What about my father?"

"He was trying to save people. But Liv, they completely surrounded the town. No one got out."

"*You* got out." She didn't believe him; he could see it on her face.

"I was lucky."

"My father is one of the most talented drafters of his generation. Don't tell me that you made it out and he didn't."

"They had drafters and Mirrormen, Liv. I watched the Delclara family get run down. All of them. The whole town was on fire. I watched Ram and Isa and Sanson die. I watched my mother die."

"I don't care about your drug-addled mother. I'm talking about my father! Don't you tell me he's dead. He's not, damn you. He's not!"

Liv left the room in a whirlwind and slammed the door behind her.

Kip stared at the door, his shoulders slumped, tears that he didn't even understand in his eyes.

Well, that went well.

Chapter 47

Seven years, seven great purposes, Gavin.

Gavin held his right hand out and counted up from his thumb, drafting each color in turn: thumb to pinky, to ring finger, to middle finger, to index finger, back to middle, to ring, to pinky. A seven count, each color in turn, from sub-red to superviolet, feeling the little thread of emotion from each.

For Orholam's sake, I'm the Prism. I am the whole man. Master of all colors. In my prime. Stronger than any Prism in living memory. Maybe the strongest for hundreds of years. Most Prisms only lived seven years after their ascension. Only four had made it to twenty-one years. Always in multiples of seven—of course, they could be killed or die of natural causes too, but none burned out except on the multiple years. Gavin had made it to sixteen, so he had at least five years left. In fact, if any Prism could make it past twenty-one years, he would be the one to do it. He felt strong. He felt stronger and more in control of his colors than he had in his whole life.

Of course, it could all be an illusion. He'd been exceptional in other ways; perhaps he'd pitch over and die tomorrow.

He felt that familiar tightness in his chest again at the thought. He wasn't afraid of death, but he was afraid of dying before he accomplished his purposes.

He stood outside his father's apartments in the Prism's Tower. His father's slave—Gavin knew the man's name was Grinwoody, though it was rude to use a slave's name if they didn't reveal it to you themselves—was waiting, holding the door open. It was a door into darkness of more than one kind. There was sharp pain in Gavin's chest. It was hard to breathe.

Andross Guile didn't know Gavin wasn't Gavin. He didn't know his elder son was rotting under the Chromeria. He thought Dazen was dead, and he'd never seemed concerned about it, much less sorry. Traitors were to be dismissed and never spoken of.

"Lord Prism?" the slave asked.

Gavin shook the last tendrils of luxin from his fingers, the waft of resinous smells a small comfort.

Andross Guile's room was kept completely dark. Thick velvet drapes had been hung over the windows, then the whole wall hung with more of the same in layers. An entry chamber had been erected around the entrance so that light from the hallway wouldn't come in with his few visitors. Gavin drew in superviolet light and then stepped into the entry.

Grinwoody pulled the door shut behind them. Gavin drew a little ball of superviolet into his hand, drafted imperfectly so it would be unstable. The instability caused it to slowly disintegrate back into light of its own spectrum. For a superviolet drafter, it was like carrying a torch whose light was invisible to everyone else. Neither Grinwoody nor Andross was a superviolet, so Gavin could have as much of the eerie violet light as he wanted.

As Gavin watched, Grinwoody pushed a heavy pillow in front of the slight crack at the bottom of the door behind them. The man paused, letting his eyes become used to the darkness. He wasn't a drafter, so he couldn't directly control his eyes. In darkness, it took a dull—a non-drafter—half an hour or more to reach full sensitivity to light. Most drafters naturally could do it in ten minutes, just from spending so much time attuned to light. A few could reach full light sensitivity in seconds. But Grinwoody wasn't trying to see. He had obviously memorized the layout of the room years ago; he was simply making sure he wasn't allowing any light into High Master Guile's chamber. Finally, satisfied, he opened the door.

Gavin was glad to be holding superviolet. Like all drafters, he'd been taught not to rely on colors to change his moods. Like most, he failed often. It was a particular temptation for polychromes. There was a color for every feeling, or to counteract every feeling. Like right now. Using the superviolet spectrum was attended by a sense of remove or alienation or otherness. Sometimes it seemed ironic or cynical. Always it was like looking down at himself from above.

You're the Prism, and you're afraid of an old man.

In the superviolet light of his torch, Gavin saw his father sitting in a high-backed padded chair turned toward a covered, boarded-up window. Andross Guile had been a tall, powerfully built man. Now his weight had dropped from his broad shoulders to form a little ball in his paunch. He wasn't corpulent; it was just that what weight he had was in his gut. His arms and legs had grown thin from years spent hardly moving from that chair, his skin loose and spotted already at sixty-five.

"Son, so good of you to come visit. An old man grows lonely."

"I'm sorry, father. The White keeps me very busy."

"You shouldn't be so supine with that wheeled wench. You should arrange for the hag to join the Freeing this year."

Gavin let that pass without comment. It was an old argument. The White said the same things about Andross, minus the derogation. Gavin sat beside his father and studied him in the eerie superviolet light of his torch.

Despite the absolute darkness of the room, Andross Guile wore blackened spectacles molded tight around his eye sockets. Gavin couldn't imagine living in utter darkness. He hadn't even done that to his brother. Andross Guile had been a yellow to sub-red polychrome. Like so many other drafters during the False Prism's War, he'd pushed himself to his absolute limit. And beyond. He'd fought, of course, for his eldest son. Using too much magic, he'd finally destroyed his body's defenses against it. But after the war, when so many drafters had taken the Freeing, Andross had instead withdrawn to these rooms. When Gavin had first come to visit Andross here, there had been blue filters set on the windows. With his own power at the opposite end of the spectrum, Andross had felt safe with blue light. Since then, the chirurgeons had told him he needed complete darkness if he was to keep fighting the colors. If he was taking such extreme precautions, he must be very close to the brink indeed.

"I hear you're trying to start a war," Andross said.

"I rarely try without succeeding, I'm afraid," Gavin said. He didn't bother marveling that his father already knew. Of course Andross Guile knew. The man owned the loyalty or the fear of half of the most powerful women and men in the tower.

"How?"

"I received a letter that I had a natural son in Tyrea. When I arrived, the town was burning. I stumbled across some Mirrormen about to murder a child and I stopped them."

"Killed them."

"Yes. The child turned out to be my natural son, and the men turned out to be Rask Garadul's. He was making an example of the town for refusing to send levies. He claimed a special interest in the boy, but I'm not sure if that was just because he thought it would hurt me."

"A special interest? I thought he was there to punish the village."

"He said Kip had stolen something from him."

"And had he?"

"The boy claimed his mother had given him a jewelry case just before dying from injuries she took during the attack. He didn't steal it, though."

"But you have the dagger? Is it the white luxin?"

A chill shot down Gavin's spine. He'd thought the worst part of this interview would be his father picking through the details of affairs that Gavin hadn't actually had and thus couldn't remember. A white luxin dagger? White luxin wasn't possible, and for Andross Guile to speak about it like this meant he thought that it was. Or knew that it was. That he'd seen such a thing, and that he thought Gavin should know what he was talking about.

His brother had mentioned a dagger too. Gavin's chest tightened.

If he wasn't very careful, he was going to ruin his disguise. This was why he avoided his father as much as possible. Andross Guile was one of the few people who would know exactly which memories Gavin would have and which Dazen would have. Others who knew had been alienated or killed during the war. The feeble excuse that the severity of the brothers' fight to the death had made Gavin forget things would only go so far. Andross, in particular, might forgive him for misremembering things that happened in the run-up to the final battle, but surely Gavin would remember things that had happened years earlier, wouldn't he?

"I didn't see the dagger," Gavin said. "It was in a box. It didn't even occur to me it might be the white luxin." White luxin was impossible. Gavin would know. He'd tried to make the mythic material himself—and as a Prism, he would be the one who was able to do it if it could be done at all.

"Idiot boy, I don't know why I always favored you. Dazen was smarter by half, but I always took your side, didn't I?"

Gavin looked at the ground and nodded. The first kind word he'd heard from his father about himself in years, and it was delivered as a rebuke.

"Are you nodding your head or shaking it? In case you'd forgotten, I'm blind," Andross said bitterly. "Never mind. I understand your own secrecy in hunting the dagger—even my spies haven't heard of you bumbling about, so bravo for that—but when you stumbled across a suspicious dagger that some halfpenny king wanted badly, that didn't send shivers up the back of your neck?"

"I was surrounded by thirty hostile drafters, Mirrormen, and an extremely put-out king. I had plenty of shivers."

Andross Guile waved his hand, like none of that was worth considering. "With no Blackguards guarding you, I suppose. Stubborn, fool boy. What was the box made of?"

"Rosewood, maybe?" Gavin said honestly.

"Rosewood." Andross Guile sighed deeply. "Alone it proves nothing, of course. But it tells you what you have to do."

"I was planning to rally the Seven Satrapies, speak to each directly, see if I could sway them," Gavin said. "The Spectrum, of course, will do nothing." He knew how this went. His father would announce what Gavin would do and run right over everything Gavin threw in his path. For Orholam's sake, I'm the Prism.

"And by the time you've done that, King Garadul will have taken

Garriston. You were right in everything you told the Spectrum, though you drew the wrong lesson and the wrong course of action. Which is why you have me. If you'd spoken with me as soon as you returned, I'd have told you this. By withdrawing unilaterally and giving a jewel into Tyrean hands—"

"Hardly a jewel, father—"

"You dare interrupt! Come here."

Woodenly, Gavin sat across from his father. Andross Guile extended a hand and found Gavin's face. He traced Gavin's cheek almost gently. Then he drew his open hand back and cracked it across Gavin's cheek.

"I am your father, and you will give me the respect you owe me, understood?"

Gavin trembled, swallowed, mastered himself. "Understood, father."

Andross Guile's chin lifted as if he was sifting Gavin's tone for anything displeasing. Then, as if nothing had happened, he continued. "Garadul covets Garriston, so even if it's a tower of feces built on a plain of ordure, giving it to him is weakness. The right course would be to raze the city, enslave the inhabitants, and sow the fields with salt—and leave before he arrived. But you've destroyed that option with your incompetence. And once King Garadul holds Garriston with twenty thousand men, you'll find it a lot harder to take back than he's going to find it to take when only a thousand are holding it."

"The Ruthgari only have a thousand men holding Garriston?" Gavin asked. It was less than a skeleton crew. If he hadn't been in such a hurry when he sculled through Garriston, he surely would have noticed.

"Troubles with the Aborneans hiking the tariff to travel through the Narrows again. The Ruthgari are making a statement with a show of force. They pulled the ships and most of the soldiers from Garriston."

"That's moronic. They have to know Garadul is massing troops."

"I agree. I think the Ruthgari foreign minister has been suborned. She's smart, she must know what she's doing. Regardless, you must go to Garriston. Save the city, kill Rask Garadul, but even if you fail those, get that dagger. Everything rests on that."

What "everything"? Here was the problem with pretending to know secrets you didn't know. Secrets, especially big, dangerous secrets, tended to be referred to obliquely. Especially when the conspirators knew spies were frequently eavesdropping on them.

Maybe I should have taken my chances with claiming to have forgotten what the dagger was.

There had been a time when Dazen had known all of Gavin's secrets, even those that were supposed to be just between Gavin and their father. Dazen and Gavin hadn't just been brothers. They'd been best friends. Though Dazen was two years younger, Gavin treated him like an equal. Sevastian was younger; they made him stay home. Gavin and Dazen had the same friends. Together, they won and lost fistfights against the White Oak brothers. Gavin missed the simplicity of those fights. Two sides, lots of fists, and once one side started bleeding or crying, the fight was over.

But Gavin had changed on the day he turned thirteen. Dazen was not yet eleven at the time. Andross Guile had come in his dress robes, looming, impressive in red-gold brocade and red-gold chains around his neck. Even then, after having been a member of the Spectrum for a decade, Andross Guile had always been referred to as Andross Guile, never Andross Red. Everyone had always known which was the more important. Andross had taken Gavin away.

When Gavin came back the next morning, his eyes were swollen like he had been crying, though he angrily denied it when Dazen asked. Whatever had happened, Gavin was never the same. He was a man now, he told Dazen, and he refused to play with him. When the White Oak brothers tried to pick a fight, Gavin filled himself with such deep sub-red that the heat emanated from him in waves, and he quietly told the brothers that if they attacked him, the result would be on their own heads.

In that moment, Dazen knew Gavin really would have killed them, too.

From then on, Gavin had spoken to their father as a confidant. Dazen had been left to fall by the wayside. For a time, he'd played with Sevastian. Then Sevastian was taken too, and he'd been alone. Dazen had hoped when he turned thirteen he'd be welcomed back into their graces, but his father had barely acknowledged the date. When it came time for it to be divined whom Orholam had chosen to be his next Prism, all of Big Jasper and Little Jasper was a whirl of speculation, but Dazen knew his older brother was the one. How it happened didn't matter. Andross had been grooming Gavin to be Prism for his whole life.

And I was groomed to be nothing. A castoff to marry Karris White Oak or some other girl to deflect some other father's ambitions. Until Gavin tried to take even that from me.

The hardest part of maintaining his disguise was here—not in pretending to be Gavin, but in being reminded of all Gavin had had and that Dazen never would.

"So, go to Garriston, save it or burn it, kill Garadul, and get the dagger. Sounds simple enough." If Gavin did things right, that would fulfill one of his purposes, and set the stage for another.

Andross said, "I'll give you letters to the Ruthgari to make sure they'll obey you."

"You're going to make me the governor of Garriston?" Every time Gavin forgot how powerful his father was—even from this little room—Andross did something to remind him.

"Not officially. If you fail it would besmirch our name. But I'm making sure that the governor does whatever you tell him."

"But the Spectrum—"

"Can, on occasion, be ignored. It's not so easy to depose a Prism, you know. When you return, we'll talk about getting you married. It's time you start making heirs. You showing up with a bastard presses the issue."

"Father, I'm not—"

"If you crush one of the satraps, even a rebel one, you're going to need to buy off one of the others. It's time. You will obey me in this. We'll talk about the bastard problem later."

Chapter 48

Liv had gone to the light garden high in the yellow tower to think, but it seemed she couldn't walk ten paces without stumbling over some young couple kissing. As the sun went down, the light garden became spectacular—and a favorite of couples. Liv should have remembered. There was something particularly jarring in the sight of young lovers when she was feeling so isolated.

She left, her emotions tumbling over each other, sorry she'd been so rude to Kip, certain she was right that her father was still alive, and scared to death she was wrong. Lonely, scared of her future, and now—hit in the face with how easy everyone else seemed to find it to find someone who liked her—lonely for a boy. Any boy. Well, practically. Liv had been at the Chromeria for three years, and the best she'd done was have a few near-misses at relationships. Being Tyrean, being the daughter of a general on the losing side, and being poor had ended most interest before it began. The one boy she'd thought really cared for her had invited her to the Luxlords' Ball and then had stood her up and gone with another girl. Apparently it had been a prank. The next year she'd briefly become the object of a competition between some of the most popular boys. For two weeks, it was glorious to be the center of attention. She'd felt like she'd finally broken through, that people were finally accepting her. One of them invited her to the Luxlords' Ball.

Then she overheard one of the others talking about a wager they had to see who could swive her first. Her revenge had been swift and terrible. She'd promised the boy escorting her to the ball—the leader of the group, a young noble named Parshan Payam—her maidenhead if he helped her fulfill a naughty dream of hers. He'd practically drooled.

At the Luxlords' Ball, they'd met in a darkened nook just off the main hall. She'd convinced Parshan to remove all of his clothes first, despite the proximity of practically the entire Chromeria dancing, talking, and drinking mere paces away. Then, pausing from kissing him while his loathsome hands wandered over her body, she asked how much he was going to win for winning the contest.

"You know? You're not mad?" he asked.

"Why would I be mad?" she asked. "Close your eyes. I've got a surprise for you."

"A good surprise?" he asked.

She trailed her fingernails down his belly. Looked down. Licked her lips. "It'll take your breath away. Promise."

He closed his eyes. She grabbed all of his clothes and stormed out into the party. He came after her with a yelp, rushing naked into the party. "This is what you get for your contest, Parshan Payam!" Liv shouted, just so that anyone who hadn't immediately seen the naked young man would notice and know who it was.

The dancers stopped. The musicians quit playing. A hundred conversations ceased. "Wagering with your friends on who can take my virginity?! You're despicable. A cad and a liar. You disgust me. You're not smart enough to fool me, you're not clever enough to deceive me, and you're not man enough to take me." She plunged his priceless clothes into the punch bowl.

Nervous titters broke out everywhere. Parshan froze. With his clothes soaking in punch, it was pointless to retrieve them to cover himself. He did his best to cover himself with his hands.

Amid silence punctuated with scattered applause, Liv stormed out of the hall and straight into Chromeria legend. Unfortunately, passing into tower lore for wreaking vengeance on a boy who'd taken a romantic interest in you—regardless of how ignoble that interest was—was not a good way to encourage interest from others. All the other boys were terrified of her.

Why am I thinking about boys? My father's dead.

No, he's not. Father's gotten out of worse things. He wouldn't allow himself to be trapped. He's smarter than that.

Still, it would be nice to have someone to talk to. Honestly, a good cry would make her feel a lot better.

Liv trudged down to Vena's room, but when she got there, *Vena* was crying. It broke Liv out of her own self-pity instantly. Vena wasn't just crying; she was bawling. Vena's usually artfully disheveled boyishly short hair was smashed down on her head as if she'd been holding her head in her hands. Her eyes were swollen.

"I can't believe it, Liv! I've been looking for you everywhere. Liv!" Vena said. "It's a disaster. Orholam, Liv, I'm being sent home!"

Looking around the room, Liv saw that all of Vena's stuff was already packed up and in large trunks. With how much stuff Vena owned and all the decorations she'd strewn over every open space in her little room, Liv knew she couldn't have packed it all herself.

"What's going on?"

It took a few minutes to get it all out in some sort of sensible order, even though the story was simple: Vena had lost her sponsorship. The Abornean lord who held her contract had lost a fortune in some business venture and needed to cut his expenses. Apparently he'd shopped Vena's contract around and found no buyers. Some other, younger drafter's lord had bought Vena's room from him, though. She was to vacate it immediately. Vena had been purchased passage home, tonight. She would have to meet with her sponsor to determine how he could best make back his investment from her.

Vena could end up as a serving girl, but she feared her lord might sell her to slavers. It was illegal—a drafter's indenture was a far cry from slavery—but there were always stories of such things.

"Liv, could you loan me some money? I could run away."

"I can't—"

"Please, Liv, I'm begging you. I know it's not a loan. I'll never be able to pay you back, but I can't face going back. Please."

Liv's heart dropped. If she'd waited just one week to meet the moneylenders, she'd have drawn one more installment of her allowance, and she'd have ample money to help out her friend. "I just paid off a debt, Vena. I've got nothing left. It cost me everything."

Vena wilted.

"Wait, we could sell some of my dresses. If you can wait until morning—"

"No, forget it. They'll be looking for me by then. And they know you're my only friend. They'll be watching you. It was a stupid idea. I need to go face this."

A knock on the door. "Miss?" a man's voice called out.

Vena opened the door and four men in slaves' clothes came in and picked up the trunks. Vena picked up her own bag. "Walk me to the docks?" she asked Liv, putting on a brave face.

Still horrified, disbelieving, Liv nodded.

They walked slowly, as if they could postpone the inevitable forever.

"This really is a great place," Vena said, as they crossed the bridge for the last time together. "It's a marvel. And I was here. For a while. My father was a servant; my mother was a servant. There's nothing wrong with going home and serving. I'm not better than they are. And you know what? I met the Prism!" Her eyes were gleaming. "He called me marvelous! He complimented my dress. Me. He noticed *me*, Liv, with all those beautiful girls there. No one can take that away from me. How many people—how many drafters never get that much in their whole lives? The Prism himself!"

Her bravery made Liv tear up. She studiously avoided looking at Vena, sure she'd lose control if she did.

But all too soon, they were at the docks. They said their goodbyes tearfully, promising to write, Liv promising that she would use any connections she could make to get Vena reinstated. Vena smiled sadly, resigned.

"Come on, ladies," the captain said. "Time and the tide wait for no man, nor for blubbering girls, neither."

Liv hugged Vena one more time and left. She'd barely stepped off the wood of the dock when she saw a familiar figure lurking in the shadows like a spider. Aglaia Crassos.

"You!" Liv said. "This is your work!"

Aglaia smiled. "I wonder, Liv, do you think we owe a debt to our friends? A debt of love, or duty?"

"Of course we do."

"But apparently your duty to your friend isn't as important as your need to defy me."

"You bitch," Liv said, quivering.

"I'm not the one who's letting her friend pay for my pride. It can stop, Liv, or it can get worse."

"You still want me to spy on the Prism."

"Vena's not going home, just so you know. I own her contract already. And I've got a deal with a rather...dubious Ilytian. He's willing to give me a good price for Vena. Most people have scruples about selling drafters. Of course, she's not a full drafter, so she won't be entitled to any of a drafter's normal privileges. But, hey, Vena loves sailing, right? Not many women on the galleys. They don't usually last very long, nor do the other slaves treat them well, so owners usually put women to other work. But I can arrange it."

Not just a slave. A galley slave. The worst of the worst. Liv wanted to vomit. She wanted to murder Aglaia. Orholam save her.

"Or..." Aglaia said, "you give me the word." She nodded toward a messenger standing across the street. "And he runs to the captain with a message, saying it's all a mistake, Vena's been reinstated, and so forth. Wonder of wonders. You are my own special project, Liv. You have my full attention."

Liv looked at the boat, despairing. It was true. She had no friends, no options, no choices. How could she fight Aglaia Crassos, with all her wealth and power? If she asked the Prism for help, he'd ask questions. He'd think she'd been spying all along. Every part of the Chromeria and the satrapies was corrupt; they were all turned against her.

"Hurry, Liv, the tide's turning," Aglaia said.

There was no way out, no time to try to come up with a third way. Maybe her father would have said no and spat in Aglaia's ugly face and held on to his honor. Liv wasn't that strong. The sharks and sea demons had her. "Fine," she said, her heart failing within her. "You win. What do I have to do?"

Chapter 49

Gavin hadn't even gotten fully out of his father's apartments when he saw trouble coming. His mother's apartments were right beside his father's, and there was no way he could leave without passing in front of her doors—and her doors were open.

Every time. Every burning time. If his father's windows hadn't all been bolted shut and covered with layers of fabric, Gavin would have jumped out of a window. In fact, it was just during one of these sorts of situations that he'd first drafted a bonnet. Every time he came back from even the shortest trip, it seemed he spent all day meeting with one important person after another. All he did was meet with people—and every one of them had demands of him.

Nonetheless, Gavin turned in as he went past his mother's open doors. The room slave was a young Tyrean girl, judging from her dark eyes and hair and kopi-colored skin. Gavin motioned to her as he passed that she could close the doors behind him. His mother had a talent for training slaves: even a girl barely in her teens like this one would wait attentively and respond to the smallest signal. Of course, Gavin wasn't so much different, was he?

"Mother," Gavin said. She stood as he came close. He kissed her many-ringed fingers, and she laughed and embraced him, as she always did.

"My son," she said. Felia Guile was a handsome woman in her early fifties. She had been a cousin of the Atashian royal family, and in her youth the Atashian noble families rarely married foreigners. Andross Guile, of course, had been a special case. He always was. She had the classic, striking Atashian pairing of olive skin and cornflower blue eyes, though her blue eyes bore a wide halo of dull orange around the iris. She had been an orange drafter—though she wasn't greatly talented, Andross would never have married a woman who couldn't draft. Slim despite her age, Felia was regal, fashionable, comfortable in herself, commanding without being domineering, beautiful, and warm.

He had no idea how she could stand being married to his father.

She flicked two fingers of her left hand, dismissing the room slave without taking her eyes off Gavin. "So, I hear a rumor that you have a...nephew."

Gavin cleared his throat. How fast did word travel in this place, anyway? He looked around the room. The slave was gone. "That's correct."

"A natural son," Felia Guile said, her lips pulling taut momentarily. She would never say "bastard." With her huge palette of facial expressions, she didn't have to. Over the years, orange had made her both more empathetic and more suspicious. With her natural intuition and intelligence, it made her quite formidable.

"That's right. He's a good young man. His name's Kip."

"Fifteen years old?" She didn't say, So you cheated on your fiancée, whom I've been urging you to marry for the last sixteen years. Felia loved Karris. Andross Guile had been dead set against Gavin marrying a woman whose family had nothing, like Karris's, after the war. It was one of the few areas where Gavin's mother had continued to defy his father. Usually when they disagreed, she would let her objections be known with force and eloquence, and then concede to whatever Andross decided. Not a few times, Gavin had seen Andross change his mind after his mother so artfully surrendered. The disagreement over Karris White Oak, however, had involved screaming, shattered porcelain, and tears. Gavin thought sometimes that if he hadn't been present during that fight, Andross would have given in, but the man couldn't lose face in front of anyone, much less his boundary-pushing son.

"He is," Gavin said.

Felia folded her hands and studied his face. "So, is his existence as much of a surprise to you as it is to everyone else, or more?"

A shiver shot down Gavin's spine. His mother was no fool. She was as careful to guard against eavesdroppers as anyone, but she had ways of getting to exactly what she meant. After Sundered Rock, when Gavin had staggered alone out of the magical conflagration, wearing his brother's clothing and his brother's crown and his brother's scars under layers of soot and blood, everyone else had taken him to be Gavin unquestioningly. Despite the age difference, the brothers had been mistaken for twins dozens of times, and their mannerisms were uncannily similar. And Gavin had been careful to emulate his brother's idiosyncrasies of vocabulary and expression. Any differences that had emerged after the war ended had been written off as Gavin having been changed by having to kill his own brother.

But Gavin woke the morning of his first night back at the Chromeria to find his mother sitting on the foot of his bed. Her eyes were red and puffy from weeping, though her cheeks were dry. She'd been careful to do her weeping before he woke.

"Did you think I wouldn't know my own boy?" she had asked. "You're the blood of my blood. Did you think you could deceive even me?"

"I didn't think it would work this long, mother. I expected any of a hundred people to see through this farce, but what else can I do?"

"I understand why you've done what you've done," she said. "I just had braced myself against your death, not your brother's, and now to see you...It's like having to choose which of my remaining sons I'd prefer to die."

"No one's asking that of you."

"Just tell me this," she said. "Is Gavin dead?"

"Yes," he'd said. "I didn't want...He gave me no...I'm sorry."

Her eyes had streamed tears, but she ignored them. "What do you need, Dazen? I've lost both of your brothers; I swear to Orholam I won't lose you."

"Tell them I'm convalescing. Tell them the battle nearly killed me. When the time is right, tell them it changed me. But don't make me look weak."

And so she'd become his only true ally in the Chromeria. And after she left, he'd barred the door and opened the chest where his drugged brother lay, not a foot from where their mother had stood. He studied the unconscious figure minutely, and then himself in a mirror. Taking note of every difference, he set to work. His brother's hair had a cowlick that stuck out whenever he cut it short; the new Gavin would have to wear his hair long so no one noticed this disparity. Gavin was a little shorter than Dazen, and had liked to wear boots with more heel; the new Gavin would wear flatter shoes. He began writing lists of his brother's mannerisms, the way Gavin liked to pop his neck to the left and right. Or was it right and left? Damn it, Dazen didn't even know how to pop his neck. Gavin liked to shave every day, even twice a day, to keep his face smooth; Dazen had shaved a few times a week, finding it too much bother. Gavin always wore a particular scent; Dazen had never bothered. He'd have to send a servant to fetch it. Gavin cared about his clothing and made sure he was at the forefront of every trend; Dazen didn't even know how he did that. He'd need to look into it. Had Gavin plucked his eyebrows? Dear Orholam.

Other changes were harder to make. Dazen had a mole on the inside of one elbow. Grimacing, he sliced it off. It would become a little scar. No one would notice.

His mother helped, coming every day, handkerchief in hand for her silent tears, but back ramrod straight. She pointed out quirks Dazen never would have remembered, like the way his brother stood when he was thinking, and what foods Gavin loved and what he hated.

But the biggest reason for his success had been the real Gavin himself. Gavin had painted Dazen as a False Prism. He'd sworn that Dazen deceived his retainers with parlor tricks that would never convince anyone who wasn't criminal or insane or who stood to benefit by standing with a False Prism. Everyone knew there was only ever one Prism every generation, so they'd believed the old Gavin implicitly. So from their first glance at Dazen's prismatic eyes, they *knew* he was Gavin. Those who knew better, who knew that Dazen had never needed parlor tricks, who knew he was as much a Prism as Gavin—in other words, Dazen's closest retainers and friends—had been scattered to the four winds after the Battle of Sundered Rock. He'd betrayed them, and if it was a betrayal for the greater good, it still kept him up nights to know that Ilytian pirates were selling his people for slaves in a hundred ports. He drew up his first list of seven great purposes, and he did what he could.

And through it all, his mother had saved him a dozen times. She deserved the truth.

"More," he told her now. It was more of a surprise to him than to anyone that he had a son. He and his men had been living in caves and on the run, and even if he'd had the energy for entertaining some of the camp followers, he'd been heartsick over Karris's engagement to Gavin. Dazen hadn't slept with anyone during the war.

She stood and walked to the door, opened it to see that no one was eavesdropping, and returned. Quietly, she said, "So you've adopted your brother's natural son. Why?"

Because you're always bothering me about giving you a grandson, he almost said, but he knew that would wound her. Because it's the right thing to do? Because Gavin would have? No, he wasn't sure that Gavin would have. Because the boy had nothing and he deserved a chance? Because Karris was there watching and there was something perversely pleasurable about wounding her by doing what was right? "Because I know what it's like to be alone," Gavin said. He was surprised that it was the truth.

"You don't give Karris enough credit," his mother said.

"What's she got to do with anything?"

His mother just shook her head. "She didn't take it well?"

"You might say that," Gavin said.

"What are you going to do if your father refuses to recognize the boy?"

"He's not moving me on this, mother. I don't do very many things that are right. He's not taking this one away."

She smiled suddenly. "Did it make your list of seven purposes this time? Defying him?"

"My list only has things that are possible."

"So it's harder than stopping the Blood War? Harder than destroying the pirate lords?"

"Twice," Gavin said. "And yes."

"You get that from him, you know."

"What?"

"Your father always made lists, goals to check off. Marry a girl from the right family by twenty-five, join the Spectrum by forty—he made it by thirty-five—and so on. Of course, he never had to organize his life in seven-year blocks."

"Did he never want to be Prism himself?" Gavin asked.

She didn't answer right away. "Prisms usually only last seven years."

Not long enough for my father. I see. "He wanted more sons and daughters, didn't he?" Even after Sevastian. More tools. More weapons, in case more went bad.

She said nothing. "I want to go home, Gavin. I've wanted to join the Freeing for years. I'm so tired."

For a moment, Gavin couldn't breathe. His mother was the very quintessence of life. Beauty, energy, cleverness, good nature. To hear her speak as if she were broken down, as if she wanted to quit, was like a blow to the stomach.

"Of course, your father will never allow it," she said, smiling sadly. "But whether he allows it or not, sometime in these next five years, I'm joining. I've buried two sons. I will not bury you." So she was just giving him warning, giving him time to prepare. Dear Orholam, he didn't even want to think about it. His mother had been his only companion, his best adviser, the one person who sniffed out threats from leagues away and loved him no matter what.

"So, what were your seven purposes? Accomplished any of them yet?" she asked, bringing the conversation back to safe ground, even though she knew he would dodge.

"I learned to fly. Took me most of the last year."

She looked at him like she couldn't tell for once whether he was joking. "That could prove handy," she said carefully.

Gavin laughed.

"You're serious," she said.

"I'll have to take you for a ride—a flight?—sometime," Gavin said. "You'll love it."

"And you think the idea of that is a good enough distraction to sidetrack me from getting the rest of your goals out of you?"

"Absolutely," Gavin said, in mock seriousness. "I learned from the best."

"Very well," she said. "Now get out of here." He was halfway out the door when she called. "Gavin!" She called him Gavin now, always, even when her eyes called him Dazen. "Be careful. You know how your father is when someone won't do what he wills."

Chapter 50

Kip woke with a dead arm from a dream about his mother holding his head in her lap. It wasn't a dream; it was half memory. He'd been young. His mother was running her fingers through his hair, her eyes red, swollen. Red eyes usually meant she'd been smoking haze, but this morning she didn't smell of smoke or alcohol. I'm sorry, she said, I'm so sorry. I've quit. It's going to be different from now on. I promise.

He cracked open one sleep-snot-encrusted eye and moaned. That's nice, mother, can you just get off my arm? He rolled over. He'd slept on the ground? On a carpet? Oh! As the blood slowly flooded back into his arm, it started hurting. He rubbed it until feeling returned. Where was he? Oh, Liv's room. It was barely dawn.

Sitting up, Kip saw a woman coming in the room. Maybe the opening door had woken him. Liv must have slept elsewhere. The covers of the bed weren't even disturbed.

"Good morning, Kip," the woman said. She was a dark woman, with heavy eyebrows, frizzy hair, and a flamboyant gold scarf around her neck. She was thick, hugely tall, with great heavy shoulders and a bold-patterned green dress draped over her like a sheet over a galleass. "It's dawn, and time for your first lesson. I'm Mistress Helel."

"You're my magister?" Kip said, still rubbing his hurting arm.

"Oh yes." She smiled, but the smile didn't touch her eyes. "And you'll remember today's lesson for the rest of your life. Get up, Kip."

Kip stood. She walked past him and opened a door to a small balcony outside Liv's room.

"Come quickly," she said. "You need to see this before the sun is fully over the horizon."

Hair squashed, mouth full of cotton, breath foul, arm throbbing, Kip licked his dry lips and stepped past Mistress Helel. Her eyes were dark and intense—so dark that he couldn't even tell what color of a drafter she was.

Weird. Here I'm supposed to see minute differentiations in colors undetectable to most people, and I couldn't even see the color in her irises. He stepped onto the pure yellow luxin balcony. Aside from streaks of water or dirt, the entire thing was eerily clear.

Despite his experience yesterday learning that the yellow was one of the strongest materials known, Kip tested his weight on the balcony gingerly. It was, of course, solid. Due to the way the towers all leaned out, as if blossoming, if Kip fell from here, he'd smash on the rocks several hundred feet below, just shy of the water. It was even worse for the floors above them, which leaned even farther out. He gulped and tried to pay attention to the rising sun.

"We don't have all day, Kip," Mistress Helel said. There was something in her voice, a tension.

Kip turned as she stepped out onto the balcony with him. At first he thought she was tripping, because she lunged forward so suddenly. He moved toward her to catch her. If there was one thing good about being fat, it was that he could stop big weights.

But Mistress Helel extended both of her hands like battering rams. Kip's move forward brought him between her arms. Her thumbs scratched across his chest and off both sides. She cursed as they crushed together in an awkward hug.

"I've got you," Kip said. "Don't worry, you're not going to—"

The big woman stood to her full height, regaining her balance. She was much taller than Kip, and the move pressed big flat breasts onto either side of his face. Somehow his chin got caught in her dress's gaping neckline as she stood and for a brief—but not nearly brief enough—moment, Kip's face was fully engulfed in flabby cleavage.

"Gah!" Kip blurted.

Mistress Helel was already bending over, mercifully freeing her neckline of Kip's chin, but then bending farther, her body pressing against his. After an experience that he was doubtless going to relive in dreams—and not the good kind—he sidled out of the way.

The woman's big meaty hands slapped on Kip's right and left legs. His move to the side made her left hand slip off his right leg, though. Then she lifted.

"What are you—" Kip stopped as soon as he saw her eyes.

Dead concentration, complete lack of emotion. She pushed forward hard into Kip, lifting. He put it all together far too slowly.

The intensity, the story, the lack of color in her eyes, the stumble that hadn't been a stumble. It had been a lunge. The lack of embarrassment at Kip being pressed against her breasts—because you don't let the touch of a little flesh deter you. Not when you've come to kill.

Kip's hands slapped against the edge of the balcony behind him. With only one leg in her hands, Mistress Helel lifted sharply. She was so strong that Kip's weight was no problem for her.

If he'd been a brave man, Kip would have fought her. If he'd been flexible, he would let her pick up the one leg while he stood on the other and beat her to a bloody pulp. Instead, Kip took the fatty's way. He went limp, floppy, making all his weight dead weight, seeking the ground the way he'd done when Ram would try to show off by picking him up and throwing him on the ground. If Kip collapsed, Ram could never lift him, where if he held himself rigid, Ram could hold his weight easily.

Mistress Helel brought one hand off Kip's left leg, seeking a grip anywhere on his round body. Kip wriggled like a fish, pushing off the balcony, trying to push himself back into the tower. She pinned him against the corner of the balcony with her own substantial weight and drew back her left hand to punch him.

But the floor called him, and without her strong arm to hold him, Kip answered. Her fist descended and landed a glancing blow, but Kip fell. She lost her hold and he went turtle, barely keeping a grip on his pant leg. Cursing, she tried to lift him by that alone.

His pants ripped, and then slipped off his waist. They tangled around his knees, but however his baggy pants hampered his movements, they did nothing to help the assassin lift him either. She cursed him and punched his leg, taking a wide stance to pound him. He yelped. Then she slugged him in the stomach, taking his breath away. She snarled. "Take your death like a man."

Kip bit her ankle.

The assassin cried out and fell on top of him. She recovered enough to land knee-first on his chest. Then she angled her fall so she crushed and trapped him. Apparently Kip wasn't the only one who knew how to use his weight to good advantage. She landed with her head toward his feet.

She trapped one of Kip's legs in one iron hand. Then she punched his thigh. She caught it dead center. It was like being kicked by a horse. He screamed. Then she grabbed his other leg. No amount of thrashing could break her grip. It was hard to even breathe with her on top of him, her legs crushing his face. She pummeled his other leg, and it too went dead. She pushed herself up and punched him in the groin.

Stars flashed in front of Kip's eyes. Any thought of counterattack fled. He just wanted to curl into a ball. Her weight shifted, crushing him again, and then she stood. She had one of his ankles in each of her hands, and she lifted him easily. She was going to toss him over the balcony, dear Orholam. There was nothing he could do to stop it.

Eyes squinted in pain, weakly thrashing, Kip saw a thin beam of superviolet luxin stick to the assassin's head.

"Stop it! Drop him now!" a young woman screamed from inside the room. Liv?

The assassin snarled a curse and turned toward Liv just as a yellow luxin ball blasted from her hands, zipped along the superviolet line, and exploded in a blinding flash against the assassin's face. Mistress Helel dropped Kip, lifting a hand to protect herself too late, and staggered backward.

She was so tall that the rail of the balcony caught her below the waist. She hit it hard and tottered. Her meaty hands slapped onto the rail as she went on tiptoe, feet seeking purchase. Kip, lying on the ground, slid a hand under her foot and lifted. Not hard—he was in so much pain he could barely move—but it was enough.

The assassin felt herself going over the edge and scrambled. She fell—and caught herself on the rail of the balcony. Through the clear yellow of the balcony, she swung face-to-face with Kip. Each balcony had a small gap for rainwater to sluice off so it wouldn't fill with water, and the big woman's face was barely a foot from Kip's own.

Kip looked at her. He knew how this ended. Some skinny woman might be able to pull her weight up, but not a woman this size. Kip was strong—he could lift heavier things than Sanson or even Ram— but when you were really big, heaving your entire weight over a ledge was impossible. And this woman was much bigger than he was. Mistress Helel heaved, and for one terrifying moment Kip thought he was wrong. Her elbows bent and her body lifted. She swung one heavy leg to the side, trying to reach it high enough to reach the rain-gap in the balcony.

Then her strength gave out and she swung back to vertical. She was finished. Kip could see it in her eyes. "Light cannot be chained, Little Guile," she said. "Anat blind you. Mot smite you to the tenth generation. Belphegor blight your sons. Atirat spit on your mother's grave. Ferrilux corrupt your father's—"

Kip punched her through the rain-gap. Her nose crunched in a spray of blood. She must have been expecting the blow, because she tried to snag his fist—but missed.

She fell, flailing all the way, screaming something, but Kip couldn't make out the words. She slammed into a sharp boulder not five paces from the crashing waves of the Cerulean Sea, and her body actually burst asunder, a piece—a leg?—shearing off and flying to splash into the water as the rest of her crunched in one long bloody smudge.

It didn't seem real. Part of Kip knew that could have been him, maybe should have been him, but he was suddenly aware of Liv standing just inside her apartments. "Kip, Kip, we killed her," Liv was saying. Kip was more aware that his balls were aching and he was pretty much naked in front of the only girl he knew, and he was fat and gross and should cover himself immediately.

He'd barely hiked up his pants by the time Liv lurched to the balcony rail and vomited. Kip hated throwing up. He hated himself throwing up, and he hated other people throwing up. But worst, he discovered, as the wind blew across the yellow tower and carried mist through the rain-gap, Kip hated being thrown up *on*. Little misty wetness stuck to his face and in his open mouth.

He rolled over, spitting and coughing and slapping at his own face to wipe off puke-mist. He rolled to his feet, balls still aching, face scrunched.

"Oh no," Liv said, her face gray and mortified, realizing she'd thrown up on him. She looked from him, to his crotch where his pants were torn, and then to the rocks so far below. She struggled for words and found none.

"You know, I'm glad things aren't awkward between us," Kip said. Did I really just say that? It was like part of him couldn't help being totally inappropriate. He'd just killed someone, and he was so terrified and pained and embarrassed and mortified and thankful to be alive and he didn't even know what all else, he couldn't help himself.

Liv's mouth twitched up for half a moment, and then she leaned back over the rail and vomited again.

Always something to say, never the right thing. Well done, Kip.

Chapter 51

"Midsummer is coming," the White said. "Sun Day."

Gavin stood in front of her on the top of the Chromeria. Together, they were waiting for the sun to rise. Midsummer, as far as Gavin was concerned, was always coming.

"I've started preparations for the Freeing," she said. "Do you think your father will commune this year?"

Gavin snorted. "Not this year. Not ever." He rubbed his temples. He hadn't slept.

"It's not natural," the White said quietly. "I used to marvel at his self-control, you know. Living in that awful room, keeping his mind sharp, keeping the nightmares at bay."

"Nightmares have to keep *him* at bay."

"I live half in darkness, Gavin," the White said as if he hadn't interrupted. "That's how it feels to live without drafting. But to live fully in darkness? Is that not a denial of Orholam himself? 'They love the darkness, for their deeds are dark, and the light shames them.'"

"I leave the state of my father's soul to my father. Are we not to honor our fathers, rendering obedience unto the authority the Father of All has entrusted to them?"

"You're not just a son, Gavin. You're the Prism. You should honor Orholam by practicing the authority he's given you, not just the power."

"Maybe it's time for you to be Freed," Gavin said bitterly. He had these conversations at least once a year. He was sick of it. The White asked after his father, his father suggested the White go first. Both pressured him to pressure the other.

The White held her hands out, palms up. "If you command it, my Prism, I will join the Freeing. Gladly."

Her words stopped him cold. She meant it.

"I also obey," the White said. "It might surprise you to learn it, Gavin, but I drew the straw to become the White before I began to understand what it was to even be a drafter, much less a Color, much less the White. But perhaps it is not a lesson that can be taught, only learned."

"What are you talking about?" Gavin asked.

"Do you know why faith is harder for us, my Lord Prism?" The White grinned. Sometimes despite her years, she seemed a mischievous girl.

"Because we know Orholam sleeps a hundred years for every day he wakes?" Gavin asked. He was tired, and not just from the insomnia.

She refused the bait. "Because we know ourselves. Because others obey us as though we were gods, and we know we're not. We see the fragility of our own power, and through it we see the fragility of every other link. What if the Spectrum suddenly refused my orders? Not hard to imagine, when you consider the scheming and lust for power it takes to become a Color. What if a general suddenly refuses his satrap's orders? What if a son refuses his father's orders? What if that first link in the Great Chain of Being—Orholam Himself—is as empty as every other link before him? Seeing the weakness of each link, we think the Great Chain itself is fragile: surely at any moment it will burst if we don't do everything in our power to hold it together."

Gavin swallowed involuntarily. He'd never really universalized the thought as she was doing, but he always thought his whole life was like that. His deceptions, his authority, his imprisoned brother, his relationships. A chain of wet paper, drooping under its own sodden weight. A chain to which he added new weight every day.

"Here's what I've learned," the White said. "Orholam doesn't need me. Oh, I can do good work for him, work that pleases him, and if I foul it, others will suffer. You see, what I do still matters, but in the end, Orholam's will prevails. So I think I still have work to do. I see unfinished business everywhere I look. But if you tell me that I should be Freed this Midsummer's, I will do so gladly, not because I have faith in you, Gavin—though I do, more than you know—but because I have faith in Orholam."

Gavin looked at her like she was a visitor from the moon. "That was very...metaphysical. Can we talk about the Freeing now?"

She laughed. "Here's the thing, Gavin. You remember everything. I know you do. You think I'm crazy now, but you'll remember this, and someday it might make a difference. And with that, I can be content."

Madwoman or saint—but then, Gavin didn't think there was any difference.

"I'm going to Garriston," he said.

She folded her hands in her lap and turned toward the rising light.

"Let me explain," Gavin rushed to say. Then he did, ignoring the beauty of the sunrise. Ten minutes later, he was almost finished when the White raised a finger. She held her breath, then sighed as the sun itself mastered the horizon. "Do you ever watch for the green flash?"

"Sometimes," Gavin said. He knew people who swore they'd seen it, though no one could explain what it was or why it happened, and he knew others who swore it was a myth.

"I think of it as Orholam's wink," the White said.

Is everything about Orholam with her? Maybe she is fading.

"You've seen it?" Gavin asked.

"Twice. The first time was...fifty-nine years ago now? No, sixty. It was the night I met Ulbear." Gavin had to reach to remember the name. Oh, Ulbear *Rathcore*, the White's husband and quite a famous man in his day. Dead now twenty years. "I was at a party, quite disgusted with the drunk young gentleman who'd escorted me there and most certainly wasn't going to be escorting me home. I went outside to get some air. Watched the sun set, saw the green flash, and was so excited I jumped. Unfortunately this very tall fellow was leaning over me to grab his wineglass that he'd left on the balcony, and I broke his nose with the back of my head."

"You met Ulbear Rathcore by breaking his nose?"

"The woman he was escorting that night was none too pleased. She was beautiful, graceful, prettier than I was by half, and somehow she couldn't compete with little clumsy me. Though I can't imagine she would have been happy if she'd married Ulbear, your grandmother didn't forgive me for two years."

"My *grandmother*?"

"If I hadn't seen the green flash at that instant, your grandmother would have married Ulbear, and you wouldn't be here now, Gavin." The White laughed. "See, you never know what you'll learn when you let old women prattle."

Gavin was left speechless.

"You can go to Garriston, of course, Gavin, but no one else can perform the Freeing, and it can be done at no other time. So there's only one option: I'll send all those to be Freed to Garriston. I'll have to send our fastest ships to intercept theirs so they can arrive in time."

"We're talking about war," Gavin said.

"And?"

"What do you mean 'and'?" he demanded. "I'm not going to have time to throw parties and set off fireworks and give speeches."

"The list I have so far is only perhaps a hundred and fifty drafters. Not a large flight this year. A good proportion of those definitely won't make it to next year. You want another eighty or ninety color wights?"

"Of course not."

"The parties are nice, Gavin, but understand what you are. This is the flip side of your first purpose." She'd figured out that he'd sworn to wipe out color wights because of Sevastian. Like everything she learned, she used it to control him. "Even if you don't believe the Prism is Orholam's gift to mankind, *they* do. The minutes each drafter spends with you being Freed are the holiest moments of her life. You can take that away, but it would be the worst thing you could do. I for one can forgive you much, but I'd never forgive you that."

That stung.

"Now, tell me how you dropped off Karris in Tyrea, killed a giist, and brought back a son, all within a few days. The trip alone should have taken you two weeks."

Well that was quick. He'd known she would learn of the skimmer and the condor as soon as he'd shown Karris, but he hadn't been able to stop himself. Maybe he was impulsive. So he told her about the skimmer and the condor. Her eyes lit up. "That would be something to see, Gavin. Flying! And the speed! I suppose you'll want to go back to Garriston the same way?"

"Yes, and I'm taking Kip with me."

Again she surprised him and didn't protest. "Good," she said. "It will be good for you to learn about a father's love."

Because I sure as the evernight didn't learn about that from my own father. Then Gavin realized that was exactly what she meant, and he bristled. But there was no point fighting over his father again.

"So what was the second time?" he asked instead.

"Second time?"

"The second time you saw the green flash. The second time Orholam winked." He kept the sarcasm out of his voice. Mostly.

She smiled. "I look forward to the day when I tell you that, my Lord Prism, but that day is not today." Then her smile passed. "When you return, we need to talk about Kip's testing."

"You noticed the wall crystals. I thought I stopped it in time."

"Old? Yes. Addled? Not yet."

"You want to hear me admit it? Kip nearly broke the test," Gavin said. "Like Dazen did."

"Or worse, passed it," the White said.

Chapter 52

Karris knew she was even deeper in trouble than she'd feared within five minutes of being captured. King Garadul's Mirrormen walked her at gunpoint over to a wagon. They didn't bind her hands, which she thought was curious and gave her a momentary hope. Then the Mirrormen handed her off to half a dozen drafters, all women. Two Mirrormen stayed, their pistols leveled at her head, barely blinking.

The women—two reds, a green, a blue, and a super—stripped her naked and searched her and her clothes, quickly finding her eye caps. The two Mirrormen barely even glanced at her body, and though men around the camp turned to see whatever they could between all the drafters surrounding her, there wasn't a single ribald comment.

Disciplined. Damn it.

Crossing her arms over her breasts, Karris looked down, feigning embarrassment. Well, maybe not completely feigning.

"Eyes up!" one of the reds commanded.

Karris looked up. They wanted to see her eyes so they would know as soon as she tried to draft. Smart too, damn it twice.

In rapid order, they went through all her clothing, scrunching every seam to look for hidden pockets. Then they went through her bag, one carefully cataloguing all the items in a codex. After they'd found everything, Karris hoped they'd give her back her clothes.

No such luck. Instead, they opened the door of the wagon and threw a violet dress and shift inside.

"Get in," the same red who'd spoken before said.

Karris got in and the door slammed behind her. She heard a bar being lowered and chains pulled into place. The inside of the wagon was fairly spacious. There was a pallet to sleep on, a chamber pot, a cup of water, several blankets and pillows—all violet, the deepest into the blue spectrum they could find. And from the noxious smell, all freshly painted. The windows were fitted with bars and violet glass, draped on the outside with violet cloth. Apparently they were taking her drafting seriously, and from their study of her eyes and the mag torches, they knew she could draft green and red. Rather than risk a color that was between her colors, they'd picked the one farthest to the end of the spectrum she didn't draft.

It was a strange kindness. They could have just blindfolded her, of course, but blindfolds slip. But most captors would have painted the wagon black and made her live in darkness. This was just as effective, but a lot more work. If a drafter couldn't see her color, or didn't have lenses and white light, she couldn't draft. Karris was about as close to helpless as she got. She hated the feeling with a passion.

She threw on the slip and the shapeless violet dress, and immediately scratched the paint. It had been heat-dried by a sub-red. She would be able to chip it eventually, but with the only light coming in through the violet curtains and violet glass, it wasn't going to matter anyway. Still, she tried. She couldn't help herself. Under the layer of violet paint was a layer of black. Under that, the wood was a dark mahogany. No luck.

The wagon began rolling within minutes.

That night, after she was fed a hunk of black bread and given water in a blackened iron cup, two drafters came in, their skin already full of red and blue luxin respectively. Behind them came, of all things, a tailor. She was a tiny woman who barely came up to Karris's shoulder. She took Karris's measurements rapidly, never writing them down, just committing them to memory. Then she stared at Karris's body for a long time, studying her like a farmer studying a rocky sidehill that he needed to plow. She double-checked her measurement of Karris's hips, and then left without a word.

Over the next five days, Karris learned little. Apparently her wagon was close to the cooking wagons, because all she heard all day was the rattle of pots at every bump in the road. The shadowy figures of horsemen, maybe Mirrormen, sometimes passed close enough to her covered windows for her to see their silhouettes. If they spoke, though, she could never make out the words. At night, she was given food in a blackened iron bowl, with a blackened iron spoon and black bread and water, never wine—damn them, they even thought of the red of wine. A Mirrorman accompanied by a drafter took her chamber pot, bowl, spoon, and cup each night after sunset. When she kept the spoon one night, hiding it under a pillow, they didn't say a word. Neither did they give her water the next day. When she surrendered the spoon, she was given water again.

The boredom was the worst. There were only so many push-ups you could do in a day, and anything more strenuous was impossible. There were no musical instruments, no books, and certainly no weapons or drafting to practice.

On the sixth night, two blues came in. "Choose a position that's comfortable," one of them said. Karris sat on her little pallet, hands folded in her lap, ankles crossed, and they bound her arms and legs in about five times the amount of luxin necessary. Then they put violet spectacles over her eyes and left.

King Garadul entered the wagon, carrying a folding camp chair. He wore a loose black shirt over his shirt, which Karris could barely see, and voluminous black pants over his pants. Karris understood being careful around her, but this was ridiculous. The king settled into the camp chair. He stared at her wordlessly.

"I don't suppose you remember me," he said. "I met you once, before the war. Of course, I was just a boy, three years younger than you, and you were already head over heels for...well, one of the Guile boys, I can't remember which. Maybe you can't either. There seemed to be some confusion for a time, wasn't there?"

"You're a real charmer, aren't you?" Karris asked.

"You might be surprised," he said. He shook his head. "I always thought you were a beautiful girl, but the stories of you took on a life of their own. A tragic love triangle between the two most powerful men in the world sort of demands a beautiful girl, doesn't it? I mean, otherwise, why would two men tear the world apart? For her insights about history? Her witty repartee? No. You were a pretty girl made beautiful by the bards' need to make some sense of what you wrought. Don't get me wrong," he said, "I was so in love with you it kept me up nights. You were my first great unrequited love."

"I'm sure you've had many. Or do women pretend to find you attractive, now that you're king?" Karris asked.

Temper, Karris, temper. But the truth was, it wasn't the red that made her say that. She'd always hated to perform for others, to do just what they wanted.

He scowled. "The shrewish tongue somehow was omitted from the panegyrics. Or is that a new addition?"

"I feel a bit freer to speak my mind these days. I already destroyed the world, what's one man's ego?" Karris said.

"Karris, I was on my way to pay you a compliment before you made us descend to this unpleasantness."

"Oh, dear. Please do go on then, there's nothing that would mean more to me than to hear praises from the Butcher of Rekton."

He rubbed his palms together thoughtfully. "I'm sorry you had to see that, Karris." He kept using her name. She didn't like it. "I hope you know I took no joy in what I ordered there, but I also hope you understand that that small monstrosity will forestall larger ones in the future. You're familiar with the manuscript called *The Counselor to Kings*?"

"Yes," Karris said. "Loathsome advice and cruelty that not even he had the stomach to countenance, when he himself ruled." The Counselor asked whether it was better for a ruler to be loved or feared. Both was best, he decided, but if a ruler had to choose, he should always choose to be feared.

"His advice was good. He was simply personally weak. I don't hold that against him. The fact is, Karris, when kings aren't feared, they end up having to instill fear eventually, at grievous prices. That's what happened at Ru. That's what happened at Garriston. Those men you loved—or at least bedded—learned the lesson eventually, but because they learned it late, what they had to do was far worse than destroying one little village. So tell me, how can you hold the death of a thousand against me, but not the death of tens of thousands, hundreds of thousands, against them?"

Karris hadn't been allowed to see the royal steps at Ru, stained with the blood and shit of hundreds murdered coldly one at a time and thrown down the steps to the gaping, horrified crowds below. She'd been kept from going to Garriston even after the war, where tens of thousands—they didn't *even know* how many—had perished in the red luxin fires of the besieged city. That was Gavin's and Dazen's doing. Somehow, it had never seemed possible that men she knew so well would have done such things. Men she thought she knew so well.

"The people of this land are my people. I am no mere satrap, no guardian of some other man's land; I am king. These people belong to me. To kill a thousand of my own was to cut a chunk out of my own flesh. But cancers have to be cut out. I am this land. My people work this land and bring forth crops at my good pleasure. I protect them and provide for them, and they in turn must render to me of their crops and of their sons. Those who would not are rebels, traitors, thieves, and heretics, apostates. They defy the holy compact. To defy me is to defy the gods' order. I had to do this because my father wouldn't. If he had hanged half a dozen mayors when they first defied him and refused to send levies, that thousand would be alive now. He was weak and wanted to be loved. No one may acknowledge it during my life, but by killing that thousand in Rekton, I saved many more. This is what it is to be a king."

"You're awfully passionate in your defense of decapitating babies and stacking their heads." The gods' order, not Orholam's?

"Karris, you're making me understand why men beat their wives." King Garadul rubbed his black beard, but made no move to strike her. "By making the display so awful, I ensured it would be seared into every mind that saw it. Do you think the dead care what happened to their bodies? Better that their example save the living than that I bury them all in a hole and my descendants have to kill their descendants. That monument will stay for a dozen generations. That is the legacy I will leave to my children's children, a secure rule, without the need to commit such massacres themselves. And the reason I

342 • *Brent Weeks*

tell you, Karris, is that I had hoped you of all people might understand. You're a woman now, not some frightened little girl surrounded by great men. You're a woman who's seen great men and terrible deeds. I had hoped you might understand the burdens of greatness. At least a little. Perhaps I give you too much credit."

Karris swallowed, trembling with rage and maybe a little fear. There was a sick logic to everything he said, but she had seen the bodies. The blood. The piled-up heads.

"As I wanted to say earlier," King Garadul said. He took a deep breath, clearly pushing away his frustration, and continued. "You were a very pretty girl, but only pretty, despite the tales. But you, to my great delight and surprise, are one of the few women I've ever seen who's gotten more beautiful as you've aged. You look better at thirty than you did at twenty, and I wouldn't be surprised if you look better at forty than you do now. Of course, I'm sure it helps that you haven't squeezed six or ten brats out of your crotch. Most pretty girls do manage to find a husband before they get so old, but let's not look a gift horse in the mouth."

Real charmer. What was it with King Garadul, did he just say everything that popped into his idiot head?

"Yours is, indeed, a face to inspire poets. This, however"—he gestured to her vaguely, she wasn't sure what he meant—"this must change. You have shoulders like a man." The bastard! How did he know how much she hated her shoulders? Whenever the fashions were such that she could hide her shoulders, they showed off her upper arms, or vice versa. And he'd said exactly what she said to herself at least once a week: I have shoulders like a man. But the king wasn't done. "Your ass looks like a ten-year-old boy's. Maybe it's that dress. We'll hope so. And your breasts. Your poor magnificent breasts. Where have they gone? They were bigger when you were fifteen! Your training ends now. I'll allow you to resume dancing and riding when you no longer resemble a starved Dark Forest pygmy."

"I won't be here that long," Karris said. She frowned. Had she just admitted she looked like a starved pygmy?

"Karris, my dear. I've waited for you for fifteen years. And whether or not you know it, you've been waiting for me, too. You and I don't settle for second best. Why else would you still be unmarried? So we can wait a few months. I'll come visit you when your dress is done." He glanced around. "Oh, and I noticed you've nothing in here to entertain you. It must get boring. It's good for a woman to excel in the pleasant arts. I'll have my mother's psantria brought in for you. That's what you play, isn't it?" He smiled and went out.

The worst part of it was that Karris *did* feel thankful. A little. The bastard.

Chapter 53

Kip and Liv went straight to the Blackguards watching the lift. "We need to see the Prism," Liv said.

"Who're you?" the man asked. He was short, Parian of course, and built like a cornerstone. He looked at Kip. "Oh, are you the Prism's bas—" He coughed. "Nephew."

"Yes, I'm his bastard," Kip said angrily. "We need to see him now."

The Blackguard looked over at his compatriot, a man just as muscular, but toweringly tall. "We've had no orders on how the Prism wants his... nephew treated," the man said.

"He just went to sleep not twenty minutes ago," the other said. "After being up all night."

"It's an emergency," Liv said.

They seemed unmoved, a little of a who-the-hell-is-this-girl creeping into their faces.

"Someone just tried to kill me," Kip said.

"Stump, get the commander," the tall one said. Stump? The short Blackguard's name was actually Stump? Because the Blackguards were both Parian, who traditionally had descriptive names like Ironfist, Kip had no idea if that was a nickname or really his name.

"He took third watch last night," Stump said, his mouth twisting.

"Stump." Pulling rank.

"Awright, awright. I'm going."

Stump left and the taller Blackguard turned and rapped on the door, three times, pause, two times. Then, after five seconds, he repeated it.

A room slave opened the door almost before the Blackguard finished knocking. A pretty woman with the unsettlingly pale skin and red hair of a Blood Forester, she was fully dressed and alert despite the early hour and the darkness of the chamber behind her.

"Marissia," Liv said. "So good to see you again." Her voice didn't sound totally sincere.

The slave appeared none too pleased to see Liv. Kip wondered why Liv had used the slave's name, then. He thought you were only supposed to do that with slaves with whom you were friendly.

From deep in the chamber, they heard Gavin's voice, deep and scratchy from just waking, "Ummgh, give me a—" Whatever else he said, it was lost in bass and pillows. A moment later, all the windows banged open and light streamed in from all sides, nearly blinding everyone, and eliciting a loud groan from the Prism on his bed.

"That's brilliant magic!" Liv said. "Look at that, Kip!" She pointed at a dark purplish-black strip of glass around the glass walls that encircled the whole chamber.

"What are you— Are you forgetting why we're here?" Kip asked.

"Oh, sorry."

Gavin was squinting at them. "Marissia, kopi, please."

The woman bobbed. "First closet, third from the left." Then she left.

"Kopi's in the closet?" Gavin asked. "What the hell? Who puts kopi—and why aren't you serving me?" The door closed behind her. "And where's my favorite shirt—oh, closet. Damned woman."

"Clearly a morning person," Liv said under her breath.

Kip snorted before he could stop himself.

Gavin had been looking down as if feeling trapped, but now he shot Kip a look. "This had better be important." He threw off his covers and walked toward the closet. He wasn't wearing anything.

Kip had seen Gavin's forearms, with hemp ropes for muscles, and he'd known his father was lean, but seeing his whole body was half awe-inspiring and half a slap in the face. Kip's shoulders were as broad as Gavin's, and his arms were probably as big around as Gavin's, but even now—not after exertion, not filled from hard labor—but now, after sleeping, Gavin's body was one smooth curving muscle meeting another, over and over, without an ounce of softness anywhere. Apparently sculling and skimming around the entirety of the Seven Satrapies did that to a man.

How did *I* come from *this*?

Next to him, Kip grew aware of Liv staring, openmouthed. She didn't avert her eyes, even as Gavin had to rummage through the closet.

"*Liv*," Kip said under his breath.

"What?" she asked, glancing away, her cheeks bright. "He's the Prism. It's practically my religious duty to give him my full attention."

Gavin, who'd seemed oblivious to them, grabbed some clothing and said, without looking at them, "Ana, staring is rude."

Liv blushed harder and sank into herself, horrified.

"Her name's Liv," Kip said.

"I know her name. Now what is it?" Gavin demanded, pulling on a dazzling white silk shirt with gold piping.

The door opened behind Kip, and Marissia and Commander Ironfist stepped into the room. Ironfist stopped at the door, while Marissia brought in a tray with a silver service on it and three cups. She poured a dark, creamy, steaming brew into one cup and handed it to Gavin, whose pants and sleeves were still unlaced. "Commander? Kip?" Gavin asked, motioning to the other cups. "I think Liv is quite alert enough already."

Liv looked like she wanted to fall through the floor. Kip grinned.

Ironfist helped himself to the kopi while Marissia took over dressing Gavin. Kip picked up a cup too. But as he picked up the carafe, his hands started shaking so badly he couldn't even try to fill his cup.

"Someone tried to throw me off the balcony," Kip said.

It was like the words made it real. One moment ago, he'd been joking with Liv, thinking about how unlike his father he was, and grinning when Liv got embarrassed. Now the reality of how close he'd come to getting thrown to his death came crashing in on him. He could see himself falling, twisting, helpless, like in an awful dream, and then his body bursting like a juicy grape.

And who would have suspected anything? The woman could have

slipped into his room, thrown him off the balcony, and then simply left. Even if they'd figured out who was on the floor at the time, who would expect a big woman as an assassin? People would have thought Kip had broken after his testing and jumped. No one would have known.

And who would have cared?

Kip felt a great gnawing emptiness in his chest.

He'd never been part of anything. Even back in Rekton, he hadn't belonged. Too fat and awkward for Isa, too smart to feel a connection to Sanson, who seemed a whisker away from simple, relentlessly mocked by Ram, too young for Liv. He'd thought that being part of the Chromeria would make him be part of something for the first time in his life. He was going to be different here, too. He would be different and alone, no matter where he went.

Orholam, why had he even stopped that woman from throwing him over? Two moments of terror, sure, and a mess of exploded Kip on the rocks. But the terror would end, everything would end, and the sea would wash away the mess.

Someone slapped him. Kip staggered. Rubbed his jaw.

"Make the words, Kip," Gavin said.

So Kip told them everything. Liv stared woodenly at the floor when he told of her leaving after he'd told her that he thought her father was dead.

Commander Ironfist said, "General Danavis has been living in some backwater village all this time?" He glanced at Liv. "Sorry, I knew we had a Danavis at the Chromeria, but I didn't think you were related." He cleared his throat and shut up.

"I wouldn't be surprised if he did get away," Gavin said. "The general was always a wily bastard, and I mean that in the best possible way."

Liv grinned, weakly and briefly. Kip told them the rest of it.

After he finished, Gavin and Ironfist shared a look. "The Broken Eye?" Ironfist asked.

Gavin shrugged. "Impossible to know. Of course, that's the point."

"The what?" Kip asked.

"My magisters told us that was a myth," Liv protested. The Prism and the commander of the Blackguard turned to look at her. She swallowed hard and stared at the floor.

Ironfist said, "Your magisters are partly right. The Order of the Broken Eye is a reputed guild of assassins. They specialize in killing drafters. They've been rooted out and destroyed on at least three separate occasions, if not more. No satrap or satrapah enjoys losing drafters who've cost them so much before the end of their natural span. We believe that each time the order has reformed, it's been without any connection to any of the previous orders."

"To put it plainly," Gavin said, "some thug rounds up a few more thugs, hoping to make a lot of money from backstabbing a few drafters, and they name themselves the Order of the Broken Eye so they can demand hefty payments. It's pure pretense."

"How do you know?" Kip asked.

"Because if they were real, they'd be better at their job."

Kip scowled. His assassin had been pretty good.

"It's not to say they're all equally incompetent, Kip," Gavin said. "That's the whole point. We shouldn't even have brought it up. It doesn't get us any closer to the real problem. Whether or not the order is real, someone sent an assassin to kill you. You haven't been here long enough to make any enemies, so it's clearly an enemy of mine. There's only one thing for us to do."

Kip bit. "What?" He didn't want to admit that he had already made an enemy. Surely that tester, Magister Galden, wouldn't have sent an assassin after him, would he?

"We run away." Gavin grinned, a reckless, boyish grin, eyes dancing.

"What?!" Kip and Liv asked at the same time.

"Meet me at the docks in an hour. Liv, that means you too. You'll be Kip's tutor. We're going to Garriston."

"Garriston?" Liv asked.

"Pack quick," Gavin said. "You never know where the order is lurking." He grinned again, teasing.

"Oh, thanks," Liv said.

"Pack?" Kip asked as Gavin swept out of the room. "I don't even own anything!"

Chapter 54

The prisoner studied the dead man. "I'm going to kill you," he said quietly.

"I don't die easy," the dead man said, his mouth twitching. He was seated opposite Dazen, in his wall, knees folded, hands in his lap, his pose a mockery of Dazen's own. He glanced at the carefully woven rag in Dazen's lap. "Who would have thought?" the dead man mused. "Gavin Guile, so patient, so quiet, so content doing women's work."

Dazen studied his handiwork. Woven of his own hair as tight as he could manage with calm cool blue flowing through his body, he wasn't even sure how long he'd spent on it. Weeks, maybe. It made almost a skullcap, a small bowl. He studied the shiny interior. Finding, perhaps, a flaw, he took a long but perfectly round fingernail and scraped it around his nose, over his forehead in methodical strokes. Harvesting the accumulated skin and, more importantly, the precious oil with another fingernail, Dazen smeared the oil carefully onto the flaw.

He was only going to get one chance. After years and years, he wasn't going to mess it up.

With a steady hand and skin filled with blue, he gathered more oil and smeared it on the wall directly over the dead man's face.

"This doesn't change anything, Gavin," the dead man said.

"No, not yet," he said.

He stood and drafted a blade. He cut off a hank of his greasy hair.

He spat on it and scrubbed it against his dirty skin, getting it as foul as possible.

"You don't need to do this," the dead man said. "It's madness."

"It's victory," Dazen said. He drew the blue luxin blade smoothly across his chest.

"If you're going to kill yourself, the wrist or the neck would work better," the dead man said.

Dazen ignored him. With dirty fingers, he pulled the cut open and tucked the putrid mass of hair and dirt under the flap of skin. Blood cascaded down his chest, the red almost tempting him to try drafting directly, but it wasn't enough, he knew that from experience. He put a hand to his chest and pressed on the wound, holding it closed, slowing the bleeding.

In a few sleeps, the cell would be cleansed with Dazen's weekly bath. Soon thereafter, depending on how well he had planned and guessed, he would either escape or be dead.

As long as he held the blue, he found he didn't care much one way or the other.

Chapter 55

Liv cleared her throat awkwardly as she stuffed clothing into a bag. "I, um, came back here this morning to apologize," she said.

"Huh?" Kip said. The clothes in her hand were some lacy undergarments. Distracting.

"You know, when you were busy trying to get killed."

"Oh, um, apology accepted?" Kip asked. What was she apologizing for? He shifted the weight on the pack that Commander Ironfist had given him before disappearing. Apparently it had taken Ironfist almost no time to gather some spare clothing, a waterskin, tools, and even a short sword for Kip. Kip still hadn't figured out how to get the pack to sit comfortably on his shoulders, though. He'd come to Liv's room to help her pack, but she wasn't making things any easier. He glanced at the short pants again.

"They're just underclothes, Kip." Ack, caught!

"They're *see-through*," Kip said. How could such a small bit of cloth actually fit a person inside it?

Liv looked down and colored a little, but played it off. She tossed the short pants to Kip, who caught them instinctively, and instantly felt awkward. "Would you check if those are clean?" she asked.

Kip's eyebrows shot off his face and stuck somewhere three floors up.

"I'm *teasing*. I just moved and they gave me all new clothes. Everything here is new."

"Except my gullibility, apparently," Kip said. That was twice in as many days she'd fooled him.

She laughed. "You're great, Kip. It's like torturing the little brother I never had."

Oh, the little brother comparison. Just what every man wants to hear from a beautiful woman. I've just been castrated. "So would I feel more or less awkward holding my sister's underclothes?"

Liv laughed again. "Would these be better or worse?" She held up some black lace that looked like little more than two strings tied together artistically.

Kip gaped.

Then she held them up to her hips and cocked a saucy eyebrow at him. Kip coughed.

"I think I need to sit down," he said. She laughed like he hoped she would, but he wasn't completely kidding. He backed up toward a chair—and instantly bumped into someone.

"Watch it," Commander Ironfist said. "You don't want to run into someone with that little sword sticking out."

Kip was too mortified for words. Little? Liv saw the look on his face and burst out laughing so hard she fell on the bed. She laughed so hard she snorted, a decidedly unladylike sound, and then that made her laugh harder.

Turning around, Kip felt Ironfist's firm hand guiding his pack away from him so he didn't stab him with the scabbarded short sword on top of it.

Oh, *that* little sword. Relief flooded Kip, until he saw Ironfist glance down at the sheer short pants in his hands.

"You need me to find some in your size?" Ironfist asked drily.

Liv snorted again, giggling so hard she was gasping for breath.

"Aliviana," Ironfist said. "You're done packing? Because we're leaving in five minutes."

Liv's laughter stopped instantly. She popped off the bed and began rummaging through her things at great speed. Ironfist let a small, satisfied smirk steal over his face briefly, then he dropped another pack next to Kip's and walked out. Before Kip could ask him about it, Ironfist said, "Move it, boy genius. If you haven't figured out the straps on your pack before I get back..."

He didn't complete the threat. He didn't need to.

Soon they were striding onto the docks together. Despite his threats, Ironfist had helped them with some settling of the packs. Mostly, that meant moving things from Liv's pack to Kip's. When Kip asked the silent question—why are you making me carry her stuff?—Ironfist had said, "It's more complicated to be a girl. You got a problem?" Kip shook his head quickly.

As they walked down the docks, past fishermen unloading catches, apprentices of various trades running back and forth, loiterers, merchant women arguing with captains about prices for goods or transit—basically, all the normal business of the day—many people stopped whatever they were doing for a few moments. It wasn't to watch Kip, of course. It was to watch Commander Ironfist. The man was big, and imposing, and handsome, and he strode with a total self-awareness, but it wasn't his sheer physical presence that got him so much attention. He was, Kip realized, famous.

As Kip turned to see the faces looking at Commander Ironfist, he could see Gavin walking onto the docks. And if for Commander Ironfist, business slowed, for the Prism, it stopped entirely. Gavin walked through smiling and nodding to people automatically, but they treated him like he was nearly a god. No one tried to touch Gavin himself, but not a few brushed his cloak as it floated past.

What am I doing with these people?

A week ago, Kip had been cleaning puke off his mother's face and hair while she lay passed out from another binge. In their hovel. With a dirt floor. No one in their backwater town had paid him the least mind. The addict's boy, that's all he was. Maybe the fat boy. I don't belong here.

I've never belonged anywhere. Mother told me I ruined her life, and now I'm ruining Gavin's.

Kip couldn't help but think of his mother's last words, and the promise he made as she was dying. He'd sworn to avenge her, and he'd hardly done anything to keep that oath.

They said Orholam himself watched over oaths. Kip hadn't learned anything, and now they were going back.

"Hey," Liv said, "why so glum?" She laid a hand on his arm, which tingled from the contact. They'd stopped at an empty place on the dock, down a ramp low to the water, and Commander Ironfist was drafting a luxin platform onto the water, the first building block of a scull.

"I, uh, I don't know. Thinking about Tyrea makes me think about—" And from somewhere that Kip didn't even know he had, tears tried to come up at the thought of his mother, dying. He pushed them away, diverted them to someone more worth mourning. "You know, I hope your father's well, Liv. He was . . . he was always good to me." He was the only one.

Yet even with Master Danavis, there had been a wall, a point past which he wouldn't let Kip in. Was it just because of his own history that he had to keep secret? Or was there something deeper, something wrong with Kip?

"Kip," Liv said. "It's going to work out."

He looked over at her and couldn't help but smile. Orholam had never made a more beautiful woman. Liv could shame the sunset with her radiance. He fell into her dimples, hopeless. He looked away.

Little brother, he sneered at himself. Fun to joke around with, but not a man. The despair threatened to choke him completely.

"Thanks," he managed to push past the lump in his throat. "Can I have a snack?" he asked Ironfist.

"Yes, of course," the big man said.

"Great!"

"When we get back."

"Hey!"

"Now shut it, the Lord Prism is here."

All eyes still on him, Gavin stopped in front of Commander Ironfist. He looked at Ironfist's pack. Neither said anything for a long time.

"You can't come, I'm not taking a bodyguard," Gavin said finally.

"I'm not coming with you," Ironfist said.

"Then get off my scull."

"I'm coming with Kip. He's a member of the Prism's family, and he's entitled to protection."

"You're the commander of the Blackguard, you can't possibly—"

"I can do what I deem appropriate to discharge the duties of the Blackguard. None may interfere with that. None."

"You *are* a wily bastard, aren't you?" Gavin said.

"It's why I'm still here," Ironfist said. "And quite possibly why you are, too."

Gavin grunted. "You win, but let me remind you of your oaths."

Ironfist looked offended.

"You'll understand soon," Gavin said. "Everyone, load up."

With a quick, practiced hand, Gavin drafted a set of the special oars he used to propel the scull, but he clearly left room for Ironfist to draft his own, which he did, albeit much more slowly. Meanwhile, Gavin drafted a bench for Kip and Liv to sit on, and straps to hold all the bags in the boat.

Ironfist wrinkled his nose at that, as if wondering why the bags would need to be strapped in, but he didn't ask. In moments, they were off. Gavin manned his oars, and Ironfist manned his, and they sped out into the bay.

The scull began veering to port almost immediately. It was Gavin's side. Kip realized Ironfist was rowing faster than Gavin, and the imbalance was driving them to port. Gavin looked over at Ironfist, who grinned back at him, continuing to sweep huge long strokes with his arms and legs. Gavin sped up. So did Ironfist. So did Gavin. Soon they were sculling across the water at a nice pace.

Liv looked over at Kip. "Can you believe this? I've never gone this fast!"

Kip laughed.

"What?" she asked.

"You'll see."

The men settled into a rhythm. They were going fast, competing, but neither trying to bury the other. "When are we going to meet your ship?" Ironfist asked, raising his voice to be heard over the wind.

"We're going to cross the sea on this," Gavin said.

Ironfist laughed. "Right. You've got more endurance than I thought!"

Kip grinned. The big Parian clearly didn't believe Gavin, but was willing to play along.

After twenty minutes, they were out of sight of any other ships. Barely slowing in his rowing, Gavin lifted one hand up and drafted one of the great tubes Kip had seen him use to propel the skimmer earlier. Ironfist looked at it quizzically.

"This is what I meant about your oath," Gavin said. "Secrecy."

"A tube attached to another tube. Your secret is safe with me, O Prism," Ironfist said, grinning. "I hope it gets us out of this port turn, though."

Gavin dropped the tube into the water. The deck shuddered as the first luxin ball hit the water streaming through the tube, then, as it quickly settled into the *whup-whup-whup* that was familiar to Kip, the skimmer shot forward. The whole skimmer rose up, and Ironfist almost fell over as his oars came free of the water.

The skimmer sped up slowly and began to skip from one wave peak to the next, then the skips got longer and longer, and soon the platform stopped hitting the waves at all. After a time, the astounded Ironfist joined in and they skimmed even faster.

The water was so clear, Kip could see the tube cutting through the waves below them. Gavin had given each tube little wings. It was on those wings that the whole skimmer was flying above the surface. The wind was incredible, but Kip could hear Ironfist whooping over it.

Hours later, when the sun was halfway to the horizon, Gavin decided to switch back to sculling before they came in sight of Garriston. As the skimmer settled back on the waves, Ironfist stepped away from his tube.

His face was a writ of wonder, awe. He actually physically trembled. Then he swept into an elaborate bow before Gavin. "My Lord Prism," he said, "you have made the world small."

Gavin bobbed his head, acknowledging the bow. "Small, maybe. Safe, no. Did you see a corvette over that way?"

Ironfist shook his head. Their watercraft, no longer lifted up by the action of the tubes, sat low in the water. But by the time Ironfist had drafted new oars, a corvette appeared, a league away, plowing right toward them. Ironfist cursed.

Gavin grinned recklessly. "So Kip, Liv, you ever fought pirates?"

Chapter 56

"Surely you're joking," Ironfist said. "My Lord Prism," he added belatedly and not enthusiastically.

"Let's go hunting," Gavin said.

"My lord!" Ironfist said. "I can't let you put yourself in that sort of danger. We can outrun these Ilytian scum. They're not threatening our mission or us."

"Do you know what this summer is, Commander?" Gavin asked.

"I'm not sure what you're asking."

"It's time for the Ruthgari handover of Garriston," Liv said as if the words left a bad taste in her mouth.

"Do you know why she sounded so happy about that?" Gavin asked Ironfist.

"I've never served on this side of the Cerulean Sea," Ironfist said.

"I'm sure you know that each country that sided with me during the False Prism's War has rotating stewardship of Garriston."

"Two years or something for each country, so no one gets long term designs on Tyrea. Can we have this conversation at a safer distance?" He glanced at the pirates. They were making good progress in the afternoon wind.

"That's what it was supposed to do," Gavin said. "Instead, each governor has taken it as a personal chance to get rich. The Parians had the first rotation, and they stripped Garriston of everything that survived the fires. Every governor since then has followed their lead."

Liv spoke up. "During the first year, most governors try to keep the Umber River clear of bandits so the crops can get through. But most of the crops come in too late on the second year. The governors don't want to lose men killing bandits just to enrich the next governor from some other satrapy, so they withdraw into Garriston. Only the most optimistic farmers even bother planting on the second year anymore."

"While repeated sacking of Garriston and the surrounding country is tragic, it doesn't have much to do with these pirates," Gavin said. "The handover happens after Midsummer's, two weeks from now. The Ruthgari merchants and craftsmen and wives and whores are busily loading their ships to take whatever plunder they've managed to steal this time home. Or just whatever they brought with them. I suppose just because every governor so far has been corrupt doesn't mean the smiths who shoe their horses are, too."

"This is fascinating," Ironfist said, "but can't some long guns shoot eighteen or nineteen hundred paces?"

"It's farther away than that," Gavin said. "Point is—"

"Finally, thank Orholam," Ironfist muttered.

"Ahem. Point is, there'll be an armada heading back to Ruthgar in two weeks. The pirates descend like wolves, and they take any ships that get separated from the main fleet."

"Serves them right," Liv said.

Gavin stared at her, and she scowled defiantly, but couldn't handle the eye contact, so she scowled at the waves.

"Some merchants try to beat the rush and get out before the rest of the fleet, hoping they'll avoid the pirates."

"But here they are," Liv said.

"Exactly," Gavin said. "And if there's war this summer, especially—Orholam forbid—if we lose, there'll be chaos. Dozens of ships, maybe hundreds, all going their own direction, fleeing. A lot of the people in those ships will be Tyrean, Aliviana."

She looked chastened.

"Smoke," Kip said.

All conversation on the little scull stopped cold. Everyone turned to look.

"It would take an extremely skilled gunner to come within a hundred paces of us at this distance," Gavin said, but Kip noticed he didn't take his eyes off the corvette either.

"Maybe it was an empty charge, just to let us know—"

The water erupted twenty paces in front of the scull. The sound of the shot reached them only afterward.

"That was quite a shot," Gavin said. "The good news is that very few corvettes have more than one gun mounted on the front, so we should have at least thirty seconds while they're—"

"Smoke!" Kip said.

"I hate this part," Gavin said. He and Ironfist scrambled onto their oar apparatus.

This time, the splash was fifty paces in front of them.

"Good to know the first one was lucky," Liv said.

"Unless the second was *unlucky*," Kip said.

Gavin looked at Ironfist, a momentary worry line pressed between his eyes. "Let's go."

"Right!"

They began rowing and quickly picked up speed. "What can I do?" Kip asked. He hated feeling useless.

"Think!" Gavin said.

Think? Kip looked at Liv to see if she had any idea what Gavin meant. She shrugged.

"Smoke!" she said.

Excruciating seconds passed, then Kip heard an odd whistling hum. The water exploded fifty paces behind them.

"Didn't expect us to come straight at 'em!" Gavin shouted. "Next one'll be closer!" He cackled.

The man had gone quite mad.

Smoke. This time, Kip counted. One. Two. Three. He strained his eyes. Surely he should be able to see something as big as a cannonball. Five. Si— *Boom!* The water exploded not fifteen paces to the left—port?—of the scull. Kip actually felt spray.

"See?" Gavin said. "Talented gunner!"

Mad. Totally mad. "It's a six count between the smoke and the splash," Kip announced.

"Good!" Gavin shouted. "Ironfist, hard starboard as soon as they—"

"Smoke!" Liv said.

The men cut hard to starboard and the next shot splashed harmlessly a good distance away, albeit probably perilously close to where they would have been.

Another shot, and they turned even more to starboard. Again, the shot was at least thirty paces off target. Kip looked at the wind and the sails of the Ilytian ship. They were cutting at a hard angle, sails full, wind steady. It looked like a good platform to shoot from, but as for how Kip could use what he was seeing to help them survive, he had no idea. He just didn't know anything about sailing. They were getting closer, though. Now the lag between the smoke and the shot was less than five seconds.

The scull cut back and forth, sometimes even stopping, and though Kip's fear never really shrank, he saw that Gavin was right. Their scull was simply too fast, too small, too maneuverable to get hit— unless the gunner made both a skillful and lucky shot. And though as they got closer to the Ilytian ship they had less time to move between the cannon being fired and the shot landing, the gunners were also having to change their angle more and more.

There was a long pause between shots.

"What's going on?" Kip asked.

"Maybe they're tired of wasting powder?" Liv asked hopefully.

Ten seconds later, they had their answer as twin columns of smoke erupted from the cannons.

"Port!" Gavin shouted.

He'd guessed right. Water erupted both where they would have been if they'd gone straight and where they would have been if they'd turned to starboard. Though it was longer between volleys, now the pirates could make two guesses of where the scull was headed instead of one.

"Clever bastard!" Gavin said. "Time to cheat! Kip, switch me." He clambered off the oars, and Kip jumped in.

"Straight," Gavin said. Blue flooded his skin and he drafted a propulsion tube into the water. As before, they leapt forward. Kip and Ironfist almost fell as Gavin cut their oars smooth. But if he hadn't,

Kip realized, they'd have been ripped apart by the inexorable turning of the gears.

Gavin's teeth gritted under the strain of pushing the entire boat by himself, muscles knotting, veins standing out on his neck, but after a moment as they gained speed and it became easier, he said, "Ironfist, put fire grenadoes in all the cannon holes and the sails. Liv, cut the rigging. Kip, you…" He paused like he couldn't think of anything for Kip the Inept to do. "You call out anything you think I don't see. Take my pistols." Gavin pulled his hand from one of the tubes and drafted a basin and filled it with red luxin in moments. Ironfist instantly began drafting blue projectiles and filling them with the flammable goo.

They traversed the last five hundred paces before the men scrambling on deck could reload the front cannons. Only one man seemed unfazed by their impossible speed.

"Musketeer!" Kip shouted. One of the gunners, whether or not it was their cannoneer with the preternatural aim Kip didn't know, stood at the bow, calmly tamping powder down his musket with a ramrod. With smooth, fast motions, he drew a square of cloth, reached into another pocket for a bullet, and then tamped those. He held a smoking slow match in his teeth.

As they got closer, Kip saw that the gunner was Ilytian, with skin as black as gunpowder, aboriginal features, a scattered dark beard, short loose trousers cut off below the knees, and an incongruously fine royal blue jacket over his lean frame with no shirt. His wiry black hair was bound in a thick ponytail. His knees were bent, compensating for the rolling motion of the deck as naturally as breathing. He fixed the burning fuse into place.

"I said, musketeer!" Kip shouted. They cut the water right beside the corvette as the cannon portholes opened and the ship turned hard away from them.

Gavin just turned with the bigger vessel. No one was going to do anything. Kip cocked the hammers of Gavin's dagger-pistols, trying not to skewer himself on the long blades.

The musketeer pivoted smoothly, aiming at Gavin. Kip raised both pistols.

The musketeer shot first. His gun exploded in his hands, knocking him off his feet. Kip pulled both triggers. The pistol in his right hand scraped the flint against the frizzen, but didn't throw a spark. Nothing happened. The pistol in his left hand roared. It kicked back at Kip with far more force than he'd expected.

Kip spun, tripped, and slid toward the back of the skimmer, rolling, scrambling. He saw Liv flinging both of her hands forward, then turning, her pupils tiny pinpricks as she drafted superviolet. Then she dove for him.

Tumbling facedown, Kip lost sight of Liv, the ship, the drafters, and the battle. All he saw was the slick blue of the skimmer's deck, sliding away below him. His face slid over the edge. His forehead skipped off the water blurring past them, making his whole head bounce up, just about tearing his head off his neck. On the second bounce, he wasn't so lucky. His nose went under, and positioned off the back of the skimmer as he was, his nostrils acted as twin scoops, jetting water up into his sinuses at great speed.

Liv must have grabbed him, because there was no third bounce, but Kip could see nothing, think of nothing. He was coughing, retching, crying, blind, spitting up salt water.

By the time he propped himself up, the Ilytian corvette was two hundred paces behind them. Its sails sagged, cut and burning. Smoke billowed out of all the cannon portholes on the starboard side, and fire was visible on the decks. And the whole ship was sitting low in the water. Men were leaping off the decks on every side.

Commander Ironfist, who'd barely said two words the entire time, said, "Men jumping off that fast means the fire must be headed for the—" The middle of the corvette exploded, sending wood and ropes and barrels and men flying every direction. "—powder magazine," Ironfist finished. "Sorry bastards."

"Men like those kill and rape and steal and enslave. They don't deserve our pity," Gavin said, slowing the skimmer. He was talking to Liv and Kip, who both sat almost equally wide-eyed. "But Ironfist's right. It's no easy thing to be the hand of justice." He dropped the tube into the water. "We'll row the rest of the way. By the by, nice shot, Kip."

THE BLACK PRISM • 363

"I hit him?"

"Blew the captain right off his wheel."

"The wheel's at the...uh, back, right?" The musketeer had been at the front.

"Stern?" Liv suggested.

A dubious look. "You weren't aiming at the captain, were you?" Gavin asked.

"Aiming?" Kip asked, grinning.

"Orholam have mercy, the nut doesn't fall far from the tree," Ironfist said. "However, luck is a—"

" 'Luck' is not dropping your father's priceless, one-of-a-kind pistols in the sea," Gavin said.

"I dropped your pistols?" Kip asked, heart dropping.

"Whereas 'slick' is catching said pistols at the last moment," Gavin said, producing the weapons from behind his back. He grinned.

"Oh, thank Orholam," Kip breathed.

"You still almost lost my pistols," Gavin said. "And for that, you get to row. Liv, you too."

"What?!"

"You're his tutor. He's your responsibility. Everything he does wrong is on you."

"Oh, *perfect*," she said.

Chapter 57

"It looks so...dirty," Kip said. After seeing the wealth of Big Jasper and the magical edifices of the Chromeria, Garriston looked decidedly unimpressive.

"Dirt is the least of it," Gavin said.

Kip wasn't sure what that meant, but he was sorry that he'd been unconscious when he'd floated through the city the first time with Gavin. If he had seen Garriston then, it would have doubtless been impressive. It would have been the largest gathering of humanity he'd seen in his life, at least, if not the cleanest. Rekton's alcaldesa would never have tolerated the heaps of trash Kip could see pushed into the alleys just off the docks, sitting right next to crates often holding food. Disgusting.

The docks had perhaps forty ships, half-protected by a seawall with great gaps in it. Liv saw Kip looking at the holes, wondering if there was some purpose for them. "The occupiers never really want to break their backs helping out us backward Tyreans," she said. "The moorages opposite the gaps in the seawall are given to locals. You should see the captains scurry when a winter storm comes. The soldiers gather up in the towers and take bets on whether individual ships will break up."

The scull, powered by Liv and a hard-breathing Kip, cruised past galleys, galleasses, corvettes, and fishing dories full of locals mending their nets. The men and women stopped their work at the sight of a scull, much less a scull with such an exotic crew. It warmed Kip just to see Tyrean faces again. It made him feel at home. Only as they went past did he see the hostility on those faces.

Ah, not much for foreign drafters. Guess that makes sense.

"Where are we going?" Kip asked.

Commander Ironfist pointed to the most magnificent, tallest building in the city. From here, all Kip could see was the perfect egg-shaped tower with a spike pointing to heaven. A wide stripe around the widest part of the tower was inlaid with tiny round mirrors, none bigger than Kip's thumb. In the afternoon sun, the tower seemed to be on fire. Above and below that stripe of mirrors, similar stripes of other colors of glass were inlaid as well.

"I sorta figured," Kip said. "What I meant was, where should we dock the scull?"

"Right there," Gavin said, pointing to a blank wall at the point nearest a gate. It wasn't a docking spot, and the level of the streets was a good four paces above the level of the water.

Nonetheless, Kip and Liv steered—fairly expertly, Kip thought—toward the wall. The scull's nose dipped lower in the water as blue luxin bloomed on the front of the boat and snaked out. It solidified as soon as it touched the wall and became steps, locking the scull in place and giving them easy egress.

"I'm still not used to this whole magic thing," Kip said.

"I'm thirty-eight years old," Commander Ironfist said, "and I'm not used to it. Just a little quicker to react. Grab your packs."

They did, and climbed the stairs to street level while locals looked at them curiously. After they were all off, Gavin touched a corner of the stairs. All the luxin in the scull lost coherence and dissolved, falling into the water as dust, grit, and goo depending on its color. The yellow even flashed a little, much of its mass translated back into light, and the water popped up a little, suddenly freed of the weight of the scull. Gavin, of course, paid it all no heed.

This is normal for him. What kind of world have I stepped into? If Gavin were at dinner and misplaced his knife, he'd draft one rather than get up and look. If his cup were dirty, he'd draft a new one rather than clean the old. That gave Kip a thought.

"Gavin—er, Lord Prism, why don't drafters wear luxin?" Kip asked.

Gavin grinned. "They do, sometimes. Obviously, yellow breastplates and such are highly valued in battle, but I'm guessing you mean as clothes."

"*You* use magic for everything," Kip said.

"That's me," Gavin said. "A normal drafter isn't going to shorten her life just so she doesn't have to dock her scull another fifty paces out. Well, some would, of course. The truth is, there was a fashion of wearing luxin clothing once, when I was a boy. With the application of enough will, even some kinds of sealed luxin can become fairly flexible. Soon, there were drafter-tailors who specialized in the clothing. But most people couldn't afford them, and if you make your own, there are any number of mistakes you can make. Some are fairly harmless, like making your pant legs too stiff. But if you made a mistake in the drafting, your shirt might dissolve into dust in the middle of a day. Or"—Gavin cleared his throat—"certain mischievous boys might learn how to unseal the luxin that the tailor-drafters had woven. These boys might have caused some chaos at a memorable party, where the ladies who'd gone to the expense of even having luxin undergarments found themselves in particular distress." His mouth tightened, hiding a grin at a memory. "Sadly, the fashion ended rather abruptly after that."

"That was you? I heard about that party," Liv said.

"I'm sure whatever you heard was much exaggerated," Gavin said.

"No," Ironfist said. "It wasn't."

Gavin shrugged. "I was a bad child. Fortunately, I've come a long way since then. Now I'm a bad man." He smiled, but it didn't touch his eyes. "Here we go," he said as three Ruthgari men approached.

The three all wore what looked to Kip like wool sheets with a hole cut for the head, carefully folded so there were pleats at their wide leather belts. The garment—a tunic?—then fell to the men's knees. Though their legs were bare, the wool seemed entirely inappropriate for Tyrea's climate, and all three were sweating freely. All wore leather sandals, though the guards' laced up into shin armor. The guards each carried a pilum, and a gladius and a crude pistol at their belts. The man in the lead, apparently in charge, had his tunic embroidered at the hem and on each breast. He carried a scroll, a large bag slung over one shoulder, and a heavy purse at his belt. He wore a pair of clear spectacles low on his nose.

Clear spectacles? What kind of drafter would want clear spectacles?

But as the men came close, Kip realized the man wasn't a drafter at all. His eyes were clear brown. The men were also all pale, a common Ruthgari trait, Kip guessed. With their skin barely bronzed, they weren't pale or freckled like Blood Foresters, but they still seemed pretty ghostly. Their hair was a normal dark hue from brown to black, but straight, and fine. They walked with either authority or hauteur. Kip glanced at Liv. She was definitely taking their attitude as the latter. She practically sneered at them. Kip thought she might spit at their feet.

"I am the assistant portmaster," the man said. "Where's your vessel? The tax is levied according to size and term of stay."

"I'm afraid the size of our vessel is negligible at the moment," Gavin said.

"I'll be the judge of that, thank you. Where'd you dock?"

"Right about there," Gavin said, pointing.

The assistant portmaster looked, then glanced up and down the wall, squinting. There were no ships within fifty paces. He folded his arms, his jaw setting as if Gavin were making fun of him. "The tax isn't heavy, but let me assure you, the penalty for attempting to evade taxation is."

One of the guards tapped the assistant portmaster's shoulder, but the man ignored him.

"As it should be," Gavin said, still polite. He handed over a letter.

The man held the letter low, so he was looking through his spectacles, like he was going to draft the letters right into words. "Oh," he said quietly. "Oh, oh!"

The man's head snapped up, and he peered at Gavin's eyes through his spectacles. "Oh! My Lord Prism! A thousand pardons! Please, my lord, let us accompany you to the fortress. It would be a great honor to us."

Gavin inclined his head.

"I sort of thought you'd pick them all up with magic and shake them or something," Kip said, once they all fell in behind the guards and the assistant portmaster.

"There's a time to toss idiots around," Gavin said. "But this man's just doing his job." They walked into the shadow of the fortress, whose northern wall nearly overhung the harbor. Both of them looked up. There were archers walking along the top of the wall, looking down at them. "Besides," Gavin said, "you start throwing luxin around, you never know who's going to answer with gunfire."

The assistant talked to the men guarding the gate. Lots of furtive glances at Gavin followed. Kip was busy looking at the fortress. The gate, and the entire fortress, was carved travertine. Mellow green, incised with a crosshatched pattern to make the stone look woven rather than carved. There were a number of murder holes cut in the gate. As the soldiers opened the gate, Kip saw that it led to a short killing ground, entirely enclosed, with murder holes everywhere, then another gate. The guards at the second gate, which was open, carried muskets with almost bell-shaped muzzles. These guns were also shorter than the muskets the guards at the Chromeria carried.

Kip was next to Ironfist now, so he asked, "Why are their muskets so short?"

"Blunderbusses," Ironfist said. "Instead of a ball, they load them with cobblers' nails or chain. At short range you can hit four or five men. Or blow a good hole in one. Good for rioters. A man cut in half isn't any less dead than one with a small hole in his heart, but he's a much greater deterrent to everyone else in the crowd."

"Nice," Kip said, swallowing.

After a few more checkpoints, at which they accrued a few more senior guards, they climbed several floors. When they were on the third floor, they passed an open door to chambers overlooking the sea. Gavin stopped abruptly. Their escorts didn't notice immediately. Ignoring them, Gavin walked into the room.

Ironfist, Kip, and Liv followed him. The room was a suite of apartments, filled with paintings, pillows, screens with ornate paintings of hunts, fireplaces, several chandeliers, and great long-handled fans for room slaves to waft their masters. Everywhere Kip looked, things sparkled, shined, and gleamed.

"This," Gavin announced as his escorts hurried in, "will be sufficient..."

"Yes, Lord Prism, of course, this is the guest of honor's suite. We'll get—"

"For my servants," Gavin finished. "Kip, Liv, I trust you can stay out of trouble while I get our accommodations arranged?"

"Yes, of course, my Lord Prism," Liv said, a formality and maturity in her voice that Kip wasn't familiar with.

"Start Kip's drafting lessons. I'll check up on you after I'm finished with a few things."

"Of course," Liv said, curtseying. Kip half-bowed, and instantly felt deeply foolish. He didn't know how to bow. No one bowed where he grew up.

"Ironfist?" Gavin said.

Ironfist raised an eyebrow—oh, *now* you want me to go with you?

"Best chance you'll have to see a pompous Ruthgari governor get kicked out of his rooms. More if you're lucky. Might even be someone you know."

The corner of Ironfist's mouth twitched. "It's the simple pleasures that make life beautiful, isn't it?"

Chapter 58

The door closed behind them, and abruptly Kip and Liv were alone, away from the important people and the matters of state. Children once more.

Liv looked at Kip for a long time.

"What?" Kip asked.

"Sometimes it's really strange to me that you are who you are. A week ago I would have blushed just at seeing Commander Ironfist. Now I'm sitting in the finest rooms in the Travertine Palace—and they're mine?"

"I've given up trying to understand it all," Kip said. "I think if I stop and think too much—" I'll become a blubbering baby. "Things will just fall apart."

In a moment, Liv's face changed. Her eyes softened, compassion etched on every feature. "You were there. In the village. When it happened."

"At Green Bridge with Isa and Sanson. And Ram, of course." He still wanted to sneer at the very thought of Ram, but that seemed cruel and small now. "Ram and Isa were killed. Sanson and I got away. But eventually they killed him too." Kip's voice was wooden and distant even in his own ears. He couldn't even look at Liv. If he saw her compassion, he'd break. He already looked weak and foolish and young and fat in her eyes, a boy to be pitied. He didn't need to make it worse by crying. "My mother made it out but her skull was smashed. I was with her when she..."

"Oh, Kip, I'm so sorry."

He pushed that down, pushed it aside. "Anyway, I really do hope your father got out. He was always good to me. In fact, if he hadn't made me leave when he did, I'd be dead."

Liv said nothing for a time. Kip couldn't decide if it was an awkward silence or not. "Kip," she said finally, "I've been trying to work up the nerve to... Things can be really complicated now. With who your father is, and the way things are at the Chromeria... Sometimes things don't really go the way we want, and we—"

"Am I supposed to have some idea what you're talking about?" Kip asked. " 'Cause..."

She opened her mouth and looked at him again. Then he saw the gates come down. "I'm just really glad you made it out, Kip."

"Thanks," he said. Thanks for not trusting me enough to say whatever you just wanted to say. "Should we get started?"

She smiled wanly, like she wanted to say more but didn't know how. "Sure. Come out to the balcony."

They walked out onto the balcony, which hung literally over the sea. From above, they could hear the muffled voices of men speaking on top of the Travertine Palace. Kip stood looking out at the sea, trying to put himself in a frame of mind to concentrate, and said, "What do I do?"

"To draft you need four things," Liv said. "Skill, Will—"

"Source, and Still," Kip said. "Er, sorry, I have picked up a thing or two."

"Right. So there's basically modifications and nuances to each of the big four, but that's where it all starts. Let's start with source."

Kip thought that he'd picked up a lot of what she was going to say, but one doesn't interrupt a beautiful girl unless one is going to be funny. Liv rummaged through her pack and pulled out a rolled-up green cloth and then a white one.

"We'll hold off on the color theory as much as we can," she said. "We know you've drafted green. So your source can either be something reflecting green light in the world or you can take something that has green as a component color and look at it through a lens."

"Huh?" Kip said. So much for this all being a repeat. "What do you mean reflecting green? You mean something green?"

"Something you'll learn the further you go in the Chromeria is that your experience of a thing and the nature of the thing itself are often different things."

"Sounds…uh, metaphysical," Kip said. Hadn't Gavin said something like that?

"Some take it that way, too, but I'm speaking strictly physically. Look at this." Liv pulled out another cloth. It was a red spectrum, but instead of flowing smoothly from the deepest to the lightest red, there were parts that took steps back. "When you look at this, Kip, you can tell that it's off. It generally goes right, but there are sub-colors out of sequence. Most men can't see that. They think it's right. They can differentiate these four spectral blocks here, but not these blocks inside. It doesn't matter how hard they try, or how long they study it. Their experience of it is less nuanced than yours or mine. Now, quite honestly, we don't know if what you and I see is the total-ity of what is actually there, or if some people from beyond the Great Desert might think we're as blind as we think the men are who can't tell this from this."

"That's weird."

"I know. In class, the magisters usually have every boy come to the front and attempt the test, just because so many of the girls who can see the differences can't believe that everyone else can't see them too. It's pretty humiliating. Actually, I think it's worse for the girls who can't see it either. The boys aren't expected to pass. The girls who can't see it feel awful." She shook herself. "Tangent. The point to remember, even if you don't believe it now, is that color doesn't inhere in a thing. Things reflect or absorb colors from light. You think this cloth is green. It's not. Really it's a cloth that absorbs all colors except green."

"This is us saving color theory for later?" Kip asked lightly.

She paused, then she saw he was teasing and she smiled. "No you don't, I'm not going to get drawn into more tangents. The point is, light is primary. This cloth, in a dark room, is worthless to you. Obviously, you can take the religious significances pretty deep, but you and I are only going to talk about the physical, not the metaphysical. You can draft green light. There are only a couple of ways for you to do that. The best is to have green things around you. Especially if you have lots of them. Especially if you have lots of different hues and tones available."

"So, like a forest."

"Exactly. That's why before the Unification, the green goddess Atirat was worshipped in Ruthgar and the Blood Forest more than anywhere else. Green drafters flocked to the forests and the Verdant Plains because they were more powerful there than anywhere else. In turn, those lands were dominated by the green virtues and the green vices, either simply because of the sheer amount of green being drafted there or because Atirat was real. Take your pick."

"That I don't understand."

"We'll worry about all that later. The second-best way to draft is to have spectacles. Like these." She reached into her pack and pulled out a little cotton pouch. Loosening the drawstring, she withdrew a pair of green spectacles.

"You don't draft green," Kip said.

"No, I don't," Liv said, smiling.

"They're for me?" Kip asked. Tingles shot down his spine.

Liv smiled broadly. "Usually there's a little ceremony, but it amounts to a congratulations."

Kip took the spectacles gingerly. They had perfectly round lenses set in a thin iron frame. He put them on his face. Liv stepped close and measured where the arms of the spectacles passed over his ears. Kip could smell her. Somehow, after a full day skimming across the entire sea and fighting pirates and then baking in the sun, she smelled wonderful. Of course, Kip hadn't been this close to a woman very often—except his mother, usually covered with sweat or vomit on the nights he was unlucky and had to carry her home. Isa had smelled good too, but different than Liv.

Isa had barely crossed Kip's mind in the last days. He'd thought about her, but there was something hollow there. He'd let himself daydream about kissing Isa someday, but maybe that had been more because she was there than that she was perfect for him. Or because she was there and Liv wasn't, and Kip needed something to distract him from thinking about Liv.

And now here she was. She'd measured both sides, and she took his spectacles off and was carefully bending the arms to fit behind his ears.

"Hmm," she said. "Your right ear's higher than the left."

"My ears are lopsided?" Kip said. *As if I didn't have enough to be self-conscious about.*

"Don't worry, mine are too! Really, most people's are off a little bit." She paused. "Just not quite *so much.*" She shook her head in disbelief.

"I've got freakish *ears?*"

Liv grinned wickedly. "Gotcha."

"Orholam's ba— Ahem, beard." Kip scowled. *Every time. Every stinkin' time.*

She smiled, self-satisfied, and gave the nose pieces a final bend, then propped the spectacles on his face. "There. You might have to play with them to make them more comfortable, but they aren't really meant to be on your face all day long anyway."

He looked around, and was not terribly surprised to see that most everything had a greenish tinge through the green glass.

"What you're seeing is white light from the sun reflected off of surfaces, then filtered through your lenses. So if you're surrounded by white marble walls or something, you'll be able to draft almost as much as if you were in a forest. The lenses aren't as good as drafting from natural greens, but it's better than nothing. You can't just look at anything, though. Look around. You see how some things really look green, and others don't? Like if you look at this cloth, what color does it appear to be?" She drew another cloth out of her bag.

"Uh, red." Kip thought he could hear Gavin's voice from the floor above them, getting louder, angry.

"It is red."

Refocusing his attention on Liv, Kip looked over his glasses, and though the cloth's tone was changed a little, it was indeed red. "So how does that work?" he asked.

"The spectacles will only help if there are surfaces that are reflecting green to you. White surfaces work best because white is all the colors together. Much less good, but sometimes possible, will be drafting through your lenses when looking at yellow or blue surfaces, since green is a secondary color."

"Lost me there."

"So now you *want* the color theory?" She grinned, joking. "For your purposes, if you need to draft, the spectacles will help most if you can find things that are either white or light-colored. Ripe wheat would work, a spruce tree won't," Liv said.

"I think I can remember that," Kip said. The whole things-aren't-the-color-they-are thing really didn't make sense, but he suspected he could wrestle with that later.

"Good, so that covers source. For the time being."

You mean we still have to cover skill, will, and still?

Liv said, "I don't want to beat this to death, and I'm sorry you don't get to have the ceremony, because maybe that helps this sink in. Those spectacles are now your most important possession. Not only do most drafters have to save up for months or even a year to afford one pair of spectacles, but everyone then immediately saves for a spare pair. If you get rich, or if the Prism orders it, I suppose, you can have a custom pair made by the lens grinders. They can give you a darker or lighter green or adjust the frame for fit or looks. But without your spectacles, you're close to powerless. I know you've been with the Prism, but he's the exception. He doesn't need spectacles. His eyes don't halo. He can use as much magic as he wants. The rules don't apply to him. Even the rules for Prisms don't seem to apply to him. Can you imagine anyone else coming in here, alone, and simply taking over? From the Ruthgari? And the funny thing is, they're going to take it. They won't like it, but they'll—"

A man's voice from the roof interrupted her. "I don't give a good god's damn what your paper says, there's no way you're—" The man cut off with a yelp.

Kip looked up just as a man plunged past their balcony. He landed far below with a huge splash in the bay, and Kip saw him struggle to the surface, spluttering, his rich clothes billowing in the water. He started crying for help.

"This is outrage—!" someone started to shout, then Kip saw another man plunge past the balcony. He splashed in the bay, almost on top of the governor.

There was a gigantic burst of light. "So help me, the next one of you isn't going to land in water," Gavin said, his voice ringing.

Kip expected to hear gunshots—surely the governor had guards—but there was nothing. They took it.

That's my father. That's my father?

Gavin imposed his will, and the world took it.

"So," Kip said, feeling very much like the men floundering in the bay beneath him, barely able to swim and desperate to be pulled out. "So. Will. That's next, right?"

Chapter 59

Corvan Danavis approached Garriston as the sun set. The outer walls of Garriston, of course, had long ago been demolished. During the Prisms' War—Corvan never thought of it as the False Prism's War—he had set men to working on rebuilding them, but there just hadn't been time. The outer walls had been built to shield a city of hundreds of thousands. At the time of the war, there had been perhaps ninety thousand. There had been no way to protect them all.

The irrigation canals that could have been watering all the land between the outer walls and the inner walls were broken, except for one or two. But the inner walls still stood, as did the Ladies.

The Ladies, mostly now stripped of associations with the goddess Anat, guarded each gate. Each was an enormous white statue, incorporated into the wall itself. Each had represented an aspect of Anat: the Guardian was the colossus standing astride the entrance to the bay; the Mother guarded the south gate, heavily pregnant, defiant, dagger bared; the Hag guarded the west gate, leaning heavily on a staff; the Lover lay across the river gate to the east. For reasons Corvan had never understood, the Lover was depicted perhaps in her thirties while the Mother was depicted as very young, perhaps still in her teens. Each was carved of the most expensive, faintly translucent white marble, such as was only available in Paria—Orholam alone knew how they'd shipped so much this far. The statues, luckily, had been coated in the finest sealed yellow luxin—all of one piece.

Astounding work. The city had been invaded at least three times, and still the Ladies were unmarked, even after the fiery devastation of the great conflagration.

Anat, the Lady of the Desert, the Fiery Mistress, the sub-red, had been the goddess of all hot passions: wrath, protection, vengeance, possessive love, and furious lovemaking. When Lucidonius had taken the city for Orholam and eliminated the cult, his followers had wanted to tear down the statues, which, granted, would have taken some powerful drafters. Famously, Lucidonius had stopped them, saying, "Tear down only what is false." Several times in the intervening centuries, zealous Prisms had wanted to tear down the pagan relics anyway, but each time the city had threatened war. Until the Prisms' War, Garriston had had enough military power that a threat of going to war with her was daunting.

Corvan had never approached the Lover at sunset. As with the other Ladies, her body was incorporated into the gate. She lay on her back, back arched over the river, feet planted, her knees forming a tower on one bank, hands entwined in her hair, elbows rising to form the tower on the other bank. She was clad only in veils, and before the war a portcullis could be lowered from her arched body into the river, its iron and steel hammered into shape so that they looked like a continuation of her veils. But in the war the portcullis had been broken and never replaced.

The sight of her still took Corvan's breath. With the sun setting, the thin yellow luxin sealing the statue, usually nearly invisible, was set alight. The yellow was like golden bronze skin, fading slowly as Corvan walked and the sun sank, finally leaving only a welcoming silhouette—a wife waiting abed for her long-absent husband.

It sent a pang through him. He could never come here without thinking of Qora, his first wife. Liv's mother. Qora had greeted him like that once, lying abed, clad only in veils, deliberately mimicking the Lover when Corvan had returned to her. Even now, eighteen years later, grief and remembered desire and joy and love twined in his breast. Corvan had remarried in Rekton, two years after Qora's death, but marrying Ell had been more to give Liv a mother than for love. Three years later, Ell had been murdered by an assassin who'd finally tracked Corvan down. Corvan had considered moving, but the alcaldesa begged him to stay, and Kip was there, so he'd stayed. But he'd not remarried again, not even with the overwhelming number of women for every man in Rekton and the constant carping of the would-be matchmakers. He couldn't love as he had loved before. Losing another woman he loved as much as he'd loved Qora would kill him, and it wasn't fair to ask another woman to act as mother to his daughter if he wasn't willing to love her with his whole heart. Corvan no longer had a whole heart to give.

He trudged on, past farms with their thin but ripening crops of spelt and barley, trying not to look at the Lover stretched luxuriously before him. Reaching the gate, which opened through the spilling tresses of her hair, he joined the line of men and women heading back into the city, brushing past those heading back out for the night. He kept his eyes down as he passed between two Ruthgari guards who had still been on their mothers' knees during the war. They were barely paying any attention to the stream of people passing by them, however. One was leaning against the Lover's cascading hair, his foot propped against the rippling stone, his straw *petasos*, the characteristic Ruthgari broad-brimmed hat, thrown back to hang from his neck now that the sun wasn't beating down on them. "...think he's here for?" he was asking.

"Scorch me if I know, but they say he threw Governor Crassos into the bay. I suppose we'll..."

Corvan couldn't hear any more without pausing, and pausing meant inviting attention. Inviting attention might mean making eye contact, and with Corvan's red-haloed eyes, that wasn't a good idea.

So someone powerful has come to Garriston, but who was powerful enough to throw a governor in the bay? Corvan didn't know anything about this Governor Crassos, but the Ruthgari royal family had half a dozen young princes. Most likely one of them had been sent to help oversee the withdrawal from Garriston. No one else would dare throw a Ruthgari governor into the sea.

An impulsive prince actually might be better for Corvan's purposes than a comfortable governor. Harder to deal with at first, but more likely to prepare for war, and war was what Corvan was bringing, like it or not.

As he passed through the city, he found himself analyzing it like the general he used to be. King Garadul might be a monster, but the Ruthgari were the occupiers. Who would the people of Garriston join, and would they join enthusiastically or not? As Corvan walked, he paid particular attention to the Ruthgari soldiers. At times, the men walked singly, running errands for their commanders or simply heading back to barracks or out to taverns. He saw a soldier get jostled on accident by a vendor closing his carpet stall who backed up too quickly. The soldier pushed past like it was an annoyance, but never checked his back. The vendor, a native Tyrean, apologized respectfully, but without fear.

This wasn't a city on the verge of revolt. The Tyreans had grown accustomed to being occupied. The Ruthgari were the fourth satrapy to do so, and this was their second time around. Not every nation got a turn in the occupation and spoils. Paria had had the first two years, and if they'd had the richest spoils to steal, they'd also had the task of putting down the most rebels. The Ilytians had ostensibly fought on Dazen's side, and had no central government anyway, so they didn't get a turn. The Aborneans had preferred to trade with both sides, and had entered the fight only after the Battle of Sundered Rock. They didn't get a turn either. That left the Parians, the Atashians, the Blood Foresters, and the Ruthgari. In that order, if Corvan remembered correctly. It made sense that the people of Garriston would have their favorites, or at least those less hated, among their occupiers.

It took Corvan only a bit of mental shuttling to figure that with the Parians replacing the Ruthgari, this would be the third time Garriston had endured the Parians. The most easily tolerated occupiers were about to be replaced by the most hated ones.

But the question his observations didn't answer was just how much fear was mixed with the hatred of the Parians. The Parians had put down rebels both times they'd ruled. Maybe their cruelty meant the Tyreans would think twice before taking up weapons. It might mean they would take them up more quickly. Corvan didn't know, couldn't know without spending a lot of time in the city. Time he didn't have.

The city was more cosmopolitan than it had been the last time he had visited, some ten years ago. Before the war, Garriston had been as populous and diverse as any rich port city in the world. After the war, everyone who could leave had left, especially those who looked like they were from elsewhere. Tensions had run high. During that time, the only people in Garriston were native Tyreans and their occupiers of the moment. Apparently, with each round of occupation, a few traders and soldiers had stayed and intermarried with locals. Corvan saw two shopkeepers chatting as they swept out their open stalls with straw brooms. One woman had the traditional Tyrean caramel skin and dark full brows and wavy hair, while the woman next to her had skin like honey, and ash blonde hair, rare even for the Ruthgari. They were dressed almost identically, bangles on their wrists, long flax skirts, hair tied back with scarves.

Corvan passed an alley where children played *gada* together, kicking and passing a ball of wrapped leather. There were more obviously Tyrean-blooded children than any other kind, but the teams were mixed. A few mothers had gathered to watch, and they stood close to each other regardless of what Corvan would have guessed were their origins, gossiping or shouting encouragement.

Not a powder keg. That was good. A radical shift in power and lawlessness in a city where neighbor hated neighbor would have invited wanton bloodshed. Garriston had seen enough of that.

The water market, basically an outsized version of what Rekton had, was nearly empty except for a few food vendors offering quick meals to passing soldiers and those who had otherwise missed dinner. Corvan bought a few skewers of rabbit and fish marinated in a fiery Ilytian pepper sauce and kept walking.

Before he headed to the Travertine Palace, Corvan walked to the Hag's Gate. Here, like the Guardian's Gate and the Lover's Gate, the statue was worked into the wall. But this time Corvan had no interest in the statue. He had come to watch the soldiers. The gates had closed for the night, though it had doubtless been a long time since raiders had dared move against the city itself. The soldiers who stood at the top of the wall were joking, laughing, talking loudly, even drinking when their superiors left. Corvan had seen archers atop the Hag's Crown and at the top of the Hag's Staff—the two towers on either side of the gate—but after the two women settled in, quivers laid down, bows unstrung, they never made a circuit of their respective posts.

So, soldiers with little discipline. Soldiers who had become city guards, through no fault of their own. In the first year of an occupation, the soldiers might be sent against raiders and brigands or patrol the river's length. After that, they retreated to the city and became guards. The soldierly duties came to seem extraneous, and discipline slipped. Sitting watch in towers where there was never anything to watch for soon became a post where soldiers gambled and drank.

Corvan headed toward the Travertine Palace. Of course, there was no way they were going to let some peasant walk in off the street and meet their prince, so when he got close to the front gate, he ducked into an alley. After Karris had been captured, Corvan had scouted King Garadul's camp enough to decide that any attempt at rescue would be suicide. Then, as they'd rendezvoused with other generals, swelling the army—most likely with forced levies—they'd turned south. Corvan had headed back to a cave outside of Rekton.

He was almost disappointed that thieves had never found his cache. When Rekton's alcaldesa had told Corvan that he and his daughter could stay, he'd hidden away everything that could connect him to the war, both for his new home's sake and his own. He'd shaved off his distinctive beaded mustache and traded rich clothes and weapons for flaxen pants and a dyer's shop. What had seemed meager gold in his pockets then was now a fortune in his eyes, but in the intervening years it had all been unspendable. No one in Rekton had gold coins, especially not stamped with a Blood Forester satrap's face.

So now he pulled out the long folded samite tunic, swept off a portion of the ground with his hand and laid it on it. Next came a broad leather belt embossed with crocodiles with tiny ruby eyes in emerald-dotted swamps with diamond-eyed herons. Last, he drew out Harbinger, the sword that had passed to him only when the last of his elder brothers died. A young boy sat on the curb opposite him, silently watching, quizzical. Corvan tried to ignore him. He stripped off his long shirt and pulled out a mirror. With mirror and a skin of water, he did his best to clean himself up. Then he dried himself with the dirty shirt and pulled on his rich clothes. There was nothing to be done about his boots or pants, but the samite tunic and the stress was going to have him sweating enough as it was. After packing his things and strapping Harbinger onto his belt and pushing his hair into something resembling order, he took a deep breath and rounded the corner, approaching the gate.

"I need to see whoever's in charge," Corvan said to the guards, walking like a man with purpose.

"Uh..." one of the guards said, looking confused and glancing at the other guard. Apparently they didn't know if he meant the governor or the prince.

"Whoever threw the governor in the bay," Corvan said. "It's an emergency."

The guards shared a look. "Got no reason *not* to waste his time," one guard said to the other. "He's not exactly given us cause to screen his visitors carefully."

The other Ruthgari soldier grinned. "We'll take you right to him, sir."

They didn't even ask his name. Corvan followed them, astounded by his good fortune. Apparently the prince—presumably a younger prince or the Ruthgari wouldn't dare behave this way—hadn't been endearing himself to the common soldiers. Even more incredibly, the soldier marched him straight to the counsel room. Corvan hadn't been there in sixteen years. The man rapped a quick code on the door, and the guards inside opened it. He whispered something about emergency, looks important, to the guard, and then beat a hasty retreat.

The counsel room guard, a tall, serious Ruthgari, ushered Corvan in. "Name?" he asked quietly.

Corvan stepped inside. The Ruthgari prince was leaning over a table in the counsel room, his back to Corvan. "Corvan Danavis," Corvan said quietly. There was a huge—both tall and thickly muscled—ebony guard standing across from the prince, his eyes hard, studying Corvan, taking note of the sword at his side. He wore all black. This prince had some nerve, pretending to have his own Blackguard. When the Chromeria found out about that, it would not be pleased.

"Corvan Danavis," the guard announced loudly. "He says he has an emergency message, my Lord Prism."

It was like lightning hit all three men at once. The Blackguard—an actual, real Blackguard, for Orholam's sake—had two pistols out and his blue spectacles on half a breath after Corvan's name was announced.

The Prism—not a princeling, Gavin Guile himself—stood and turned. His lip curled. "General Danavis, it's been too long."

Chapter 60

Gavin kept his face carefully neutral. After sixteen years, Corvan Danavis still looked fit, healthy, and sharp as ever. His skin was deeply tanned, no doubt to try to cover the freckles and look as Tyrean as possible, and there was no sign of his famous beaded mustache. His blue eyes were only about half-haloed with red, not much more than when Gavin had last seen him. The lines, both smile lines and deeper worry lines, were new, however. His eyes flicked to Ironfist, and then he looked dismayed.

Consummate actor, Corvan Danavis.

"Commander Ironfist, please relieve this man of his weapons, and reprimand the guards. Carefully, yes?" Ironfist would understand instantly. The Ruthgari guards couldn't be too harshly treated or it might inspire general fury at the new boss. But if Gavin let such lax—or possibly insolent—duty stand uncorrected, the Ruthgari soldiers wouldn't respect him. Ironfist would put the fear of Orholam into the guards, without actually making them hate Gavin.

"You wish me to leave you with this traitor, Lord Prism?" Ironfist knew as well as Gavin did that the original guards who'd allowed Corvan into the palace would have beaten a hasty retreat, which meant he'd have to go after them and wouldn't be close if things got out of hand.

Gavin nodded curtly.

Ironfist lowered the hammer of one pistol and tucked it into his

386 • Brent Weeks

belt without taking his eyes or the other pistol off Corvan. He walked forward and took Corvan's sword, eyes flicking only briefly to it in appreciation. After putting the sword and Corvan's bag in a small closet off the main room, he put away his other pistol and frisked Corvan briskly.

Before turning to go, Ironfist looked one more time at Gavin. Are you sure? You know this is a bad idea, right?

Gavin nodded fractionally. Go.

The door closed behind Ironfist. Gavin looked around the room. He hadn't been here long enough to know if there were peepholes or eavesdropping tunnels behind the walls. Corvan stood, hands folded, waiting patiently. "Come out onto the balcony, General."

"Please, I've not been a general for many years," Corvan said, but he followed Gavin out. Gavin closed the double doors behind them. The balcony was spacious, with a number of chairs and tables spread out so the governor and his visitors could enjoy the view over the bay. It made Gavin glad he'd flung the governor a long way. Dropping the man off the roof onto this wouldn't have been quite as humorous— and he hadn't remembered this balcony protruding quite so far. Lucky, Gavin.

Funny that I always think of it as luck, rather than Providence.

Corvan glanced over the edge. "Bay looks deep enough here," he said, the corner of his mouth twisting wryly.

Gavin leaned on the balcony's railing. The sun was just touching the horizon, setting the sea alight, pinks and oranges threaded through thin clouds. Suddenly, the lost years were rolling down his cheeks and he was holding the railing like a drunk, simply to be able to stand. "It cost too much, Corvan."

Corvan glanced around for spies, checking the docks, looking back into the counsel room, up at the roof. He said, "It's good to see you too. Now quit that or you're going to get me started."

Gavin glanced at him. Corvan wore his quirky grin, but his eyes betrayed him. That grin was him trying to give his face something to do so the depth of his emotion didn't overwhelm him.

Suddenly, appearances didn't matter. Gavin embraced his old friend.

"It's good to see you...Dazen," Corvan whispered. That broke open the floodgates for both of them. They wept.

The grand deception had been Corvan's idea from the beginning, sixteen years ago. It had been a throwaway idea when he'd proposed it. Neither had really believed Dazen could beat Gavin. One night, when they'd had a rare respite from the battles and had been sharing one too many skins of wine, Corvan had said, "You could win and simply take Gavin's place."

"That's sort of the point of a Prisms' War, isn't it? Last man standing?" Dazen had said. "Last Prism shining?"

Corvan ignored the joke. Dazen was a little further gone than he was. "No, I mean you could *be* Gavin. You two look almost the same. For years, every time the two of you played *scrum*, the only way anyone could tell you apart was Gavin's prismatic eyes. You have those now."

"Gavin's a peacock. And I'm taller."

"Clothes can be changed. And he wears lifts in his shoes to make himself as tall as you are. Which would actually make things easier."

"He's got that scar. Which you gave him, I might add," Dazen had said.

"I could give you one too. Nice symmetry to that, huh?"

Now Dazen was taking it seriously. "I've gone a while without a haircut. The scar's right along the hairline. I could hide the cut while it was healing."

"If I can remember which side I cut him on," Corvan said. "Pass me that skin, I'm getting parched."

A few days had passed, and Dazen had asked Corvan to stay after another council of war. After dismissing everyone from the tent, he'd handed Corvan a piece of paper. On it was written a precise description of Gavin's scar.

"I was joking," Corvan said, looking into Dazen's serious eyes.

"I'm not. I've got a chirurgeon waiting outside the tent to stitch me up. If anyone notices, we were sparring and had an accident. I'm embarrassed about my clumsiness, so I asked you not to say anything about it."

Corvan had said nothing for a long time. "Dazen. Have you thought about what this would mean? You'd have to maintain a charade for years, maybe the rest of your life. Everyone who loves you now would think you dead. Karris—"

"I lost Karris when I killed her backstabbing brothers."

"Are you prepared to be Gavin in her eyes?" Corvan had asked.

"Corvan, look at our allies," Dazen had said, tense, lowering his voice. "I've practically sworn a port in every satrapy to the Ilytians. I've promised the Atashian throne to Farid Farjad. The cultists joined us in hopes that their strength would help us shatter the Chromeria. Once we win, they'll turn on us. And the Blue-Eyed Demons have been too valuable to us to be content with mercenaries' wages. I expect Horas Farseer to come to me on the eve of the battle with some outrageous demand: lands, titles, permanent bases. I'll have to agree. After we win, I might renege with one group, but not with all of them. I don't know how it got to this, but however things started, we're the bad guys now."

"We're the bad guys. After what they did to Garriston," Corvan said bitterly.

"In terms of what will happen to the Seven Satrapies if we win? Yes."

A long silence. "You'll be discovered eventually," Corvan said. "You must know that. It can't last forever."

"I don't need to fool them for long. A few months. Enough to consolidate the victory. Even if the Spectrum found out, they wouldn't expose me until our enemies are crushed. Some morning, I won't rise from my bed. I can accept that."

"We're not without options," Corvan said. "I mean, if we win. These problems can be handled. We don't know what will happen after we win. If we can take Gavin's army relatively intact and get the Chromeria to capitulate quickly, we could counter—"

"Do you see the White capitulating quickly?"

Corvan opened his mouth. Closed it. "No."

"It's not a good plan," Dazen said. "I know that. But it may be the least bad."

"We may still lose, I suppose," Corvan said.

"You always do look on the bright side," Dazen had said.

Now Corvan pushed Gavin back, wiping his own tears away with the backs of his hands. "I've missed you, friend."

"And I you. Now, what the hell are you doing here?" Gavin asked.

The joy at their reunion leached from Corvan's face. "I came to warn the governor that King Garadul's marching here. His army will arrive within five days, a week at most. And they captured Karris White Oak."

Gavin sucked in a breath. Karris captured?

There was nothing to be done about it now, even if it did tear a hole in his stomach and hollow him out. "I knew about King Garadul," he said. "Not...the other."

"I figured. Why else would you be here?" Corvan said.

"You think he'll attack just after Midsummer's?" Gavin asked.

"The day after," Corvan said. "Ruthgari will have withdrawn, but the Parian regiments won't have landed."

It was what Gavin had guessed. It gave him almost no time. "I can't believe that Governor Crassos never got word of Garadul's army."

"Don't believe it. He did know," Corvan said. "The Ruthgari have been withdrawing early. It's a skeleton crew now, so they make sure they all get out of the city before Garadul attacks. Why should they fight to save the city for the Parians?"

"Bastards," Gavin grunted.

"And cowards and opportunists." Corvan shrugged. "What do you intend to do about it?"

"I intend to hold this city."

"And how do you hope to do that?" Corvan asked.

"Put someone in charge who's an experienced hand at lost causes," Gavin said.

A pause, then Corvan raised his hands. "Oh, no. You can't. It's impossible. Lord Prism, I'm the enemy general!"

"And since when don't the conquered sometimes join the victor's army?" Gavin asked.

"Not as generals. Not right away."

"It's been sixteen years. You're a special case," Gavin said. "Corvan Danavis, held in high esteem by both sides of the False Prism's War. The man who ended the war honorably. A man of unimpeachable integrity and intelligence. It has been a long time, why could people not believe that we had put it all behind us?"

"Because I'm the one who put that scar on your temple, and you were none too happy about it. And Gavin's men killed my wife."

Gavin's brow wrinkled. "There is that."

"You don't need me," Corvan said. "You're no slouch at command, Lord Prism."

It was true. Gavin had seen good leadership and practiced it enough to know his own abilities. He also knew his weaknesses. "With equal armies and terrain and me without magic, who would win between us, Corvan?"

Corvan shrugged. "If you had a good cadre of support staff, and your field commanders would tell you the truth, I think—"

"Corvan, I'm the Prism. Men don't tell me the truth. I ask them, can you do this? And they say yes, no matter what. They want to think the righteousness of obeying the Prism himself will magically help them overcome any obstacle. When I ask for objections to my most flawed plans, I get silence. It took months and several disasters to get our armies even halfway past that back in the war. We don't have that time now." It took a certain kind of mind to understand exactly how each branch of his forces would react, what kind of combat situations they could handle and what ones they would buckle under. Gavin was good at that. He was good at judging enemy commanders, especially those he'd met, and figuring out what they might do.

But making snap judgments about the disposition of enemy forces from fragmentary scouts' reports and getting thousands of men in various branches into position was something else entirely. Splitting your forces and getting them to take different paths to an objective, each under its own commander, and having them arrive simultaneously—that was a skill very few men had. Instilling discipline in men to continue maneuvering during the battle itself, for men to disengage *right now* when they could kill their opponent with just one more thrust, and to get men to communicate so lines could open just a second before a cavalry charge came through the ranks themselves—that was almost impossible. Gavin was good at men and magic. Corvan understood numbers and time and tactics. And sixteen years ago, he'd certainly been Gavin's master in the art of deception. Together, they'd been unstoppable.

"Of course, Rask did massacre my village." Corvan said it dispassionately. He wasn't working through his fury at losing everyone he knew; he was working through the story people would tell: I thought the Prism and General Danavis hated each other! They do, but the Prism needed a general, and Danavis's village was just butchered by King Garadul, he wants revenge.

It worked. It would seem odd, but not incredible. It had been sixteen years.

"So we're both using each other," Gavin said. "I need your tactical genius, you need my army to effect your revenge. I could check in on you openly, making it clear I didn't quite trust you."

"I could grumble about slights in front of the men. Nothing to undermine their confidence, but enough to make it clear I wasn't comfortable with you."

"It could work."

"It could," Corvan said. He turned from looking at the bay. "Deception comes quickly to you these days."

"Too much practice," Gavin said, sobered from his initial joy at the chance to work with his friend once more. "You know, if this works, we can be friends again in a year or two. Even in public."

"Unless I can serve you better as your enemy, Lord Prism."

"I've got enough of those. But fair enough. Now I've got a surprise for you."

"A surprise?" Corvan asked, dubious.

"I can't be seen giving you something you enjoy, so you'll have to go downstairs without me. The room directly below this one." They stepped back toward the counsel room, but Gavin stopped. "How is she?"

Corvan knew who he was talking about and what he really meant. "Karris once seemed like a wilting flower, bowing to her father's every command. And she became a Blackguard, the White's left hand. If anyone can make it, she will."

Gavin took a deep breath and, masks of seriousness and distrust replaced, they stepped into the counsel room. Commander Ironfist had already returned. He stood by the main doors in the loose, casual readiness of a man who spent much of his life guarding, waiting, watching. He was accustomed to inactivity and prepared for violence.

"Commander," Gavin said. "Corvan Danavis and I find ourselves with a common enemy. He has agreed to help us coordinate Garriston's defenses. Please notify the men that they will be overseen by General Danavis, effective immediately. The general will answer only to me. General, you can take it from there?"

Corvan looked like a man who'd swallowed vinegary wine and he wasn't doing a good job of hiding the fact. "Yes, my Lord Prism."

Gavin waved his hand in dismissal. Abrupt, slightly imperious. Let Commander Ironfist take it as Gavin asserting his dominance. Corvan's jaw tightened, but he bowed and left.

Go, my friend, and may finding your daughter repay a tiny measure of the misery you've endured because of me.

Chapter 61

"Will is what makes the Chromeria scary, even for us," Liv said. The sun was just touching the horizon outside, and room slaves entered as if on cue and began lighting lamps and a fire.

"Who is this Will, and how do we stop him?" Kip asked.

"Kip." Liv tilted her head down. "Focus."

"Sorry, go ahead." She was ignoring the room slaves, so Kip tried to do so as well.

"Will is just what you think it is. You impose your will on the world. You will magic to happen. Will can cover over the gaps in flawed drafting. That's especially important for flailers."

"Flailers?"

"All men drafters and the half of the women drafters who aren't superchromats," Liv said. She paused. "Well, *most* men, huh?"

The term was a bit nasty, really. A little bit, We're better than you are, you helpless hacks. You try, we succeed. But that was how the Chromeria worked, wasn't it? Everything was about power and dominance. "Right," Kip said, "flailers. Those sad sacks. Pitiful." Even if Kip found himself in the elite group, it didn't mean he had to like how the others were demeaned.

Liv flushed and shot back, "Look, Kip, you don't have to like it, but you have to deal with it. And you'll probably do better if you don't have a chip on your shoulder about everything. It's not like back home. Because guess what? We don't have a home now. The Chromeria is all we get, and we've got it good. So grow up."

It was like he'd been slapped. She was right, but he hadn't expected so much vehemence out of nowhere. He averted his eyes. "Right. Sorry."

She expelled a breath. "No, I'm sorry. That…I don't know…I guess I'm still adjusting to this whole life myself. There's a hierarchy to everything at the Chromeria, Kip, and it's not easy to adjust to. I don't even know if it's good to adjust to it. But once you know your place, you can figure out how you're supposed to deal with everyone else, even people you don't know. It does simplify things. I just—after the last three years as a monochrome in an obscure color, and a Tyrean on top of that, I never liked the whole hierarchy. But I'd finally come to terms with my place in it, and I was almost finished with my training and ready to head out into my shitty life. Now I'm a bichrome and everything's different, overnight. I'm going to have to stay at the Chromeria for another couple of years, and my life will be totally different. People see me now." She smiled ruefully, sadly. "I guess you know all about having everything change in a blink. The thing is, I like my new life. I have new clothes, jewelry, an allowance. A room slave. I guess what I'm seeing is that maybe I didn't hate the hierarchy, maybe I just hated being at the bottom of it. So every time I enjoy something, it feels like confirmation that I'm a hypocrite."

"I'll promise to make your life as difficult as possible, if it'll make you happy," Kip said.

She hit his shoulder playfully, but it nailed a sensitive spot. "You're a real lifesaver, Kip." She grinned, though, as he rubbed his shoulder. Then her smile faded again. "I guess I should take my own advice and start dealing with how things are. You're the Prism's son, I'm your tutor. I shouldn't hit you. Orholam, you're the Prism's son, how dare I?"

Kip's chest tightened. "No!" he almost shouted. The room slaves shot looks at him. He lowered his voice, embarrassed. "Liv, swear to me you won't. I—"

What were you going to say, Kip? I've been in love with you since I can remember? Right.

"I couldn't bear losing my last anchor to Rekton," he said instead, all the words tripping over each other. "You're the only one who knew me before all this."

Great, good job making it seem like it's totally impersonal. I don't care about you, I just care about Rekton.

"I mean...Liv, you know me, you're—" You're my friend? That sounds a little presumptuous, doesn't it? What if she's never thought of you as a friend?

"You're from Rekton, too," he said instead, lamely. Impersonal again. Damn! "I need someone to talk to, and I've always...admired you."

Admired? Like she's a painting?

"I mean, I appreciate—"

Appreciate. Kind of the same as admire, isn't it? Like she's a good cook?

Orholam's balls, this is agony! Ah, a way out! Not appreciate her, but appreciate how she does something.

"I appreciate how you—" How she whats?

How she looks in that one too-small green shirt she used to—shit!

"—have always been so nice to me."

Now you're the pleading, awkward child again. Well done. Kip Silver Tongue, they ought to call you.

I'm never going to speak to another woman again.

Kip could barely stand to look at Liv after that performance, but she waited until he met her eyes, leery.

"Why, Kip, are you flirting with me?!" she asked.

It was like Kip had stepped into that nightmare where he walked to the Midsummer's Dance on the green, barely registering the curious glances until he stepped up on the stage and the music stopped, every dancer missed their steps, and everyone turned to look at him. And then he noticed he was naked. And then everyone started laughing. Pointing. Making jokes.

No, this was worse. He wasn't going to wake from this. All the blood had drained from his face. Evernight, it had drained from everywhere. He had no idea where it had all gone, but it had taken his ability to speak with it.

"Kip, I'm kidding," Liv said.

His mouth moved. Blood coming back. Thoughts slower.

"Not often that you're left with nothing to say," Liv said, poking him. His thoughts on that must have shown, because she smirked. "If you don't watch it, I'll ruffle your hair."

"That's it, I'm shaving my head!" Kip declared.

Liv laughed. "Enough, enough! No more digressions! I'll never teach you anything if we keep on like this."

"So," Kip said, "will. Not the bad man. See? At least I remember where we got off track."

Liv shook her head, amused. "Not so fast. First, Kip, you've got a deal. I'd love to be your friend. Maybe we can remind each other every now and again where we came from."

Kip felt his ears getting hot. As if they'd ever cooled. "I'd like that a lot," he said.

"Now, *finally*, will. Will covers a multitude of flaws, just as—"

"Love covers a multitude of sins," a familiar voice declared from the door.

Both Kip's and Liv's heads snapped around. It was Master Danavis, Liv's father, alive.

"Father? Father!" Liv literally shrieked. She jumped up and ran to her father and threw herself into his arms. Corvan laughed and squeezed her hard.

"I heard you were dead!" Liv said.

Um, yes, that was me. Kip, bringer of false bad tidings. "I didn't believe it, but I was so—" Liv started crying.

Corvan closed his eyes, just holding his daughter. Kip wondered if there were some way he could escape.

And go where? This is my room.

But after a few moments, Corvan gently pushed his daughter back. "I am surprisingly durable. You look more lovely than ever, Aliviana."

"I'm all cryey," Liv protested, wiping her eyes.

"Perhaps even a smidge more beautiful than your mother. A claim I'd not have tolerated until this day, seeing the truth with my own eyes. She'd be so proud of you."

"Father," Liv said, her cheeks coloring, but pleased.

"Don't you think she's beautiful, Kip?"

Kip spluttered, making some kind of sound like he was drowning. Seriously, if embarrassment were a muscle, I'd be huge.

"Faather!" Liv said, horrified.

Corvan laughed. "My day wouldn't have been complete without my daughter thinking I was embarrassing. Your pardon, Kip."

"Erm," Kip said eloquently. So he hadn't been the target after all. Liv had. Kip was seeing where she got her wicked sense of humor.

"It's wonderful to see you well, Kip...Kip Guile." Corvan shook his head, astounded. "Liv, Kip, I'd love to catch up with you both, but the Prism has just given me work."

"Work?" Liv asked.

"I've been put in charge of the defense of Garriston, under only the Prism himself."

"What?!" Liv said. "You're a general again?"

"Not as enviable a position as you might think. A softer bed doesn't make for easier sleep when ten thousand lives rest in your shaking hands. King Garadul's army will be here in about five days. They'll attack the day after Midsummer's. If we're to hold this city, I'll have to devise a more brilliant defense than I've ever seen. I need to go set some things in motion now, but Liv, I'll come find you sometime after midnight. Kip, maybe tomorrow?"

"I'd like that, Master Danavis. *General* Danavis?"

Master Danavis smiled. "Yes. Hadn't noticed how much I'd missed that. Despite everything. Say, Liv, do you know anything about Karris White Oak?"

Liv shrugged. "Only Blood Forester Blackguard, astounding fighter, bichrome who was nearly a poly, maybe the fastest drafter on the Jaspers. Why?"

The new general said, "She was captured by King Garadul. The Prism won't admit it, but I know it's going to drive him to distraction. He cares a great deal about her. I doubt it will be possible to rescue her, not with the limited assets I have, but I'm going to learn all I can to see if there's any hope at all."

And just like that, a stupid, mad, impossible idea took root.

Chapter 62

"Wake up, Kip," a voice said.

Kip was usually a heavy sleeper, but he sat upright instantly at that voice. "My Lord Prism?" he asked, blinking. It felt like it had barely been ten minutes since he went to bed.

Gavin said, "Get dressed. We're going for a walk." He turned toward Commander Ironfist, who was standing by the door. "You're invited."

A grin flashed over Ironfist's face, visible only because his teeth were so starkly white against his ebony skin. He would have accompanied them regardless.

Kip pulled on his clothes. Within minutes, they were walking the streets of Garriston. Kip was playing his part of the gawker once more, still a little overwhelmed by being in a city of this size, despite that it wasn't nearly as impressive as the Jaspers. The construction, of course, wasn't all towering minarets. Like back home, the buildings were square, with flat roofs where people could relax in the evenings or sleep during the unbearably hot nights. Even with the sea breezes, it got stiflingly hot here. But the buildings here weren't solely the stone construction that was used in Rekton. Interspersed with the stone, often on the same building, were mud bricks and date palm wood, all stuck together with gypsum mortar. Even the whitewash, helpful in cooling homes and preserving the mortar and mud bricks from the sun, was applied haphazardly. The buildings were, however, three and four stories tall. Only a few buildings in Rekton rose to three stories. People in the streets looked dirty, and there was garbage everywhere.

Gavin, Kip noticed, was wearing a worn, faded cloak with a single button holding it closed in front. Disguising his status? Indeed, Commander Ironfist was getting more stares than either Kip or Gavin.

"Hey, Ironfist, you think you could be a little less conspicu—" Gavin started, then traced his eyes from Ironfist's feet up, until he had to tilt his head back to take in the huge, hugely muscled man. "Never mind."

Kip smiled. "Where are we going?" he asked.

"You'll see," Gavin said. "How are your studies?"

"I don't know that anything I've done yet counts as studying," Kip said. He scrunched his face. "Liv was barely beginning to explain how drafters' dependence on will makes for a lot of dangerous men when her father came in."

"What'd she say?"

"Well, nothing. I didn't really understand it, and she didn't get the chance to explain."

Gavin turned into an alley to help them bypass the crowded streets surrounding the water market. "Very few men are superchromats, Kip. Even I'm not a superchromat, though Dazen was, so apparently it runs in the family. If you want to draft something that will endure, you have to draft the exact middle of the spectrum you're working with. You want to make a blue sword that will last years after you draft it? It has to be perfect, and of course, you have to keep it out of light, but that's a different topic. Because men, aside from the few exceptions, can't do that—can't draft in the exact middle of a color, not can't keep it out of the light, obviously. Ahem, that is, if men want to make anything permanent, they have to add will. Makes it sound like it's meat you add to a stew, doesn't it? Hmm. I don't teach much, obviously. Let me try this." Gavin appeared perfectly heedless of the dark corners they were passing and the acquisitive eyes that followed them. But then, once any acquisitive eyes alit on Ironfist, they found other things to study in a hurry.

"Every time you draft, you use your will. You have to decide that something totally outlandish, weird, unnatural-seeming is going to happen, and you're going to make it happen. In other words, you decide to do magic. Now, the more outlandish it is, the harder it is to believe you can really do it. Or to put it another way, the more will it takes. You with me?"

"Makes sense so far," Kip said.

"Good. Now, blue sword." Gavin lifted a hand from beneath his cloak. His hand was solid blue, and as Kip watched, blue luxin blossomed from it. Gelled, solidified, hardened into the form of a blue sword. Gavin handed it to Kip.

Kip took it, feeling self-conscious as they passed through an intersection with another alley and he was bearing the blade like he was following it to his destiny. "Uh," he said, but then he felt the hilt go slippery. A moment later, the blade drooped, broke off the hilt of its own weight, and splatted on the dirty cobblestones of the alley. There was a light shimmer of blue, and then nothing but blue dust. The same happened moments later to the hilt in Kip's hand, leaving only that gritty blue dust.

"What's the dust?" Kip asked.

"A later lesson," Gavin said. "I'm having trouble teaching the basics as it is. The point for you is to imagine I'd drafted you a plow instead of a sword. Great, it works while the drafter is at your farm, but ten minutes after he leaves, all you've got is dust, literally. Not helpful. This is why superchromats are heavily recruited by all satrapies."

"So they can make plows?"

"Not all magic is for fun and dismemberment, Kip. In fact, most drafters spend their whole lives doing practical things like making plows. For every artist, there's ten men who repair roofs with green luxin. Anyway, men—and the women who aren't lucky enough to be superchromats—can cover their failings with will."

"You mean just by trying harder."

"Pretty much."

"That doesn't sound so bad. So they try harder. Liv was making men among drafters sound like slaves compared to the freeborn."

"More like dogs, I'd say," Gavin said.

"Huh?"

"Well, they are second-class because using will constantly wears you. It's exhausting. And will isn't just effort, it's belief and effort together. So if you need belief to do magic, what happens to the man who loses all his belief in himself?"

"He can't do magic?" Kip guessed.

"Exactly. That's half of what all the hierarchy among drafters is about. Satraps and satrapahs treat drafters like they're Orholam's gift to the world not just because they *are* Orholam's gift, but because if the drafter doesn't believe he's special and you call on him to do magic, he won't be able to do it. Drafter who can't draft? Useless."

"I never thought of that." So the rigid hierarchy wasn't simply because they could? Kip guessed that this wasn't the way Liv's tutors had explained things to her.

"Of course, it's a circle that spirals on itself. You're a satrap, you've paid a fortune for a bichrome drafter, well, now you've invested so much in him that you can't afford for him to fail you, so you have to reinforce his feelings of superiority and pamper him, give him slaves and so forth. It makes the more powerful drafters more and more difficult to manage."

There was a cough from behind them. Ironfist.

"Commander," Gavin asked, "you have something to add to this discussion?"

"Little dust in my throat. Apologies," Ironfist said, sounding not at all apologetic.

"Problem with will is, we think that the more will a man or woman expends in their life, the faster they die. Or it could merely be that men or women with great will tend to draft a lot more. Either way, their careers are spectacular. And short. It's probably why male drafters don't tend to live as long as women do, expending will all the time in order to have their drafting be useful. Side effect is that among the most powerful drafters, we have a lot of people with titanic will. Or, to put it bluntly, a lot of arrogant assholes. Especially the men. And madmen. Delusional people tend to believe in what they're doing. Makes them powerful."

"So I'm going to be spending my time with crazy, arrogant bastards."

"Well, many of them are of the finest blood."

Oh, that's right, I'm the only bastard around here. "I thought being a drafter was going to be fun," Kip said.

"Grunts never get to scull," Gavin said.

"Grunts?"

"Grunts, mundies, norms, grubbers, clods, shovelslingers, blinders, dulls, scrubs, mouth breathers, slumps, the benighted—there's lots of names. Most of them not as nice as those. They all mean the same thing: non-drafters."

"So what about you?" Kip asked, as they finally left the alleys. They crossed a wide, peaked stone bridge over the Umber River.

Gavin looked at him. "You mean what nasty names do they call me?"

"No!" Oh, Gavin was teasing. Kip scowled. "Your eyes don't"— he looked for the right word—"halo. So does that mean you can draft as much as you want?"

"I tire like anyone, but yes. For a time I can draft every day as much as I can handle and it won't burn me out. Someday, most likely five years from now, I will start to lose colors. It will take about a year, and then I'll die."

"Why five years from now?" Kip asked. It was still odd to him how matter-of-fact drafters were about their impending deaths. I guess they have time to get used to the idea.

"It always happens on multiples of seven from when a Prism begins his reign. I've made it sixteen years, so I have until twenty-one. Long time for a Prism."

"Oh. Why multiples of seven?"

"Because there's seven colors, seven virtues, seven satrapies? Because Orholam likes the number seven? Truth is, no one knows."

They walked on through streets swelling with people starting their morning errands, and those eager to get as much work done as possible before the heat of the day. They approached a long line of workers bottlenecked at the Lover's Gate, heading out to work outside the city. Though Kip didn't even see him draft, Gavin turned and handed him a green rock. Not a rock. Green luxin, perfectly the size to fit in Kip's palm. Kip took it, confused.

"You bring your specs?" Gavin asked. He handed Kip a square board, not a foot on each side, perfectly white.

Kip produced them. Smiled weakly. I have a bad feeling about what he's going to tell me next.

"Your turn. You can have lunch—or dinner or possibly break-fast—when you make a green luxin ball of your own. You've got the spectacles, a white reflector, plenty of sun, and an example. I couldn't make it easier if I tried."

"But I need Skill, Will, Source, and Still. I don't have skill. Any skill. At all."

Gavin looked at him sardonically. "And how do you think you get skilled? Skill is the most overrated of the requisites. Will covers a multitude of flaws."

I keep hearing that. Kip hadn't even had breakfast, and he wasn't going to get to eat until he made a magic ball? Fantastic.

They came upon the back of the line. Gavin glanced at Commander Ironfist. Without further prompting, Ironfist said, "Looks like a wagon broke down. It's blocking half the gate."

Gavin swept a hand forward, as in, You go first. Commander Ironfist went first, and the impatient farmers and craftsman parted easily for him. Or at least those who looked furious at being pushed aside quickly hid it once they saw the size of the man towering over them. "We're going to help," Gavin said.

"Sure, you Parian scum," someone said, spitting. Gavin stopped and scanned the crowd for who'd spoken. As men met his eyes and saw those prismatic orbs, they quieted, confused, stunned.

"You can have my help, or you can have my enmity," Gavin said loudly. He unbuttoned the nondescript cloak and threw it back over his shoulders, exposing the almost blindingly white coat and shirt he wore underneath, worked with gold thread and jewels.

He walked on, and Kip scooted close to him. The crowd parted around them, murmuring questions and imprecations. In a minute, they were at the front of the line. At least a dozen men were straining to move a wagon. Apparently, the horses had spooked and veered to the side as they passed through the gate. The wagon's wheel had smashed into the gate's support—here actually the Lover's hair. The wheel was completely shattered, as was the wagon's axle, and the whole thing was still stuck against the wall, making normal efforts at repair impossible. The men were straining to lift the wagon by sheer brute strength, with a few using long poles to try to crank the mass off the wall.

"We're going to have to bring up an empty wagon and unload this before we've got a chance," one of the guards was saying.

To Kip's admittedly inexperienced eye, the man was right. The combined muscle of all these laborers was barely budging the wagon. But the assembled crowd groaned, a few complaining aloud.

"Bring an empty wagon? From where? Through that whole mess behind us? It'll take hours!"

"You all are going to have to use the other gates today," the guard said.

That met similar protests. With how thickly crowded the street was, none of the men at the front of the line would be able to leave until everyone at the back dispersed. It would take hours.

"What?" the guard shouted. "I didn't do this. I'm just trying to fix it! You have a better idea?"

"I do," Gavin said.

"Oh, sure, you smart— Lord Prism!" the guard said.

That sent a ripple of murmurs through the crowd.

Gavin ignored it. He gestured to the men to step back. They did, some in awe, others more peeved, some hostile. He simply walked to where the wagon was smashed against the wall. "I see why you had trouble," he said. "But I have a few extra tools available to me."

Kip, still holding his green luxin ball and the white board, realized Commander Ironfist had disappeared.

He's gigantic. How does he disappear? Kip looked around, and finally found him. The commander was standing behind a man in the crowd whose hand had dropped to the big work knife at his belt. Commander Ironfist's huge hand enveloped both the man's hand and his knife. The commander himself, towering over the man, was quietly speaking in his ear.

As he spoke, the man's face blanched and his whole body slackened.

Commander Ironfist gave the man a friendly pounding on his shoulder—which nearly crushed him—and stepped back toward Gavin.

"Always running off when I need you," Gavin said.

Commander Ironfist grunted.

Kip couldn't help himself. "I think he might have just saved your—" He saw the look on Gavin's face belatedly. Gavin knew. "Oh. Um. Never mind." Clever Kip.

But Gavin was back to work already. "I need ropes." He held a hand up over his head and a bar of yellow luxin formed in his hand and snapped out in both directions, until it was three times the height of a man. He handed it to one of the stunned workers. "You and you, get this in position, I'll need you to lever the wagon off the wall."

The man bobbed his head. He and the other man started jamming the pole as deep between the wall and wagon as they could.

Gavin walked as far around the wagon as he could, sending out thin jets of luxin in a number of places under the axles. "Now," he told the men with the lever.

They strained and moved the wagon less than a hand's breadth. After a three count, they relaxed and set their shoulders to try again.

"Not necessary," Gavin said. "You gave me enough already. Well done." And indeed, there was luxin even behind the wagon, encasing the whole in a shimmering web of various colors, mostly greens and yellows.

Gavin rolled his shoulders, braced himself, pointed at the arching luxin-and-stone of the gate, and shot out a stream of blue and yellow. In moments, it congealed into a pulley. He took coils of rope from a nearby farmer and shot out another bolt, anchoring one end of the rope to the ceiling. Then he threaded the rest of the rope through the pulley. He pulled some slack into the rope between the fixed pulley and the attached end and drafted a free-rolling pulley onto that, which he then fixed to the web of luxin around the wagon. He beckoned the farmer, apparently the wagon's owner, and tossed him the rest of the rope. "It'll still take all of you helping," he said.

Kip swallowed. "Please tell me he isn't designing those off the top of his head," he said to Commander Ironfist, who was silently watching the crowd.

"He's not. You'd be surprised how often wagons break down when your army is pursuing another army across half the Seven Satrapies. I've seen him lift heavier loads by himself. Albeit with lots more pulleys."

Which meant the real question was why Gavin didn't just do this himself. He could draft luxin better than any hemp rope. He could draft another four pulleys and make the burden so light he could lift the wagon himself. But as soon as Kip asked himself, he knew. Gavin was building rapport with the townsfolk. If he marched in and did it all himself, they'd be awed, but they'd not be a part of it. This way, he was simply enabling them to help themselves. His power might still be awesome, but it was power in service of them.

The men heaved on the lines, and Gavin called some men to him. As the wagon lifted off the ground it swung away from the wall, and Gavin and a few others braced it so it didn't swing wildly and hurt anyone. Finally they stabilized the swinging, and Gavin shouted, "Okay, hold it there!" Then he slid under the wagon, scooting on his back under the broken back axle.

That was no light wagon, and the men were straining to hold the load—these men of a city Gavin's army had nearly obliterated sixteen years ago. And yet Commander Ironfist didn't seem perturbed.

"Aren't you worried they'll drop it on purpose?" Kip whispered.

"No."

Kip was. But Gavin appeared unafraid. He grabbed the ends of the broken axle and brought them together as close as he could. It was no use, they were twisted and bent, but Gavin brought them as close as he could and then bound them by degrees with yellow. The wagon wheel followed in short order. He repaired what he could, and replaced what he couldn't.

He scooted out and gestured. The men lowered the wagon and it settled on the road, easily taking the weight. A shout of triumph went up from those who'd been helping. Gavin clapped the farmer on the shoulder. "Those'll be good for about three days, then you'll need to get real repairs, but it'll hold you until then."

"Thank you, sir, thank you ever so much. I thought they were going to lynch me for sure. A day's lost wages for all these men. You've saved me, sir."

Gavin smiled and said, "You're welcome. Now get those horses hitched up."

Only as he saw the smiles did Kip understand fully what Gavin had done. With ten minutes of effort and a little subtlety, he had turned an annoyance into an opportunity to win over not just the men he'd helped, but all those to whom they would repeat the story. The incongruity of the Prism himself joining in the starkly physical labor of lifting and moving and stabilizing the wagon, heedless of soiling his expensive white clothing, joining them muscle to muscle, communicated something to these men. A ruler who would sweat with them was a ruler who might understand men who won their bread by the sweat of their brow. That man was easier to trust than some dandy in silks who might be all kinds of noble-smart but didn't know the real world.

"It's why you hardly ever hear anyone call him Emperor Guile," Ironfist said quietly, reading Kip's mind. "At heart, he's not an emperor; he's a promachos. It's not always the best way to fight, but it's his only way. It's why men will die for him."

"Why didn't he stay promachos, then?" Kip asked, wondering if it was a dangerous question.

"I could list a dozen reasons. Truth is, I don't know."

With a gesture—completely for show, of course—Gavin released all the luxin and it dissolved, shimmering, until it was nothing but dust. He nodded to his fellow laborers and then gestured Kip to follow.

As Kip joined Gavin and walked through the gate, Gavin said, "You have that green luxin ball for me yet?"

"What?" Kip protested. "I can't believe—I didn't even have a chance—"

Oh. He got me again. Gavin was grinning.

"Look, Kip," Kip said, "gullible's written on the sky!" He gazed up as if clueless. "Huh? Where?"

Gavin laughed, and if Kip didn't misjudge, he thought even Ironfist was smiling. "A little slow at the starting line, but watch out when he picks up speed. Reminds me of someone." His smirk told Kip the someone was himself. He put his hand on Kip's shoulder.

Kip felt a thousand things he couldn't identify at that touch. That touch claimed him: That's my boy, it said. His mother had said those words a few times—always after Kip messed up. She'd never said them with pride.

Gavin Guile wasn't just a great man. He was a good man. Kip would do anything for him.

Chapter 63

"General, I need to speak with you." Liv Danavis had found her father on the roof of the Travertine Palace, checklists and reports spread all over a table. It wasn't yet dawn, and he was bundled against the chill of the morning. He was standing, ignoring his work for the moment, his butt against the edge of his table, looking toward the east.

"'General' this morning, not 'father.' I must be in trouble," he said. The corners of his mouth twitched. "Come here."

She came to his side and he pulled her close so they could watch the sun rise together.

"Moments of beauty sustain us through hours of ugliness," her father said. She watched him as he watched the sun rise. His blue eyes—outside the red halo, of course—looked tired. Corvan Danavis had always had the capacity to survive on less sleep than anyone Liv knew, so she knew it wasn't the early hour that had him weary. It wasn't the first time she'd seen this look on his face, but she thought it might be the first time she understood it.

All those times she'd seen this look pinching his eyes and squeezing the joy out of her usually jovial father, he was reliving battles. Today, he was preparing to see more men die—and fighting *for* the very man who'd killed his people in the past, Gavin Guile. It must be tearing him apart.

The sun rose in magnificent pinks and oranges mirrored in the waves, and slowly the tension leaked out of her father's eyes. She could see the freckles under his caramel skin around his eyes, and the faint red highlights in his hair were set afire by the sunlight. She'd inherited neither, nor the blue eyes that would have helped her be a more powerful drafter.

Corvan's lips moved faintly, mouthing words. Oh, he was praying, she realized. Finished, he made the triangle, splaying three fingers: touching his thumb to his right eye; his middle finger to his left eye; and his forefinger to his forehead, the spiritual eye. He completed the gesture by touching mouth, heart, and hands. The three and the four, the perfect seven, sealed to Orholam. What you behold, what you believe, how you behave.

He didn't turn from the risen sun. "You came to demand how I can fight for my old enemy," he said.

"He killed mother." Liv's voice was icy.

"No, Aliviana, he didn't."

"His people did. Same thing."

"The situation is more complicated than you realize."

"What's that supposed to mean? Don't treat me like I'm a child!"

"I'm sorry, Aliviana, I have to protect—"

"I'm seventeen. I've been surviving without your protection for three years! You don't have to protect me anymore."

"Not protecting *you*," Corvan said. "Protecting others from you."

What? It hit Liv like a shot in the stomach. Her father didn't trust her?

"You know who was seventeen when he upended the world?" Corvan asked. "Dazen Guile."

"But—but—that's not even close to the same thing."

"Aliviana, I'm asking you to trust me. I've seen fathers who abuse their position and demand slavish obedience of their children. I've never done that with you, have I? When you wanted to go to the Chromeria and I didn't want you to go, when I told you that I could teach you everything about drafting you needed to know, what happened?"

"You let me go." Eventually.

"And it was awful for you there, but you showed me how strong you are, and here you stand. I'm proud of you, Aliviana. You swam with sea demons and survived. But I'm asking you to trust me on this. I'm doing the right thing. I promise. I haven't forgotten your mother. I haven't forgotten you."

She couldn't maintain the eye contact or her righteous indignation in the face of her father's open, honest refusal to be more open and honest. He was standing on his record, and more than anyone, she knew that his record was unimpeachable. She also knew that he wouldn't be moved once he made a decision like this. If she was stubborn, she'd come by it honestly.

She gave in. "It was so much easier to admire him when he wasn't making war in our country. I mean, I didn't even think about the war when I was around him."

"A little infatuated?" her father suggested.

A flush crawled up her cheeks. "Maybe a little," she grumbled.

"I'd wonder if you weren't. He is what he is," Corvan said, shrugging.

"He really isn't responsible for mother's death?" Liv asked, feeling weak.

"Responsible? That's tricky. If the Guiles hadn't gone to war, would your mother still be alive? Probably. But I can tell you two things: Gavin didn't order or desire your mother's death in any way, and he is utterly and forever besotted with one woman, and that's not you."

"That's three things, isn't it?" Liv asked, shooting her father a grin.

He grinned back. "You get one free for being my daughter."

"What's he doing here? The Prism's men burned this city, killed tens of thousands. He's showed no interest in Garriston since then, so what does he want now? Like it didn't matter when no one wanted it, but now that someone does, he can't lose it?"

"There weren't two Guile brothers, there were three. The youngest one, Sevastian, was murdered by a blue wight when Gavin was about thirteen. Gavin's first purpose is to protect the innocent from color wights. Or, if you want to look at it uncharitably, to kill color wights wherever he finds them. King Garadul is using color wights, or at least the Prism believes he is. So he must be stopped."

"A blue wight? That doesn't make sense. Blues are rational, aren't they?"

"Liv, people talk about breaking the halo like you go instantly mad, like it's as clean a separation as between living and dying. It's not. Some color wights hold on to something like sanity for weeks or even months. Some are fine during the night, but in light, they're fully in the grip of their color. The madness is different every time. A blue can go into a murderous rage; a red can seem calm and philosophical. It's why they're so dangerous. Now, are you going to help me?"

"Fine, what can I do?" she asked.

"Do you know how to make luxin grenadoes?"

"What? No."

"What are they teaching you dims at the Chromeria these days?"

"Hey!"

Corvan smiled. "You have your specs?"

"Of course," Liv said.

"Good, I could use a yellow."

"I'm not a very good yellow. I mean, I can't make a solid brightwater."

"That's not what I need," Corvan said. "Do you know what happens when you mix red and liquid yellow, seal it airtight in a blue shell, and then shatter it against something?"

"Uh, something good?" Liv asked.

"Boom!" Corvan said. "You could use superviolet for the shell, too, but it makes throwers nervous."

Picking up an explosive when you couldn't see whether the shell was intact? Liv could see how that might make someone nervous.

Corvan tossed her a blue luxin ball. She caught it and was surprised that it rattled. She looked closer. The ball had round shot inside it, like small musket balls. For some reason, it stunned her. "These, these…"

"Those are what make grenadoes kill. That's what we're doing, Aliviana. We're killing people. Right here, right now. We're using

Orholam's gift to kill Orholam's children. Most of whom are fools who could be our friends at any other time. It's a hard world. You want me to lie about it? You want to be protected after all?"

Liv felt the blood drain out of her. Her father's words were a sponge, sucking up her illusions, blotting up the thin joy she'd gotten from being in his presence again, in trusting someone to make her decisions for her. Something snapped.

"Father, I can't do this," she said. "I can't kill Tyreans, not for the Chromeria, not just because you say so."

For a moment, she saw keen sorrow in her father's eyes. He looked—for the first time she'd ever seen in her whole life—*old*, haggard. "Liv." He paused. "At some point, you have to decide not merely what you're going to believe, but how you're going to believe. Are you going to believe in people, or in ideas, or in Orholam? With your heart, or with your head? Will you believe what's in front of you, or in what you think you know? There are some things you think you know that are lies. I can't tell you what those are, and I'm sorry for that."

It seemed to Liv that this was his long way of explaining Fealty to One.

"What did you choose, father? Ideas or men?" Liv asked. Though she had just seen him praying, she knew her father wasn't very religious. That part of him had died with her mother. His prayer had likely been something along the lines of: "Well done, sir. This is a beautiful sunrise." Her father rejected the idea that Orholam actually cared about individual men or women, or nations, for that matter.

She saw him blink. His mouth opened, closed rapidly. Set in a line, eyes pained. "I can't say," he said finally.

Can't say because you never actually made the choice? How can you lecture me, then? But that didn't make sense. Her father was the best man she knew.

No, that wasn't it. Her father had lived his life because he believed in certain ideas. That was what had led him to fight against Gavin Guile, to give up everything in that fight. He'd been a man of ideals. Those ideals were what had made him stay away from the Chromeria himself, what had made him oppose his daughter going to the

Chromeria. He'd been afraid that she would be corrupted by the Chromeria's lack of ideals.

A wise fear, as it turned out, Liv thought guiltily. She had been corrupted. She had agreed to spy on Gavin. She was just as bad as everyone else at the Chromeria.

But that didn't explain why her father was suddenly fighting for the man he should hate. The ideals hadn't changed. If anything, Gavin being here, fighting Tyreans, should have made her father fight him all the more fiercely.

Orholam, maybe her father had been corrupted too. Maybe he'd been bought. Maybe he'd sold out his ideals just like everyone else. Her heart hurt at the very thought, but why else wouldn't he tell her the answer to what was an obvious question? Because it would make his hypocrisy undeniable.

The whole swiving Chromeria was corrupt. It defiled everything it touched. Liv had been at the bottom. She'd seen how monochromes were treated; she'd seen how Tyreans were treated. And she'd become part of the power, too. She'd become almost a friend to the Prism himself—and she'd loved it, loved talking with a powerful man, basking in his attention. She'd loved the beautiful dresses and being treated as special and worth attention. And to keep her power, she'd sold herself—so easily, so easily. But that was how things worked at the Chromeria. It had even corrupted her father.

"Liv," her father said. "Liv, trust me. I know it's hard, but please."

"Trust you? When you won't trust me?" she asked, pained.

"Livy, please. I love you. You know I wouldn't do anything to hurt you."

And then it all became clear and it took Liv's breath away. How could the Prism get her father to betray everything he held dear? Why would her father evade simple questions? Because he loved her. Corvan had been corrupted, but not by money or power or sex. She knew he wouldn't sell his soul so cheaply. So what did the Prism have over Corvan? He had Liv.

Gavin Guile was using Liv to suborn her father. She didn't know what exactly the threat and the bribe had been, but it didn't matter. Liv was being bribed and threatened exactly the same way, but by the

Ruthgari. She knew how the game was played, now. She had betrayed her principles because she loved Vena. Her father was betraying his principles because he loved Liv.

Corvan had chosen that his fealty would be to his family only. That meant Liv. And it meant he couldn't tell her. Because if he told her, she'd ruin it and make his sacrifices worthless.

Liv's heart broke. She had to clamp down hard on her emotions to keep from bursting into tears. Cruel. So cruel. How could Gavin do such a thing and then smile at her?

Because that's how the Chromeria is. Vipers and villains, all of them. And Corvan had done everything he could to try to keep Liv out of the Chromeria—everything short of ordering her not to go, because he wasn't so imperious. It was her fault. Liv swallowed the sudden lump in her throat. Her father had been debased because of her. He deserved better than for her to expose his shame.

She smiled as bravely as she could, pretending to acquiesce. "I understand, father. I do trust you. Just tell me everything when you can. Fair enough?"

"Fair enough," Corvan said, his relief obvious. "I love you, Livy."

"I know you do, father."

And Gavin Guile was going to pay for turning that love against him.

Chapter 64

It's simple, Kip. You're not being asked to draft a pulley or a scull. One little green ball. It's nothing.

He was sitting cross-legged, green spectacles on, white board in his lap, willing something to happen. He'd been doing this for two hours. And what exactly was he doing? Nothing. How were you supposed to even keep your mind on drafting when nothing happened for hours? His stomach was complaining again. It was constant now as the sun approached noon.

No food until I draft? It's cruel. It's torture. It's impossible.

Kip looked up. Gavin had brought them only a few hundred paces outside the Lover's Gate to the ruins of the old outer walls. When they'd arrived, there were already hundreds of men at work, and since then, many of those who'd been stuck in the line that they'd passed had joined them. They were excavating the roots of the wall down to bedrock, which was at least four paces down in the few places Kip could see. The excavation, though, went faster than he would have thought possible, between the sheer number of men working and the sandy soil, with only thin vegetation on top.

Gavin was poring over drawings with Master Danavis. General Danavis, Kip supposed, and the natural manner with which the general commanded men to do this or that—exactly how he'd told Kip to go do this or that—made Kip wonder why he'd never wondered about Master Danavis before. The man was obviously too big for a little town like Rekton, but Kip had never even thought about him. Children only think about themselves, Kip.

"It's not good enough," Gavin was saying. "No, the detail's fine. The detail's perfect. But the old wall didn't stop us, so why rebuild something that's faulty?"

Rebuild the wall? Hadn't Gavin said that King Garadul's army was arriving in four or five days?

"We'll be *lucky* if we can get something that's merely faulty," General Danavis said. "We'll be lucky if we can finish anything at all."

"Bring me the drawings of Rathcaeson," the Prism said.

"You're seriously going to build a wall based on artists' renditions of a mythical city?"

The muscle in Gavin's jaw twitched with irritation.

"Understood, Lord Prism," General Danavis said. He bobbed a bow.

"Bring your daughter," Gavin said. "I could use a superviolet."

A slight hesitation. "Of course." The general left, mounting his horse and galloping toward the city, his Ruthgari personal guards trailing in his wake.

Then, though he'd been speaking nonstop with foremen, Ruthgari guards, and General Danavis all morning, Gavin was suddenly alone. He looked over at Kip. Oops, I think I'm supposed to be drafting.

Gavin cocked an eyebrow at him. "Not hungry yet, huh?"

Kip grimaced. "Thanks for reminding me."

"Kip, more than any other color, green can be summarized in one word. All the others require at least a few, a bit of hedging, some qualifiers. Green is wild. Everything both good and bad associated with wild is what green is. That's why I can tell you that you only need will, because will and wildness go so naturally together. If you were an incipient blue, I'd have to explain the sense of drafting, the harmony, the order, how it fits with the world. That's not you. Any questions?"

Not about drafting. "What happened to that gunner?"

"What?" Gavin asked.

"The one on the Ilytian boat, who nearly killed us. Right before I shot him, his gun blew up."

"It does happen," Gavin said. "You overcharge your shot, the musket can't handle the charge."

"That gunner, who nearly hit us from five hundred paces? He misjudged a musket?"

Gavin smiled. He turned his palm over. There was nothing in it. Oh. Kip tightened his eyes. A superviolet ball rested in Gavin's hand. "See it?" Gavin asked.

"I see it."

Gavin extended his hand. A little pop, and his hand jumped back. The superviolet ball streaked out like it was a musket ball itself. "I blocked his musket barrel," Gavin said, shrugging. "You can use any color to do it. Yellow only if you can make solid yellow, of course, but pretty much anything else."

"Why not kill him?"

"I may have," Gavin said. "A musket exploding in your hands is no joke." He shrugged. "I recognized him. Freelancer during the war. Sometimes fought for me, sometimes for my brother, sometimes for any captain that would pay him enough. He's a drunk and a scoundrel and the finest artist of the cannon in the Seven Satrapies. Whatever name he was born with, now he's simply known as Gunner. It's everything he is. His first underdeck command as cannoneer was on a ship called the *Aved Barayah*, the Fire Breather."

"The Fire Breather? *The* Fire Breather?" Kip asked.

"Only ship in memory to ever kill a full-grown sea demon. Gunner was maybe sixteen years old." Gavin shook his head, dispelling a memory. "I've killed a lot of people, Kip. Sometimes you hesitate, and as bad and as dangerous as that is, I like to think it's proof that I've still got some humanity left. Besides, I knew making his gun blow up in his hands would really infuriate him. If I know Gunner, he made that musket himself, and he's probably wondering who the hell overcharged his precious musket." He glanced over to a richly dressed Ruthgari approaching, flanked by guards and slaves carrying a mobile pavilion to shade the light-skinned man. "I'll leave you to your work," Gavin said. "You might want to hurry, the servants should be bringing lunch anytime."

Just when I'd sort of forgotten my stomach. Thanks.

Kip pushed the spectacles up his nose—they kept slipping down, and they weren't even close to comfortable—and stared at the white board. Wild. Wild, unbridled, growing. The Ruthgari noble—Kip gathered it was the governor—was complaining shrilly to Gavin about something or other, and he stood as if he was going to take his time about it. Kip tried to block him out.

Green. Come on, let's suck up some wildness.

Wild, now there's a word for me. Kip the wild. I was pretty wild when Ram used to call me Tubby, huh? I was pretty wild when he made me back down over Isa. She'd be alive if I'd been a little wilder. To be wild is the opposite of being controlled, and I've been controlled for my whole life. Controlled by Ram, by *Ram*! A village tough. A boy! Barely a bully.

If Kip had told Ram to go to the evernight, if he had shredded Ram with his tongue, what could Ram have done except beat him? Ram's muscles weren't half a match for Kip's brain.

Well, they're not a match for anything now that they're rotting.

The thought made Kip queasy. He didn't want Ram dead. There'd been plenty of good things about the boy. A few, anyway. And if Kip didn't feel terrible that Ram was dead, he did wish the boy were alive so he could face him now.

I've talked with Gavin Guile. I sank pirates with him! Well, mostly I tried not to drown while *he* sank pirates, but still.

Kip looked at his hands. Still no luxin. The governor was still complaining loudly. Orholam, how was Gavin standing it? The man had the most nasal voice Kip had ever heard. Kip wanted to bean the man in the head with a big old ball of green luxin. He glanced at his hands again. Nothing.

I'm going to fail Gavin. Again. Like I failed Isa. Like I failed Sanson. Like I failed my mother a thousand times.

Hunger gnawed Kip's belly. That's all I am, a fat failure. A new life's been handed to me on a plate. Gavin Guile's son, bastard son, sure, but he hasn't once treated me like an embarrassment. And I can't even summon the will to reach out and take this new life. In return for all the good he's done me, I'm going to humiliate the man who saved my life, who gave me a second chance.

It was like bands of iron were being laid across his chest, and now they tightened, tightened. Kip could barely breathe. His eyes welled with tears. Baby. Failure. Disappointment. His mother's face, twisted, dangerously high from smoking ratweed laced with ergot: You ruined my life! You're the worst mistake I ever made. I gave everything and you took it all and gave me nothing! You make me sick, Kip.

Kip, you can throw off those chains. Stop believing those—

"Lies!" the governor shouted. Kip shivered, his skin tingling. The sun was nearly at its zenith. Orholam's eye pressed down on the land like a physical weight, but to Kip it was a caress. Light, energy, warmth, love, light in dark corners. He looked at the white board, and in the green filtered through his spectacles, he saw one face of Orholam. Kip wouldn't call it wildness. It was freedom. He wanted to shout, dance for joy, to hell with what anyone thought. There was freedom from all of that, and freedom from the prison of his own head, freedom from the nagging voices of doubt, from the running commentary about everything he saw and did. It was action, and it was as powerful as a redwood springing up in the cracks of a boulder. Life would win. The roots would reach and heave and strain.

Kip could feel those bands of iron around his chest burst asunder. He felt more alive than he had in his whole life. An animal strength and joy.

So this is what they mean by wild.

The yapping governor's voice shrilled. Kip drew a ball of green luxin into his hand. Just like that? Just by deciding to do it? It seemed too easy. The ball was thick, dense, but flexible to his squeezing fingers. Kip made it bigger, hollow, about twice the size of his own head. Now the flexibility was exaggerated. Soft enough that it wasn't going to kill anyone.

With the biggest grin on his face, Kip held it in his palms. How had Gavin shot out luxin? Kip had seen Ironfist do it too. He wrinkled his nose. Maybe I just will it.

A tiny part of his mind was protesting: You can't assault the governor! He's the *governor*, for Orholam's sake. You think his bodyguards are going to appreciate that you don't really mean to hurt him?

But in the grip of green, words like "governor" were bled of meaning. What was that? What was the difference? The trappings of human rituals and human titles seemed artificial, thin.

Kip willed the ball to shoot out of his hands. Still seated, grinning like a fool, he could feel energy coiling up behind the ball. How long did he let that build before he let it go? Oh well, that felt like long enough. A muffled crack and the ball jetted out of Kip's hands, fast.

Still seated on the ground, he was blasted ass over elbows.

Rolling to his knees, laughing, Kip looked to see what had happened to the yapping man.

The governor was laid out, and apparently the green luxin ball had bounced around some, because the palanquin was collapsing, two of the slaves tumbling away from it. The palanquin dropped right on top of the governor, and Kip heard him shrieking—but his view was blocked as one of the bodyguards charged Kip, sword out.

Spectacles askew, Kip couldn't draw any more green, but he still had a good amount in his body. He began drawing another, smaller ball. Too slow, too slow!

The air shimmered between him and the swordsman as he raised his hands. There was a crack from his hands and a tiny green ball shot out, snapping both hands back painfully from the kick.

A wall of blue luxin unfurled between Kip and the swordsman in the blink of an eye. The swordsman's sword struck the blue wall in midlunge toward the kneeling boy. The blade screeched as it was forced downward, peeling off layers of blue. The swordsman himself smacked bodily into the blue a split second later, grunting. There was a sound like glass cracking, and a high-pitched whine.

The swordsman recovered, then stopped. The blue luxin right in front of his face was cracked from Kip's shot, spiderwebs centered where his head would have been, a musket-ball-sized crater in the blue luxin.

"Enough," Gavin said. He didn't raise his voice, just injected it in a moment of silence. His blue wall had saved both of them.

Kip felt shaken, weak. Oh, *shit*. What did I just do?

The governor, still protesting, was pulled from the fallen palanquin by two of his bodyguards. He stood, nose bleeding, face flushed from embarrassment rapidly giving way to rage, and stormed over to Gavin.

"Your slave has assaulted me, I demand satisfaction!" The governor drew the decorative blade hanging at his hip and pointed it at Kip.

A muscle jumped in Gavin's jaw. "That's no slave. Kip is my natural son."

"This, *this* is your bastard?"

Stony silence from Gavin. Finally, "Kip, apologize."

Kip swallowed and stood, unable to conceal his trembling. "I'm terribly sorry, sir. I was practicing drafting for the first time. I really didn't know what I was—"

"An apology? No, Lord Prism, first you assault me, and now this outrage? I demand satisfaction."

"You'll demand nothing," Gavin said. He never broke eye contact. "You're corrupt if not treasonous, Governor Crassos. You've been colluding with King Garadul, and if I can find just a little more evidence of it, I swear when you return to Ruthgar, your head will have a pike waiting for it. Unless Satrapah Ptolos decides to hand you over to the Parians instead. You're incompetent, contemptible, a liar, a thief, and a coward. If you want satisfaction, you can duel with me. Sword to sword. On my word of honor I won't draft, but we'll do it right now."

The governor blinked and the sword point trembled. He blinked again. Sheathed his blade. "I'll leave brawling with swords to the benighted." He snarled and turned on his heel, storming off.

Kip became aware that someone was right behind him. He turned and saw Ironfist looming over him. "How long have you been there?" he asked.

"Long enough to protect you from your foolishness, if not long enough to stop it. I wasn't aware you had your family's knack for getting into trouble in the blink of an eye."

Oh, the blue wall had been Ironfist's. Was that twice over now that Kip owed his life to the huge Blackguard?

"Commander," Gavin said, "I need you to go speak with our spies. Crassos is rattled. He may run. Make sure the crews manning the cannons at the harbor's entrance are men who will obey the order to fire, if it comes to that. And that he doesn't plunder the treasury. I need to be able to pay our army."

Ironfist frowned. "I'd prefer not to leave Kip. I'm a Blackguard, Lord Prism, not a messenger. My duty is here."

Gavin said, "I can't do it. Kip can't do it. It needs doing. This is my fault for forbidding you to bring more Blackguards, but the point remains."

Commander Ironfist hesitated only one second more. "Very well, Lord Prism." He bowed and headed for the horses someone had brought for them.

When he had gone, there was a conspicuous silence. Dozens of workmen had seen what had happened, and humiliating the governor had clearly earned Gavin some goodwill, but no one appeared to want to come close either, lest Gavin was angry. Gavin rubbed his forehead. "You're probably wondering why we're going to fight a war for assholes like that governor," he said.

Actually, the thought hadn't occurred to Kip, but now that Gavin brought it up, it did seem odd.

"Because Rask Garadul had the stench of a fanatic, Kip. That's all. Hundreds, or if we're unlucky, thousands of people will die because I met Rask for a few minutes and I thought he was crazy." Gavin expelled a breath. "He wants this city, and honestly, he's got a right to it. If I could simply give this city back to Tyrea's people, I would. They deserve it. They—you—have paid too high of a price for a war in which they took the only side they could. If there were anyone else who would take over after we left, I'd do it, and damn the Spectrum. But with Rask in power... It's a little more complicated than that, of course, but that's why I'm here, and my presence is what will make this a near thing. If we left, Rask would march in unopposed, close the harbor before the Parians could land, and that would be pretty much the end of it. The Parians would be furious, but the profits here aren't so great that they want to march an army here. Eventually, Rask would offer an exclusive shipping contract on all the citrus from Garriston for a few years, and they'd take it. What do you think? Is it worth it?"

He's asking me like my opinion is worth something. Kip hadn't had that many adults care what he thought. "I think King Garadul should die and save us all this trouble."

Gavin laughed ruefully. "If only. Maybe Karris will work a miracle and do just that."

"You really miss her, don't you?" Kip asked before he could stop himself.

Gavin looked at Kip sharply. Then he looked away. Relented. After a minute, he expelled a long breath, and it was like Kip was watching Gavin's hope leak out of him. "That obvious, huh?" Gavin asked.

"You think they'll kill her?" Kip asked.

A number of emotions flitted over Gavin's face, settling in resignation, sorrow too deep for tears. "She'll live until Rask sees if I'll trade the city for her. Then he'll kill her. Either way."

No. No they won't, Kip thought. I swear it.

Chapter 65

The empty feeling in Kip's stomach didn't go away when they served lunch. Gavin and General Danavis—even though it was weird to think of him as General Danavis rather than Master Danavis, it was too weird for Kip to think of him as just Corvan—and even Liv were poring over the drawings and plans with architects and artists while they ate. Kip sat to one side, out of the way. He had no idea what they were doing, and space around the table was limited. He ate fresh oranges with gusto, and tore into the intriguing spiced fresh javelina. It tasted amazing, but even he couldn't keep his mind on food for long.

"I'd ask if you're serious," General Danavis was saying, "but you have that look."

"The problem isn't the drafting," Gavin said. "I can handle that much luxin easily—"

"Easily?" General Danavis interrupted, dubiously.

"Fine, not easily, but I can do it. The problem is the weight. I can't lift this much, much less throw it into place."

Liv cleared her throat gently, as if unsure she really wanted to intrude.

"Aliviana?" Gavin asked.

She colored. "Please, Liv." She brushed her hair back nervously. "How about this?" She drafted something onto the table. It was, of course, superviolet, and thus invisible to most people.

General Danavis scowled. Apparently, most people included him.

"Sorry, father," she said. "I can't control yellow enough to make models with it."

Kip tried to see what she'd drafted, but the table was obscured by bodies.

Gavin chuckled. "It looks ridiculous," he said, and Liv blanched. "But it'll work. Perfect. Fine. What do our architects think of the design?"

For a moment, Kip thought Gavin was being pretty rude. Obviously, General Danavis and everyone else around the table was curious about what Liv had designed. But this was Gavin as leader. All the rest of them didn't need to know, and there was work to be done. He understood the solution to the problem, and that was all that was necessary. On to the next problem.

Which is what I should be doing. Kip had finished lunch. He could now draft a little bit, and on purpose. He knew what he had to do.

"My Lord Prism, none of us has ever built a wall of this magnitude, or, or—or a wall at all, to tell the truth," a nervous architect said, "but these old drawings you've shown us of Rathcaeson are clearly flawed. Too much fantasy, not enough function."

"This empty desert doesn't have enough function," Gavin said sharply. "Tell me what we need to do to fix it. I need to start building now, today."

The architect blinked. Swallowed. "Uh, here." He drew a line with his finger. "This interior passage isn't wide enough. You're going to have men rushing back and forth in armor, with guns, cannons being rolled into position, or replaced for repair. This passage must be wide enough for men to run past each other and past carts or cannons."

"How wide?" Gavin demanded.

"I'd say, uh..." He held his fingers apart on the drawing.

"For Orholam's sake, write on it," Gavin said.

"Sir, those drawings are hundreds of years old, priceless relics of—" another man, perhaps an artist, protested.

"Priceless is being alive next week," Gavin snapped. "Continue."

Kip didn't know why he'd been so slow, but it only dawned on him now that Gavin was seriously planning on building a wall, here. Before King Garadul's army arrived. In four days.

Oh, maybe because it's impossible?

Of course, crossing the Cerulean Sea in a morning was impossible too.

But seriously, did Gavin mean to draft the entire thing by himself? Kip didn't know all that much about drafting and how much a drafter could safely use in a day, but the mere fact that the world wasn't bursting with luxin buildings and bridges and walls told him that it had to be incredibly difficult. In fact, the only luxin buildings he'd seen had been at the Chromeria, and he had to guess that the seven towers had been the product of a huge collaborative effort.

The architect, a squinting little man, after puffing out his cheeks a number of times, deep in thought, began drawing quickly. "The cut-outs on these murder holes don't give sufficient range of fire. If you modify the top of the wall like this, scaling ladders won't be able to hook onto the wall—at least not as easily. A railing on the back, like so, will save more of your own men from falling off the wall than theirs. These areas on top of the wall need to be bigger so you can store more powder for the cannons. There's no place in these drawings for taking the wounded. I think you could incorporate that here. If you can set sleds like this right into the wall of the interior passage, it'll be easier to move materiel around. There are also no lantern hooks in this plan. Your wall will be entirely dark if you don't fix this. You'll need cranes here, here, and here to lift supplies."

"You've never built a wall before, huh?" Gavin asked.

"I have studied a few," the architect said.

"How much am I paying you?"

"Uh, nothing yet, Lord Prism."

"Well, double it!" Gavin ordered.

The architect looked befuddled, obviously doing the arithmetic and not liking the result, but not wanting to call the Prism himself out on it.

"He's joking," General Danavis told the man.

Gavin's eyes sparkled.

428 • Brent Weeks

"Oh." The man looked relieved. Then Kip could see the question cross his face: joking about giving me nothing, or joking about giving me more for doing a good job?

Gavin said, "Keep working. This man here will take notes. I'm going to go lay the foundation."

"He means that metaphorically, right?" the architect asked, squinting at the receding figure of the Prism.

"Our Prism's a bear for metaphors," General Danavis said.

"Huh?" the architect asked.

Kip stood, feeling heartsick. Now was going to be as good of a chance to escape as he was going to get.

"Kip!" Gavin's voice rang out, drawing everyone's eye to Kip. Kip felt a surge of panic and embarrassment at having been caught so easily. "Well done today. It's not many boys who can draft consciously on their first day of trying."

A flush of pleasure went through Kip, only doubled by the impressed look that flitted over Liv's face.

"Liv!" Gavin called out, making her head whip around. "I want you to make models: lay out the curvature of the halls, widths for the top of the wall, whatever the architect tells you."

"Yes, Lord Prism!" she said, her eyes turning back to the table and her work.

Now or never. If he waited, Ironfist would be back, shadowing him wherever he went. Kip looked at General Danavis, head down, making suggestions; Liv, listening intently; and finally at Gavin. These were the only people in the world who meant anything to him, and incredibly, they accepted him. Tolerated him, anyway. With them, for the first time in his life, he felt like he was part of something.

Kip turned his back and walked toward the city.

Chapter 66

It was only as Kip approached the Lover's Gate that he understood why Gavin was attempting to build a new wall. The old wall was encrusted with homes, shops, and inns like a ship with barnacles, except here the walls were covered both inside and out. In places, people's roofs were almost level with the top of the wall. If Gavin wanted to make that wall defensible, he'd have to level hundreds of homes. The demolition itself would have taken four days.

Clearly, the effect on the people's opinion of demolishing the homes of perhaps a fifth of the city's population would be ruinous. Gavin had only a few days in which to make the people who remained in the city want to fight for him rather than for his enemy. He'd been caught between impossible choices: leave the people's homes propped against the inner walls and have a militarily indefensible wall, or tear the houses down and risk turning an already divided populace against him. So Gavin had decided to build his own wall.

Unbelievable. How must it have been during the Prisms' War, when people had to choose which brother to fight beside? It would have been like fighting beside giants, knowing that their slightest move might crush you, but knowing that standing in the no-man's-land between them would be even worse.

Kip found his way back to his rooms and packed what he guessed he'd need. Cloak and food, and more food, and short sword, and a stick of tin danars in a money belt. It was more than he thought he'd need—he hoped they'd forgive him for that, but he might need money for bribes. Then he decided he'd need to leave a note so they didn't waste precious time searching for him.

There was a quill and parchment on the desk in his room, so he scratched out the letters laboriously. "I'm Tyrean and young. More help as a spy than here. No one will suspect me. Will try to find Karris." He signed the note, folded it after the ink dried, and stuck it under the covers in Liv's bed.

Then he scratched out another one. "Went to buy some food and watch minstrel shows. Shaken after drafting. Will be back by midnight."

That one he left on the desk. They would find it first and give him a head start. They wouldn't find out he was truly gone until after nightfall. At that point, they'd know he would be too far gone for them to catch him.

With what he felt must have been suspiciously overloaded saddlebags, Kip made his way past the gate guards and to the stable.

"I need a horse," Kip told the stableman imperiously.

The man returned his gaze, not moving from his position leaning against one wall. "Right place," he said.

Kip had a sinking feeling. The man wasn't buying that he was anyone who could give orders. If Kip couldn't get a horse, he couldn't do anything. It would be the shortest attempt at running away in history. He hadn't even gotten out of the house. "Uh, I need something not too ostentatious, and not too...spirited."

"Not much of a rider, huh?" The man's tone said, Must not be much of a man.

Confess your ineptitude and fall on his mercy, Kip. "What's your name, shit shoveler?" he demanded instead. Oops.

The groom blinked and stood up straight unconsciously. "Gallos...sir," he added uncertainly.

"I don't ride these stinking meat barrels much, but I need one that's reliable, that can handle my fat ass, and that won't panic when I use magic, you understand? And I don't have time for your superciliosity." Was that even a word? Kip bulled forward. The groom probably didn't know either. "There's a war on. Get me my damned horse and save the shit-packing for your stable boys."

The groom moved with alacrity, saddling an old draft horse. "Best I got for what you've asked, sir," the man said.

A *draft* horse? I'm not that fat.

"Sorry, sir, only one I got."

"It'll do," Kip said. "Thank you." No need to press his luck. The stirrup did look impossibly high, however. Instead of humiliating himself by trying to mount and most likely failing, he took the reins and led the beast out into the city, taking care to tip the groom.

Orholam, I really was an asshole. Kip didn't know what made it more disconcerting: that being an asshole had promptly gotten him his way, or that he had enjoyed exerting mastery over another man. Back home, he would have been whipped, and he would have deserved it.

In the streets, he kept his eyes peeled until he found a man roughly his own size, wearing a coat despite the heat. It looked old, worn, and cost maybe as much as one of Kip's coat's pockets. Kip traded with the man. Then he bought wine and water in one of the streets leading to the water market and was convincing a shopkeeper that he really did want to trade his fine cloak for a plain woolen one when he heard loud voices. He turned.

Some old man was standing in the back of a wagon, exhorting the crowd heading into the water market, most of whom were ignoring him. "—to have our own nation again. With our own king! You all want to writhe under the bootheel of the Parians again? Do you remember what they did last time? Have you no memory?!"

"They killed hundreds for listening to nonsense like yours!" someone shouted.

"And I say we don't have to let them ever do it again," the old man snapped back. That got some murmurs of agreement.

"Everyone who wanted to listen to your shilling for King Garadul has already left!" a shopkeeper yelled.

"The king isn't willing that any should perish. Come, join him, and fight!"

"We don't want to fight. We don't want to kill. We don't want to be killed. We want to live."

"Cowards!" the old man said. Then he shuffled off to look for a more sympathetic audience.

Kip was about to head out of town when something caught his eye. There was a new ship in the bay, a galleon flying a white flag with seven towers. The Chromeria's flag. Almost at the moment that he identified the flag, he saw a line of men and women walking through the streets led by at least a dozen Blackguards. He froze. Guilty conscience. They didn't know him, and he didn't see the only two Blackguards he'd seen before, Stump and whatever the other one's name had been.

The people behind the Blackguards were perhaps more interesting, though, and Kip studied them as they passed half a block away and turned down a street to head toward the Travertine Palace. There were perhaps two hundred of them, and Kip was sure that every last one was a drafter. A few had eyes light enough that he could see their irises were solid blue or green or red, but some of the lighter-skinned among them actually had a visible tint to their skin. Some concealed that with long sleeves. Others didn't seem to care. "...be true, but it looks better than the last time we were here, Samila," a blue-tinged man said. Despite his light-enough-to-show-color skin, the man had his hair in dreadlocks almost to his waist. The woman was stunning, perhaps forty years old, with solid blue irises, high cheekbones, and the olive skin of the western Atashian upper classes. Both wore rich clothing.

Samila Sayeh and Izem Blue? No, surely not. Those names were just from stories. Surely there were plenty of drafters their age who happened to be blues and reds who had special relationships with each other.

Next came more Blackguards, helping infirm drafters or wheeling them in chairs. Kip decided not to wait to see if Stump were with them.

He turned to slip through the crowd—and found himself face-to-face with Liv. She stood with her hands on her hips, her jaw tight. She flicked her eyes to the horse and back to Kip. Gulp.

"I can explain," Kip said.

"You already did. Twice." There was no amusement in her tone. She'd found both notes. Oh hell.

"Don't stop me, Liv, please."

"What do you think you're doing?" She lowered her voice. "You think you're going to spy? You're going to find Karris? And do what?"

His jaw set. "I'm going to save her."

She made no effort to hide her incredulity. "That is one of the more ridiculous things I've heard in my life, Kip. If you want to run away because it's too dangerous here, you don't need to pretend—"

"Go to hell!" he said, stunning even himself. Her eyes shot wide. He couldn't believe he'd said that to Liv—Liv, for Orholam's sake! "I'm sorry!" He said it too loud and some people around them looked at him. He lowered his voice sheepishly. "I'm really sorry, that was stupid to say, and mean. I didn't mean it. I—Liv." He paused, then bulled ahead. "I'm *nothing*. I've been a nothing for my whole life. And I'm being catapulted into having people treat me different because of something I had no control over? Because of my father?" He could see on her face that she understood. She knew exactly what he meant. "Liv, I owe Gavin everything, and he hasn't asked anything of me."

"He will," Liv said darkly.

"Has he ever asked you to do anything wrong, Liv?"

"Not yet," she admitted. "I'm just saying that you have to look out for yourself when it comes to people from the Chromeria."

"And what? You're not one of them? If you make me go back, you'll be making me break my word."

"What?" Liv looked like he'd just slapped her face.

"I swore that I was going to save Karris. Don't you see, Liv? I'm perfect precisely *because* I'm a nothing. Look at my eyes!" Still confused, she looked at his eyes. "No color, no halo," Kip said. "But I can draft. Liv, for the first time in my life, I know exactly what I have to do. No one is making me do this. I'm doing it because it's right. There's something tremendously—" He clenched his hands, trying to pull in the words. "Freeing. Powerful. I don't know what, but I know it feels good."

"Even if you go to your death?" Liv asked.

He chuckled joylessly. "I'm not being a hero, Liv. I just don't like myself that much. So what if I die?"

"That's the most awful thing I've ever heard," Liv said.

"I'm sorry," Kip said. "I'm not trying to be pitiful. I'm just say-ing—I've got nothing. I'm an orphan, at best a bastard. A shame. I just don't have that much to lose. If I can do something good with my life—or even with my death—then how could I not try?"

He could see her wavering. For the first time, he had hope that he could actually get away with this.

"Please, Liv. If I fail in this—if I can't even get out of the city—I really am a nothing. Please. Don't make me fail in the most impor-tant thing I've ever tried to do."

She blinked, then grinned. "I never thought what might happen if you turned that wily tongue against *me*. You ought to be an orange."

"I do resemble one in general shape, but I'm not sure—"

"A drafter, not a fruit!" she said, laughing.

Oh, he was like a slippery drafter.

"Does this mean you're not going to stop me?" Kip said.

"Worse," she said.

"Huh?"

"You have to do what's right; I have to do what's right. You're my responsibility, Kip."

"Oh no you don't."

"Yes. I'm going with you—or you're not going."

"Liv, you don't understand—" She doesn't understand what? That you're totally smitten with her? That she's beautiful and smart and wonderful and amazing and your whole soul longs just to be with her, but you can't imagine putting her in danger?

"I don't understand what?" she asked. Damn it.

"You're light to me." It slipped out. He couldn't believe he'd said it out loud. His eyes went wide even before hers did.

He'd been nearly physically naked before her when that assassin had tried to kill him. This was worse. He was paralyzed. His lips failed him.

"Very funny, Kip, but you're not going to fool me and slip away when I'm not looking or something. You might be wily, but I wasn't born yesterday."

Oh, thank Orholam! She thought he was joking! A wave of relief passed over him, leaving his knees weak.

"I'm going with you," Liv said, "and that's final. You're right: what you're trying is a good thing. I know Karris is worth saving, and what she's learned could change the whole war. And if you want to succeed, you're going to need my help, and you'd be making *me* break *my* oath to look after you if you don't let me come."

He had used that "don't make me break my oath" thing as the whole linchpin of his argument. He didn't particularly like having it turned against him, but with his whole brain in a fog—his heart was still pounding hard—he couldn't exactly counter it.

"Besides," Liv said more quietly, "even if you're not running away from anything, maybe one of us is."

"Huh?" Kip said. "Huh" is the best I can manage? Great.

"I'm coming. Let's go," Liv said.

Together, they found the old man who'd been shouting at the crowd earlier, and got directions to King Garadul's army: "Head south and follow the tracks. Thousands have gone already. If you want to join the army rather than be useless like the rest of the camp followers, tell the recruiting sergeant that Gerain sent you."

The guards at the Hag's Gate didn't even look at them twice. Outside the city, Kip found a rock, stood on it, and wiggled his way into the saddle. Liv took his hand and climbed up behind him. The huge draft horse seemed to have no trouble with the weight. Kip willed himself to relax as Liv put her arms around his waist to hold on.

Still, Kip hesitated, looking north, looking back at Garriston. Come on, Kip, you've done dumber things and lived to tell the tale.

Not so sure about that. Still, Kip prodded the big horse and they began the long trip.

Chapter 67

It started as a dull throb. It always did. For a while, Karris hoped her stomach was reacting to the food King Garadul was practically forcing down her gullet. Karris hadn't had her moon blood in six months. Like most of the women of the Blackguard, her flow was irregular at best. Their level of training simply precluded it. But when Karris had hers, it was like her body was making up for lost pain.

Damn King Garadul. This was his fault. The enforced boredom was driving Karris mad—sitting in the wagon, unable to do much, and constantly checked on. When they'd found her doing strength exercises, they'd sent in three drafters and two Mirrormen. The six barely all fit in the little wagon. Karris had been seized by the Mirrormen and laid over the knee of one of the drafters. *Literally* laid over her knee.

The woman had produced a man's leather belt and beat Karris's bottom raw. Like she was a recalcitrant child. She'd been caught three times, and the punishment never changed, but gradually her will to resist did. It had seemed like too small and inconsequential a rebellion to keep up.

Now she wished she had. The throbbing was already spreading to her back. Not long now for the diarrhea to start.

Love being a woman.

The other women of the Blackguard took advantage of their relative freedom from moon blood as also granting relative freedom from worrying about pregnancy. Karris just enjoyed her relative freedom from pain. It had been years since she'd had sex with anything more than her pillow. Not that she wanted to think about that right now. In fact, she thought if she even saw a man she'd tear his eyes out.

It was for men that women suffered this. As the old saw said, a woman has to bleed to fertilize man's seed. Chronologically confused, but true enough.

They brought her the dress in the morning.

It wasn't the kind of clothing one would expect to be asked to wear for one's execution. It wasn't an exact copy of the dress she'd worn when she'd finally given in to her father's demands and joined Gavin at the head of his armies when they'd reclaimed Ru, but it was close. For one thing, it was black silk rather than green. King Garadul's tailor had obviously been working either from memory or a painting of the day or they had simply decided to alter the dress for the changes of sixteen years of fashion.

The fit would be perfect, of course.

Karris stared at the dress with loathing all day, as cramps wracked her guts, as the inevitable diarrhea came, as she nearly passed out a couple of times. That dress symbolized more than giving in to Rask Garadul's childish fantasy. That dress was Karris's youth. It was the girl she'd been. It was femininity, softness, yielding. The desperate grubbing for people's eyes, for the jealousy of the other girls, for the envy of older women, for the attention of men. Karris had been weak and petty and stupid, hopelessly dependent.

They would force her to wear the dress, of course. She could wear it now, or be beaten until she gave in and wore it. Of course, she could tear it to shreds. While satisfying, that would only delay the inevitable. Besides, they weren't going to let her out of here without the dress. She was certain of that much. What she didn't know was if they would let her out even with the dress. Still, it was a better chance than nothing. And how was she going to kill Rask Garadul from in here?

She put on the dress.

She wanted to hate it. She wanted to hate it with a passion. But she hadn't worn anything that fit her so well in years. Her Blackguard garb, of course, fit like a glove, but those were work clothes. This, the whisper of fine silk on skin, was altogether different. It fit like a sheath. If it hadn't been so perfectly tailored, she wouldn't have been able to breathe, much less move. The dress was curve-hugging around her hips and stomach, and the more generous scalloped neckline drew attention to both the liquid dazzle of folds of fine silk and to her cleavage. Surely her old dress hadn't been so low-cut in the back, the few thin interlaced ties only emphasizing her back's essential nakedness. Looking down at her chest—there was no mirror in the room—she hoped she didn't get cold. If she did, everyone was going to know it.

Had her dress been unlined when she was that stupid sixteen-year-old? Had she not even noticed? She honestly couldn't remember. All she could remember was loving that dress. She'd felt like the goddess Atirat standing next to Gavin in it, long hair caught up in a diamond-and-emerald-encrusted tiara, people practically worshipping them. She'd convinced herself that she could love Gavin. At first, before the Luxlords' Ball, she'd felt more attraction toward him than toward Dazen. Surely she could blow that coal back to flame.

Dazen had been perpetually in his elder brother's shadow, and he seemed content with it. Gavin had been so confident, so masterful. She'd been drawn to him irresistibly, as everyone was. But after that night at the Luxlords' Ball, everything had changed. After she got to know Dazen, suddenly there hadn't seemed to be much depth to Gavin. Dazen had never understood his own strength. He had worshipped Gavin, projected all his own virtues onto his older brother, been blind to his faults and exaggerated his qualities. Gavin had fed on all the adoration and grown fat on it.

But Gavin was still gorgeous, stylish, commanding, and admired. To the sixteen-year-old Karris, other people's regard had been very important. She'd always wanted to please her father, her mother, Koios and her other brothers, her magisters, everyone. Gavin was everything good. He was the Prism, his brother by that point a disgraced runaway and a murderer. Karris remembered convincing herself she could be content with the Prism. *Content*—with the most admired, feared, desired man in the Seven Satrapies. Besides, after what Dazen had done, she had to marry Gavin or what was left of her family would be ruined.

On the platform announcing their betrothal, Karris had thought she really was going to be happy. She *had* admired her fiancé. Gavin always cut a fine figure. She had enjoyed every minute of the attention.

At dinner that night, Gavin had made a jest to her father about taking Karris back to his rooms and not sleeping a wink. Karris's father, ordinarily so traditional, the man who'd always sworn his daughter wouldn't give milk until some young satrap bought the whole cow, the man who had beaten Karris for giving her virginity to Dazen, that man, that hypocrite, that coward, had chuckled nervously. Until that moment, Karris had been able to stave off her rising panic. At least I won't have to sleep with him until we're married, she'd thought. I'll be able to fall in love with him in the coming months. I'll forget Dazen. I'll forget my shivers when he kissed the back of my neck. I'll forget that swelling in my chest I felt every time he gave that reckless grin. Everyone else is right, Dazen isn't half the man Gavin is. I can't love Dazen after what he did.

But there had been no escape. Karris had chosen her own kind of cowardice and gotten roaring drunk. Her father had noticed too late—or just in time, depending on how you looked at it—and forbade the servants from giving her more wine before she could pass out at the table. She couldn't even remember what she'd said at the table, but she did remember Gavin half-carrying her back to his room. Her father had watched her go with empty eyes; he said nothing.

She'd thought being drunk would help her be docile, quiet, malleable. It had worked, and she didn't know why she was so bitterly disappointed about that. When she'd turned her face away from his kisses, he'd mistaken it for shyness and kissed elsewhere. When he'd pulled off her slip and she'd covered herself with her hands, he'd mistaken it for modesty. Modest? When she'd been with Dazen, she'd gloried in his eyes on her. She'd been bold, shameless. She'd felt like a woman—though now she knew she'd only been playing at being a woman in so many ways. With Dazen, she'd felt beautiful. With

Gavin, she was filled with such unutterable despair it choked her cries in her own throat. She couldn't remember if she even protested, if she'd asked him to stop. She'd wanted to, but her memory was fogged. She didn't think she had. She'd kept thinking of her father saying, "Our family needs this. Without this marriage, we're ruined." And she hadn't fought.

She remembered crying, though, during. A gentleman would have stopped, but Gavin had been drunk and young and horny. There was no gentleness in him. When she wasn't ready and he was hurting her, he'd ignored her protests and thrust with a young man's need.

Far from keeping her awake all night as he'd bragged, he'd soon finished. Then he'd told her to leave. The casual cruelty of it had taken her breath away. And she'd taken it. She should have clawed his eyes out.

He hadn't wanted Karris. He'd wanted to show that Dazen couldn't have what rightfully belonged to him. Karris might as well have been a tree for him to piss on after the last dog, reclaiming his territory.

She'd stumbled through the halls in that beautiful dress with half its buttons undone—the damned thing required the help of servants to button. She'd been seen, of course. Somehow she got home, not their home on Big Jasper that had burned to the ground, but to their apartments nearby. Her father had been waiting up, but he didn't say a word, just stared at her. Her room slave had undressed her with trembling fingers, and when Karris had finally fallen in bed, the doorway of her room was darkened with her father's silhouette. He wobbled, leaned against the doorframe.

"I could challenge him to a duel," he said. "But he'd kill me, Karris, and then you'd be ruined. Hopeless. We'd lose everything our fathers have fought for for fifty generations. Maybe tomorrow will look better."

She'd been winesick for two days, and when she'd emerged, Gavin had kissed her in public, seated her at his right hand, and treated her like a queen. It was like the night had never happened. Or like it had been beautiful.

Later she'd decided it was because everyone had been talking about the two of them as such a perfect couple, of how beautiful she was, and Gavin had decided she suited his image. So instead of casting her aside, he'd decided to go through with the marriage. But then he'd left and soon after fought the final battle at Sundered Rock.

When he came back, he seemed like a different man. He treated her with a genuine warmth, respect, so unlike the man who'd banished her from his bedchamber after he took his pleasure of her. It made Karris doubt that the night had happened at all. She could have convinced herself that it had all been a nightmare—until she found out she was pregnant. The very day she'd become aware of it, before she could tell him, Gavin had broken their betrothal.

She'd been sixteen, pregnant, and without any prospect of marriage. In other words, her father's perfect nightmare. As soon as she was certain she wasn't going to miscarry, she'd told her father. He demanded she see the chirurgeons and get it taken care of.

For the first time in her life, she'd refused her father. To hell with him. He moved to strike her. She pulled out a pistol. She told him she'd hollow out his skull if he dared to strike her. She told him he was a coward. She was going to bear Gavin's bastard and let the world know it was his. To hell with him, and to hell with her father, and to hell with everyone. Bearing that child would be her first free act, and her revenge.

Her father had gotten down on his knees and begged. Literally begged. Please save our family, we can't be the ones who let down all the generations of White Oaks who sacrificed everything to get us here. We and us, he said. He meant, I and me. He was the one who had destroyed the family and he knew it. He looked so small and weak, cold sweat gleaming off his balding head. Abruptly, she despised him. He'd been the absolute lord over her, and he was disgusting. She refused his pleas, and she felt pleasure at the sick, slack despair in his eyes.

Two days later, her father kissed the double barrels of a pistol and blew out his own brains. His ledger books were all in order. That was how he'd spent those two days. All the family properties had been sold to pay off their debts, leaving Karris enough to live on quietly for the rest of her life, enough to support her illegitimate child. Her father had taken care of everything. His suicide note had simply explained where the remaining monies were and told Karris where to go if she wanted to bear her child in secret. It didn't beg her to do so. Indeed, there was no emotion in the note whatsoever. No curses, no forgiveness, no regrets. It was as empty as his skull after the musket balls passed through them. Just gore and black powder residue. Ordure and death. Hollow, messy.

She couldn't stand to stay on the Jaspers, couldn't endure the pity and the awkward glances. So she'd left, going to a distant cousin's house deep in the Blood Forest. She'd borne the child and given it up immediately, not even hugging it, asking not even to know its gender, and learning only through her hosts' indiscretion that it was a boy. The family adopting Gavin's get lived nearby, and Karris couldn't bear to stay, so she'd gone back to the Chromeria. She'd lost the baby weight in short order, and her young skin barely even showed any stretch marks. It was like nothing had happened, except for the memories clinging to her like hellstone eating her soul.

Fitting that my new dress is black then, huh? A little piece of midnight, like what's inside me.

Thought you left the melodrama behind, Karris.

Go bend over a fence.

I think that's what the king is hoping for.

That'll be a treat for both of us. Hope he enjoys blood.

So, what? I'm supposed to be thankful that I'm flowing now? Not much chance—

A cramp wracked her in midthought. Karris hunched. Not much thankfulness here.

While she was hunched over, a slip of paper was pushed under the door. Karris picked it up. It was no bigger than her finger.

"Orders: assas. KG. Dark. Can't help." There was an old Dayric rune at the bottom. It was the agreed symbol to show it was from the agent Karris had been sent to meet. Not well drawn, but correct.

It wasn't much of a code, but they'd never figured Karris would need a code. She was supposed to have met the agent in person. He was to identify himself by idly tracing part of the rune on any surface: a table, dirt, whatever. Karris's orders were to assassinate King Garadul. Secretly. And her contact wouldn't be able to help her.

Perfect. Karris couldn't even burn the note, and though small, it was grimy. She popped it into her mouth with a grimace and swallowed it.

Her contact wouldn't be able to help her. Damn it, Karris, you've been thinking so much about the past, you haven't thought about the present. In one moment, Corvan had understood that someone must want Karris dead. Of all the White's agents, Karris had to be the worst person to send here. Either the White wanted Karris dead, or...

There was no other possibility. Or she hoped I'd be kidnapped and maybe raped? Ludicrous.

She knew she frustrated the White at times, but she'd thought the stubborn old woman liked her. Then again, the White always played a deep game. Maybe she thought she could use Karris's death to accomplish something else.

Karris felt sick to her stomach. It was possible. She wouldn't have thought it before, but she'd sworn to give her life for the White if necessary. Maybe the White had decided it was necessary.

There was a knock at her door. It was the same routine as before, lots of drafters, lots of guards. This time, however, several women bearing tins of powders and glosses came in. With the efficiency of professionals, they made up Karris, fixed her hair, and applied perfume. But they didn't apply any powder to her eyes or lashes.

And soon enough, Karris found out why as one of the slaves took out violet eye caps. Blind them, they'd thought of everything.

"If you tear these off, you'll certainly rip your skin," one of the slave women said. "And possibly tear off your entire eyelid. If you leave them alone, the king may give you greater freedom, and it won't hurt your eyes. In a few days, they will loosen and come off by themselves."

"At which point you'll reglue them," Karris said.

"Yes."

"What if I get something in my eye?" It would be impossible to get it out.

"Try not to."

They tried the fit over her eye sockets. The caps weren't a perfect fit. The slave woman, eastern Atashian from her features, scowled. "To make the caps fit, we're going to have to use extra glue. Extra glue means if you blink, your eyelashes will get stuck. King Garadul wants you for your beauty, so I don't want to cut off your eyelashes if I can help it. But once we set the caps on your face, they'll be there for days. You really don't want your eyelashes globbed with glue—or stuck in it. So, do you want to be blind, irritated, or lashless?"

"Lashless, and to hell with Rask," Karris said.

The slave pursed her lips. "You're right. The king might be annoyed. We'll have to take our chances. Blink right now as much as you can, because you're going to have to not blink for as long as possible." With great care and globs of glue, they put the eye caps on. The glue globs took care of the gaps left in the fit.

Karris barely dared breathe, holding as still as possible, forcing herself not to blink. When she finally broke down and had to blink, her lashes caught for a moment in the drying glue, but pulled free.

"Oh, and try not to cry," the slave said. "Or you'll be up to your eyeballs in tears. Literally." She smiled unpleasantly.

Hilarious.

They put more makeup around her eyes after the glue was fully dried.

Then, bracketed by drafters and Mirrormen, Karris was whisked through camp. The sun had set perhaps an hour before, and Karris welcomed the fresh, dry air. Over the smell of her own perfume, she was finally able to smell horses, men, campfires, butchered raw meat, cooking meat, sagebrush, oil. Oil? She looked around and saw a supply wagon nearby. Oh, oiled swords and gunmetal.

With the number of wagons surrounding her own, Karris couldn't see enough of the army to get a good idea of how many men were marching on Garriston. Even the number of wagons didn't help her. She didn't know how heavily or lightly packed they were, and even if she did, the last time she'd traveled with an army, she hadn't paid any attention to such things. Young, pampered, terrified, and stupid, it hadn't occurred to her that such simple things might be useful to her someday.

There were a large number of women diffused throughout the

army, carrying fresh-cut wood for the fires, standing on the butcher's wagon, shouting at men to make sure the skinned wild javelinas were dispersed fairly, tending the minor injuries inevitable in moving thousands, taking in weapons and armor that needed repair for the blacksmiths, rejecting those that they deemed reparable by the men trying to get someone else to do it. Most of the women seemed to be in service roles, however, which either meant that King Garadul didn't think much of women or that most were new recruits. From the wide variety of their dress, Karris guessed they came from all over the social spectrum. That meant they were newer recruits, and willing ones. These people weren't all servants he'd brought from Kelfing; they were locals. King Garadul had significant support from the Tyrean people.

From the glimpses out into the growing darkness punctuated by fires scattered randomly as stars, it seemed the army sprawled wherever it willed, but Karris was brought quickly to an area where perhaps fifty wagons were circled, leaving only a few avenues between them at the points of the compass where horses would be able to pass, each guarded by ten Mirrormen with matchlocks. In the middle there was an open space for defense, small falconets pointed out everywhere like a porcupine ready to fire its quills, and then a number of large striped pavilions of every color.

A cramp caught Karris as she was ushered to the central pavilion. She hunched, breath taken away. She squeezed her eyes tight shut, and the luxin caps cut into her brows and cheeks painfully. She smoothed her expression and waited until the fury of the cramp passed. She took a slow breath, mastering the pain. Then she gestured to one of her guards, as if she were a queen and ready to enter now, thank you.

The man pulled back the pavilion's flap, and Karris entered.

It must have been some dress. Because as soon as Karris stepped inside, conversation ceased.

There were perhaps seventy people in the pavilion: slaves, tumblers, jugglers, and musicians surrounding perhaps thirty noblemen and -women seated on cushions around a lower table piled high with delicacies and wine. Everyone was colorfully dressed, so much so that Karris could tell even through the muting of her dark eye caps. King Rask Garadul sat at the head of the table, of course, rings sparkling from fingers wrapped around a wine goblet. He had stopped, midsentence, and was staring at her, openmouthed.

But Karris barely even saw the king, because at his right hand sat a man like none she'd ever seen. She forced herself to continue walking toward the king, hips rolling, skirt swishing, head up, shoulders loose, as if she weren't unnerved.

The man was a Tainted, a color wight. Karris had only ever seen one, and that one had been in the early stages of his madness. This man wasn't in the early stages, but neither did he appear mad. He wore a simple luxiat's robe, but it was dazzling white rather than the customary black of Orholam's luxiats, that color an admission that they needed Orholam's light most of all. Nor did his face bear any trace of a luxiat's humility.

But at least his face was mostly human—skin and bone and blood. Threads of green luxin lay submerged beneath burn-scarred skin like faded tattoos, rising close to the surface at his cheekbones and brow. At his neck, his body changed. The skin was pure luxin of every color of the rainbow. The inside of his elbow, visible as he raised his wine goblet in a mocking salute to Karris, was flexible green luxin, as were his other joints and his neck. Blue luxin plates sat on every surface that didn't need to move. It made plate armor on his forearms, formed gauntlets from his very hands, his knuckles spiked, his shoulders unnaturally broad under that blasphemous luxiat's robe, the V of his chest visible through the robe shimmering with reflected light like the sea at sunrise. Not plates of blue luxin, then, but actually woven blue luxin, which tripled its strength and made it much less likely to shatter, if one had the skill and patience to make it.

Everywhere, yellow luxin flowed between or beneath the other colors, constantly renewing whatever was lost to sunlight or natural breakdown. Where plates came together, lubricative orange luxin made them slide smoothly past each other. Red luxin formed archaic designs of runes and etchings of eight-pointed stars in thin layers on top of the blue plates. Karris couldn't see if he had incorporated superviolet into his skin, but was certain he had. After all, in the middle of each palm he'd embedded a flame crystal. Flame crystals, the physical, sealed manifestation of sub-red, usually only lasted a few seconds. Exposure to air made them burst and flame out.

This monster had somehow sunk one into each hand and sealed it from the air with blue luxin so that you could literally see through each of his hands, albeit as though through a mirage, the image wavering from the heat, which was the signature of a flame crystal. And yet he still retained the use of his fingers, meaning he was either a miracle-working healer or it was some illusion. It had to be. The whole thing was impossible.

Karris saw his eyes last, as she came to stand before King Garadul. The Tainted's eyes were shattered. The halo was broken everywhere. Colors leaked everywhere from the iris, staining the white of his eyes with every color. The colors themselves swirled constantly, blue coming to the fore as the Tainted studied Karris, green wriggling like a snake through a maze of orange and red.

"You," King Garadul said, "are a vision, Karris. A sight for sore eyes."

"And you're a sore sight for eyes," she replied, smiling sweetly.

He laughed. "Not only more beautiful than you were as a girl, but sharper, too. Karris, join us. I have a gift for you, but first, I'd like you to meet my right hand." He gestured to the Tainted. "Karris White Oak, meet the Crystal Prophet, the Polychrome Master, Lord Omnichrome, the Color Prince, the Eldritch Enlightened."

"Long name," Karris said. "Must take your mother forever to call you to dinner."

"You can pick your favorite," the Color Prince said. His voice was disconcertingly...human. Strong, confident, amused if husky like a longtime haze smoker's.

"The Motley Fool then."

Red snapped to the surface of his eyes, quickly replaced by cool, amused blue. "Now, Karris, is that the way your father taught you to speak? You used to be so concerned with pleasing him. So ladylike, so sweet. So tame for a green drafter."

"That ended a long time ago," she said. "Who the hell are you? You don't know me."

"Oh, but I do," the Color Prince said. He glanced over at the king.

"Oh, sure, go ahead, let her open her present early," Rask Garadul said, pretending exasperation.

"Look at me, Karris," the Crystal Prophet said. "Take a moment. See beyond your fear, your petty disgust, your ignorance."

Karris bit her tongue. There was something genuine in that raspy voice, some wish to be known. So she looked, silently. The body, of course, was no help, so she studied his face. The luxin-stained skin obscured the features, as did the burn scars. One eyebrow had grown back in white, whether reacting to fire or luxin, she didn't know. But there was something familiar.

Orholam. The fire. The burn scars. A fist clamped tight around her heart and squeezed. She couldn't draw a breath. It couldn't be him, he was dead these sixteen years. But as soon as she saw it, she knew it could be no other. "Koios," Karris said. So this was why the White had sent her. Her enemy was her brother. Her knees gave out and she sat heavily on the cushions next to the king, lest she suffer a very ladylike fainting spell.

Chapter 68

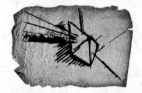

Gavin stopped drafting as the sun sank below the horizon. He could use the ambient reflected light if he wished, but he was already exhausted. He looked over the scrub brush plain to the south. Karris was out there, somewhere. In all likelihood, he would never see her again, never get the chance to tell her the truth. It saddened him more than he would have imagined possible.

He turned back and studied the day's handiwork with disappointment. He'd hoped to erect half a league of wall today, at the least. Instead, he'd laid nothing more than foundation, albeit a full league of it. Surprisingly enough, it had been Aliviana Danavis who'd solved the hardest problem so far. Or maybe not surprisingly, given how smart her father was. Gavin had been walking along the trench the workers were digging, spraying yellow into it. Where there was existing wall, he'd let the yellow flow over it like water, sinking into every crack, reinforcing stone and mortar with magic. Where even the old wall's foundation was gone, he drafted the yellow into solid luxin directly, giving the wall a foundation seven paces wide. Everywhere, he anchored the yellow to bedrock with a half-evaporated, tarry thick red luxin.

But not only was walking slow, but as soon as the luxin reached the level of the ground, Gavin had to throw it. Like every other color, yellow had mass. It weighed about as much as water, and with the amounts that Gavin was moving, he was getting crushed. His muscles would give out far before his drafting ability. Of course, it would only get worse as the wall got taller.

He'd begun using scaffolding, but within half an hour it was clear that that wouldn't get the wall finished in a month, much less the five days he had.

That was when Liv had sketched out her idea, and like most great ideas, it seemed simple, obvious—after she said it.

Gavin laid two tracks on either side of the wall, and drafted arms to connect them. With the addition of wheels and a harness to hold him, he was able to hang suspended in the air over the wall. The wheels glided along the tracks, so instead of having to move a scaffolding every twenty paces, his scaffolding moved with him. Instead of throwing luxin, he could drop it. It took almost all the physical effort out of the project.

By the time he'd properly drafted the harness so that he wasn't swinging crazily every time he threw more luxin, it was late afternoon. Gavin had rolled slowly along his tracks, sealing the yellow luxin at twenty-pace intervals and laying more yellow over the sealed points. With the amount of time left before sunset, he'd focused on the brute drafting, so rather than tackle the intellectual challenges of drafting the interior of the wall, he'd decided to draft as much foundation as he could.

He made huge progress, but it was still hard to say whether he was going to finish the whole project in time. If he finished an entire tall, impregnable wall by the time Rask Garadul's army arrived, except for two hundred paces in the middle, the entire endeavor would be vanity.

Gavin lowered himself to the ground. He wobbled a little as he approached Corvan Danavis, who was holding their horses. Corvan looked concerned. "Just a long time off my feet," Gavin said.

Corvan accepted that silently. A few blocks later as the sun was fading out of the sky, he said, "So...Karris was captured."

"Mm-hm," Gavin said, not making eye contact.

"So you've put all that behind you?"

Gavin said nothing.

"Good. I always thought she was the biggest threat to your plan. Enough reasons to hate both of you, and rash enough to tear it all down without thinking. So you'll antagonize Rask and hope he kills her to show he's serious?"

"Damn you," Gavin said.

"Oh, not past it, then?" Corvan asked.

He wasn't serious about getting Karris killed. Gavin knew that. Corvan might always understand the cutthroat thing to do, but that didn't mean he always did it.

"So she still doesn't know?"

"No. That's why I broke our betrothal."

"Because she was the most likely to see through you, or some other reason?" Corvan asked.

"We destroyed her. Dazen burned down her home and the war took the rest. I didn't realize she had nothing—and I should have. By the time I offered to restore her family's fortune, it seemed like an insult. She spat on me and disappeared for a year. When she came back, she was different."

"I noticed. A Blackguard. An astounding achievement. But you didn't answer my question."

Though it was getting darker, the streets were comfortably warm, and if anything, the crowds were getting thicker, people lighting lamps outside their own homes or shops. Others were relaxing, drinking on the flat roofs of their houses. It was almost as if doom weren't impending.

Gavin looked around and made sure his voice was low enough not to carry. "I've lied to everyone. I've lied so much sometimes I forget who I was. With everything my brother and I did to Karris...I couldn't— well, shit, she's seen us both naked, hasn't she? If anyone would know, she would. It would be the quickest way to destroy everything."

"True enough, but you were going to say something else," Corvan said, looking down at his saddle, giving Gavin that shred of privacy.

"I thought about it, you know? How to marry her and still deceive her. Or, failing that, how to show her that she had no choice but to keep my secret. In the end, she was the one thing I wasn't willing to defile. After I ran away, she fell in love with my brother. If she figured out the truth and decided to destroy me..." Gavin shrugged.

Now Corvan did look him in the eye. "I don't know whether to admire you all the more, or to be horrified that you'd be so stupid."

"I usually opt to admire me all the more," Gavin said, grinning.

Corvan gave a grudging smile, but didn't laugh.

They rode through the streets as quickly as they could without crushing anyone, and arrived at the Travertine Palace as darkness set in. Ironfist was standing at the gate. Uncharacteristically, he had a huge grin on his face.

"High Lord Prism," he said. "Dinner awaits."

Gavin scowled. If Ironfist was grinning, it meant something awkward, unpleasant, or vexing was coming. But he wasn't going to ask. With that grin, Ironfist would just grin bigger and enjoy being mysterious. Fine. Gavin started walking toward the private dining hall.

"High Lord," Ironfist interjected. "The great hall."

It was only a few steps away. Gavin barely had time to think why they might possibly need the great hall for dinner before he was inside the antechamber to the great domed hall.

The great hall of the Travertine Palace, though perhaps only a third the size of the Chromeria's great hall, was one of the wonders of the old world. The doorways were enormous bulbous horseshoe arches, striped green and white, speaking of the days when half of Tyrea had been a Parian province. Travertine and white marble alternated everywhere: in the chessboard pattern of the floor, in intricate geometric shapes on the walls, and in old Parian runes that decorated the bases of the eight great wooden pillars that supported the ceiling, their layout an eight-pointed star. Each pillar was a full five paces thick—*atasifusta*, the widest trees in the world—and none narrowed perceptibly before reaching the ceiling. The wood was said to have been the gift of an Atashian king, five hundred years before. Even then it had been precious. Now they were extinct, the last grove cut down during the Prisms' War. Gavin had never found out who had done that. When he arrived in Ru, the grove was simply gone. His commanders—Dazen's commanders—had sworn the last trees were standing when they left the city. Gavin's commanders after the war had sworn the trees were gone when they arrived.

What made the atasifusta unique was that its sap had properties like concentrated red luxin. The trees took a hundred years to reach full size—these giants had been several hundreds of years old when they'd been cut. But after they reached maturity, holes could be drilled in the trunk, and if the tree was large enough, the sap would drain slowly enough to feed flames. These eight giants each bore a hundred twenty-seven holes, the number apparently significant once, but that significance lost. On first look, it appeared that the trees were aflame, but the flame was constant and never consumed the wood, which was ghostly ivory white aside from the blackened soot smudges above each flame hole. Gavin knew that the flames couldn't be truly eternal, but after allegedly burning day and night for five hundred years, these atasifustas' flames gave little indication of going out anytime soon. Perhaps the flames nearer the top were a little duller than those lower as the sap settled in the wood, but Gavin wouldn't have bet on it.

When the wood wasn't mature, it made incredible firewood. A bundle that a man could carry in his arms would warm a small hut all winter. No wonder it was extinct.

No torches were necessary in the great hall, of course, but outside the stained glass windows, each also a horseshoe arch, torches burned so that the colored glass would glow day or night, white or green or red.

Again, the colors, the shape itself, all were meaningful to the people who'd built this wonder, and Gavin had no idea what any of it meant. It gave him a sense of insignificance. He didn't think anything he made would survive five hundred years after he was gone. Indeed, it was mostly luck that his brother Gavin hadn't razed this very wonder when he'd destroyed this city.

As Gavin walked in, his eyes were pulled from the majesty of those atasifusta pillars to the men and women seated at the great table, every face turned toward him. He was distracted briefly as he stepped past twin shadows flanking the halls. His head snapped to the side, expecting an assassin. No, it was a Blackguard. One on either side of the doorway, and dozens more around the hall, all of them familiar to him. Blackguards? Here?

Oh, the ships of those to be Freed have come. Ironfist must have commanded all these Blackguards to come along.

His eyes returned to the table. There were at least two hundred drafters waiting for him. A small class, as the White had told him. What she hadn't told him was who was in this class. Gavin knew all of them by face, and most of them by name. He recognized Izem Red and Izem Blue, Samila Sayeh, Maros Orlos, the discontiguous bichrome Usef Tep whom they called the Purple Bear, Deedee Falling Leaf, the Parian sisters Tala and Tayri, Javid Arash, Talon Gim, Eleleph Corzin, Bas the Simple, Dalos Temnos the Younger, Usem the Wild, Evi Grass, Flamehands, and Odess Carvingen. Everywhere he looked, heroes from the Prisms' War, from both sides. These were some of the most talented drafters in the Seven Satrapies, and they represented every single one of the Seven Satrapies too; even the Ilytians were represented, albeit only by Flamehands, and Eleleph Corzin was Abornean.

Gavin stopped in his tracks, disbelieving. Every year, some drafters from the war were Freed, but Gavin hadn't had this many of the greats since immediately after it, when so many had been pushed to the brink by the amount of power they'd handled in fighting.

These drafters had all been young during the war, and Gavin had known and dreaded that they'd start passing, but so many, all in one year?

"We had us a pact," Usem the Wild said, answering Gavin's obvious confusion. "Some of us who fought together. Said once the first of us had to go, we'd all go together. Wanted another year or two, myself, but better to go out on top, isn't it?"

"Better to go out sane," the Purple Bear growled.

"Better to go together," Samila Sayeh said. "And stop making Deedee feel bad."

Indeed, Deedee Falling Leaf did look worse than most of them. Her skin was tinged a permanent green, and the halo of her eyes was straining under the green that had overwhelmed her formerly blue

irises. She smiled weakly. "Lord Prism, it's an honor. I've been looking forward to this Freeing for a long time." She curtsied, choosing to
ignore, as most of the old warriors did, that she had been on the
other side of the war than Gavin.

The rest of them followed her example, bowing or curtseying in
the formal style of their homelands. Gavin bowed formally, meeting
their eyes, careful that he too gave equal respect to drafters from
each side.

Inside, as it always did, his heart broke. He wanted to tell those
who'd fought beside him that it was him, that he wasn't Gavin, that it
had all been for the best. Instead, he sat with them, finding himself
next to the irascible Usem the Wild as the slaves brought out steaming platters of food and cool flagons of citrus juices and wine.

"When I told some of the others"—Usem nodded grudgingly over
at the Izems and Samila, who'd fought for Gavin—"they thought it
would be a good year for them too."

"We wished, Lord Prism, to perhaps help the Seven Satrapies put
the...war behind us," Samila Sayeh said, diplomatically stopping
herself from calling it the False Prism's War. "We've actually become
good friends."

"Personally," Maros Orlos, the shortest Ruthgari Gavin had ever
seen, said, "I'm glad to have a Freeing without all the trappings. The
fireworks and speeches and posturing by satraps and satrapahs and
upstart lordlings who won't ever have to fulfill the Pact themselves. A
Freeing's holy. It ought to be between a man, the Prism, and Orholam. The rest is distractions."

"Distractions? Like dinner with the Prism and your Freeing class?"
Izem Red asked. He was Parian, lean as a whip and with a wit to
match. He still wore his ghotra folded so it resembled a cobra's hood,
a style he'd picked up as a seventeen-year-old drafter, and endured
incessant teasing for it. He'd been called a poser until the first battle
when his lightning-like strikes, fireballs as fast as an arrow, and deci-
mation of the enemy's ranks had silenced all teasing once and for all.

Maros opened his mouth to protest, realized he was about to spar
with Izem Red, and turned his attention back to his food.

Tala, an older Parian woman with short white hair and red halos compressing brown irises, said, "You know, High Lord Prism, Commander Ironfist told us you have a little project you're working on. Something about that reminds me of that old poem about the Wanderer. How does it go, some work...?"

It was a famous poem; they all knew it. She didn't even need to say the whole thing. She was offering their help on Gavin's wall. "That would be wonderful—" Gavin began.

Bas the Simple, the odd Tyrean polychrome, interrupted, his head cocked to the side. " 'Some work of noble note may yet be done, not unbecoming men that strove with gods.' Gevison, *The Wanderer's Last Journey*, lines sixty-three and sixty-four." He looked up, saw everyone looking at him, and looked down shyly.

"That would be marvelous," Gavin said. "I understand if anyone has objections and doesn't wish to join me, but if you would like to...I'd really appreciate it." It was a total gift, and one that wouldn't cost most of them anything. Not all of these drafters were at the edge of death, most of them were ridiculously powerful, and many were wonderfully subtle in their chromaturgy. Their help would make all the difference.

Of course, these were also all the people who had known Gavin and Dazen best. If anyone were likely to discover that Gavin was a fraud, he or she was in this room. And with their Freeing looming, the discoverer would have little or nothing to lose in exposing him.

Gavin's chest tightened and he smiled over his fear, as if he were smiling at how brilliant and strangely simple Bas was. Smiles returned to him from every side of the table. Some of those smiles, Gavin knew, must surely be serpents' smiles, but he had no way of knowing which ones. Who would be more likely to destroy him? Those who thought he was the man who had been their friend and learned he had usurped Gavin's place, or those who'd fought for him and had believed him dead and now learned that he'd betrayed them?

Bas the Simple was staring at Gavin, not smiling, his head cocked to the side, oddly perceptive eyes studying everything.

Chapter 69

"The boy's gone," Ironfist said. It was almost midnight. They were standing on the roof of the Travertine Palace, looking over the bay. "Kip," he said, as if there were some other boy. He didn't say "your son," though.

Great how everyone has to dance around my misdeeds. *My* misdeeds. Right. Thanks, brother. "Why wasn't I told?" Gavin asked. He'd spent all night pretending to be his brother with drafters who knew them both, and having to pretend to be enjoying himself. It was disconcerting. He'd enjoyed his old enemies' company, and felt constantly like his vision was blurring. The men and women he'd hated when he'd been Dazen had been quite pleasant. A few of Dazen's old friends, though not all, had had an edge on all their interactions that made them unattractive. Gavin looked at men and women whom he had arranged to live and work far from the Jaspers just so they wouldn't endanger him and thought, I ruined you and you never even knew it. And I missed you.

"We just discovered it a few minutes ago. This note was sitting out. The other was tucked under the bedsheets."

Smart. Kip accomplished exactly what he was trying to do: he bought himself time. Kept us from looking for him all day. Gavin extended his hand, knowing Ironfist would have the notes. Ironfist handed them over.

The important one read, "I'm Tyrean and young. More help as a spy than here. No one will suspect me. Will try to find Karris."

A spy? Orholam strike me. "Any other news?" Gavin asked.

"He took a horse and a stick of coins."

"So he could get himself into even more trouble than simply heading into an enemy camp armed only with delusions," Gavin said.

Ironfist didn't respond. He generally ignored statements of the obvious. "The Danavis girl is gone as well. The stableman says she asked him for a horse, but he turned her down. Sounds like she found the notes and went after him."

Gavin stared out over the bay. The Guardian, the statue guarding the entrance of the bay, and through whose legs every sailor passed, held a spear in one hand and a torch in the other. The torch was kept by a yellow drafter whose entire job was to keep it filled with liquid yellow. Special grooves cut in the glass slowly exposed the yellow luxin to air and caused it to shimmer back into light. Mirrors collected and directed the light out into the night, spinning slowly on gears driven by a windmill when there was wind and draft animals when there wasn't. Tonight, the beam illuminated the misty night air, cutting great swathes in the darkness. It was what every drafter was supposed to do: bring Orholam's light to the darkest corners of the world.

It was what Kip was trying to do.

Ironfist said, "If he came into my camp and kept a low profile, *I* wouldn't suspect him as a spy."

Because he'd make a marvelously bad spy, perhaps? "About our spies, what have you learned?"

"Governor Crassos very innocently came to inspect the docks, carrying a very innocent-looking and strangely heavy bag. He looked awfully pleased to see me," Ironfist said.

"You only get sarcastic when you're mad," Gavin said. "Go ahead. Let me have it."

"I swore to protect Kip, Lord Prism, but first, the spies—"

"You can call me Gavin when I've been stupid," Gavin said flatly.

"The spies report—"

"Out with it, for Orholam's sake."

Ironfist clenched his jaw, then willed himself to relax. "I need to go after him, Gavin, which means I can't be here, helping with the defense and directing my people."

"And you're Parian and huge and pretty much the opposite of inconspicuous, so if you go after him—as your honor demands— you'll most likely be killed, which will not only mean that you're killed, which you don't particularly desire, but it also means you will have failed to protect Kip, which would be the only point of going after him in the first place. And you can't delegate the mission to any-one else because you promised to protect him personally, and besides, any other Blackguard would stand out nearly as much as you do." It wasn't that Blackguards were darker-skinned than Tyreans and had kinky rather than wavy or straight hair. There had been enough mix-ing over the centuries that quite a few Tyreans had both traits. Even Kip could still make a good spy despite his blue eyes; Tyreans were used to minority ethnicities from all the people who'd stayed after the war. The problem was that ebony-skinned, extremely physically fit drafters who exuded danger from their very pores were going to stand out anywhere. Blackguards would stand out among an army of Parian drafters.

"That's pretty much it," Ironfist admitted, the edge of his anger blunted by Gavin acknowledging exactly why he was angry.

"What else did you learn from our spies?" Gavin asked, shunting aside Ironfist's concerns for the moment.

Ironfist seemed just as happy to not be talking about his dilemma. "Some of them have come from King Garadul's camp, and I think our problems are bigger than we realized." He pushed his ghotra off his head, scrubbing his scalp with his fingertips. "It's religious," he said.

"I didn't think you were much for religion," Gavin said, trying to inject a bit of levity.

"Why would you think that? I speak with Orholam constantly."

"'Orholam, what did I do to deserve this?'" Gavin suggested, thinking he was kidding.

"No. Seriously," Ironfist said.

"Oh." Ironfist, devout?

"But you know how that is. You speak with him all the time as well. You are his chosen."

"It's different for me." Very very different, apparently. "But sorry to jest. Religion?"

"This isn't just some political matter of calling himself a king. Rask Garadul wants to upend everything we've accomplished since Lucidonius came. Everything."

An indefinable dread settled in Gavin's stomach. "The old gods."

"The old gods," Ironfist said.

"Get Kip back, Commander. Do whatever you have to. If anyone complains about your methods, they'll have to go through me. If you can, save the girl too. I owe her father a debt I can never explain."

Gavin slept little and fitfully. He never slept much, but it was always worse as the Freeing approached. He hated this time of year. Hated the charade. His chest felt tight as he lay in his bed. Maybe he should have let his brother win. Maybe Gavin would have done a better job of all of this. At the very least, he wouldn't be here now.

Nonsense.

And yet he couldn't help but wonder if Gavin would have been a better Prism than he was. Gavin had always borne burdens of responsibility better than Dazen had. It didn't even seem like a weight to his older brother. Like the man had been without self-doubt. Dazen had always envied Gavin that.

The morning came none too soon. Dazen sat up and put on his face, Gavin once more. He felt that stab of pain radiating through his chest, tightening his throat. He couldn't do this.

Nonsense. He was just missing Kip, and Karris, and was worried for Corvan's daughter and dreading the exhausting drafting he was going to have to do all day long. There was nothing to do but get on with it.

After taking his time with his ablutions—why had Gavin had to be such a dandy?—he ate and rode to the wall. He was greeted by a young orange drafter.

The drafter was one of the tragically young who couldn't handle the power. An addict. He couldn't have been twenty years old, mountain Parian, but he didn't wear the ghotra, instead wearing his hair in dreadlocks, bound back with a leather thong. The rest of his clothing spoke of similar rejection of traditional attire—any tradition. Oranges tended to see exactly how others liked things to be. In most cases they used that to their advantage, becoming as slick as their luxin. But in some cases they defied every convention they saw, becoming artists and rebels. Given how the man's clothes somehow worked together to look good despite their disparate origins, and that all the colors and textures complemented each other, Gavin guessed this one was an artist. This young man's orange halo was thin with strain, though. He definitely couldn't have made it until the next Freeing.

"Lord Prism," the young man said. "How can I help?"

The sun had barely cleared the horizon, and all the drafters who were capable of drafting without hurting themselves or losing control had gathered at the wall. The local workmen seemed stunned to be surrounded by so many of them.

"What's your name?" Gavin asked. He didn't think he'd even seen this young man before.

"Aheyyad."

"So you *are* an artist," Gavin said.

Aheyyad smiled. "Not much choice, with the grandmother I had."

Gavin tilted his head.

"Sorry, I thought you knew. My grandmother is Tala. She knew I was going to be an orange and an artist by the time I was four years old. She forced my mother to rename me."

"Tala can be very, ahem, persuasive," Gavin said.

The boy grinned.

A boy going to the Freeing at the same time as his grandmother. There was a tale of woe just under the surface there, a family's grief, the loss of two generations at once, but no need to prod that now. All things are brought to light in time. "I need an artist," Gavin said. "Can you work fast?"

"I'd better," Aheyyad said.

"Are you any good?" Gavin already knew that Aheyyad was or Corvan wouldn't have sent him. He wanted to know whether the young man would be bold or tentative when faced with something so vast.

"I'm the best," Aheyyad said. "What's the project?"

Gavin smiled. He loved artists. In small doses. "I'm building a wall. Work with the architect to make sure you don't screw up anything functional, but your task is to make this wall scary. You can commandeer any of the old drafters to help you. I'll give you some drawings we have of Rathcaeson. If it can resemble those, do it. You'll tell the blues how to hold the forms. I'll fill them with yellow luxin. I'm doing functional things first. We can attach and integrate whatever you design in two or three days."

"How big can I make...whatever I make?"

"We've got a couple leagues of wall."

"So you're saying...big."

"Huge," Gavin said. Having the artist only design the forms would also keep the young man from having to draft anything at all, which with how close Aheyyad was to breaking the halo would possibly save his life.

It took until noon before they were ready to start the drafting. Gavin had asked all the old warriors to look at the plans of the wall, and not a few of them had come up with suggestions. Those suggestions had covered everything from expanding the latrines—and making sure the raw sewage could be routed onto their enemies by emptying the pots suddenly through chutes out the front of the wall—to reworking the mounts for the cannons and adding furnaces to heat the shot at several of the stations. Heated shot was wonderful for setting fire to siege engines. Someone else suggested texturing the floors and providing gutters not only outside for rainwater, which had already been considered, but also within the wall itself for blood.

Many good suggestions, and quite a few bad ones. The wall should be bigger, smaller, wider, taller. There should be space for more cannons, more archers, more beds in the hospital, the barracks should be within the wall, and so on.

At noon, Gavin was rigged back into his harness and lifted off the ground. The others swarmed around him, drafting forms, steadying his harness. Then he set to work.

Chapter 70

It wasn't until two days later, as Kip and Liv came within sight of King Garadul's army, plopped over the plain and fouling the river like an enormous cow pie, that he realized how deeply, incredibly, brilliantly stupid his plan was.

I'm going to march in there and rescue Karris?

More like waddle in there.

At the top of a small hill, they sat on the horse, which seemed grateful for the break, and scanned the mass of humanity before them. It was immense. Kip had never tried to estimate a crowd, and never seen one this large.

"What do you think, sixty or seventy thousand?" he asked Liv.

"More than a hundred, I'd guess."

"How are we going to find Karris in that?" he asked. What did I expect? A sign, perhaps? "Captured drafter here"?

Most of the camp was chaotic, people pitching lean-tos against wagons, those who had tents screaming at each other over who got which spot, children running around, clogging the spaces between tents and wagons and livestock. The sky was still light, though the sun had gone down, and campfires were being started all over the plain. Kip could hear people singing nearby. Men were swimming and bathing in the river, downstream of where some soldiers had hastily erected a corral. The animals dirtied the water, but no one seemed to care. Other men stood on the bank, urinating directly into the water. The color of the river upstream and downstream of the camp was distinctly different. People were carrying buckets of water everywhere, taken directly from the river.

Maybe I'll only drink wine.

More importantly, the smell of meat cooking permeated the air.

Kip's stomach complained. They'd gone through his food faster than he'd thought—mostly, *he* had gone through it faster—and now he had nothing. Well, except for a stick of danars I stole with half a year's wages on it.

Oh. That.

"We split up," Liv said. "You head directly for the center of the camp. I imagine that's where the king will have his tents. She's important, so they might be keeping her close. I'll go look for where the drafters are camping. A captured drafter will probably be watched by other drafters. She's got to be in one place or the other. We'll meet back here in, say, three hours?"

Kip nodded his acquiescence, impressed. He would have been lost on his own.

And almost instantly, she slipped off the horse and was gone. No hesitation, no second-guessing. Kip watched her go. He was hungry.

Leading the big, docile horse, tugging and pulling the beast as it tried to munch grass to the right and left, Kip approached at one of the larger fires. Not one but two javelinas were roasting on spits over the fire, and as Kip stared, swallowing, one of the fattest women he had ever seen sawed off a fully cooked leg with a few deft strokes at the joint. The smell was rich, succulent, savory, mouthwatering, lovely, astounding, mesmerizing, debilitating. Kip couldn't move—until he saw her raise the meat to her lips.

"Pardon me!" he said, louder than he meant. Others around the fire looked up.

"Didn't smell it," the fat lady said, then she sank her teeth into greasy ham. Kip died a little. Then more as the hard men and women around the fire laughed at him. The fat woman, leg in one hand, long knife in the other, grinned between bites. She had at least three chins, her facial features disappearing into the fat that encased her like an awkward child surrounded by a crowd of bullies. Her linen skirt could have served as a tent. Literally. She turned away from Kip, slipping the knife back into a sheath and putting her hand back to turning the spit. Her butt was more than a jiggly haunch; it was architecture.

"Pardon me," Kip said, recovering. "I was wondering if I could buy some dinner. I've got money."

Ears perked up all around the fire at that. Kip wondered suddenly if he'd picked a good fire to stop at. Were the men everywhere in the camp as scruffy as these ones?

Kip looked around. Uh, yes, actually they were.

Oh shit.

He fumbled with the leather money belt holding the stick of tin danars. He'd grabbed the money belt because it already had money in it and would be easier to transport than loose coins. The stick was a great way to carry money. Cut square to fit the square hole in the middle of danars, and of uniform length so people could rapidly count their own money—scales were still used to count others' money, of course—it was convenient and kept your money from jangling at every step as they did in a purse. Plus the sticks could be bound in leather for attaching to a belt or hiding inside of clothes, as Kip's was. He'd seen the gleam of this stick and grabbed it.

But as Kip pulled the open end of the money stick out to pull off one tin danar coin, he saw something was very wrong. He froze. The weight had been right, or at least close enough that he hadn't thought about it, but the coin he pulled out wasn't tin. A danar was about what a worker would make for a day's labor. An unskilled laborer like his mother would only make half a danar a day. He'd assumed the stick he grabbed was full of the tin coins, each worth eight danars.

Instead, he'd grabbed a stick of silver quintars. Slightly wider in circumference, but only half as thick, and the metal slightly lighter than tin, the silver coins were worth twenty danars each. A stick of silver quintars held fifty of the coins, twice as many as the twenty-five tin coins that would fit on the same stick. So instead of stealing two hundred danars from the Travertine Palace—an already princely sum—Kip had stolen a thousand. And he'd just pulled out one right in front of everyone, making it clear he had more.

Conversation ceased. In the dancing light of the fire, more than a few eyes gleamed like wolves'.

Kip tucked the rest of the money belt away, praying no one had seen how full it was. What did it matter? His life might be worth less than even the *one* silver quintar. "I'll take the other leg," he said.

The fat woman let go of the spit and reached her hand out.

"I'll need nineteen danars back," Kip said. A full day's wages should be more than three times what the javelina leg cost.

She chortled. "We run a charity house here, we do. Look like luxiats, huh? Ten."

"Ten danars, for a meal?" Kip asked, not believing she was serious.

"You can go hungry if you wanna. You ain't gonna starve," the woman said.

The injustice of this *whale* calling him fat and the impossibility of doing much about it paralyzed Kip. He gritted his teeth, glaring around the fire, and handed over the quintar.

The leviathan took the quintar and held it between her teeth, bending it slightly. If it were a counterfeit, tin coated with silver, it would give the curious crackling sound unique to bending tin. Satisfied between the weight and the texture that it was real, she tucked the coin away. She took a swig from a glass jug, set it down, and then sawed a leg off the javelina. While she was working, Kip noticed that some of the men around the fire had disappeared.

No doubt he was going to find them in the spreading darkness, waiting for him. Orholam, they had seen the rest of the stick.

Nor were the remaining men and women looking at him in a terribly friendly manner. They sat on their bags, on stumps, or on the ground, mostly watching him quietly. A few drank from wineskins or aleskins, murmuring to each other. A glassy-eyed woman was lying with her head in a long-haired, balding, unshaven man's lap, stroking his thigh. Both were staring at him.

The whale handed Kip the javelina leg.

Kip looked at her, waiting.

She stared blandly back at him from beneath her layers of blubber.

A few weeks ago, Kip would have backed off. He was used to people treating him like dirt. Ignoring him or bullying him. But he couldn't imagine Gavin Guile being bullied, not even when the odds were stacked against him. Kip might be a bastard, but if he had one drop of the Prism's blood, there was no way he could knuckle under. "I need my ten danars," Kip said.

The drunk woman across the fire laughed suddenly, uncontrollably, until she started snorting and laughing harder. Not just drunk, then.

"Do I look rich enough to have ten danars?" the whale asked.

"You can cut that danar in half."

She drew her knife and shrugged, stepping close to Kip. She reeked of grain alcohol. "Sorry, got no knife."

Kip understood instantly. Several of the men were sitting up, not only paying more attention, but getting ready to hop to their feet. They weren't waiting only to laugh at him, knowing this whale would cheat him. They were waiting, knowing the whale would cheat him, to see if he was a victim. Would Kip meekly accept being cheated? If he was a victim, he was a mark. If he had one quintar, he might have more.

But what could he do? Give back the food? No, she wouldn't give him the quintar back regardless. If he left, he'd confirm his weakness. Someone would be waiting for him in the darkness. What would they do if he attacked her? If, without warning, he punched her in her blubbery face as hard as he could?

They'd attack him, of course. And after they beat him, then they'd rob him.

If he ran away, even if he got away, he'd lose his horse, and he had too much trouble mounting the beast to leap into the saddle and ride away—even if it hadn't been the most placid creature on earth, unlikely to gallop even with hell on its heels.

"Fine," Kip said. He turned as if to go, but instead grabbed her glass jug. "I'd like to have a drink with dinner. You keep the rest. For the great service." He smelled the jug. As he thought, it was grain alcohol. He took a swig to look tough and had to school his face to stillness when it set his mouth on fire. Then his throat. Then his stomach.

The men who'd been shifting to get up settled back down.

"Mind if I sleep here tonight?" Kip asked.

"It'll cost you," the man who was balding up front and had hair halfway down his back said.

"Sure," Kip said. He wasn't nearly as hungry as he'd been a few minutes ago, but he forced himself to eat the greasy javelina leg. As the rest of the javelina cooked, the other men and women came and took slices.

As Kip finished, he sucked his fingers and walked toward his horse. He got far enough that he began to hope that they would simply let him leave.

"What are you doing?" the balding man demanded.

"I need to rub down my horse," Kip said. "It's been a long day."

"You don't need to go anywhere, and I don't want you near my horse."

"Your horse," Kip said.

"That's right." The man bared blackened teeth at Kip—not quite a smile, not quite like he was going to bite him—and drew a knife.

"We'll be needing that coin belt, too," another man said.

The women around the fire simply watched, impassive. No one moved to help. Several other men joined the two already facing Kip. Kip looked into the darkness, his vision spoiled by the fire, but still he could see several dark shapes waiting for him.

Give them what you have, and maybe you'll escape with a beating, Kip. You know you're not getting out of here with everything. Stall for time, maybe there's some kind of camp guards here who might save you.

"Evernight take you," Kip said. He smashed the top off the jug of grain alcohol on the edge of a wagon wheel.

"Fool boy," the balding man said. "Most people keep the handle if they do that, not smash it off."

Kip lunged, splashing grain alcohol over the man. The balding man grimaced, rubbing stinging eyes, switching his knife to his left hand. "You know what? I'm going to kill you for that," he said.

With a yell, Kip charged.

It was the last thing the man expected. He was still rubbing his eyes. He raised an arm to fend off a blow, but Kip dove at his stomach, past the knife, spearing the top of his head into the man's gut. With a *whoof!* the man staggered backward and tripped right at the edge of the fire.

For a moment, nothing happened. Then the grain alcohol on his hands ignited. He lifted his hand with a yell, and his hair ignited. His beard ignited. His face. His yells pitched to tortured screams.

Kip bolted, straight past the flaming man.

No one moved for a blessed moment. Then someone dove for him, missing his body but clipping his heel. Kip went down heavily.

He hadn't even gotten three paces from the fire.

Some run, Porky.

He rolled over in time to see the flaming man, still screaming, run straight into the fat woman. She shrieked, an oddly shrill sound to come from such a big woman, and started whacking at him with her big knife.

Then three men were on Kip, the fire behind them making them huge grotesque shadows. A kick caught Kip in the shoulder, then one from the other side hit his kidney. Pain lanced through him, taking his breath away. He curled into a ball.

Kicks rained on his back and legs. One of the men was leaning over him, punching his hip, his leg, trying to hit him in the crotch. Someone stomped on his head. It was a glancing blow, but it caught his nose. Hot blood exploded over his face and his head caromed off the dirt.

Only a single thought won through the fog suddenly wreathing Kip's brain. They're going to kill me. This wasn't going to be punishment. It was murder.

So be it. They'll have to kill me on my feet. He struggled to all fours.

That opened his ribs to attack and a kick hammered his side. He absorbed it with a groan.

Three grown men, attacking a boy who'd done nothing to them. Something about the injustice of it tapped an iron reserve of will. No, not only three now. More had joined. But the additional numbers only infuriated Kip further. He hunched into his own bulk, gathering his strength, tucking his head between his shoulders. Burn in hell, I can take it.

With an inhuman roar, a sound like Kip had never heard, a sound he didn't even know he was capable of, he shot to his feet, taking a wide stance. The suddenness of his movement seemed amplified by his previous slowness.

Bellowing, bleeding, with his yell he sprayed blood into the face of a man who'd been running forward to kick him. Kip was like a cave bear, suddenly standing on its hind legs. The man's eyes went wide.

Kip grabbed the man's shirt and pulled, spinning, screaming, and hurling him the only direction that wasn't blocked by bodies.

Into the fire.

The man saw where he was headed. He grabbed for the spit arcing over the fire to catch himself, missed, caught it with his elbow instead. It spun him sideways into the fire, his head dropping right into the heart of the flames, the spit collapsing.

Kip didn't watch, didn't listen to the new screams. Someone hit him in the stomach. Ordinarily the blow would have folded him in half. But now the pain didn't matter. He found his attacker—a big, bearded man easily a foot taller than him, looking at him like he was stunned the boy hadn't fallen. Kip grabbed the man's beard and yanked it down toward him as hard as he could. At the same time, he lunged forward, head like a ram. The big man's face crunched as they collided. He went down in a spray of blood and flying teeth.

Something like hope glimmered through Kip's rage. He turned again, looking for another victim just as something cracked across his head.

Kip went down. He wasn't even aware of falling. He was just on the ground, staring up at another grinning ghoul of a man carrying a piece of firewood in his hand. Behind that man were four others. Four? Still? Between the tears and the dizziness, Kip wasn't even sure he was counting right.

He clambered to all fours again, and promptly fell over, spots exploding in front of his eyes. He had no balance.

"Throw him in the fire!" someone yelled.

There were other words, but Kip couldn't sort them out. The next thing he knew, he was being lifted, one man taking each limb. He was facedown. The heat of the fire beat at the top of his head, his face.

The men stopped. "Don't push *us* in, you assholes!" one of the men at the front said.

"On three!"

"Orholam, he's big."

"Don't have to throw him far."

"Gonna sizzle like bacon in the pan, ain't he?"

"One!"

Kip swung a little over the fire, close enough that he swore his eyebrows curled from the heat. Fear strangled him. The dizziness disappeared.

He swung back away from the fire.

"Two!"

Enough. The odds were just too bad. I tried. What do I have to fear when I have nothing to lose? I despise myself. So what if I die? A little pain, so what? Then the pain's gone forever. Then oblivion.

Kip swung farther over the fire, closing his eyes, welcoming the heat. His eyebrows and eyelashes melted. The fire licked his face like a cat.

A Guile wouldn't give up. They accepted you, Kip. Expected you to pull your weight. Gavin, Ironfist, Liv, they let you belong for the first time in your life. And you're going to disappoint them?

And like that, the fear was gone. No.

They swung him back away from the fire; one last time. Four men. Four Ramirs. Four of his mother, treating him like shit and expecting him to take it.

Hell no. The sudden, implacable heat of Kip's hatred matched the heat of the fire.

"Three!"

The men swung him forward.

Kip kept his eyes open and felt them go wide—but not with fear, fear was gone. His eyes widened at the sight of the fire like a lover's eyes widen at the sight of his beloved. Yes, beautiful. Yes, mine.

A rushing sound like a mighty wind roared out of nowhere. The fire deformed, leapt toward Kip—*into* Kip. And disappeared. The entire fire went out in an instant, plunging the camp into darkness.

The men dropped Kip with a shout.

And Kip barely noticed.

He'd fallen among the embers. He caught himself with his left hand, and heard a sizzle as his hand closed around a burning faggot. Though he'd sucked up the whole fire, the embers were still red-hot.

And Kip barely noticed. Rage was a sea and he merely floating in it. He wasn't himself, wasn't aware of a self. There were only those he hated, who must be struck down.

He screamed, throwing a hand heavenward. Heat gushed out, becoming fire a foot away from his hand, painting the sky blue, yellow, orange, and red. He stood, heat roaring through his veins. Unbearable heat. Despite the darkness, he could see the men who'd been holding him clearly. He saw their warmth. One had tripped and was staring at him, openmouthed.

Kip flung a hand at him. Fire enveloped the man from head to foot.

The others fled.

Kip threw his left hand toward one. He felt skin crack as he opened that hand, but the pain was a distant echo. He aimed with his right hand, too. *Pop, pop, pop.* Three fireballs, each the size of his hand, flew into the night, almost pushing him back into the fire with the recoil. But each found its target, burying itself in a man's back, gutting him with fire, cooking him from inside even as he fell.

Falling to his knees, still hot, so hot, so overwhelmed, Kip raised his hands once more. Fire poured into the sky from both hands, even his crippled left hand. Then his vision returned to normal. He heaved deep breaths, like some demon had just released him, leaving him empty, hollow, part of his humanity burnt away.

The fire was burning once more, much smaller, the heat of the coals slowly returning the wood to flame, illuminating the wagons and the faces of the fearful crowd gathering to see what had happened.

In the light of the lanterns and torches and the reawakening fire, Kip saw the scene with sane eyes. Scores of people were staring at him from a wide circle around the fire, all looking ready to bolt. There were bodies strewn about: the four men who'd tried to throw him in the fire were dead, one a charred meaty skeleton, the others with holes the size of Kip's hand in their backs.

Somehow, the others were worse. The man Kip had doused with grain alcohol had skin sloughing off his face and chest and knife wounds all over his arms and body. He lay moaning softly, a few tufts of hair still protruding from his burnt scalp. The fat woman lay next to him, openly weeping. The flaming man must have run head-first into her, because her face was scorched, blistered on the right side, her eyebrow gone, her hair melted back halfway up her head, and somehow her own knife had been plunged to the hilt low into her right side. Blood dribbled down her cheek. The man Kip had flung into the fire was the worst, though. He'd caught the spit to stop himself, and only his head had dropped into the fire, falling directly onto the hottest coals.

He'd dragged himself out of the fire, and by some dark miracle he was still alive and still conscious. He was crying softly, as if even weeping hurt, but he couldn't stop. He'd rolled over, exposing the burnt side of his head. His skin hadn't just sloughed off—it had stuck to the coals like burnt chicken sticking to a pan. His cheekbone was exposed, his cheek burned through, exposing teeth now washed red with coursing blood as he wept, his eye burnt a chalky white.

The only one who might survive was the bearded man whose teeth Kip had smashed. He was unconscious, but so far as Kip could see, still alive.

Kip tottered toward his horse, unfeeling. He didn't have a plan. He just had to get away. He was so ashamed. He got all the way to the beast before he saw the soldiers. They had surrounded the camp, but were staying back in the crowd. Kip looked at one of the soldiers who was mounted, an officer, he guessed.

"I'm sorry, sir, but we can't let you leave," the officer said. "One of the Free will be along for you shortly."

"They attacked me," Kip said, exhausted. "Tried to rob me. I...I didn't mean..." He leaned against the horse. Stupid beast hadn't run away. Oh, it didn't have a line of sight, and it had been tied up so it couldn't leave if it wanted to. Still, he would have expected it to be going crazy. Instead, it stood, placid as ever. Kip leaned against it.

With his left hand. Orholam. The skin cracked and tore open and started bleeding at every joint. Kip gave a little cry. But even the thought of his own agony dragged his eyes back to the fire, to the people he'd killed, and those who weren't dead yet but would be. His heart felt wooden, like he should feel more, but he just couldn't.

Looking back, though, he saw a young man moving among the bodies, checking them. The young man—no, boy, for he couldn't have been more than sixteen despite his splendid clothing—was pulling white fawnskin gloves off his hands. Large hooked nose, light brown skin, dark eyes, dark unruly hair. Over his white shirt, his forearms were covered with multicolored vambraces with five thick bands of color against a white background. His cloak echoed the pattern, from a band outlined in black that looked fuzzy—sub-red?—to red to orange to yellow to green. There was no blue or superviolet. It didn't take a genius to guess he was a polychrome.

But that wasn't what arrested Kip's attention. Out of all the thousands of people in this camp, and out of the hundreds of drafters they must have, Kip recognized this one. He'd been part of the force that massacred Rekton. He'd personally tried to kill Kip at the water market. Zymun, the boy's master had called him. Kip's heart plummeted like a child jumping off a waterfall.

Zymun put on a pair of green spectacles. "Hello, firefriend," he said. "Welcome to our war. I assume you've come to join the Free?"

"Right," Kip said, finding his voice. The Free?

Emerald smoke swirled down into Zymun's hands. "Just so you know," he said, "you can kill who you must—though Lord Omnichrome prefers it not be so indiscriminate—but when you do, please clean up your messes." He swept his arms in a martial circle, slowly, bending his knees, giving the impression of gathering energy. Then his hands snapped across each other, flashed out. *Pa-pop, pa-pop.* Four spikes of green luxin, each as long as a finger, shot out in two volleys. Around the fire, almost simultaneously, four heads burst open with wet splatters. The wounded. Their moans stopped instantly.

Kip goggled.

Zymun looked pleased with himself. He folded his green spectacles and tucked them in a pocket.

He's showing off. He's showing off by *killing people*.

Zymun frowned suddenly as Kip stepped close. "What's your name?"

"Kip," Kip said, before thinking that it might be a poor choice to use his real name.

"Kip, you have a tooth in your head."

Huh? Kip showed his teeth and pointed. "Actually, I have *all* my teeth in my head." Play it like you don't want to throw up, Kip. Push through this.

"No, not *your* tooth," Zymun said. He gestured to his own scalp like he was being a mirror.

Kip reached up and, sure enough, there was a tooth sticking in his scalp. What the hell? He pulled it out, wincing, and fresh blood dribbled down his face.

"Hmm," Zymun said. "Maybe we'll take you by the chirurgeons first and get you looked at."

"First?" Kip asked.

"Yes, of course. Lord Omnichrome insists on meeting all of our drafters. Even the sloppy ones."

Chapter 71

As darkness fell over the vast host, Liv wandered through campsites, becoming more and more aware that she was alone and female, surrounded by rough men. Lots of rough men. Men who were laughing too loud, drinking too much, afraid of the coming battle. And if being Tyrean had made her an outcast and studiously ignored back at the Chromeria, here she had no such protection. Most of the men looked at her subtly enough that if she hadn't been so intensely aware of being alone and not wanting to be looked at, she would never have noticed it. Others stared at her so blatantly that she checked her neckline. Nope, it was quite modest.

Just a few jackasses who've been away from their wives for too long.

She was practically starving, and though she didn't want to stop at any campfire, it was the only way to get not only food, but information.

Liv picked a campfire with some kind-looking farmers huddled around a pot of stew. She couldn't see everyone before she entered the circle, of course, but a few of them looked kind, and it was the best she could do.

"Good evening," she said, a little more cheerily than she felt. "I'd give half a danar for some stew. You have any extra?"

Eight heads swiveled toward her. An older man spoke. "It's a mite thin to call it a stew. One rabbit, a couple tubers, and the leavings of a javelina leg between nine mouths." He smiled, self-effacing. "But Mori did find a grapefruit tree the soldiers missed somehow."

Feeling reassured, Liv came closer. The man looked at her eyes, blinked, and said, "If you're getting hassled, you should put on your spectacles, young lady."

"Hassled? Why would you think that?" Liv asked. "And it's Liv, thank you."

"You look as skittish as a deer at a watering hole, that's why." He handed her a tin cup of broth with a few chunks. He waved off her attempt to pay him. She ate the thin stew and the small, underripe grapefruit they gave her, and mostly sat and watched.

After a time, the men returned to their talk of war and weather and crops they hadn't bothered to plant this year, citrus trees they hadn't bothered to prune because if they bore more fruit, it only meant the bandits would spend longer close to their village. They weren't bad men. In fact, they seemed quite decent. They had their complaints about King Garadul, and one muttered darkly about a "Lord Omnichrome" before remembering that a drafter was present, but they reserved their hatred for their occupiers.

The nuances of the rotating rule of Garriston were lost on them. They didn't differentiate between the better and worse occupiers. They hated them all. One had lost his daughter a number of years before when a patrol had passed through their village and an officer had simply taken her. He'd gone to Garriston afterward to try to find her, but never did. The others had come partly for their friend, partly because they had nothing else to do and taking a city might drop a few coins into their hands, and partly because they hated the outlanders.

And so men will die and kill for an offense ten years old, committed by some other country.

There was no point reasoning with them, even if Liv had cared to. Fools who could be our friends at some other time, her father had said. After she finished eating, she put on her yellow spectacles, drafted a few luxin torches that would last for a few days to thank them for the soup and the fruit, asked directions to where the drafters were camped, and then headed out.

No one bothered her on her way. Once a man called out to her as she passed, but the comment dried up on his lips as he saw her colored spectacles—even now, in the darkness, they respected drafters.

The drafters' tents were separate from everyone else's—not because they were guarded or staked off, but evidently no one wanted to camp too close to them. Liv slipped her spectacles off, but kept them in hand, in case someone challenged her.

She moved past a wagon surrounded by Mirrormen and painted all violet—odd, but she didn't slow, she moved with purpose, as if she had orders. It was a trick she'd learned in the Chromeria. If you stood around, someone would find something for you to do. If you looked busy, you could get away with almost anything.

She passed a number of fires with drafters being served a lavish dinner by cooks and wine or ales by a large number of slaves. The drafters all wore their colors on their wrists in either cloth or metal vambraces or in large bracelets for some of the women. The hem of their cloaks or dresses also echoed the color. Other than that, everyone wore his own style. In general, though, these drafters were much more interested in loudly proclaiming their colors in broad swathes across their clothes than was common at the Chromeria, where a woman might have a single green hairpin to let others know she was a green.

They were a raucous, privileged group, but as Liv watched from the shadows, she saw that the men and women here often glanced to the south—not to the huge pavilion guarded by drafters and Mirrormen alike that Liv assumed was King Garadul's residence, but to another set of bonfires. She grabbed a pitcher of wine from one of the slaves' tables and headed over. In the dark, her own apparel didn't look too different from the slaves'.

What she saw, beyond the forms of the slaves, took her breath away. People—or monsters shaped like people—were talking, drinking, cavorting, drafting.

Nearest to Liv, a circle of blue drafters, half of them wearing blue spectacles, and all filled with blue luxin, tinting their skin in the firelight, were talking with a woman who seemed made of crystal.

For long moments, Liv had no idea what she was seeing. They were drafters, though, obviously, and there was luxin everywhere. Oathbreakers. The mad. The broken. Color wights. Liv could barely take it in.

These were people who'd violated everything Liv had been taught.

She caught only fractured details. A broken-haloed eye. The crystalline woman drafting a matrix in the air as the other blues listened. Greens laughing, dancing around one fire, bouncing on unnaturally springy legs, jumping higher than any man Liv had ever seen, doing flips and backflips over each other. A man and a woman, skin permanently green but not yet transformed, were standing, holding each other, grinding their hips together, dancing in a manner so lascivious that—wait, no, the woman's skirt was bunched around her waist. In full view of everyone, including some cheering drafters, they were actually—

Liv tore her eyes away, her cheeks suddenly hot. A yellow was tossing little luxin balls into the air while a blue shot blue bullets at them, each little target exploding in a flash of light when he connected.

But Liv's eyes were drawn to the full color wights. Even here, there weren't many. She'd only heard rumors about such things at the Chromeria. They said almost everyone who broke their halo simply went mad and died—or went mad and killed others, more often. That danger was what made the Pact necessary. Orholam made magic to serve men, and a drafter swore to serve her community. Oathbreakers served only themselves, and they endangered everyone.

But there were always the legends of those who remade themselves. Now, here, Liv was seeing that they weren't wild tales. Now, here, these drafters were teaching each other how to do it. Liv looked at the crystal blue woman. She was oddly beautiful. Crystal hair, and diamond-shaped eye caps close over her eyes, flawed crystal skin, broken into a thousand facets, covering every natural curve of her body. She'd conquered the problem of how to deal with drafting hard, unbending blue luxin onto a body that had to be able to move and to bend by making thousands—tens of thousands—of small crystals. Her body glimmered, shimmered, coruscated in the firelight as she shifted her upper body like a dancer to show her disciples what she'd done. She laughed, showing strangely white teeth against those gleaming blue lips. Then she shifted suddenly into a fighting stance, spiky guards springing up along the edges of her forearms, and plates of blue luxin congealing over her skin to make armor.

Shit!

"Hey, caleen! I said wine!" a voice said.

Liv turned and found herself face-to-face with a man with hideous burn scars all over his body. A sub-red, with the odd shimmering of fire crystal broken through his halos. He held out a glass to Liv, and she filled it with wine, trembling, averting her own eyes until he looked away. The man held a haze pipe in one hand, and there were fresh burns all along his skin. As Liv looked, she realized the burns were deliberate. He was trying to scar all of his skin deeply enough to lose feeling in it. Until then, he was deadening himself to the pain any way he could.

It had to be incredibly dangerous to even be in close proximity to a mad fire drafter. He couldn't control himself normally, and now he was drunk and high on haze.

The man had barely left when Liv saw a gout of flame blast into the night sky a few hundred yards away. She stopped, and so did a few of the color wights, nudging those around them and pointing.

Whatever it had been, the drafter who'd done it had been powerful. That was a lot of fire to throw into the night. Where had he gotten the light to do that? From one of the bonfires?

Then it happened again, fire painting the sky for several seconds. Liv felt her throat tighten with fear. Kip! No, that was ridiculous. Kip was green/blue. Fire, sub-red, was at the opposite end of the spectrum. It couldn't be Kip. The color wights just laughed, as if it were one of their own out there, having fun.

Orholam, Kip could be getting killed out there in the night. Liv needed to go.

She turned and headed out of camp. She almost ran into a dozen Mirrormen who were escorting a woman clad in a gorgeous black dress and wearing violet eye caps out of the king's pavilion. Liv stopped. Karris.

They hustled past, but Liv had no doubt where they were going. Karris was being held in that odd violet wagon she'd seen, held captive. Liv should have figured it out earlier.

Still, any elation Liv had felt about finding Karris—actually finding her, on the first day, in a camp of maybe a hundred thousand souls if not more—was quashed by her fear for Kip.

When she got out of the drafters' area, she put on her yellow spectacles. No one bothered her. She arrived at the place she and Kip had agreed to meet just in time, but he wasn't there. He never came.

The next day, she learned a heavy boy with Tyrean skin and blue eyes had been attacked and had killed five men—or ten or twenty, or five women too, depending on the rumor—and then thrown fire into the air. He'd been taken away by drafters and Mirrormen. Despite the impossibilities—Kip couldn't draft sub-red—her intuition confirmed it. It had been Kip. She was sure. Someone had drafted fire, someone else had killed those people, and Kip had been taken.

She searched for him for two days. She found nothing.

Chapter 72

As the sun dragged its feet toward the horizon, Gavin gave the signal, and the teamsters' whips cracked. The draft horses surged forward. Their leads drew taut, and the ropes connected to the great yellow luxin supports strained for a moment. Then the supports fell, the great straining mass of the horses snatching them away from the dropping wall.

The final layer of yellow luxin hit the ground with a boom, shaking the earth. Gavin quickly moved to inspect that everything had gone according to plan.

"One league out!" Corvan called. He was standing on top of the wall, looking out toward King Garadul's vast army.

"Shit!"

"Here, Lord Prism!" one of the engineers called.

Gavin hurried over. The last of many big problems he'd run into in crafting a wall almost entirely of yellow luxin was that all the luxin had to be sealed. The seal was always the weakest point. If you could melt through that one area—no mean feat, but still—the whole structure would unravel. That his wall was made in sections just meant that each section had multiple seals. If any section failed, it would be catastrophic—an entire section of wall, fifty paces across, would splash into liquid light in moments.

It was probably the reason no one before Gavin had been idiot enough to make an entire wall of yellow luxin.

The solution had been simplicity itself: two layers of luxin, each protecting the other, the seals to the inside. That part was common enough among drafters, but the seal was always the last thing you touched. So you *couldn't* really tuck it inside, not on something as big as a wall. You could protect one seal by covering it with more luxin and sealing that, but one seal would always be external. Most drafters would have covered the seal and covered that seal and covered that one and left it at that.

It wasn't good enough for Gavin. He'd built the entire second layer of the wall up on supports. Then he'd built each side, sealing them on the inside. When the draft horses pulled out the supports and the second layer of wall fell into place, it left a structure where the seals—for the first time that Gavin had ever heard of—were truly protected, not just by yellow luxin, but by the vast weight of the wall itself. And as each section locked to the next, it became more and more difficult for anyone to ever lift the wall to access the seals.

Gavin was building something monumental, something pure, and it felt great. This edifice would stand long after he was dead. There weren't many men who could claim the same. The locals were already calling it Brightwater Wall.

Hurrying over to the engineer who'd called out, Gavin found that one of the supports hadn't been pulled all the way free. The wall had dropped on it, pounding the two-pace-wide support almost halfway into the earth, and keeping the wall from fitting the next section perfectly.

"Three minutes until our artillery will be in place!" Corvan called down.

Sonuvabitch! Gavin dropped on his knees next to the broad yellow support and brushed dirt away hurriedly. The support, unlike the wall sections, was sealed right at the surface for just this eventuality. Right…there! Gavin sent some sub-red into the seal and the entire support dissolved, the yellow luxin abruptly liquid. The wall settled with a deep rumble.

Gavin had made the tolerances too tight. He should have made those joints able to hook together even if they weren't so well aligned. The tight joints gave the wall more strength and would keep soldiers inside dry even during rainstorms, but still.

Taking his attention off the wall for the first time in hours—it felt like days, though it was only early evening—he looked to the people assembled, looking for who he needed.

There were thousands assembled. Most of the people of Garriston wanted to see the wall being built. Vendors had set up their wagons and stalls. Minstrels wandered through, playing and prodding people for coins. Soldiers kept avenues clear and began ferrying gear and powder and ropes and shot for cannons and firewood for furnaces and additional armor and arrows and muskets. Others operated the cranes as soon as the second layer settled in place. Drafters were pouring through the inside of the wall, sealing any cracks, looking for flaws that they could fix, or larger ones that needed Gavin's hand. The Blackguards—nearly a hundred of them—also stood nearby.

They'd told everyone to leave already, but they didn't have the men to spare to enforce the order. The people were too curious; they knew they'd never see anything like this again in their lives. Gavin couldn't worry about them right now. He was already feeling the tightness of impossibility squeezing his chest.

"Captain!" Gavin called. "You've seen the process. Get the teamsters moving as fast as they can. We've got sixteen more sections. Send half the teams all the way to the east side, and have half work from here out. Take six drafters. You four, you, and you. You've seen what I've done. Go do it.

"General Danavis, talk to me!" Gavin shouted. Less than a league now. It should be enough.

Gavin moved to the inside of the great arch that would hold the gate. There were open holes, tubes running down the great curving length of the wall. Gavin filled himself with light and blasted green luxin down each tube. It would give the wall some flex, but also strength to recoil from any battering ram blow. He sealed each green luxin tube at the end.

"Lord Prism," Corvan called, holding a fresh-drafted telescope up to one eye. "It looks like they have teams pushing their artillery out in front of the army. They know we don't have the skirmishers to go out and smash them. Damn spies! I can't see the culverins, but we know they have half a dozen. If they fire from greatest random—"

He paused, doing mental calculations. Greatest random was literally the greatest distance gunners could reach, but at almost two thousand paces for the biggest culverins, there was no such thing as aiming. "They could begin their bombardment anytime now if their crews are practiced. Within minutes, even if they're not."

It wasn't the culverins Gavin was worried about. Because of the trajectory of those big guns, their shots would hit the front of the wall. Brightwater Wall could take as many direct hits as they wanted to give it. They would have to come substantially closer for the higher-trajectory howitzers and closer still for the mortars that would absolutely wreak havoc on the stubborn crowds behind the wall. Garriston's cannons would have to knock out those guns before they could be placed, bagged, and loaded.

"Damn it, find someone who's not doing something more important and get these damn people back," Gavin ordered. "This isn't a Sun Day outing! Shells are going to be landing where they sit in ten minutes!" Gavin turned back to General Danavis. "Start firing as soon as you can. Buy me time, General!"

Gavin felt more than heard the next section of wall fall into place. People were rushing everywhere, but he pushed it out of his mind and confronted the new biggest problem of all, now that the wall was actually taking shape.

He hadn't built the gate.

He ran over to one of the cranes hoisting supplies to the top of the wall. It was already lifting off the ground as he approached, rising fast. Gavin jumped, throwing out two hooks of blue and green luxin, snagging the sides of the load. He rose fast and pulled himself up. He jumped off as soon as the load settled on top of the wall, startling the soldiers operating the crane. They froze.

"To work!" he roared. They jumped, and then jumped to it.

Gavin ran across the top of the wall, dodging men to get back to the arch above the gap where he needed to draft the gate.

Tremblefist was barking orders, sending up a small number of Blackguards to stand with Gavin—as if they could do anything to protect him from incoming shells—but not so many that they would get in the way of the defenders trying to set up the wall for any of a hundred tasks. The rest of the Blackguards took up positions in front of the empty gate.

As in all battles, there was simply too much to see, too much happening all at the same time to put everything together. Gavin looked toward the sun, poised above the horizon.

Two hours. All I need is two hours. Protecting these people is one great purpose I have that you *must* approve of. So if you're up there, would you please get off your holy ass and help me?

General Danavis had been organizing, training, promoting, firing, and training Garriston's defenders for the past week. Twenty hours a day, sometimes twenty-two. It was inhuman, and yet it wasn't enough. Gavin was accustomed to the discipline and ease of working with veterans. By the end of the Prisms' War, his men had worked together fluidly. Stocking this wall with supplies would have taken his veterans literally one-third of the time it was taking these men. His veteran cannoneers would already be sighted in, with distances marked off. These men barely knew each other, much less trusted each other. It made everything painfully slow, and Gavin was slow to adjust to how slow they were.

We're doomed.

But then he drafted a quick platform to walk out on in front of the open arch—necessary to gather some of his open threads of luxin—and he caught his first sight of the wall as his enemies would see it.

That damned boy artist had made his masterpiece.

Gavin had been the one who filled the forms, but he'd always been hovering above them, and while he was getting the sections to fit together he'd always been on the other side of the wall. Now he saw the whole.

The entire wall—the entire great curving league of it—glowed the color of the sun when it first shows its face. That glow came from the liquid yellow—a hair's breadth from being perfect, hard yellow—that floated behind the first layer of perfect yellow. The liquid yellow would mend any damage that did scar the outer wall. But then, within that thin layer, Gavin saw that his old drafters, doubtless under the direction of Aheyyad, had added their own touches. As an enemy approached, he would see that the entire wall was swarming with loathsome things. Spiders the size of a man's head appeared to be crawling across the wall, stopping, little jaws clacking. Small dragons appeared to swoop and spin. Disapproving faces swirled up out of the gloom. A woman ran from some many-fanged thing and was torn to pieces and devoured alive, her face painted with despair. A man who appeared to be walking along the base of the wall was seized by hands that swirled out of the mist and yanked him in. Beautiful women turned into monsters with forked tongues and huge claws. Blood seeped and pooled on the ground. And those were just the things Gavin could see in a cursory glance. It was as if the drafters had gotten together and taken every nightmare any of them had ever had and put it into the wall. They were illusions, all of them mere images within the wall, but an enemy wouldn't know that at first, and even if they did know it, it was scary as the evernight itself. Better, it would certainly distract enemy archers and musketeers from making accurate shots at the murder holes hidden by those images.

And that was just the wide blank sections of the wall. At every corbel, the scowling, forbidding figure of a Prism looked down on the attackers. As Gavin looked, he saw that *every* Prism for the past four hundred years had been crafted into the wall, with Lucidonius at the right hand of the figure who dominated all and Gavin himself at the left hand. Above them, over the huge gate gap, loomed the scowling figure of Orholam himself, radiant and furious, his planted arms making the arches of the gate. Anyone attacking this gate would be attacking Orholam himself, and all his Prisms. A brilliant little trick to make the attackers feel uneasy. Each figure, including Orholam, had cunningly hidden machicolations to drop stones or fire or magic on attackers.

Gavin bit off another curse. He'd paused for a good five seconds, admiring his own damned wall. He didn't have time.

For a moment, he thought of simply closing the gate gap, just making pure wall. But at this point, that wouldn't be any faster. The forms were already shaped to make a gate. All he had to do was fill them and tie them—just on one side, the cleverness he'd use for the rest of the wall would have to wait. Tomorrow, if they lived that long.

Gavin gathered the spools of superviolet that connected the whole superstructure of the wall and began pouring in yellow luxin.

Orholam, he was exhausted. He'd been drafting to his absolute limit every day for the last five days, and all through this day in particular since the first rays of dawn. If he'd been a normal drafter, he'd have gone mad long ago. Even most Prisms would have killed themselves with the amount of drafting Gavin had done. The others knew it too. If anything, Gavin had gotten more powerful since the war, and far more efficient. He'd seen women like Tala—whom he'd never seen impressed by anything in her life—shoot glances his way during unguarded moments like he was downright frightening. But there was only so much even he could draft.

Nonetheless, he poured perfect yellow luxin into the forms. The real Gavin couldn't have done this: he wasn't a superchromat, he couldn't draft a perfect yellow. But Gavin couldn't go halfway. There was no "good enough" with yellow luxin; if it weren't drafted perfectly, it would dissolve. Simple as that.

Something rocked the wall, and Gavin almost fell from his perch. Someone steadied him, and he saw that Tremblefist was standing beside him, holding him up. A moment later, he heard the delayed rumble of distant artillery.

"I've got you," Tremblefist said. He wasn't quite as big as his older brother, but he too had worked with Gavin a long time. He must have seen the glazed, stupefied look in Gavin's eyes, because he said, "Our own cannons will start in a moment. Don't be...distracted." Don't be alarmed, he meant. Don't be frightened. Don't botch the gate and get us all killed.

More of King Garadul's artillery began landing in the field, most of it far short of Brightwater Wall. The sound of the enemy culverins became a thunderstorm in the distance. Gavin gathered his will and kept drafting. He didn't realize that he was weaving on his feet until he felt Tremblefist's big hands close on his shoulders. Several other Blackguards pressed close.

"Raise the cowl!" General Danavis yelled.

As yellow luxin splashed from Gavin's hands into the forms below him, he felt the wall shudder as each section of the cowl swung into place on counterweights. The cowl was his architect's invention. Basically, it was a removable roof for use during artillery bombardment. There were plenty of times when an open roof was preferable—to gather rainwater, when it was unbearably hot, or when men had to carry great loads or carts had to pass down the length of the wall. But during a bombardment, it would shield defenders from howitzers and mortar fire. The wall's own artillery was left free to fire on the same basic defensive design as an arrow slit—easy to fire out at a wide angle, but requiring a direct hit from the other side to put it out of commission.

"What the hell is that?" Tremblefist breathed. Gavin wouldn't have even heard him except that the man was basically holding him up. And Tremblefist didn't talk to himself much.

Gavin looked up, giving himself a small break, and looked over the plain.

The army was rumbling ever closer, catching up with their culverins. In front of them were teams setting up the howitzers—the defenders *still* hadn't fired a single shot, a fact that had General Danavis screaming at the nearest crews.

But that wasn't what had Tremblefist cursing. In front of the main army, drawing even with the advance cannon emplacements, were more than a hundred men and women, some riding, and some simply running. All were dressed in brightly colored clothing. Gavin could tell that by the way the greens moved, sprinting with huge bouncing, league-devouring strides that they weren't just drafters. They were color wights, and they were headed straight for the gate.

They would be at the wall within four minutes at the most.

Four minutes. Gavin looked at his half-formed gate. If he didn't worry about hinges, if he just sealed the damn thing to the wall itself, it was possible. Maybe. He looked up at the sun, gathering power. It was less than an hour until sunset. The festivities for Sun Day's Eve would start as soon as the last ray of sun disappeared from the horizon. Whether the attackers were heretics or pagans or faithful, they wouldn't fight during Sun Day. Sun Day was holy even to the gods Lucidonius had driven out.

If they could hold off the attackers for that one hour, they had a chance. And Sun Day would give them the time they needed to reinforce the gates and get supplies and guns in place.

One day. One hour. Four minutes that would determine the course of this war. It came down to this. Gavin was not going to quit. He had four minutes left in him.

The culverins on the wall finally answered those out in the field, but the shots were wild, not even close to the field artillery emplacements or the charging color wights. And more of King Garadul's shots were hitting the wall itself, each rebounding off the yellow luxin with a crunch and a whine and a splay of yellow light as the wall absorbed the blow and healed itself.

The forms Gavin was filling with luxin were three-quarters full, washing him in the invigorating scents so close to mint and eucalyptus, but he was tiring anyway. He looked out to the color wights. Not even two minutes left.

Orholam, I'm trying to do something good here. Great purpose, Orholam. Selfless and all that. You want people to be selfless, right?

Tremblefist handed Gavin off and was shouting orders down to the Blackguards on the ground. General Danavis was ordering troops to the gate and to form in ranks behind the wall. The crowd was beginning to scatter. Everyone was shouting, but Gavin couldn't even make out the words anymore.

Flashes of magic bloomed in front of him. The color wights had spotted him. They were throwing missiles and fire and everything they could think of, but his Blackguards were deflecting it all.

Gavin kept drafting. The color wights were only two hundred paces out now, running at a full sprint. He had only seconds left. A cannon roared to Gavin's right and tore through a dozen of the color wights, shredding them. But the color wights behind them leapt through the blood and smoke and flying limbs, faces snarling, inhuman, glowing.

Drafting the last of the yellow luxin to fill the last form, Gavin pulled the threads together in his hand. He was going to make it! He was sealing the luxin when a cannonball smashed into the forms. All the force of the impossibly lucky shot went straight into Gavin's hands. It was like holding a rope and having someone drop an anvil tied to the other side.

The luxin was yanked out of Gavin's hands instantaneously. Gate and cannonball slammed into the ground beneath the arch, the cannonball blasting through Blackguards and a dozen still-gawking civilians behind them. The gate—abruptly unheld, unsealed yellow luxin—hissed and seethed into light before Gavin could stop it.

In two seconds, the gate flashboiled into nothingness and disappeared—and so did Garriston's hope.

Chapter 73

Gavin collapsed. Or he would have, if two Blackguards hadn't caught him and dragged him away from the brink. He wanted to fight them, to stand up, but he was so lightheaded he couldn't even make words.

He missed the first clash, right below his perch, but he heard it, felt it. The yells of men and women bracing themselves, giving voice to fear and rage, honing their will for their drafting. Then waves of heat and the shock of impact, armor popping, men and wights grunting. Then, screams, always screams.

"Where are my muskets?! I ordered those brought here two hours ago!" General Danavis was screaming. Swearing. He was standing ten paces from Gavin, looking through the murder holes and machicolations at the battle beneath the arch of the gate. His soldiers were blinking at him. Out of twenty men, only two had muskets. "Fire, damn you!" he shouted at them. "You, and you, go find muskets. Now!" Then he was gone, screaming at the artillery crews.

The Blackguards pulled Gavin to the edge of the wall. The cowl on the wall meant there were only a few places open on either the front or the back. They found one where the cranes pulled in goods. A Blackguard bichrome drafted a blue-green slide all the way to the ground.

"What are you doing?" Gavin managed.

"We're taking you to safety, sir." Then the man jumped onto the slide.

Gavin was looking through the bright hallway formed by the bon-

net to one of the culverin teams. They had fired a ball and were looking downfield—the sign of an inexperienced crew. Only one man
needed to watch so they could adjust their aim. The rest should be
reloading already. But after a moment, they cheered. "Got it!" Gavin
couldn't see what they'd hit, but as they turned back to their task, he
saw a flash of movement.

"It's safe!" the Blackguard called up from the ground at the base
of Brightwater Wall.

Green claws latched onto the wall just in front of the artillery
team. What? Gavin had known green wights to infuse their legs with
the springiness of green luxin, but he'd never seen one jump even half
the height of this wall. He cried out, pointing, but not before the
beast flung itself upon the artillerymen. Its hands, grown into huge
claws, tore through four men before they even knew it was there.
Blood was flung in broad arcs, splattering against the walls. The last
three men saw the beast, but froze. Only one even made an attempt
to grab a musket from the wall.

The green wight clove the man's head in three, two broad claws
descending halfway through his head.

The Blackguards hesitated for only half a second. None of them
had ever seen a color wight either. Four Blackguards stepped forward, almost simultaneously. The two in front went to one knee,
clearing firing lanes over their heads. Their hands dipped in unison,
one hand coming up to draft, the other coming up with a pistol.

Triggers clicked, and flints struck, but in the two seconds it took to
fire a pistol, luxin was already streaking out from every drafter. A
ball of blue luxin like a fist hammered the green wight toward a wall.
A glob of red luxin splattered across its side and back and made it
stick to the wall. Slick orange smeared the floor in case it pulled away.
But that wasn't necessary. The green wight's claws were still stuck in
the unfortunate gunner's head, and it had no time to react before the
last Blackguard's flames hit the red luxin and set it alight.

The next moment, three guns roared. All three hit the green wight's
chest. Green luxin and all too human red blood burst from the
wounds. The wight would have collapsed, but the red luxin held it to
the wall, even as it burned.

"Black out!" one of the Blackguards yelled. She stepped forward, already pouring more powder in her flashpan. Apparently hers had been the gun that misfired. She cocked the gun, aimed, and pulled the trigger. A second later, it blew the still-burning green wight's head apart.

The Blackguards were already reloading their pistols. For most of them, Gavin knew, it was their very first battle. First blood. Yet each reloaded his or her pistol without looking. It was something they were taught to do only when there was extreme and pressing danger—visually inspecting a pistol was usually a good idea to prevent misfires and double-charging—but it was worth it to not have to take your eyes off the battlefield sometimes, and all of them had the presence of mind to do it correctly.

"Tell General Danavis to withdraw the cowl," Gavin said. The cowl was keeping the green wights from getting in anywhere except at the artillery stations, but it left those men totally vulnerable. And while the Blackguards had all hit their target—now slumped on the floor, bleeding out and barely smoking—the other defenders wouldn't be so accurate. The cowl transformed the top of the wall into a yellow luxin tunnel. That meant ricochets. Ricochets meant anyone who missed a shot at an attacker would probably kill a defender. It wasn't worth the tradeoffs, especially because King Garadul's culverins and howitzers had stopped firing so they wouldn't kill the color wights.

General Danavis must have realized the same thing, though, because before the Blackguards could argue that they couldn't send even one of their own away from Gavin, the cowl slid back. The sudden motion knocked several defenders off the wall, the fall guaranteeing maiming or death. But it had to be done.

It also snapped the slide that the Blackguards had made for Gavin. But in moments they remade it and threw him unceremoniously down. He couldn't even catch himself. The sheer amount of luxin he'd drafted today had left him with nothing.

The Blackguards at the bottom of the slide caught him and lifted him to his feet. He was able to stand.

"Take me to the gate," Gavin ordered.

The Blackguards looked at each other.

"Damn you! Lose the gate, lose the wall. We lose the wall, we lose the city."

"This city isn't our concern. Your safety is," a voice shouted. Tremblefist. He'd appeared from nowhere. "You can stand, can you run?" he asked Gavin.

"I'm not running!"

"We can't hold the gate!" Tremblefist shouted. "My Guards are getting slaughtered, and for what? We're not your personal army. We protect your life, not your whims. You're making our job impossible!"

Gavin's failure spun out before him. This was his own fault. It wasn't his drafting that had failed, it was his leadership. He'd never told these men and women why they fought. He'd demanded obedience unto death without even telling them why it was important. He'd been divided in his own mind and now he was surprised that they didn't want to die for that? A lie would have been better.

All he could see through the press of the soldiers between himself and the gate was flashes of fire, and smoke, and blood splashed high against the arch. The Blackguards were doubtless still in the front line—only the Blackguard could have stood for so long against the number of color wights Gavin had seen coming. The crackle of musket fire was constant but slow. The soldiers between Gavin and the fight had no idea about establishing fire lanes, so men farther back didn't shoot for fear of striking those in front of them. But so far, no one was turning back.

Of course, that would change when they saw their best fighters retreat, abandon them. The Blackguards were the linchpin.

With a roar of frustration, Gavin grabbed a nearby soldier's musket and ran toward the gate. He could hear Tremblefist's curse, and had no doubt the big man would be hot on his heels. He pushed and weaved through the crowd, his size slowing him, but not as much as Tremblefist's even bigger size.

Gavin was cursing, screaming at men and women to move out of his way, when he heard a crunch of impact. A moment later, there was a surge from the gate, pushing everyone back a good five paces.

Gavin cut across a line of soldiers to the wall. He grappled across a section where the image of a huge warrior stood, stoic, unmoving except for breathing, little puffs of steam escaping from his mouth. He touched a few sections—damn it, he should have done something to demarcate the appropriate place—until he found the one he was looking for. He touched it—anyone could touch it, it activated from the heat in a man's hand—and a little window of the wall went transparent.

He was right. The crunch had been the impact of the regular soldiers arriving. There were tens of thousands of them pressed against the wall right now, already hefting scaling ladders and ropes. He couldn't wait for them to find his little surprise—but none of that mattered if they couldn't hold the gate.

Looking to the sun, Gavin saw it was touching the horizon. Not long now. If they could make it until the sun had fully set, the drafters' power would be more than halved. They could still draft from diffracted light, but not nearly as strongly. He started running again, pushing through men and women directly against the wall. He heard the whistle of an incoming mortar.

The pitch was familiar, horribly familiar. A sound that replayed in his nightmares. You could hear death coming, but other than cowering on the ground, there wasn't anything you could do to avoid it. The thump and boom of the shell landing and exploding going *Thboom*, shattering eardrums and blasting men off their feet. This one was getting really really loud—

Gavin dropped to the ground and covered his head with his arms. Something heavy crushed him farther into the ground, and the world outside went blue.

Thump!

Tremblefist rolled off Gavin and dissolved the blue shield he'd drafted over them both. Gavin stared at the cannon shell, embedded in the earth not ten paces away. It hadn't exploded. It hadn't even crushed anyone. It had landed right between two lines of soldiers. One man was dancing around, shaking his hand. His crushed musket lay beneath the mortar itself, knocked out of his hand by the shell. It was right about where Gavin had been before he cut toward the wall.

"Orholam's hand is on you indeed, you damn fool Prism," Tremblefist said.

Gavin was already up and pushing toward the heaving, bulging lines in front of him. The men here had already fired their muskets and there was no way to reload. Some had fixed bayonets, the knife handles set inside the open barrels. Others had drawn swords. Others were using muskets as clubs.

Over their heads, musket fire rang out from the murder holes and stones the size of a man's head were thrown through the machicolations in the arch. But no luxin poured down. Either the drafters above had exhausted themselves long ago, or they'd been killed, or they had never made it to their positions.

One more day, Orholam. One more day, and this wall would have been impregnable. One more hour.

Gavin pushed into the melee at last. The area around the gate was a charnel house. The stench of magic and gore mingled. Blood covered the ground thickly enough that the combatants splashed it up around their legs as they fought. The bodies of men and monsters mingled, tripped up attackers and defenders. A pile of bodies filled the area directly beneath the gate, and as King Garadul's men climbed up and over them, that made them targets for the soldiers farther back in Gavin's army who otherwise couldn't shoot for fear of hitting their own men. Gavin saw a Blackguard fall, her leg ripped open by a glasslike jagged foot claw of an exhausted blue wight.

His musket roared and the wight's head exploded in red mist. Gavin flung the musket at a burning red wight that was moving to embrace a wounded soldier who was backed up against the wall, weaponless. He didn't see what happened. He grabbed the wounded Blackguard and tried to haul her to her feet.

She was far heavier than she should have been. Gavin blinked, his exhaustion coming back to him in a rush. No, he was just weak. Someone grabbed the wounded woman from him and hauled her off, and the sounds of the battle took on an eerie, tinny quality. He could hear incoming mortars—too distant to matter, but several of them. He could hear men screaming, the wordless roars of those running to what they knew was likely death. He heard the whimpers of the wounded, saw a woman in that great pile of bodies at the gate trying to crawl away, wounded but not dead. Next to her a man was clawing at the air, blind because he was missing half of his face. Luxin fires burned on a dozen corpses, and luxin dust was everywhere. Gavin caught a glimpse of the faces of his Blackguards. He could see their delight, their sudden purpose—where were the rest of them? They were rushing over to him.

He pulled his pistols from his sash. The red wight, body covered in pyre jelly, his entire form burning, ran toward him. If Gavin hadn't arrived so late to the battle, it would have drafted instead and incinerated him. He pulled the trigger. His dagger-pistol, being Ilytian make, fired instantly. The ball punched into the red wight's chest but didn't stop its momentum. Gavin stepped to the side and slashed the blade of the dagger across the wight's throat as it fell. He stumbled, almost went down.

He was more aware of than actually saw the two Blackguards streak past him. By the time he recovered and was standing once more, one Blackguard had been impaled on a great blue luxin sword that a blue wight had drafted in the place of its right arm. Even dying, the Blackguard had latched on with both hands to keep the wight from throwing him clear. The other Blackguard—Gavin thought his name was Amestan—had circled the creature and hacked a sword at its neck. Once, twice—blue luxin shards exploding at each great impact. The creature struggled to free itself but couldn't. On the third cut, Amestan's sword broke through the blue luxin and went into its neck. That wight's will was broken, and Amestan's fourth cut severed its head.

One of King Garadul's Mirrormen—what the hell were they doing here?—came over the top of the bodies piled chest deep, scrabbling, using his hands, his drawn sword awkward. He saw Amestan's back to him and charged.

Instinctively, Gavin tried to lash out with luxin, but even the touch of magic made him want to vomit. It was like offering drink to a man with a hangover. He weaved, almost lost consciousness, leveled the pistol, fired.

At the last moment, Amestan spun to face his attacker—and moved directly into the line of fire. Gavin's shot blew off the back of his head. A second later, the Mirrorman ran Amestan through, but he was already dead.

"No!" Gavin yelled. An entire line of Mirrormen appeared over the pile of bodies. King Garadul had realized the same thing Gavin had. The gate had to be taken tonight, or the wall would never be taken at all. So the king had sent his own personal guard to get it done. There were only maybe thirty Blackguards left, and the appearance of the dazzling Mirrormen would easily be enough to make the defenders break. Especially without the Blackguards.

It wasn't right that so much valor should result in failure. So much death. Gavin wasn't thinking clearly. He knew that. He didn't care.

As the sun's last rays kissed the earth, Gavin drafted. It was like drinking vomit. It was like diving headfirst into sewage. It was too much for his body. He didn't care. He threw everything he had into this. This wasn't for Gavin Guile. To hell with Gavin Guile. This was for everyone who'd fought and died for him. They'd stood for him. He couldn't fail them, not even if it meant his life.

The magic was like a second sun being born within the gate arch. In moments, it was born, stood, and leapt forward. The Mirrormen became radiant, their mirror armor reflecting light a thousand directions. But mirror armor was to magic like normal armor was to weapons: good for deflecting glancing blows, but nowhere close to invincible. A rushing wind filled Gavin's ears an instant before a cone of pure magic swept through him and blasted forth, exploding to the width of the entire gate. The gate became like the barrel of a vast cannon. The Mirrormen went incandescent, standing for a moment longer than seemed possible, their armor glowing, then glowing red-hot, then glowing white-hot, then ripping apart like everything else.

A concussion rocked the earth at the power of the blast, and only Gavin didn't fall. He rode the earth, magic bursting forth like he was nothing more than the tip of a volcano, the barrel of a musket.

Then, not five seconds after it started, it was gone.

The gate area was scoured clean. The bodies were gone, and a wide area around the gate on King Garadul's side was scorched and blackened.

There was stunned silence—either that, or Gavin had gone deaf. He stood, looking out, and a figure stumbled into his view. A big man, dressed in rich clothes, now blackened. King Garadul. Evidently the man hadn't just sent his personal guards to attack the gate; he'd come with them.

Gavin and Garadul stood, facing each other, forty paces away. Gavin could read the awe and uncertainty in the big man's very stance.

Then Gavin's body gave out. He collapsed. There was something white in the dirt near his face, or he was going blind. Spots swam in every color before his eyes.

Men were lifting him, carrying him away, and he heard the distant sounds of renewed battle. As the Blackguards lifted him, surrounding him with their bodies and withdrawing from the field, he saw King Garadul through the open gate, charging the gate—alone. Whatever else Gavin had done, he'd destroyed the barricade and every other impediment in that area. A few men joined their king. The dirt around Rask was exploding in little puffs as snipers tried to kill him, but none hit. It was like the man was charmed, blessed, protected by some old god mightier than Orholam.

Then Gavin saw Tremblefist's bloodied, gunpowder-streaked face. "Forgive me, Lord Prism," the Blackguard was saying. "You did everything you could. More. Now—" Then Gavin lost consciousness.

Chapter 74

As night fell, the plain didn't darken. At first, Liv had no idea why. She had been walking all day, stuck behind the wagon, wearing an old petasos with the brim low so her drafter's eyes would be less conspicuous. She'd heard the rumble of guns earlier, but assumed it was posturing. There was no way the army was at Garriston yet. Along with what appeared to be half of the entire camp, she went forward to see what was so bright.

There were so many people covering the plain that Liv almost missed the signs of the battle that had concluded mere hours before, obvious as they were. Trenches where cannonballs had landed simply became ditches for the wagons to avoid. Slippery, muddy, bloody areas next to those cannon scars, with fragments of armor littered about, were just places to watch your footing in the near-darkness. The pungent aroma of gunpowder was already dissipating.

The last of the great lines of soldiers were marching through the gate even now, forcing all the camp followers to wait until after they'd gone inside and set up camp. Liv heard wild rumors of huge magical conflagrations, an epic battle, but she was skeptical. King Garadul's army had taken the wall in an afternoon. It couldn't have been much of a fight. Her father was a great general. He'd only lost one battle in his life, and that barely. He must have decided that they wouldn't finish the wall in time and had withdrawn to the city walls. He'd probably just had some cannoneers stay to inflict some easy damage on King Garadul's men and then withdraw.

The thought made Liv feel better. If her father had chosen to make his stand elsewhere, then he surely wouldn't have been in danger today. The idea that he might have fought and died less than a league away and that she hadn't had so much as a sick intuition was too terrible to entertain. She'd been so caught up in looking for Kip that she hadn't even realized they were this close to the city.

But all thoughts and worries and distractions faded as she pushed through the crowds lined up looking at the wall. No one went within fifty paces of it. As Liv finally pushed to the front, she saw why. An enormous spider, larger than a man, had strung up a dozen corpses—no, not corpses, at least one of the web-wrapped bundles was struggling. As Liv watched, the man tore his head free, his hands bound tight up against his chest. Upside down, the man wriggled, trying to free his arm, setting himself swinging gently. The spider didn't notice as it tended to another bundle ten paces away.

Liv saw a sword stuck in the ground not far from the man. He tore his right arm free and began clawing at the rest of the webs holding him, but couldn't rip them open. Then he saw the sword. He swung, reaching for it. Didn't quite reach it.

"Orholam save him!" someone breathed in the crowd.

"Look at the spider!"

The spider had frozen as if it heard something. Then it turned, just as the man swung farther. It turned, eyes glowing a sickly green.

The man's hands closed on the sword hilt just as the spider pounced. He swung, missed, and the spider's jaws closed on his neck. For one terrible instant the man's entire body tensed, face contorting in pain. Then those awful jaws scissored together, and his head fell to the ground and rolled. His free arm—still holding the sword—spasmed for several long moments as blood gushed out of his neck onto the ground. Then he dropped the sword. It speared into the ground, right where he'd left it.

The spider latched onto his bleeding neck and began feeding.

Liv heard someone retch. Others muttered prayers and curses.

She was transfixed, as was everyone else. Eventually, the spider pushed the man's arm back against his chest and wrapped him in webs once more. Then it picked up his head and put it back with his body.

While the spider was fixing the webs, wrapping the man's head back in place, one of the other bundles began moving.

"I been watching for two hours," a man next to Liv said. "They don't none of them get away. This fella gets about thirty paces before she rips out his guts. Them two try to fight her together. It's the same every time. I know it, but I can't stop watching."

The same every time? Liv looked back to the first man and position of the sword below him. It was the same as before—exactly the same. The blood that pooled beneath his severed head had slowly receded to nothingness. This wasn't a murder; it was a mummer's show. Which actually didn't make it any less impressive.

"What are you doing?" someone called out behind Liv.

She hadn't even realized she was walking forward, but she didn't stop. As she got closer, it became more and more apparent that she'd been right. She walked closer as—sure enough—the second man tore free and ran away. But then the spider stopped in its pursuit, froze, and turned. The crowd behind Liv gasped. The spider bounded back with great speed, going straight for Liv.

Liv froze, her heart leaping into her throat. The spider stopped, right in front of her, great pincer jaws snapping together, forelegs lifted to grab her. Too frightened to move, Liv watched those jaws clack-clack together, not ten paces away. *Clack-clack…*

Soundlessly?

Liv let out a breath she hadn't realized she was holding. She tightened her eyes and saw that the ground around her was laced with superviolet triggers. Brilliant. She stepped to her left, and the spider didn't move until she stepped into the next zone, and then it was there, fast. And now that she was this close, she could see that the cavern behind the spider looked all wrong. It wasn't nearly as deep as it appeared from fifty paces out. It was like a painting, with light and shadow used to make it appear that there was an entire cave where there was none. And the spider itself was crafted entirely of primary, stable luxin colors, layered so that it wouldn't be obvious that it was a luxin creation.

As Liv moved past the triggers, the spider went bounding after the man who had "escaped," but somehow hadn't taken advantage of the last thirty seconds to actually run away. The spider ripped out his guts, just as the man had said.

Liv touched the luxin of the wall and immediately forgot about the genius of the spider mummery. The yellow luxin was flawless. It was perfection.

Forgetting where she was, she drafted directly from the yellow glow of the wall. Drafting from yellow luxin had once been pursued as the perfect source of light—at least for yellows—but it had never panned out. Something was always lost, it was always inefficient. But with an entire wall, leagues long, inefficiency didn't matter. Liv drew a little torch of solid luxin into her hand to better see the wall when illuminated by a second source of light. Sometimes drafters hid things in their construction that—

"Hey! Mistress! What are you doing out here? All drafters are supposed to be inside the walls already."

Startled, Liv saw a grizzled old soldier coming toward her, wearing the uniform of a Tyrean sergeant, a brace of nice wheellock pistols at his belt and an empty scabbard. His face was smudged with gunpowder or smoke and there were light bandages wrapped around his hands. He glanced at Liv's forearms as he approached.

"I, uh—" She tried desperately to remember the lie she'd prepared in case someone asked her about her lack of the colored vambraces.

"You're dazzled by Brightwater Wall. I know, all the drafters is. Where're your arms?"

Arms? Liv guessed he meant the color vambraces all the other drafters wore. "I, ahem, was invited to the color lords' party last night and I had a bit much to drink, I'm afraid. I fell asleep behind a bush and my unit either didn't find me or thought it would be funny to leave me there mostly, ahem..."

"Naked?"

Liv blushed as much from the brazenness of her lie as anything.

"I'm lucky I still have my specs," she said, showing him her yellow spectacles tucked in a pocket.

"I'd probably drink a lot if I were asked to that party myself. Put on your specs and go to the gate. They'll let you through. Then go to Quartermaster Zid. He's a real bastard and he'll give you all sorts of trouble, but... Ah, hell. Come with me, I'll take you. That's me, Master Sergeant Galan Delelo, sucker for a pouty lip and a clueless gaze."

"Hey!" Liv said.

"Joking, joking," Galan said. "You actually remind me of my daughter. And if she's clueless, she got it all from her father. Come on." He turned. "And you, all you damned fools, it ain't real. It's just a show. Stop piddling yourselves." He slapped the wall to emphasize his point and half the crowd ducked at the sharp sound.

Mumbling to himself, he took her to the gate. Even the soldiers continued to march through. They'd left a narrow two lanes on one side for messengers and nobles and drafters to pass, and the guards there knew the master sergeant and let him right through.

Inside the wall, he weaved quickly between tents, walking fast, and cut to the front of a line of lower-ranking soldiers to speak with the quartermaster. "Need yellow rags for this girl here," Galan announced to the quartermaster's back as the big, hunchbacked man was collecting half a dozen swords to give to some young soldier.

Quartermaster Zid turned. "I don't recognize her. She's not with the units I supply. Forget it."

"You're going to give me hell? Tonight? You crazy old ninny, do I need to put my foot up your arse?"

"Ninny? You come harping on me like a harridan and you expect roses and wine? I ought to pound that ugly nose of yours flat," the hunchbacked man said.

Galan laughed, rubbing a nose that had obviously been broken many times. "I seem to recall you trying that a time or two."

The quartermaster grinned, and Liv's terror faded as she realized the two were good friends.

"I know you're happy to see I'm alive," Galan said. "So just do me a favor and give the girl the rags."

"Yellow?" Zid asked. He poured the swords onto the counter, ignoring the young soldier who tried and failed to grab all of them and almost skewered himself trying—unsuccessfully—to keep them on the counter.

"Yes," Liv said.

He grabbed a list. "Name?"

"Liv."

He scanned quickly. "No Livs, sorry. There's not a yellow drafter named Liv in the entire army."

Liv's mouth went dry.

"You and you," Zid said, pointing to some soldiers waiting, irritated, in line. "Arrest this woman. We'll need to report an impostor—"

"Oh for Orholam's sake, Zid, whaddaya think she is, a spy? She's probably barely sixteen! What kind of a swiving fool would send a baby to spy on us?"

At the word "spy" Liv's knees turned to water.

"Maybe a very cunning fool, who thought we would discount her for that very reason," Zid said, suspicion leaking out of his very pores. "They say Gavin Guile did. They say some boy over in the chirurgeons' tents is his own bastard. Who'd send a child? Those wily bastards, that's who." He nodded vaguely toward Garriston.

"I'm seventeen," she said instead. What? Kip was in the chirurgeons' tents? Was he sick? Wounded? She was too flustered and scared to rejoice that she'd just heard her first lead to Kip's whereabouts.

"Come on, Zid, those lists are barely good enough to wipe your arse on once the fighting starts, you know that. It's like you've never done this bef—"

"Gotcha," Zid said. He threw back his head and laughed. He threw some yellow sleeves across the table. "That was for the 'ninny' crack. Now we're even."

"Even, oh, we're not even close to even," Galan said, but he was smiling. "Meh, duty calls, nice to meetcha, Liv, and if you ever can, knock this fella down a notch or three, wouldja?"

"Gladly," Liv said, smiling over the sick feeling in her stomach, as if she were glad to be in on the joke.

In minutes, she was alone and, donning her sleeves for the first time, she was in. Now all she had to do was save Kip and Karris. And really, how hard could that be?

Not for the first time in the last few days, Liv wanted to swear and throw things and whine and complain, and—maybe just a little— she wanted to cry. Instead, she took a deep breath and headed deeper into camp.

Chapter 75

When Gavin opened his eyes, it was bright out. There was a figure sitting beside his bed. He looked at her. His mother.

"Oh, thank Orholam. I thought I was awake," Gavin said.

Felia Guile laughed, and he knew he wasn't dreaming. His mother's laughter sounded somehow freer than it had in years. "It's almost noon, son. I know I hardly have to lecture you on duty, but you really should get up."

"Noon?" Gavin sat bolt upright. It was a mistake. His whole body hurt. His head hurt. His eyes hurt. He held himself still while the hammer blows to the back of his head receded from ten-weight sledges to five-weight sledges and his eyes found focus once more. He usually didn't get lightsick—but then, he'd never used so much magic as he had yesterday, either. Not since Sundered Rock, and he'd been young then. "It's almost noon on Sun Day?" he asked.

"We thought it best to spare you greeting the sun and the dawn processional. It was going be a more informal Sun Day this year, regardless. Orholam will forgive us."

"Mother, what are you doing here?"

"It's time...Gavin."

"Time?"

"For my Freeing."

Gavin felt a wave of cold dread course down his body from head to toe. No. Not his mother. She'd said sometime in the next five years.

She'd given him time to prepare, but it couldn't be this early. "Father?" he asked instead.

She folded her hands in her lap, her voice holding quiet dignity. "Your father has made far too many decisions for me. The Freeing is between a drafter and Orholam."

"So he doesn't know," Gavin said.

"I'm sure he knows by *now*," she said, a little sparkle in her eyes.

"You *ran away*?" And that would have been what it was, too. She would have slipped out at night, bribed a ship captain some obscene amount, and gone before Andross Guile's spies could even report back. She would have chosen the fastest ship in port so that even if Andross sent a ship with the next tide, his men would still arrive too late. It was, Gavin had to admit, brilliant.

And it would not go over well with Andross Guile. Not at all.

She was quiet for a long moment. "Son, I've told your father I wished to join the Freeing every year for the last five years. He forbade it. I can feel myself slipping away. I haven't drafted for three years, and my life feels gray. I love your father dearly, but he's always been a very selfish man. Andross wants to hold on to his life and his power forever, and he doesn't want to be alone. I...pity him, son, and I've given him these years for the love we once shared. You know I'm loyal, but we both know he'll see this as a betrayal. And I know that he'll blame you rather than himself, but if I have to choose between my duty to your father and my duty to Orholam..."

"Orholam wins."

She patted his knee. "I've sent a courier to Corvan Danavis—"

"Corvan's alive? At the wall, I was afraid..."

She smiled sadly. "He's well. But your defenders lost the wall, despite your heroics."

My heroics. Only his mother could talk about his heroics without a hint of irony in her voice. What would you think about that, down in your prison, brother?

"Anyway, I've sent a courier to let him know you're awake. I'm glad to see him again. He's a good man." She knew, of course, that Corvan had taken a life in exile in order for Gavin's masquerade to work, but as always, she was circumspect, just in case there were spies eavesdropping. Gavin's mother had always had a gift for figuring out how to live her life and let her opinions be known despite the pressures of court life and the demands of protocol, secrecy, and discretion. "I'll see you tonight, son."

Gavin got dressed slowly after she left, testing his body to see if he'd done any permanent damage with yesterday's exertions. He was sore, but he surely deserved worse. His muscles would loosen up as the day progressed, and he thought he'd be ready to draft the necessities this evening. Past noon on a Sun Day.

There was a quick little flurry of light knocks on the door, the tempo of an old song he and Corvan used to enjoy. The door opened.

Corvan came in. "You're up." He sounded surprised.

"Not much the worse for wear. Thanks for letting me sleep in, but you know you need my help today. What's the situation?" Gavin was lacing up his shirt.

Corvan grabbed Gavin's face in both of his hands and stared in his eyes. Gavin slapped his hands to knock them away, but Corvan held him firmly.

"What the hell are you doing?" Gavin demanded.

"You should be dead," Corvan said. "Do you remember how much you drafted yesterday?"

"I remember it vividly, thank you, including quite a headache that you're not making any better."

After staring for a few more moments, Corvan released him. "I'm sorry, Lord Prism. They say there are signs when a Prism starts dying. I have no idea what they are, but I figured if anything would break you, it would be what you did yesterday. Even a Prism shouldn't be able to draft that much. But your eyes look fine."

Gavin shrugged it off. "How did we lose the wall?"

Corvan blew out a breath. "Rask Garadul is either brilliant and crazy, or just crazy, that's how."

"So no one shot that moron as he charged the gate?"

"They got lucky. I think you scared both sides half to death with... with what you did. The snipers were shaking so hard they couldn't hit an easy target. Then, when the men saw that Rask was charging and you had fallen, they thought you were dead—that he'd somehow defeated you. The Blackguards pulled out to take you to safety and most of the best Tyreans we had had already been killed in the fighting." He pinched his nose between his eyes. Tension headaches. Gavin had forgotten how Corvan always got those when there was fighting to be done. Gavin could imagine it now—the Prism down, the elite Blackguards suddenly pulling out, and the enemy charging as if unfazed by all Gavin had done. No wonder the Tyreans had lost courage.

"So King Garadul's men joined his charge and what...our men melted? Got massacred? What?"

"They actually held the gate for a few minutes. They bungled the troop refresher maneuvers I tried to teach them, though." That was when fresh musketeers with loaded weapons would switch with the frontline troops. "But they were passing loaded muskets up the ranks, handing back fired muskets to be reloaded. They were losing ground, but not fast, and the wall defenses were holding. It was getting dark—I thought we were going to hold it."

"And then?"

"They ran out of powder." He sighed. Gavin could tell that the general took it as a personal failure. "There was plenty elsewhere, of course. I'd sent men to take care of it, but...war happens." Confusion, or spies, or the couriers being killed, or the wagon men who were supposed to bring the black powder forward deserting, on top of officers not checking back in and double-checking that the orders had been followed, either through their own inexperience or cowardice or death. Any link in the entire chain could break with an army in which few men had trained at all, and few units had trained together. It was simply that the supply of black powder was the link that had broken.

Of course, that wouldn't have mattered if Gavin had built the damned gate first. Or if he'd been stronger. Or if that cannonball hadn't crashed through his forms. But second-guessing was futile.

"Our defenders broke and ran," Corvan said. "King Garadul didn't send anyone after us. I managed a fairly orderly retreat for the men in the wall. I suppose Garadul thinks we'll surrender. Maybe he thought mercy would accomplish his objectives more quickly than wiping out as many men as he could. Or he didn't want his men killing each other in the darkness. Or he's devout and this new religion of his forbids night fighting."

"Old religion, I think," Gavin said.

"They're not giving any sign of attacking today."

"Sun Day is holy even to pagans," Gavin said.

"So we have until tomorrow. What do you want to do, Lord Prism?"

"When you thought I was incapacitated, what did you decide to do?"

"Whatever goodwill King Garadul gained in the city by sparing the men who fled yesterday, he more than lost by using color wights in battle. The city is wild with tales of monsters. They're terrified. Two days ago, I was worried they would turn against us in a heartbeat. They watched you build a wall to protect them, and they saw what you were protecting them from. So now they trust you and they revile the man who slaughtered their friends with the help of abominations. This whole city is yours. If you show your face, they'll follow you to the gates of the evernight."

"Corvan. The question."

Corvan rubbed his neck. Hesitated. "We can't win. The old stone wall around the city couldn't keep out a determined mule. Rask took most of our gunpowder when he took the wall, and all of our cannons. Half our muskets were left on the field as men dropped them when they fled. We'd be lucky to kill a few thousand before they took the inner wall, and once we start fighting street to street, we could kill quite a few at some choke points, but eventually their numbers guarantee it will be a slaughter. With their numbers and our lack of matériel, this city is indefensible. There's no strategy I can imagine in which we win. We can hurt them badly while we lose, but that's not the same." He grimaced. "I was preparing a retreat."

"A retreat." Corvan Danavis had never lost a battle—well, if one didn't count Sundered Rock as a loss, which Gavin didn't. If you mean to lose, and you do, in exactly the way you intended, it's not really a loss, is it?

"Even a retreat is beset with unforeseen difficulties, Lord Prism. The presence of the 'monsters' that put everyone in the city on our side also means *everyone* in the city wants out. They think they'll be slaughtered and eaten if they stay, and there's no way we can evacuate so many people with the ships and the time we have."

Gavin rubbed his forehead. Threw on his ceremonial white cloak. Stalled, basically. "Have our spies reported anything about Karris?" he asked, trying to sound disinterested. Not that Corvan would be fooled.

"Still alive as of yesterday. I imagine he was planning to use her to barter with, if he needed to." Which now, of course, he wouldn't. Meaning Karris had become expendable. Corvan didn't have to say it aloud.

"Kip or Liv or Ironfist?" If Gavin had been thinking, or a little less self-centered, he'd have asked about Corvan's daughter first.

"No word," Corvan said. His jaw was tight.

"Which could be good news, right? If they'd done anything disastrous, our spies would be more likely to hear about it, right?"

Corvan didn't say anything for a while, refusing to take such weak solace. He wasn't a man to grasp after straws or to believe that tragedy couldn't befall him. The deaths of two wives had cured him of idealism. "Our spies did report that there's some kind of king of the color wights, a polychrome wight. They're calling him Lord Omnichrome. No word on who he was before breaking the Pact—unless he's a true wild polychrome."

Gavin shrugged. Just another problem among hundreds, but he knew Corvan was laying all the potential problems on the table so Gavin could make his own choices about what was and was not important.

"What do you want to do, Lord Prism?"

He meant about the battle or the evacuation, of course.

"I want to kill Rask Garadul."

Corvan said nothing, didn't move to order an assassination or something similarly stupid.

Damn him, but Gavin's father had predicted even this. If you lose the city, kill Rask Garadul, Andross Guile had said. Gavin had been sure he could save the city—and hadn't arranged assassins to kill Rask. He should have done both. Too late now, unless Rask charged him tomorrow as foolishly as he had done yesterday.

Gavin moved to speak, but the words wouldn't come. He cleared his throat, trying to remove the taste of failure. "I'll help as much as I can while performing my religious duties, but..." He cleared his throat again. *Seven years, seven great purposes. Here I was trying to do something good for once.* "I've failed, Corvan. Order the evacuation."

Chapter 76

Judging from the cold air licking his skin, it was well after midnight when Kip was escorted through some kind of gate. He had to judge from the temperature because he was wearing a blindfold, along with a black sack over his head, a noose around his neck, hands bound behind his back.

One of the guards who was accompanying him was cursing, quietly but constantly, awed by something apparently called Brightwater Wall. They passed through slowly, stopping and starting, some military sounding voice barking, "Don't stand there and pick your butts. Move deeper into camp. You're blocking everyone else." Kip heard the crack of a whip like a pistol shot, and the line started moving again.

The last couple of days had been like this. Kip had woken in darkness—darkness that turned out to be a blindfold, his hands bound at his sides. When he struggled to get it off, men had come. They removed the blindfold, one stared at his eyes, pulling them wide open with rough fingers, then they blindfolded him again. His left hand was agony. That first day—if it was just a day—they had dosed his wine with something foul that dulled his pain and his senses.

They'd taken him to see Lord Omnichrome, withholding Kip's dosed wine so he would be lucid, but they never removed the blindfold. They'd sat in a tent with many voices for hours, with Kip in agony, and then they'd left. Apparently the lord was too busy to see him.

After a while, Kip heard his guards arguing. A clever man would have figured out some way to exploit their divisions. Kip just stood quietly, wondering when his next dose would be. His hand was throbbing.

They handed him off to someone else—literally handing over the noose around his neck.

"Aren't you going to give him the poppy wine?" one of his guards asked.

"Why waste good poppy on bad blubber?" the other guard asked. "I like poppy wine my own self."

"Oh, that stuff tastes foul," the first said. Kip could agree with that.

"I don't drink it for the *taste*," the guard said, laughing. Kip could agree with that too. "Let's go. I saw some women a ways back. With your charm and my poppy wine..." He laughed again.

Kip was pulled into a wagon. He stumbled up the steps and nearly strangled on the noose, but soon found his seat. The door was closed behind him.

Someone loosened his noose, pulled it off, took off his hood, pulled off his blindfold. "Kip?" she asked.

Kip blinked. Though the light in the violet room was dim, after two days in total darkness it made his eyes water nonetheless. But through the blear of his tears, he made out Karris White Oak.

"Karris?" he asked. Stupid question. Of course it's her, you're looking at her, you idiot.

"Kip, what are you doing here?"

"I'm here to rescue you," he said. Then he laughed.

"Kip, how much poppy wine did they give you?"

It had been hours since they'd given him wine, but he just laughed harder.

Karris guided Kip to her pallet in the wagon. He fell asleep instantly. She stared at him. A hard, mean part of her wanted to hate him.

My son would be Kip's age. Hell, Kip could *be* my son. He does have blue eyes, and my grandmother was Parian.

What, you think brown skin and kinky hair skips a generation? Like twins?

Karris rubbed her face. It was an idle fantasy and she knew it. The son she'd abandoned was Kip's half brother, but any similarities they shared would be because they shared Gavin as a father. And what a father he'd been, to both boys.

She had to get out of here. She was thinking too much.

Karris watched Kip sleep, seeing the Guile blood in the shape of his brow and his nose, and she couldn't even name the feelings in her heart.

Eventually, she covered him with her blanket.

Chapter 77

Gavin survived the noon rituals. The luxiat, a perfectly well-intentioned young green, was shaking like a leaf through the whole thing. Garriston wasn't exactly a prime posting, so no doubt the young man hadn't expected to ever catch a glimpse of the Prism, much less meet him, much less be responsible for performing the Sun Day ritual with him. They muddled through, Gavin prompting the young man with his lines two or three times. It took an hour and a half—and that was with Gavin cutting short the list beseeching Orholam's blessing on every noble in the Seven Satrapies and every official in the Chromeria.

"If even Orholam can't remember their names, maybe they aren't all that important, eh?" he told the luxiat, leaving the young man gawping.

It was early afternoon before he could escape. Escape being relative, of course. He had a dozen Blackguards, a secretary, four messengers, and a dozen city guards accompanying him. He went to the docks.

He found Corvan there, ably directing the mess. The crowd wasn't as bad as he had assumed it would be. Perhaps people were holding out hope that Gavin would save them. Perhaps after seeing him build an impossible wall, they thought his powers were unlimited. Perhaps some were simply religiously observant—only absolutely necessary work was supposed to be done on this holiest of days.

Good thing staying alive doesn't count as absolutely necessary.

Many nobles were bartering with ship captains. Boxes of goods were piled on the docks—and plenty of goods that weren't in boxes. Rolled-up tapestries that must have hung in families' great halls, furniture with gold leaf paint, artwork, a maze of trunks packed with Orholam knew what.

"Lord Prism," General Danavis said, coming up to Gavin quickly. "Perfect timing."

Which means you're about to hand over some truly unpleasant duty.

"I gave the order yesterday that no ships were to leave the harbor, in case an evacuation became necessary. I let it be known that disobedience meant seizure of the ship for the captain, and death for whoever hired him."

It was a harsh sentence, but war called for harsh sentences. Whoever took a ship out of the city early was condemning dozens to death if Garriston were overrun and a massacre began. The problem with harsh sentences was that someone always tried to call your bluff—once. "Who was it?" Gavin asked. He thought he knew already.

"Governor Crassos. His men fired on the Blackguards who went to stop them."

Blackguards? How'd Corvan get Blackguards to obey a "fetch me that prisoner" order? "Any hurt?"

"No, Lord Prism."

"He's here?" Gavin asked. He needed to get out of here. His entourage was blocking Corvan's people from coming and going through the street as they needed to, and they were blocking access to the docks as well. But this he wouldn't dodge. It was better to handle these things in a way that reinforced the solemnity of the law, but it was best to handle them quickly before others disobeyed the same law and you ended up having to kill more. When the sands were running out of the glass, delayed justice was as bad as injustice. "Bring the sailors too, and whatever cargo he was taking," Gavin told Corvan quietly.

Governor Crassos was, indeed, barely ten paces away. He'd just been surrounded by guards much taller than he was, blocking him from sight. His hands were bound behind his back and one eye was swelling. A motley collection of smugglers were brought forward with him, scruffy, hard-edged men who'd taken on the job knowing the risks.

Gavin raised both hands over his head, throwing out a small fan of sparks. Anyone who hadn't been looking before was now. "I hereby convene this adjudication in the light of Orholam's eye. Let justice be done."

Heads bobbed all around the docks in acknowledgment of the sudden prayer. The accused were pushed roughly to their knees. Humility before justice.

If I'm going to block the docks, I might as well accomplish something while I'm here.

"Governor, you're accused of hiring a ship to flee the city, against the orders of the general in charge. Is this true?"

"General? I'm the governor of this shithole! No one tells me what to do!"

"Not even I?" Gavin asked. "The general was acting in my name, given explicit authority to do so. Did you hire this crew to leave the city?"

"You've got fifty witnesses who'll tell you I did. So what? We helped you. My family stood by you in the war. You wouldn't be here without us!" Governor Crassos's voice trailed to a whine. "You're going to put these *peasants* in front of me?"

"Captain," Gavin said, turning away from the governor, "you acknowledge your attempt to flee?"

The captain looked around, defiant, unbroken, but not quite daring to meet the Prism's eye. Apparently everyone on the docks had seen the attempt. He had the air of a man who knew he was going to die and wanted to die well. He was holding his courage in a tight grip. "Yessir. The guvnor hired us last night. I already wanted out." *Of course he did. Every man with a ship wanted out, and wanted out yesterday.*

"It is an old tradition," Gavin said loudly, for the assembled crowd, "to grant one pardon on Sun Day. As Orholam is merciful, so should we be merciful."

"Oh, thank Orholam and his Prism among us," Governor Crassos said, struggling to his feet. "You won't regret this, Lord Prism."

Gavin drafted superviolet for its invisibility and smacked it across the back of Crassos's knees, never even looking at him. The man dropped. Gavin addressed the captain. "Captain, by rights I should lock you in a cell and leave you there to whatever fate might find you. Instead, I'm going to release you, and I'm going to give you my ship—the ship you forfeited—and your crew. I'll be watching you, Captain. Serve well."

The captain looked poleaxed. Then, embarrassingly, his eyes welled with sudden tears.

"What?!" Crassos demanded.

"Governor Crassos, you have disobeyed my order and demeaned your office. A governor is to bear up his people, not weigh them down. You have stolen from the people Orholam gave you the duty to lead. You are a thief and a coward. I hereby strip you of your governorship. You wanted to take your riches and leave? So be it."

Gavin selected a trunk from among those Crassos had taken with him. It was full of rich clothing, large, and so heavy that one man would have trouble holding it. He shot large holes in the top, bottom, and sides. He gave orders and guards put the trunk in Crassos's arms and then bound it to him with ropes.

"You can't do this," Crassos said.

"It's done," Gavin said. "Your only choice now is how you face it."

"My family will hear of this!" Crassos said.

"Then let them hear you died like a man," Gavin said.

It was like Gavin had slapped the man across the face. His family obviously meant everything to him.

Gavin drafted a blue platform out into the water. "You wanted to flee, Lord Crassos? Go."

Without hesitation, Lord Crassos walked down the steps of blue luxin and out onto the water, carrying his trunk. He got out about fifteen paces before the luxin cracked and he fell into the water. In moments, he was kicking to keep the buoyant chest from bobbing over his head and drowning him.

The tide was just turning, so he merely sloshed back and forth, neither pushed in closer to shore nor washed out toward the other piers or toward the Guardian and the open sea.

A thousand pairs of eyes watched him, silently. In a minute, he wasn't having to kick so hard to keep the trunk from pushing him under—because the trunk wasn't floating as high in the water. He was trying to stare defiantly toward the dock, toward Gavin, but his wet hair was falling in front of his eyes, and he couldn't seem to shake his head enough to get it out of them.

He screamed something right before he went under. Gavin couldn't understand him. More death. He hadn't liked Crassos, hated his attitude, hated the type of noble he represented, who took and took and never thought to give a crumb back. But he'd just killed a man, made enemies of his family—and this in the midst of a war that would have done the job for him.

Gavin watched for the bubbles and didn't see any. Crassos had floated too far out. Gavin raised his hands, and then brought them in. "Orholam have mercy," he announced, bringing the adjudication to a close. He'd already spent too much time here. He turned.

Behind him in the bay, a shark's fin cut the water like an arrow headed for its target.

Chapter 78

At sunset, Gavin had finished the most public of the rituals of the day. It was a big show, and he did his best to make each one special. It was one part of the day he could feel good about. He always performed nearly naked. Colors bloomed and raced through his body, out of his body, and gave the appearance of going back into him.

It hurt a little to use so much magic after yesterday's fight, but it was one thing he wouldn't compromise.

All too soon, however, it was over, and people were retiring to their parties. The parties would go all night. Sun Day lasted until the next dawn. The parties of those to be Freed would begin at full dark. He was sitting in a little chapel in the fortress. He had a few minutes, supposedly to pray.

There was a time when he had used it to pray. No more. If Orholam was real, he was busy, he was asleep, he didn't care, he was taking a shit. Time was different to Orholam, they said. That would explain why he'd been doing it for Gavin's entire life.

Gavin's chest felt tight. He was having trouble breathing. The chapel seemed too small, too dark. He was sweating, cold, clammy sweat. He closed his eyes.

Get some balls, Gavin. You can do this. You've done it before. This is for them.

It's a lie. It's *all* a lie.

It's better than the alternative. Breathe. This isn't for you. You want to go out there and tell those drafters waiting for you that their entire lives are a fraud? That their service is a waste? That Orholam doesn't see their sacrifice? That what they've done, what they've given, doesn't matter? Everyone dies, Gavin, don't rob it of meaning for these people. Don't make them see themselves as worthless. Their sacrifice as empty. All life as meaningless.

It was the same debate he had with himself every year. He'd even brought a bucket with him into the chapel, along with extra incense. He threw up, some years.

There was a knock at the door of the chapel.

"Lord Prism, it's time."

Kip wasn't blindfolded the next night. Instead, they gave him darkened glasses, bound them around the back of his head, pulling them tight against his eyes, and ripped the sleeves off his shirt. It would be hard to draft, and anyone around him would have ample warning.

"Apparently there's something they want us to see," Karris said as the guards, Mirrormen and drafters, hustled them out of the wagon they'd been sharing.

They were brought to a security perimeter out away from the tents. It was oddly separate from the rest of the camp, given far too much room. The perimeter itself was simply a rope strung between posts pounded quickly into the ground, but it was huge—and no one from the camp even came close to violating the circle. Inside, looking tiny compared to the size of the circle, was a crowd gathered before a platform. The sun had fully set, but it wasn't yet dark.

"They don't want to be overheard," Karris said. "Tells you how crazy they are. They're going to rally the troops with some idiocy any norm would mock outright."

Norm? Oh, a person who couldn't draft. Wait, that meant...

As they were walked closer, Kip saw that his inference was correct: every single person here was a drafter. There had to be eight hundred or a thousand drafters here!

"Orholam," Karris breathed. "There must be five hundred drafters here."

So I can't count, so what?

But even Kip's bravado melted away as they got closer. His and Karris's tenders pushed them into the crowd, and the first person they pushed out of the way stared at them with wild green eyes. His halos were cracked, snakes of green wriggling through the whites of his eyes.

Kip felt like he was passing through a menagerie. It seemed almost everyone light-skinned enough for it to show had skin stained by luxin. Green, blue, red, yellow, orange, even purple. When he looked into the superviolet, the superviolet drafters stood out like beacons. They'd worked designs into their cloaks, their armor, even their skin—all invisible to anyone but other superviolets. Adjusting his eyes, Kip saw that the sub-reds had done the same, etching dragons, phoenixes, whorls, and flames onto their clothes. Blues wore spikes curling like rams' horns, or knife edges along their forearms. They passed an orange. The man looked normal except he'd slicked back his hair with orange luxin as if it were hair oil, and the whites of his eyes were solid orange, leaving no differentiation from white to iris, only the tiny black dots of his pupils marring that perfect color. A green clad only in leaves hissed at them; then she laughed. A menagerie indeed, except Kip was in the cage with the animals.

They were brought all the way to the front. The crowd was arrayed in front of a stone rising out of the ground, its surfaces worn smooth by wind and rain, but tall enough to be a platform. As Kip and Karris arrived, a man climbed up on the rock wearing a hooded cloak. He reached the top of the stone, threw back his hood, and tore off the cloak, throwing it aside as if it disgusted him.

The man's entire body glowed in the gathering dark. He stood, defiant, silent, legs braced. He extended a hand toward the crowd, and at every five paces, in a wave, torches burst into flame, bathing them in light. Last, torches ringing his stone platform caught fire, and Kip saw that the man was made entirely of luxin. And he was glowing from within.

All around, drafters were dropping to their knees before Lord Omnichrome. But not all of them. Those who stood looked awkward, conflicted. For those who bowed weren't just bowing, they were pressing their faces to the ground. This was pure religious devotion.

"Don't bow," Karris said. "That's no god."

"What is he?" Kip whispered.

"My brother."

Lord Omnichrome extended his hands. "Please, no. Brothers, sisters, stand. Stand with me. We have fallen prostrate before men for far too long."

The orange drafter, the artist Aheyyad, fell prostrate before Gavin. He was to be the first of the night. It was an honored place, and Aheyyad deserved honor. Real honor, not this travesty. But there was no way out. There never was.

Gavin stepped forward. "Stand, my child," he said. Usually, when he called the drafters "my child" he felt sardonic. But Aheyyad was a child, or at least barely a man.

Aheyyad stood. He met Gavin's eyes, then quickly looked away.

"You have something to say," Gavin said. "This is the time." Some drafters felt the need to confess sins or secrets. Some made requests. Some just wanted to express a frustration, a fear, a doubt. Depending on the number of drafters to be Freed before dawn, each year Gavin took as much time with each drafter as he could.

"I failed you, Lord Prism," Aheyyad said. "I failed my family. They always said I was the son who could have been great. Instead, I'm a waste. An addict. I'm the gifted one who couldn't handle Orholam's gift." Bitter tears rolled down his cheeks. He still couldn't look Gavin in the eye.

"Look at me," Gavin said. He took the young man's face in his hands. "You joined me in the greatest work I have ever done. You did what I, the Prism, couldn't do. Any man who has seen a sunset knows that Orholam values beauty. You made that wall as beautiful and terrible as Orholam himself. What you did will stand for a thousand years."

"But we lost!"

"We lost," Gavin acknowledged. "My failure, not yours. Kingdoms come and go, but that wall will protect thousands yet unborn. And it will inspire hundreds of thousands more. I couldn't have done that. Only you could. You, Aheyyad, have made beauty. Orholam gave you a gift, and you have given a gift to the world. That doesn't sound like failure to me. Your family will be proud. I am proud of you, Aheyyad. I will never forget you. You have inspired *me*."

A quick grin flickered over the young man's face. "It is a pretty great piece, huh?"

"Not bad for your first try," Gavin said.

Aheyyad laughed, his whole demeanor changed. He was a light indeed. A gift to the world, beautiful and so burning with life.

"Are you ready, son?" Gavin asked.

"Gavin Guile," the young man said. "My Lord Prism. You, sir, are a great man, and a great Prism. Thank you. I am ready."

"Aheyyad Brightwater, Orholam gave you a gift," Gavin began. The last name was the invention of the moment. In Paria, the only people given two names were great men and women, and sometimes their children. From the sudden tears welling in Aheyyad's eyes and the deep breath he took, his chest swelling with pride, Gavin knew he'd said the perfect thing. "And you have stewarded well the gift he gave you. It is time to lay your burden down, Aheyyad Brightwater. You gave the full measure. Your service will not be forgotten, but your failures are hereby blotted out, forgotten, erased. Well done, true and faithful servant. You have fulfilled the Pact."

"They say we take a Pact! We make an oath! And with that oath, they bind us, they bury us," Lord Omnichrome said.

Liv was pushing carefully through the throng, moving toward the front. She swore she'd seen Kip led there, black spectacles bound to his head. But everyone else was paying rapt attention to the freak up front, so she couldn't move too quickly. Instead, she pretended to listen, too, and moved slowly.

"Like this," Lord Omnichrome said. He gestured to the rounded stone on which he stood. "This is all that's left of what was once a great civilization. You have seen these relics scattered throughout this land. Statues of great men, broken by the pygmies who followed." Liv's ears perked up. Rekton had had a broken statue, out in an orange grove. No one had ever said anything about where it came from. She thought that was because no one knew.

"You think these statues are a mystery?" Lord Omnichrome asked. "They're no mystery. You think it was a coincidence the Prisms' War ended here, in Tyrea? You think the Guiles simply wandered the Seven Satrapies until their armies found each other? And it happened to be here? Let me tell you something you already know, something that all of you have believed but no one dared to say: the wrong Guile won the Prisms' War. Dazen Guile was trying to change things, and they killed him for it. The Chromeria killed Dazen Guile. They killed him because they were worried he would change everything. They feared him, because Dazen Guile wanted to Free us." There was some consternation in the crowd at that phrase. They all knew what day it was, and that the Prism was in Garriston, not even a league away, performing the Freeing this very night.

"You see?" Lord Omnichrome said. "You feel that uneasiness? Because the Chromeria has twisted our very language against us. Dazen wanted to Free us. Dazen knew that light cannot be chained."

"Light cannot be chained," some of the drafters echoed. It was an almost religious refrain.

"The Freeing, they call it. Lay your burdens down, the Prism says. I give you absolution and freedom, he says. Do you know what he gives us? Do you know?!"

"I give you absolution," Gavin said, his heart in his throat as Aheyyad knelt at his feet, eyes up, right hand on Gavin's thigh. "I give you freedom. Orholam bless you and take you to his arms." He drew his knife and buried it in Aheyyad's chest. Right in the heart. He withdrew the blade. A perfect thrust. But then, he'd had a lot of practice.

He didn't look at the wound, didn't watch the blood bloom on Aheyyad's shirt. He held the boy's eyes as the life went out of them. And when it did, Gavin said, "Please forgive me. Please forgive me."

Gavin had sheathed the dagger, and he was scrubbing his hands on the blood rag he carried—though they were clean. He stopped.

"They *murder* you!" Lord Omnichrome shouted. "They stick a knife in you and watch you die. As you beg, they watch—and they say their god smiles on this! Tell me, is this any way to treat our elders? Under the Chromeria, we barely *have* elders. They've killed them all. Oh, except for the White. Except for Andross Guile and his wife. The rules don't apply to them, but you and me, and *our* mothers and *our* fathers—we should be killed. They say this is Orholam's will. They say it is the Pact. Like something we swore to as ignorant children makes their murder of our parents good and right. What insanity is this? A woman serves the Seven Satrapies for all her life, and then as a reward, she's murdered? Is this freedom? This is what they call 'Freeing' her?"

Liv caught sight of Kip, but she wasn't pushing toward him anymore.

"You know it's wrong. I know it's wrong. They know it's wrong. That's why they speak about it in hushed tones and euphemisms. It's not just. It's not a Freeing, it's a murder, let's be clear about that. And then they don't even have the decency to give your body back to your family. They use it in some dark ritual instead. Is that what our fathers served so long to get? Is that just? The Chromeria soils everything it touches. And do you think that all who are 'Freed' have volunteered?"

Lord Omnichrome laughed derisively.

As the Blackguards took Aheyyad's body out of the room, careful not to spill any blood, there was a single knock on the door. One strike, followed by nothing. It took Gavin a moment to remember: Bas the Simple had never really understood knocking.

"Come in, Bas," Gavin said. Children and idiots. This is who I kill? I bathe in the blood of innocents.

The man came in. He was actually quite handsome dressed in his finery. Unlike other simpletons Gavin had known, there was no sign of Bas's difference in his facial features.

"I am sorry for coming out of turn, Lord Prism. I have a question, and I did not wish to interrupt my Freeing to ask it."

That he was interrupting someone else's Freeing to ask the question didn't occur to him, of course.

"Please, ask," Gavin said.

"I heard Evi Grass talking about Brightwater Wall. Evi is a green/yellow bichrome. She's from the Blood Forest, but I don't think she's scary at all. My mother used to tell me that anyone with red hair is just as like to set you on fire as look at you, but Evi isn't like that."

Gavin knew Evi well. Not classically bright, she was incredibly intuitive but rarely trusted herself. At least she hadn't years ago.

"Evi once saved me from a charging—"

"What did she say, Bas?" Gavin asked.

"She didn't say anything, she just saved me. I guess she might have yelled. I couldn't tell you for sure—"

"What did Evi say about Brightwater Wall?"

"I don't like it when you interrupt, Lord Prism. It makes me nervous."

Gavin stifled his impatience. Pushing harder would make Bas completely incapable of speech.

Bas saw that Gavin wasn't going to push and then thought for a moment. Gavin could see him find the mental path once more. "Evi said the brightwater was drafted perfectly. She said she didn't remember you being a superchromat. I can't see the color differentiations myself, of course, but I don't think she'd lie, and Gavin Guile wasn't a superchromat. His brother Dazen was. And you're taller than Gavin. He wore boots to make himself look taller, but Dazen was taller by his thirteenth birthday. I remember that day. It was sunny. My grandmother said that Orholam had always smiled on the Guiles. I was wearing my blue coat..."

Gavin wasn't listening. He felt like the floor had dropped out from under his feet. He'd known this moment was coming. He'd expected it for sixteen years. He'd gone into his first meetings as Gavin expecting anyone, everyone, to point and scream, "Impostor! Counterfeit!" Others had figured it out, but never in a way he couldn't contain. He couldn't discredit Bas. The man was immune to political currents, and everyone knew it. And if asked, Bas would point out a hundred differences between Gavin and Dazen. By the time he was done speaking, the Gavin mask would be destroyed.

And yet he'd come alone. On this night, of all nights.

"So my question was...my question was, why are you lying, Dazen? Why are you pretending to be Gavin? Dazen is bad. He kills people. He killed the White Oaks. All of them. They say he went from room to room in their mansion, even killing the servants, and then he burned it all down to hide his crimes. The children were trapped in the basement. They found their little bodies in a pile. They were hugging each other. I went there. I saw them." Bas stopped speaking, evidently consumed by that old image. With his perfect memory, it must have been vivid indeed. "I told those little charred bodies that I would kill Dazen Guile," Bas said.

Gavin felt an old dread, like the sting of an old master's lash. Bas was a green/blue/superviolet polychrome. Every drafter was changed over time by his colors. Only the wildness of green would make the formerly order-obsessed Bas skip his place in line. But the orderliness of blue was making him crazy to know why, to see how things fit together. "Bas, I'm going to tell you something I've only told one other person in the world. I'm going to answer your question. You deserve it." He lowered his voice. "When I was sixteen years old, I had a...a vision. A waking dream. I was in front of a presence. I fell on my face. I knew he was holy, and I was afraid—"

"Orholam himself?" Bas asked. He looked doubtful. "My mother told me that people who say they speak for Orholam are usually lying. And Dazen is a liar!" His voice pitched up at the end.

The last thing Gavin needed was Bas shouting something about Dazen. "Do you want to hear my answer or not?" he asked sharply.

Bas hesitated. "Yes, but don't you—"

Gavin stabbed him in the heart.

Bas's eyes went wide. He grabbed Gavin's arms. Gavin withdrew the dagger.

Coldly, so coldly, Gavin said, "You gave the full measure, Bas. Your service will not be forgotten. Your failures are forgotten, erased. I give you absolution. I give you freedom."

By the time he said "absolution," Bas was dead.

Gavin lowered the man to the floor carefully. He went and knocked at the side door. The Blackguards came in and took the body, and just like that, Gavin got away with murder.

Chapter 79

The man was a liar. Kip didn't know exactly what was lie and what was truth, but Lord Omnichrome was King Garadul's right hand. They'd massacred his village. For nothing. If murder was nothing to them, what was a lie?

But there was truth here, like all the best lies. That really was what the Pact meant. No wonder they talked about it in sidelong conversations, hushed tones. You got old, you broke your halo, you became like a mad dog. They had to put you down. Kip remembered when Corvan's dog had been bitten by a raccoon and later started foaming at the mouth. Corvan, the alcaldesa, and some of the other men loaded muskets and went after it. Corvan himself blew its brains out. He hid his face afterward, and everyone pretended not to see his tears. It had been a year before he talked about that dog, but when he did, it was never of its madness, never of killing his dog. This was the same. No one talked about the Freeing because no one wanted to dishonor the dead: "Kip was a great man, right until he went crazy and started trying to kill his friends. Right until we had to put him down."

So it was a hard truth. That didn't make it a lie. Indeed, it probably made it more likely that it was true.

But no one in this crowd wanted to accept that. They wanted someone to blame for the death of their parents. They didn't want to die themselves. They could dress that up in some holy-sounding bullshit, but Kip had seen behind the veil. These people were murderers. Gavin was a good man. A great man, a giant among dwarfs. So he had to do hard things. Great men made the hard choices, so everyone could survive. So he held people to the Pact, so what? Everyone swore to it. Everyone knew what they were swearing. There was no mystery, no con. They made a deal, and they liked the deal until they had to pay the price.

These people were cowards, oathbreakers, scum.

I have got to get out of here.

He turned and saw the last woman he expected to see here.

"Ilytian water clocks claim this is the shortest night of the year," Felia Guile said from the doorway. "But it's always been the longest for you."

Gavin looked up at her, gray-faced. "I didn't expect you until dawn."

She smiled. "There was some disturbance with the order. Bas the Simple cut in earlier than he was supposed to. Some withdrew until later." She shrugged.

Withdrew? So maybe they know. It's all falling apart.

Maybe it's best this way. I kill my own mother now, and she doesn't have to see it all come crashing down.

"Son," she said. "Dazen." The word was almost a sigh, a release of pent-up pressure. Truth, spoken aloud after years of lies.

"Mother." It was good to see her happy, but terrible to see her here. "I can't—I didn't even take you on that flight I promised you."

"You really can fly?"

He nodded, his throat tight.

"My son can fly." Her smile lit her face. "Dazen, I am so proud of you."

Gavin tried to speak, but failed.

Her eyes were gentle. "I'll help you," she said. She knelt at the rail, opting for more formality. With his mother, Gavin should have known. "Lord Prism, I have sins to confess. Will you shrive me?"

Gavin blinked back sudden tears, mastered himself. "Gladly... daughter."

Her attitude of simple piety helped him play his part. He was not her son, not here and now. He was her spiritual father, a link to Orholam on the holiest day of her life.

"Lord Prism, I married unwisely and lived fearfully. I let myself be owned by my fear that my husband would put me aside, and didn't speak when I knew I should. I let my sons be pitted against each other, and one is dead because of it. Their father didn't foresee it because he was a fool, but I knew."

"Mother," Gavin interjected.

"*Daughter*," she corrected firmly.

Gavin paused. Acquiesced. "Daughter, go on."

"I have spoken cruel words. I have lied a thousand times. I have treated my slaves without regard to their welfare..." She spoke for five minutes, not sparing herself, blunt and forthright, not condensing her answers for her sake, but for Gavin's—he had others to shrive this night. It was surreal.

Gavin had heard stunning admissions and seen darker sides of people with saintly reputations for the last sixteen years, but hearing her confess beating an innocent slave in her rage minutes after finding Andross in bed with another woman was heartrending. Dislocating. To hear his mother confess was like seeing her naked.

"And I have killed, thrice. For my son. I lost two boys; I couldn't bear to lose my last," she said. Gavin could hardly believe her. "Once I got a Blackguard who suspected him reassigned to a dangerous post during the Red Cliff Uprising, where I knew he would be killed. Once I directed pirates to the ship Dervani Malargos was taking home after having been lost in the wilds of Tyrea for years. He claimed to have been closest to the conflagration at Sundered Rock and to have seen things no one else had. I tried to buy him off, but he slipped away. And once I hired an assassin during the Thorn Conspiracies, using the cover of someone else's fight to murder someone who was about to blackmail my son."

Gavin was speechless. In the first year of his masquerade, he'd killed three men to protect his identity and exiled a dozen more. Then two in the seventh year. He hadn't killed anyone in cold blood since—until Bas. He'd known his mother had protected him, but he'd always thought she'd done it by passing on information she learned. His mother had always been fiercely protective, but he'd never imagined how far she would go. How far he would force her to go because he'd supplanted Dazen.

Dear Orholam, how I wish I believed in you, that you might forgive me for what I've done.

"Each time," she said, "I told myself I was serving Orholam and the Seven Satrapies, and not just my family. But my conscience has never been clear."

Shaken, he intoned the traditional words, offering her forgiveness.

She stood, looking at him intently. "Now, son, there are a few things you should know before I lay my burdens down." She didn't wait for him to say anything, which was good, because he didn't think he was capable of it.

"You are not the evil son, Dazen. You were errant, but never mean-spirited. You are a true Prism—"

"Errant? I murdered the White Oaks! I—"

"Did you?" she interrupted, sharp. Then, softer, "I've seen that poison eating you for sixteen years. And always you've refused to talk. Tell me what happened." His mother really was a Guile, if not by blood, by temperament. She'd wanted to talk about this all along.

"I can't."

"If not me, who? If not now, when? Dazen, I'm your mother. Let me give you this."

His tongue felt like lead, but the images were there before his eyes in an instant. The leering faces of the White Oak brothers, the surge of fear paralyzing him. Gavin licked his lips, but he couldn't force the first words out. He felt the hatred once more, fury at the injustice. Seven on one, more. The lies. "Things were already bad with Gavin. Blue and green awoke for me early, but I was starting to suspect I could do more. I told him. You know, we hadn't been close since he'd been announced Prism-elect, and somehow Sevastian's murder only made things worse. I guess I thought telling him my gifts were growing would bring him back. Like we could be best friends again. But he didn't like it. Not at all." From nowhere, a wash of tears came to Gavin's eyes. He missed his brother so much it tore his soul. "I understand now how threatening it must have been for a young man to lose the one thing that made him special. I didn't, then. The day after I told him I was a polychrome, I heard him urging father to betroth him to Karris. It was the greatest betrayal I could imagine. Her love was the one thing that made me special. It was some time before I saw the symmetry to that.

"Anyway, I thought Karris was as in love with me as I was with her. When father announced her betrothal to Gavin, we decided to run away together. She must have told someone. Maybe it was an accident. Maybe Gavin seemed a better prize. Karris and I were supposed to meet just outside her family's mansion after midnight. She wasn't there. Her maid told me she was inside. It was a trap, of course. The White Oak brothers knew I'd been trysting with Karris, and they wanted to teach me a lesson. Said I'd dishonored them, turned their sister into a whore."

They'd grabbed him as soon as he stepped inside. All seven brothers. They'd torn off his cloak and snatched away his spectacles and his sword. He remembered the great, enclosed courtyard, servants peeking out from doors and windows. There was a great bonfire in the courtyard—plenty of light, but none for a blue/green bichrome without spectacles. "They started beating me. They'd been drinking. Several were drafting red. It got out of hand. I thought—still think—that they were going to kill me. I got away once, but the gate I tried was chained shut."

"*They* chained the gates?" Felia Guile asked. It had become part of the story that Dazen had done that. Out of cruelty. Karris's father had known better, but had said nothing to combat the lie.

"They didn't want me to get out or any guards or soldiers from the outside to be able to get in to interfere before they were done." Gavin got quiet. Glanced at his mother. Her face was all tenderness. He looked away.

"I split light for the first time that night. It felt... wonderful. I'd thought I might be a superviolet to yellow polychrome, but that night,

I used red. A lot of red. Maybe I wasn't ready for what red does to you when you're already furious." He remembered the shock on their faces when he started drafting. They knew he was a blue/green. They *knew* what he was doing was impossible. There was only one Prism each generation. Images of fireballs streaking from his bleeding hands, of Kolos White Oak's skull smoking while he still stood, of the White Oak guards slaughtered by the dozen, limbs sheared off, blood everywhere. "I killed the brothers and all the White Oak guards. The fires were spreading. The front gate collapsed as I got out. I heard people screaming." He'd gone, staggering, left empty and numb, to find his horse.

"There was a maid at the side door. The woman who'd lured me into the trap. She looked through the bars and begged me to open it. It was the same door I'd tried when I was trying to get out. It was chained on the inside, but she didn't have the key. I told her to burn, and I left. I didn't realize—I didn't even think that all the other doors were chained too. I just wanted to get away. They couldn't find the keys in time, I guess. With that casual cruelty, I consigned a hundred innocents to death." Like it was better for the guilty to die than for the innocent to live.

Funny thing, he could weep about not being friends with his brother, but he had nothing inside himself for all those dead innocents. Slaves and servants bound to the White Oaks not by choice. Children. It was just too monstrous.

And most of the men who'd joined Dazen in the war later hadn't even asked what had happened that night. They'd been happy to fight for a man whom they thought had killed an entire mansion full of people—because it meant he was indestructible. How he despised them.

His mother came and held him. And now, silently, he wept. Perhaps for those dead. Perhaps only selfishly, because he was losing her.

"Dazen, it isn't mine to absolve you of what happened that night, or of all that happens in war that you carry still. But I do forgive you of all that I can. You are no monster. You are a true Prism, and I love you." She trembled, tears streaking down her cheeks, but she glowed. She kissed Gavin on the lips, something she hadn't done since he was a boy. "I'm proud of you, Dazen. Proud to be your mother," she said. "Sevastian would be proud of you too."

He held her, weeping. There was no absolution for him. Sevastian was still dead, and her other son rotted in a hell Gavin had created for him. She wouldn't have forgiven that. But he wept and she held him, soothing him like a child once more.

Then, all too soon, she pushed him back. "It's time," she said. She took a deep breath. "Is it...is it acceptable for me to draft one last time? It's been years."

"Absolutely," Gavin said, trying to put himself back together. He gestured to the orange panel of the wall.

She drew in orange luxin. Shivered. Sighed. "It feels like life, doesn't it?" She knelt gracefully. "Remember what I said," she said.

"Everything," he swore. Even if I don't believe it.

"It's all right," she said. "You'll believe it someday."

He blinked.

Felia Guile chuckled. "You don't get all your smarts from your father, you know."

"I never doubted it."

She drew her hair back over her shoulders to give him a clear path to her heart. She placed her hand on his thigh, looked up at him. She let the orange luxin go. "I'm ready," she said.

"I love you," Gavin said. He took a deep breath. "Felia Guile, you gave the full measure. Your service will not be forgotten, but your failures are hereby blotted out, forgotten, erased. I give you absolution. I give you freedom. Well done, good and faithful servant."

He stabbed her in the heart. Then he held her, kneeling with her, kissing her face as she died. It was several long minutes before he had the strength to stand and summon the Blackguards.

When they opened the door, he saw that there were a hundred drafters in the hall, waiting for him. They weren't smiling. The enormous Usef Tep, the Purple Bear, stepped forward. "We didn't want to cause a disturbance while you were with your mother, but sir, we need to talk."

Sir. Not Lord Prism. Not Gavin.

So begins the end.

Chapter 80

"Kip, whatever happens, stay close to me," Karris whispered, leaning close.

She said it with a tension and certainty that told Kip something *was* going to happen. Soon. Though he wanted to, he didn't ask. Their guards were close, though everyone's attention was focused on Lord Rainbow up front and his verbal feces about duty and justice. Kip had long ago stopped paying attention. He was staring at a girl, not ten paces away. Liv.

He could have sworn she'd been pushing closer to him and Karris for a while, but for the last ten minutes she'd stood as though frozen, listening to Lord Rainbow. The crowd between them moved, and he saw that she was wearing yellow cloth vambraces. Liv was a yellow. It had to be her.

Kip craned his head around, looking toward Brightwater Wall.

"Stop acting suspicious," Karris said through gritted teeth. Which left Kip with absolutely zero places to look. If he stared at Liv, that would draw attention to her, the speech disgusted him, he couldn't look at the wall, and when he looked at Karris, he couldn't help but notice her dress. Karris had been thought-freezingly gorgeous when Kip had seen her wrapped in a heavy black cloak over her Blackguard garb. In the thin black dress she was wearing, her beauty ripped Kip's breath out of his chest, stomped on it, and set it on fire. She stood straight, imperious, regal, elegance personified. No one had given her a shawl despite the coolness of the night. In the rising light, Kip could see the gooseflesh on her arms.

"Cold out, huh?" he said.

One of their guards snorted.

"I *will* beat you to death if you ask for it," Karris said, still staring straight ahead.

Kip had no idea what she was talking about, or why the guard was laughing. "What did—" He looked down at her chest. Her nipples were clearly defined against the thin silk. Kip gaped just as she looked over and caught him looking.

"Kip. Dark spectacles are not a license to ogle."

Will the earth please open and swallow me now? She thought he'd been being snarky about...Oh, Orholam. He was the stupidest boy in history.

The speech ended without anything special happening. Kip glanced carefully at Karris. She looked toward the east, where the sky was lightening.

"He's waiting until it's almost dawn," Karris whispered, as their guards pushed them to start walking. "Be ready."

"He?" Kip asked.

"Shut it!" the Mirrorman to Kip's left said. He smacked Kip with the butt of his musket.

Oh, I can make inappropriate jokes on accident, but you've got a problem when I'm just trying to escape?

At first, Kip couldn't see very well where they were going through the vast crowd. Gradually, though, he saw that the drafters were joining a much larger group that was being addressed by King Garadul.

Kip lost sight of Liv quickly. The dark spectacles he was wearing made him almost blind. He could see out of the sides if he strained, but it made it impossible to search the crowd. With his hands tied behind his back, there was no way to fix that either.

Tens of thousands of soldiers surrounded King Garadul. The man was waving his arms, shouting, but Kip could only hear snippets as the drafters joined the outskirts of that group: "cleanse this city... Take back what has been stolen from us...punish..." It sounded pretty grim.

Again, Kip seemed to be the only person who wasn't hanging on every word, so as the sun rose, first touching Brightwater Wall behind them because it was higher than the plain below, he saw movement on the wall.

He couldn't see it well around the frame of the spectacles, but the forms of five men—a cannon crew—became three, then in a violent motion two, then just one. The cannon on the wall had been pointed at a high trajectory toward Garriston, but the man was angling it down and down.

A quick spark.

Boom!

The cannon spat fire. Kip didn't see the shell hit, but he felt it. The earth seemed to jump.

For a moment, no one did anything, thinking it must have been a mistake. Screams of fright and pain. Then Karris collided with him, knocking him off his feet.

Kip smacked his head as he fell, so at first he wasn't sure if the second explosion was just his imagination.

"Canister shot!" Karris said. "Shit! We have to move! Ironfist's aiming for that wagon."

Wagon? Ironfist? Why was Ironfist shooting at them?

Kip was blinking. Something was strange about his vision—oh! Smacking his head against the ground had knocked one of the black lenses out of the frame of his spectacles.

"Grab that lens and cut my hands free!" Karris barked.

They were both lying on the ground, hands bound. The crackle of musket fire filled the air.

One of the Mirrorman guards grabbed Kip, trying to haul him to his feet.

Despite lying flat on her back, Karris kicked the back of the man's knee with her left foot. He folded, and by the time he landed on his back her right foot had swept up and then down in an ax kick across his throat. There was a crunch and blood sprayed through the mail flap over the man's mouth.

Kip could hardly believe what he'd just seen, but Karris was already moving on. She scrambled over the dying man, lying right on top of him. With her hands still behind her back, she drew the man's belt knife a hand's breadth and cut her wrists free.

"Stop!" a Mirrorman yelled, his musket pointed at Karris's head.

There was still screaming everywhere. Chaos. Shouting and gunfire and the screams of the dying.

Kip lashed out, kicking for the Mirrorman's knee as Karris had done seconds before.

The Mirrorman saw it coming and swung the butt of his musket for Kip's leg—

—and was flung away like Orholam's own hand had slapped him.

A concussion, a roar, a pressure so vast Kip's vision went black for an instant. Everyone standing was torn off their feet. Things—Kip couldn't even tell what they were—blasted overhead.

He must have lost a few seconds. He rolled over, tried to stand, fell. His wrists were bloody, but no longer bound. The acrid aroma of gunpowder filled the air. Bits of wood rained down on the ground.

When Kip tried to stand again, someone helped him. Not even a hundred paces away where the powder wagon had been, he saw a crater in the ground a good ten paces across and at least two paces deep. Everyone in a huge circle around it was dead.

Karris turned him around, her mouth moving, skin smudged with powder. He couldn't hear her.

He saw her mouth a curse as she realized the same thing. He was pretty sure she was mouthing "Ironfist" and a series of curses. She put a musket in his hands and said, slowly enough that Kip could read her lips, "Can you walk?"

Kip nodded, not sure how much he was hearing her and how much he was reading her lips. She pulled at him and they started jogging. He was still disoriented, but he saw that he wasn't the only one. Dozens of men and women with powder-darkened skin and clothes were staggering around, some of them bleeding from their ears. A man was carrying his left hand in his right hand, looking for the rest of his arm as blood pumped out of his mangled shoulder.

Teams of soldiers were forming up now and running toward the wall. Others stood back and were firing their muskets at the gun emplacement, but Kip didn't see anyone on top of the wall returning fire.

Someone was shouting at Kip. Good, so he could hear. He turned.

He didn't recognize the soldier standing in front of him. "Form up, soldier!" the man shouted. "Move it!"

They thought he was a soldier because he had a musket. But then, with his powder-blackened clothes, it was no wonder.

"Come on, soldier, we've got a city to take!"

There were at least twenty soldiers with the man, and only the officer had a real uniform. Kip shot a glance at Karris. She was wobbling back and forth, holding her hands over her eyes like she was blind, just another wounded person. Kip realized that if they saw the violet caps over her eyes, they'd capture her immediately. Or kill her outright. With that dress, it was best not to let their attention alight on her any longer than necessary.

If Kip refused, the man could summarily execute him. And he looked grim, ready to do it. "Yes, sir!" Kip said. He joined the lines, glanced at Karris, looked once more for Liv and didn't see her, and then ran with the soldiers toward the city and the sound of guns and the flash of magic.

Chapter 81

Gavin squared his shoulders and confronted his accusers. A hallway in the Travertine Palace. It wasn't exactly where he would have picked to die, but he supposed it was better than some dungeon somewhere. *Better than I gave you, Gavin.* At least he could face this with dignity.

"What do you want?" he demanded.

"We know what you're doing," Usef Tep said. "Sir." The "sir" was belated. It always was with the Purple Bear.

Samila Sayeh came forward, put a hand on Usef's meaty arm. "We've come together to stop you, Gavin Guile."

"And how do you propose to do that?" Gavin asked.

"By volunteering."

Huh? Gavin tottered on the edge of drafting everything he could. Stopped. Tried to keep his idiot perplexity off his face.

"It's noble, Lord Prism, but it's not wise."

What? Well sometimes when you don't know what the hell someone's talking about, the best thing to do is play along.

"I don't know what the hell you're talking about," Gavin said. Oops.

"The Freeing is the holiest moment in a drafter's life," Samila said. "You're trying to protect that for us. And we thank you for that. But we're warriors. All of us fought in the war. We're willing to fight again."

"I die this day," Usef said. "It's my duty to make an end, and I accept that. But I've got no patience for all this Orholam this and Orholam that. I'd rather go down fighting."

"Lord Prism," Samila Sayeh said, "we have to hold the city long enough for everyone to escape. Holding the walls is a death sentence. Why not give it to us? We're dead anyway."

Their talking had given Gavin a few moments to think, to recover his balance. "If I send you out there, you'll all break the halo. That's why you're here. Next year I'll have to face you fighting for him. They don't put down color wights. It's not just your souls we're talking about here. It's your sanity. And you're right, you're all warriors. That makes you ten times as dangerous when you break."

"We'll fight in teams. Each with a pistol and a knife. When we break, we'll do as the Blackguards do."

When a comrade broke the halo on the battlefield, the Blackguards considered them dead—and indeed, it did usually render a person unconscious temporarily. The Blackguards would check the eyes of a fallen comrade, and if the halo was broken, they'd slit their throat.

"Except when a team's down to one, we end ourselves too," Samila said. It was, for some, a thorny theological point, though not without precedent. Was suicide a sin when you knew you were going mad and would likely hurt or kill innocents? "You *are* the Prism, you could make a special dispensation."

"Future generations would believe that implied special dispensation is needed," Talon Gim said, scowling. He had always had very definite theological views.

Maros Orlos stepped forward. "Lord Prism, we've already sent to be Freed all the drafters we knew were too far gone to be any use on the battlefield. What is the greater good here? That we do things as they've always been done, or that we save an entire city?"

There was no contest, of course. Gavin was trembling. "I think such a sacrifice would honor Orholam. I will give each of you a... special blessing as you take up this burden. I am...deeply humbled by this act of devotion. Deeply grateful."

That much was no lie.

After making the decision to let the Freeing class fight to the death instead of be Freed on his knife, Gavin still met with each of them. He shrived them, listened to their concerns about dying, and blessed them. It was exactly the same as he would have done otherwise— minus the killing. But to Gavin, it was entirely different. Usually, he was so sickened by what he had to do that he couldn't give their words his full attention. He tried. He pretended. He knew they deserved his best.

But today, he did it. They weren't really talking to him as they spoke; they were talking to Orholam. Gavin was simply an instrument to make their confessions easier than addressing an empty room. What they were doing was an act of devotion. It was an act of sacrifice.

To others, it wouldn't seem that different than what some did every year at the Freeing. It would end with a dead drafter who'd gone to death bravely. But without the burden of shedding their blood, Gavin was able to see it clearly for the first time. These people were heroes.

If Gavin hadn't pulled one over on the whole world and on Orholam himself by masquerading as his own brother, perhaps the Freeing would have seemed this holy every year. It was supposed to be something to celebrate, but Gavin had dreaded it. Always.

Now, as he prayed with each drafter, he could almost believe Orholam listened.

Samila Sayeh was the last. She was, Gavin was reminded, a woman whose beauty withstood scrutiny. Her skin, even in her forties, was nearly flawless. A few smile lines, but clear and glowing. Slim. Stunning blue eyes against Atashian olive skin. Impeccably dressed.

"I had an affair with your brother, you know," she said.

Gavin froze. He knew that he, Dazen, had not had an affair with Samila Sayeh—which could only mean one thing: she knew. "Sometimes a man likes to pretend that nothing has happened between him and an old lover," Gavin said quickly. "Especially when it was a great mistake."

She laughed. "I've wondered often over the years, are you just so good that you've never been discovered, or does everyone who could expose you have an ulterior motive for not doing so?" She stared at him, but he said nothing. "You know, Evi was looking at your wall.

She said, 'I don't remember Gavin being a superchromat. He shouldn't be able to craft a yellow this perfect.' And do you know what she said after that? She said that Orholam must have blessed your effort. That it was proof you were doing his will. And everyone nodded their heads. Can you believe it?"

Gavin felt a chill.

"Gavin would have made a wall that would last a month and bragged it would last forever. You made a wall that will last forever, and said it might last a few years. You just couldn't stand to make an inferior product, could you, Dazen?" Someone who'd been drafting blue for twenty-five years would be pleased to see the order in this: Dazen was a perfectionist, so even though he could make his mask better with imperfection, it didn't match his personality to do so.

"No," he said quietly.

"I fought for your brother. I killed for him," Samila said.

"We all did an awful lot of that," Gavin said.

"I felt so betrayed by you, that you wouldn't even acknowledge me after what we'd had. I felt a glimmer of hope when you broke your betrothal with Karris. When I finally figured it all out, I still wasn't sure of myself. Gavin told us things about you, about what you would do if you won. And you weren't doing them. Was your brother a liar all along, or did you change? You were supposed to be a monster, Dazen."

"I am a monster."

"Glib, still. The snot-nosed younger brother with a quick tongue. I mean it." She looked at him long and hard. Looked at the Freeing knife that he hadn't drawn. "How well do you know yourself?"

He thought about the years, the goals he'd achieved, and the ultimate goal it was serving. "The Philosopher said that a man alone is either a god or a monster," Gavin said. "I'm no god."

She stared at him for one moment more, those intense blue eyes unreadable. She smiled. "Well then. Maybe the times call for a monster." She knelt at his feet, and he blessed her.

Chapter 82

Kip had always pictured a charge as being somehow glorious. Whatever he'd pictured, it wasn't this. He held his pants up with his wounded left hand and the musket in his right. And the musket was heavy! His heart was heaving and everyone else was running faster than he was.

He had little sense of what was happening anywhere else. A man who roared that the soldiers could call him either god or Master Sergeant Galan Delelo ran at the front, urging his men on. The backs of the other soldiers filled the rest of Kip's vision, and the pain of running distracted him from all else except for the intermittent whistling, which he couldn't place at first—until he realized it was the sound of musket balls flying past, and then he could hardly think of anything else.

For a moment he saw the city walls as the men in front of him disappeared in a ditch before scrambling up the other side. He remembered dismissing these walls not even a week ago. Now they looked pretty impressive. The side of the wall was encrusted with slums like barnacles, and King Garadul's men were already swarming there, trying to use the low buildings and rough shelters as a ladder. But even in the brief glimpse Kip had, one of the slum buildings on which the men were climbing teetered and then collapsed, crushing men and sending up a cloud of dust.

Something wet and chunky splattered across Kip's face as he ran.

He turned, vaguely saw a man dropping beside him—and then the ground suddenly wasn't where it was supposed to be.

He went down hard in the dry irrigation ditch. He skidded on his face, flipped over, rolled, the wind knocked cleanly out of him. As he moaned, struggling to regain his breath, he realized he wasn't alone. The irrigation ditch was full of men cowering inside its marginal cover.

Master Sergeant Galan Delelo appeared back on the lip of the ditch. "Get up, you pathetic rats! They've got an angle right into this ditch from the wall, you damn fools. Get up! If you're anything less than dead, get up or I'll shoot you myself!"

For a second, no one moved.

"You wouldn't," a man said.

The master sergeant drew a pistol and shot him in the belly. "Who's next?" he yelled. He pointed his other pistol at a man carrying a large robin's egg blue sack.

"I'm a messenger!" the man screamed.

"You're a soldier now," Master Sergeant Delelo shouted. He was either unaware or just didn't care about the musket fire raining around him, sending up little puffs of earth. "Now, move!"

The man dropped his messenger sack, grabbed Kip's musket, and ran forward, along with everyone else.

Lying on the ground, Kip was left with the other corpses. When he had his breath back, he touched the side of his face. Gore, gray-red chunks of...He didn't want to think about it. What mattered was that he was free. At least until the next officer commandeered the cowards who filled up this ditch again.

There wasn't much time. If Kip thought too much or waited too long, he wouldn't move, and he needed to move now. The master sergeant was right, this ditch wasn't out of the line of fire. If Kip waited, he was going to get killed.

He wanted to see more of the battle, make a good plan. He didn't know what kind of a judge he would be of whatever he saw, and he didn't even know which way to run.

He grabbed the messenger's sack and slung it over his shoulder. He saw the wreck of a wagon farther back away from the wall.

Did we run right past that? Kip hadn't even noticed. Regardless, the oxen who'd been pulling the wagon were dead or mewling, screaming in pain, bloodied. Kip ran for it.

He ducked into the shadow of the wagon and found two other men already there. They looked at him with wide, fearful eyes. "Move!" he shouted.

Kip climbed up on the wreck and looked out on the plain. At first all he saw were the dead bodies. Several hundred perhaps. Mostly he couldn't see any blood, so it looked like people sprawled about sleeping. It wasn't so great a toll, considering how big the army was, Kip thought, but seeing so many dead wasn't really something he could merely think about. Those people were dead. He could have been one of them. He could still be.

He tore his eyes away, tried to look for something useful. In a few spots at the wall, King Garadul's men had actually reached the top of the wall. There was fighting in three or four places, defenders and attackers alike being thrown off, grappling, puffs of black smoke erupting everywhere from musket and pistol fire.

To Kip's left, there was a slight hill, out of range of musket fire from the wall. There were several hundred horsemen and drafters around the hill. In front of the hill, drafters were crafting a bridge over the irrigation ditch. Kip saw then that the original bridge had been destroyed by the retreating people of Garriston. It had slowed King Garadul's advance, probably more because they'd stopped to talk about it than if they had simply charged the horses through.

At the top of the hill, Kip saw standard bearers and a figure who might have been King Garadul himself. He was shouting, making huge animated movements toward Lord Omnichrome, who was unmistakable because he literally glowed in the early morning light.

Kip didn't realize he'd made a decision until he found himself running. He snatched a musket from the ground next to a woman curled in the fetal position, moaning, and kept running. His vengeance was this close.

As Kip approached the hill, movement began on the hill and rapidly spread, horns sounding orders. It was a few seconds before Kip saw the horses moving. King Garadul was advancing on the wall—personally, right toward the Mother's Gate. Was he trusting that his men would open the gate by the time he got there, or was he just an idiot?

Kip was halfway up the hill when he saw a woman whose form seemed familiar. He stopped.

Karris White Oak had flagged down one of the horsemen heading after King Garadul. The man slowed down for her, and she swung up into the saddle behind him with surprising grace. The man turned in the saddle to ask her a question, and then tumbled out. Kip saw the quick gleam of a dagger, then it was sheathed, and Karris kicked the horse's sides and went speeding after King Garadul. She was going by herself, and with her eye caps still on. She wouldn't be able to draft, but she was still going to try to kill him. Even if she were successful, it would be suicide.

I swore to save her. And I swore to kill him.

Kip was a terrible rider, but there was no way he could catch up without a horse. Seeing horses tied up near the crown of the hill, he headed straight for them.

"...through the Lover's Gate. You'll have to swim. Join the refugees. He'll—"

Kip rounded a tent in time to see the young drafter Zymun swing up into a saddle. He was taking orders from Lord Omnichrome himself. Kip's heart leaped. They weren't twenty paces away.

"You need a horse?" someone said, right at Kip's elbow.

Kip almost jumped out of his skin. He blinked stupidly at the groom.

"Rough work out there, huh?" the groom said.

"Message!" Kip said, remembering he was carrying a messenger bag. "Message for the king! Yes, a horse! I need a horse."

"I figured," the man said. He went off to find a beast large enough.

Kip looked back toward Lord Omnichrome and Zymun. He missed whatever else they said, but he saw Lord Omnichrome hand a box to the mounted drafter.

That box. Kip couldn't believe it.

That was his box. Right size. Right shape. That was his inheritance. The only thing his mother had ever given him. And Zymun had it.

Zymun bowed to Lord Omnichrome. Kip sank back as the young drafter pulled his horse around and galloped away to the east. Lord Omnichrome strode back toward the crown of the hill. The groom brought Kip a horse and helped him mount and stash the musket in a sleeve beside the saddle.

Kip looked, torn. Lord Omnichrome was disappearing up the hill, rejoining his entourage. He was the heart of this; Kip knew it. He should kill him. Orholam, his chance was passing through his fingertips. But to the south, Karris was charging to her death, and to the east, that snake Zymun was stealing the only thing Kip had to remember his mother by. Kill Lord Omnichrome and stop the war. Kill Zymun and take the knife. Or save Karris and have a chance at King Garadul. Kip couldn't get them all.

Kip had made his oaths to the living and to the dead. He gritted his teeth, sure he was making the wrong decision—and making it anyway. It's better that the innocent should live than that the guilty die. Gavin loved Karris, and he deserved another chance at happiness. Kip rode after her.

Chapter 83

Karris had never fought in a full-scale battle before, but she had watched several with Gavin's general Running Wolf. In another age, he would have been revered as a great leader. Instead, he'd faced Corvan Danavis, and been thrice bested by smaller forces commanded by the mustachioed genius. Regardless, he'd been a kindly older gentleman with a soft spot for Karris, and he would explain to her what he was seeing as the distant lines clashed. Of course, he was often too busy to tell her much, but at other times it seemed to help him to think out loud. So now as Karris galloped down the hill and headed toward the fray, she was able to piece together more than she would have otherwise.

The buildings propped against both sides of the wall—the feature that would eventually doom it, Karris was sure—were actually helping in the short term. They were like a talus slope, wide enough that it encumbered anyone bringing forward siege ladders, and too unpredictable to charge men straight up at any one place. Eventually, King Garadul's men would figure out which places were stable and how much weight they could support, but until then the collapsing buildings killed and slowed the men attacking the wall.

As Karris rode in, drafters appeared at the top of the wall en masse for the first time. The wall wasn't high, but it was wide enough for the defenders to move along the top at great speed, and they'd seen King Garadul's cavalry coming here.

Reds and sub-reds worked in teams from the top of the walls, one flinging sticky pyre jelly down onto the attackers, and the other setting it alight. King Garadul had a line of his own drafters up front, blues and greens attempting to divert the pyre jelly in midair and throw it back at the wall. Reds threw their own luxin up at the defenders on the wall, though Garadul's teams weren't as good at getting it alight every time. On both sides, musketeers did their best to pick off drafters.

The defenders were getting the best of it, but there were simply so many attackers, Karris didn't see how they could possibly hold out for long. And why had King Garadul brought his cavalry here now? Directly against the wall, their maneuverability was negated and they made easy targets for the blue drafters at the top of the wall, who would pop up from behind the crenellations, fire off a few daggers of blue, and then duck back down.

All Karris had to do was muscle her way through the crowd—not hard when you were mounted—steal a musket, stay alive long enough to get close to King Garadul, and blow his head off. In the heat and fury and blood and confusion and cacophony of battle, it was quite possible no one would even realize the killing shot had come from behind him.

Karris heard a yell behind her, somehow different from the rest of the screams. She turned her head, still leaning low over her galloping horse. A dozen Mirrormen, coming after her on their gigantic chargers. Her heart convulsed.

So the subtle approach isn't going to work.

She picked at the eye caps again. The skin at the corner of her eye was tearing, but she wasn't any closer to pulling the damned things off. If she could draft, she would have a chance. She pushed down the sudden flood of red fury with effort.

Eighty paces out, she saw a line of musketeers reloading. She scanned the crowd for anyone bearing a flintlock—a matchlock wouldn't work for this. Then, slowing her horse to get the timing right, she swept in just as one of the officers finished reloading and hefted the musket up to his shoulder. She snatched it right out of his hands.

Commander Ironfist had often chided her for her trick riding, for practicing things they both knew had no use beyond impressing the Blackguard's new recruits. A vision of the big man's head shaking in amused surrender went through her head as she jammed the musket into the saddle sleeve. She was wearing this damn dress that left her half naked and half totally restricted. She wasn't really going to—Karris kicked her feet free of the stirrups, turned her wrist behind her back to get a firm grip on the cantle, tucked the reins between horse and pommel, and dismounted as the horse continued at a canter. She hit the ground and instantly leapt, twisting, feeling the sleeves of her dress rip. She'd always practiced this with a better cantle, but she'd also practiced on taller horses, and she almost flung herself over the side of the saddle on her way back up. It took a half a moment, but she settled into the saddle, backward. She drew the musket, leveled it, trying to absorb as much of shock of the horse's cantering in her knees as she could, trying to time how long it would take between trigger pull and musket fire. She aimed at the lead Mirrorman forty paces behind her and pulled the trigger.

She'd aimed perfectly, timed everything right, but the musket didn't fire. She cocked the flintlock again, checked the mechanism. No flint. It had fallen out, probably during her impressive trick riding. Bollocks!

Karris threw the musket away, reversed her hands, turned her head over her shoulder to make sure she'd be leaping off flat ground, and dismounted. The reverse dismount and remount was actually much harder than the original trick, but she did it perfectly, both feet hitting the ground, pushing off in tandem just as the pull of the horse's forward motion catapulted her into the air. Except as she was pulled up and forward, half of her horse's head was torn off by a musket ball and its body dove for the earth. If she'd still been holding the reins, she'd have been flung to earth too. Instead, she became a human cannonball. The force of her jump and the horse's sudden dive had her twisting like a cat. She was flying, upside down and backward.

Time only for one thought: Roll when you hit.

But when she hit, there was no time for anything at all. Whatever it was, there were multiple levels, and it was mercifully soft—which didn't stop it from whipping her head and limbs in different directions. When she finally hit ground, she couldn't move for a few long seconds.

Someone was cursing. She saw feet. She was lying on top of a man, and he was struggling to get out from under her. She must have crashed into the backs of half a dozen soldiers—and taken them all out with her. One man had his leg twisted at a nasty angle. Another turned to look at her, his nose fountaining blood, cursing.

A huge explosion took away whatever he was saying. Perhaps sixty paces away. Everything seemed to freeze for a moment on the battlefield, then things began moving too fast to take them all in at once.

Karris jumped to her feet—and almost collapsed. She was so lightheaded that it took all of her concentration not to fall. She checked herself quickly. There were stinging abrasions on her arms and legs, dress in pathetic shape, but no serious wounds. She touched her eyes. The eye caps were unbroken, of course. *And* smudged with blood so they were harder to see through. Just perfect.

Now that she was in the midst of the battle, the world narrowed. There were images like little paintings, but no whole. Karris saw a drafter up on the Mother's Gate—Izem Blue? What was he doing here? He stood, skin fully blue, both arms extended, shooting blue daggers in rapid succession—an absolutely stunning display to work so fast, keeping his will focused, shooting from both hands. He was like a dozen musketeers—three dozen, despite the hazy quality of the morning's misty sunlight. Everywhere he turned, men went down. He turned toward the Mirrormen, and Karris saw those blue blades shearing off in every direction from the mirror armor, chewing through everyone around the Mirrormen, but sometimes catching a chink or hitting the mirror armor flat enough that a knife punched through.

A body stood in front of Karris, headless, its neck spraying blood in time with the last beats of its heart.

The sound of muskets firing and the roar of blood in her ears melded together, a pulse, life and death twined together.

The Mirrormen surged toward a hole in the wall, perhaps seven paces across. So that was where the explosion had been.

A red drafter—one of King Garadul's Free—had gone mad. He was cackling, throwing pyre jelly on everyone around him. The men splattered with the stuff were shouting in fear. Someone was begging him to stop.

A man was falling off the shattered edge of the wall, slipping, screaming.

Off to one side atop the wall, the sun gleamed off a man's copper hair. Karris's eyes locked on him. Gavin! He leaned close to another man, issued an order. Corvan Danavis. So the man really was a general. And he was here? Gavin clapped the man on the shoulder, and they parted.

Karris turned, remembering the pursuing Mirrormen, perhaps too late.

The leader was twenty paces back, horse surging through the lines, shouting at men to move aside, sword drawn. He was alone, his men cut off behind him by a sudden sideways surge in the line, but he was too close. Karris was unarmed and still wobbly on her feet.

Ten paces away, her pursuer seemed to jump in his saddle. Karris could see the whole front of his body, so he hadn't been shot from the wall, but nonetheless, he tumbled out of his saddle.

Someone had killed the man from behind. What the hell? Karris looked behind the man.

Kip.

Kip? The young man was riding at a full gallop behind the Mirrormen, following the path they'd pushed open through the ranks of soldiers. But he didn't have a musket.

Instead, he was carrying a big green ball, larger than his own head. His skin was green, and he had a wild look in his eyes—and he looked like he was going to tumble out of the saddle at any moment.

Not seeming to care that he was guiding his horse directly into other horses, Kip drew the green globe backward like he was throwing a ball—classic tyro misperception, they always thought that because a ball had mass, you had to muscle it. Kip's arm came forward, and then with an audible pop he shot the green globe out at the Mirrormen.

It caught one in the side of his mirrored helmet. The mirror armor sheared luxin easily, but it still had to deal with the momentum of what was hitting it. A breastplate might withstand a bullet, but the man inside was still going to have some broken ribs. Here, the man's head snapped to the side, blasting him out of the saddle, and the green globe ricocheted off, hitting another Mirrorman's shoulder and not quite dismounting him, then caromed into a third Mirrorman's horse, catching the animal on the side of its head and knocking it off its feet.

The force of the shot blew Kip out of his own saddle, almost halting all of his forward motion. His horse shied, trying not to collide with the others at the last second, but they had been startled by riders falling and a giant green ball flying past their heads, and one dodged directly into its new path. Animal collided with animal at great speed, crunching a Mirrorman's leg that was trapped between them.

Both horses went down, but Karris was more concerned about Kip. She lost sight of him when he fell. Soldiers were still a river, pressing past the Mirrormen, not knowing or caring much what this fight was about. They just wanted to get out of the shadow of these deadly walls and into the city.

Karris snatched a sword off the ground and ducked through the crowd. Three riders had wheeled around and were pushing toward a spot farther back. She couldn't get there in time.

One was drawing his musket from the saddle sheath to kill her when his head exploded in a burst of yellow light and pink mist. Karris was sure this time the shot hadn't come from the wall. It had to have come from the opposite direction—from the hill? And what the hell could have done that? An explosive musket ball?

She was still too far away. She saw two Mirrormen pulling muskets out, aiming down.

Twin green spears—pillars, almost, they were so thick—erupted from the ground where the riders were pointing and impaled them. The first one was hit square in the chest. Green light fractured out in a spray as the mirrored breastplate held for a moment, and then burst—and still the green spear shot up, lifting the Mirrorman up into the air. The other man was no more lucky. That spear hit the top of his breastplate, again shearing some luxin away into a flash of green light. Then the spear rode up, catching him under the chin and going into his head, ripping his helmet off his ruined head like a child popping the head off a dandelion.

Each was lifted several paces into the air before the green luxin spears cracked and dropped them to the ground and dissolved to nothing.

Kip jumped to his feet, looking a lot less dead than he deserved.

Karris arrived a moment later. He gave her a curious look, and she said, "Kip, it's me. Do you recognize me? It's Karris." Despite that astounding display of power, Kip was a new drafter, and the mental and emotional effects of the colors were always greatest when you first started. The wildness of green could make a drafter dangerous.

He lifted a hand quickly and she flinched. "Kip, it's me, Karris," she said, all too aware that there was still a battle going on, though the amount of musket fire from the top of the wall had dwindled to almost nothing.

"Hold still," he said, staring intently at her face. He brought up a single finger and moved it as if to poke her in the eye. She could feel the heat radiating from it. What? Kip was a sub-red, too?

There was a hiss as he touched the eye cap, and he must have hit the fuse point because the eye cap dissolved. Then he did the other.

And like that, Karris could draft again.

Oh, hell yes.

"What do you say?" Kip asked.

What was he talking about? "Thank you?" Karris asked.

"I say we go kill us a king," Kip said, grinning recklessly. When they were in the grip of their color, greens didn't tend to be real big on common sense.

Karris looked and saw that Rask Garadul was just getting to the gap they'd blown in the wall. Half of his men were already through. It was the perfect time to attack—well, other than the fact that Karris and Kip were on the side of the wall with King Garadul's entire army.

Drafting some red off the pools of gore around them, Karris felt the comforting wash of red rage. She felt strong. "Let's go kill us a king," she said.

Chapter 84

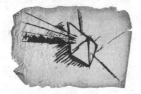

I'm not important enough for this, Liv thought as Lord Omnichrome came back to the top of the hill where she was tied up. From her vantage point, she could see a familiar form taking a big red stallion from a groom, then mounting. Kip. If he turned around, he couldn't help but see her.

For a moment, Liv wasn't sure if she wanted him to see her or not. She had no doubt what he would do if he did. He'd come charging up the hill, and to hell with the odds. That was Kip. That was who he was and who he always had been. Not always smart, but always ferociously loyal.

She ducked her head. There was only death here for Kip. And sure enough, he turned for one second as he sat unsteadily atop the big horse. Then he kicked his heels in and almost tumbled out of the saddle as the animal surged forward.

Liv almost grinned at the sight, but the looming figure of Lord Omnichrome wiped away any thought of amusement. As he came close, she realized he wasn't as big as he seemed from a distance. His white robes and the white cape hanging off great blue horns rising from his shoulders made him seem bigger than a mortal man, but he wasn't even as tall as Gavin Guile. But he glowed. It was like yellow luxin filled his veins instead of blood. His hair had been sculpted into a spiky crown with yellow luxin, so it dazzled, as if he'd been crowned by the sun itself, and his eyes beneath were a constant riot of colors. And he was staring at her.

I'm not important enough for this, she thought again. Her cheek was throbbing, still dribbling blood. The powder wagon's explosion had knocked her unconscious, and shrapnel had cut her in a dozen places. She didn't know how they'd found her among all the bodies. She didn't know why they would want her.

"How did you come to be here, Aliviana Danavis?"

"I walked, mostly," she said. Danavis, so that was it. They knew her father was commanding the enemy army. And she'd stupidly delivered herself into their hands. Well done, Liv.

Lord Omnichrome's retainers surrounded them: broken-haloed drafters of every type, soldiers, messengers, and a few high-ranking officers from King Garadul's camp who looked decidedly uneasy around all the drafters, much less Lord Omnichrome. Lord Omnichrome picked up a strange musket as long as he was tall. He lifted it, fitted its leg into a slot on the barrel, propped it up in front of himself, and aimed down the hill toward the fighting.

"Dead center on that green door," he said.

"Third house from the left?" a spotter asked.

Liv didn't know much about muskets, but she knew you couldn't make a shot that accurate at three hundred paces. Not that you'd want someone shooting in your direction, but past one hundred paces aiming was more a general hope. Nonetheless, Lord Omnichrome took a deep breath, sighted down the barrel through the mists, fired.

The musket roared.

"Three hands high, one hand left," the spotter said.

Lord Omnichrome handed the musket to an attendant, who began reloading it. He turned to Liv. "I want you to join me, Liv. I saw you, last night, listening. You understood. I could tell you did."

Orholam, she thought he'd looked at her, but then she'd dismissed it as her imagination. There had been thousands listening last night. And how did he recognize her?

"You love your father, don't you, Liv?"

"More than anything," she said. How did he know her name, much less her nickname?

"And how old is he?"

"Maybe forty?" she said.

"Old, then. For a drafter. If he weren't a drafter, he could live another forty years. But as a drafter loyal to the Chromeria, he's an old dog already, isn't he? Most men don't make it to forty. Your father must be very disciplined, very strong."

"Stronger than you know," Liv said. She felt a surge of emotion. Who was this bastard, talking about her father? She wouldn't let anyone speak badly of him. He was a great man. Even if he had made mistakes.

The attendant handed the long musket back to Lord Omnichrome. He raised it, stabilized its significant weight on its leg, and said, "Blue drafter, just right of the gatehouse."

Liv watched, horrified, as Lord Omnichrome waited. The blue drafter was ducked behind a crenellation, popping up to throw death down on the men below and ducking down again. He popped up, Lord Omnichrome said, "Heart." The musket roared.

A burst of light and blood and the drafter disappeared from view.

"Shoulder, your left," the attendant said. "One hand left and three thumbs high."

Lord Omnichrome handed the musket back to the man with a polite thank-you. "When the time comes, will you tell them?" he asked Liv.

"Tell them? Tell them about my father?" Liv hesitated. "I'll do what I need to do."

"What you need to do. Interesting how they make it that, isn't it? What if you couldn't make it back to the Chromeria in time? Would you kill your father yourself, with your own hand? What if he asked you to stop? What if he begged you?"

"My father isn't such a coward."

"You're dodging the question." Lord Omnichrome's eyes were swirling orange. Liv had never liked oranges much. Always unnerved her. When she didn't speak for a long moment, he said, "I understand perfectly. When I started my own Chromeria, I followed them blindly at first, too. Despite what I am. One of my students broke the halo and I murdered her with my own hands. She wasn't the first to die for the drafters' ignorance nor the last, but she was the beginning of the end. When I killed her, I knew what I did was wrong. I couldn't shake it."

"Drafters go mad. Like you. They turn on their friends. They kill those they love."

"Oh, absolutely. Sometimes. Some people can't handle power. Some men seem decent until you give them a slave, and soon they're a tyrant, beating and raping the slave in their charge. Power is a test, Liv. All power is a test. We don't call it breaking the halo. We call it breaking the egg. You never know what kind of bird is going to be hatched. And some are born deformed and must be put down. That is tragedy, but not murder. Do you think your father could handle a little extra power? The great Corvan Danavis? An immensely talented drafter who's nevertheless had the discipline to make it to forty?"

"It's not that simple," Liv said.

"What if it is? What if the Chromeria has perpetuated this monstrosity because this is how they keep themselves in power? By scaring the satrapies, saying that only they can train the drafters born among them—for a price, always for a price—and only they can restrain the drafters who go mad, which is all of them. By doing that, they make themselves forever useful, forever powerful, and by divvying out drafters to the satrapies, they make themselves the center of everything. Tell me, Liv, when you judge the Chromeria by its fruit, do you find it a place of love and peace and light—as one might expect from Orholam's holy city?"

"No," Liv admitted. She didn't even know why she was defending it, except out of stubbornness. The Chromeria was everything she hated, and it defiled all it touched. Including her. She owed debts there, and she couldn't lie to herself so much that she would believe her flight to Tyrea and to follow Kip wasn't partly a flight from her debt to Aglaia Crassos and Ruthgar.

"The truth is, Liv, you know I'm right. You're just afraid to admit you've been on the wrong side. I understand. We all do. There are good men and women who fight against us, good people! But they're deluded, deceived. It hurts to leave a lie, but it hurts more to live one.

Look at what I'm doing. I'm freeing a city that's ours, by rights. Garriston has been passed around like a whore to be abused by every nation in turn. It's not right. It has to end, and since no one else will end it, we will. Does not this land deserve freedom? Should these people pay because two brothers—neither of whom was born here or cared a whit for this land—fought here? For how long should they pay?"

"They shouldn't," Liv said.

"Because it isn't just."

He took the long musket from the attendant again. "Red drafter, top of the gatehouse. Head."

Liv watched. The battle in front of the Mother's Gate was hard to see clearly through all the smoke and flashes of magic. But she saw King Garadul's cavalry reaching the gate, loading their muskets and firing at the men at the top of the wall, but seeming to wait for something, frustrated it hadn't happened yet. Lord Omnichrome's musket roared, and an instant later there was a small bright flash at the top of the gate tower. Liv was glad she hadn't seen all of it.

"Dead center, Lord Omnichrome," the attendant announced. "Excellent shot!"

"Begone! Leave us." The top of the hill cleared quickly of everyone save the musket attendant, whom Lord Omnichrome gestured to stay. Lord Omnichrome turned toward Liv. He wasn't smiling. "I don't like killing drafters. I hate it," he said. "What I do here is what must be done. I want you to join me, Aliviana."

"Why? Why me? I'm barely a bichrome, not that powerful, no influence."

He snorted. "Are you ready for the answer to that question? You want to be an adult, Aliviana? You want hard truths? Because that's the only kind I've known for the past sixteen years."

"I'm ready," she said.

"I want you because you're a drafter and every drafter is precious to me. And because you're Tyrean, and this country will take a lot of reassuring after we win, and I'm not Tyrean. And because you're Corvan Danavis's daughter."

"I knew it!" she spat.

"Listen, you half-wit! Listen or you're unworthy of the role I have for you anyway."

That shut her up.

"As Corvan's daughter, I have some hope that you're half as intelligent as he is. If so, you'll be a formidable ally. I need bright leaders. But I won't lie to you. I hope that your coming to our side might free your father from the Chromeria's grip. I suspect that he only serves the Prism because they held you hostage. If that's true, Corvan might come over to us, and having a general of his standing on our side might prevent any further war from even being necessary. That's how much fear your father inspires. Men won't even take the field against him. During the Prisms' War, his enemies would use spyglasses to see which general was directing a battle. If it was your father, they would retreat and fight another day. That's how good your father is, and I'd be a fool to ignore him when he might fight for me. If you think that's me manipulating you, you're right. I'll use you. You're important. The Chromeria will use you too. Already has. Grow up and realize it. I'll be honest about it, that's all. And my honesty gives you a choice. That's better than they'll give you." His eyes were threaded with red and orange, like flames.

He was right. It was true. And if that was true, what if all of it was true?

"King Garadul slaughtered my whole town."

"Yes. He even took some of my drafters and made them help him."

Liv had expected him to deny it, excuse it.

"And yet you'd have me serve him?"

Lord Omnichrome lowered his voice. "Kings don't live forever. Especially reckless ones."

A huge explosion rocked the wall to the left of the gatehouse. It was powerful enough that it threw many of the combatants off their feet, and more than a few people off the wall itself, but as the smoke gradually cleared, to Liv it seemed that the charge must have been planted on the other side of the wall—the damage that she could see there was much more extensive, rows of houses simply obliterated. A cheer went up among the cavalry, though, as the clearing smoke showed a gap blasted in the wall itself.

"You see, the people of Garriston are working with us. They want to be free."

But Liv barely heard him. She'd just seen something through the mists on the battlefield that took her breath away. Kip. And not just Kip. Kip and Karris both were riding into the fray. For a moment, Liv didn't understand. Kip and Karris had switched sides? They were fighting to free Garriston? Then her eyes followed the path they were taking. The path led straight to King Garadul.

King Garadul, who Kip hated for wiping out their town and killing his mother.

And they were being pursued by half a dozen mounted Mirrormen.

"How much am I worth to you?" Liv said.

"I've already told you."

"Then I'm yours, on one condition."

The red swirled out of his eyes, replaced by orange and blue.

"Save my friends. Him, and her. The ones those Mirrormen are after." She pointed.

Lord Omnichrome beckoned his attendant sharply, and the man came running with his long musket. "You wish me to kill several allies in order to gain one," Lord Omnichrome said. "You barter lives like—"

"Like an adult," Liv said sharply.

"And a formidable one indeed. But I'm not in the business of buying loyalty. I'll do my best to save your friends. As a gift, regardless of what you decide." He sighted down his musket and fired. A Mirrorman riding toward Karris died in a flash of light and blood. Lord Omnichrome handed the musket off to be reloaded.

"So take that out of your calculations, Liv, but tell me now, whom will you serve? Me, or the Chromeria?"

Fealty to One. And to one only.

There was no good choice. There were no good guys. Trying to do the right thing had led Liv to spying on her greatest benefactor. The Chromeria corrupted even people's love for each other. Everyone she knew said Lord Omnichrome was a monster, but everyone she knew had been corrupted by the Chromeria. So maybe Lord Omnichrome wasn't perfect. Neither was Gavin. The only people innocent here were the people of Tyrea. They deserved to be free. If Liv had to fight, she wasn't going to fight for their oppressors. Fealty to One? A Danavis had to choose whom she would serve? So be it.

Taking a deep breath, Liv gave a full Tyrean formal curtsey. "Lord Omnichrome," she said, her voice even, her eyes meeting his. "I'm yours. How may I serve?"

Chapter 85

"Traitors!" Kip heard a woman say. His head snapped toward Karris. She spat on the dead Mirrormen. Imperious, masterful.

What is she doing?

Karris grabbed a musket and powder horn and began reloading it, as if she were a simple soldier. When Kip saw the looks on the faces of the soldiers near them, he finally understood. They'd just seen her and Kip fight Mirrormen, but none of the surrounding men knew who was fighting on which side or if they should interfere. It looked like these soldiers had lost all of their officers—not surprising, since the defenders on the wall would try to kill officers first. That was probably the only reason Kip and Karris were still alive.

"Well, drafter?" she said, finishing her reloading. She was as fast at that as she was at everything. Her skin was the color of blood. Her eyes were no longer capped with the violet eye caps that kept her from drafting. Wait, had he done that? He was feeling shaky, drained. Her bluff had worked, though. The soldiers were turning back to the fighting, determined not to get in the way of this virago.

She was talking to him.

That's right, genius, seeing how you're the one who just drafted two huge spikes and impaled a couple of Mirrormen.

Which made Kip look toward the men he'd killed. Mistake. One had a frothy gore-hole in his chest the size of Kip's fist. The other's head was torn in pieces, chunks of white bone mixed amid red in a picture that refused to coalesce into a face.

"Kip, ordinarily this is a bad idea when you're as new as you are, but I want you to draft more green. I need you with me," Karris hissed.

He was staring at the smear of head on the ground. The soldiers pushing toward the gate were trampling right over the pieces of brain and bone, giving more room to the two drafters than they did to the men Kip had killed.

"Kip!" She slapped him, hard. "Cry later. Be a man now." The red diamonds in her emerald eyes blazed. She cursed, cast about for a moment, looking for something, then a few threads of green wove their way from her eyes to her fingertips through the ocean of red that colored her pale skin, and she drafted something small in her hands.

Spectacles. Spectacles entirely of green luxin. She put them on his face, adjusted them, did something to seal them, and then stepped away. "Now draft!" she ordered.

Kip was a sponge. It was like going outside on a hot day, closing his eyes, and basking in the heat. Everywhere he looked there were light-colored surfaces, homes and shops whitewashed against the sun, and every one of them gave him magic. He soaked it in, feeling potent. Free. The throbbing in his burned hand faded to nothing.

He joined the stream of soldiers heading toward the gap in the wall. The musket fire from atop the wall had all but ceased. It was turning into a glorious morning, bright, crisp, slowly burning off the mist. It would be hot soon.

Where before, when he was unmoving, the stream of men had parted around him like a boulder as they saw that he was a drafter, as soon as he joined the stream he was jostled about just like everyone else. The lines compressed the closer they got to the wall, and men trying to stay with their units pushed hard. As it got tighter and tighter, more and more constrained, Kip started to rebel against it. He wasn't sure how much of the agitation was his, and how much was the green luxin's influence on him, but he could tell that there was more to his reaction than his own psyche.

With the confluence of horses and men in armor—though only a small fraction of King Garadul's army was armored or uniformed, those soldiers were intent on going in first—Kip lost sight of King Garadul himself. Karris had slipped into the line in front of him, and she was using her slender form and muscles to slip in between rows and push forward. Kip soon lost sight of her too. It was all he could do to keep on his feet as the crowd packed tight together right at the wall.

"You!" someone shouted.

Kip looked. A horseman, ten paces away, was staring at him. Kip had no idea who the man was.

"You!" the officer repeated. "You're not one of us!"

At first, Kip had no idea who the man was. He thought maybe it was one of the soldiers who'd escorted him with Zymun after Kip had blown up the fire. But even that was only a guess. Unfortunately, it didn't matter. The man recognized him.

The officer tugged at his musket, trying to pull it from the saddle sleeve, but there were other horses pressing in on either side of him, and it was stuck.

"Spy! Traitor!" the officer shouted, pointing at Kip. "He doesn't have the sleeves! He's not one of us! Murderer! Spy! That green drafter is a spy!"

Kip had been pushed up the rubble pile to the gap in the wall itself. It put him at a high point. Everyone was able to see him.

The officer finally pulled his musket free and kicked his horse savagely to come after Kip. Turned backward looking at the man, not really believing he would fire into a crowd of his compatriots, Kip lifted his hands to draft something, anything. His foot slid on the rubble, and the surging crowd, some pulling away, some reaching toward him, threw him off balance. He went down in stages. The people were packed so tight that he didn't fall all at once, but neither could he stop himself once he started.

The gap in the wall vomited them into Garriston. Kip fell and rolled.

Someone stepped on his burned left hand. He screamed. Feet were hitting his sides, someone tripped over him, someone stepped on his belly, someone kicked the side of his head. He tumbled, rolling down the slight hill of rubble, tried to gain his feet, and got smacked with the stock of a musket. He ended up on his back, head ringing, left hand on fire with pain, eyes having trouble focusing. Without meaning to, he'd gone turtle again, as he had when Mistress Helel had tried to kill him—and again, he was about as effective as a turtle on its back.

It was like the world knew Kip needed to take the coward's way, and it conspired together to land him here.

The next thing he knew, there were people on every side of him, kicking, kicking. Some were trying to slam musket butts down on him, but there were so many people packed in so tightly around him that he only felt a few glancing blows on his legs. Back in the old days, he would have rolled over on his stomach and buried his head in his hands, rolled into a ball and waited until Ram had asserted his superiority again and tired of the game and left him. Doing that here would be death.

Do you expect me to take a whipping lying down?

Yes, Kip. It's your way.

You expect me to die lying down?

Face it, Kip, you're not much of a fighter, not when it matters. Why don't you curl up in a ball and quit?

Part of him expected Karris to save him. She was a fighter. A warrior. A drafter. She was quick and decisive, nimble and deadly with magic or blade.

The crowd was like a beast, a seething, teeming, roaring mass that had lost all individuality. And Kip hated it. He ducked his head as someone tried to stomp on him. He saw leering faces. Brief images of snarling mouths. Visages twisted with hatred.

Part of him expected Ironfist to save him. The man had swept in out of nowhere twice before and done that. Ironfist was huge, strong, intimidating. He was as quiet and as unmoving as steel. A guardian.

Part of him expected Liv to save him. Why not? She'd come in at the last minute to save him from the assassin Mistress Helel.

Part of him expected Gavin to save him. What good was a Prism if he couldn't save his own bastard? Gavin was here. Somewhere. He

had to be close. He had to know the wall had been breached. He had
to be hurrying here even now.

A kick caught Kip in the kidney, sending lances of pain through
his whole body. As he lurched, a fist caught him in the face. His head
bounced off the stones. Blood shot out of his nose, drenching his
mouth and chin.

No one was coming. Like when his mother had locked him in a
cupboard when he was eight years old because he'd complained or
talked too much or—he didn't even remember what he'd done wrong.
He just remembered the look of disgust on her face. She despised
him. She threw his soup at him and locked the door and went out to
get high. And forgot about him. Because he was worthless.

After a day, the rats had come. He woke to one licking the dried
soup off his neck. Its little claws dug into his chest, its weight terrify-
ingly heavy. He'd screamed, jumped to his feet, thrashed. Screamed
and screamed, and no one heard. That rat ran away, but soon, in the
darkness, more had come. They dropped into his hair, bit his bare
toes, scrambled up his pant legs. They were everywhere. Dozens of
them. Hundreds, for all he knew. He'd screamed until his throat was
raw, thrashed and hit at them until his hands were bleeding, twisted
his ankle on some old boxes crammed into the cupboard. And no one
had come.

His mother had found him on the morning of the third day, curled in
a ball, head tucked in his arms, whimpering, dehydrated, long bloody
wounds all over his head, shoulders, back, and legs, not even trying to
dislodge the rats covering him like a cloak. There were a dozen dead
rats with him and more live ones. She'd given him water, eyes haze-
glazed, begrudgingly cleaned his wounds with the last of her harsh
lemon liquor, and then wandered out to find more haze. All without a
word. She seemed to have forgotten it all when he next saw her. He still
had scars on his shoulders, back, and butt where the rats had bitten him.

No one's coming, Kip. Another kick. You always were a disappointment. Another kick. A failure. Kick. You're not good at anything. Kick.

"Enough! Enough!" someone shouted. The officer finally pushed
through the crowd, carrying his musket. "Move back!" he shouted.

He hefted the musket, pointing it at Kip's head.

What can I do? Draft little green balls? Fine.

Kip drafted a green ball and threw it up into the yawning barrel, willed it to stay.

The officer pulled the trigger. A moment, then the musket exploded in his hands. The breech of the musket blew out, throwing flaming black powder into the man's face, setting his beard alight. He screamed, fell back.

"Kill him!" someone shouted.

Kip saw steel being drawn on all sides, flashes of the sun on blades. And he started laughing. Because he was good at something.

He was good at taking punishment. He was a turtle. Or maybe a bear. A turtle-bear. Orholam, he was an idiot. He laughed again, slapping his hands to his shoulders as he lay on the ground. Green luxin jetted out, covering him like he'd seen it cover the green wight back in Rekton.

As Kip watched, a sword descended and hacked into the green luxin over his arm. It cut in two finger's breadths, but the luxin was thicker. It stopped, quivering like an ax in wood. Kip flipped over, pulling in more green from every light surface, not even knowing how he did it, pulling and pulling, drafting light from Orholam's endless tap.

It filled him with that same wildness. Wildness chained, hemmed in, trapped. The luxin covering him grew thicker. Kip gathered his feet beneath himself and stood, roaring.

He was crazy. He was crazy, and he felt great. He smashed a green forearm into a wide-eyed man holding a sword. It flung the man back. Kip paused for a second, and spikes sprouted from his green armor everywhere. He threw his weight back and forth, crashing into the crowd like they were rats to smash against cupboard walls.

Blood was flying in red ropes. Kip wasn't human anymore. He was an animal, unwilling to be caged. He was a mad dog. Some dim, thinking part of him thought that he shouldn't have been able to move so well with such a heavy suit on him. He was strong, but not this strong.

He had no sense of the battle beyond the little circle around him.

Even that was a blur—sharp motions to the left and right, gleams of light off blades and rising muskets to be crushed before they could fire. He slashed and hacked and pounded with unreasoning fury. He could hold only one thought: I will not be stopped.

In moments, or hours, Kip had no notion of time—he saw fear in every eye. A continual flood of men spilled in through the gap, thrust forth hard by the mass of bodies behind them, all pushing them forward and into Kip, but his very presence was slowing the flood, men pushing back as soon as they saw him, others leaping to the sides, hoping to avoid his fury.

Their weakness inflamed him further. Like rats willing to bite in the darkness but scattering in the light, they were cowards. He clubbed them, smashing heads, ripping open bellies. He charged the gap where they couldn't flee, impaled them, flung gore left and right.

A thought won through his brain. Among all the shouting and screams and fear and mist and musket fire and clash of arms, someone was screaming a word: "Kip! Kip! King Garadul! That way!"

Kip couldn't see who was shouting. He stretched, found himself taller, the luxin swirling under his feet, boosting him several hand's breadths. Looking into the city, he saw Karris, skin red and green entwined, holding a sword, pointing it deeper into the city still.

King Garadul was rallying his Mirrormen around him there, pulling them together after they'd been separated coming through the gap. He was screaming orders. Seemed furious about something. Hadn't seen Kip.

Before he even knew what he was doing, Kip was charging, all his will focused, intent, implacable. This one thing remained: King Garadul had to pay for what he'd done. He had to die.

Chapter 86

When Gavin heard the explosion, he knew immediately what it was. He was almost back to the wall on his way from the docks, where he'd been using the first light to help draft boats for the refugees. The evacuation was entirely possible if people would be reasonable. Gavin had told the city's elders that nobles could bring three chests, armorers and apothecaries could bring three as well, rich merchants could bring two, and everyone else could only bring what they could carry.

It was a simple rationale, if a hard one. The fleeing Tyreans would need medicine, and they didn't want to leave any arms that King Garadul could use to arm his troops and spread his aggression. And though it stuck in Gavin's throat to help the rich more than the poor, the rich would bring their riches out of the city. Those riches, if left, would again be used by King Garadul and would help him kill others. If people did everything according to orders, there would still be room for everyone to escape who wanted to.

Except, of course, everyone cheated. Everyone. Nobles brought six chests. Rich merchants brought five. Others lied and claimed to be armorers or apothecaries who were not.

Gavin put a local guild head in charge, went to draft on the barges, and when he came back found the man letting his own guild members bring extra baggage. Gavin drafted a scaffold off the side of the pier in five seconds, and had the man strangling on it in ten. He put someone else in charge before the first man was dead.

"Make decisions fast and as justly as you can," Gavin told the deeply frowning, pockmarked cooper he was putting in charge. "And my whole authority is behind you, even if you make mistakes. Take one bribe, and I'll take my time making your death as much worse than this as I can imagine." Then he left. He didn't have time for this.

He was at the base of the wall when he heard the explosion. It was exactly what he'd been afraid of. It had been why he'd drafted Bright-water Wall in the first place. With all the homes and shops built directly against the city wall, it was hard to defend from enemies out-side, but impossible to defend from enemies within. Anyone who owned a shop could be given barrels of black powder, tunnel under the wall a little bit, and set a charge. They could work in full privacy, uninterrupted—could, and had.

Blackguards in tow, Gavin dug his heels into his horse's flanks. But he didn't head for the gap. A hole in the wall was a prize, of course, but it would immediately attract defenders, and it might not be big enough for the army to come through. It might become a choke point, a killing zone. Better to use the distraction of a breach in the walls to open a gate elsewhere.

Gavin dispatched messengers to the Hag's Gate and the Lover's Gate and headed toward the Mother's Gate. At the top of the wall, he ran into General Corvan Danavis with his entourage. Doubtless, Corvan was going to direct the defense at the breach in the wall personally.

Corvan paused only to say, "They're holding back their drafters and color wights. I don't know why. But if we lose a gate in the next twenty minutes, we won't make it until noon." That was Corvan, condensing the information to the absolutely vital.

"If it falls," Gavin said, "be at the ships an hour before noon."

Corvan nodded his head. No fighting to the death. Gavin clapped Corvan's shoulder. Then the general was gone.

At the top of the gate, Gavin looked over the teeming mass on the other side. Hardly anyone was firing at the invaders from the wall anymore, but the army pushed forward like a blind beast, black fin-gertips reaching up to grab the wall.

Many of the homes outside the wall had been demolished in just a few hours, but of those that remained, the army had found which places were easiest to scale. At half a dozen places, a slow trickle of men were clambering up onto the wall itself and engaging the few defenders.

Farther out, King Garadul's men were setting up their mortars. Too late, really. There was no point in them bombarding the city at all, and doing so now would probably kill as many of their own as it would kill defenders. Nonetheless, they were already loading the mortars. Gavin had found that lots of men liked to be safe from the fighting, but they wanted to be able to say they'd taken part. Those idiots would fire some rounds and later brag how they'd turned the battle.

Good to see that King Garadul's got discipline problems too.

And where was the king?

From the gate's highest point, looking back into the city, Gavin spied him despite the mists. King Garadul had pressed into the city himself. Idiot! Sure, Gavin had done the same more than once, but he was armed like few others. Gavin's presence on a battlefield wasn't simple morale-boosting. King Garadul was leading the attack, sur-rounded by perhaps a hundred Mirrormen. As Gavin caught sight of him, he saw the king yelling at some messenger, gesticulating angrily.

He wants his drafters.

And why isn't he getting them?

Gavin moved to the front of the Mother's spear, stared out to the hill, some five hundred paces away. On the crown of the hill there were banners and a crowd. He drafted lenses, adjusted the distance necessary between the two to get the focus right, and studied the image above the low-hanging mists. A multicolored man was lifting a musket, pointing it right at him. Insanity. No musket could fire so—

The musket fired—a huge charge from the cloud of black smoke. Gavin couldn't hear it over the rest of the sounds of battle, of course. One of the mortars fired. Gavin continued to study the man. He drafted the two lenses together to keep the focus steady. A poly-chrome wight. Probably a full polychrome, or at least pretending to be one, from all the colors he'd drafted into his own body. Curious. The man was studying him too.

Around Lord Omnichrome, there were not just the usual complement of generals and lackeys, but dozens of drafters. They were clearly not going anywhere.

Someone handed the musket back to Lord Omnichrome. Lord Omnichrome took the musket, aimed quickly, and fired. A second later, something hit the Mother's spear two paces above Gavin's head and exploded, taking a chunk out of the rock. Luxin projectiles? From five hundred paces? Gavin was still thinking about it as the Blackguards pulled him away and to the back of the spear.

Lord Omnichrome wanted King Garadul dead. So simple, so bold. He probably had even egged on King Garadul at Brightwater Wall, daring him to be a promachos, getting the young king to lead from the front, hoping he'd get killed.

If your enemy wants it, deny it.

Gavin drafted a small yellow tablet, making it read, "Capture Garadul, not kill. At all costs." He covered it in blue and liquid yellow luxin and shot it into the path where he believed Corvan was going.

But Gavin's intuition told him the main strike was going to happen elsewhere, while the defenders focused their efforts here. "To the Hag's Gate," he told his Blackguards. "We run!"

Chapter 87

Karris snatched a second sword from a man lying on the ground, bleeding from a stomach wound. She didn't know what side he was fighting for; she didn't care. The city smelled of gunpowder, sewage, and men's sweat, the kind of stench that gets into leather armor and never comes out. As she ran, she drafted a thin sheen of green luxin down the swords, sealed it, then ran red luxin on top of that and sealed that too.

This entire area was a tangle of alleys. The buildings were thrown down haphazardly with seeming intent to vex one's neighbors and make straight lines of sight impossible. The good news was that it made it impossible for King Garadul to rally his men in any numbers here.

The bad news was that—oh shit! Karris rounded a corner and almost ran into three Mirrormen, lost, peering down different alleys and looking like they were about to start arguing which way to go. Karris careened into them before any of them could react. She threw her weight into the smallest one and, catching him flat-footed, managed both to stop herself and to fling him off his feet. She spun, left sword swinging in a red arc.

The second Mirrorman was moving his sword into guard position, but too slowly, with no leverage. Her blade beat right through his and cut into his neck above his gorget. Not a deep cut, but deep enough, right there. Red luxin splattered on the outside of his armor, and as she yanked the blade back, red blood splattered the inside to match. He was still standing for the moment, but to Karris he was already dead.

Between colliding with the first Mirrorman and cutting the second, Karris had lost sight of the last one. She spun around, ducking, blocking with both swords, left down, right up in a reversed grip. The cut would have beaten right through her weak right-hand guard if she hadn't ducked too. Instead, her own blade slapped into her shoulder. She couldn't tell if it cut—what kind of moron went into battle without armor?

She came up cutting, but the Mirrorman blocked her strike. Then his eyes went wide. A low red flush of light washed them both. His sword had struck sparks off of hers, setting the red luxin aflame— and not only on her sword. Where the two blades had met, his sword had scraped off red luxin too, and the same sparks had set his alight. She'd intended the flames for later, but it worked as well for now.

Karris swung her right-hand, flaming sword in a quick arc and stabbed the Mirrorman in the face with her left.

If you're going to wear heavy armor, never open the visor while you're in battle.

She kicked him off her blade in a spray of broken teeth and exhaled blood, spun again, and saw the Mirrorman she'd collided with and sent sprawling crawling for his blade. She stomped on his hand as he lunged for it, and punched her blade through the mirror armor. It took a strong, direct strike to push through plate, but she'd practiced it a hundred times with the Blackguard, who trained assuming assassins would bear every advantage, including mirror armor.

Pulling the blade free again, she quickly wiped the last of the flaming red luxin off the sword with one of the men's cloaks and reapplied the red luxin. She'd set herself alight if she wasn't careful. She lifted a sturdy bow and a half-empty quiver from one of the dead.

Now where the hell was she? And where was Kip?

Karris had taken a shortcut, she thought. She knew there was a market on the south side of the city, and she'd thought she remembered roughly where it was. She'd pointed Kip after King Garadul hoping he would wreak some havoc by following, which would allow her to circle behind the king and kill him.

Maybe it had been a bad choice. Orholam, she'd abandoned Kip. A baby drafter.

Not that she could have done much to help him. At the Chromeria, they called what Kip had done going green golem. At one time, they had taught it as a war magic. No longer.

There were three problems with going green golem. First, you couldn't seal the green luxin. If you did, you couldn't move. Some drafters got around that by making big sealed plates and just holding the joints in open green. What Kip was doing was much harder. He was holding all the magic at once. It took enormous focus, and the armor was only as hard as his will. If someone broke his focus, he'd lose his armor instantly. Second, using that much green luxin burned out drafters fast. In the False Prism's War, Karris had heard of green drafters breaking the halo after going green golem only three or four times. Third, you had to be strong as a bull. The suit—the armor, the golem, whatever it was—had weight. For the drafter, it was less because their will took part of the weight, but they still had to move an enormous hunk of luxin. That said, using open green in the legs did mean that a skilled user could make enormous bounds, and once they got moving, they were nearly impossible to stop.

It all meant that Kip was more likely to get himself killed than anything. And Karris had abandoned him. Damn it. What kind of woman abandons a child?

Karris double-checked the position of the sun from the shadows. The sun was still low in the sky and these alleys were swaddled in shadows and mist. As she looked up, she was struck by it. The rooftops rose from the mists like distant, square mountain peaks reigning over the clouds. Then she saw the retreat flares. It was the color Gavin or the Blackguards were supposed to use, and she was sure that was how he was using them now. But retreat to where?

The docks. They knew they were going to lose the city. They were just trying to make King Garadul pay as heavy a price as possible.

Karris didn't have much time to make sure that price was the ultimate price.

She ran into an empty house—she was pretty sure all the houses were empty here. Pushing past the leavings of chickens and several dogs, and one live skinny cow—lots of people brought their animals inside during the night, both for safety and to warm the house—she found the stairs, ran up to the family's quarters, which had been hurriedly emptied, and found the ladder to the roof.

The square, squat houses of Garriston all had these flat roofs. The roof became a third room for most families. A perfect place to cool down on the hot, long summer evenings, the commoners' only chance of catching a breeze off the Cerulean Sea. The buildings were packed tight, but by no means uniform. Not every building was three stories, and even of the many that were, the stories were different heights.

All the same, as Karris reached the roof, for one moment she was struck by the beauty of the scene. The whitewashed roofs, little squares and rectangles, gleaming in the sun, with mist curling up around every edge, churches and a few mansions rising like mountains out of the clouds, and the Travertine Palace dominating everything. Farther south, she could just see Brightwater Wall, like a golden belt around the city. Nearer, there was black smoke rising from the city wall, flashes of magic from the gates.

She shut it out. Found the market she'd been heading for. With the mist, she couldn't see enough to tell if her guess had been correct.

You've already bet Kip's life on this course, might as well see if it pays off.

Cursing herself for a fool, Karris drafted a green weapon harness, sheathed both blades on her back, messed with the harness for a second to get it to set right with the quiver and bow, cursed the torn, tight sleeves on her dress, cursed her muscular shoulders, and tore the sleeves off. She breathed. Then she sprinted to the edge of the roof and leapt.

The houses here were so close, it was an easy jump. Some homes even had planks between them so neighbors could visit each other. So long as she didn't want to cross the street, it was easy going. She ran as fast as she could. One street to clear, then another block of houses, then the market. Her eyes bounced back and forth as she approached the larger gap of crossing the street.

There! One of the houses on the other side had a significantly lower roof. Karris veered left and leapt, passing over the heads of thirty or forty Mirrormen. She hit the lower roof, rolled, popped to her feet just in time to have to leap again—to a higher roof. She hit the next roof with one foot extended. She pushed up, trying to push herself just a little higher but not stop her forward momentum.

Her body popped up, but not forward enough. She landed with half of her torso on flat, whitewashed stucco, then slid down, scrambling, trying to find purchase.

She dropped to her fingertips, on dirty, cracked, crumbling stucco. She swung sideways, lost one handhold for a second as the stucco ripped away. She latched her hand back onto the roof, a clean grip this time, and swung back the other way. Her foot reached the edge, tearing the slit of her dress up even higher. She pulled herself up quickly, not trusting that the rest of the stucco wouldn't crumble at any moment.

No time to be elated at being alive. Karris checked her swords and bow, glanced once down at the twenty-foot drop onto an uneven surface below—a broken leg there if she'd fallen, at least. Then she ran again.

She reached a roof overlooking the market and stopped. King Garadul was coming, with hundreds of Mirrormen and a few drafters—and Kip was hot on their heels. Literally.

This was going to get messy.

Karris smiled.

Chapter 88

Kip was on fire. Someone had doused him in red luxin and lit him up.

It didn't stop him. He simply thickened the green that encased him so the red wouldn't burn through. The pyre jelly stuck to the green. He couldn't rub it away from his face, it was glued in place, implacable. But he could move the green luxin itself, so he made it swirl outward, until his eyes were clear and he could see again. Using the same technique, he swirled all of the pyre jelly to his arms and shoulders, then along his sides, so he was outlined in flame. It all took only a few moments. He thought it, and the luxin did it. Or more precisely, he willed it, and it happened.

The wildness within him was so strong that he wanted to break free of the city and run away. But he wouldn't allow it. He harnessed the wildness. The wildness would serve him. It would help him destroy the man who held the lash and the leash, the man who wanted to control him: King Garadul.

He wasn't sure that he was going the right way, but he followed the flow of King Garadul's soldiers. Kip himself was like a beacon, burning as he was in the misty morning. But the light made his vision lousy. It was like holding a torch: if you held it over your head, you might see into the darkness, but if you held it between yourself and the darkness, you weren't going to see anything at all. Kip *was* the torch. He couldn't see much, and he didn't care. He could see the men streaming away from him, some of them seeing him and just running like hell, but others seemed to be running toward something. A meeting place, a rallying point. Where King Garadul would be.

Kip barreled around a corner into the backs of half a dozen soldiers. They hadn't seen him and he couldn't stop. He ran right over them in a mess of screams and burning flesh and curses and blood and a struggle just to keep from falling as he stepped on body parts. He swung his arms in big sweeping motions, fire and blood and blades unleashed into a crowd.

And it was a crowd. Kip had made it. There were hundreds of soldiers here. He could see dim flashes of the winking armor of the Mirrormen on the other side of the square. Then he was subsumed, folded into the loving arms of battle. There was no morning mist. No counting of his foes. No deciphering the shouts of his enemies into plain language, orders that might help him know what was coming. There was only the roar coming from Kip's own throat, the hammering of his own heart, the pulsing life that was his magic. There was only the burning in his muscles, the resistance his arm felt as a bladed arm cut into a man's torso, and the freedom as he pulled it all the way through.

The world closed in on Kip. He could barely see, barely turn his neck within the green armor. It drove him crazy. He needed freedom. He couldn't be trapped. He was an animal. He crashed through ranks of soldiers as they formed against him. His sweeping arms snapped spears like nothing. He bludgeoned heads with his closed fists. Tore men off his back and snapped their spines in his hands.

Then, abruptly, the ranks parted in front of him. All except one man, who didn't move aside in time, and Kip saw two rows of ten musketeers each. The first row was kneeling, the second row standing, all muskets pointed at him. Someone shouted, his voice a command. And Kip saw the one soldier between him and the musketeers. The man heard too, and understood. Kip saw the panic on his face.

The musketeers loosed a volley. Fire and smoke leaped like a pouncing, snarling lion from their muskets. Kip saw the soldier cut down, even as he steeled himself against the blast.

The musket balls hit him like a fist, many striking at the same time, and a few instants behind the first, carrying him like a punch's follow-through. He was swept off his feet.

A cheer went up. Kip's head swam and he felt the green luxin going soft all around him.

No! I can take punishment. That's my gift. That's my talent.

A musketeer ran over to Kip, pointed a blunderbuss at his head. Something streaked by the man's head—an arrow?—but missed. Kip grabbed the yawning mouth of the blunderbuss and pulled it to himself, stuck it right to his forehead, and pressed green luxin down the barrel. The man pulled the trigger and the breech exploded.

Kip jumped to his feet with inhuman strength. He stomped on the screaming musketeer and looked at himself. He could see the lead musket balls, flattened, inside his green armor. Like they'd shot a tree. The bullets had penetrated, but been stopped. Kip laughed, damn near insane. He was bulletproof.

Ignoring the musketeers, several of whom were running away while the rest were reloading furiously, fumbling with their ramrods and powder horns, trying to ready another shot, Kip looked for King Garadul. These men were no threat. They couldn't bind him. But he couldn't see. So he pulled green luxin around him and made himself taller. Simple.

And there he was. Surrounded by his Mirrormen, King Garadul was mounted, shouting at a drafter beside him, pointing at Kip. The drafter's skin was bright blue, but even as she gathered her magic, something streaked out of the sky. The woman's hands opened limply and blue poured out of her, puddled on the ground. She toppled out of her saddle.

King Garadul stopped in midsentence, looked around. The drafter on his other side, a red, fell out of her saddle. This time Kip—and all the Mirrormen—followed the arrow's path back to its source. Up on a rooftop. Karris, skinny, muscular, bloody, wearing a torn dress and already drawing another arrow. One of the Mirrormen tackled King Garadul out of his saddle. Karris's third arrow cracked a Mirrorman's greave and pinned his leg into his horse. The stallion went crazy, bolting, knocking down half a dozen men and trampling them before it tripped and rolled over on the Mirrorman.

Kip ignored the havoc. He had his target now. He could feel his strength ebbing. He had to do this now. There would be no second chance. He bulled forward, men and women dodging out of his way, slowly reaching full speed.

I'm crazy.

Kip laughed. If this was insanity, so be it. He collided with the first ranks of Mirrormen before they had all recovered from looking for Karris. Some were turned, some were mounted, others had dismounted, some were still drawing or reloading muskets to fire at the rooftop assassin. Kip bowled over a horse, smashed men, deflected weak strikes.

Swinging one big luxin fist, he crushed a Mirrorman's helmet, but the blow also sheared off half of Kip's green hand. Elsewhere, he saw that the spikes and blades he'd drafted onto his body had been cut or broken off where it collided with mirror armor. He smashed left and right, but even as he crushed men, his armor was disintegrating. He was hacking parts of himself off with every blow he inflicted.

The Mirrormen, recovering, formed up behind the front row. Kip burst through the row and found himself staring at dozens of pistols, all roaring. It knocked him back once more, even though he braced himself. He felt hot lines against his skin—the luxin was thinner now. Some of the shots must have gotten through.

I will not fail. Not now. Not so close. Damn it, where's the king?

Kip lashed out at the nearest Mirrorman, shooting a ball of green luxin at the man. It hit the Mirrorman's chest and split in half, gobs of green luxin flying off in either direction, leaving no more damage than if Kip had thumped the man's chest lightly with his fist, scored only because a musket ball had been carried unintentionally inside the green luxin Kip had thrown.

The rest of the Mirrormen dropped their muskets and drew sharp, mirror-bright swords as one. Kip was looking at his chest, studded with those flattened musket balls suspended in green luxin, some of them surrounded by blood where they had cut him. He was drawing in more luxin to replenish his armor and he saw the little balls swirling around like little boats under a waterfall.

Luxin doesn't hurt? How about lead?

Kip drew one of the lead balls up from his chest into his hand. He extended his hand and shot out a tiny ball of green luxin carrying the musket ball with all his will.

A little hole lined in green goo appeared in one of the Mirrormen's chest plates. His mirror armor cracked in splintery, spidery lines around the hole, and then crimson blood joined the emerald luxin and he toppled backward.

It was like Orholam had breathed new life into Kip. He was exhausted, broken, elated, and free. He was laughing again. Totally insane. Totally unstoppable. Lead bullets swirled through his armor and into his palms and he fired them like he was a musket himself. The weight of green armor, which had been so crippling before, now allowed him to shoot the little bullets so hard that if he had been doing it without the armor it would have bowled him over.

He extended right hand, left hand, right hand, left. Shooting everywhere. At each place, men died. Kip wasn't accurate in the least, but this close, he didn't need accuracy. He pointed at a chest and might hit a neck or a belly or someone else in the second rank. Either way, it killed, and ranks disappeared before him. He emptied all the musket balls from his chest and found more in his back and arms, and new ones added every moment. He cut a gory path through the Mirrormen. He couldn't see King Garadul, but he figured that wherever the resistance was greatest was probably the right way. Nothing good is easy.

Through the ranks and chaos, Kip saw a flash of something. Royal garments. Garadul.

He burst through just as King Garadul was pulled up onto a platform at the back of the market square. His men were trying to hustle him down some narrow alley there. Kip bounded forward, and found that his green luxin legs bounced him much farther than he'd intended. He landed between King Garadul and the alley, crushing two of the king's men, including his last drafter. The ground was littered with dead drafters, but Kip didn't care how they'd died. He had eyes only for the king. He extended a hand behind him and shot out a dozen musket balls toward the remaining Mirrormen.

King Garadul tripped over a body on the platform. In an instant,

Kip was on top of him. He kicked at Kip. Kip brought a big fist down and broke the king's leg like kindling. The man screamed. Kip grabbed his head, latching big luxin fists together on either side and lifting. The rattle of musket fire stopped. Kip was too close to the king; no one would dare.

"You killed my mother!" Kip shouted in the king's face.

The king's eyes focused on Kip's face within the green armor. "You?" he said. "Lina's brat? She's not worthy of vengeance and you know it."

"Kip!" Someone was shouting, but Kip barely heard it. The king was trying to draw a bich'hwa from his belt, but he was in too much pain.

"Go to hell!" Kip screamed. "You go to hell!" He lifted the king high and squeezed with all his strength and all his will.

"Kip! Stop! This is just what Lord Omnichrome wants—"

Nothing could penetrate the madness, the sheer fury. Kip wasn't even sure whether it was more at this man for massacring his village or at his mother. He loved her. He hated her.

King Garadul screamed and Kip screamed and together they drowned out Corvan Danavis's scream. Kip's hands clapped together and the king's head popped like a grape, like a watermelon dropped from a great height, splattering juice all over.

"Kip! No! It's just what they want you to do!" Corvan Danavis's voice penetrated Kip's iron skull as he dropped the king's limp corpse onto the platform.

Looking up, stunned, Kip saw Corvan Danavis, mounted at the head of perhaps a hundred men riding into the square. The invaders, already broken and leaderless without King Garadul, scattered at the sight of so many fresh soldiers.

Kip heard a body fall behind him, and turned to see a Mirrorman with an arrow in his heart. Someone had saved him. Again. He hadn't even seen the man. His brain was swimming. He felt like he was shrinking. He was standing on his own feet again, the green luxin was gone. He tottered, and felt someone steady him on his feet. He turned. Karris had come down from the roofs and was taking the bich'hwa from the king's body. Karris? He'd meant to save her, hadn't he?

That turned out well.

He looked at King Garadul's body and felt nothing but emptiness. When he looked up, Corvan Danavis was there, swearing. Kip had never heard Master Danavis swear.

"Do you have any idea what you've just done?" Corvan asked.

"Go to hell," Kip said, empty, dry, lifeless. "He killed our whole town. He deserved worse."

Corvan stopped and looked at Kip with a new respect in his eyes. He didn't say anything for a moment, then said, "Mount up. We have to get out of the city. Now."

"But I killed him. Don't we win?" Kip asked. His head felt so thick and fuzzy. And the light was hurting his eyes. He wanted nothing so much as a blanket and a dark room. They had won, hadn't they? "Why do we have to go?"

"Look at that," Karris said, coming close. She was already mounted. She was pointing toward the wall.

Lord Omnichrome stood on top of the Mother's Gate, perhaps four hundred paces distant, and when he spoke, through some trick of magic, they could hear him perfectly. "They've killed King Garadul! Avenge the king! Drive out the foreigners!"

The gate opened, revealing hundreds of drafters—*hundreds*— and dozens of color wights. They were followed by thousands more soldiers.

"That's why," Karris said.

Chapter 89

Gavin's intuition was wrong.

On arriving at the Hag's Gate, he'd become like a man trying to plug a leaky hull with his fingers and toes. He could only reach so far. He and the Blackguards had held the Hag's Gate alone, with no other support, against thousands of soldiers, for ten minutes now. At this point he could hold it by simply standing here behind the bullet shield his Blackguards had drafted in front of him.

They weren't fighting him. Everywhere he went, the army facing him withdrew. If the city had only had one gate, that might have been helpful. But with three gates and a crumbling three-quarters circle for a wall, it was hopeless. No one would face him. They simply sent men around the sides and waited. If he held these men up for long, the armies would simply enter through the other gates. By this time surely all the gates had fallen.

So his enemy was canny. He wasn't wasting his men throwing them against Gavin. Time would deliver the victory into his hands, so he was preserving his strength. No need to rush the victory. Send the men around Gavin and advance everywhere but where Gavin was. Then Gavin would either be rendered totally ineffectual, dashing from one place to another fighting men who melted away, or he would become separated from the main body of his army—at which point Lord Omnichrome would throw away as many lives as he needed to to kill him. Or capture him.

The campaigner in Gavin was furious. During the war, he would have gone for the throat. They wanted to melt in front of him? He would have gone for the king and killed him and let the chips fall where they may. Doing such a thing would put him in the most peril possible, but he wouldn't have cared. Which is why fortune favors the young. He snorted. If he got killed, the refugees wouldn't make it two leagues out of the harbor.

Cursing, Gavin drafted the retreat flares and shot them high into the sky.

"Any news from the docks?" he asked.

"No, sir."

Gavin hadn't expected any messengers to be able to find him, but it still would have been nice. "Let's go."

A red Blackguard laid down a thick carpet of red luxin across the broken opening of the gate and set fire to it as Gavin turned and started jogging. They'd lost their horses earlier, and hadn't grabbed any replacements. Horses that weren't trained to musket fire and magic were often as dangerous to their riders as they were useful. Being mounted also made you a nicer target for muskets and drafters. The city wasn't that big, they'd run.

Odd, running through an empty city. Almost everyone was simply gone, and there wasn't yet that air of abandonment and layer of dust that settled over cities soon after their inhabitants had left. Garriston was the kind of empty that happened when people left food burning on the fire and simply ran. The burnt smell hadn't even dissipated yet. In fact, they were lucky no one had burned the city down. Empty alleys. Empty homes. Little potted flowers abandoned in windowsills and not yet withered.

Death will come for you too, little flower.

They made it to one of the bridges when the ambush was sprung. Two dozen drafters and several color wights popped up from the roofs and began hurling magic. No hesitation, no warning. Of course. They'd circled Gavin to cut off the most obvious route out. The flat roofs gave them an excellent platform from which to attack, and the open area of the bridge made a perfect killing field.

But the Blackguards were Blackguards. Every one of them knew his task and how the tasks would shift depending on which of them were killed. They practiced for this. This is what they were. Shields of green luxin, blue luxin, and more green luxin, three layers thick, enfolded Gavin. He knew exactly where they would land, and each shield had holes in it, so that he could fight too.

He stuck a hand outside of his shield and pointed at every one of the attackers he could see. He shot narrow tendrils of superviolet luxin at them, sticking it to each drafter, leaving dangling ropes of superviolet. Two of the Blackguards were superviolet/blue bichromes. Their first action was to shield Gavin, second to shield themselves, and third—if possible—this. They could see Gavin's superviolet threads, and they drafted blue along those shining paths as they pulled grenadoes from their bandoliers. They hurled the grenadoes, which followed the arcing superviolet tracks unerringly. One, two, three, four, five, six. They had even bolstered the arcs of luxin so they followed a natural throwing path.

But the ambushers were moving too. Three Blackguards went down in the first wave of fire missiles. In defending Gavin first, they couldn't fix their own shields in time. A gout of red luxin jetted in from four sides, trying to drench the entire bridge so they could set it alight. Blue and green Blackguards threw up shields to divert the flows off the sides of the bridge while a yellow threw light-burst grenadoes at everyone she could see.

Gavin looked forward and saw that the ambushers weren't blocking the way across the bridge. There was only one reason for that. They wanted Gavin and the Blackguard to flee headlong into something worse.

Projectiles were sparking and whining off his shields, grenadoes' explosions were rocking the rooftops, and huge blue knives like icicles were being fired by two of the color wights behind them. The Blackguards were compressed tight around Gavin, using their shields and, if that failed, their bodies to keep him safe.

"Let's move! Cross the bridge!" the commander said. She was young. Orholam, had they lost so many that this young woman was in charge?

All this was according to the Blackguard training, too. Protect, secure, decide, act. No hesitation.

"No!" Gavin shouted. He pointed off the side of the bridge and drafted a new walkway in green from the middle span to a point thirty paces down.

"Flash!" one of the Blackguards yelled. She was a yellow. She launched a flash bomb a mere ten paces into the air. Gavin and the Blackguards covered their faces as it exploded with so much force that Gavin could feel it rock his shields.

Then they ran across the new green bridge, even as the bridge behind them, no longer protected from the red luxin streams, went up in flame.

One of the blue wights dropped into the street in front of them as they made it back to land, determined to steer them back into the secondary ambush. A dozen Blackguard hands went up and the beast was riddled with luxin bullets and cudgeled aside instantly.

A Blackguard fell, though Gavin hadn't seen what cut him down. "No! No! No!" the man was yelling. His partner split away from them. The Blackguard who had fallen rolled over onto his back. His partner, a woman near forty, Laya, Gavin thought her name was, stood over him.

"I'm sorry," the fallen Blackguard said. "Too much. Too much."

Laya pulled an eyelid up to get a good look at the fallen Blackguard's halo. She whispered something, kissed her fingers, touched them to the fallen man's eyes, mouth, and heart. Then she cut his throat. The rest of the Blackguards didn't wait.

They ran past an alley and found themselves looking at the backs of dozens of musketeers, all in formation, muskets up, pointed the other way where the ambush had originally tried to steer Gavin. The men were so intent on waiting for their quarry to appear in front of them that they didn't see Gavin behind them. As they ran past, Laya slopped red luxin over them. A lot of red. The whoosh of flame was so intense as she set it alight that Gavin saw shadows half a block away—which meant the flames had leapt for a moment above the rooftops. The screams followed. Men burning to death.

One more river crossing. This time, Gavin led the Blackguards to a blank section and drafted his own green span across. No need to risk another ambush.

They made it to the docks and found hundreds of soldiers there, muskets loaded, facing out. The boats were still being boarded, mountains of luggage pushed aside, left behind, now gathered for use as barriers. There was a stream of boats already heading out, a line disappearing into the distance, going through the Guardian's legs as she stood guard. Every ship in the entire harbor had been used. And most were already gone. Two huge barges crafted of blue and green luxin and wood had been constructed and were already heading out too. That left one luxin barge that was rapidly filling even now, with far too many men to fit in it.

The soldiers here were locals mostly—where the hell had all the Ruthgari soldiers gone? Boarded earlier ships no doubt. Someone would pay for that, but not now. The soldiers who remained looked resolute, and their countenances lifted as they saw Gavin. These were men who thought they were going to die to give their families a chance to get away. Men who were willing to pay that price.

"Who's in charge?" Gavin asked.

"I am, sir. Lord Prism. Sir." A mousy Ruthgari with oddly kinky hair for his pale complexion and a look in his eyes like he was scared to death stepped forward. In another time, Gavin would have laughed to see the awkward little man. "We've got almost all the ships we have loaded. Men gathered who will fight. We need room for another three hundred, if no one else comes from the city."

"Any sign of General Danavis or Commander Ironfist?" Gavin asked.

"No, sir. Lord Prism. Sir."

"Sir is fine," Gavin said. "Blackguards, any of you who can draft without breaking the halo, help me. We'll make one more barge while we wait."

"Wait, sir?" a Blackguard asked.

"General Danavis is coming. We finish one more barge. Then we go. He'll be here by then."

A trumpet sounded. The pale Ruthgari shouted, "Enemies coming! Ready!"

"Can you hold while we make a barge?" Gavin asked.

The man was still small, still mousy, but his face was resolute, and anything comical about his appearance was gone. "We'll hold, sir. To the last man."

Chapter 90

Karris selected one of the Mirrormen's horses that looked like it still had some wind and spirit left. Its barding was mirrored, and it shone in the morning sun. She might as well paint a target on her back. Well, she wasn't exactly inconspicuous herself.

They didn't have long. The four hundred paces between Lord Omnichrome's color wights could only be crossed through a maze of alleys or rubble-strewn streets. It would slow them, but not much. Some things, though, had to be done. Karris moved to check King Garadul's body, gritting her teeth against the gore.

He was definitely dead. She felt a peculiar emptiness. She'd wanted him dead. He deserved it. Now he was just gone. And, quite possibly, it hadn't accomplished anything. She saw her bich'hwa on the ground next to him. Sonuvabitch. She picked it up, and scanned the ground, but there was no sight of her ataghan.

No more time. Corvan Danavis's men were finishing collecting gunpowder and shot or replacement weapons from the dead and forming back up. Kip looked as bad as Karris would have expected. Corvan said, "It's called being lightsick, Kip, and it might do *anything* to you. Make you feel weak as a puppy or strong as a sea demon. I've seen modest men tear off all their clothes because they couldn't bear anything touching their skin. And shy women, well, never mind."

"Hey, that was just the one time," Karris protested, mounting up.

When you could, it was good not to let a drafter sink too deep into themselves after drafting too much.

Corvan laughed. "I don't know that I'd call you 'shy,' on any day, Karris White Oak." He glanced down at her leg. "Certainly not today."

Karris followed Corvan's eyes. Oops. She'd managed to tear the slit in her dress practically to her hip, and sitting on a horse didn't help. Well, what was she going to do? Go change?

"Time's up!" Corvan shouted to his men. "We head for the docks! Catch up or die." One of his officers came to him with a question, and he was swallowed up by his duties.

Which left Karris with Kip. She would prefer to be unencumbered during a battle, but she wasn't going to abandon him, not again. There were things more important than her freedom. She sidled her horse over to the platform. "Come here, Kip," she said with a little more edge than she meant.

Obviously dazed, Kip clambered up, and they were off.

At first, Karris thought they were going to get away cleanly. Then they came to the bridge. The far end was blocked with wagons and carts that must have just been set on fire moments before Corvan's men arrived or they would have seen the smoke.

The men at the front of the column skidded to a stop, and the men who'd been running behind them collided with them, collapsing the column and causing chaos. Corvan, mounted near the front, was trying to extricate some drafters from the crush to get them to work on clearing the flaming barricades. It would only take a minute or two, in normal circumstances.

Near to the back of the column, Karris pulled up sharply and started shouting at the men near her to form a rear guard. "Load muskets, affix matches!" She wheeled around in time to see the first of the color wights pursuing them.

Karris had never seen anything like it. She'd known green wights could change their joints to give their legs immense springiness, but the greens weren't the only color wights leaping from roof to roof behind them.

A yellow wight, limbs all aglow, ran straight toward the edge of a flat roof, gathering luxin in both hands. She leapt off the edge, and threw her hands down, releasing a jet of yellow at the ground, using the recoil to throw her up high enough to make it to the next roof. Like she was playing leapfrog in midair.

A flash of green, much closer.

Karris shot a ball of green up, intercepting the green wight as it descended. Her shot blasted the green wight off its trajectory, lifting it so that instead of landing among the terrified soldiers, it collided with the side of a building. The soldiers around it recovered before the wight did. Karris heard a rattle of musket fire.

Damn! Veterans would have dispatched it with their blades, saving precious shots for more active enemies.

Another green wight streaked through the air, and Karris missed it. It crashed through the back ranks, scattering men. Others, terrified, leveled their muskets and fired, most of them missing the wight and hitting their own friends.

By the time they put that one down, wights of every color were converging on them. Lord Omnichrome's army was rounding a corner, not three hundred paces away, jogging, picking up speed for a charge. Half a dozen of Omnichrome's red and sub-red drafters were mounted. They closed within two hundred paces and lobbed great flaming missiles toward Corvan's massed, trapped men.

A blue wight, all glittering angles and blades, was the next across the rooftops to the left. A sub-red was leaping across roofs on the right, bald, her whole body literally aflame.

Out of nowhere, a big drafter dropped into the street straight in front of Karris, his back to Corvan's men. He stood, arms spread out as if he were holding ropes and expecting a heavy load. His arms snapped out just as the blue wight and sub-red wight leapt to attack.

Both color wights jerked hard as the invisible superviolet luxin ropes around their necks went taut. The blue wight's body went abruptly horizontal, all the luxin it had held going to jelly in an instant as it lost concentration. It crashed to the ground in front of the rear guard.

The sub-red wight, without the benefit of blue armor around her neck, barely changed directions. Her body landed on the next roof and fell, and her flaming head rolled right into the river.

The drafter who'd saved them shot a glance back, making sure the color wights were dead. It took Karris's breath away. It was Usef Tep, the Purple Bear himself, the hero of the False Prism's War. Even as Karris registered the fact, she saw the flaming missiles that were arcing toward the rear guard suddenly veer left and right in the air, exploding at a safe distance.

Another green wight she hadn't even seen crashed into the ground, riddled with blue luxin knives. Karris saw Eleleph Corzin, skin luminous blue, step out of an alley.

"We've got your backs. Go!" a woman yelled.

Karris turned to see at least a dozen drafters stand on the last rooftop. It was like Karris had stepped into a heroes gallery. The woman who'd yelled was Samila Sayeh. Deedee Falling Leaf stood next to her, skin wrapped in vines of pure green luxin. Flamehands stood on the corner of the building, a steady stream of fireballs popping from each hand. Sisters Tala and Tayri to the right. Talon Gim bleeding heavily, left arm useless, but going to stand beside Usef Tep in the street. And others that Karris recognized from her youth, or who'd fought for Dazen and whom she'd heard described in vivid detail.

"Damn you! You and that boy are the only ones who can save Gavin. Take him and get the hell out of here!" Samila Sayeh yelled, her eyes flashing.

Corvan's men surged as the barricades gave way. Karris felt Kip stirring behind her. Lord Omnichrome's army was like an onrushing tide. Karris spurred her horse on, only shooting glances back at the magical conflagration behind her.

It was enough. All of Corvan's men made it over the bridge. From there, it was a straight adrenaline-fueled shot to the docks.

Karris made it with the last group. Corvan, up at the front, was moving toward Gavin down on the docks. Gavin was working, drafting barges, it looked like. Someone alerted Gavin, and Karris saw a flash of his crooked smile toward Corvan.

And in that moment, Karris knew. It was like she'd been clubbed. Her throat tightened. The pieces spun together. A thousand pieces from the past sixteen years, and the last few in the past few days: That grin. Patting Corvan's shoulder on the wall this morning. If Karris hadn't spent more than a decade in the Blackguard, she wouldn't have caught it. But Gavin and Corvan should hate each other. That could be explained away. They were professionals, sure. They had reasons to work together, right. But seamless command and instant obedience come only with time and trust. How could these men trust each other?

Who comes back from war a better man?

Gavin had said, "What's in that note, it isn't true. I swear it isn't true." Why would Gavin double down on a lie that he knew was going to be exposed minutes later?

Because it wasn't a lie.

Oh shit.

Chapter 91

Shaken from his torpor by Karris dismounting, Kip looked from one side to the other, squinting, head pounding. One moment, he'd been holding on to the woman, more concerned that as he clung to her his arms were touching her breasts and she was going to think he was groping her than worried about the exploding guns and coruscating magic.

He was, by any rational account, a moron.

And then, abruptly, they were at the docks. Kip couldn't follow things well. At first the men were challenging Corvan, and then welcoming him, and Corvan was giving orders and disappearing into the men, talking with this person and that. Kip felt simultaneously dizzy and as strong as a bear. Karris cursed aloud, but he didn't understand why. She pulled at his arms, still clamped around her waist. He released her, and almost fell when she slipped out of the saddle.

"I'll be back for you in a little while." Karris patted his arm. Suddenly, her face came into tight focus. Like he was looking through her, like he was understanding her. She looked...vulnerable.

Vulnerable? Karris White Oak? At another time, Kip would have laughed at the thought. Now his focus was too great. Her eyes were tight. Some of that was concern for Kip, but that pat of his forearm was a "You'll be fine in a little while" pat. She wasn't worried about Kip. She was nervous about something else.

Karris turned and Kip saw her square her shoulders. Her shoulders lifted—she was taking a deep breath. Then she strode down the dock as if she were as confident as always in between soldiers, drafters, sailors, and scared civilians. Despite the bustle and the nerves and the not-so-distant fighting, the crowd parted for this vision of war and beauty: knotted muscles and femininity, the luxin sword on her back still smoking, soot on her naked shoulders and cleavage, a clawed bich'hwa in her fist, barefoot, black hair windblown, her stride fearless.

She stopped behind a copper-haired drafter who was working on a great barge. Spoke. The man's head whipped around like it was on a swivel. Not just any man. The Prism.

Gavin swept Karris into a huge hug immediately. Relief.

Karris's body was stiff, her arms still at her sides, either shocked or repulsed, Kip couldn't tell. Then, slowly, the stiffness in her arms and shoulders seemed to melt by degrees. Her arms were moving, coming up to Gavin's back to return the embrace.

Then Gavin saw Kip. Surprise. He released Karris, said something.

Karris's open hand cracked across Gavin's cheek.

Gavin's hands turned up. What did I say?

But Karris was storming off, not answering.

Gavin looked from her to Kip to the unfinished barge behind him. Threw his hands down. Kip could swear he heard the curse all the way from here. He wanted to shrink into himself. It was like he'd just seen his parents fighting. All he wanted was to be gone.

He turned toward the city. His vision was still intensely focusing on one thing at a time, losing the wholes for the parts. The lightsickness. He knew it was an army there in front of him, but he only saw this man checking the fuse on his matchlock; this one with half of his mustache burned off fiddling with his musket's ramrod, spinning it in its rest; this man with his plug bayonet out, using it as a back-scratcher and joking with his comrades as if he were totally unafraid, while his tight, dead eyes told otherwise; this man talking nonstop while no one paid him any attention.

Kip looked over empty slips at the dock. Not a single ship left. Even the smallest dory was gone. Almost on the dock parallel to theirs, he saw a huge swarthy man chased down and surrounded by a dozen Mirrormen. Something defiant was written in the man's stance, but the Mirrormen had muskets on him from every angle.

Ironfist.

"Have I gone mad or is that Commander Ironfist?" Kip asked.

"Sir?" a man standing next to Kip's horse asked.

"Move!" Kip shouted. "Move!" With a few curses, the men parted for him.

"Kip! What are you doing?" Corvan Danavis shouted. From his angle, he couldn't see Ironfist.

Kip barely heard him. He dug his heels into the horse and held on for dear life. Breaking free of hundreds of nervous men, the horse ran. Kip was tossed around like a sack of pomegranates being crushed to juice and seeds. The horse galloped along the edge of the docks, going in the right general direction—but it wasn't slowing down. Kip pulled hard on the reins, but the horse had its bit in its teeth. And it wasn't letting go.

The Mirrormen saw Kip coming and yelled. A few had time to discharge shots. Kip swore a musket ball licked his ear with a hot tongue.

I am the stupidest person I have ever met. As the horse streaked toward Ironfist and his captors, still not slowing, Kip kicked his feet free of the stirrups and jumped out of the saddle, diving for the Mirrormen.

Whatever he'd done before with all the green luxin that had cushioned everything—this time he didn't do it. He missed the Mirrormen and hit the ground hard, flipping over and over, smacking his cracked, burned left hand hard against something. It felt like fire traced through every joint in his hand. He smacked his head, skidded on his back, clothes tangling him up, and tried to stand.

He was facing the city. There was no one that direction. He turned toward Commander Ironfist, got his feet tangled, fell. Caught himself with his left hand. Tears sprang out of his eyes unbidden. Agony.

"No!" Ironfist screamed.

Kip was tottering on one knee, dizzy, propped up only by his shrieking left hand. He wanted to fall on his back, show these men he wasn't a threat, beg them not to hurt him.

I spend more time on my back than a rent girl. Enough.

One of the men had his bayonet fixed. He was stepping toward

Kip. Kip pushed himself up—off his left hand. The fire of pain shot up his arm.

Kip just pointed his ruined left hand at the Mirrorman and made that fire shoot back down, propping himself up on his good hand. Flame roared out and engulfed the man. He baked, his mirror armor useless.

Staggering to his feet, Kip threw more and more fire into the guards. And then he found out why Corvan had said he wouldn't want to draft for a month when you were lightsick. His stomach boiled; he puked.

He couldn't keep his feet. The dizziness and nausea dropped him like he'd been cut off at the knees. His stomach cramped so hard he bent in half, curling into a fetal position, still puking, splattering vomit on his own pants.

Once again, Kip the Charging White Knight manages to do nothing.

He was dead. He knew he had to be dead. The men had been charging at him and he'd killed at least one of them. They should have killed him by now.

"Let go of the rest of the luxin. It'll make you sick again, but it's better, I promise. Now, boy! I can't carry you and draft at the same time!"

"Ironfist?"

Kip cracked his eyes open, saw dead men scattered around and Ironfist standing over him, his fists bearing spikes of bloodied blue luxin. Ironfist had cuts and dried blood and powder burns everywhere. He wore blue spectacles close to his eyes, the earpieces tied tight around the back of his head. His ghotra had been knocked off his head, and his hair was singed on one side. How had the man gotten away after commandeering a cannon? Surely the whole of King Garadul's army had fallen on him.

Nonetheless, here he was. Bruised, exhausted, injured, but not so hurt that he couldn't save Kip one more time.

"Now!" Ironfist demanded. "I'm lightsick myself. I know what I'm asking!"

Kip let go of the rest of the luxin and threw up again, his insides heaving, all of his viscera trying to rush out of his mouth.

But then, miraculously, he did feel better. Almost able to stand.

Ironfist grabbed the shoulder of his shirt and lifted him bodily to his feet.

"Idiot boy, I did all this to save you, and you nearly throw it away. What the hell were you thinking?"

But Kip was in no state to answer.

He was staring at the army, back on the other dock.

Orholam's balls.

A full-scale battle was being waged just two hundred paces away. Perhaps a hundred soldiers and drafters were holding the dock against thousands of soldiers and dozens of drafters. The confined space was all that kept Gavin's men from being overwhelmed. The front lines were a mess of bayonets and swords, a few spears and hoes and scythes and long-handled orange limb shears and magic being thrown and blocked each way. Behind the front lines, Gavin and some other drafters were just finishing the last barge, unable to join the fighting because their drafting talents were needed for shipbuilding.

The mass of invaders was pushing Gavin's men steadily backward, their sheer weight unstoppable. To Kip, it looked like they were already too late. And he was still sick, still dizzy, still feeling stronger than ever in his life, torn between wanting to lie down and feeling like he needed to go running or he would burn up.

"Follow me," Ironfist said. "Stay as close as you can. It doesn't float for long."

With no more explanation—float? what was floating?—Ironfist ran straight off the side of the dock, one hand spraying blue luxin out in a wide stream.

Kip followed, charging down the slick surface, holding his pants tight in his left hand and praying he didn't fall. The blue path dove off the end of the dock steeply and then leveled out at the water, floating on top of the surface like a very unsteady boat.

"Keep running!" Ironfist said.

In front of them, the defense was crumbling just as the great luxin barge pushed off the dock. The last remnants of the defenders were trying to fight and retreat at the same time. Some turned and were cut down as they tried to run to make the jump to the barge. Others abandoned the idea of making it to the ship themselves and stood their ground.

Lord Omnichrome's army, though, was so huge and had so much pent-up pressure that without a hundred soldiers pushing it back, it burst down the dock, the men behind shoving the men in front of them so hard and so relentlessly that both defenders and the front lines of Lord Omnichrome's men were pushed straight off the edge of the dock. Dozens, perhaps a hundred men and women splashed into the bay.

We're not going to make it. There's nowhere for us to go!

But Ironfist merely turned his blue path over the waves out. By Orholam, they were going to run all the way out to the barge?

Kip couldn't make it. He was too dizzy. It was too far.

"Faster, Kip! Damn you! Faster!" Ironfist shouted.

Water jumped up into the air to their right. Kip glanced that way, saw nothing, found himself running right along the edge of the blue path, almost falling in the water, and curved back. More water jumped to each side of them.

They're shooting at us!

Lungs heaving, head swimming, in front of them Kip saw magic setting the air alight between the barge and the dock. Gavin was standing at the stern of the boat, throwing out great swathes of flame, darts, light grenadoes—a veritable artillery barrage of chromaturgy. A space cleared around him on the barge as everyone else shrank back, stunned, awed, afraid of anyone who could handle so much magic. Gavin was fighting all the drafters on the dock—by himself. And winning.

That's my father. I can't let him down. I've screwed up everything else. I'm going to get to that damned boat.

"I can't keep this up," Ironfist shouted, his voice strained. "I've got to make it narrower, Kip, or we won't make it!"

"Do it!" Kip yelled.

The platform abruptly shrank to barely three hand's breadths wide. It sank into the water even as Kip ran across it, his feet splashing water.

But they had only thirty paces to go. The path started arching up, out of the water to attach to the side of the barge, out of the way of all the magic going back and forth.

Kip looked up at Gavin, and saw that someone had stepped into the empty circle behind the Prism. Though the boy wore peasant's garb, Kip recognized him instantly. Zymun! Zymun had snuck onto the barge with the rest of the refugees, and he was holding a box. Kip's box. The last thing Kip's mother had ever given him. The only thing she'd ever given him.

Gavin was still hurling magic and deflecting magic. Everyone was either watching him or had crowded to the side of the barge and was watching Ironfist and Kip come in. Ironfist was looking down at the path he was drafting, intent on the magic. Kip was the only person who saw a gleaming knife come out of that box.

Kip's next step missed the narrow luxin platform. He plunged hard into the water. Clumsy Kip. Stupid Kip. His huge splash would make even more of a distraction for Zymun to take advantage of.

Lord Omnichrome had sent Zymun to assassinate Gavin. Kip had seen it—and he'd decided to go somewhere else. He'd had a dozen chances to do the right thing, and he'd missed them all. Even five minutes ago, if he hadn't gone after Ironfist, he would have been on the barge. He could have stopped Zymun.

Kip wouldn't fail again. He refused. He threw his hands down, opened his eyes despite the water, and started sucking in light. It hurt like hell. He didn't care. He sucked it in like he was the mouth of one of Gavin's great skimmer engines. And threw it down.

He shot out of the water. By Orholam's own hand, or by all the luck that had gone against him for his whole life now finally reversing course, he shot in the right direction. He flew onto the barge's deck, blasting through half a dozen people gathered at the railing looking for him—and he kept his feet, though he was at a crazy angle and had to run as fast as he could just to not fall down.

He burst into the opening around Gavin just as Zymun closed on the Prism. Zymun sank the great white dagger into Gavin's back an instant before Kip collided with him, the top of Kip's head smashing Zymun's nose. His momentum carried them both off the opposite side of the barge.

They landed with a great splash. Kip got a breath before they went under and immediately began tearing at Zymun, punching him, ripping at the dagger in his one hand and the sheath in the other. Zymun hadn't taken a breath. He let both go and flailed, trying to get away from Kip with panicky motions. Kip tried to slash the other boy, still underwater, and missed.

With a gasp, Kip surfaced. Zymun surfaced five paces away, blood streaming from his broken nose, staining the water.

Kip heard screams beyond Zymun. The sharks had come and were turning the water between Zymun and the docks to white froth in the frenzy.

"Kip! Grab the rope! Grab the rope!" someone shouted. A coil hit the water close to him.

Zymun gave Kip one hateful glance and started swimming for shore. He was a good swimmer, too. Faster than Kip. It would be madness to go after him. And he was bleeding.

"Kip!"

Kip felt the first tremor of lightsickness hitting him. Oh shit.

But he'd lost his dagger before. It was everything. He wouldn't lose it again. Bobbing in the waves, trying to ignore at least another score of triangular fins cutting the water headed for the dock, he sheathed the blade and tucked it inside his pants, and only then did he grab the rope.

Good thing there was a loop on the end. Kip managed to pull it over his head before he threw up the first time. There was nothing in his stomach, so he dry heaved as the barge towed him along for a way until the men on deck could haul him out of the water.

"Let go of the rest of the luxin, Kip," someone was saying to him.

"I can't, I can't." He knew it was going to be bad. He couldn't take any more pain. He couldn't even open his eyes.

"Come on, Kip, do it for me," Gavin said gently.

Kip let go of the last of the luxin. The last thing he was aware of was pain shooting through his head, lances of light blotting out darkness, only to leave more behind.

Chapter 92

The prisoner was full in the fever's grip. The gash he'd cut across his chest and the foul hair he'd packed into the cut had done their work. Death or freedom. It was time.

He tried to stand, but couldn't. He was shaking too hard. Maybe he'd waited too long. He'd wanted—needed—to wait until the fever was at its hottest in order to have any chance at all. If he'd miscalculated, he would simply die, and end all of Dazen's problems for him.

That would just be tragic.

He propped himself up, found his dirty little hair bowl close at hand, tried to inspect it for flaws for the thousandth time. He couldn't tell. He felt like weeping, the fever throwing his very emotions into disarray.

"I'm sorry, Dazen. I failed you," he said aloud. Meaningless words. From nowhere. The part of him that had marinated in blue for so many years found that curious. Not unexpected, but still strange. Why should he feel emotions simply because his blood was literally hotter than normal? Strange, but inconsequential.

He pulled the cut on his chest open, pulled out the chunky, dirty, blood-clotted wad of filth, and threw it aside. It didn't all come out together. Some was stuck in the wound. With a grimy fingernail, he scratched out the remaining filth. It made him gag with pain.

Stupidity. He'd used his fingernail? When trying to clean a wound?

He should have drafted tweezers. He wasn't thinking straight. He blinked, his body tottering. No, there was no failure. Lesser men might fail. Not him. Not without trying his plan.

Gavin scooted over to the shallow bowl he'd scraped with his own hands over the course of sixteen years.

Well, some men might have *nothing* to show for sixteen years of labor.

He laughed aloud.

The dead man in the wall looked concerned. Keep it together, Dazen. Gavin. Whatever. Whoever you are, today you're a prisoner, today you can be a free man. Or a dead man, which is a freedom of its own, isn't it?

Dazen took his finely woven hair bowl and laid it inside the stone bowl he'd dug over the years. It fit perfectly, as well it might. He'd made it to fit, and checked it a thousand times as he crafted it. Sitting right in front of the bowl and its depression, Dazen untied his loincloth and shifted awkwardly until he could set it aside.

"If only Karris could see us now, huh?" the dead man said. "How could she choose him over this?"

Dazen barely glanced at the dead man, sitting in his shiny blue wall, mocking him, seated with legs spread grotesquely in front of a hair bowl and a shallow hole. "You can't debase me," Dazen told the dead man. "I do what I must. If that's depravity, so be it." He licked dry lips. He hadn't been drinking water. He needed to be nearly dehydrated for this. His tongue felt thick.

The dead man said something in response, but Dazen ignored him. For a moment, he forgot what was next. He needed to make water. He wanted to lie down. Orholam, he was tired. If only he could rest, he'd have the strength...

Slapping! That was what was next. A little more pain, and then freedom, Dazen. A little more. You're a Guile. You can't be chained like this. You're the Prism. You've been wronged. The world needs to know your vengeance.

Seated still—there was no reason to move from here, he wouldn't be able to make it back if he moved—he studied every surface of his body that was visible.

Then he started slapping himself. Everywhere that he would be able to see. Hard.

"This strikes you as rational?" the dead man asked. "Maybe sixteen years in blue hasn't been enough for you."

Gavin—Dazen, damn it—ignored him. He slapped his forearms, his stomach, his chest everywhere except where the cut was—he didn't want to pass out this close to victory—and his legs. Every surface of his body that he could see he slapped until it was insensitive, numb to the pain and, more important—red.

Gavin was only human. Though he was a superchromat, even he made tiny errors. That was Dazen's bet. That was why Gavin hadn't let anything with color down here. If he'd made the blue light perfectly, all in only one incredibly tight spectrum, there would have been only blue light to reflect from any item. Gavin wouldn't have had to worry even if his prisoner had red or green or yellow spectacles. But the tiny flash of green Dazen saw every time he pissed into his bowl before it was leached of color told him that there was some spectrum bleed.

Now everything depended on how much and how fast he could draft.

Shivering, trembling hard from fever and from beating his skin nearly bloody, he pissed. Not straight into the depression. Not straight into the hair bowl. If he pissed too hard, he was worried he'd break right through the oil that he'd so painstakingly smeared around the inside of the hair bowl. So he pissed into his hand, and let the warm liquid flow gently into the hair bowl.

You've made me an animal, brother.

But if animal he was, Dazen was a fox. The dehydration had made his urine as shockingly yellow as his body could produce, and the woven, oiled hair bowl held. Dazen's heart leapt—he wanted to weep—as he saw yellow for the first time in sixteen years. Yellow! There was spectrum bleed! By Orholam, it was beautiful.

He drafted off of it. Just a tiny amount, it was like trying to suck water through a bag, even as the bowl slowly drained. He drafted a yellow ball, not even as big as his thumb, into the palm of his left hand.

It immediately started shimmering into light—but yellow light. For the first time, Dazen saw his cell in something other than blue light. He saw his body in something other than blue light. And yellow, being in the middle of the spectrum rather than at the opposite end, made red a hell of a lot easier to see. And it had spectrum bleed both up and down.

And Dazen's whole body was red from him slapping it.

Dazen drafted red hard, as hard as he could, even as the little yellow marble sputtered out and disappeared. It was enough. It had to be enough. The skin down to his right arm looked dull in the blue light that once again dominated the cell, but he knew it was red.

And now the whole reason he'd given himself a fever.

Dazen drafted heat from his own body. It was incredibly inefficient. It had never worked before. He was shaking, the fever was so bad he couldn't think. Surely...surely...

He drew on his body's heat, tried to imagine it rising in waves as from a desert. A tiny flame, a spark was all he needed. He had as much as he could get. Like an old man, Dazen propped himself up. Magic had weight, and with as much as he was planning to throw, he needed to not fall over as soon as he started. He got up to his knees and grinned at the dead man.

The dead man grinned back, like he'd been expecting this. Like he'd been waiting for it for years.

Dazen brought his hands together. He threw a tiny starter stream of red out of his right hand, directly at the dead man's face. His left hand let all the heat he'd gathered go at once—

And made a tiny spark.

The spark caught. The red blazed, and suddenly the blue cell was flooded with red light and heat. Dazen drafted more and more and released it in a hammer blow, straight at the dead man, straight at the weak spot in the cell wall.

The concussion bowled him over despite his attempt to brace himself. He'd thrown his fireball with so much will there'd been no way he could take the force in his weakened body.

He didn't think he lost consciousness, but when he opened his eyes, the world was still blue. Failure. Dear Orholam, no.

Dazen rolled over, expecting to see the dead man leering at him. But the dead man was gone. A hole stood in his place. Jagged, broken in the wall, the edges smoldering, glowing with sludgy low-burning red luxin. A hole, and a tunnel beyond.

He couldn't stop himself. Dazen started weeping. Freedom. He couldn't stand, he was too weak, but he knew he had to get out. He had to go as far as he could from here before Gavin discovered he was gone. So he started crawling.

As he crossed out of the blue luxin cell, he held his breath, sure there would be some trap, or some alarm. Nothing. He breathed deep, fresh, clean air filling his lungs with strength, and began crawling to freedom.

Chapter 93

Kip woke in a little blue room. Every surface was blue luxin, even the pallet where he was sleeping, though it had been softened with a heap of blankets. From the faint rocking motion, he realized he was on one of the blue barges.

And his back hurt like hell. In fact, most of his body hurt. His left hand was bandaged heavily and he could feel that a thick poultice had been spread all over it. His shoulders and both arms were bruised everywhere, he felt like someone had beaten both of his legs with a board, his head was throbbing, and he was sore pretty much any other place on his body he could think of. He wiggled a pinky toe. Yep, that was sore too.

And he was hungry. Unbelievable.

You're on a refugee ship, Kip. There ain't gonna be any food.

He tried to go back to sleep. That was the best thing for it. He'd feel better when he woke up. And they might catch some fish or something by then. He rolled over, and his lower back still hurt. What the— He shifted, and realized he was lying on something.

Reaching down to his waistband, his fingers brushed something. His eyes shot open. The knife. His inheritance. If it didn't hurt so bad, he would have laughed about it. Clearly, he'd been carried in here wrapped in blankets, and left. No one had even noticed. In an armada of ships with thousands of refugees and soldiers and maybe a hundred boats, with pirates and everything else to worry about, apparently Kip hadn't been the first thing on Gavin's mind. Well, what did I expect? They couldn't strip me and get me dry clothes—there *are* no dry clothes.

Kip rolled off the knife and sat up. He groaned. He really was sore. And hungry. But that didn't matter now.

A figure passed the door, and Kip hid the knife by his leg hurriedly.

Gavin poked his head in. "You're awake!" he said. "How do you feel?"

"Like an elephant sat on me," Kip said.

Gavin grinned and came and sat on the edge of Kip's pallet. "I heard you were trying to be Ironfist for a while out there. He's pretty steamed. He's supposed to be the one who saves my life, you know."

"He's mad?" Kip asked, worried.

Gavin sobered. "No, Kip. No one's mad at you. He won't admit it, but he's proud of you."

"He is?"

"And I am, too."

"I thought I was too late." Gavin was proud of him? His mind couldn't really register the thought. His mother had always been ashamed of him, and the Prism himself was proud? Kip blinked quickly, looked away. "You're really fine?" Kip asked.

Gavin smiled. "Never felt better," he said. "Oh, did you ... did you know that boy? The assassin?"

Kip felt a lump in his throat. "He was one of the drafters who wiped out Rekton. Zymun was his name. He tried to kill me there. Did he get eaten?" Kip remembered the boy bleeding profusely, swimming toward all those sharks.

"I don't know," Gavin said. "My rule is, if you don't see an enemy dead with your own eyes, assume they're still alive." He grinned, almost grimly, at a private thought. "But," he said, shaking himself out of it, "I guess that explains this." He pulled out the rosewood box that had held Kip's dagger.

Gavin handed it to Kip. "It's empty," he said. "But I thought it looked like that box your mother tried to give you. Either your Zymun stole it from King Garadul, or this is a common style. Looks like it held a knife, but I guess that went into the waves. I'm sorry."

Kip wanted to rush to confess, but the knife was his. Gavin might take it away from him. Kip hadn't even gotten to see it yet, not really.

"Anyway," Gavin said, "you rest up. I've got work to do. I'll have someone send in some food to you, and we'll talk later. All right?" He got up, stopped at the door. "Thank you, Kip. You saved my life, son. Well done. I'm proud of you."

Son. Son! There was pride in Gavin's voice as he said it. Kip had made the Prism proud. It was like light bursting over hills to illuminate places in his soul that had never seen it.

The lump in his throat grew huge, his eyes filled with tears. Gavin turned to go. "Wait! Father, wait!"

Kip froze, as did Gavin, outlined in the door. The last time Kip had used the word he was being a snot, and things hadn't gone well.

And then it got worse, as Kip suddenly realized Gavin had meant "son" like "young man." Kip wished he could go jump back into the water for the sharks. "I'm so sorry," he said, "I didn't—"

"No!" Gavin cut him off with a hand. "Whatever else you did, you proved yourself a Guile today, Kip."

Kip licked his lips. "Did Karris...I saw her hit you. Was that because of me?"

Gavin laughed gently. "Kip, a woman is the mystery you'll never stop investigating."

Kip paused. "Is that a yes?"

"Karris hit me because I needed hitting."

That didn't really help.

"Get some sleep...*son*," Gavin said. He paused, as if he was tasting the word. "We're done with that 'nephew' nonsense. The world will know you're my son. And to hell with the consequences." A little reckless grin. And then he was gone.

Kip didn't sleep. He propped his back against one blue wall and pulled out the dagger. The blade was a dazzling strange white metal with a spiraling core of black threaded from point to hilt. There was little ornamentation except for seven clear, perfect diamonds on the hilt. Well, six diamonds and maybe a sapphire. Kip didn't really know his jewels, but six stones were clear as glass but brilliantly refractive. The seventh matched the others in size and clarity, but it glowed a brilliant, magical blue. Kip sheathed the dagger.

How did my mother get such a thing? How did she not pawn it for haze?

Kip opened the rosewood box to put the dagger away, and with his bandaged left hand he fumbled it, dropping it upside down in his lap. He turned it over and saw that the silk lining was loose, not attached to the box itself but to a frame that filled the box. He pulled on the frame, lifting it out. Underneath was a thin compartment that held extra laces that matched the color of the sheath to tie it to different sizes of belt. It wasn't a secret compartment, but obviously Zymun hadn't noticed it, nor had King Garadul, because there was a note there.

With trepidation, glancing at the door to make sure no one was passing, Kip read the note, written in his mother's hard, deliberate strokes: "Kip, go to the Chromeria and kill the man who raped me and took away everything I had. Don't listen to his lies. Swear you won't fail me. If you ever loved me, if you've ever wanted to do anything good in this world, use this dagger to kill your father. Kill Gavin Guile."

Kip felt locked up, paralyzed. Someone was lying to him, betraying him. Kip felt those deep, sucking pools of rage stirring. It had to be his mother. Addict. Whore. Liar. Kip's mother would lie for haze: she would abandon Kip in a closet. Gavin had been hard on him, but he'd never lied to him. He never would. Never. He was Kip's family. The first Kip had ever had.

But his mother had kept the dagger, and even the box. She could have sold either for a mountain of haze. She would have thought of them every time the madness of craving had been on her. If this was more important to her than haze, why would she lie?

Kip shivered, feeling like he was being ripped out of his moorings. He didn't know the truth. But he would. He swore it.

He folded the note and saw a quick scribble on the back he'd missed before, written looser and faster than the rest, but undeniably in his mother's hand: "I love you, Kip. I always have." She'd never said those words. Not once. Not in his whole life.

He threw the note away like it was a serpent. Pushed his face into the blankets so no one could hear. And bawled.

Chapter 94

Dazen was crawling through darkness. This was death, but life lay beyond, somewhere. The floor was sharp, cutting his hands and knees cruelly. He'd sucked up as much red luxin as he could before he'd left the blue cell, and if he hadn't been fevered, he would have kept a flame alive, but his thoughts were still sluggish, stupid. All he could do was hold on to his anger, and the red had helped him do that at first.

I will have my vengeance, he thought, but it was passionless. There was only the pain in his hands and knees and the crawling. He refused to stop. This tunnel had curved and curved again, but it couldn't go on forever. Soon, he would sleep, and either die or wake stronger. Strong enough to gather his strength and bring down Gavin. He laughed weakly and kept crawling.

Damn this sharp rock. What had his brother done? Carved his prison out of pure hellstone?

Son of a bitch, that was exactly what Gavin had done. Spent a fortune simply to cut Dazen up. The hateful bastard. But Dazen wasn't so easy to stop. He kept crawling. Freedom would not be denied him so easily.

Still, obsidian was so rare that lining an entire tunnel with the stuff would have cost more than the Guile family made in a year. Why would Gavin have done such a thing? The magic properties of the stuff meant that with pure darkness and a direct connection—such as through blood or an open cut—it could drain the luxin out of a drafter. No wonder the red luxin wasn't helping Dazen feel hatred anymore. It had all been drained away.

Something niggled at Dazen's mind. The bends in the tunnel, maybe that was it. The tunnels had bent so that no blue light would spill from the blue cell into the tunnel. Thus the tunnel would be totally dark. So the obsidian would work.

Damn Gavin to the evernight. He's not stopping me. I don't care if I'm a bloody wreck. I'm getting out of here.

Part of Dazen was telling him to stop, to think. That blue, rational part of him. But he couldn't stop. If he didn't keep moving, he'd never get anywhere. He was so sick, so fevered that if he stopped he might never move again. Gavin wanted to paralyze him.

No. No no no. Dazen pushed on. The floor here felt different. Not obsidian. He'd gotten past it. He crawled farther. He could swear there was a glow ahead of him. Dear Orholam, there was—

The floor dropped out from under him, swinging open on hidden hinges. Dazen tumbled down, rolling over and over, unable to stop himself, down a chute that snapped shut behind him. He rolled over, bathed in green light.

Green?

An entire, round chamber, with green walls like trees. A hole up top for water and food and air, and a hole in the bottom for waste. Dazen looked desperately at his skin for the red luxin. It was gone. All gone, all sucked up by the obsidian tunnel.

Dazen started laughing stupidly, desperately, madly. A green prison, after the blue prison. He laughed until he was sobbing. There wasn't one prison. There weren't two. He knew it now. He had no doubt. There were seven prisons. One for every color, and in sixteen years, he had only escaped the first.

He laughed and sobbed. In one luminous green wall, the dead man laughed with him. At him.

Chapter 95

"Not bad for a defeat," said Corvan Danavis, coming into Gavin's cabin.

Gavin sat up, blinking the sleep from his eyes. His "quick nap" after talking to Kip had left him wooly. But he'd drafted so much over the past week, it was no wonder he felt off. He said, "We lost a city, three-quarters of the Blackguard, and hundreds if not thousands of soldiers. My natural son—whom I just acknowledged—publicly murdered a rightful satrap, which will make the other satraps worry I'm trying to rule the world again. We have thousands of refugees that we have to put Orholam knows where; there's some pagan army in charge of Garriston; and I've built them a damn near unassailable wall, which will now protect my enemies. Oh, and your daughter has joined our foes. If that's not bad for a defeat, I'm not really sure what is."

"Could be worse," Corvan said.

Gavin rubbed his cheek where Karris had slapped him. It was worse, Corvan, he wanted to say. He'd been so delighted to see Karris alive that he'd hugged her without thinking. He'd deserved the slap for that alone. But she'd clung to him, for half a moment. Maybe she just felt relieved to be safe, away from King Garadul's army, but he'd hoped it was something more.

Then she'd whispered, "I know your big secret, you asshole. Why couldn't you be man enough to tell me yourself?"

Big secret? His heart froze up in his chest. Which big secret?

She released him and stared into his eyes. Unable to take it, he'd glanced away—and saw Kip. Kip, whom he'd thought was most likely dead. Like a moron, he said, "Kip?"

He hadn't meant Kip was his big secret. That would be stupid. Of course she knew about Kip. But his brain wasn't working. Her closeness, the battle, the effects of his drafting so much, and the sudden sense of exposure throttled his thoughts.

She'd slapped him. He'd deserved it.

Gavin said to Corvan, "It can always be worse. Is the weather holding?" He sat up. If he had to make these barges weather a storm, he was going to have a lot of work to do.

"Hold up," Corvan said. "Your attitude when you go out there matters."

Gavin stopped. Corvan had talked to him like this before, but not since the war. "What are you talking about?"

"I mean this Lord Omnichrome doesn't care about Garriston. The only thing Garriston was to him was a chance to take a victory from us, and frame you for murdering a satrap so he could mobilize people to fight you. What he wants is to destroy the Chromeria. He wants to drive out the belief in Orholam and set up a new order. And we don't even know what that new order is yet."

"So let's rephrase 'defeat' as 'crushing defeat,' huh?" Gavin knew he was being childish, but Corvan was the only person around to whom he could complain. It felt good to have his friend back.

"We have to get ready for war," Corvan said. "A bigger war than over one little city."

"You think people are going to join him?"

"In droves," Corvan said. "My daughter did, and she's not stupid. So we have to believe he's charismatic, and we've already seen that he's smart enough to defeat us and get all he wants. So we have to look at what we have, and prepare."

"I'm sorry she joined him, Corvan. She seemed like such a sensible girl. I should have watched out for her better while she was—"

"She *is* a sensible girl. I'm not worried about her. She'll come back," Corvan said. There was an edge on his voice, as well there should be. He was trying to convince himself too. But Gavin knew not to push it.

"So what do we have?" Gavin asked.

"We have you and me. We got Karris back and Kip back and Iron-fist back, when we could have easily lost all three. We have the devotion, loyalty, awe, and motivation of thirty thousand people who now believe in Gavin Guile to the core of their souls. I call that the start of an army. You're the Prism. How is some pagan king going to stand up to you?"

Gavin laughed, because both of them knew that there were about a thousand ways. It was also a little scary, how Corvan thought. How he saw through things. Gavin would have to be careful. There are things you can't tell even your best friend. Great purposes best achieved by misdirection.

Pensive, Gavin said, "You know, I came up with a list of things I want to accomplish before I die, and the best thing on that list was to free Garriston. What I let happen there after the war was...I don't know if it's the worst thing I've done, that's a crowded field, but I let what was happening in Garriston *keep* happening. For sixteen years. With all my power, I could never get the Spectrum to stop it."

"I knew a man once who had a knack of changing the rules when he couldn't win. He didn't give up when others said he'd already lost," Corvan said. "So...Garriston is a collection of ramshackle buildings with indefensible walls."

"So I built new walls, I changed the rules. I tried, Corvan! I lost!" Gavin grimaced, light dawning. "Oh, and you're going to say next, 'You lost a collection of ramshackle buildings.' And I'm going to say, 'Yes! We've established that.' And you're going to point out that when I decided to free Garriston, I probably wasn't worried about the misery of the buildings, but the misery of the people."

"And then I'll point out that all those people you wanted to free *are here*. And then you'll admit my superior wisdom."

Gavin laughed. In some moments, it was like a day hadn't passed since they'd been separated. "Well, we know one of those things isn't going to happen."

Corvan grinned. He was right, though. "So," he said, "go out there and smile, and pat your soldiers on the back, and act like an emperor with a great purpose before him—a promachos who *will* accomplish that great purpose. You *have* freed these people. You *are* going to protect them, and you *will* give them a new home. You will give them justice. And they're going to help you."

"Sometimes I think you should have been the leader, not me," Gavin said.

"Me too," Corvan said. He grinned. "Orholam's ways are mysterious. In some cases, *very* mysterious."

"*Thanks,*" Gavin said. Then they laughed together. It felt good. Food for a hungry soul.

"By the by, how's your back? I could've sworn that little weasel stabbed you. Kip's being hailed as a hero for stopping him, you know."

"He got him right in the nick of time, I guess," Gavin said, though he must have taken a shot in the kidney from the boy's fist as Kip had tackled him, because he had felt a searing pain. He pulled his shirt around and showed it to Corvan. The shirt was cut over his kidney, but his skin was unbroken. "A near thing," he said.

Corvan whistled. "Orholam's hand must be on you, my friend."

Gavin grunted. From how his head felt, he wished Orholam's hand were a little gentler. "Well, time to go play emperor, then," he said. Together, they walked to the door of the cabin—and who had drafted cabins onto the barge?

Gavin paused. "Corvan, something was bothering me."

"Yes?"

"All those years you spent in that little town. Seems like an awful coincidence that both you and Kip were in the same place."

"Not a coincidence," Corvan said soberly.

"You tracked him down. You were looking out for him. Watching him." Gavin didn't need Corvan to confirm it. He knew. "But you never got very close to him."

"Tried not to, anyway. He's a good boy. But he is who he is," Corvan said. He meant, He is your brother's son. Corvan looked down at his hands and lowered his voice, so that even if someone had been eavesdropping just outside the room, they couldn't have made out the words. "I knew you might need me to kill him someday. I didn't want to make it harder than it had to be."

Neither said anything for a long moment.

The Danavis motto was Fealty to One. Corvan didn't believe in Orholam, or the Chromeria, or any creed. He believed in Gavin. Sometimes it was frightening to have someone believe in you like that. For a second, Gavin considered telling Corvan his seventh and final purpose. Trusting him. But no. Safer this way. He'd tell him when the time came.

"Some world," Corvan said finally.

"Some day," Gavin said, looking out on the gray skies. Blah.

Corvan grunted. "At least it's nice out," he said, and went on his way.

Sometimes Corvan's sarcasm was so deadpan.

Gavin shrugged and went around patting shoulders, checking on the wounded, asking about supplies and their course, mostly being seen and being seen to care and to be in charge. Karris watched him the whole time, but never said a word to him. There was another problem he'd have to address.

He checked in on Kip. The boy was curled up, asleep. As well he might be. Gavin was still sorting out the tales. According to the stories, Kip had drafted green, blue, red, and maybe yellow. At fifteen years of age. Gavin had hoped to buy them both some time by falsifying the testing stone; Kip's road was going to be hard enough as it was. Too late now. Smart, brave, and now a polychrome, the boy had more than proven himself a Guile—Gavin would have to work twice as hard to keep the truth from him.

There was a lot of work to do.

Not least of which was facing his father and telling him his wife was dead, that his bastard grandson had killed a satrap, and trying to fend off a conversation about marrying some satrap's daughter in order to patch things up—a conversation Gavin was going to lose.

He went to the side of the barge to draft a scull to head over to the other barge. He looked around for something blue to draft from. There was nothing. He looked up. There were no clouds. He was on a barge on the sea under a bright sky. But something was wrong.

He tried to draft blue. He was a Prism; he could split white light into anything.

But nothing happened.

A bolt of panic flashed through Gavin. He counted off his colors on his fingertips, thumb to forefinger first, down then up. Sub-red, red, orange, yellow, green, bl— Nothing. He stared at his offending middle finger as if this were its fault. There was no blue. He couldn't draft it. He couldn't even *see* it. It was starting. Not on the seventh year. Now. He'd never even known how a Prism knew when the end began. Now he knew. He was losing his colors. He didn't have five years left; it was starting now. Gavin was dying.

Acknowledgments

Two years ago, I sent my Night Angel trilogy into the world with the typical triumph and terror. I've burned to be a novelist since I was thirteen. This was my shot, my chance to run the gauntlet of the masses. A hundred things can bury a debut, and just to push off the necessity of getting a real job, I needed my debut to do better than most. But dreams burn to the ground every day. Tragedies happen.

But so do miracles.

So my first thank-you is to you readers who gave an unknown guy with some ninja novel a chance. And thank you especially to you readers who then handed my book to a friend and said, "Try this. No, really, try it." And a double especially with whip and a chocolate-covered espresso bean to those of you who work at bookstores who did that, from Albuquerque to Perth. You all have changed my life. It is a huge privilege to get to write for a living, so thank you.

Kristi, you are grace and tenacity. I wouldn't be living the dream without you, and I wouldn't want to. Thanks for having that crazy impractical streak where it comes to me, an inch wide and a mile deep.

Don, thank you for not just wrangling deals, but also knowing when to say no to them. Thank you for steering me to work with people who will be passionate about my books. Cameron, thanks for foisting my books on the unwary all over the world.

Devi, thank you for using the fierce Eye of Sauron—no, not on me!—but secretly on my behalf. And to you and Tim, Alex, Jack, and Jennifer, I promised you this book would be my shortest, and it turned into my longest, causing headaches for everyone. Rather than beating me to get the next product in the supply chain, you've allowed me a huge amount of autonomy. I appreciate your faith in me and all you do to make me successful. You guys are fearless and brilliant, and it's great to work with you.

Thanks to all the other folks at Hachette, from the nameless unpaid interns (hang in there!), to the guy who keeps the computers running, to Gina (I really owe you *several* nice dinners, don't I?), to the patient production people who have good reason to hate me. But I pass all hatred along to my editor, Devi. (She also likes unsolicited manuscripts! Here's her home phone number ████████████ and personal email ████████@████████████.)

Heather and Andrew, thank you for all your work in managing the forum. You've allowed me to connect with my fans—and still have time to write. Thank you thank you thank you.

I'm afraid I've rewarded the friends and family who tolerated many email updates over the years (how many words can you use to say "still no book sale"?) by being so busy in the last two years that I hardly ever update them at all. If you were in the first acknowledgments, thank you again.

Cody L., your enthusiasm is better than coffee. Shaun and Diane M., thank you for your wise counsel and friendship. Scot and Kari-ann B., thanks for the trips to Red Robin every time we sold a foreign right. (Italy, huzzah!) Dr. Jacob K., thanks for awesome impromptu lectures, gentle translation corrections, and "promachos." Thank you to Dr. Jon L., who once said, "Wouldn't it be cool if instead of [genre trope], the hero [inverse of genre trope]?" That seed niggled at me for years, Jon. I have since found the very good reasons why more writers haven't done that—and had a blast doing it anyway. Thank you to Seiei, who changed this whole book with a couple of tweets. Thank you Nate D., for genius brainstorming, and Laura J. D., for insights into two things I will probably never truly understand: women, and being incredibly fit. Any errors in this book are theirs.

Thank you Rockstar Energy Drink. Those years you took off my life were probably the bad ones anyway.

And last, thank you to you unshakably curious readers who *still* read acknowledgments though you aren't looking for your name. What, the book wasn't long enough for you? Go on, get outta here and go tell someone, "You gotta read this! No, really. C'mon, there's a maa-aap."

Character List

Aheyyad: Orange drafter, grandson of Tala. A defender of Garriston, the designer of Garriston's Brightwater Wall; dubbed Aheyyad Brightwater by Prism Gavin Guile.

Amestan: A Blackguard at the Battle of Garriston.

Arana: A drafting student, a merchant's daughter.

Arash, Javid: One of the drafters who defended Garriston.

Arien: A magister at the Chromeria. She drafts orange and tests Kip on Luxlord Black's orders.

Ariss the Navigator: A legendary explorer, discoverer.

Atiriel, Karris: A desert princess. She became Karris Shadowblinder before she married Lucidonius.

Bas the Simple: A Tyrean polychrome (blue/green/superviolet), handsome but a simpleton, sworn to kill the killer of the White Oak family.

Blue-Eyed Demons, the: Mercenaries who fought for Dazen's army.

Carver Black: A non-drafter, as is traditional for the Black. He is the chief administrator of the Seven Satrapies. Though he has a voice on the Spectrum, he has no vote.

Carvingen, Odess: A drafter and defender of Garriston.

Corzin, Eleph: An Abornean blue drafter, a defender of Garriston.

Counselor, the: A legendary figure. Author of The Counselor to Kings, which advised such cruel methods of government that not even he followed them when he ruled.

Crassos, Aglaia: A young noblewoman and drafter at the Chromeria. She is the youngest daughter of an important Ruthgari family.

Crassos, Governor: Elder brother of Aglaia Crassos; the last governor of Garriston.

Danavis, Aliviana (Liv): Daughter of Corvan Danavis. She is a yellow and superviolet bichrome drafter from Tyrea. Her contract is owned by the Ruthgari, and she is supervised by Aglaia Crassos.

Danavis, Corvan: A red drafter. A scion of one of the great Ruthgari families, he was also the most brilliant general of the age and the primary reason for Dazen's success in battle.

Danavis, Ell: The second wife of Corvan Danavis. She was murdered by an assassin three years after their marriage.

Danavis, Erethanna: A green drafter serving Count Nassos in western Ruthgar; Liv Danavis's cousin.

Danavis, Qora: A Tyrean noblewoman; first wife of Corvan Danavis, mother of Aliviana Danavis.

Delara Orange: The Atashian member of the Spectrum. She represents Orange and is a forty-year-old orange/red bichrome nearing the end of her life. Her predecessor in the seat was her mother, who devised the rotating scheme for Garriston.

Delarias: A family in Rekton.

Delauria, Katalina: Kip's mother. She is of Parian or Ilytian extraction and is a haze addict.

Delclara, Micael: A quarryman and a Rekton villager.

Delclara, Miss: The matriarch of the Delclara family in Rekton. She had six sons who are quarrymen.

Delclara, Zalo: A quarryman, one of the Delclara sons.

Delelo, Galan: A master sergeant in the Omnichrome's army. He escorts Liv to the gates of Garriston.

Delmarva, Gad: A young general of Dazen's army who took the city of Ru and publicly massacred the royal family and their retainers.

Elos, Gaspar: A green color wight.

Falling Leaf, Deedee: A green drafter. Her failing health inspired a number of veteran drafters to take the Freeing at Garriston.

Farjad, Farid: A nobleman and ally of Dazen's once Dazen promised him the Atashian throne during the False Prism's War.

Farseer, Horas: Another ally of Dazen's, the bandit king of the Blue-Eyed Demons. Gavin Guile killed him after the False Prism's War.

Flamehands: An Ilytian drafter and defender of Garriston.

Galden, Jens: A magister at the Chromeria, a red drafter.

Galib: A polychrome at the Chromeria.

Gallos: A stableman at Garriston.

Garadul, Perses: Appointed satrap of Tyrea after Ruy Gonzalo was defeated by the Prism's forces in the False Prism's War. Perses was the father of Rask Garadul. He worked to eradicate the bandits plaguing Tyrea after the war.

Garadul, Rask: A satrap who declared himself king of Tyrea; his father was Perses Garadul.

Gerain: An old man in Garriston who exhorted people to join King Garadul.

Gevison: A poet (long deceased).

Goldeneyes, Tawenza: A yellow drafter. She teaches only the three most talented yellows each year at the Chromeria.

Goldthorn: A magister at the Chromeria. Barely three years older than her disciples, she teaches the superviolet class.

Gonzalo, Ruy: A Tyrean satrap who sided with Dazen during the False Prism's War.

Grass, Evi: A drafter and defender of Garriston. She is a green/yellow bichrome from Blood Forest, and is a superchromat.

Greenveil, Arys: The Sub-red on the Spectrum. A Blood Forester, she is cousin to Jia Tolver, the Yellow. Her parents were killed in the war by the Green's brothers.

Grinwoody: Andross Guile's chief slave and right hand.

Guile, Andross: Father of Gavin, Dazen, and Sevastian Guile. He drafts yellow through sub-red, although he is primarily known for drafting red, as that is his position on the Spectrum. He took a place on the Spectrum despite being from Blood Forest, which already had a representative, by claiming that his few lands in Ruthgar qualified him for the seat.

Guile, Dazen: Younger brother of Gavin. He fell in love with Karris White Oak and triggered the False Prism's War when "he" burned down her family compound, killing everyone within.

Guile, Felia: Married to Andross Guile. The mother of Gavin and Dazen, a cousin of the Atashian royal family, she is an orange drafter. Her mother was courted by Ulbear Rathcore before he met Orea Pullawr.

Guile, Gavin: The Prism. Two years older than Dazen, he was appointed at age thirteen.

Guile, Kip: The natural Tyrean son of Gavin Guile and Katalina Delauria.

Guile, Sevastian: The youngest Guile brother. He was murdered by a blue wight when Gavin was thirteen and Dazen was not yet eleven.

Gunner: An Ilytian pirate. His first underdeck command was as cannoneer on the Aved Barayah. He later became a captain.

Helel, Mistress: She masqueraded as a teacher in the Chromeria and tried to murder Kip.

Ironfist, Harrdun: Commander of the Blackguard, thirty-eight years old, a blue drafter.

Isabel (Isa): A pretty young girl in Rekton.

Izem Blue: A legendary drafter and a defender of Garriston under Gavin Guile.

Izem Red: A defender of Garriston under Gavin Guile. He fought for Gavin during the False Prism's War. A Parian drafter of red with incredible speed, he wears his ghotra in the shape of a cobra's hood.

Jorvis, Ana: A superviolet/blue bichrome, student at the Chromeria.

Kadah: A magister at the Chromeria; a green drafter who teaches drafting basics.

Klytos Blue: The Blue on the Spectrum. He represents Ilyta, though he is a Ruthgari through and through. A coward and Andross's tool.

Laya: A Blackguard who drafts red, present at the Battle of Garriston.

Lightbringer, the: A controversial figure in prophecy and mythology. Attributes that most agree on are that he is male, will slay or has slain gods and kings, is of mysterious birth, is a genius of magic, a warrior who will sweep, or has swept, all before him, a champion of the poor and downtrodden, great from his youth, He Who Shatters. That most of the prophecies were in Old Parian and the meanings have changed in ways that are difficult to trace hasn't helped. There are three basic camps: that the Lightbringer has yet to come; that the Lightbringer has already come and was Lucidonius (a view the Chromeria now holds, though it didn't always); and, among some academics, that the Lightbringer is a metaphor for what is best in all of us.

Lucidonius: The legendary founder of the Seven Satrapies and the Chromeria, the first Prism. He was married to Karris Shadowblinder and founded the Blackguards.

Lunna Green: The Green on the Spectrum. She is Ruthgari, a cousin of Jia Tolver. Her brothers killed Arys Greenveil's parents during the war.

Malargos, Dervani: A Ruthgari nobleman, Tisis Malargos's father, a friend and supporter of Dazen during the False Prism's War. He is a green drafter who was lost in the wilds of Tyrea for years. When he tried to return home, Felia Guile hired pirates to kill him so that he wouldn't reveal Gavin's secrets.

Malargos, Tisis: A stunningly beautiful Ruthgari green drafter. Her father and uncle fought for Dazen.

Marissia: Gavin's room slave. A red-haired Blood Forester who was captured by the Ruthgari during Dazen's war, she has been with Gavin for ten years, since she was eighteen.

Marta, Adan: An inhabitant of Rekton.

Mori: A soldier in the Omnichrome's army.

Naheed: Satrapah of Atash. She was murdered by General Gad Delmarta during the False Prism's War.

Nassos: A Ruthgari count in western Ruthgar. Liv Danavis's cousin serves him.

Navid, Payam: A handsome and popular magister at the Chromeria.

Omnichrome, Lord (the Color Prince): The leader of a rebellion against the rule of the Chromeria. His true identity is known by few, as he has re-formed almost his entire body with luxin. A full-spectrum polychrome, he posits a faith in freedom and power, rather than in Lucidonius and Orholam. Also known as the Color Prince, the Crystal Prophet, the Polychrome Master, the Eldritch Enlightened, and the Lord Rainbow. He was formerly Koios White Oak, one of Karris White Oak's brothers. He was horribly burned in the fire that triggered the False Prism's War.

Orholam: The deity of the monotheistic Seven Satrapies, also known as the Father of All and the Lord of Light. His worship was spread throughout the Seven Satrapies by Lucidonius, four hundred years before the reign of Prism Gavin Guile.

Orlos, Maros: A very religious Ruthgari drafter. He fought in both the False Prism's War and as a defender of Garriston.

Payam, Parshan: A young drafter at the Chromeria who attempts to seduce Liv Danavis as part of a bet. He fails in spectacular fashion.

Philosopher, the: A foundational figure in both moral and natural philosophy.

Ptolos: Satrapah of Ruthgar.

Pullawr, Orea: See White, the.

Rados, Blessed Satrap: A Ruthgari satrap who fought the Blood Foresters although he was outnumbered two to one. He was famous for burning the Rozanos Bridge behind his army to keep it from retreating.

Ramir (Ram): A Rekton villager.

Rathcore, Ulbear: The late husband of the White, he has been dead for twenty years.

Running Wolf: A general for Gavin during the False Prism's war. He was thrice bested by smaller forces commanded by Corvan Danavis.

Sadah Superviolet: The Parian representative, a superviolet drafter, often the swing vote on the Spectrum.

Sanson: A village boy from Rekton.

Sayeh, Samila: A blue drafter for Gavin's army. She fought in the defense of Garriston under Gavin Guile.

Sendinas, the: A Rekton family.

Shadowblinder, Karris: Lucidonius's wife and later widow. She was the second Prism. See also Atiriel, Karris.

Spear: A commander of the Blackguards when Gavin first became Prism.

Stump: A Parian Blackguard.

Sworrins, the: A Rekton family.

Tala: A drafter and warrior in the False Prism's War. She was also a defender of Garriston. Her grandson is Aheyyad Brightwater, and her sister is Tayri.

Tarkian: A polychrome drafter.

Tayri: A Parian drafter and defender of Garriston. Her sister is Tala.

Temnos, Dalos the Younger: A drafter who fought in both the False Prism's War and the defense of Garriston under Gavin Guile.

Tep, Usef: A drafter who fought in the False Prism's War. He is also known as the Purple Bear, because he is a discontiguous bichromein red and blue. After the war, he and Samila Sayeh became lovers, despite having fought on opposite sides.

Tolver, Jia: The Yellow on the Spectrum. An Abornean drafter, she is a cousin of Arys Greenveil (the Sub-red) and Lunna Green.

Tremblefist: A Blackguard. He is Ironfist's younger brother.

Usem the Wild: A drafter and defender of Garriston.

Varidos, Kerawon: A superchromat, magister and head tester of the Chromeria. He drafts orange and red.

Vena: Liv's friend and fellow student at the Chromeria; a superviolet.

Wanderer, the: A legendary figure, the subject of Gevison's poem The Wanderer's Last Journey.

White Oak, Karris: A Blackguard; a red/green bichrome; the original cause of the False Prism's War.

White Oak, Koios: One of the seven White Oak brothers, brother to Karris White Oak.

White Oak, Kolos: One of the seven White Oak brothers, brother to Karris White Oak.

White Oak, Rissum: A luxlord, the father of Karris and her seven brothers; reputed to be hot-tempered, but a coward.

White Oak, Rodin: One of the seven White Oak brothers, brother to Karris White Oak.

White Oak, Tavos: One of the seven White Oak brothers, brother to Karris White Oak.

White, the: The head of the Spectrum. She is a blue/green bichrome, but currently abstains from any drafting in order to prolong her life. Her name is Orea Pullawr, though it is rarely used. She was married to Ulbear Rathcore before his death.

Wit, Rondar: A blue drafter who becomes a color wight.

Zid: Quartermaster of the Omnichrome's army.

Zymun: A young drafter and member of the Omnichrome's army.

Glossary

Aghbalu: A Parian city.

alcaldesa: A Tyrean term, akin to village mayor or chief.

Anat: Goddess of wrath, associated with sub-red. See Appendix, "On the Old Gods."

Aslal: The capital city of Paria.

ataghan: A narrow, slightly forward-curving sword with a single edge for most of its length.

Atan's Teeth: Mountains to the east of Tyrea.

atasifusta: The widest tree in the world, believed extinct after the False Prism's War. Its sap has properties like concentrated red luxin, which, when allowed to drain slowly, can keep a flame lit for hundreds of years if the tree is large enough. The wood itself is ivory white, and when the trees are immature, a small amount can keep a home warm for months.

Atirat: God of lust, associated with green. See Appendix, "On the Old Gods."

Aved Barayah: A legendary ship. Its name means *The Fire Breather*.

aventail: Usually made of chain mail, it is attached to the helmet and drapes over the neck, shoulders, and upper chest.

balance: The primary work of the Prism. When the Prism drafts at the top of the Chromeria, he alone can sense all the world's imbalances in magic and can draft enough of its opposite (i.e., balancing) color to stop the imbalance from getting any worse and leading to catastrophe. Frequent imbalances occurred throughout the world's history before Lucidonius came, and the resulting disasters of fire, famine, and sword killed thousands if not millions. Supuerviolet balances sub-red, blue balances red, and green balances orange. Yellow seems to exist in balance naturally.

beams: See Chromeria trained.

Belphegor: God of sloth, associated with yellow. See Appendix, "On the Old Gods."

belt-flange: A flattened hook attached to a pistol so it can be tucked securely into a belt.

belt knife: A blade small enough to be tucked in a man's belt, commonly used for eating, rarely for defense.

bich'hwa: A "scorpion," a dagger with a loop hilt and a narrow, undulating recurved blade. Sometimes made with a claw.

bichrome: A drafter who can draft two different colors.

Big Jasper (Island): The island on which the city of Big Jasper rests just opposite the Chromeria, and where the embassies of all the satrapies reside.

Blackguard, the: The White's bodyguard. The Blackguard was also instituted by Lucidonius both to prevent the Prism's overreaching power and to guard the Prism from external threats.

Blood Plains, the: An older collective term for Ruthgar and Blood Forest, so called since Vician's Sin caused the Blood War between them.

Blood War, the: A series of battles that began after Vician's Sin tore apart the formerly close allies of Blood Forest and Ruthgar. The war was seemingly interminable, often starting and stopping, until Gavin Guile put an end to it following the False Prism's War. It seems there will be no further hostilities. Also known as the Blood Wars among some scholars who differentiate between the various campaigns.

Blue-Eyed Demons, the: A famed company of bandits whose king Gavin Guile killed after the False Prism's War.

blunderbuss: A short musket with a bell-shaped muzzle that can be loaded with shrapnel. Useful at short distances only, such as against mobs.

brightwater: Liquid yellow luxin.

Brightwater Wall: Its building was an epic feat. This wall was designed by Aheyyad Brightwater and built by Prism Guile at Garriston in just days before and while the Omnichrome's army attacked.

Broken Man, the: A statue in a Tyrean orange grove. A Ptaru relic?

caleen: A diminutive term of address for a girl or female slave, like "girl" but used regardless of the slave's age.

Cannon Island: A small island with a minimal garrison between Big Jasper and Little Jasper.

cavendish: Tobacco-like fruit leather.

Cerulean Sea, the: The sea at the center of the Seven Satrapies.

cherry glims: Slang for red-drafting second-year students.

chirurgeon: One who stitches up the wounded and studies anatomy.

Chosen, Orholam's: Another term for the Prism.

Chromeria, the: The ruling body of the Seven Satrapies; also a term for the school where drafters are trained.

> **Chromeria trained:** Those who have or are training at the Chromeria school for drafting on Little Jasper Island in the Cerulean Sea. The Chromeria's training system does not limit students based on age, but rather progresses them through each degree of training based on their ability and knowledge. So a thirteen-year-old who is extremely proficient in drafting might well be a gleam, or third-year student, while an eighteen-year-old who is just beginning work on her drafting could be a dim.
>
> - *darks:* Technically known as "the supplicants," these are would-be drafters who have yet to be tested for their abilities at the Chromeria or allowed admission to the school.
> - *dims:* The first-year (and therefore lowest) rank of the Chromeria's students.
> - *glims:* Second-year students.
> - *gleams:* Third-year students who are fairly advanced.
> - *beams:* Fourth-year students.

Colors, the: The seven members of the Spectrum. Each originally represented a single color of the seven sacred colors, and could draft that color, and each satrapy had one representative on the Spectrum. Since the founding of the Spectrum, that practice has deteriorated as satrapies have maneuvered for power. Thus a satrapy's representative, though usually appointed to a color corresponding to his abilities, could be appointed as Luxlord Green, but not actually draft green himself. Likewise, some of the satrapies might lose their representative, and others could have two or even three representatives on the Spectrum at a time, depending on the politics of the day. The term is for life.

color matchers: A term for full-spectrum superchromats. Sometimes employed as satraps' gardeners.

color-sensitive: See superchromat.

color wight: A drafter who has broken the halo. They frequently remake their bodies with pure luxin, rejecting the Pact between drafter and society.

Counselor to Kings, The: A manuscript, noted for its advocating ruthless treatment of opponents.

Cracked Lands, the: A region of broken land in the extreme west of Atash. Its treacherous terrain is only crossed by the most hardy and experienced traders.

Crater Lake: A large lake in southern Tyrea where the former capital of Tyrea, Kelfing, sits. The area is famous for its forests and the production of yew longbows.

Crossroads, the: A kopi house, restaurant, tavern, the highest-priced inn on the Jaspers, and downstairs, allegedly, a similarly priced brothel. Located near the Lily's Stem, the Crossroads is housed in the former Tyrean embassy building, centrally located in the Embassies District for all the ambassadors, spies, and merchants trying to deal with various governments.

cubit: A unit of volume. One cubit is one foot high, one foot wide, and one foot deep.

culverin: A type of cannon, useful for firing long distances because of its heavily weighted cannonballs and long-bore tube.

dagger-pistols: Flintlock pistols with a blade attached, allowing the user to fire at distance and then use the blade at close range or if the weapon misfires.

Dagnu: God of gluttony, associated with red. See Appendix, "On the Old Gods."

danar: The currency of the Seven Satrapies. One danar at an expensive inn on Jasper Island buys a cup of kopi. The average worker makes about a danar a day, while an unskilled laborer can expect to earn a half danar a day. The coins have a square hole cut in the middle, and are often carried on square-cut sticks. They can be cut in half and still hold their value.

tin danar: Worth eight regular danar coins. A stick of tin danars usually carries twenty-five coins, that is, two hundred danars.

silver quintar: Worth twenty danars, slightly wider than the tin danar, but only half as thick. A stick of silver quintars usually carries fifty coins, that is, one thousand danars.

den: One-tenth of a danar.

darks: See Chromeria trained.

Dark Forest: A region within Blood Forest where pygmies reside. Decimated by the diseases brought by invaders, their numbers have never recovered, and they remain insular and often hostile.

Dazen's War: An alternate name of the False Prism's War, used by the victors.

dey/deya: A Parian title, male and female respectively. A near-absolute ruler over a city and its surrounding territory.

dims: See Chromeria trained.

discipulae: The feminine plural term (also applying to groups of mixed gender) for those who study both religious and magical arts.

drafter: One who can shape or harness light into physical form (luxin).

drafter-tailor: A profession that disappeared overnight during the Guile brothers' childhood. These tailors could, with enough will, craft luxin flexible enough to be fashioned as clothing and seal it.

Embassies District: The Big Jasper neighborhood that is closest to the Lily's Stem, and thus is closest to the Chromeria itself. It also houses markets and kopi houses, taverns, and brothels.

evernight: Often a curse word, it refers to death and hell. A metaphysical or teleological reality, rather than a physical one, it represents that which will forever embrace and be embraced by void, full darkness, night in its purest, most evil form.

eye caps: A specialized kind of spectacles. These colored lenses fit directly over the eye sockets, glued to the skin. Like other spectacles, they enable a drafter to see through their preferred color, allowing them to draft more easily.

False Prism, the: Another term for Dazen Guile, who claimed to be a Prism even after his older brother Gavin had already been rightly chosen by Orholam and installed as Prism.

False Prism's War, the: A common term for the war between Gavin and Dazen Guile.

Fealty to One: The Danavis motto.

Ferrilux: God of pride, associated with superviolet. See Appendix, "On the Old Gods."

firefriend: A term sub-red drafters use for each other.

foot: Once a varying measure based on the current Prism's foot length. Later standardized to twelve thumbs (the length of Prism Sayid Talim's foot).

Free, the: Those drafters who reject the Pact of the Chromeria to join the Omnichrome's army, choosing to eventually break the halo and become wights. Also called the Unchained.

Freed, the: Those drafters who accept the Pact of the Chromeria and choose to be ritually killed before they break the halo and go mad. (The closeness of this term with "the Free" is part of the linguistic war between the pagans and the Chromeria, with the pagans trying to seize terms that had long had other, perverted, they thought, meanings.)

Freeing: The ritual release of those about to break the halo from incipient madness; performed by the Prism every year on Sun Day.

frizzen: On flintlocks, the L-shaped piece of metal against which the flint scrapes. The metal is on a hinge that opens upon firing to allow the sparks to reach the black powder.

gada: A ball game that involves kicking and passing a ball of wrapped leather.

galleass: A large merchant ship powered by both oar and sail. The term later referred to ships modified for military purposes, which included adding castles at bow and stern and cannons that fire in all directions.

Garriston: The former commercial capital of Tyrea at the mouth of the Umber River on the Cerulean Sea. Prism Gavin Guile built Brightwater Wall to defend the city, but his defense failed, and the city was claimed by Lord Omnichrome, Koios White Oak.

gemshorn: A musical instrument made from the tusk of a javelina, with finger-holes drilled into it to allow different notes to be produced.

ghotra: A Parian headscarf, used by many Parian men to demonstrate their reverence for Orholam. Most wear it while the sun is up, but some wear it even at nighttime.

giist: A colloquial name for a blue wight.

gladius: A short double-edged sword, useful for cutting or stabbing at close range.

Glass Lily, the: Another term for Little Jasper, or for the whole of the Chromeria as a collection of buildings.

gleams: See Chromeria trained.

glims: See Chromeria trained.

gold standard: The literal standard weights and measures, made of gold, against which all measures are judged. The originals are kept at the Chromeria, and certified copies are kept in every capital and major city for the adjudication of disputes. Merchants found using short measures and inaccurate weights are punished severely.

Great Chain (of Being), the: A theological term for the order of creation. The first link is Orholam himself, and all the other links (creation) derive from him.

Great Desert, the: Another term for the Badlands of Tyrea.

great hall of the Travertine Palace, the: The wonder of the great hall is its eight great pillars set in a star shape around the hall, all made of extinct atasifusta wood. Said to be the gift of an Atashian king, these trees were the widest in the world, and their sap allows fires to burn continually, even five hundred years after they were cut.

Great River, the: The river between Ruthgar and Blood Forest, the scene of many pitched battles between the two countries.

great yard, the: The yard at the base of the towers of the Chromeria.

Green Bridge: Less than a league upstream from Rekton, drafted by Gavin Guile in seconds while on his way to battle his brother at Sundered Rock.

green flash: A rare flash seen at the setting of the sun; its meaning is debated. Some believe it has theological significance. The White calls it Orholam's wink.

Green Forest: A collective term for Blood Forest and Ruthgar during the hundred years of peace between the two countries, before Vician's Sin ended it.

Green Haven: The capital of Blood Forest.

grenado: A flagon full of black powder with a piece of wood shoved into the top, with a rag and bit of black powder as a fuse.

grenado, luxin: An explosive made of luxin that can be hurled at the enemy along an arc of luxin or in cannon. Often filled with shot/shrapnel, depending on the type of grenado used. Smaller grenades are sometimes carried in bandoliers.

Guardian, the: A colossus that stands astride the entrance to Garriston's bay. She holds a spear in one hand and a torch in the other. A yellow drafter keeps the torch lit with yellow luxin, allowing it to dissolve slowly back into light, acting as a kind of lighthouse. See also Ladies, the.

Guile palace: The Guile family palace on Big Jasper. Andross Guile rarely visits his home in the time Gavin is Prism, preferring to reside at the Chromeria. The Guile palace was one of the few buildings allowed to be constructed without regard to the working of the Thousand Stars.

habia: A long man's garment.

Hag, the: An enormous statue that comprises Garriston's west gate. She is crowned and leans heavily on a staff; the crown and staff are also towers from which archers can shoot at invaders. See also Ladies, the.

Hag's Crown, the: A tower over the west gate into Garriston.

Hag's Staff, the: A tower over the west gate into Garriston.

Harbinger: Corvan Danavis's sword, inherited when his elder brothers died.

haze: A mind-altering drug. Often smoked with a pipe, it produces a sickly sweet odor.

hellstone: A superstitious term for obsidian, which is rarer than diamonds or rubies as few know where the extant obsidian in the world is created or mined. Obsidian is the only stone that can draw luxin directly out of a drafter if it touches her blood directly.

Idoss: An Atashian city, ruled by a council of city mothers and a corregidor.

Jasper Islands/the Jaspers: Islands in the Cerulean Sea that hold the Chromeria.

Jasperites: Residents of Big Jasper.

javelinas: Animals, good for hunting. Giant javelinas are rare. Both species have tusks and hooves and are nocturnal.

Kelfing: The former capital of Tyrea, on the shores of Crater Lake.

kopi: An addictive stimulant, a popular beverage. Bitter, dark-colored, and served hot.

Ladies, the: Four statues that comprise the gates into the city of Garriston. They are built into the wall, made of rare Parian marble and sealed in nearly invisible yellow luxin. They are thought to depict aspects of the goddess Anat and were spared by Lucidonius, who believed them to depict something true. They are the Hag, the Lover, the Mother, and the Guardian.

league: A unit of measurement, six thousand and seventy-six paces.

lightsickness: The aftereffects of too much drafting. Only the Prism never gets lightsick.

lightwells: Holes in the Chromeria's towers that are positioned to allow light, with the use of mirrors, to reach into the interior of the towers late in the day or on the dark side of the towers.

Lily's Stem, the: The luxin bridge between Big and Little Jasper. It is composed of blue and yellow luxin so that it appears green. Set below the high-watermark, it is remarkable for its endurance against the waves and storms that wash over it.

Little Jasper: The island on which the Chromeria resides.

Little Jasper Bay: A bay off Little Jasper Island. It is protected by a seawall that keeps its waters calm.

longbow: A weapon that allows for the efficient (in speed, distance, and force) firing of arrows. Its construction and its user must both be extremely strong. The yew forests of Crater Lake provide the best wood available for longbows.

Lord Prism: A term of address for the Prism.

Lover, the: A statue that comprises the eastern river gate at Garriston. She is depicted in her thirties, lying on her back arched over the river with her feet planted, her knees forming a tower on one bank, hands entwined in her hair, elbows rising to form a tower on the other bank. She is clad only in veils. Before the Prisms' War, a portcullis could be lowered from her arched body into the river, its iron and steel hammered into shape so that it looked like a continuation of her veils. She glows like bronze when the sun sets, and the entrance to the city comes through another gate in her hair.

luxiat: A priest of Orholam. A luxiat wears black as an acknowledgment that he needs Orholam's light most of all; thus he is commonly called a blackrobe.

luxin: A material created by drafting from light. See Appendix.

luxlord: A term for a member of the ruling Spectrum.

Luxlords' Ball, the: An annual event on the open roof of the Prism's Tower.

magister: The term for a teacher of drafting and religion at the Chromeria.

mag torch: Often used by drafters to allow them access to light at night, it burns with a full spectrum of colors. Colored mag torches are also made at great expense, and when made correctly give a drafter her exact spectrum of light, allowing her to eschew spectacles and draft instantly.

match-holder: The piece on a matchlock musket to which a slow-match is affixed.

matchlock musket: A firearm that works by snapping a lit slow match into the flash pan, which ignites the gunpowder in the breech of the firearm, whose explosion propels a rock or lead ball out of the barrel at high speed. Matchlocks are accurate to fifty or a hundred paces, depending greatly on the smith who made them and the ammunition used.

matériel: A military term for equipment or supplies.

Midsummer: Another term for Sun Day, the longest day of the year.

Midsummer's Dance: A rural version of the Sun Day celebration.

Mirrormen: Soldiers in King Garadul's army who wear mirrored armor to protect themselves against luxin. The mirrors cause lux into disintegrate when it comes in contact with it.

Molokh: God of greed, associated with orange. See Appendix, "On the Old Gods."

monochromes: Drafters who can only draft one color.

Mot: God of envy, associated with blue. See Appendix, "On the Old Gods."

Mother, the: A statue that guards the south gate into Garriston. She is depicted as a teenager, heavily pregnant, with a dagger bared in one hand and a spear in the other.

mund: A person who cannot draft. Insulting.

murder hole: A hole in the ceiling of a passageway that allows soldiers to fire, drop, or throw weapons, projectiles, luxin, or fuel. Common in castles and city walls.

Narrows, the: A strait of the Cerulean Sea between Abornea and the Ruthgari mainland. Aborneans strangle trade between the Narrows by charging high toll fees to merchants attempting to sail the silk route, or simply between Paria and Ruthgar.

near-polychrome: One who can draft three colors, but can't stabilize the third color sufficiently to be a true polychrome.

non-drafter: One who cannot draft.

norm: Another term for a non-drafter. Insulting.

Odess: A city in Abornea that sits at the head of the Narrows.

old world: The world before Lucidonius united the Seven Satrapies and abolished worship of the pagan gods.

Order of the Broken Eye, the: A reputed guild of assassins. They specialize in killing drafters and have been rooted out and destroyed at least three times. They are thought to have re-formed each time with no connection to the previous incarnation of the Order. Some say paryl drafters worked with the Order hundreds of years earlier. Shimmercloaks were the pride of the Order, always working in pairs.

Pact, the: Since Lucidonius, the Pact has governed the Seven Satrapies. Its essence is that drafters agree to serve their community and receive all the benefits of status and sometimes wealth in exchange for their service and eventual choice to die just before or after breaking the halo.

parry-stick: A primarily defensive weapon that blocks bladed attacks. It sometimes includes a punching dagger at the center of the stick to follow up on a deflected blow.

petasos: A broad-brimmed Ruthgari hat, usually made of straw, meant to keep the sun off the face.

pilum: A weighted throwing spear whose shank bends after it pierces a shield, preventing the opponent from reusing the weapon against the user and encumbering the shield greatly. They are becoming more rare and ceremonial.

polychrome: A drafter who can draft more than two colors.

portmaster: A city official in charge of collecting tariffs and the organized exit and entrance of ships into his harbor.

Prism: There is only one Prism a generation. She senses the balance of the world's magic, can balance the magic, and can split light within herself. Her role is largely ceremonial and religious, not political, except for her balancing the world's magic so that wights and catastrophes don't result.

Prism's Tower, the: The central tower in the Chromeria. It houses the Prism, the White, and superviolets (as they are not numerous enough to require their own tower). The great hall lies below the tower, and the top holds a great crystal for the Prism's use while he balances the colors of the world. The annual Luxlords' Ball is held there.

promachia: The institution of a person named to the office of promachos. It gives great, nearly absolute powers during wartime.

promachos: A title given the Prism during war. It allows for his absolute rule and can only be instituted by order of the entire Spectrum. Among other powers, the promachos has the right to command armies, seize property, and elevate commoners to the nobility. It is an ancient term meaning He Who Fights Before Us.

Providence: A belief in the care of Orholam over the Seven Satrapies and its people.

psantria: A stringed musical instrument.

Rath: The capital of Ruthgar, set on the confluence of the Great River and its delta into the Cerulean Sea.

Rathcaeson: A mythical city, on the drawings of which Gavin Guile based his Brightwater Wall design.

ratweed: A toxic plant whose leaves are often smoked for their strong stimulant properties. Addictive.

Red Cliff Uprising, the: A rebellion in Atash after the end of the False Prism's War. Without the support of the royal family (who had been purged), it was short-lived.

Rekton: A small Tyrean town on the Umber River, near the site of the Battle of Sundered Rock. An important trading post before the False Prism's War.

Rozanos Bridge, the: A bridge on the Great River between Ruthgar and the Blood Forest that Blessed Satrap Rados burned.

Ru: The capital of Atash, once famous for its castle, still famous for its Great Pyramid.

Ru, Castle of: Once the pride of Ru, it was destroyed by fire during General Gad Delmarta's purge of the royal family in the Prisms' War.

Salve: A common greeting, originally meaning "Be of good health!"

Sapphire Bay: A bay off Little Jasper.

satrap/satrapah: The title of a ruler of one of the seven satrapies.

Skill, Will, Source, and Still/Movement: The four essential elements for drafting.

> **Skill:** The most underrated of all the elements of drafting, acquired through practice. Includes knowing the properties and strengths of the luxin being drafted, being able to see and match precise wavelengths, etc.
>
> **Will:** By imposing will, a drafter can draft and even cover flawed drafting if her will is powerful enough.
>
> **Source:** Depending on what colors a drafter can use, she needs either that color of light or items that reflect that color of light in order to draft. Only a Prism can simply split white light within herself to draft any color.
>
> **Still:** An ironic usage. Drafting requires movement, though more skilled drafters can use less.

*slowmatch:*Another term for a slow fuse.

spectrum: A term for a range of light (for more information on the luxin spectrum, see the Appendix); or (capitalized) the council of the Chromeria that is one branch of the government of the Chromeria(see Colors, the).

spyglass: A small telescope using curved, clear lenses to aid in sighting distant objects.

star-keepers: Also known as tower monkeys, these are petite slaves(usually children) who work the ropes that control the mirrors of Big Jasper to reflect the light throughout the city for drafters' use. Though well treated for slaves, they spend their days working in two-man teams from dawn till after dusk, frequently without reprieve except for switching with their partner.

subchromats: Drafters who are color-blind, usually men. A subchromat can function without loss of ability—if his handicap is not in the colors he can draft. A red-green color-blind subchromat could be an excellent blue or yellow drafter. See Appendix.

Sun Day: A holy day to followers of Orholam and pagans alike, the longest day of the year. For the Seven Satrapies, Sun Day is the day when the Prism Frees those drafters who are about to break the halo. The ceremonies usually take place on the Jaspers, when all of the Thousand Stars are trained onto the Prism, who can absorb and split the light, whereas other men burn or burst from drafting so much power.

Sun Day's Eve: An evening of festivities before the longest day of the year and the Freeing the next day.

Sundered Rock: Twin mountains in Tyrea, opposite each other and so alike that they look as if they were once one huge rock cut down the middle.

Sundered Rock, Battle of: The final battle between Gavin and Dazen near a small Tyrean town on the Umber River.

superchromats: Extremely color-sensitive people. Luxin they seal will rarely fail. Far more common among female drafters.

tainted: One who has broken the halo, also called a wight.

thobe: An ankle-length garment, usually with long sleeves.

Thorn Conspiracies, the: A series of intrigues that occurred after the False Prism's War.

Thousand Stars, the: The mirrors on Big Jasper Island that enable the light to reach into almost any part of the city for as long as possible during the day.

Threshing, the: The initiation test for candidates to the Chromeria.

Threshing Chamber, the: The room where candidates for the Chromeria are summoned to test for their abilities to draft.

Travertine Palace, the: One of the wonders of the old world. Both a palace and a fortress, it is built of carved travertine (a mellow greenstone) and white marble. Notable for its bulbous horseshoe arches, geometric wall patterns, Parian runes, and chessboard patterns on the floors. Its walls are incised with a crosshatched pattern to make the stone look woven rather than carved. The palace is a remnant of the days when half of Tyrea was a Parian province.

Tree People, the: Tribesmen who live (lived?) deep in the forests of the Blood Forest satrapy. They use zoomorphic designs, and can apparently shape living wood. Possibly related to the pygmies.

Umber River, the: The lifeblood of Tyrea. Its water allows the growth of every kind of plant in the hot climate; its locks fed trade throughout the country before the False Prism's War. Often besieged by bandits.

Unchained, the: A term for the followers of the Omnichrome, those drafters who choose to break the Pact and continue living even after breaking the halo.

Unification, the: A term for Lucidonius's and Karris Shadowblinder's establishment of the Seven Satrapies four hundred years prior to Gavin Guile's rule as Prism.

urum: A three-tined dining implement.

vambrace: Plate armor to protect the forearm. Ceremonial versions made of cloth also exist.

vechevoral: A sickle-shaped sword with a long handle like an ax and a crescent-moon-shaped blade at the end, with the inward bowl-shaped side being the cutting edge.

Verdant Plains, the: The dominant geographical feature of Ruthgar. The Verdant Plains are favored by green drafters.

Vician's Sin: The event that marked the end of the close alliance between Ruthgar and Blood Forest.

warrior-drafters: Drafters whose primary work is fighting for various satrapies or the Chromeria.

water markets: Circular lakes connected to the Umber River at the center of the villages and cities of Tyrea, common throughout Tyrean towns. A water market is dredged routinely to maintain an even depth, allowing ships easy access to the interior of the city with their wares. The largest water market is in Garriston.

widdershins: A direction; counter-sunwise.

Appendix

On Monochromes, Bichromes, and Polychromes

Most drafters are monochromes: they are able to draft only one color. Drafters who can draft two colors well enough to create stable luxin in both colors are called bichromes. Anyone who can draft solid luxin in three or more colors is called a polychrome. The more colors a polychrome can draft, the more powerful she is and the more sought-after are her services. A full-spectrum polychrome is a polychrome who can draft every color in the spectrum. A Prism is always a full-spectrum polychrome. Merely being able to draft a color, though, isn't the sole determining criterion in how valuable or skilled a drafter is. Some drafters are faster at drafting, some are more efficient, some have more will than others, some are better at crafting luxin that will be durable, some are smarter or more creative at how and when to apply luxin.

On Disjunctive Bichromes/Polychromes

On the light continuum, sub-red borders red, red borders orange, orange borders yellow, yellow borders green, green borders blue, blue borders superviolet. Most bichromes and polychromes simply draft a larger spectrum on the continuum than monochromes. That is, a bichrome is most likely to draft two colors that are adjacent to each other (blue and superviolet, red and sub-red, yellow and green, etc.).However, some few drafters are disjunctive bichromes. As could be surmised from the name, these are drafters whose colors do not border each other. Usef Tep was a famous example: he drafted red and blue. Karris White Oak is another, drafting green and red. It is unknown how or why disjunctive bichromes come to exist. It is only known that they are rare.

On Outer-Spectrum Colors

Full discussion of Outer Spectrum colors is currently considered heterodox and will have to wait for another era, or special permission. Our reportage on chi, paryl, black, and white luxin is merely telling what is said in popular myths.

On Subchromacy and Superchromacy

A subchromat is one who has trouble differentiating between at least two colors, colloquially referred to as being color-blind. Subchromacy need not doom a drafter. For instance, a blue drafter who cannot distinguish between red and green will not be significantly handicapped in his work. Superchromacy is having greater than usual ability to distinguish between fine variations of color. Superchromacy in any color will result in more stable drafting, but is most helpful in drafting yellow. Only superchromat yellow drafters can hope to draft solid yellow luxin.

On Luxin (with sections on physics, metaphysics, effects on personality, legendary colors, and colloquial terms)

The basis of magic is light. Those who use magic are called drafters. A drafter is able to transform a color of light into a physical substance. Each color has its own properties, but the uses of those building blocks are as boundless as a drafter's imagination and skill. The magic in the Seven Satrapies functions roughly the opposite of a candle burning. When a candle burns, a physical substance (wax)is transformed into light. With chromaturgy, light is transformed into a physical substance, luxin. Each color of luxin has its own properties. If drafted correctly (within a tight allowance), the resulting luxin will be stable, lasting for days or even years, depending on its color. Most drafters (magic-users)can only use one color. A drafter must be exposed to the light of her color to be able to draft it (that is, a green drafter can look at grass and be able to draft, but if she's in a white-walled room, she can't). Each drafter usually carries spectacles so that if her color isn't available, she can still use magic.

PHYSICS

Luxin has weight. If a drafter drafts a luxin hay cart over her head, the first thing it will do is crush her. From heaviest to lightest are: red, orange, yellow, green, blue, sub-red,* superviolet, sub-red.* For reference, liquid yellow luxin is only slightly lighter than the same volume of water.

(*Sub-red is difficult to weigh accurately because it rapidly degenerates to fire when exposed to air. The ordering above was achieved by putting sub-red luxin in an airtight container and then weighing the result, minus the weight of the container. In real-world uses, sub-red crystals are often seen floating upward in the air before igniting.)

Luxin has tactility.

Sub-red: Again the hardest to describe due to its flammability, but often described as feeling like a hot wind.

Red: Gooey, sticky, clingy, depending on drafting; can be tarry and thick or more gel-like.

Orange: Lubricative, slippery, soapy, oily.

Yellow: In its liquid, more common state, like bubbly, effervescent water, cool to the touch, possibly a little thicker than seawater. In its solid state, it is perfectly slicked, unyielding, smooth, and incredibly hard.

Green: Rough: depending on the skill and purposes of the drafter, ranges from merely having a grain like leather to feeling like tree bark. It is flexible, springy, often drawing comparisons to the green limbs of living trees.

Blue: Smooth, though poorly drafted blue will have a texture or can shed fragments easily, like chalk, but in crystals.

Superviolet: Like spidersilk, thin and light to the point of imperceptibility.

Luxin has scent. The base scent of luxin is resinous. The smells below are approximate, because each color of luxin smells like itself. Imagine trying to describe the smell of an orange. You'd say citrus and sharp, but that isn't it *exactly*. An orange smells like an orange. However, the below approximations are close.

Sub-red: Charcoal, smoke, burned.

Red: Tea leaves, tobacco, dry.

Orange: Almond.

Yellow: Eucalyptus and mint.

Green: Fresh cedar, resin.

Blue: Mineral, chalk, almost none.

Superviolet: Faintly like cloves.

Black: *No smell/or smell of decaying flesh.*

White: *Honey, lilac.*

(*As stated in our curtailed note On Outer Spectrum Colors, these are mythical. This is a restatement of smells as reported, not espoused or verified.)

Metaphysics

Any drafting feels good to the drafter. Sensations of euphoria and invincibility are particularly strong among young drafters and those drafting for the first time. Generally, these pass with time, though drafters abstaining from magic for a time will often feel them again. For most drafters, the effect is similar to drinking a cup of kopi. Some drafters, strangely enough, seem to have allergic reactions to drafting. There are vigorous ongoing debates about whether the effects on personality should be described as metaphysical or physical.

Regardless of their correct categorization and whether they are the proper realm of study for the magister or the luxiat, the effects themselves are unquestioned.

Luxin's Effects on Personality

The benighted before Lucidonius believed that passionate men became reds, or that calculating women became yellows or blues. In truth, the causation flows the other way.

Every drafter, like every woman, has her own innate personality. The color she drafts then influences her *toward* the behaviors below. A person who is impulsive who drafts red for years is going to be more likely to be pushed farther into "red" characteristics than a naturally cold and orderly person who drafts red for the same length of time.

The color a drafter uses will affect her personality over time. This, however, doesn't make her a prisoner of her color, or irresponsible for her actions under the influence of it. A green who continually cheats on his wife is still a lothario. A sub-red who murders an enemy in a fit of rage is still a murderer. Of course, a naturally angry woman who is also a red drafter will be even more susceptible to that color's effects, but there are many tales of calculating reds and fiery, intemperate blues.

A color isn't a substitute for a woman. Be careful in your application of generalities. That said, generalities can be useful: a group of green drafters is more likely to be wild and rowdy than a group of blues.

Given these generalities, there is also a virtue and a vice commonly associated with each color. (Virtue being understood by the early luxiats not as being free of temptation to do evil in a particular way, but as conquering one's own predilection toward that kind of evil. Thus, gluttony is paired with temperance, greed with charity, etc.)

Sub-red drafters: Sub-reds are passionate in all ways, the most purely emotional of all drafters, the quickest to rage or to cry. Sub-reds love music, are often impulsive, fear the dark less than another color, and are often insomniacs. Emotional, distractible, unpredictable, inconsistent, loving, bighearted. Sub-red men are often sterile.

Associated vice: Wrath

Associated virtue: Patience

Red drafters: Reds are quick-tempered, lusty, and love destruction. They are also warm, inspiring, brash, larger than life, expansive, jovial, and powerful.

Associated vice: Gluttony

Associated virtue: Temperance

Orange drafters: Oranges are often artists, brilliant in understanding other people's emotions and motivations. Some use this to defy or exceed expectations. Sensitive, manipulative, idiosyncratic, slippery, charismatic, empathetic.

Associated vice: Greed

Associated virtue: Charity

Yellow drafters: Yellows tend to be clear thinkers, with intellect and emotion in perfect balance. Cheerful, wise, bright, balanced, watchful, impassive, observant, brutally honest at times, excellent liars. Thinkers, not doers.

Associated vice: Sloth

Associated virtue: Diligence

Green drafters: Greens are wild, free, flexible, adaptable, nurturing, friendly. They don't so much disrespect authority as not even recognize it.

Associated vice: Lust

Associated virtue: Self-control

Blue drafters: Blues are orderly, inquisitive, rational, calm, cold, impartial, intelligent, musical. Structure, rules, and hierarchy are important to them. Blues are often mathematicians and composers. Ideas and ideology and correctness often matter more than people to blues.

Associated vice: Envy

Associated virtue: Kindness

Superviolet drafters: Superviolets tend to have a removed outlook; dispassionate, they appreciate irony and sarcasm and word games and are often cold, viewing people as puzzles to be solved or ciphers to be cracked. Irrationality outrages superviolets.

Associated vice: Pride

Associated virtue: Humility

LEGENDARY COLORS

In accordance with the Office of Doctrine, these paragraphs have been removed.

COLLOQUIAL TERMS

Students at the Chromeria are encouraged to use the proper names for each color, but the impetus to name seems unstoppable. In some cases, the names are used technically: pyrejelly is a thicker, longer-burning draft of red that will burn long enough to reduce a body to ash. In other cases, the reference becomes precisely the opposite of the technical definition: brightwater was first a name for liquid yellow luxin, but Brightwater Wall is solid yellow luxin.

A few of the more common colloquialisms:

Sub-red: Firecrystal
Red: Pyrejelly, burnglue
Orange: Noranjell
Yellow: Brightwater
Green: Godswood
Blue: Frostglass, glass
Superviolet: Skystring, soulstring, spidersilk
***Black:** Hellstone, nullstone, nightfiber, cinderstone, hadon
***White:** Truebright, starsblood, anachrome, luciton
(* As before, etcetera.)

On the Old Gods

Sub-red: Anat, goddess of wrath. Those who worshipped her are said to have had rituals that involved infant sacrifice. Also known as the Lady of the Desert, the Fiery Mistress. Her centers of worship were Tyrea, southernmost Paria, and southern Ilyta.
Red: Dagnu, god of gluttony. He was worshipped in eastern Atash.
Orange: Molokh, god of greed. Once worshipped in western Atash.
Yellow: Belphegor, god of sloth. Primarily worshipped in northern Atash and southern Blood Forest before Lucidonius's coming.
Green: Atirat, goddess of lust. Her center of worship was primarily in western Ruthgar and most of Blood Forest.
Blue: Mot, god of envy. His center of worship was in eastern Ruthgar, northeastern Paria, and Abornea.
Superviolet: Ferrilux, god of pride. His center of worship was in southern Paria and northern Ilyta.

On Technology and Weapons

The Seven Satrapies are in a time of great leaps in understanding. The peace since the Prisms' War and the following suppression of piracy has allowed the flow of goods and ideas freely through the satrapies. Cheap, high-quality iron and steel are available in every satrapy, leading to high-quality weapons, durable wagon wheels, and everything in between. Though traditional forms of weapons like Atashian bich'hwaor Parian parry-sticks continue, now they are rarely made of horn or hardened wood. Luxin is often used for improvised weapons, but most luxins' tendency to break down after long exposure to light, and the scarcity of yellow drafters who can make solid yellows (which don't break down in light), means that metal weapons predominate among mundane armies.

The greatest leaps are occurring in the improvement of firearms. In most cases, each musket is the product of a different smith. This means each man must be able to fix his own firearm, and that pieces must be crafted individually. A faulty hammer or flash pan can't be swapped out for a new one, but must be detached and reworked into appropriate shape. Some large-scale productions with hundreds of apprentice smiths have tried to tackle this problem in Rath by making parts as nearly identical as possible, but the resulting matchlocks tend to be low quality, trading accuracy and durability for consistency and simple repair. Elsewhere, the smiths of Ilyta have gone the other direction, making the highest-quality custom muskets in the world. Recently, they've pioneered a form they call the flintlock. Instead of affixing a burning slow match to ignite powder in the flash pan and thence into the breech of the rifle, they've affixed a flint that scrapes a frizzen to throw sparks directly into the breech. This approach means a musket or pistol is always ready to fire, without a soldier having to first light a slow match. Keeping it from widespread adoption is the high rate of misfires—if the flint doesn't scrape the frizzen correctly or throw sparks perfectly, the firearm doesn't fire.

Thus far, the combination of luxin with firearms has been largely unsuccessful. The casting of perfectly round yellow luxin musket balls was possible, but the small number of yellow drafters able to make solid yellow creates a bottleneck in production. Blue luxin musket balls often shatter from the force of the black powder explosion. An exploding shell made by filling a yellow luxin ball with red luxin (which would ignite explosively from the shattering yellow when the ball hit a target) was demonstrated to the Nuqaba, but the exact balance of making the yellow thick enough to not explode inside the musket, but thin enough to shatter when it hit its target, is so difficult that several smiths have died trying to replicate it, probably barring this technique from wide adoption.

Other experiments are doubtless being carried out all over the Seven Satrapies, and if high-quality, consistent, and somewhat accurate firearms are introduced, the ways of war will change forever. As it stands, a trained archer can shoot farther, far more quickly, and more accurately.

extras

meet the author

Travis Johnson Photography

BRENT WEEKS was born and raised in Montana. After getting his paper keys from Hillsdale College, Brent started writing on bar napkins, then on lesson plans, then full time. Eventually, someone paid him for it. Brent lives in Oregon with his wife, Kristi. He doesn't own cats or wear a ponytail. Find out more about the author at www.brentweeks.com.

introducing

If you enjoyed
THE BLACK PRISM,
look out for

THE BLINDING KNIFE

Lightbringer: Book 2

by Brent Weeks

Chapter 1

Gavin Guile lay on his back on a narrow skimmer floating in the middle of the sea. It was a tiny craft with low sides. Lying on his back like this, he'd once almost believed he was one with the sea. Now the dome of the heavens above him was a lid, and he a crab in the cauldron, heat rising.

Two hours before noon, here on the southern rim of the Cerulean Sea, the waters should be a stunning deep blue-green. The sky above, cloudless, mist burned off, should be a peaceful, vibrant sapphire.

But he couldn't see it. Since he'd lost the Battle of Garriston four days ago, wherever there was blue, he saw gray. He couldn't even see that much unless he concentrated. Robbed of its blue, the sea looked like thin, gray-green broth.

His fleet was waiting. Hard to relax when thousands of people were waiting for you and only you, but he needed this measure of peace.

He looked to the heavens, arms spread, touching the waves with his fingertips.

Lucidonius, were you here? Were you even real? Did this happen to you, too?

Something hissed in the water, a sound like a boat cutting through the waves.

Gavin sat up on his skimmer. Then stood.

Fifty paces behind him, something disappeared under the waves, something big enough to cause its own swell. It could have been a whale.

Except whales usually surface to breathe. There was no spray hanging in the air, no whoosh of expelled breath. And from fifty paces, for Gavin to have heard the hiss of a sea creature cutting through the water, it would have to be massive. His heart leapt to his throat.

He began sucking in light to draft his oar apparatus—and froze. Right beneath his tiny craft, something was moving through the water. It was like watching the landscape speed by when you're riding in a carriage, but Gavin wasn't moving. The rushing body was huge, many times the width of his craft, and it was undulating closer and closer to the surface, closer to his own little boat. A sea demon.

And it *glowed*. A peaceful, warm radiance like the sun itself on this cool morning.

Gavin had never heard of such a thing. Sea demons were monsters, the purest, craziest form of fury known to mankind. They burned red, boiled the seas, left fires floating in their wake. Not carnivores, so far as the old books guessed, but fiercely territorial—and any interloper that disrupted their seas was to be crushed. Interlopers like ships.

This light was different than that rage. A peaceful luminescence, the sea demon no vicious destroyer but a leviathan traversing the seas, leaving barely a ripple to note his passing. The colors shimmered through the waves, grew brighter as the undulation brought the body close.

Unthinking, Gavin knelt as the creature's back broke the surface of the water right underneath his boat. Before the boat slid away from the swell, he reached out and touched the sea demon's skin. He expected a creature that slid through the waves to be slimy, but the skin was surprisingly rough, muscular, warm.

For one precious moment, Gavin was not. There was no Gavin Guile, no Dazen Guile, no High Luxlord Prism, no scraping sniveling dignitaries devoid of dignity, no lies, no satraps to be bullied, no Spectrum councilors to manipulate, no lovers, no bastards, no power except the power before his eyes. He felt small, staring into incomprehensible vastness.

Cooled by the gentle morning breeze, warmed by the twin suns, one in the sky, one beneath the waves, Gavin was serene. It was the closest thing to a holy moment he had ever experienced.

And then he realized the sea demon was swimming toward his fleet.

Chapter 2

The green hell was calling him to madness. The dead man was back in the reflective wall, luminous, grinning at Dazen, features squeezed skeleton-thin by the curving walls of the spherical green cell.

The key was to *not* draft. After sixteen years of drafting only blue, of altering mind and damaging body with that loathsome cerulean serenity, now having escaped the blue cell, Dazen wanted nothing more than to gorge on some other color. It was like he'd eaten breakfast gruel morning, noon, and night for six thousand days, and now someone was offering him a rasher of bacon.

He hadn't even liked bacon, back when he'd been free. Now it sounded lovely. He wondered if that was the fever, turning his thoughts to sludge and emotion.

Funny how he thought that: 'Back when he'd been free.' Not 'Back when he'd been Prism.'

He wasn't sure if it was because he was still telling himself that he was the Prism whether he was in royal robes or rancid rags, or if it simply didn't matter anymore.

Dazen tried to look away, but everything was green. To have his eyes open was to be dipping his feet in green. No, he was up to his neck in water and trying to get dry. There was no hope of dryness. He had to know that and accept it. The only question wasn't if he was going to get his hair wet, it was if he was going to drown.

Green was all wildness, freedom. That logical part of Dazen that had basked in blue's orderliness knew that sucking up pure wildness while locked up in this luxin cage would lead to madness. Within days he'd claw out his own throat. Pure wildness, here, would be death. He would finally accomplish his brother's objective for him.

He needed to be patient. He needed to think, and thinking was hard right now. He examined his body slowly, carefully. His hands and knees were lacerated from his crawl through the hellstone tunnel. The bumps and bruises from his fall through the trapdoor and into this cell he could ignore. They were painful, but inconsequential. Most worrisome was the inflamed, infected slash across his chest. It nauseated him just looking at it, oozing pus and promises of death.

Worst was the fever, corrupting his very blood, making him stupid, irrational, sapping his will.

But Dazen had escaped the blue prison, and that prison had changed him. His brother had crafted these prisons quickly, and probably put most of his efforts into that first, blue one. Every prison had a flaw.

The blue prison had made him the perfect man to find it. Death or freedom.

In his reflective green wall, the dead man said, "You taking bets?"

Chapter 3

Gavin sucked in light to start making his rowing apparatus. Unthinking, he tried to draft blue. While brittle, blue's stiff, slick, smooth structure made it ideal for parts that didn't undergo sideways stresses. For a futile moment, Gavin tried to force it, again. He was a Prism made flesh; alone out of all drafters, he could split light within himself. The blue was there—he knew it was there, and maybe knowing it was there, even though he couldn't see, might be enough.

For Orholam's sake, if you could find your chamber pot in the middle of the night and, despite that you couldn't see it, the damned thing was still there, why couldn't this be the same?

Nothing. No rush of harmonious logic, no cool rationality, no stained blue skin, no drafting whatsoever. For the first time since he was a boy, he felt helpless. Like a natural man. Like a peasant.

Gavin screamed at his helplessness. It was too late for the oars anyway. That son of a bitch was swimming too fast.

extras

He drafted the scoops and the reeds. Blue worked better to make the jets for a skimmer, but naturally flexible green could serve if he made it thick enough. The rough green luxin was heavier and created more drag against the water, so he was slower, but he didn't have the time or attention to make it from yellow. Precious seconds passed while he prepared his skimmer.

Then the scoops were in hand and he began throwing luxin down into the jets, blasting air and water out the back of his little craft and propelling himself forward. He leaned far forward, shoulders knotting with the effort; then, as he picked up speed, the effort eased. Soon his craft was hissing across the waves.

The fleet arose in the distance, the sails of the tallest ships first. But at Gavin's speed, it wasn't long before he could see all of them. There were hundreds of ships now: from sailing dinghies to galleasses to the square-rigged three-masted ship of the line with forty-eight guns that Gavin had taken from the Ruthgari governor to be his flagship. They'd left Garriston with over a hundred ships, but hundreds more that had gotten out earlier had joined them within days for protection from the pirates who lay thick in these waters. Last, he saw the great luxin barges, barely seaworthy. He himself had created those four great open boats to hold as many refugees as possible. If he hadn't, thousands of people would have died.

And now they would die regardless, if Gavin didn't turn the sea demon.

As he sped closer, he caught sight of the sea demon again, a hump cresting six feet out of the water. Its skin was still placidly luminous, and by some good fortune it wasn't actually cutting straight toward the fleet. Its path would take it perhaps a thousand paces in front of the lead ship.

Of course, the ships themselves were plowing slow furrows forward, closing that gap, but the sea demon was moving so quickly, Gavin dared to hope that it wouldn't matter. He had no idea how keen the sea demon's senses were, but if it kept going in the same direction, they might well make it.

Gavin couldn't take his hands away from the skimmer's jets without losing precious speed, and he didn't know how he would deliver a signal that said, "Don't Do Anything Stupid!" to the whole fleet at once even if he did. He followed directly behind the sea demon, closer now.

He'd been wrong; the sea demon was going to cut perhaps five hundred paces from the lead ship. A bad estimate, or was the creature turning toward the fleet?

Gavin could see lookouts in the crow's nests waving their hands violently to those on the decks below them. Doubtless shouting, though Gavin was too far away to hear them. He sped closer, saw men running on the decks.

The emergency was on the fleet far faster than any of them could have expected. In the normal order of things, enemies might appear on the horizon and give chase. Storms could blow out of nowhere in half an hour—but this had happened in minutes, and some ships were only seeing the twin wonders now—a boat traveling faster across the waves than anyone had ever seen in their lives, and the huge dark shadow in front of it that could only be a sea demon.

Be smart, Orholam damn you all, be smart or be too terrified to do anything at all. Please!

Cannons took time to load and couldn't be left armed because the powder could go bad. Some idiot might shoot a musket at the passing form, but that should be too small a disturbance for the monster to notice.

The sea demon bulled through the waters four hundred paces in front of the fleet and kept going straight.

Gavin could hear the shouts from the ships now. The man in

the crow's nest of Gavin's flagship was holding his hands to his head in disbelief, but no one did anything stupid.

Orholam, just one more minute. Just—

A signal mortar cracked the morning, and Gavin's hopes bellyflopped in the sea. He swore that all the shouting on every ship in the fleet stopped at once. And then began again a moment later, as the experienced sailors screamed in disbelief at the terrified idiot captain who'd probably just killed them all.

Gavin had eyes only for the sea demon. Its wake went straight, hissing bubbles and great undulations, another hundred paces. Another hundred. Maybe it hadn't heard.

Then his skimmer jetted right past the entire beast as the sea demon doubled back on itself faster than Gavin would have believed possible.

As it completed its turn, its tail broke the surface of the water. It moved too fast for Gavin to make out details. Only that it was burning red-hot, the color of iron angry from the forge, and when that span—surely thirty paces long—hit the water, the concussion made the signal mortar's report sound tinny and small.

Giant swells rolled out from the spot its tail had hit. From his dead stop, Gavin was barely able to turn his skimmer before the waves reached him. He dipped deep into the first wave and hurriedly threw green luxin forward, making the front of his craft wider and longer. He was shot upward by the next swell and flung into the air.

The skimmer's prow hit the next giant swell at too great of an angle and went straight into it. Gavin was ripped off the skimmer and plunged into the waves.

The Cerulean Sea was a warm wet mouth. It took Gavin in whole, chomped his breath out of him, rolled him over with its tongue, disorienting him, made a play at swallowing him, and when he fought, finally let him go.

extras

Gavin surfaced and quickly found the fleet. He didn't have time to draft an entire new skimmer, so he drafted smaller scoops around his arms, sucked in as much light as he could hold, threw his arms down to his sides, and pointed his head toward the sea demon. He threw luxin down and it threw him forward.

The pressure of the waves was incredible. It obliterated sight, blotted out sound, but Gavin didn't slow. With a body made so hard by years of working a skimmer that he could cross the sea in a day, and a will made implacable by years of being Prism and forcing the world to conform to his wishes, he *pushed*.

He felt himself slide into the sea demon's slipstream: the pressure suddenly eased and his speed doubled. Using his legs to aim, Gavin turned himself deeper into the water, then jetted toward the surface.

He shot into the air. Not a moment too soon.

He shouldn't have been able to see much of anything, gasping in air and light, water streaming off his entire body. But the tableau froze, and he saw *everything*. The sea demon's head was halfway out of the water, its cruciform mouth drawn shut so its knobby, spiky hammerhead could smash the flagship to kindling. Its body was at least twenty paces across, and only fifty paces now from the ship.

Men were standing on the port rail, matchlocks in hand. Black smoke billowed thick from a few. Others flared as the matches ignited powder in the pans in the instant before they fired. Commander Ironfist and Karris both stood, braced, fearless, glowing luxin forming missiles in their hands. In the gun decks, Gavin saw men tamping powder into the cannons for shots they would never get off in time.

The other ships in the fleet were crowding around like kids around a fistfight, men perched on gunwales, mouths agape, all too few even loading their muskets.

Dozens of men were turning from looking at the monster approaching to see what fresh horror this could be shooting into the air—and gaping, bewildered. A man in the crow's nest was pointing at him, shouting.

And Gavin hung in midair, disaster and mutilation only seconds away from his compatriots—and threw all he had at the sea demon.

A coruscating, twisting wall of multicolored light blew out of Gavin, streaking toward the creature.

Gavin didn't see what it did when it struck the sea demon, or even if he hit it at all.

There was an old Parian saying that Gavin had heard but never paid attention to: "When you hurl a mountain, the mountain hurls you back."

Time resumed, unpleasantly quickly. Gavin felt like he'd been walloped with a club bigger than his own body. He was launched backward, stars exploding in front of his eyes, clawing catlike, twisting, trying to turn—and splashing in the water with another jarring slap, twenty paces back.

Light is life. Years of war had taught Gavin never to leave yourself unarmed; vulnerability is a prelude to death. He found the surface and began drafting instantly. In the years he'd spent failing thousands of times while perfecting his skimmer, he'd also perfected methods of getting out of the water and creating a boat—not an easy task. Drafters were always terrified of falling in the water and not being able to get out again.

So within seconds Gavin was standing on the deck of a new skimmer, already drafting the scoops as he tried to assess what had happened.

The flagship was still floating, one railing knocked off, huge scrapes across the wood of the port side. So the sea demon must have turned, must have barely glanced off the boat. It had slapped its tail down again as it turned, though, because a few of the small sailing dinghies nearby had been swamped, and men were jumping into the water, other ships already heading toward them to pluck them from the sea's jaws.

And where the hell was the sea demon?

Men were screaming on the decks—not shouts of adulation, but alarm. They were pointing—

Oh *shit*.

Gavin began throwing luxin down the reeds as fast as possible. But the skimmer always started slow.

The giant steaming red-hot hammerhead surfaced not twenty paces away, coming fast. Gavin was accelerating and he caught the shockwave caused by such a massive, blunt shape pushing through the seas. The front of the head was a wall, a knobby, spiky wall.

But with the swell of the shockwave helping him, Gavin began to pull away.

And then the cruciform mouth opened, splitting that entire front hammerhead wide in four directions. As the sea demon began sucking water in rather than pushing it in front of it, the shockwave disappeared abruptly. And Gavin's skimmer lurched back into the mouth.

Fully into the mouth. The open mouth was easily two or three times as wide as Gavin was tall. Sea demons swallowed the seas entire. The body convulsed in rhythm, a circle that squeezed tighter and then opened wider, jetting water past gills and out the back almost the same way Gavin's skimmer did.

Gavin's arms were shaking, shoulders burning from the muscular effort of pushing his entire body, his entire boat across the seas. Harder. Dammit, harder!

The sea demon arched upward just as Gavin's skimmer shot out of its mouth. Its tetraform jaws snapped shut, and it launched itself into the air. He shut his eyes and screamed, pushing as hard as he could.

He shot a look over his shoulder and saw the impossible: the sea demon had breached. Completely. Its massive body crashed back down into the water like all seven towers of the Chromeria falling into the sea at once.

But Gavin was faster, up to full speed. Filling with the fierce freedom of flight and the luminous lightness of life, he laughed. Laughed.

The sea demon pursued him, furious, still burning red, moving even faster than before. But with the skimmer at full speed, Gavin was out of danger. He circled out to sea as the distant shapes of men cheered on the decks of every ship of the fleet, and the creature followed him.

Gavin led it for hours out to sea; then, circling wide in case it headed blindly in the last direction it had seen him go, he left it far behind.

As the sun set, exhausted and wrung out, he returned to his fleet. They'd lost two sailing dinghies, but not a single life. His people—for if they hadn't been his before, he owned them heart and soul now—greeted him like a god.

Gavin accepted their adulation with a wan smile, but the freedom had faded. He wished he, too, could rejoice. He wished he could get drunk and dance and bed the finest-looking girl he could find. He wished he could find Karris somewhere in the fleet and fight or fuck or one and then the other. He wished he could tell the tale and hear it retold from a hundred lips and laugh at the death that had come so close to them all. Instead, as his people celebrated, he went belowdecks. Alone. Waved Corvan away. Shook his head at his wide-eyed son.

And finally, in his darkened cabin, alone, he wept. Not for what had been, but for what he knew he must become.